Possessions

JUDITH
MICHAEL

POSEIDON PRESS
New York

2   3   4   5   6   7   8   9   10

Library of Congress Cataloging in Publication Data

Michael, Judith.
Possessions.

I. Title.
PS3563.I254P6   1984   813'.54   84-3454

ISBN 0-671-50421-5

We dedicate this book to
Harry Barnard
Whose boundless love and encouragement we deeply miss

Part I

CHAPTER 1

"**K**ATHERINE!" The voices echoed in the brightly lit rooms. "Wonderful party . . . terrific food! . . . so *good* to be here . . ." And to one another, still at the top of their voices, they shouted, "Didn't know they threw these parties . . . did you?"

The voices rose above the music from the record player and swept through the house and out to the terrace where couples danced in the warm June night or stood on the low stone wall to view the spectacle of Vancouver's skyline across the bay. And Katherine, with Jennifer and Todd's help, opened new bottles at the small bar and moved back and forth between the kitchen and dining room, keeping the steaming casseroles and platters on the buffet heaped with food.

"The guest of honor salutes a terrific hostess," said Leslie McAlister, lifting her glass. "And," she added with a small bow, "Jennifer and Todd. Your mother should hire you out to friends when they entertain." She put her arm around Katherine. "Very impressive, being the reason for such a party. Why didn't you tell me you threw such terrific affairs? If I'd known, I wouldn't have let three years go by since my last visit. On the other hand, why haven't you come to San Francisco so I could give a party in *your* honor?"

"You should have come sooner," Katherine agreed. She was trying to twist the cork out of a champagne bottle. "Craig does this so easily, but I can't seem to—"

"Let me." Leslie took the bottle from her. "It's one of the first skills single women learn." With a flourish, she pushed up the cork with her

9

thumbs, at the same time covertly studying Katherine, comparing her to the plain, shy Katherine Fraser she'd seen only sporadically for the past ten years. She was still shy—slightly alarmed at the boisterousness of her party and looking surprised when her guests praised her—but she was a little prettier, especially now, with the excitement of her party brightening her wonderful hazel eyes and giving her pale skin some color. And though she and Leslie were the same height, she was slimmer; she doesn't worry about her hips, Leslie thought ruefully.

Still, her educated eye saw that Katherine wasn't nearly as attractive as she could be. Her heavy dark hair was pulled back and held tightly by an elastic band, stretching the skin at her temples, her lipstick was the wrong shade for her skin, and her dress was too plain for a figure that demanded drama. Leslie, who worked at being stunning and sophisticated, making a virtue of kinky red hair and a sharp jaw, felt her fingers itching to redo Katherine. Silently she laughed at herself. Never content; not only did she spend her days as an executive of an exclusive department store that catered to the whims of wealthy customers, but she also couldn't wait to go to work on a friend who seemed perfectly satisfied with herself.

The cork popped neatly from the bottle, trailing misty tendrils of champagne vapor. "Oh, well done!" cried Sarah Murphy, small, round, with black alert eyes. "Men always spray it everywhere, but you have such finesse! You must entertain a great deal. Katherine, on the other hand" —she tapped Katherine playfully— "never entertains, yet here she is giving *such* a lovely party. And without a husband in sight. Where *is* Craig, my dear? Usually I see him leave like clockwork every morning, but I haven't seen him since Tuesday."

"He had to go to Toronto—"

"With a party coming up? It must have been terribly important to make him disappear and expect you to—"

"Cope," Leslie finished smoothly. "And isn't she admirable? One might be envious—if one were the type." She smiled sweetly. "Katherine and I were catching up on our news; do you mind if I monopolize her before I leave for the airport?"

"Oh, my, no," said Sarah. "Of course not; Katherine's been so anxious to see you—" She followed them, still talking, until they hid behind a cluster of guests at the piano. Beneath the noise of the party, they burst out laughing.

"Thank you," Katherine said. "She's a wonderful neighbor and she'd do anything to help us if we needed her, but she's a little hard to get rid of."

"Hinting," Leslie scorned. "I can't stand people who haven't the guts to be honestly nosy."

"Or honestly anything," Katherine added as they went through the glass doors to the terrace. "You never liked anyone who lied."

"That's why we latched on to each other: the two of us, so damned stubborn about the truth. So how come we don't see each other more often?"

A shout from the living room broke in, rising furiously above the sounds of the party. "You son of a bitch, you have to accommodate the Quebecois—"

"Accommodate the French!" came an outraged response. "We're already taxed up to our necks to pay for them. Our money should stay in the west—"

"So that's what you want, eh? You'd do anything to get out of paying taxes!"

Katherine's face was frozen with panic. "They can't fight; it would ruin everything."

The outraged voice rose higher. "Pretty free with accusations, Doerner! You're known for that, aren't you? Especially false ones!"

"What the hell—! Listen you bastard, that was two years ago. And when I found out I was wrong, I paid the costs and it was over. Who do you think you are—"

"Oh, shit!" someone else cried. "Do you two have to come to blows at every party?"

Leslie looked at Katherine's face. "Shall I try to break it up? Sometimes a stranger is a good distraction."

Katherine shook her head. "I should do it. Damn, why isn't Craig here? He'd know what to do; one of those men is his partner. Well—" She straightened her shoulders. "I'll be right back."

In the living room she made her way through a crowd surrounding two men, their faces contorted with anger as other guests held them apart. Katherine drew a shaky breath and, forcing a smile, raised her voice. "It's like an American Western, isn't it? But shouldn't we have a saloon and a dusty street where you can pace off?" She heard a ripple of laughter and the two men reluctantly smiled. She put her hands on their arms. "We do have a bar; can I offer you drinks instead of bruises?"

"Far more civilized," one of them said. "Mrs. Fraser, I apologize. If some people weren't so free with accusations—"

"The bar! The bar! Drinks, not bruises!" came cries from the guests. A short, gray-haired woman mouthed an apology to Katherine and took the other man's arm, turning him toward the bar. In a moment, Katherine slipped out and returned to the terrace.

Leslie was watching from the doorway. "The perfect hostess," she said admiringly. "I thought you said you don't give many parties."

"We don't give any parties. We used to, years ago, but we haven't lately; Craig doesn't like them." Katherine was trembling but a feeling of pride swept over her. "I did stop them, didn't I?"

"You did. Without making anyone angry. Who are those guys, anyway?"

"Carl Doerner, Craig's partner in Vancouver Construction; I have no idea who the other man is. My house is full of people I don't know."

"Katherine! You're not serious."

"Yes I am. We don't have many friends, and I wanted to impress you. So we invited Craig's business acquaintances and people I'd met at Jennifer's and Todd's school."

"But they came to your party."

"They wanted to meet my friend, the vice-president of Heath's of San Francisco. You're a celebrity."

"If I am, it's the first time. And I didn't make this terrific party; you did."

"If I did, it's the first time." They grinned at each other and Katherine felt the warmth of Leslie's closeness. It had been almost the only warmth in high school and two years of college, and afterward, until she met Craig. Leslie, brash and curious, had breached her shyness and given her a chance to know how good a friend she could be. But then, on a vacation in British Columbia, Katherine met Craig Fraser and, within a month, married him. And Leslie, returning to San Francisco after the wedding, decided to make herself the first woman vice-president in the fifty-year history of Heath's of San Francisco.

"The years disappeared," Katherine said, thinking back, trying to answer Leslie's question of why they saw each other so seldom. "And you haven't visited us very often."

"Look who's talking!" Leslie retorted. "You've never come back to San Francisco. Ten years, and never one visit."

"Craig wouldn't go. I asked him so many times; he just refused and wouldn't talk about it." Katherine gazed unseeing at the lights of Lions Gate Bridge, strung across the bay, fastening West Vancouver to the glittering Vancouver skyline. "Do you remember the time I called you, when I was so lonely? We'd been married about three years and had only a couple of friends, and Craig was starting with Carl Doerner's company, and I was always alone with the babies—it was when you were breaking up with what's-his-name—and we nearly drowned our telephones in problems and tears. What *was* his name?"

"I have no idea. Seven years ago? How could I possibly remember?"

"You were so miserable, I thought it was an undying love."

"It probably was, at the moment. I haven't found one that lasts. I don't see many, either. You and Craig; a few others. Though don't you think you *could* find someone else if he suddenly— Sorry, ghoulish question."

"Well, it is, but everyone thinks about it. And I suppose I could love someone else if something happened to Craig." She smiled at Jennifer, who came on to the terrace carefully balancing two plates of steamed shrimp. "Thank you, sweetheart. Would you and Todd like to go upstairs now? I can take over; you've worked so hard and it's getting late."

"Todd's already goofing off," Jennifer said resignedly. "He's talking about Atari games with some computer guy. I *like* being the hostess. See you later."

Amused, Leslie said, "Seems you've been displaced as hostess. Speaking of computers, my wild oats brother has become a computer whiz. In fact, I hired him a while back, figuring a good job might make him an upright citizen. Fingers crossed and daily prayers; so far he seems to be making it." She paused. "So do you. You look happy, Katherine."

"I am." Through the open doors, Katherine heard fragments of conversation and a chorus reviving old folk songs to a piano accompaniment. She felt she was floating on the bright lights and colors of her beautiful house, and wished Craig were there, to share it. We've got to stop being so solitary, she thought; we should make more friends, entertain more.

"I'm sorry I won't see Craig," Leslie said, as if picking up Katherine's thoughts.

"I am, too. I can't imagine why he isn't back; he promised he'd be here to help with the party. Can't you stay over? He'll probably get here just when you leave."

"I really can't. A couple of odd things have come up at the store and I ought to earn my salary by looking into them. I wouldn't even have come up for the conference, if you weren't here. You'll just have to bring the whole family to San Francisco."

"I will. I don't know what Craig has against it, but we'll—"

"Katherine." Carl Doerner was in the doorway. "Could I see you for a minute?"

"I'll get some more wine," Leslie said, and left them alone.

"I apologize," he said. "No excuse for such childish behavior. I'm on edge, lots on my mind, but still...Katherine, have you heard from Craig?"

"No, have you? I thought he'd be back by now."

"I just called him at the Boynton. He's not there."

"Of course not. He's on his way home."

"They don't have a registration for him."

"They must have; that's where he stayed. But it isn't important, is it? He's on his way home."

"Katherine, have you heard from him? All week?"

"No, he's probably been busy. So was I, with the party—"

"Does Craig use other hotels in Toronto?"

"No. Carl, what is this? Craig is on his way home; there's no mystery about it."

"Probably not. But when he gets here, will you have him call me? Right away."

Something in his voice finally reached her. "Are you *worried* about Craig?"

"Of course not. Just—have him call me. All right?"

She nodded, frowning slightly as he walked away. Behind her, someone said, "Wonderful house, Katherine. So much room to move around."

"We built it," she answered. "Three years ago. It is beautiful, isn't it? Craig and the architect worked out every inch."

What does that mean—no registration at the Boynton?

"Talented fellow; he and Doerner built our office building."

"And that new motel in Burnaby? Didn't they do that?"

Of course he was registered. Carl was impatient and didn't ask them to check.

"Mom!" Katherine looked down at Todd's mischievous grin. "There's a whole bunch of chocolate cake in the kitchen. It's for us, isn't it?"

She smiled. "How much have you eaten?"

"Just a taste. Jennifer said I better ask you."

"How much is 'just a taste'?"

"Uh... two and a half pieces? Jennifer only had two."

"Quite a taste." She kissed the top of his head. "One more small piece. And don't forget to brush all that chocolate off your teeth before you go to bed."

"Sure. When's Dad coming home?"

"I guess tomorrow. He'll probably call and let us know."

He would have told me if he'd changed hotels.

"He promised me a balsa airplane model."

"Then he'll bring you one. Good night, Todd. Sleep well."

Unless he changed his plans at the last minute.

"Nice boy, Katherine. The picture of his father."

But whenever he changes his plans, he calls me.

"Katherine." Leslie was carrying her overnight bag. "I've got to go or I'll miss my plane." They walked to the front door and she looked at Katherine appraisingly. "A sudden problem?"

"Why?"

"Furrowed brow, faraway look. Can I help?"

"No, it's not serious, just something that I can't explain. I wish you could stay longer."

"Next time. Or you'll stay longer in San Francisco. You will come? Promise?"

"Promise. As soon as Craig can get away."

"Don't wait too long; I really have missed our talks."

"So have I. I didn't realize how much until now."

"You could come alone, you know."

"Oh. Yes I could. I'd rather not, though; and wouldn't you like a visit from the whole family?"

"Of course. Come soon, then. I'll give you the key to the city." They put their arms around each other. "So damn good to see you. Letters and phone calls aren't enough. Why the hell we let ourselves get so wrapped up in our own lives—" And she was gone, waving from the front gate as she got into the taxi.

Just as Craig did when he went to the airport on Tuesday.

Three days earlier. Tuesday morning. He held her to him as the taxi pulled up, but he was looking off in the distance, already thinking of Toronto. He kissed her, told her he loved her, and was gone, waving as the car pulled away. An ordinary trip, no different from the dozens he took every year to meet with suppliers, architects, other contractors with whom he and Carl did business. Back on Friday, he had promised at breakfast, to help with the party. An ordinary trip. *But why wouldn't he be registered at the Boynton?*

Her exhilaration had vanished; her party had changed. Her guests still gesticulated and smiled, talking rapidly, but the sound and brightness had dimmed, as if muffled by a curtain. I'll find out for myself, she thought, and ran upstairs to call the hotel. "No, Mrs. Fraser, he didn't register," the clerk said. "We certainly wouldn't make a mistake about one of our regulars. That's what I told Mr. Doerner when he called, and if he hadn't gotten angry and hung up on me, I would have told him that Mr. Fraser did have a reservation but he didn't arrive. We assumed he'd changed his plans. I wish I could help you, but I can't. He isn't here, Mrs. Fraser, and he hasn't been, all week."

He isn't here, Mrs. Fraser. He hasn't been all week. Katherine sat on the bed and looked blankly at the wall. He hasn't been all week. Laughter drifted up the stairs, glasses clinked, and the chorus at the piano belted out "The Big Rock Candy Mountain," but the sounds were far off, the air dark. He isn't here, Mrs. Fraser. He hasn't been all week.

CHAPTER 2

O N Saturday morning, the debris of the party lay strewn about the house. Katherine sat at the kitchen telephone, watching her children clean up the dining room. "We need a *maid*," Todd grumbled, stacking plates precariously on the floor. "*We're* the maid," Jennifer responded. "If Dad was home," Todd said, "Mom would do it with us, like she always does." "She's waiting to hear from Daddy," said Jennifer. "She's worried." Todd looked up from his stack of plates. "She didn't say she was worried. She just said Dad would be late because he got busy in Toronto." "He always calls, doesn't he?" Jennifer demanded. "He calls in the middle of the week and he calls if he's going to be late and this week he didn't call at all." "Mom!" Todd yelled. "Has something happened to Dad?"

Katherine came to the door. Her legs felt heavy, her eyes scratchy from being up all night, waiting, watching the blazing porch light grow feeble as the sun rose. She was too tired to lie convincingly, and her children were expert at catching her in contradictions—and anyway, she thought, they deserve to know what's happening. "I don't know where he is, Todd. He's probably tied up with some business people and he'll call us as soon as he can."

"But where *is* he?" Todd insisted.

"I said I don't know," Katherine snapped. More gently she said, "I'm waiting for him to call."

The telephone rang and she flung herself across the kitchen to answer it. "You haven't heard from him?" Carl Doerner asked without preamble.

"No." In her disappointment, her legs gave way and she sat on the

16

stool at the counter. "But if he's really busy . . . Couldn't something important have come up at the last minute? Something in another city—?"

"He's heard of telephones, hasn't he? Katherine, tell me the truth: you have no idea where he is?"

"Why would I lie to you? Carl, I'm *worried*; Craig always calls on business trips, and he promised to be back on Friday. I'm going to call the Toronto police."

"Well, hold on a minute now, slow down. Craig's a big boy; we don't have to panic just because we're not sure where he is. Something unexpected probably did come up. Chances are he'll walk in any minute and we'd feel pretty silly, wouldn't we, if we had half of Canada out looking for him?"

"Half of Canada? I only said—"

"I know, I know, but I think you should wait. You watch, he'll waltz in safe and sound, wondering what the fuss is all about. I think we ought to give him time to finish his business and get home. But have him call me as soon as he gets in, will you?"

Jennifer was beside her. "What did he say?"

"That we shouldn't worry." Katherine turned on the burner beneath the tea kettle. "And he's right; Daddy can take care of himself. I think we should get to work. What would he say if he came home to a house that looked like it was hit by a cyclone?"

But all day, and into the evening, as the three of them cleaned the house, all Katherine could think of was Craig lying in the street, victim of a mugging or a hit-and-run driver or a heart attack. But wouldn't someone have found him and called her? Not if a robber had taken his wallet; that happened all the time. So she had to call the police. And if Carl didn't think she should, that was just too bad.

Still, she waited a little while longer, until Jennifer and Todd went to bed. "Wake us up when Daddy comes home," Jennifer pleaded.

"We both will," Katherine said. "Don't you think he's anxious to see you too?" But when she dialed the Toronto police, her voice failed. She felt ashamed, as if she were calling Craig a criminal—someone to be searched for, hunted down, his name bandied about by strangers. An anonymous officer at the other end was saying, "Yes? Hello? Yes?" and at last, knowing she had to do it, she forced out the words. "My husband is missing."

"Yes, ma'am," he said, so matter-of-fact Katherine wondered how many missing husbands he dealt with each week. "When did you last see him?"

"Tuesday morning when—"

"He was coming here? Toronto?"

"Yes, he went there often, on business, and he—"

"What airline did he fly?"

"Airline? I don't know; he didn't tell me. Probably Air Canada."

"And his hotel in Toronto?"

"He always stays at the Boynton. But I called them and—"

"Did he have a reservation?"

"Yes, but he never . . . he never got there."

"Never got there. When did you expect him home?"

"Friday. Yesterday afternoon. We were having a party for a friend of mine from San Francisco—"

"He didn't call or write?"

"No! If he had, I wouldn't be calling you!"

"All right, ma'am, I know this is a strain, but if you'll just be calm. We have to ask these questions; it's our job. Give me a description now."

Katherine pictured Craig, sitting at his desk, organizing neat piles of paper and binding them with rubber bands or string. "Six feet tall," she said. "Light brown hair and beard, brown eyes—"

"Weight?"

She paused. How odd, she thought. "I don't know."

"About—?"

"I guess . . . about one seventy? He takes a size forty sweater."

"Scars or distinguishing features?"

"A scar next to his right eyebrow, not a big one but you can see it. That's all. He's really—he's not unusual—just nice-looking."

"Shoe size?"

"I don't know." He must think I'm a terrible wife not to know these things. "I don't buy his shoes."

"Right." He went on and on, asking about the people Craig went to see, companies, banks—"I don't know, I don't know," Katherine repeated—and then for their charge card numbers, and she read them to him. "All right, Mrs. Fraser. We'll get back to you as soon as we can."

"Tonight?"

"Or tomorrow morning. Sit tight, ma'am; give us time to check everything out."

That night again, as the hours dragged by, Katherine huddled in a corner of the couch, drinking tea, listening for the sound of Craig's key in the front door. The house creaked and shifted in the dark and she held herself rigid, afraid to investigate the sounds. At dawn she put her head back to rest her aching neck, and fell asleep—to be awakened two hours later by the furious sibilance of Todd's and Jennifer's whispers.

"He must have called," Todd said. "And Mom's waiting for him here instead of upstairs in bed."

Jennifer bit her knuckle. "She said she'd wake us up if he called. She's down here because she doesn't like to sleep alone. Parents don't like to be in bed by themselves."

"I'll bet he called and he's on his way home with my balsa model."

"Who cares about your balsa model? I just want Daddy!"

We all want him, Katherine thought, her eyes still closed. And he hasn't called. Sunday morning and Craig hasn't called. She opened her eyes and stood up, aching as if she had not slept at all. "We all want him," she repeated aloud. "And it's hard for us, not knowing where he is. I think when he gets home we should ask him to be more considerate next time he goes away."

Todd scowled. "Maybe a truck hit him. Or a train. Or a meteor."

"Meteors don't hit Toronto," Jennifer scoffed.

"They do too. They hit everywhere. Even Vancouver. One of them could smash into our house and wipe us all out."

"Cheerful thought." Katherine smiled. For a brief moment everything seemed normal: Todd and Jennifer, the morning sun slanting into their bright living room, a beautiful ordinary June day. Soon Craig would walk in, just as Carl had predicted, apologizing because he got so busy he forgot to call, explaining his change in hotels, telling her she should know better than to worry; he could take care of himself just as he took care of his family. "I think we would have heard if a meteor had smashed into Toronto," she said. "Now, look: I'm going to take a shower and I think you'd better do the same. Isn't this the day for that picnic on Grouse Mountain? What time are you being picked up?"

"We're not going," Jennifer declared. "We're going to stay home and wait for Daddy."

"You are going," said Katherine firmly. "If he gets home before you, we'll come up and find you. Come on, now, let's get moving. Todd? Jennifer? *Please.*"

But after all it was not an ordinary day and as soon as they were gone, Katherine rushed to the telephone to call the Toronto police again. It rang as she reached it.

"Yes!" she cried. "Craig?"

"No, Mrs. Fraser," the Toronto officer said. "I'm sorry. And I'm sorry we took so long getting back to you; we wanted to be sure—"

"What? Of what?"

"That there's no trace of your husband. He's not in any hospital in the area; he's not in jail; he's not in the morgue. He didn't register at any hotel other than the Boynton. He didn't charge any meals or rent a car. Mrs. Fraser—" The officer cleared his throat. "He probably wasn't even there. We checked with the airlines. Mr. Fraser didn't fly to Toronto last Tuesday."

"That's impossible." Katherine's throat was tight.

"No, they have no record of—"

"Of course he flew to Toronto." Her voice rose. "I saw him leave for the airport on Tuesday."

"Mrs. Fraser, don't you understand? *He never used his ticket.* Either something happened to him in Vancouver, before he got to the airport, or he never intended to take that flight."

"How dare you—! How dare you accuse my husband of lying to me! Who do you think you are—" She put down the telephone, trying to draw a breath. She heard the officer repeatedly calling her name, but his voice in the receiver was so tiny and distant she knew it had nothing to do with her. She hung up on it.

But in a minute, with frantic urgency, she dialed the Vancouver police. Craig never lied to her. Something terrible had happened to him, and if the Toronto people were telling the truth, it had happened in Vancouver. Right here, and all week she had had no idea of it. She'd been happy and busy, planning the party, and the only time she'd thought of Craig was when she felt annoyed with him for not being there to help her. And all that time he was ill, or injured, or dead. I should have known, she thought. When he didn't call.

"My husband is missing," she said when a policeman answered, squeezing the words once more through her locked throat, and then nervously paced her living room, waiting for someone to arrive.

Two young officers came, carrying clipboards and printed forms, and they checked off categories and carefully wrote Craig's description as Katherine recited it for the second time that day. They asked for a recent picture and Katherine gave them one and then, synchronized and efficient, they took turns asking questions and writing answers. As she told them what the Toronto police had said about the airlines, Katherine caught a look between them. "What is it?" she asked. "If there is something you haven't told me—"

"No, ma'am," one of them said. "We were wondering what you haven't told *us.*"

Katherine shook her head. "Nothing." A wave of exhaustion from two sleepless nights engulfed her and she closed her eyes. If she could just sink into bed and turn away, shut out everything... But the officers were rustling impatiently and she forced her eyes open. "Nothing. What else could there be?"

"Ah . . . your husband's lady friends?" the officer suggested. "Any you know of, that is. Lots of wives don't, so you shouldn't feel ashamed if . . ." His voice trailed away at Katherine's look.

"What we mean," the other one put in helpfully, "is that people don't just vanish without a reason. Husbands have *reasons* for disappearing. It wouldn't necessarily be a lady friend. You understand" —he was so earnest, Katherine thought, and so clumsy; why were boys sent to do this job?— "we're not suggesting anything in particular. Maybe the two of you were having problems? Or your husband piled up gambling IOUs? Maybe he's been despondent lately. Have you looked for a suicide note? They have *reasons*, Mrs. Fraser, that's all; we're certainly not here to criticize you or your husband—that's the way things *happen*."

"Not to us." Katherine's lips were stiff and she was too tired even to be indignant, as she had been with the Toronto officer. "My husband and I have been married for ten years and I know he wouldn't stay away if he could help it. You don't know anything about him; you don't know what happened to him."

"No ma'am; that's true. But *did* he like the ladies?"

The telephone rang and Katherine raced to the kitchen, her heart pounding. "My dear," said Sarah Murphy, her voice rippling with curiosity. "Is everything all right? I just glanced out my window and saw the police car."

Katherine's shoulders slumped. "Sarah, I can't talk now."

"It's not a heart attack, is it? Craig, I mean? Katherine? Is Craig all right?"

"Craig isn't home. Sarah, I have to go—"

"But he did get back. Didn't he?"

"Sarah, I'll talk to you later—"

"Yes, you don't want to keep the police waiting. But Katherine, I'm here, you know, if you need me."

"Yes—"

"I'm always here, always available."

"I know. I'll call you later, Sarah."

The police officers were at the front door. "We'll send out a bulletin on your husband, Mrs. Fraser, and we'll let you know if we hear anything. But you really ought to look around for clues; that's probably the only way we'll find him."

Don't they understand that my husband may be dead? Katherine watched them walk past her flower gardens and disappear beyond the hedge. Then, without planning it, she found herself sitting at Craig's desk. Not looking for clues, she thought; that was ridiculous. But perhaps he'd left a schedule of appointments; places she could call. That was all she was looking for.

She felt like a trespasser. It was Craig's desk; she never used it. Superstitiously, she thought she might be making it more likely that he was dead. "Oh, don't be stupid," she said aloud, and quickly pulled open all the drawers.

Gradually, she stopped feeling guilty as her puzzlement grew. Going through drawers and pigeonholes, lifting and putting back neat folders and packets of papers, she found Craig's notes on buildings Vancouver Construction had built, sketches for the wood carvings he made in his spare time, copies of expense forms he had submitted for business trips, including frequent trips to Calgary (he'd never told her he had a long-term job in Calgary), past-due membership notices from his private club, a batch of unpaid department store bills, and lined pads of paper covered with scribbled numbers—added, subtracted, multiplied, crossed out with angry X's, then repeated in different combinations.

Katherine pondered the numbers. Craig always paid the bills; he'd never even hinted about debts. We'll have to talk about it, she thought, as soon as he gets home... Then, behind a box of business cards in the bottom drawer, she found a small picture, torn raggedly from a larger one. Disquieted, she gazed at the lovely girl laughing into the camera; someone she had never met. *I didn't know Craig kept a picture of an early love. Something else he never told me.*

"Mom!" Todd cried, throwing open the front door. "Mrs. Murphy says the police were here. What happened to Daddy? He isn't dead, is he?"

Jennifer jabbed him with her elbow. "Don't *say* it." She looked at Katherine. "What did they want?"

"I asked them to find out if Daddy's been in an accident." Katherine steadied her voice. "They can check hospitals faster than we can. That's all they're doing. How was your picnic? Tell me about it while we make dinner."

They were subdued, but they talked and helped her as they did every evening and once again, for a few peaceful moments, Katherine thought that everything would be fine; how could anything bad happen when her house seemed so normal? And then they heard the front door open and with a yell Todd and Jennifer tore through the dining and living rooms with Katherine just behind them. But it was not Craig; it was Carl Doerner.

"The door was open," he apologized, striding in. "I didn't hear from

Craig; did you forget to tell him to call me?" He stopped in the middle of the living room, his back to Katherine. When she was silent, he let out a long sigh and turned to face her. "Nothing? Not a word?"

She shook her head.

"Damn, damn, damn." His large head, with its mane of gray hair, moved slowly back and forth. "I'm sorry, Katherine. I hoped it wasn't true."

Uneasy, Katherine turned to Todd and Jennifer. "Would you set the table? I'll be there in a few minutes." Jennifer made a disgusted sound but the two of them left the room. "What does that mean?" Katherine asked Carl.

"He's skipped. I wish I could spare you this, but—"

"What are you talking about? Skipped? You mean ran away? He had nothing to run away from. And he wouldn't anyway. You know him, Carl; he's not the kind of man to run away from anything."

"Katherine, I'm sorry." Restlessly, Doerner moved about the room, shoving furniture out of his way. Katherine thought how out of place he looked in the bright room with its flowered furniture and drapes—like a shaggy bear in a summer garden. "I'm sorry," he repeated, his voice heavy and slow. "But Craig's been stealing company funds for over two years."

"Stealing! Carl, are you mad?"

"Nearly seventy-five thousand dollars. The accountant caught it, and Craig and I had it out and he admitted it: he made up fake companies, sold them fake materials, authorized payments to himself—it's complicated, but I can show you how it worked if you want. He asked me to give him a week and—"

"It's not true!"

"He asked for a week to raise some money, and I believed he meant it, so I promised not to go to the police."

"I don't believe it; there's been a—"

Doerner pulled a thick envelope from his pocket and held it out to her. "Statements. From the accountants, the solicitors—" When she did not move, his hand dropped. "God damn it, Katherine, why would I make this up? Craig was more a son to me than a partner; I was going to retire and sell him the company in a couple of years. Now what the hell am I going to do?"

"Craig stole?" Katherine asked numbly. "He stole from the company?"

"That's what I said."

"Well, you're wrong. Why are you so sure it was Craig? Why are you blaming him—?"

"I'm not blaming him; *he admitted it*. Said your house set him back more than he expected, and there were other things—he wouldn't say what—but he said he'd pay it back, every damn cent. And I trusted him! I let him go!"

"When?"

"What?"

"When did you and Craig talk about . . . about the money?"

"Monday. Last Monday. He said he'd have some of it by Friday and a plan to pay off the rest. He was crying. Damn it, so was I. Now what the hell can I do? I don't *want* to charge him with embezzling!"

"Wait, please, just wait a minute." Katherine was dizzy. Doerner had pushed the furniture out of place and the room seemed to be shifting, like the deck of a ship in a storm. Monday. And on Tuesday, even though she asked him to stay home that week, he rushed off to Toronto.

He kissed me goodbye and said—I'm sorry; I love you.

She clasped her hands. "What are you going to do?"

Doerner grunted. "Up to now I've kept my word. But damn it, he betrayed me! Don't you see that I've got to report this? Too many people are involved—the insurance company, our solicitor, the accountant— I have no choice; I have to go to the police!"

Like a missile, Todd flung himself across the room at Doerner. "You can't go to the police about my Dad, you bastard; you're a *liar*—!"

"Todd!" Katherine pulled Todd's battering hands away from Doerner and knelt to hold him against her. As he buried his face in her shoulder, crying noisily, she saw Jennifer watching stonily from the doorway.

"Just a minute," she said to Doerner. Taking Jennifer and Todd by the hand, she led them upstairs. "I promise we'll talk about this in a few minutes." Her voice was shaky and she cleared her throat. "But I want you up here. I do not want you downstairs. Is that clear?" When they nodded, their eyes wide and blank, she went slowly downstairs. Doerner was still in the middle of the room.

"Betrayed his kids, too." His face was dark. "Son of a bitch. Bad enough he let me down, but to do that to you and the kids . . . by God he deserves whatever he gets! I treated him like a son but now he's going to pay—!"

"Carl, don't go to the police. Please. Can't you wait? One more day, just until tomorrow. Craig must have been on his way home when something happened . . . he's ill or hurt . . . you don't know! If he really did take that money he wouldn't run away; he'd make it up to you. We'd both make it up to you. Please, Carl. You've waited this long. Please."

Doerner flung out his hands. "What the hell. One more day. To-morrow's Monday; I'll call you at noon. I can't wait any longer than that." Katherine nodded. "Well, then." He sighed. "He really left you in the lurch. I wish there was something—" He waited but Katherine was silent. "Well, then—" Another moment and he was gone, passing beneath the porch light that was blazing for the third night in a row.

A few more hours for Craig, Katherine thought. I don't even know if he needs them. Or what else he might need. *Not knowing* was a leaden weight inside her, so heavy it made her feel sick. She thought of the dinner they had made and could not imagine eating it.

But they all picked at it while Katherine told Jennifer and Todd, sketchily, what Doerner had said. "We only have his word for it," she finished, refusing to think about the envelope he'd offered her; it could have been anything. "We won't know the real story until Daddy gets back. All we can do is wait. We'll hear from the police, or Daddy will walk in the front door and explain everything."

"Daddy wouldn't run away," Jennifer said.

"Of course not." Katherine remembered the jokes she'd heard about wives who preferred to think that an overdue husband was injured rather than unfaithful. Which do I want, she wondered grimly. Craig in an accident or Craig running from a crime?

It kept her awake for another night in their cold bed. *Craig, I want you home.* She was crying. *Please come home. I want you safe, and everything the way it used to be.* But the next day, when Doerner called exactly at noon, she had nothing to tell him. And so he called the police.

An hour later, a different pair of officers appeared at her door, older than the first two, with different questions and a keener scrutiny of Katherine and her house.

"Nice," said one, pacing off the living room and admiring the view through the curved wall of windows. "My wife," said the other, "always wanted to live in West Vancouver. Too expensive for us; too expensive for most people." When Katherine did not respond, they sat down and asked questions, hammering at her husband's purchasing habits, travel, debts, gambling, women, gifts, drinking, drugs... But Katherine had become cautious. She did not mention Craig's desk with its unpaid bills, scribbled numbers and overdrawn notices from the bank. Instead she told them, truthfully, that her husband had not changed in the ten years they'd been married; that he was generous to his family but careful with money; that he did not gamble, drank very little, dressed simply and did not use drugs.

After an hour, the policemen exchanged glances. "We have to know about his private life, Mrs. Fraser," said one. "We've issued a warrant for his arrest, and of course we'll find him if he's alive, but it would be easier, especially for you and your children, if we had the names of his friends."

"You mean women."

"That's what it usually comes down to."

"There are no women," she said without emotion. She seemed to have none left. Like an automaton, she repeated her denials, looking at her hands, feeling the room slide away as waves of sleep lapped at her.

"Well, we'll be off," they said at last. "Unless there's something more you want to say." Katherine did not move. "You know where to reach us if you think of something." She nodded. "Well, then, we'll be talking to you. And Mrs. Fraser." At the altered voice, she looked up. "We'd appreciate it if you didn't leave town."

In less than an hour the first reporter rang her doorbell. Katherine, as wary now as a trapped animal, stood in the doorway, keeping him on the front porch. "I have nothing to tell you," she said.

He waved his pencil as if conducting with a baton. "Mrs. Fraser, did you and your husband quarrel? Did you have—um—intimate problems? Did your husband buy jewelry? Give gifts to friends? Did he travel often? Where did he stay when he traveled? Hotels, or—um—with a friend?"

Katherine clung to the doorjamb, shaking her head. "It's none of your business," she said and slammed the door in his face.

But on Tuesday morning, her husband's picture with his faint, sad smile looked up at her from the front page of the *Vancouver News*. "Craig Fraser," she read, "a partner in Vancouver Construction, a firm that has built some of Vancouver's major office buildings and residences, is wanted by the police for questioning in connection with a seventy-five-thousand-dollar embezzlement from his company. He has been missing since last Tuesday, when, according to his wife in a statement to the police, he said he was going to Toronto. Mrs. Fraser refuses to speak to reporters. Police in Canadian provinces and the border cities of the United States are searching for him; an arrest, they say, is expected shortly."

The stark words and Craig's picture—a public figure, a wanted man— were like a strong wind slamming shut a door Katherine had tried to keep open. For the first time she let the thought form and settle within her. *He is not coming home.*

CHAPTER 3

Ross Hayward put down his newspaper and looked out the window as the plane descended over Vancouver. Bordered on two sides by water, the city's skyscrapers seemed to float in the early morning sun with a haze of mountains on the horizon. It reminded Ross of the city he had just left; someone from San Francisco could feel at home here. The thought made him glance again at the newspaper in his lap. He had read and reread the story of embezzlement and flight, but it was the photograph that he had been studying for two days: the bearded man with his faint, sad smile. "Possibly," he murmured. "But probably not; too incredible to believe..."

In the terminal, he found a telephone directory and looked up Craig Fraser's address. He did not call ahead; he had to surprise the wife and watch her face; otherwise, he'd have had no reason to make the trip.

"You must go there," Victoria had said the day before. "Telephoning won't do." She had burst into his conference room just ahead of his protesting secretary, stopping the staff assistant to the mayor of San Francisco in the middle of a sentence. "Ross, I must talk to you. Now." Her hair was windblown and the silk scarf at her neck askew—the first time in his thirty-five years that Ross had seen his grandmother even faintly disheveled or permitting herself to show emotion in public.

He pushed back his chair at the head of the conference table. "I think you all know my grandmother," he said, aware that Victoria was on first-name terms with many of these men and women, dining and sitting on boards of directors with them, and entertaining them in her home. She

27

greeted them brusquely and Ross took her arm. "If you'll excuse me a moment—you can criticize my plans without the static of my biased opinion."

The city director of planning waved a hand. "We haven't discussed rents—"

"The figures are on page forty. If you'll go over them, I won't be long." Ross ushered Victoria through a door into his office, leaving behind San Francisco's top government officials, who'd been studying and debating his architectural plans for months. And it would be months more before they approved every detail so that work on the three-hundred-million-dollar project, called BayBridge Plaza, could begin. He wanted to be with them, defending his ideas, speeding the process along, but his grandmother demanded his attention. He sat beside her on the couch. "Tell me what's happened."

"Look at this." Her trembling hand held out a copy of the *Vancouver News.* "Tobias saw it at one of those international newsstands. Craig's picture—"

Her voice broke on Craig's name. Ross looked at the front-page picture, read the story and looked again, remembering Craig. Slowly he shook his head. This was a stranger, with a high forehead, full face and deep lines on either side of his nose, disappearing into a heavy beard. Not Craig, who had been thin and boyish, hair falling over his forehead, shadowed hollows in his cheeks. Still, there was something about the smile, and the clinging sadness of the eyes...

"Of course there's the beard," said Victoria. "And he's much older. But the eyes! And that smile! Ross? Isn't it Craig?"

Ross shook his head, anxious to get back to his meeting. "I doubt it. There is a resemblance, but only a suggestion of one; it's interesting, but—"

"*Interesting!* What is the matter with you?" She sat straight, her eyes blazing at him. "Do you think I don't know my own grandson? And even if, perhaps, I had some doubt, I thought I could count on your curiosity and stubbornness—but all you do is wave aside this *interesting* resemblance. What in heaven's name is wrong with you?" She saw him glance at the door to the conference room. "Well—you want to get back. Why don't you simply agree to do what I ask? Then I'll leave you alone."

Ross laughed and gently adjusted the scarf at his grandmother's throat. "All right; what is it you're asking me to do?"

"Go up there. Find out the truth for me."

"To Vancouver? My dear, you can't ask me to drop everything to search out a stranger just because he seems to resemble someone you haven't seen for fifteen years."

"Will you stop being so cautious! I don't think this is a stranger and I'm asking you to find out for me. For heaven's sake, who else can I ask?"

"Tobias," Ross suggested. "Claude—"

"For some favors. Not this one. Ross, I *must know.*"

Ross was rereading the story. "He's disappeared, it says. I wouldn't be able to see him."

"His wife. His children. Photographs. Good heavens, boy, are you going to make me beg?"

"No." Ross smiled and took her hand. Of all the family, he felt closest to Victoria. He would not make her beg. "But I can't get away this week—" His private telephone rang and he made a gesture of apology as he answered it.

His brother's voice charged at him. "Someone just called to tell me Craig's picture is in yesterday's *Vancouver News.*"

Ross tensed. "It's hardly that certain."

"You've seen it?"

"Yes. There's a curious resemblance. Nothing more."

"I'm going up there to find out. Read me the story so I'll have all the information."

"Derek, wait a minute. I've already made arrangements to go and there's no need for both of us to be there. I'll call you when I get back."

"*You're* going to Vancouver? To check out a long shot on Craig?"

"I'm going to Vancouver—"

"What the hell for? It's nothing to you if he—"

"—and I'll call you when I get back."

Victoria smiled serenely as he hung up the telephone. She straightened her scarf and ran a small brush through her white curls. "Thank you. How clever of you to keep Derek out of it. What a dreadful mess he might have made."

Ross bent down to kiss her cheek. "I would have gone anyway. For you."

"I never doubted it, my dear. When will you go?"

"Tomorrow."

From his taxi, driving through the city streets and across Lions Gate Bridge to the suburb of West Vancouver, Ross noted the buildings that had gone up since his last visit, six years earlier. He had just opened his own firm in San Francisco and had been meeting with Vancouver city planners about the restoration of decaying neighborhoods. At the end of the day, he'd gone back alone to the European boutiques of Robsonstrasse to shop for Melanie and the children. Might Craig have been here then— even, perhaps, passing him on the street? For God's sake, he thought; of course he hadn't. Craig had been dead for fifteen years, and this trip was a waste of time.

The houses of West Vancouver were built into wooded hills. Set back from the road, they offered passersby glimpses of natural wood and stone, wide windows, and terraced yards. As Ross opened his window to let in the scents of June, the taxi came to a stop beside a boxwood hedge. Beyond it, at the crest of a gentle slope, was a house smaller than its neighbors but skillfully designed to look larger by taking advantage of the contour of the land. Two children, a boy and a girl, ran down the walk and stopped a short distance away, watching gravely while Ross paid the driver. Turning, he got a good look at the boy and drew a sharp breath. Everything else faded; only the boy was clear: his compact body, his thin face tilted in curious examination, and the impatient gesture with which he pushed blond hair away from bright brown eyes.

"I guess you're not a detective," the boy said. "They all have cars. And you're not a policeman. So what are you?"

He was about eight, Ross thought, and it might be nothing more than coincidence.

"What *are* you?" the boy repeated.

"Not a detective," Ross said to the boy. "Have detectives been here?"

"Not yet—I don't think—but my dad was supposed to be home last Friday and lots of people are looking for—"

"We don't answer questions from strangers," the girl broke in.

"But you ask them," Ross said, smiling at her. She was about nine, his son's age, and she promised to be a beauty, with heavy dark hair and high cheekbones in a delicate face. Her mouth was more determined than her brother's and her enormous hazel eyes were bold. For the first time, Ross wondered about their mother.

"It's our house," the girl said firmly. "We're supposed to ask questions. I'll bet you ask plenty when strangers come to your house."

He smiled again, liking her spirit, wanting her to like him. "You're right, I do. Especially when they don't introduce themselves. My name is Ross Hayward. I'm an architect, I live in San Francisco and I've come to see your mother, to talk to her about your father. I'd like to help," he added, though he had not intended to say any such thing. "If there's anything I can do."

They studied him, shading their eyes against the noon sunlight. The girl made the decision. "I'm Jennifer Fraser. This is my brother, Todd. Mother is in the house and I think it's all right if you come in. You can follow us."

"Thank you." Ross followed them up the curving walk, thinking,

Jennifer. Her name is Jennifer. As they reached the front door he slowed. The children had left it open and for a fleeting moment it seemed to be an entrance to a mysterious cave.

"Don't worry," Jennifer said impatiently. "I said it was all right for you to come in. I'll get Mother." She ran off as Todd led Ross through an arch into the living room.

After the shadowed entrance hall, the brightness was striking. A curved wall of windows looked south and west, across the deep blue of the bay to the city of Vancouver and, beyond it, Vancouver Island. Though the house was only about two hundred feet above the water, the expansive view gave an illusion of greater height and also made the living room seem twice as large as it really was. Ross, the architect, the builder, scanned the room, running his hand along the window frames. "Well done," he murmured, admiring the vision of another architect and builder.

"I beg your pardon?" a voice said behind him, and he turned as Jennifer came in with her mother.

"I was admiring the windows," he said. "They're very fine."

"My husband designed them." She stopped, keeping the length of the room between them. "I trust Jennifer's instincts, but I'd rather not have visitors right now, so if you'll just tell me why you've come—"

He walked to her and held out his hand. "Ross Hayward," he said, watching for her reaction as she briefly put her hand in his, but there was nothing; either she did not recognize the name or she was so exhausted she could not respond. He could see her exhaustion: an aching weariness etched in her face, her body swaying slightly as she took her hand from his and rested it against the doorjamb, her neck muscles tense with the effort of holding up her head. But the architect and artist in him saw, beneath her pale exhaustion, the delicate structure of her face—high cheekbones, a broad, clear forehead, long-lashed eyes with a faint upward turn at the corners, a generous mouth. Her dark hair was pulled carelessly back, but a few tendrils escaped the rubber band that held it and clung to her cheeks. In better times, Ross thought, she could be a lovely woman, and he found himself wanting to help her, to ease the strain in her face, to see her smile.

Instead, she frowned, meeting his searching look with her own puzzled one. Twice she began to say something, then caught herself. Finally, she said, "I asked why you've come. If you won't tell me, you'll have to leave."

"Mrs. Fraser," he said. "Does my name mean anything to you?"

"Your name?"

"Hayward."

She shook her head. "Why should it?"

"Your husband never mentioned it?" Again she shook her head and Ross, watching her closely, said, "He never . . . used it?"

"Of course not; why would he? He has his own name."

Ross nodded. He looked at Jennifer and Todd, standing silently behind their mother. "I think—" he began gently.

"That's not fair!" Jennifer cried, knowing what was coming. "We let you in! You can't tell us to leave!"

Katherine felt a chill of warning. "Maybe we should go along with this," she said slowly to Jennifer. "I don't know what it's about, but— why don't you and Todd wait in the front yard? I'll call you as soon as Mr. Hayward finishes all his secrets."

"Mother, it's not fair!"

"I know. I want you to do it anyway."

Jennifer shrugged glumly. She took Todd's hand. "Come on. Nobody wants us."

Ross and Katherine watched them leave. "I like them," he said. "I have two of my own, about their age—"

"Do you," she responded distantly, and Ross fell silent, feeling the awkwardness of his intrusion. Why should she be interested in anything about him, except why he had come?

"Could we sit down?" he asked and led the way to the couch where they sat at opposite ends, facing each other. Katherine could not take her eyes off him. Tall, broad-shouldered, with an easy stride, he had a narrow, tanned face that was stern in repose, then suddenly lightened by the warmth of his smile. His dark eyes were deep-set beneath heavy brows and unruly dark blond hair, and he wore his clothes with the confident air of a man accustomed to wealth. He was everything that Craig was not—and yet, somehow, the longer Katherine looked at him, the more he reminded her of Craig.

"I'm sorry," she said, turning away, picking up a thread from the carpet. "I know I'm staring, but you remind me of . . . something about you reminds me of my husband. I don't know what it is, you're really quite different from Craig, but something about you . . ." She faltered. "It's absurd, I know; I suppose I'll see Craig everywhere, now that—" She stopped again and took a breath. "What is it you want?"

Ross opened his briefcase and took out the newspaper folded at the picture he had been looking at on the plane. "I saw this yesterday in San Francisco." He held it out, but Katherine, recognizing it, made no move to take it. A little awkwardly, he put it on the couch between them. "I have a cousin," he began. "Or I had one. Craig Hayward." From an inner pocket he pulled out a small photograph and laid it beside the newspaper. "This was taken in 1966, when he was twenty-two. He was home from college for the summer, in San Francisco. A month later he was killed in an accident. At least, we thought he was killed. But when we saw this newspaper, it seemed a good idea to talk to you."

There was a silence. "Yes?" Katherine said politely. Relief was sweeping through her and she barely glanced at the picture. He had nothing important to tell her. "I still don't know what you want from me."

"Some of my family," Ross said carefully, "think the two pictures are the same man."

Katherine frowned. "I thought you said your cousin is dead."

"We thought he was dead."

"Well, it doesn't matter whether he is or not. My husband has nothing to do with him. He has a different name; he comes from Vancouver, not San Francisco; and he doesn't look anything like your picture. Even if he did, what would it mean? The world is full of people who look like other people and no one thinks anything of it. I'm sorry you've had a trip for nothing, but you're wasting your time, and mine, too, so if you'll please go—"

"You're probably right," Ross agreed, but he stayed where he was, looking from the photograph to the newspaper picture and then around the room. "But as long as I'm here, I'd appreciate it if you'd answer a few questions. If you don't mind."

"I do mind." There was something about his voice, too, that reminded her of Craig, and she was becoming uncomfortable.

"Mrs. Fraser," said Ross quietly. "Do you really believe your husband told you everything about himself? Isn't it possible that he had some secrets from you, that he kept a part of himself separate—"

"No!" Abruptly, Katherine stood up, hating him for making her lie. "It is not possible and it is none of your business; nothing here is any of your business!"

He sat still, looking up at her. "I want a few answers. Then I'll leave. The more you help me, the sooner that will be."

"I can't help you! Can't you understand that? Can't you understand that I have no interest in you or your cousin? You said yourself there was probably nothing in it; what more do you want? You walk in here and accuse my husband of being someone else, which is ridiculous; you show me a picture that doesn't look at all like him; and you expect me to let you talk all day about it? I have other things to think about and I want you to go. I don't even know why you came here, trying to upset us—"

"I'm not here to upset you. I'm here because my grandmother sent me."

The unexpectedness of it caught Katherine in mid-flight. She tried to picture Ross's grandmother—how old she must be!—sending him to Vancouver on a wild goose chase. Ross leaned forward. "You see, Victoria is absolutely certain this is *her* Craig, her grandson, and she asked me—instructed me," he added with a private smile of such tenderness that for a moment Katherine liked him. "Instructed me to drop everything and come to Vancouver to confirm it."

"And if you found it wasn't true?"

"I would tell her that and she would accept it. After all, she'd already lost him once."

"Lost him." For the first time, Katherine picked up the picture and really looked at it. A thin young man, clean-shaven, wearing a sports shirt open at the neck, tilting his head and smiling, but with an air of sadness, as if a thought or a memory haunted him. Shakily, she sat down. The eyes were like Craig's. The face was Todd's.

Ross was watching her. "You see why I wanted answers."

Stalling while she tried to think, Katherine asked, "What does that mean—lost him?"

"He disappeared. There was a sailing accident in San Francisco Bay and we never saw him again. We assumed he drowned and was swept away. The current is especially strong near the Golden Gate Bridge, where it happened. But he was very strong—a champion long-distance runner in high school and college. It's possible that he was able to swim to shore. And then walk away."

"But why would anyone do that?"

"I don't know. Shock, perhaps. He'd jumped in the water to save his sister when she fell overboard."

"And—did he?"

Ross shook his head. "She died."

"That's . . . terrible. But still—"

"Her name was Jennifer."

"Oh." It was like a long sigh.

"And Craig never could face his own failures. He always ran away from them."

The way your husband did. The unspoken words hovered in the quiet room. But we don't know that, Katherine argued silently; we don't even know if he's alive. She thrust the picture at Ross. "Your grandmother is wrong. It's nothing more than a resemblance. My husband didn't even have a grandmother, at least none that he knew. He had no family at all; he was an orphan, just as I was. It was one of the things we talked about: how much we wanted a family."

"No family. Who brought him up?"

"Oh, foster parents, but we meant we wanted a loving family. The Driscolls fed and clothed him but they didn't—"

"The Driscolls? That was the name he gave you?"

The note in his voice stopped her. "Do you know them?"

"My cousin and I used to play a game—that we were kidnaped and gave our kidnapers such a hard time they paid us to escape from them. We made it up from an O'Henry story we liked, called 'The Ransom of Red Chief.' One of the kidnapers in the story, and in our game, was named Driscoll."

In the silence Katherine heard the pounding of her heart. It's because he's so serious, she thought; he makes these coincidences sound more important than they are. "I'm not interested in your childhood games," she said, making a move to stand up. "And if that's all you have to say, you'll really have to leave. We have so many things to do—"

"You have nothing to do but wait," Ross said coldly. "Look, damn it, I don't like this any better than you do. I didn't even want to come up here—I thought it was a waste of time—but now I have the damndest feeling that it's not. In any event, there are too many things I can't explain, and I don't like loose ends. I'd think you wouldn't either; don't you want to know the truth? I want your help; whatever you can give me—"

"I can't give you anything!"

"Photographs. Letters. A diary. Didn't your husband have a desk? Craig always had one at home, with everything sorted out, alphabetized, organized into neat packs held with rubber bands or pieces of string that he'd collect and wind around his finger—"

"So what?" Katherine cried. "Millions of people organize their desks that way!"

"Or," he went on, watching her. "You can tell me what you thought when you looked at this picture. Todd. Is that right? I think it is; when I first saw him, I thought I was looking at Craig at that age. Craig and I grew up together; he was only two years older—that would make him thirty-seven now; is that your husband's age?—and we were as close as brothers, especially since neither of us liked Derek, who really is my brother. Derek is one year older than I. We all came in a rush, as Victoria liked to say. Jennifer, too: if she'd lived, she'd be thirty-three now. And Todd is the image of Craig at seven or eight. Which is he?"

"What?"

"Todd. Is he seven or eight?"

"Eight." Katherine walked to the arch that led to the entrance hall. Through the open front door she saw Todd and Jennifer sitting cross-legged on the grass, not talking, not moving. Waiting. For their father, for news of their father, for something to happen. She shivered. Something was happening. She turned back to Ross, thinking that she liked his face, its strong lines, the steady, absorbed way he looked at her, his smile when he talked about his grandmother. Briefly she wished they could like each other, because she had no one to talk to. No one had called, no one had come by, not even Sarah Murphy, since the newspaper story about the embezzlement had appeared two days ago. But there was no way Ross could be their friend.

"I want you to leave," she said again. He was silhouetted against the wall of windows and she could not see his face; when he did not answer she went on. "You've told me your story, this crazy story that you're determined to believe, no matter what I think. Well, I'll tell you what I think. I'm sure there was a Craig Hayward who resembles my son, but it's just a coincidence and that's your problem, not mine. I married Craig Fraser, I've lived with him for ten years and I *know him*. You can't walk in here and tell me I don't know my own husband, that he's kept a lifetime of secrets from me about San Francisco and a grandmother and an entire family I never heard of. Do you think I'm a child? I'm sorry you're disappointed, but not one word you've said is the truth...well, I suppose you do have a cousin named Craig, or you did, but nothing else is true, nothing else, *nothing else*..."

Her words fell away in the silent room. Ross walked toward her and she saw his dark eyes, oddly gentle in his stern face. His voice, when he spoke, was so quiet it took her a minute to feel the impact of his words. "My cousin, Craig Hayward, his sister Jennifer, my brother Derek and I grew up in San Francisco, in a neighborhood called Sea Cliff, and spent our weekends swimming or sailing or hiking in the mountains. Craig always said that someday he would build a house high up, with a curved wall of windows overlooking mountains—or water."

Instinctively, Katherine looked past him, through the curved windows, at the sunlit bay at the base of their hill.

"He read a lot," Ross went on. "Mostly spy stories and histories. He was good with his hands and liked to make wood carvings, especially figures of people. But his favorite carvings were the soapstone ones made by Eskimos. Like this one." He picked up an eight-inch black whale that Craig had bought a year ago from Hank Aylmer, a friend who bought carvings in Eskimo villages to sell in the United States.

Katherine closed her eyes, wishing Ross Hayward gone. He waited, and in the dense silence, she felt the force of Craig's absence. She had been too bewildered, too busy making telephone calls and talking to the police and trying to deal with Jennifer and Todd to feel the reality of it, but in that moment the full impact struck her. She stood in her house and Craig was nowhere in it. She felt him everywhere but he was nowhere. It was not the same as saying: Craig isn't in the living room or the dining room or even in Vancouver. It was as if she had to say, *Craig is not.*

Didn't this man understand that that was what she had to think about? Why did he force this relentless outpouring of information on her when she had to think about a house without Craig? She opened her eyes to tell him, but as soon as she did, he began talking again.

"And my cousin liked the construction business. We were in it together: our grandfather, Hugh, who died in 1964; his sons Jason and Curt; and the three of us—Craig was Jason's son; Derek and I are Curt's sons. Every summer we worked in our family's company; we'd done it since we were kids, sweeping out offices, doing errands, tagging along on site inspections, later helping with blueprints. Craig loved it; he couldn't wait to finish college and work full time. He was on a job with my father the summer Jennifer was killed and he disappeared. Are there any photographs in the desk in that room?"

Trembling, Katherine folded her arms rigidly to keep her body still. She didn't have to tell him anything. Without her help, he would have to leave; she would never see him again; she could forget he'd ever been here.

But she knew it was too late for that. Because he was right: she did want to know the truth. Walking around him, she went into the study and took from the top drawer of Craig's desk the picture she had found. Wordlessly, she handed it to him and together they looked at the lovely girl laughing in the sunlight.

Ross let out a long breath. "Dear God." Once again he opened his briefcase and handed Katherine another picture, this one of four people on a sailboat: Ross on deck, hoisting the sail; the young Craig of the first picture at the wheel; a stranger, handsome and aloof, in the cockpit, and beside him the lovely girl, shading her eyes as she watched the sail rise up the mast.

"Jennifer," Ross said simply. "Craig's sister."

CHAPTER 4

DEREK Hayward refilled his glass with the special Scotch his grandmother kept on hand for his visits and looked thoughtfully across the room at the woman his brother had foisted on the family: a Canadian housewife as out of place in Victoria's elegant home as a field mouse among orchids. Katherine Fraser. Wife of Craig Fraser. Who, if Ross had it straight, was in fact their cousin Craig Hayward. Long gone, long forgotten. They'd thought.

Why the hell had Ross been in such a hurry to bring her here? Without giving them a chance to talk about her, even to get used to the idea of her, he decided *on his own* to invite her and her offspring to meet them. And without a whimper Victoria went along. So here they were—a family dinner. Even Jason and Ann, coming out of hiding in Maine to meet Katherine Fraser and hear about their son, their golden boy. Who, after all, hadn't drowned fifteen years ago. Who had only run away. And now, it seemed, had done it again.

Derek smiled thinly. Trust Craig, he thought, to act like Craig. Absently swirling his Scotch, he watched Katherine as she talked to the rest of the family, and wondered what she was like beneath that drab facade. There had to be more, he thought; Craig had always liked good-looking women. But this one had no poise or sophistication, no glamour, no beauty... well, maybe. Good bone structure in her face, unusual eyes— might be interesting if she fixed herself up and stood straight instead of dragging down every line of her face and body. He shrugged. What difference did it make? If she really was Cousin Craig's wife—and the

photograph she'd shown Ross seemed to prove it—the only thing that
mattered was that she was here, a stand-in for her husband, and they'd
have to find out what she wanted from them, and what she really knew
about Craig.

The others were clustered about her at one end of the vast drawing
room of Victoria's penthouse. Almost fifteen years since they were all
together, but still they were more interested in Craig's wife than in each
other. Even absent, the son of a bitch managed to make himself the
center of attention. Something else he'd always done.

Derek looked away, giving the room a cursory inspection as he did on
every visit, to make sure Victoria was keeping the place up. It was worth
a fortune; far more than the fortune that had been spent on it since his
grandfather bought the top two floors of the building and remodeled them
twenty-five years ago. The old man had been a genius, Derek reflected.
Long before restoration became chic, he made the Hayward name famous
for the kind of expensive custom work that rebuilt without destroying the
best of the old. And everything he knew went into his own home, from
the smallest carved moldings to the huge marble fireplaces and the ceiling-
high Tiffany window. Superb workmanship. It had been at the heart of
every lesson Hugh Hayward's grandsons learned under his direction and
still remembered and used, even if it was in the modern glass and steel
towers that Derek preferred. At least, Derek amended, I remember, and
I suppose Ross does. Who knows what Craig remembers?

Craig again. Always there. Intruding. Across the room, that Canadian
housewife stood between Ross and Victoria, reminding everyone that he
was alive and could turn up any day. Possibly in Vancouver but, now
that Ross had brought her here, just as likely in San Francisco, back to
their big happy family and the construction company that Derek had
been running for years without interference.

"A fearsome, ferocious frown," Melanie commented lightly, coming
up beside him. "Who's the latest target?" She followed his gaze. "Oh.
Ross's new toy."

He took a moment to approve her sleek good looks and the curve of
her silk dress, then asked casually, "And what do you make of her?"

She pursed her lips. "A good wife never comments on her husband's
toys."

"My dear Melanie, you know better than to suggest that my brother
collects other women. Or plays with them." Shifting his glass, his hand
brushed her bare arm. "If you're looking for reasons to divorce him, you'll
have to look elsewhere."

"And if I find some?"

"It would amaze us all." He watched Ross bring Katherine a glass of wine.

"Amaze you! Haven't I told you, over and over—?"

"Over and over." He smiled at her. "Proving how easy it is to complain about a husband without giving up his bank account."

"Derek, Melanie," said Tobias, behind them. "Deep in a sinister plot?"

"Exchanging recipes," Derek said smoothly. "How are you, Tobias? Still well? Still writing your book on—what was it? Cannibalism?"

"Love," Tobias corrected cheerfully. "I think you have them confused, Derek." His blue eyes were wide and innocent above the neat white beard that quivered as he spoke. "And then of course, the family history, as you also know. Perhaps I should interview you for both books. With your unique viewpoint—"

"I think Victoria wants you," Derek cut in, seeing his grandmother look around the room. "Aren't you being her good brother and helping host this festive affair?"

Tobias shot him a quick glance, his eyes briefly penetrating, then wandering and amiable again. "Claude is helping, which he enjoys, so I can tiptoe about, listening, which *I* enjoy. How did you and Melanie resist discussing our newest family member?"

"Excuse me," said Melanie abruptly, and walked across the room, casually inserting herself between Katherine and Ross. "We've hardly met," she said to Katherine. "Everybody's monopolizing you, but after all it was my husband who found you so I should get a chance, don't you think?"

Katherine felt as if a light had flared beside her, exposing everything about her that was wrong. Next to Melanie's blue silk dress her linen suit was wrinkled and plain; her hair was dull compared to Melanie's gleaming ebony; her pale skin washed out beside Melanie's golden tan. And she knew, as she pulled her shoulders back, trying to stand straight, that Melanie's gliding walk across the room came from a confidence and wealth she did not even know how to imitate. In the luxury of Victoria's apartment, among these wealthy people, Katherine felt as strange and uncomfortable as a foreigner.

Still, she was the center of attention. Ross had told her she would be, when he invited her to meet them. "It's your family too; you should know them and let them get to know you, let them get used to the idea of you and the children. After all—" He had looked bemused for a moment, realizing anew the enormity of what had happened. "After fifteen years, to discover someone you loved is not dead but alive, and married, with children—"

"He may . . . not be alive," Katherine had said.

"I'm assuming he is. But even if he isn't, you have a family in San Francisco and everyone has a lot of catching up to do."

He had made it seem so simple. And in the two days before they flew there, as they tried to imagine that unknown family, Katherine became excited about the Haywards and Jennifer and Todd overcame their confusion enough to be intrigued by the idea of suddenly having grandparents, as well as the prospect of their first airplane trip. "But I still don't see," Jennifer said on Sunday, when they were high above the earth and she could tear herself from the window, "why Daddy never told us he had a family." "That's the nine millionth time you've said that," Todd grumbled, frustrated because he had lost the coin toss and would not get the window seat until the trip home. "Well, I want to know why he didn't tell us, even if you don't," Jennifer retorted. "He probably didn't like them," Todd said. "You don't have to like people just because they're your family. We probably won't like them either. I bet they aren't even Daddy's family; I bet it's all a stupid mistake. I wish we weren't going." "Me too," Jennifer confessed. "It's scary. Daddy would have told us if we had grandparents. Why did they invite us? We should have stayed home." "Maybe they're going to kidnap us," said Todd. "And hold us for ransom." "Who'd pay?" Jennifer demanded. "Daddy, of course," said Todd. "Only he's not here," he remembered. "So nobody will and they'll never let us go and we'll be prisoners for ever and ever."

"Oh, enough," Katherine said between weariness and amusement. "It seems pretty clear that the Haywards are Daddy's family, which means they're our family, and I'm sure they're not scary. Ross said they want to meet us, and maybe all of us together can figure out why Daddy never told us about them. Or we won't know until he comes back and tells us himself. But no more guessing, all right? Just think instead how nice it will be to have an instant family to help us."

An instant family. Waiting for them. In a way, Jennifer was right: it was scary. But, sitting on the aisle of the huge airplane, watching her children inspect their wrapped silverware and small dishes of food, Katherine recaptured her eagerness. The Haywards would be a place to belong, an anchor to cling to when everything else seemed to be collapsing. And someone to talk to about Craig. There was no one else; Katherine had tried to call Leslie, but she was out of town. With the Haywards, she wouldn't be alone anymore.

Her eagerness was in her face when Ross met them at the airport. By the time they reached Victoria's building, it was in Jennifer's and Todd's, too, though they clung to Katherine's hands in the elevator, and hung back as Ross led them into an apartment where a cluster of people waited. "Craig's family," Ross said quietly.

A circle of piercing, measuring eyes surrounded Katherine. *Craig's family.* Impossible. But no one contradicted Ross when he said it. *My husband's family. And I never knew they existed.*

"Victoria Hayward," Ross said into the brief silence. "Craig's grandmother. Katherine Fraser." The two women faced each other. Eighty years old, Victoria was as tall as Katherine and as slender. With skin like finely webbed parchment, and short, pure white curls about her head, she had a regal beauty that made Katherine nervous. Beneath that calm gaze, she felt young, and inexperienced.

Their hands met, Victoria's cool and dry, unexpectedly firm. "Welcome, my dear," she said with a faint smile. "You come as a surprise."

"And Todd and Jennifer Fraser," Ross said, bringing the children forward. Victoria glanced at them and her body went very still. Behind her, a woman gasped. Touching Todd's blond hair, Victoria said, "Your son. And you named your daughter Jennifer."

"Daddy chose it," said Jennifer. "It was his favorite name, he said."

"Yes," Victoria murmured.

Todd looked at her challengingly. "Are you our grandmother?"

"Incredible," Victoria said. "Even the voice—"

"I am." A small woman, her shoulders hunched, came forward, holding out her hands to Todd and Jennifer. "Your grandmother." She smiled tremulously at Katherine. "I'm Ann Hayward. Craig's mother. And Jason—" She gestured toward a tall man with a dark, weathered face. "His father." It was Ann who had gasped when she saw Todd and now she put her arm around him, her face radiant. "It is incredible, isn't it? Jason? The resemblance—?"

Todd squirmed in embarrassment but Katherine was watching Jason, who had not moved. His face was blank. "Yes," he said. "Craig looked like that once."

Ross continued his calm introductions. "Tobias Wheatley, Victoria's brother; my wife Melanie; our children Jon and Carrie; Claude Fleming, a friend of the family. And my brother. Derek Hayward."

Derek nodded to Katherine. She recognized him from the photograph; the handsome aloof stranger in the cockpit of the sailboat. He was still aloof, taking no part in the talk that was starting and stopping, like a reluctant motor, in the small group of people.

"There's a bunch of Atari games in the library," Jon Hayward said to Todd. He was a year older, with blond hair and his father's deep-set, dark eyes. "Do you want to play? You too," he added magnanimously to Jennifer and Carrie.

"We can beat them," Carrie whispered loudly to Jennifer. Small, blond, lively, just ten years old, she bounced on her toes. "Jon always gets impatient and plays like a gorilla."

"Mom?" Todd asked. "Can we?"

Katherine hesitated, not wanting to be left alone, and Jennifer, watching her, said, "I'd rather stay here."

Katherine shook her head. This seemed planned, as if Ross had instructed his children to clear the youngsters from the room. "Of course you should go," she said. "Have a good time."

She watched the four of them run off and followed the family into the drawing room. A few steps in, she stopped, overwhelmed by brilliant colors and textures: silk-covered apricot walls, pale yellow velvet furniture and muted Persian rugs. With the red-gold sunset flooding in through high windows, the room seemed lit from within and Katherine drew a breath of pure pleasure. "It's the most beautiful room I've ever seen," she said softly.

"Yes," said Victoria, pleased. She sat in a wing chair beside open French doors that led to a balcony, while the others stood nearby, pouring drinks, filling small plates with hors d'oeuvres from a table beside the piano, and asking questions of Katherine. Only Derek stood apart. Katherine kept glancing at him, puzzled by his aloofness, vaguely aware of the power of his separateness: he was the kind of man others would want to impress, to make a dent in his still, smooth surface.

"—Craig look like?" Ann was asking eagerly. "I couldn't tell from the newspaper picture; they're so fuzzy..."

"I brought photographs," Katherine said, taking a packet from her purse and handing it to Ann. Immediately, Ann gave it to Victoria. Katherine flushed. Everything begins with Victoria, she thought. Ross told me; I should have remembered.

Victoria went through the pack slowly, handing each picture to Ann as she finished with it. She was very pale, and her lips quivered, but she finished the pile in silence and then stared fixedly through the French doors.

"Did Craig still hike in the mountains?" Ann asked, looking at the photograph of all of them in the Grouse Mountain cable car. "Did he have a staff working for him?" she asked when she came to the picture of Craig and Carl Doerner at their desks. "I have his trophies for long-distance running," she said, holding a picture of Craig on a bicycle. "I can send them to you, if you'd like." Tobias, too, was looking at the photographs, commenting and passing them on to others, who made their own remarks. From the tangled voices, Tobias said, clearly and sadly, ". . . and wondering all the while, what stranger would come back to me."

A silence fell. "Not to me," Katherine faltered. "He's not a stranger to me."

"Oh, dear, oh, dear," Tobias lamented. "I'm so sorry; I didn't mean to upset you. I was quoting a poet. Wilfrid Gibson. I have a habit of doing that: popping up with quotations, which, alas, my family usually ignores. When I taught at the university, my students had no choice but to listen. I do miss that. You mustn't take it personally. Though Craig *is* a stranger to us, you know."

Jason walked past Tobias to Katherine. Tall and thin, he had the tough gnarled hands of a man who worked outdoors, and his gaze was restless, searching the room. "Ross said your husband is in the construction business. His own company?"

"He has a partner."

"How much does he own?"

"One-fourth."

"*One-fourth?*"

"He was going to buy more," Katherine said defensively. "In fact, Carl planned to have Craig take over when he retired."

"How much did he make?"

"I don't know." She was defensive again. "It depended on how many jobs they had each year and Craig didn't like to talk about money. We always had enough."

"Well," Jason said. Katherine held her breath, waiting for someone to say, *Enough of stolen money. He embezzled from his company.* But no one did. They won't talk about it, Katherine thought. In fact, she suddenly realized, they were asking questions, but no one was really talking about Craig at all.

And she and Jason had talked in the past tense. As if he were dead.

She looked about the room. Derek was watching her, his narrow face and deep eyes so absorbed it was as if he had erased everything else, holding only Katherine in the path of his vision. Flustered, she looked away, at Claude Fleming, who had not yet spoken, at Ross, who was more distant than he had been in Vancouver, and beyond them, through the French doors.

The kaleidoscope of San Francisco stretched from Victoria's balcony at the crest of Pacific Heights far down to the misty water of the bay. The view blended with the mirrors and tapestries on the apricot silk walls so there seemed to be no barrier between the rooms and the sky and the city below. They were suspended above the earth on the golden light of early evening. A magic place, Katherine thought, and wondered if Craig had felt the same way when he was here.

When he was here. He had spent his growing-up years in these rooms, with these people. It was impossible to understand. *Where are you?* Katherine cried silently. This is your family; I shouldn't be here without you, we should be here together...

"Katherine." Victoria motioned to her to sit beside her. "Tell me about your family." Briefly, Katherine described her father and mother, their small grocery store, and the apartment above it, where they lived together until she was three, when her parents died within a few months of each other and her aunt came to live with her.

"In Vancouver?"

"No. In San Francisco."

"San Francisco! Ross! Did you know that?"

"No." He looked at Katherine. "You never mentioned it."

"You only wanted to know about Craig."

"You should have told him," Victoria declared. "And where did you go to college?"

It's a test, Katherine decided. And I've probably failed because I grew up over a grocery store. "I went to San Francisco State College for two years; then I had to go to work."

Beneath Victoria's scrutiny, Katherine thought—She's comparing me to the women the Hayward men usually choose. Richer, smarter, more beautiful.

Ross brought her a glass of wine and Claude Fleming asked, "Where did you work?"

"I was a clerk in a jewelry store. I wanted to learn to design and make jewelry."

"And did you learn?"

"I've made a few pieces."

"That you sold?"

"No; I gave them as gifts." *I know what it is. I'm like the bride-to-be, under inspection by the groom's family. But there isn't any groom.* Dimly, Craig hovered nearby and suddenly her longing for him burst within her. It engulfed her and tears stung her eyes. *Where are you?* she cried again. *And who are you?* She wanted Craig, the Craig she knew; she wanted to be home; she wanted the four of them to be together, where they belonged.

"Mrs. Fraser." Claude Fleming stood beside Victoria's chair. "Does your husband have any distinguishing features? A scar, for example? Or a limp?"

Hope flared in Katherine. They weren't really sure it was the same man. Maybe Todd had been right: it was all a mistake. And she'd been right, too: she *knew* Craig—he would not have kept such an enormous secret from her.

Ross had been gazing across the room at Melanie and Derek, their heads close together as Tobias came up behind them. He turned. "Claude, you can't dismiss the photograph Katherine found."

"Or the son," said Victoria shortly. "I know you're trying to be helpful, Claude, but the boy is the image of Craig. And the girl is named Jennifer. We've all accepted it."

"A lawyer looks for proof," Claude said. "Not emotion."

"Lawyer?" Katherine asked.

"Family lawyer as well as friend. Did your husband have any distinguishing features?"

"A scar," she answered, thinking how curious that the Haywards should ask their lawyer to help them meet her. "Next to his right eyebrow."

"And so did Craig," sighed Victoria. "From one of Derek's acrobatic horseshoe pitches."

"It's not conclusive," said Claude. "But let it go for now. Mrs. Fraser, what did your husband tell you about the Haywards?"

"Tell me—? Nothing. I told you I never heard of the Haywards until Ross came to Vancouver."

"For fifteen years," Claude said sarcastically, "a man does not tell his wife about his family. Parents. Grandparents. A sister. Two cousins. A little hard to believe, wouldn't you say?"

Katherine flushed. "I don't know what *you* would say—"

Ross put a steadying hand on hers. "I think he kept us a secret, Claude," he said quietly.

"Then what the hell *did* he tell you?" Claude demanded.

"That he was an orphan. It was one of the things we—I thought we shared. He was brought up by foster parents in Vancouver—he said—and always wanted a family..." Her voice trailed away.

"Insane," Claude muttered. "Ridiculous."

And it was then that Melanie crossed the room, pushing between Ross and Katherine, saying, "We've hardly met," and making Katherine feel drab and out of place next to the flare of her high color and blue silk dress.

"Ah," said Victoria, relief in her voice, as she saw the butler in the dining room arch. "Dinner. Ross, will you help me? Derek, you've been avoiding us; please take Katherine in. Claude, you and Melanie. Jason and Ann, I suppose. Tobias dear, we have no one for you."

"Only the butler," said Tobias cheerfully and, leading the way, took the chair at the foot of the table, opposite Victoria at the head.

Derek sat at Victoria's right, Katherine at her left, but it was not the intimate family dinner she had imagined. Nine people, at formal place settings on hand-embroidered linen place mats, were spaced about a gleaming mahogany table where eighteen would have been comfortable.

No places for the children, Katherine realized, just as Victoria said, "The children are being served in the library. In my experience, they're happier with each other than with adults. But if you prefer having your children with you, the arrangement can be changed."

"No." Once again, Katherine felt tears sting her eyes. "I'm sure they'll be happier there." Feeling alone and troubled, she watched the butler fill wine glasses as the maid served pale green soup in fragile bowls. Except for Derek, everyone was friendly, and no one had said a word against Craig. But something was wrong, and she tried to identify it as she ate her soup and listened to the others talk about an office tower the Hayward Corporation was building in the financial district and a highway overpass they were bidding on near San Jose.

Across the table, Ross lifted his wine glass. "We should drink a toast to the newest member of our family."

"Yes," said Victoria. "Welcome, Katherine. We hope—"

She paused and there was a silence. What? Katherine wondered a little wildly. We hope Craig isn't dead or injured and lying somewhere undiscovered? That if he's alive he isn't guilty of embezzlement? That he'll come back to his wife and children and settle his financial problems? That he'll choose to come back to his first family after fifteen years of living a lie? That he'll tell his wife the truth for the first time in their marriage? That Katherine figures out what she's going to do?

"We hope Craig finds his way back to all of us," Ross finished gracefully. "Katherine, would you tell everyone about your house? It's very fine, especially the windows."

She began, but almost immediately Ross took over, explaining how the house and its wall of windows followed the contour of the tree-covered hill, facing south above the panorama of English Bay, Vancouver and Vancouver Island.

"But the view," Tobias said to Katherine. "How do you have a view with all those trees?"

"They're so tall," she said absently, preoccupied with her thoughts. "We look between them; they're like pillars, holding up the sky."

Derek looked up sharply. Tobias, too, looked surprised that she had said something interesting. "A pleasant fancy," he murmured.

"Don't you love the trees?" Ann asked. "In Maine we live at the edge of a forest."

"Craig helped clear them when we built the house," Katherine said, remembering his triumphant smile when he and the crew finally pulled out a large tree that was dying but still stubbornly clinging to the earth. "He liked—likes—heavy work."

"But aren't you tired of the forest?" Tobias asked Ann. "Fifteeen years of peace and quiet: so excessive. Why don't you move back here?" There was a glint in his eye. "Jason could rejoin the company and we'd all be together again."

Slowly Derek turned in his chair. "Have you taken up family planning, Tobias?" he asked evenly.

Melanie laughed. Tobias looked amiably vague and Claude changed the subject, and at that moment Katherine knew what was wrong with the evening. *No one was excited about Craig.* Jason seemed almost angry, and the others—even Victoria and Ann, who did seem to care that he was alive—were so restrained it was as if they had no feelings about him at all. They'd asked questions, all except Derek, but at the table everyone was behaving as if this were an ordinary family dinner, with nothing unusual to discuss.

She cleared her throat. Her heart was pounding because she was afraid of making them angry. But after all, she was here to find out about Craig. "Why did Craig disappear fifteen years ago?" she blurted into the murmuring conversations.

The conversations stopped. Everyone looked at Victoria. But Melanie spoke first. "Why," she drawled. "Most likely for the same reason he ran out on you."

"Melanie, be silent," Victoria snapped. "You don't know what you're talking about."

"They weren't married then, you know," Tobias explained to Katherine. "Melanie and Ross, that is. So she never met Craig."

"Superb roast beef," Derek said pleasantly to Victoria. "Perfectly rare. Have you hired a new chef?"

"I hired him," said Tobias. "But Claude found him."

"I also found the orchid," said Claude, touching the plant in the center of the table, its arching stems of white flowers mirrored in the mahogany. "Like the roast, it is quite rare."

"Do you grow flowers?" Victoria asked Katherine. "Or vegetables? I confess I know nothing about the climate of Vancouver."

Katherine put down her fork. She was Victoria's guest, and hopelessly inferior to all of these wealthy, self-confident people, but she was desperate to learn about Craig. With her eyes on the orchid, she said, "I was trying to find out why Craig ran away fifteen years ago. I thought you would help me. With—"

"Money," said Melanie brightly. "And didn't we all know that was coming. You said I was wrong," she told Ross. "Well, who's wrong now? The minute she found out her husband had a wealthy family—"

"No," he said flatly. "I invited Katherine, and she came—"

"For her share of the wealth." Melanie looked steadily at Katherine's lowered eyes. "Right? Veteran's pay. Or maybe—if Craig wanted to come back for a piece of the company, wouldn't it be smart to send a sweet wife to test the waters?"

Victoria was watching Katherine. Letting Melanie do the dirty work, Katherine thought. "'Blow, blow, thou winter wind!'" Tobias intoned. "Melanie, you are cold and unpleasant."

"Or," Melanie persisted, "hush money. Not to broadcast Craig's latest mess and whatever else he did in the last—"

"God damn it!" Ross pushed back his chair.

"We don't *know* why he disappeared," Tobias said hastily. "Fifteen years ago. We have trouble talking about it," he added. "Partly because we don't know. Claude worked with the police—"

"We thought he was dead." Claude spoke directly to Katherine. "It never occurred to anyone that he might deliberately have disappeared."

"We've thought and thought—" Ann exclaimed.

"Lack of information—" began Tobias.

"Trust!" stormed Jason. "Lack of trust! If that young fool had come home and told us what happened—"

"What *did* happen?" asked Katherine.

"He wasn't a fool!" Ann protested. "He was clever and dear and gentle..."

So was Craig, Katherine thought.

"The golden boy," murmured Derek.

"Who wasn't a hero," said Jason. "So he ran away, to keep from facing us."

"More likely," said Ross quietly, "he ran away because he couldn't face himself."

"*Why?*" Katherine's voice was frustrated.

"Cowardice!" Jason boomed, but Ann cried out, "He died trying to—" as Claude's courtroom voice rode over them: "It seems he didn't die."

"That is quite enough!" Victoria stood at the head of the table, her eyes blazing. "I apologize," she said to Katherine. "My family is behaving like a raucous mob." She swept them with her gaze. "It is unforgivable." At her gesture, the butler, wheeling in the dessert cart, stopped in the doorway. The room was still. Slowly, Victoria sat down and nodded permission to the butler to circle the table, offering a selection of desserts. The maid poured coffee. When everyone was served, Victoria said to Katherine. "Ross told you nothing about the sailing accident?"

Uncertainly, Katherine said, "Only that there was one."

Victoria nodded. "We do find it difficult to talk about. Even after so many years. And especially now...with the ending changed. But you shall hear the story." She took a sip of coffee and looked around the table. "Claude will tell it."

"Of course," Claude said easily. Why? Katherine wondered. He wasn't there. Ross said it was the four of them.

"The four of them," Claude began. "Craig, Jennifer, Derek, and Ross, were sailing home across the bay. It was dusk. The bay is often unpredictable, particularly at that time and especially near the Golden Gate; I am told great concentration is needed to sail it safely. But they had been at a party in Sausalito, with a great deal of drinking, and none of them was capable of such concentration. There was a sudden change in wind direction and the boom swung across the boat. It struck Jennifer, knocking her unconscious, and she fell overboard. Craig immediately jumped in to save her. Ross and Derek—though neither was an experienced sailor at that time—managed to turn the boat around and return to Jennifer. They found her dead. Craig, of course, was gone."

Again the room was still. Katherine glanced at the closed faces of Ann and Jason, trying to imagine what it would be like to lose both her children on the same day. But it was unimaginable: her thoughts skidded from the idea and she wondered if that was why they had moved to Maine.

"Odd," Tobias ruminated. "I thought there was something more to it. Of course I was living in Boston, but I seem to remember hearing that besides the wind, there was also a disagreement, one might say a quarrel, that distracted—"

"You *heard*, Tobias?" Derek asked coldly. "You never told us you heard voices. Do you also see visions?"

"Katherine should hear the whole story," Tobias said quietly.

"Craig was quarreling?" Katherine asked. "What about?"

"They'd been drinking," said Claude. "There were conflicting, and, I gather, belligerent opinions on the best way to sail the boat. For some reason, rumors about a quarrel, even a fight, cropped up afterward; no one knew why. I think it would be unwise to resurrect any of them at this late date."

There was a pause. Melanie's fingernail rang nervously against her wine glass. "If you please," said Victoria, and Melanie's finger was still.

"So," Claude went on. "Apparently Craig made his way to Vancouver. Most likely hitchhiking. Did he ever tell you, Mrs. Fraser?"

Startled, Katherine said, "How could he? I told you he never talked about—"

"Yes, I keep forgetting. Where did the name Fraser come from?"

She looked at him blankly. "I don't know."

"A suburb of Vancouver, perhaps? On the southern edge of the city?"

"Named Fraser?" Ross asked. "Is there one, Claude?"

"Not far from the U.S. border. I found it on a map. I suppose he passed through it when he was running."

"Did Craig keep up his carving?" Tobias asked Katherine. "I always loved those little people he made—so realistic."

"He went through a stage," Ann recalled, "of wanting to make carving his career. Can you imagine?"

"I can't at all," said Tobias. "I thought he was anxious to go into the company with Jason and Curt. My, my; so Ross wasn't the only one who wanted to break away."

They had done it again, Katherine thought: moved on to small talk. She turned to Tobias. "You mean you think he left to break away? You see, I'm trying to find out what kind of person he was—is—"

"You married him," Melanie said sweetly. "You must have known what kind of person he was."

"Is he dead?" asked Tobias. "I didn't know we'd decided that."

"No—!" Katherine burst out.

"It's hard to know," mused Derek. "With Craig."

"It is hardly a decision we can make," Victoria said. All through dinner she had been intent on the conversation, her eyes following the rest of them. The only time she spoke out, Katherine realized, was to stop an outburst that might have revealed something about Craig. "Port and cognac in the living room," Victoria added, and stood up.

Not everyone had finished coffee and dessert. Katherine understood that she was hurrying them through dinner. *Because she wants me gone.*

It was simple; it was obvious. Why had it taken her so long to see it? Ross had asked Victoria to give a dinner and she had done it, but not because she wanted to. None of them wanted this dinner; none of them wanted Katherine to be there. None of them wanted to talk about Craig.

Or maybe they did, but they could not confront the evidence that he had been alive all these years. And since they could hardly evade it with Katherine there, she was an interloper. And so is Craig, she thought. Even though he's not here.

What did he do, that his family can't rejoice that he's alive?

As clearly as if he sat beside her, she heard Craig say, Most families are rotten. He had said it often, when they were first married, adding that theirs would be different. Now he seemed so close she thought she could touch him. Rotten, his voice repeated.

"Please," Katherine said loudly as the others pushed back their chairs. "Please wait." They looked at her.

"In the living room," Victoria ordered.

"No, please," Katherine insisted; as long as they were together at the table, she might get them to listen to her. "I don't understand you. I have so many questions about Craig's life before I knew him, and I thought you would want to know about his life the past fifteen years. I thought we could share what we know because he never put his two lives together; he kept them separate—"

"That's *all* you want?" Claude asked. "Knowing what you do about the Hayward family and the company—"

"I don't know anything about them! Don't you understand? I don't know the man I married; I barely know his family; I don't know what to believe—I don't even know if I understand myself. Don't you see?" No one answered. "Well, then, there is something else. I thought you'd be so happy to know Craig is alive you'd do all you could to find him. You have so much wealth and power" —she ignored the triumphant look Melanie gave Ross— "I thought you might hire investigators, put advertisements in newspapers, call people you know in other cities where he might have gone...I thought you'd help me look for him. And I thought perhaps the reason he vanished before might be connected with why he's gone now, and if we knew that we might find him together much faster than I could alone."

No one spoke. They looked out the window or at Katherine or at the white orchid reflected in the dark mahogany table. Laughter from the library reached them faintly, but the dining room was silent.

Katherine stood up. She felt light-headed and dizzy, but, strangely, almost excited. She had to handle it alone, without Craig's help. And if they became angry and turned their backs on her—she would handle that alone, too.

"And I did think you might help us with a loan, just until Craig gets back, because we don't have much money and I don't know what we're going to do. But I wanted a loan, not a gift, and one of the things I wanted to do with it was hire detectives to look for him. Because we have to find him and help him—" She stopped briefly. "If we can; if he's still alive. I don't know what's happened to him, he may be in trouble, or hurt, but you act as if *you're* the ones who are hurt, that he's insulted you because he—" She stopped again. No one had mentioned embezzlement and she would not be the one to bring it up. "He's been—he *is* a wonderful husband and a wonderful father and I love him and I won't turn my back on him, even if you do, and I don't understand how you can talk about flower gardens and wood carvings and orchids when Craig—"

Victoria raised an imperious hand. "We do not need you to tell us how to behave. You know very little about us—"

"I'd know more if you'd tell me!"

"Do not interrupt me! We opened our home to you and your children; you have little cause to criticize us."

"I didn't want to." Katherine's eyes filled with tears. "But I think you'd be happier if you'd never heard of Craig Fraser at all."

"Katherine," Tobias chided, looking at Victoria's tight lips. "Too much, too much. Don't say more than we can forget."

"You don't want us here," she went on doggedly. "You don't want me and you don't want Craig. But of course it was very kind of you to invite us." She hesitated, then turned to leave.

"Young woman!" Victoria's icy voice stopped her. She heard Tobias lament, "Oh, Katherine," and Melanie murmur, "How charming; no one walks out on—" as Victoria said, "How dare you turn your back on me! And where do you think you are going? You have no one else to help you."

Katherine half-turned to see her—so beautiful in her regal anger it seemed nothing could touch her. "You don't want to help and I don't need you. Craig and I have gotten along by ourselves for ten years, you haven't existed for us, so why should I come to you now? I'll find him . . . and we'll be all right." Quickly she left the room, trembling so violently she thought she would fall.

But suddenly Ross was there, his arm lightly around her shoulders as they walked through the drawing room. "I think you should stay," he told her. "What you said about us was partly true, but Victoria was right: there are many things you don't know about us. And there's no question that we'll help you financially. I apologize for my wife's insinuations—"

"You have nothing to apologize for. But I don't want any help from your family. All I want to do is go home, where I belong, and find my husband."

He started to say something, then changed his mind as they came to the library. Jennifer and Carrie were locked in a computerized race with Todd and Jon on the television screen and it was a few minutes before

Katherine was able to pry them loose. "They have a million games, Mom!" Todd said as they all walked down a long gallery.

"They aren't ours," said Jon. "They're Great-Grandma's. But she lets us play any time we want, and when you come back—"

"*Are* we coming back?" Jennifer asked, squinting as she tried to read her mother's face.

"No—" Katherine began and that single word, louder than she had intended, met Victoria and Tobias, who were waiting in the entry hall.

Tobias took Katherine's hands in his. "We've all behaved badly; I'm quite ashamed of everyone. But you will come back, of course you will, now that we've met, now that we consider you part of the family—"

But it was clear he wasn't asking them to stay. Katherine stepped back. "Goodbye," she said to Victoria. "I'm sorry."

"So am I," Victoria responded unexpectedly. But then she said to Ross, "Are you driving them to the airport?"

The last of Katherine's fears of angering them dropped away. "That isn't necessary," she said bitingly. "We can manage on our own. We wouldn't want to disrupt your life—I mean your *dinner*—any more than we already have. Todd, do you have your jacket? Jennifer?" She opened the carved oak door and urged them ahead of her into the small vestibule. "We'll get a cab downstairs, for the airport. We're going home."

As she pushed the elevator button, she saw Ross gesture to Victoria and Tobias to stay behind. He followed her into the vestibule. "Your luggage is at the Fairmont," he said.

"We'll pick it up on the way to the airport."

"There may not be a flight for Vancouver tonight."

"We'll find out." The elevator arrived and the uniformed doorman slid open the door. Katherine held out her hand to Ross. "Thank you again. When Craig comes home, would you like us to let you know?"

There was a barely perceptible pause. "Of course," he said. "But I'll call in a day or two to see how you are."

"Your family wouldn't approve." Her courage exhausted, Katherine shepherded her children into the elevator and nodded to the doorman. The last thing she saw as he pulled shut the iron grille and started down was Ross, shaking his head, contradicting her, and Carrie and Jon, who had run out to the vestibule, peering through the grille to shout a farewell to Jennifer and Todd.

CHAPTER 5

AFTER the golden splendor of Victoria's apartment, the house in Vancouver seemed a cool and earthbound haven. But as soon as they opened the door, Katherine knew it was not. Driving home from the airport, listening to Todd and Jennifer imagine their father waiting for them, she had almost let herself be convinced, until they walked in and Todd called, "Dad! We're home!" and they came up against the silent emptiness of the dark rooms. The house was exactly as they had left it, nothing out of place, nothing changed. "God damn it!" Todd yelled, stomping down the stairs after searching the bedroom. Katherine let him. It was better than keeping it locked up inside.

But the next morning she was less patient. "Just go," she ordered, wanting to be alone, when they dragged their feet after breakfast. "Daddy will come back, or not, whether you're here or at day camp. We have to keep going; we can't sit around like run-down toys, waiting for Daddy to come along and wind us up."

That made them giggle and she was able to send them off to catch their bus, leaving her alone in the quiet rooms. Craig seemed to be everywhere—papers with his handwriting, pictures he had hung on the walls, the banister he had sanded and varnished to silken smoothness, the dent he'd made in the dishwasher when he threw a coffee mug at it in a fit of anger. What had he been angry about? Katherine couldn't remember. Maybe she had done something that reminded him of the Haywards.

If that was it, she could understand his anger. A closed private club, the Haywards. If Craig felt as uncomfortable with them as she had, no wonder he left.

But she still didn't know why he left. Sitting at Craig's desk, she knew she had bungled the evening. She hadn't been clever enough to get past their barriers, and so she lost the chance to learn more about her husband.

She shuddered, remembering how inferior they had made her feel. Forget about them, she ordered herself. Think about now. Especially about money. The top of the desk was covered with bills for roof repair, gasoline charges, summer clothes for the whole family, overdue bills, "last notice" bills, a card from a collection agency, mortgage, utilities, and at least a dozen others coming due the first of July. Tomorrow.

Craig always insisted on paying the bills. Sometimes Katherine had teased him, asking what dark secrets made him so protective. Now she knew. She wondered how long he had been juggling accounts to keep them from being canceled. Your house set him back more than he expected, Carl Doerner had said. Why didn't you tell me? Katherine silently asked Craig. Didn't you trust me?

Don't think about Craig; think about the bills. Two thousand dollars for the mortgage, due the first of the month. Fifteen hundred dollars in other bills due at the same time. Cash on hand: four hundred dollars in the checking account; one thousand in savings. Think about that. Thirty-five hundred dollars in bills. Fourteen hundred dollars on hand.

But she wasn't even sure of that. How much did he take with him? She picked up the telephone and called the bank. And was told that the checking account contained five thousand dollars.

"How much?" She repeated the account number.

"Five thousand four hundred thirteen dollars, Mrs. Fraser," the voice chirped. "A deposit of five thousand dollars was made at ten-thirty A.M. on June 16 at the Park Royal branch. Would you like us to send you a duplicate deposit slip?"

"No. Thank you." June 16. Two weeks ago. The day Craig stood with her at their front gate at ten fifteen in the morning and kissed her goodbye before taking a taxi to the airport. Only he hadn't gone straight to the airport. He'd stopped off at the bank in the Park Royal shopping center and made a deposit. To keep his family going for a while.

He never intended to be home on Friday.

He wasn't dead; he wasn't hurt. He was looking for money to pay back Carl Doerner. That was the whole story: no sexy young girl, no mugging and murder, no heart attack. He'd gone away because things got too much for him and he'd come back when he got them straightened out. And that wouldn't be long. He knew Katherine had only enough money for two months. By leaving five thousand dollars, he was telling her he would be back in two months.

Or he'd decided that in two months she'd be able to manage alone.

Or that was all he could spare.

The telephone rang and she snatched it up. It was a policeman, asking if she had heard from her husband.

"No—"

"Or anything about him?"

"Yes." All of Craig's secrets were becoming public. She told him about the Haywards. "Well, now, ma'am," he said doubtfully. "That's a very strange story. But we'll check with the San Francisco police. And you keep in touch, now; don't forget about us if you hear anything else."

Don't forget about us. Idiots, she thought, slamming down the telephone. All of them—Carl Doerner, the police, the Haywards—saw Craig's disappearance as a personal insult or challenge. No one seemed interested in her, or what she was discovering: that Craig Fraser didn't trust his wife to share his troubles, or his thoughts. He just disappeared and left her to clean up the mess.

No one seemed interested. A few friends had made perfunctory calls, duty calls, offering, not sympathy (after all, the newspapers said her husband was a criminal) but—"Help if you need it, Katherine; if things really get bad..." (How bad, she wondered, is "really bad"?)

For the first time, Katherine recognized how fragile were her friendships of the past ten years. Craig had kept people at arm's length, insisting he and Katherine needed only each other. And Katherine had gone along. Through letters and phone calls, Leslie remained her only confidante; her friendships in Vancouver were casual and pleasant, but never intimate.

Now that had come to haunt her. Most people shy away from those in trouble, as if they might catch it by coming too close, and none of Katherine's and Craig's acquaintances were close or affectionate enough to hold out a supporting hand. Well, she'd do without them; she didn't need them. She didn't need the Haywards, either, or any of her neighbors, whom she had been avoiding because she found herself feeling ashamed of being Mrs. Craig Fraser.

She didn't need Carl Doerner, either. He should have known Craig was in trouble at the company, and done something about it. Anyway, he was out of town, his secretary told her, for two weeks.

"I can always talk to myself," Katherine said aloud, but the sound of her voice in the empty house made her feel even more alone and she turned on the radio, spinning the knob until an announcer's comforting baritone filled the rooms. With his company, she sat at Craig's desk and paid the most urgent bills, putting the others aside. Signing the checks, she felt a brief surge of accomplishment, until she checked the bank balance. How had it shrunk so quickly? She might not have enough for another month. One emergency could wipe them out.

She paused, her hand halfway to the envelope she was about to stamp. *He had no right to do this to us.*

Quickly she shoved the thought away, with all the others she couldn't face, and when Todd and Jennifer came home, she was ready to think of dinner. "Not that stuff again!" Todd groaned as she took cold cuts and cheese from the refrigerator. He dropped his knapsack on the floor. "Why can't we have lamb chops or meat loaf or something *real*, like we used to?"

"You don't like to cook when it's just us, do you?" Jennifer asked. "When Daddy's on a trip, you never cook a whole dinner."

"You're right," Katherine said after a moment. "I haven't been very creative." She returned the food to the refrigerator. They'd never seemed like a family when Craig was away and those were the times she used up leftovers or made picniclike meals. But Craig had been gone for two weeks. We're the family now, she thought. It's about time I begin cooking for three. "Why don't we go out for hamburgers tonight?" she suggested. "And tomorrow we'll buy groceries for the rest of the week."

"The kind Daddy likes," Jennifer said. "So when he comes home he won't think we changed everything while he was gone."

Katherine turned away. There had been changes every day since he left: little ones, hardly noticeable at first, and big ones, like paying the bills herself. The longer Craig was gone, the less recognizable home was—as if they lost him a little more each day.

"How are we going to buy hamburgers and groceries?" Todd asked. "Daddy has all the money."

"Don't be silly," Jennifer scoffed. "Mother goes shopping every week."

"She gets the money from Daddy," Todd insisted. "So if he's not here, she doesn't have any."

Uncertainly, Jennifer asked, "We don't have any money?"

And Todd said, "Who's going to take care of us?"

The wall clock hummed, the refrigerator clicked on, a sprinkler watered the roses on the terrace. The house was alive: solid and familiar. But as if a strong wind had made it sway, the children were afraid. And so am I, Katherine thought, but that idea, too, she had to banish.

"We're going to take care of us," she said firmly. "We do have money; we just have to be careful how we spend it."

"How long will it last?" asked Jennifer.

"Until I start to earn our living." The words came out on their own. Katherine repeated them silently, wondering when she had made the decision. Writing checks, she thought; when else? Another change: the biggest so far. "I'm going to get a job," she said. "As a jewelry designer."

On Dominion Day, July first, Ann Hayward called. "We want to see you, Katherine, before we go back to Maine. We can be there this afternoon."

"Here?" Katherine asked. "Why?"

"To apologize, of course. Such a dreadful evening, and even though you can't really blame anyone—"

Oh, yes I can. "I'm sorry," she said. "We're busy all day; I promised to take Jennifer and Todd to the parade and then the fireworks—"

"*Today?*"

She thinks I'm lying because I don't want to see her. "Dominion Day. It's something like the Fourth of July, but not quite the—"

"Well, we'll go with you. Katherine, we want to get to know you. We certainly didn't have a chance the other night."

Katherine hesitated. They were Todd and Jennifer's grandparents. But then she remembered Jason's harsh questions. "Does Jason want to come?"

After a pause, Ann said, "I may come alone. He's needed at home—we have a shop, you know, for pottery and things." She fumbled for words. "And it's taking him a while to get used to the idea that Craig is alive—"

"That would please most fathers," Katherine said coldly.

"Yes. Of course. But it's hard for him to think that Craig abandoned us, let us mourn... It's very difficult. We've started quarreling again, all the old quarrels about whether Victoria and I spoiled him too much, or Jason expected too much of him... But that isn't why I called. I want to see you and I'm sure Jason won't mind if I come alone."

I don't want to be involved with your family, Katherine thought, and said, "Maybe some other time."

"But we're in California," Ann pressed. "Much closer than Maine. And I'd be representing the whole family."

"Some other time. I promised Jennifer and Todd the whole day."

"Katherine, you have no right to deprive me of my grandchildren!"

For a moment Katherine was tempted to say all right, to pretend Ann was the mother she'd never had and she was the daughter Ann had lost, to let Ann spoil Todd and Jennifer as her only grandchildren, and perhaps at last to have someone to talk to. But she couldn't do it. Ann was a member of the Haywards' private club; she had been silent, deferring to her husband and the others when Katherine asked for help. "I'm sorry," she said reluctantly. "Maybe some other time."

"Well." Ann sighed. "If you refuse to let us be friends..." Katherine said nothing. "I'm sending you some money. Not a lot, I'm afraid, but after I've talked to Jason I can send more."

"I don't want it. We're fine; we don't need it."

"It's already in the mail. Katherine, you should be more gracious; we're not as bad as you think and we can be very helpful to you and the children. It's true that we were confused when we met you; we'd had no time to get used to—"

Katherine listened as Ann repeated everything she had said before, but the evening at Victoria's had convinced her that she had her own life— hers and Craig's and the children's—and she had to hold it together by herself until Craig came back; she wasn't sure why, but she knew it was important. The only promise Katherine would make, because Ann begged her, was that she would not tear up the check when it arrived.

Two weeks later, she took it from the drawer where she had tucked it out of sight, and deposited it in the bank.

Her hand shook as she endorsed it and she wrote briefly to Ann, telling her she would repay it as soon as she found a job; as soon as she was earning her own money. The trouble was, she had almost no money, no job, and no prospects for one.

"Sorry, not now," said most of the jewelry store buyers whom she called for an appointment. "We're full up with orders. Try us in six or seven months; sometime after Christmas." Others told her to send in sketches or color slides of her jewelry. "However," they added, "we buy very little from unknown designers." Three agreed to see her.

And all three turned her down. "What is missing," they all said in one way or another, while inspecting the necklace and earrings she had brought in, "is the meticulous touch of the professional. This has been your hobby, is that right? It shows, you see. Your technique is very basic, not complex and original; there is no touch of the artist. Truly fine jewelry should make you say, 'This would be less beautiful if the design, materials and technique came together in any other way.' One cannot say that of your pieces. Look here, at this necklace..." And, like the teachers who had criticized her in grade school, each of them found fault with some part of her jewelry.

None of them suggested she come back another time. They dismissed her and turned their attention elsewhere even before Katherine was gone.

There is no touch of the artist. Katherine huddled in the corner of the couch where she sat every night, waiting for Craig amid the shadows cast by the porch light's glare. *Your hobby, is that right? It shows . . .* Craig had said she was good. Everyone said, "You're so clever, Katherine; so talented." But it wasn't true; they'd said it to please her.

I'm not talented or clever, she thought. I'm not even good.

A wind came up, slamming the screen door back and forth. In the living room, shadows swayed, creating new shapes. Everything was changing but Katherine felt bogged down. People spend years becoming jewelry designers, but I expected to walk in and find stores, customers, a salary, all waiting for me. I thought it would be easy because I love doing it. But people don't pay you for doing something just because you love it. You have to be good; you have to be professional. And I'm not.

Leslie might have some suggestions, but Katherine still hadn't been able to reach her. And she wasn't sure she really wanted to talk to Leslie. *All my failures compared to her triumphs.* No, she thought, I'll manage. She walked through the swaying shadows to Craig's desk and put her samples and sketches into a bottom drawer. And the next day she went job-hunting.

"Ah . . . no experience, Mrs. Fraser," said one personnel director after another, looking at her application. "Clerk in a jewelry store ten years ago. And since then—nothing?"

Only running a house, she answered silently. Bringing up two children. Being a wife.

"Skills, Mrs. Fraser?" They all skimmed her application. "No typing. No shorthand. No data processing. No computer experience at all?" She shook her head. "No accounting. No bookkeeping. Not even general office experience. You've never worked in an office?" Again she shook her head. "Or sold real estate?"

"No," she said.

They shrugged. "Nothing we can offer you. No skills and you haven't worked for ten years. No track record. The recession, you know; we're cutting back. The only people we might hire would be ones with experience. Sorry. Good luck."

Good luck. While all around her, doors were closing.

She curled up on the couch, tighter each night. What will I do if I can't find a job? I could borrow on the house. No I couldn't; not without a job. And anyway, how would I pay it back? What will we do if I don't find a job? Fear spun a web inside her. Of course I'll find a job. I just have to be patient. I'll find one tomorrow.

Two days later she swallowed her pride and called the friends who had offered help if she needed it, to ask if they knew of any jobs. Some worked in offices in the city; all of them were married to men who did. But they all said, "Oh, Katherine, there isn't a thing. The economy, you know; nobody's hiring. But I'm sure you'll find something; you've always been so good with your hands. And, listen, we should get together for lunch. Not this week or next—things are so busy—but one of these days we certainly will get together."

None of them said a word about Craig.

The last name on Katherine's list was Frances Doerner, and she sounded as friendly as ever. "Of course I'll talk to Carl, Katherine, and I'm sure he'll find something for you; every company needs efficient people, don't you think? He's still out of town but as soon as he calls, I'll talk to him and get back to you."

Not as friendly as ever, Katherine thought as they hung up. Once she would have invited us to dinner. But it doesn't matter. Carl will find me a job.

Still, whatever she earned would be far less than Craig had brought home. If they had been living beyond Craig's salary, how could they live on hers? She sat at the desk, adding and subtracting numbers, thinking of wild schemes that dribbled away to nothing. And the next morning, at breakfast, with no solution in sight, she forced herself to explain their finances to Jennifer and Todd, as honestly as she could. "So what we have to do," she concluded, and without warning began to cry, "is sell the house."

They stared at her, sitting stiffly in their chairs. "We *can't* sell the house," Jennifer said. "We *live* here. And we have to be here when Daddy comes back."

"We can't, we can't," Todd chimed in. "Daddy won't know where we are; he'll think we forgot him; he'll think we don't want him anymore."

"He's smart enough to find us," Katherine said. She wiped away her tears and swallowed the unshed ones. "We're going to rent an apartment in Vancouver and he'll call Information to get our new address and telephone number."

"What apartment?" they asked.

"The one we're going to find tomorrow afternoon. We'll make a list of neighborhoods we like—"

"Not me," said Jennifer. "And I'm not moving, either. I'm staying here until Daddy comes home."

"Me too," Todd chimed in. "I'm staying with Jennifer."

"You'll do what I tell you!" Katherine's voice rose. "I'm selling this house because we can't afford it, because your father didn't leave me enough money to pay for it, and since you don't know anything about that, you'll keep quiet and do what you're told!"

Jennifer and Todd burst into tears. "Why did he go away?" cried Todd. "Didn't he like us anymore?"

"If he got mad at something we did . . ." Jennifer said, her words trailing off.

"He would have told us, though," Todd asserted. "At least . . . wouldn't he?"

Katherine was slow to understand. "Told you what?"

"WHAT WE DID TO GET HIM MAD!" Todd bellowed. He scowled at Katherine. "Like, if he was mad at me and didn't want to be around me anymore—"

"Or me," Jennifer echoed.

"I could maybe fix it," Todd went on. "Or say I'm sorry or something so he'd come back. If he knew. We'd have to find him to tell him, and if we don't know where he is . . ."

"He wouldn't stop loving us, though," Jennifer said. "Would he? And leave us? I mean, he never disappeared before, and I did lots of things he didn't like, so I don't see why—"

"Wait. Wait a minute, both of you." Katherine shook her head. Where did they get such ideas? She leaned forward and held them, feeling guilty for the hurt in their eyes. They needed to believe the world was an orderly place where everything had a reason, but she had no reasons to give them. "Listen to me. You had nothing to do with Daddy's leaving. It's complicated, but you're not to blame. He loves you."

Jennifer shook her head disconsolately. "What else could it be?"

Todd frowned. "Maybe he's hiding, to test us. And we have to find him. Like the prince in that story who had to climb a hundred mountains and pick a special flower and kill a witch and slay a dragon before he could be king. Or something."

"That's dumb," Jennifer said, but softly, because Todd was trying to make her feel better. She said to Katherine, "If it wasn't us, was it because of what Mr. Doerner said that day?"

"No!" Todd shouted.

"It might be," Katherine said carefully. "Nobody knows the whole story, though. We can't make any judgments yet."

"But if he *was* mad at us," said Jennifer, "and found a family he liked better, and they didn't do anything to get him mad—"

"That's enough!" Katherine's control began to slip. "He wasn't mad at you; he didn't find another family. He'll tell you that himself, when he gets back." She hurried them through breakfast, and out of the house, to catch the bus for camp. And before she could begin to brood about whether she had handled them properly or not, she called the realtor and made an appointment for that afternoon.

He greeted her at her front door with the energy of an inquisitive terrier. "Mrs. Fraser, good afternoon, kind of you to think of us. Let's see what we have here, shall we?"

Clipboard in hand, he moved through the house, talking to himself as he took swift inventory and made notes. "Good views, good light; oh, very pleasant kitchen. This door goes to—? Ah, garage, yes, a bit messy, but the youngsters can take care of that and also—um, basement, dear, dear, we need a good bit of straightening here, too, otherwise can't see the—ah, water heater. The whole house—you'll forgive my frankness—could use a thorough cleaning. Of course you've had other things on your mind, if one can believe the newspapers, but you do want it to look its spanking cheerful best—purchasers pay more for a happy house than a sad one. Get your youngsters to clean up the garage and basement; it's good for them; help Mother sell the place, don't you know."

Katherine watched the realtor sniff about the rooms, indifferent and unsparing, enumerating their faults, ignoring the love and laughter they had held. Once the house had been a refuge; now she was handing it over to be invaded and scrutinized by strangers and bought by someone who would not know or care about the lives that had been lived within its walls.

I don't want to sell it; I don't want to leave. She followed him back to the living room. Why couldn't it wait? A week; maybe two; maybe a month. . . . And lose it all, she thought. Because I can't keep up the payments. Clenching her hands, she thrust them into the pockets of her skirt. "I was wondering about the price. And how quickly you can sell it."

"Well now, difficult to say. The market is bad; bad all over; we're all hurting. Now I'm aware that you need to sell—you have my sincere sympathies, by the way; an awkward time for you—what is it? What's wrong? Are you all right?"

Between laughing and crying, Katherine began to cough. Awkward, she thought. It is certainly awkward to be deserted. Catching her breath, she said, "I thought two hundred twenty thousand for the house. Is that about right? That's what our neighbors got two years ago."

"Two years ago, Mrs. Fraser, it was a different market. For today that's high. And this is a small house. But we can start there and come down. How low will you go?"

"I don't know. This neighborhood—"

"One of the best. But in bad times people will take other neighborhoods if they have to. Tell you what, Mrs. Fraser. Leave it to me. You clean up the place; have the kids tackle the basement and garage; they'll look bigger when they're neat. You do that and I'll get plenty of traffic moving through here. We'll have an offer in no time and I guarantee you'll be satisfied." He shook her hand, smiled brightly, and was gone.

As melancholy as they felt, it was a relief to have something definite to do. Jennifer and Todd, helping Katherine clean, began to accept the idea that they had to sell the house. "And someday build another one," said Todd. "Just like this. Only with a basketball court."

Then house-hunters came, tramping through the rooms, opening closet doors, peering into bureaus. One of Craig's favorite Eskimo carvings disappeared. But within two weeks the realtor called to say an offer had been made. "It's not as much as we'd like, Mrs. Fraser; in normal times, we wouldn't even entertain it for a house in West Vancouver. But since you're in a hurry—"

"How much?" she asked, cradling the telephone and reaching for a pencil.

"One seventy."

"Wait." Katherine scribbled numbers. One seventy minus his commission was about one sixty. Their mortgage was one fifty-two. Which left her—

"I know it's not what you'd hoped for, Mrs. Fraser, but—"

Which left her eight thousand dollars.

"—but it's a bad time to sell a house, especially if you're in a hurry. I'm sure we'd do better if you'd wait a few months or a year, but as things stand, I recommend you accept it."

Eight thousand dollars. For their wonderful house. "I'll call you back," Katherine said. Slowly she walked through the house, running her fingers along walls and doorjambs and curving windows, sitting briefly on the stone hearth where she and Craig had sat in the evenings when the house was being built, imagining the rooms that would take shape from the skeleton of studs and beams silhouetted around them. Our house, Katherine thought. We dreamed of it for years, we watched it grow, we painted and tiled and varnished, finishing it ourselves to save money. We made it. It's our house. How can I sell it on my own, without Craig? It's as if I'm cutting us apart, cutting our marriage apart.

Within her, something seemed to slip, like a cloth sliding off a table, exposing its flawed surface. *That's what Craig has done.*

In the vestibule, the mail was lying beneath the slot in the front door: more bills, an announcement of a sale at Eaton's, a letter, and two large manila envelopes from jewelry stores. Numbly, Katherine opened them. The last ones, she thought. All the photographs and sketches she had assembled so carefully and sent to jewelry buyers had come back, with polite notes. "Dear Mrs. Fraser. Thank you for sending us your designs. We regret that they do not meet our needs at present, but we wish you success in your career."

"How can I be successful," she murmured, "if I can't get a start?" She opened the letter: a paragraph from an insurance company where she had applied for a job as a receptionist. They had hired someone with more experience, but wished her success in the future. How kind of everyone, she thought, to wish me success.

The telephone rang and she ran to it, thinking, as they all did whenever it rang—this time it will be Craig. But it was not. "Katherine," Ross said. "I've been thinking about you."

Absurdly, her heart leaped. She hadn't realized how isolated she felt until she heard his deep voice and remembered his smile. But then she thought—It's been five weeks since he said he'd call to see how we are. "I've been busy," he said. "Or I would have called sooner. I owe you an apology for that fiasco at Victoria's, especially since I got you into it. We're a lot nicer than we seem, at least some of us are; I hope you'll discover that for yourself. Now tell me, how are you? What have you heard?"

"Nothing." She would have liked to tell him everything, but she couldn't: he was part of that family; he'd probably been thinking about her only because he wondered about Craig. Not much of a person to count on. "We're just waiting. But I've decided to sell the house and move to a place we can afford."

"Sell—? Isn't that a rash decision? How much money do you have?"

"Enough," she said evasively. "But not if we stay here."

"But I might . . . you haven't sold it yet, have you?"

"I think so."

"Look, you obviously think it's none of my business but—how much will you clear?"

"Eight thousand dollars. It's not—"

"Eight thousand—! On that house? Katherine, don't be a fool. That's a valuable piece of property!"

"Who do you think you are?" she cried. He was as arrogant and unsympathetic as the rest of his family. "The market is very bad here and I'm in a hurry; I can't make the payments—"

"I might make the payments. At least until you get a better price."

"I don't want any money from you."

"Damn it, it could be a business arrangement. To protect your property."

I'd like someone to protect me, she thought wryly, but aloud she said, "I don't want to be indebted to anyone."

"Especially not the Haywards."

She was silent.

"But we could help you, if you'd let us." He waited. "Katherine, you were the one who said you wanted a loan." Still she said nothing. He let out his breath in a sigh. "There's only so much we can do, from this distance. If you were here, we could—" he paused. "Katherine, what about that? If things are as bad as they sound, what about your moving back to San Francisco?"

It was so unexpected she sat down abruptly on the kitchen stool. "Moving?"

"You grew up here, you know the city, and if you were close by, we could help you. Forget what happened at Victoria's; it was one night, not a lifetime. If you were here, my kids could help yours, Melanie could introduce you to her friends—"

Melanie. Sleek, polished, disdainful. "Ross, how many of Melanie's friends have no money? How many of them work?"

"None that I know of," he conceded. "But you'd have a family waiting for you—"

Why is he doing this? "I don't have a family waiting for me. They don't want me; they don't even want Craig. And I don't see how I could leave Vancouver." The doorbell rang. "I have to go. Thank you. For calling and for thinking about me."

A policeman stood at the door. Faintly, Katherine said, "You found him."

"No, ma'am. Just stopping by to see if you've heard anything."

She let out her breath. *Not this time.* "No, I haven't."

"No sign of him, ma'am? He hasn't called?"

"No."

Whenever we talk about Craig, she thought, the word we use most often is No.

The telephone rang again. When Katherine answered it, Frances Doerner said hurriedly, "Katherine, how are you? I can't talk; I'm late for my hair appointment; I just wanted to let you know, and I *am* sorry, but I'm afraid I was wrong about a job in Carl's company."

Carl's company. It was Carl's and Craig's company a few days ago.

"There just aren't any jobs, and of course you wouldn't want them to fire anyone. I'm so sorry I misled you; Carl was very unhappy when he heard what I'd done. So that's the problem, dear Katherine; Carl is determined to keep costs down and I couldn't budge him. I'm so sorry; if there's anything else I can do—"

"No," Katherine said. "Thank you for trying. Goodbye, Fran—"

"Uh... Katherine, one more thing... Carl asked me to tell you he needs the car."

"The car?"

"The one Craig was using. It belongs to the company, you see, and Carl asked me to tell you he needs it. I am sorry—"

"It's all right. I didn't know it wasn't ours. I'll return it tomorrow."

"It's so sweet of you to take it so—"

"Goodbye, Frances."

Her budgets glared up at her—the payments that would be due in two weeks and all the money she had: three thousand dollars. She opened a drawer and took out the check from Ann Hayward. She had turned down Ross, but this was different: one check, and it was in her hand. One thousand dollars. Plus the three thousand in the bank. And eight thousand from selling the house. Enough to move to an apartment and keep going until she found a job.

Don't think about it; just do it. She called the realtor. A fool, Ross had said. Don't be a fool. But he hadn't said definitely that he'd pay the mortgage; only that he might. She wouldn't take it anyway. She'd manage alone, even if it meant selling the house.

But when she had told the realtor to accept the offer, she felt she'd made a terrible mistake. She'd been rash, just as Ross said. But he hadn't advised her; he'd only called her a fool. "Craig, I need you," she said aloud. "I miss you. *Please* call; please come back." She was crying again. It seemed everything made her cry and she was so tired of it, but there always seemed to be more tears, welling up.

She swiveled in Craig's chair and looked into her living room and beyond, to her dining room and kitchen, thinking, with a sick feeling, that they weren't hers any more. Outside, the tall trees stood like sentinels among the bushes and flowers she had planted, but they were no longer hers, either.

You shouldn't have sold it. She heard Craig accuse her. You should have waited. The room was empty, but she heard his voice. You had enough money for two months.

"I couldn't do it," she argued with his shadowy presence. "I don't believe you'll be back then. And what if I couldn't find another buyer?

Craig, I had to do this on my own." He did not answer.

Through the window she saw Jennifer and Todd get off the bus and run up the walk. Todd was disheveled, his face smudged; Jennifer's blouse was torn. What had they been up to? They were almost never rowdy. As they came in, she saw tears on their faces and jumped up to meet them. "What happened?" she exclaimed as they clung to her.

"It doesn't matter," Jennifer said vehemently. "Because we're moving away from here and we won't go to back to camp. I never want to go there again; I don't want to see any of those kids ever again."

"They're liars," Todd delcared. "I beat up Eddie and I almost broke Mack's head open, but then somebody tripped me. If he hadn't I would've killed them all."

"But why were you fighting?" Katherine asked, thinking—I know. I know why.

"They said Daddy stole money," Todd said. "And ran away, because he was afraid of going to jail. So I beat—"

Jennifer stamped her foot. "We're never going to see any of them again as long as we live!"

Damn them, Katherine thought fiercely. Damn the cruelty of children, and damn their parents who talked about us and gave them the ammunition to hurt my children.

"Tell me," she said, sitting with them on the couch. "How did they make fun of you?"

"Oh—" Jennifer tried to toss off the words. "They said we should've put Daddy on a leash till he was trained to stay home like other dogs—" The words were lost in a storm of weeping and she burrowed her face into Katherine's shoulder.

"They said their dads were home," Todd muttered. "And we should learn to keep our dad at home where he couldn't steal. But they're lying, aren't they? Just like Mr. Doerner. All those bastards are lying, aren't they? Fucking bastards, shitty bastards—"

"Todd!" Katherine said. "It doesn't help to talk that way."

"Yes it does. And they *are* bastards, Mom. They *lied!*"

With her children pressing against her, Katherine sent a silent, futile plea to Craig. What do you want me to tell them? If you're coming back I can make up something, but if you aren't, what can I do? I have to face them every day and answer their questions; they're not infants; they deserve the truth.

"We talked about this," she said at last, feeling Jennifer tense as she held her breath. "Remember? And I said there was a lot we don't know. I think those kids—stink. They're stupid and cruel and we should ignore them. But what they were saying... gets complicated, because it seems maybe Daddy did take money from the company."

"No," Jennifer said in a muffled voice.

"It seems he did. But he meant to pay it back. That's why he went away: to get money to pay back what he took. I don't know why he hasn't come home. Maybe he had more trouble getting it than he thought he would. We just don't know. And until he comes back and tells us—"

"If he's alive." Jennifer sat up and wiped her eyes with the back of her hand. "We don't know that either, do we?"

"Not for sure." What would the experts advise? Katherine wondered. Is it good or bad to burden children with the truth? She didn't have time to check; she had to decide for herself. Suddenly there were so many things she had to decide for herself. "All we can do is hope he's alive and wait to hear from him, or from someone else, if he's been in an accident—"

Once more the telephone rang and Todd dashed to answer it. "Sure," Katherine heard him say glumly. "It's for you, Mom. That lady you gave the party for."

Leslie. Katherine grasped the telephone as if it were a lifeline. "How wonderful that you called," she laughed shakily. "Perfect timing."

"My God," Leslie said. "What is it? What's wrong?"

"I've been trying to reach you..." Katherine sat down and the words poured out: everything that had happened, from Carl Doerner's first question at the party to the sale of her house and Jennifer's and Todd's fight at camp. She was crying, overwhelmed by reliving it all at once.

"Christ," Leslie said when she finally stopped. "Lousy, rotten mess... Well, now, hold on a minute; let me think." There was a comforting briskness in her voice and Katherine felt herself begin to relax. "We will ignore for the moment the fact that you didn't ask me for help, which makes me feel unwanted—"

"I tried to call; you were out of town. And then so many things kept happening—"

"—we will talk instead about my helping you now. How much money do you need?"

"Leslie, I can't borrow money." Katherine looked at Jennifer and Todd in the living room, and lowered her voice. "Craig has already done that for both of us."

"Oh. Well, I wouldn't look at it that way, but I can see how you might. So what are you doing for money? A job?"

"I'd love one. Have you got one to offer?"

"Sure. But not in Vancouver. You mean you can't find one?"

"Not yet." She'd left that out, ashamed to admit it to her successful friend, who had built a career for herself while Katherine invested herself in a man who left her. But now she related her rejections as a jewelry designer, as an office worker—"as anything; no one will hire me. There aren't many jobs to begin with and why should they take a chance on someone with no experience?"

"Because you're smart and quick and reliable."

"So I'd make a good Girl Scout."

"Well, I'd hire you in a minute. There's a job here you'd be perfect for—assistant to the guy who does our window displays. He's an ass, but you can't have everything. You want it?"

"Leslie, I live in Vancouver."

"I know." Leslie's voice was thoughtful. "But do you have to? I mean, what if you and the kids came here? You really could have that job, you know; I could arrange it. And I could find you an apartment so you'd have a place ready to move into. We could go back to our old days of gossip and chocolates. Damn it, Katherine, this is turning into one of my better ideas! Katherine? Are you there?"

"Yes." First Ross, now Leslie. But Ross had made only a casual suggestion. Leslie was offering a new life.

Gossip and chocolates. All through high school, into college and work, they would sit up all night in Leslie's bedroom, gorging on candy and bemoaning stodgy teachers, the crudity of young men, and the lack of glamour in their lives.

But what did they have in common now? Leslie was an executive with money and freedom; she was attractive and sophisticated and moved in a fast crowd of professional people. Katherine had been a housewife, but now she'd lost her husband and sold her house, so she didn't know what she was.

"I don't think so," she said. "We live here; it's home."

"Home! Listen, lady, from what you tell me, you're in hostile territory up there. No job, no friends, your kids fighting nasty little campers, and not even your own house anymore. You call that home? What about San Francisco? You lived here longer than you've lived in Vancouver; you probably remember every street sign. Right?"

She was right. Katherine remembered a feeling of homecoming the month before, from the moment Ross met their plane, and memories sprang up at every turn. *Home.* My roots and memories. And now—a job, a place to live, a friend.

"But Craig—" she began.

"Craig," Leslie echoed. "Well, what about him? First of all, until you're settled you leave my name and phone number with the Vancouver police and any friendly neighbors you can dig up. He can find you through me. Second, isn't it possible he'd go back to San Francisco instead of Vancouver? To his first family, so to speak? If you're here, too, he'll have everybody in one place, do all his explaining, end all his troubles at once. Dandy for him, don't you think?"

And for me, Katherine thought, aching for Craig and their life together. He must miss it, too—if he's alive. It meant so much to him. He'll come back to it—if he's alive. He'll find us, wherever we are.

Nothing else had worked. The closed doors of the past month surrounded her. What else is there? she thought. If I don't try something new, what else is there?

"I'll think about it," she told Leslie, but the tone of her voice had changed and Leslie heard it.

"Good," she said cheerfully. "Let me know when you decide; I'll hire a brass band to greet you at the airport."

"No," Katherine said absently, already thinking ahead. "I won't need a band. Just an apartment near a good school for Jennifer and· Todd—"

And it was only when she heard Leslie's laughter that she knew she had made up her mind.

CHAPTER 6

THE great red cables of the Golden Gate Bridge swooped low, then swung upward to the top of the four-tiered tower looming above them as Katherine parked the rented truck at the side of the road. "Last chance to be a tourist," she said gaily. "After this, we'll belong here."

"We'll never belong here," said Jennifer morosely, lagging behind as Katherine and Todd jumped from the high cab. "We belong in Vancouver."

"Jennifer," Katherine urged gently. "Come and look; it's quite wonderful."

"Wow," Todd whispered loudly, spinning in place. They were below the north end of the massive bridge, beside a small, sheltered bay where a few fishermen were casting their lines, and as they looked up, the bridge seemed to fly across the water, plunging at the far end into a thickly wooded park, with San Francisco just beyond it. "A lot bigger than Lions Gate."

"It is not," snapped Jennifer, but then she was silent, caught in the spell of the scene across the water—a city of hills, with white and pastel sun-washed houses and apartments stepping up and down the slopes, a solitary cluster of skyscrapers standing together like secretive friends, and everywhere the sparkle of water, almost surrounding the city, with hills and houses beyond. "It's a little like Vancouver," Todd said, to make Jennifer feel better, but Jennifer responded. "Vancouver is a thousand miles away."

Katherine barely heard them. She was filled with anticipation. Everything will be all right, she thought; I know where I am. We're not strangers. The city shimmered before them and she said impulsively, "It's waiting for us."

"So's Vancouver," muttered Jennifer, turning away from the shining view before it could soften her determination to be unhappy.

"Look over there," Todd called, walking along the edge of the small bay toward tall, needle-like rocks, a sandy beach, and, beyond it, a lighthouse. "Can we go look, Mom?"

"Not today," Katherine said. "We're meeting the realtor, remember? We'll come back." They looked together at the lighthouse on the point of land jutting into the water.

"Lime Point," said a fisherman standing nearby. "Great place. Out at the end you feel like you're all alone in the middle of the water. And over there" —he pointed to the left— "that's Alcatraz."

"Alcatraz—!" breathed Todd.

"Another day," said Katherine firmly. "We do have an appointment."

In the truck again, they drove back up the road to the highway, then over the bridge, between its huge arcs of red cables, watching the city grow larger. Jennifer stared gloomily out the window, wishing her mother would stop trying to be cheerful when every minute they were getting farther away from Daddy. It wasn't fair; she hadn't asked them if *they* wanted to move to San Francisco; she just made up her mind and then everything happened at once. She ordered them around, making them help her pack, and she rented the truck—Mother driving a truck!—and had half their furniture put in storage and the rest loaded onto the truck. They watched their house get emptier and emptier and when they walked through it for the last time, she and Todd had burst into tears and Mother was crying, too, kind of quietly. It was so awful—empty rooms with bare floors echoing their footsteps, the windows naked and sad without curtains, the doors like black holes in the blank walls. When Daddy came back, he'd cry, too. Why didn't you call us? Jennifer wailed silently to her father. We waited and waited till the last minute but you didn't call and now we're in this awful truck a *thousand miles* away.

Waiting at the stop light just past the thick forest of the Presidio, Katherine glanced at Jennifer: rebellious Jennifer, staring out her window. She knew she should be comforting her, but she couldn't. From the moment she sat behind the wheel of the truck and backed out of the driveway, her own feelings had overwhelmed her and she was impatient with her children's demands. Sitting high above the ground, she felt the anguish of leaving begin to ease and found herself exulting in what she had done: organized, packed, got away on schedule. By herself she had closed the house. Closed a life, she thought with a chill, but it faded in the light of her adventure: her first one alone since meeting Craig. After the fears and failures and loneliness of the past two months, the rattling truck became a chariot, bearing them away, and no matter how frightening the future, Katherine felt, for the first time that she could remember, that she was the one who would decide its direction.

The realtor led them to an apartment near Forty-sixth and Irving. Katherine vaguely remembered the neighborhood, called the Sunset, but she had forgotten how dense it was, street after street of tiny houses squeezed together in unbroken rows that sloped gradually down to the ocean. After the openness of West Vancouver, she felt hemmed in, and when the realtor stopped and she saw the building, her heart sank. In a city where the tiniest, most ordinary house was painted blue, pink, or yellow, or a gleaming white, the gray stucco building looked as unfriendly as a prison.

"You've got the ocean," the realtor recited briskly. "Just a few blocks away; see it from your doorstep. And of course Golden Gate Park, only a block away. Now let's show you inside."

"This is *it?*" Todd asked, looking into the three rooms in disbelief.

"It's ugly," Jennifer said flatly, and stomped out, to sit on the small patch of grass and scowl at the street.

The realtor spread his hands. "Miss McAlister said no more than four hundred. Not many places in the Sunset that cheap, you know. Nice place to bring up kids, lots of people want to live here. Good school nearby. And it's a clean building." Katherine nodded. "But Miss McAlister sends a good bit of business our way," he added hastily. "We wouldn't want you to be unhappy. How about we give you some paint and you and the youngsters can brighten up the place. And we'll start your rent with September. Give you two weeks free."

Katherine looked around. "This is four hundred dollars a month?"

"Right." He peered at her. "I thought Miss McAlister told you."

"She told me she would look for something between three and four—"

"Mrs. Fraser, you cannot be serious. For three in the Sunset you get nothing. Do you think this is a slum?"

Katherine walked into the dingy bedroom. Four hundred dollars was half a month's salary in the job Leslie had gotten her at Heath's. She shouldn't rent it. They could go to a hotel for a few days, until she found something cheaper. But she didn't know all the neighborhoods and this was the one Leslie had recommended. She stood, irresolute, the brief exultation of the trip draining away. Look where her direction had taken them: to three rooms for four hundred dollars a month. "All right," she said. They'd stay here while she looked around for herself. She started to write a check for September's rent.

"That'll be twelve hundred dollars," the realtor said, pulling out his receipt book.

"Twelve hundred—?"

"First month, last month, and one month security deposit. We have to protect ourselves," he added, seeing the shock on Katherine's face. "People skip, you wouldn't believe it—or they do damage."

Numbly, Katherine wrote the check. Whenever she thought she knew how much money she had, something came along to make it less. "Canadian bank," the realtor said, shaking his head. "Their dollars are worth about eighty-five cents here."

The exchange rate. Something else she hadn't planned on. "Could we settle it later?" she asked, trying to keep her voice calm. "After I open a bank account here?"

After a moment, he nodded. "I guess I can trust you for that. How about you make up the difference in next month's rent?"

"Fine." As soon as he left, she turned back to the apartment. Living room, bedroom, kitchen, bath. After what they'd had in Vancouver! Stunned by the enormity of it—giving up the space and light of their wonderful house, the terrace overlooking Vancouver, her rose garden, the huge trees and open yard—she shook her head. She had given that up... for this. How could she?

"Katherine! Good Lord, what have I done to you?"

Leslie stood in the doorway, her eyes meeting Katherine's over the grocery bags she held in her arms. "God damn it. Katherine, I had no idea. The realtor said it was perfect for a family and the best he could do with a top of four hundred..."

"It's all right, Leslie; we'll get used to it. And when we do some painting, it will be a lot brighter."

"But you ought to have more room."

"I can't afford more room."

Their different paychecks loomed between them. "In that case," Leslie said, putting the bags on the floor and holding out her arms, "welcome to San Francisco."

Katherine laughed and they held each other tightly. "Thank you. And thank you for coming; it's good to see a friendly face."

"Especially in this place." Leslie backed up and surveyed it, shaking her head. "Well." She became businesslike. "Here's the schedule. A crew of muscular young men will be here as soon as I give them the signal, to unload your truck. They do—"

"Leslie, I can't afford movers. We hired a high-school boy in Vancouver and I thought we'd do the same here."

"They aren't movers; they're maintenance men from one of our branch stores. Consider them a welcome wagon. They do whatever they're told, so have them put every piece of furniture exactly where you want before you let them get away. Then I'm taking all of you to dinner. Don't shake your head at me. It's the same welcome wagon. After this you're on your own, but to start you need something special, so we're going to Henri's at the top of the Hilton. Quite a view, decent food, and wine for the grownups. How does that sound?"

"It sounds like Christmas."

"Listen, I lured you down here; I have to keep you happy. Speaking of which, I brought you a present." She pulled something from one of the grocery bags. "Know what this is?"

"It looks like a bundle of rags."

"It is a bundle of rags. The most valuable gift a friend can bring someone just moving in. Now, I'm going to the pay phone at the corner to call the muscular young men and then I'll help you scrub what I am sure is a grimy kitchen. Jennifer and Todd should help, too, don't you think? Instead of sitting outside looking like the sky has collapsed?"

"Of course. How odd that I never thought of rags."

With Leslie as organizer, the apartment came to life. Two young men, as muscular as she had promised, unloaded the truck, while Katherine and Leslie, with a mildly grumbling Jennifer and Todd, washed the kitchen and bathroom and all the floors. In the three small rooms, they bumped and tripped over each other, but Leslie joked about it, and as Katherine heard the laughter and saw her own furniture settle into place, the anticipation she had felt that morning began to return.

"You see," Leslie said later, as they were led to a table in the restaurant. "All it takes is organization."

"Or desperation," Katherine said lightly. They sat beside a window while Jennifer and Todd toured the room to see the view from all directions, admitting it was pretty spectacular. Katherine gazed at the glowing city below and the curving panorama of lights across the bay—Oakland, Berkeley and their neighboring towns—and had a moment of pure happiness. Dinner with a friend, her children chattering happily instead of complaining, a home where lamplight and familiar furniture waited, and, in two weeks, when Jennifer and Todd started school, a job, a salary, a beginning. We've found a place, she thought as the waiter brought their shrimp and crab appetizers and Jennifer and Todd sat down to eat. Until Craig comes back, we've found a place to stay.

The small details of everyday life are invisible until they must be changed. Katherine changed almost all of them in her first two weeks in San Francisco. She arranged for a telephone and sent their new number and address to the Vancouver police, Carl Doerner, and two neighbors whom Craig might call when he found strangers living in their house. Using Leslie's recommendations, she found doctors and a dentist, and made a list of discount stores she could reach on public transportation. She opened checking and savings accounts in a bank near Heath's, filled out an application for check cashing at a neighborhood grocery store, and, borrowing Leslie's car, was first in line one morning to get a California driver's license. All her charge cards were in Craig's name, so she applied for new ones in her own name at Macy's and Sears; she had an employees' account at Heath's. Registering Jennifer and Todd at their new school, she found she'd forgotten to bring their records from Vancouver and sent to their old school for test scores, and to their doctor for their medical histories. And she spent a morning getting acquainted with a neighborhood pharmacist, the butcher at the supermarket, and the owner of a fish store down the street.

Best of all, Jennifer and Todd discovered Annie, who lived across the hall, and brought her to meet Katherine. Tall, blond, lanky, just turned sixteen, she was breezily cheerful, serious about her studies, and mad for new clothes, and therefore always on the lookout for ways to earn extra money—for instance, by keeping an eye on Jennifer and Todd when Katherine began her new job.

"Not that I'm not crazy about them," she told Katherine earnestly. "I'd do it as a favor, except... well, you know, things *cost* so much..."

Katherine knew. She also knew that since Annie lived across the hall, she could be in her own home, at least part of the time, at her own typewriter, listening to her own records, and still be earning money as long as both apartment doors were open. Once they agreed it was a good deal for the two of them, they worked out a schedule of hours and payment for after school and evenings.

Not that Katherine expected to be going out at night, but just in case something came up, it was good to know Annie was there. Especially for the afternoons. In Vancouver, she'd always been home when Jennifer and Todd arrived from school and the thought of their wandering around on their own while she was trapped at work had frightened her. Now that fright was gone.

One more arrangement made, she thought. It takes a lot of running and planning, to belong. But there was still more running ahead. They went sightseeing.

Katherine splurged and rented a car, and they left early one morning for the Muir Woods. Driving north, they drove through a tunnel with its entrance painted in a huge rainbow. A good omen, Katherine thought as Jennifer laughed with pleasure when she pointed it out, and a little later, when they stood in awestruck silence beneath the cool grandeur of towering redwoods, all of Todd's and Jennifer's grumbling and disparaging comparisons with Vancouver ended, at least for a while.

The next few days were packed with exploring: museums, parks, an old sailing ship, a chocolate factory converted to a shopping center, a zoo with a Gorilla World and a Zebra Zephyr tour train. But most exciting of all, for Jennifer and Todd, was driving on San Francisco's streets: the weird disembodied feeling that made them screech with delight when Katherine drove up one of the city's steep hills and they saw nothing ahead but sky, nothing of the other side, until the car was at the crest and then precipitously descending, giving them a stomach-clutching view down, down, past a cross street, then down past another, and still down, farther and farther, all the way to the water's edge. Then they would let out a long sigh of relief and pause before demanding, "Where's the next hill?"

At the end of the week, when school and Katherine's job were both about to begin, they listed the places they'd had to postpone. It takes a lot of running to belong, Katherine thought again, smiling. But what a good start we've made.

Heath's main store turns a cool marble facade toward Union Square. From four tall windows, haughty mannequins gaze at the comings and goings in the square across the street: couples entwined on the grass, men in tatters sleeping on benches, revival singers and fervent speakers on a stone platform haranguing anyone who pauses to listen, office workers taking a shortcut on the diagonal walks between flower gardens, clipped hedges, and tall spiky palms. Katherine stood among the mannequins in one of the windows, holding a silk scarf and a handbag, waiting for Gil Lister to ask for them. Heath's window designer for twenty years, Lister ran his little kingdom with entrenched power and a sharp tongue and only reluctantly had accepted Katherine as his assistant. Short and round, with quivering lips and smooth skin, he established his supremacy the day she arrived.

"Stand there, my dear, no, a little more to the right; now, when I ask for the scarf you will hold it up, so, and wait until I take it from you. No tossing it at me and no scurrying about so that I don't know where you are. Think of yourself as a surgeon's assistant, always alert for what I need, making sure I expend a *minimum* of effort in achieving the *maximum* of my potential. Clear? Not too difficult for you, my dear? Let's try it, then. Stand here—no, a little to the left. . ."

When she was not holding items above her head, her arms aching with the effort of keeping them extended exactly as Lister instructed, she sat at a small desk in a corner of his workroom, copying sketches of window displays, ordering mannequins and sending others out for repair, writing orders for scenery and props, and keeping files on all of Lister's designs and those he copied from designers in other stores. "It doesn't hurt them in the slightest," he told Katherine. "I'm not taking any business from them, and I could put together far more original ideas of my own, but you see how busy I am, my dear, it is appalling the way time rushes past and art suffers first, you'll discover that, art suffers when we have no time to contemplate and create. Still, we don't want competitors to be peeved at seeing their little designs in our windows, so we embellish them to give our customers the prestigious look they expect from Heath's. Hand me that table, my dear, we'll change this from a den to a living room."

Alternately amused by his tricks to impress others and furious with his tyranny over her, Katherine could not wait to get away at five thirty each day, and by the end of her first week at work, she was worn out. Still, getting off the bus on Friday, she realized that for a whole week she hadn't anguished over Craig; she'd been too busy, too tired. Is that good or bad? she wondered. I mustn't let him seem too far away; too much depends on him. And if he were here, she reflected, he'd remember that today is my birthday and I wouldn't feel so low about it.

She turned the corner, leaving behind the noisy congestion of Irving Street with its traffic, stores and restaurants from a dozen countries. Walking home, she began to feel better. It was a quiet, pleasant street of identical tiny houses, each with a garage and a bay window above it, a small patch of lawn in front, with miniature gardens and small trees or bushes, almost like a small village.

Beyond another, identical block was Golden Gate Park, its border of tangled bushes hiding museums and gardens, windmills and lakes, fields, woods, restaurants, and numberless paths to explore. Katherine saw Jennifer and Todd on the edge of the park, with Annie, waving at her, waiting to cross Lincoln Way. When they ran up to her she thought they looked conspiratorial.

"The paint finally came," said Todd as Annie went in to do her homework. "White and yellow. Pretty dull."

"Those are the colors I asked for," Katherine said. "Do I get a greeting?"

They gave her a perfunctory kiss. "When do we eat?"

"For heaven's sake!" she exclaimed. "Can I have a few minutes to be me before I become the cook?"

"Mom!" Todd stepped back and squinted at her. "You never used to talk like that."

Damn, Katherine thought, and bent to kiss them. "I'm sorry. It hasn't been the best week, you know." She saw them exchange a look. "All right, let's get dinner. Did you look in those bags to see if we got paint brushes and rollers?"

They talked about school and painting the apartment, and as they were finishing dinner, Katherine said, "You haven't told me what you did after school."

They gave each other a quick, secretive glance and shrugged. "Walked around with Annie."

"Where?"

"The park. Irving Street. You know."

"Just walking?"

"Not exactly..."

"Then what?" Katherine asked in frustration.

"This!" Todd shouted, and from beneath his chair whipped out a small wrapped package. "Happy birthday!" he shouted again.

Jennifer jumped up to give Katherine a loud kiss. "Daddy always took us shopping for your birthday so we weren't sure what to get but we hope you like it." Tears filled Katherine's eyes and Jennifer put her arms tightly around her. "We love you, Mommy. And next birthday we'll shop with Daddy again, so everything will be all right."

Katherine tried to smile. All day she had been remembering the ten festive birthdays that had gone before, celebrated with Craig's flowers, lavish gifts, a decorated cake from one of Vancouver's elite bakeries, and a rousing off-key "Happy Birthday" sung by Craig, Todd, and Jennifer. Now, as Jennifer and Todd put before her a plate of glazed doughnuts bristling with candles, it was all she could do to keep her tears from overflowing. "Happy birthday," they sang—and all of them thought what a thin chorus it was without Craig. Then Katherine blew out the candles and, with Todd and Jennifer eagerly watching, opened her present.

"Oh," she said blankly, then recovered. "Oh, how lovely; and I've been needing a new one; how did you know?"

They beamed. "It was Jennifer's idea," Todd said. "I never even heard of a blusher."

Katherine turned the small plastic square in her hand, opened it to reveal the mirror, pressed powder and small brush, then closed it and ran her finger over the tortoiseshell surface. "I'll use it all the time," she said, hugging them. "Thank you—and thank you for remembering." But she wondered, as they washed the dishes, if Jennifer had thought of a compact as a way of telling her to pay more attention to herself. She felt embarrassed, and pressured, because she couldn't rouse herself to care about her looks. Each morning, dressing for work, she knew she should try, but a wave of lassitude would sweep over her and she would give up. I'm clean and neat, she told herself; that's enough. Someday I'll do more. If—*when* Craig comes back, I'll want to. Until then— She slipped the small compact into her purse. Just as she and the children were waiting for Craig, it would, too.

Saturday morning Leslie appeared as Katherine was opening the first can of paint. "I don't believe it," Katherine said. "What good timing. Too good, in fact. How come you're here?"

Leslie sighed deeply. "Do not look a gift horse—"

"Leslie. Why are you here?"

"Long story. I stopped by this morning when you were grocery shopping and your kids were telling Annie you yelled at them last night, and worrying that you must be sick. They also told me you were painting the place today, and I decided to make it a party. Are you sick?"

"Of course not. They told Annie? They must have been more upset than I realized. I guess we all were. I didn't understand that they were in a hurry to eat so they could give me my present—"

"Present?"

"Yesterday was my birthday."

"Damn it, lady, why didn't you tell me? We could have had a party. Thirty-five?"

"Yes."

"A depressing age to reach alone. Why didn't you tell me?"

"I guess I didn't want a party." Katherine began to stir the paint. "And I had no idea Jennifer and Todd even remembered."

"Good kids," Leslie said casually. "Which reminds me—where are they?"

"At the hardware store. We needed extra brushes. Leslie, you don't have to help paint—"

"I know I don't. That's why I'm doing it. Don't argue. Four painters cut the work in half and double the fun."

And they did. With Jennifer and Todd, they gathered brushes, rags, rollers, and paint, arguing vociferously over the best way to stack furniture and divide the work, and soon the small apartment rang with banter and laughter. They worked steadily, stopping only for a sandwich at noon and by three they were almost finished.

"How are you getting along with Gil Lister?" Leslie asked from the top of a ladder.

"As long as I'm his obedient puppy, we get along fine."

"I'm sorry about that. I told you he was an ass, but I thought with your artistic eye you'd like doing the windows."

"I would."

"But Gil doesn't want your ideas? Pity you aren't a charming young boy with a taste for rotund queers."

"What's a rotund queer?" Jennifer asked, coming in from the bedroom.

"An overweight eccentric," Leslie said hastily. "I don't suppose you've met any."

"I don't suppose that's really what it means, either," said Jennifer shrewdly. "I'll ask my mother later; she doesn't think my education should be censored."

"My God," Leslie breathed. "I've been put in my place."

"Jennifer!" Todd yelled from the bedroom. "I think I spilled something!"

"Don't you *know?*" she called back in exasperation. "Wait a minute; I'll come and help."

When she left, Leslie grinned at Katherine. "I feel humbled. Is she always so damned bright and grown up?"

"Only often enough to confuse me."

"It would scare the hell out of me. Whenever I think it's about time I had one of my own, I meet one of these kid geniuses and decide I couldn't possibly cope."

"Jennifer seems pretty normal to me. What do you mean, have one of your own? Are you secretly married?"

"No. And no prospects in sight. But is that a requirement?"

Katherine cocked an eyebrow. "It's at least a convenience."

"Not always." Leslie waved her brush. "Not even necessarily. How many women shed unsatisfactory husbands long before the offspring are even half grown? How many men walk out and leave their wives stuck with bringing up—oh, shit, Katherine, I'm sorry. I am a full-fledged ass. I got carried away with speechmaking and forgot present company."

"It's all right," said Katherine absently. She had stopped painting the baseboard and was looking around, trying to figure out why she suddenly felt uneasy. From her place on the floor, she could see all three rooms at once, looking bigger and brighter in their glistening new colors. Her apartment.

How extraordinary. Her apartment, her home. Filled with her possessions, her children, and companionship. But something was wrong.

The bright rooms had the look of a doll's house: a small bedroom for Jennifer and Todd, two narrow closets, a living room with a sofa bed for Katherine, a kitchen just big enough for their oak table and captain's chairs. And then Katherine knew what was wrong.

There was no room for Craig. They had made a home for a family without Craig.

Melanie Hayward always asked for Wilma in the Empire Room of Heath's: the only saleswoman, she said, who understood her and always found clothes that were *her*. It was true that Wilma gossiped about the divorces and affairs and marital tiffs of her customers, but a word from Melanie and she was silent. And Melanie always gave the word, as soon as she learned something new about her circle.

"—taken up with Ivan something," Wilma chattered as she helped Melanie into a silk sheath with a chiffon scarf. "Macklin, I think, Ivan Macklin; they've been seen together at Carmel and Las Vegas and her husband told her to drop him or get out. 'I'm not running no motel,' he says. 'Either you—'"

"I hardly think," Melanie cut in, "that those were his words."

"No'm, maybe not," Wilma agreed cheerfully. "Now you can either loop this scarf around your neck or wear it around your shoulders..."

By the end of the afternoon, Melanie had spent just under six thousand dollars on five outfits for the winter season, had learned three new items about her friends, and had instructed Wilma to watch for something special for an April gala she was planning at the Fairmont. Humming, she browsed casually along the main floor, then stopped abruptly near the Union Square exit. Through an open door in the wall, she had caught sight of two people dressing a mannequin in a velvet evening gown. "*Hand* me the sash, my dear," the man said testily as Melanie watched, and the woman stretched her arm out for him to take a sash from her hand. What the hell, Melanie thought, remembering the last time she had seen the woman—pale, wearing a wrinkled suit, and ready to flee Victoria's dining room. What the hell is she doing here? Ross never said a word.

She watched as they put a champagne glass in the mannequin's hand and moved on to dress another in satin and lace. Not as pale, Melanie thought, and the haunted look was gone. But there was something forlorn about her as she stood waiting for the little man's orders, obediently handing him clothing and props and, once, glancing furtively at her watch. Serves her right, Melanie thought, for trying to worm her way in.

But why was she working at Heath's? Driving home across the Golden Gate Bridge, Melanie seethed over it. What was she doing in San Francisco? How long would she wait to call the family and announce that she was ready to become a Hayward and share the Hayward wealth?

Maybe she already had. Maybe they knew and hadn't told her about it. Forced to slow down in the heavy traffic, Melanie clenched the wheel. Of course little Katherine would call Ross the minute she arrived. And he kept it a secret. She swung the wheel at the Tiburon exit and a mile farther, at the base of their hill, put the car in low gear and took the steep road a little too fast all the way to the top. She wondered if he'd told Derek. Or Victoria. Or all of them. Why the hell, she demanded silently, am I the last to know?

"I saw your mousy little friend today," she told Ross at dinner. "Working at Heath's."

He looked up from contemplating a bottle of wine. "Who?"

"You know perfectly well. Your dowdy Canadian protégée, the one who told us off at Victoria's."

"Katherine? In San Francisco?"

"Don't put on an act with me. Do you think I don't know you're behind it?"

"At Heath's, you said? By God, that took courage. As a sales clerk?"

"I *said*, don't put on an act. You know damn well she's not a sales clerk. You probably got her the job. And a place to live. Without once mentioning it to me. Who *did* you mention it to? Victoria? Derek?"

"I didn't know about it." They sat across from each other. Carrie and Jon had eaten earlier, as usual, in the kitchen with the maid and the cook, and, as usual, he and Melanie faced each other with no one to break the silences between them or moderate their taut exchanges. "I haven't spoken to Katherine in weeks."

"You didn't know she was moving to San Francisco?"

"No. We did talk about it once; in fact, I suggested it, but she didn't—"

"Suggested it!"

"She grew up here; she has a close friend—in fact if anyone is helping her, that's probably who it is. And she has us."

"She doesn't 'have' us. She has nothing to do with us. If you didn't keep dragging her in—"

"I didn't drag her this time. She made up her mind by herself and didn't tell me about it. What was she doing at Heath's?"

"Window dressing. Helping a nasty little man who treated her like dirt." The maid came in to clear their plates. "What did *you* do today?" Melanie asked brightly.

He sat back. "As a matter of fact, this was a red-letter day. I was waiting to tell you about it."

"About what?"

"We got approval from the mayor's office for BayBridge Plaza."

"Oh?"

"Melanie," he said very softly. "BayBridge Plaza. I've told you about it perhaps a hundred times in the four years I've been working on it. Approval from the mayor's office is almost the last hurdle. A few more approvals—maybe another month of negotiating—and we can begin."

"I remember. You said it was a big project. Expensive?"

"About three hundred million dollars."

Her eyes widened. "Your fee is a percentage of that."

He shrugged. Reliable Melanie; he always knew what would get her attention. "My expenses are up, too. I told you I hired seventy new people, and I'll be using outside consultants. . . And I have to buy out a lease on that building I bought a few years ago, on Mission Street. It's been added to BayBridge, but the former owner's still in it. I think he's ready to sell; he was talking the other day about needing money."

"Anyone we know?" she asked idly as the maid put cups and a silver coffee server beside her.

"I don't know him. His name is Ivan Macklin; he built the building. In fact his name is on it."

"Macklin? I think I know him. Or maybe only the name. Where did I hear it?" Pouring coffee, she frowned. "Oh. Wilma."

"Wilma?"

"My salesgirl at Heath's. She heard he was playing around with some-one. Maybe that's why he needs money." The maid put a bowl of sliced peaches and *crème fraîche* in front of Melanie and left the room. "Are you going to call her?"

"Who?"

"Ross, don't be tiresome. Katherine Fraser."

"Of course."

"I'd rather you didn't."

"I know."

Tight-lipped, she spooned the dessert into two bowls and passed him one. "Are you going to buy out Ivan Macklin?"

"Do you care?"

"Not much. Not at all, I suppose. Not any more than you care that I don't want you to call that woman."

"I do care; I'm sorry it bothers you. Why does it?"

"I've told you. She doesn't belong; she . . . complicates things."

"Meaning money."

"Partly." She stirred her coffee, then burst out, "I don't want a helpless woman running around looking for protection."

"Well at least that's honest." Pushing back his chair, he stood up. "But I'm not sure she's helpless. A woman who moves her family a thousand miles and finds a way to support them seems pretty self-sufficient to me. In fact, the only thing she might need is friendship." He slid open the door to the den. "I'm sorry if it bothers you, but that much I intend to offer."

Katherine was filling out shipment forms for returning window scenery to the warehouse when Ross telephoned. She had thought about calling him for three weeks, ever since they arrived, but his voice was so unexpected that for a moment she was speechless. "How did you know?" she stammered. "I didn't think anyone knew we were here."

"I'll tell you at lunch. Can you meet me at one?"

"Today?"

"Unless you're too busy."

She looked at Gil Lister. "I only have an hour—"

"We'll try to stretch it. One o'clock then."

"No, I can't. I mean, I can only go at noon."

"Noon. Well—all right. The Compass Rose at the St. Francis. I'll be waiting."

He had chosen a place diagonally across Union Square from Heath's and Katherine was there exactly at noon. "Good heavens," she said, gaping as they climbed the carpeted stairs from the lobby to the restaurant and were confronted with a riotous conglomeration that included Ionic columns, eighteenth-century blackamoors, cobra lamps, Lebanese mirrors, and an art deco bar with huge lucite scrolls at the back and griffins at each corner.

Ross led Katherine past overstuffed chairs and couches grouped around marble and glass tables, across a small dance floor to an alcove where a velvet couch curved beneath a Chinese lacquer screen. "You've never been here?"

"I don't know how I missed it," Katherine said. "It's just the place for people who grow up above grocery stores."

He chuckled as he gave the waiter their order, then sat back and looked at her. "I'm glad to see you. How are you?"

"Not bad," she said, and thought about it. "Really not bad. I don't have that feeling all the time of being on the edge of a cliff, about to topple over."

"But you still have it sometimes."

She looked pensively at a bronze goddess reclining beneath English pewter wall sconces. "I miss being sure of what will happen tomorrow and the day after. I miss knowing the boundaries of my days—what I can or can't do, what I'm supposed to do, what the people I love can do. I know that none of it was true—nothing was certain—but it was so comforting to think it was. And I miss it. I miss Craig; I miss our times together; I miss our house. I get lonely." She sat straighter. "I'm sorry. I didn't mean to whine."

"You're not whining. Loneliness is a fact, not a complaint." She looked up at the odd note in his voice, but he changed the subject. "Why must you eat lunch at noon?"

"Because the man I work for decrees it."

"Why?"

"He didn't tell me. Don't you make rules for the people who work for you?"

"As few as possible. They work harder and more happily when they have some control over their days."

"Yes." Katherine watched the waiter serve scallops and wild rice, and fill their wine glasses. "Gil hasn't learned that."

"Gil?"

She told him about her job, making it seem more quaint than difficult and then, as he asked questions, she described their move to San Francisco.

"And all that time you didn't call me."

"I thought about it. I wanted to do things by myself. And get used to being alone."

"But you let your friend help you."

"That was different."

"Alone means without a man." It was a statement, not a question, and it startled her.

"I never thought about it. I suppose it does. Right now, anyway."

He looked at his watch. "Dessert?" She shook her head, wondering if he was offended. "You know," he mused. "I've never gone in drag, but if that's what it takes to be your friend, I'd consider it."

It was several seconds before she took it in. He had spoken so seriously, and he looked so normal as he sat beside her—handsome, successful, at ease—that the words made no sense. Then she burst out laughing. "What an absurd thing to say."

"As absurd as refusing to call a friend."

Their eyes met in laughter. "You're looking much better," Ross said, thinking how remarkable her eyes were and how laughter transformed her face. "The city suits you."

She flushed and looked away. "And your wife?" she asked. "And Carrie and Jon?"

"Fine." He wondered why she resisted compliments. "You haven't told me where you live or how I can help you."

"In the Sunset."

"*Where* in the Sunset?"

She gave him her address. "But we don't need anything. All we have to do is get used to the fog. I'd forgotten that the closer the ocean, the more fog there is. Todd and Jennifer are inventing a fan to blow it out to sea."

"How do they like school?" he asked.

"Not as much as they would if they let themselves. But they're afraid school means we really *live* here, we'll never go back to Vancouver, or—" she cleared her throat to stop the waver in her voice "—see Craig again."

And there was Craig, Ross thought, as if Katherine's words had brought his shadow to sit beside them. "You haven't heard from him? Or anything about him?"

Katherine shook her head. "Everything I do—the apartment, my job, my friends—seems to push him farther away, but at the same time he's always with me. As if he's watching to see how well I can manage alone. I know that sounds silly, but still he's *here*."

Ross signaled for their coffee. "It's not silly. It took us years to get used to the idea that Craig and Jennifer were dead."

"But Craig wasn't."

"He might as well have been. He might as well be now. If he's not with you, if he doesn't come back—"

"I don't talk about that," Katherine said abruptly. "Tell me about your work. You haven't talked about yourself at all."

"Do you have five minutes more? I'll tell you about a place I designed called BayBridge Plaza."

"Can you tell me in five minutes?"

"I can start. The other three hours will have to wait until next time." She laughed. "Please start."

"Do you know what mixed-use development is?"

"No, but I suppose—a combination? Offices and stores?"

"That's it, but BayBridge goes even further: residences, office buildings, shops, theaters, eating places, and lots of space and light—parks, atriums, fountains, gardens, tennis courts—places for people. The whole idea is people—on foot, not in cars, and not dodging cars to get around." He smiled. "We're building for pedestrians. It's a dream we've had for a long time."

Puzzled, Katherine asked, "Who are 'we'?"

"My company. The one I began six years ago."

"It's your dream, then."

"Well, yes, but my staff is made up of people with the same ideas. What we're trying to do is rebuild cities and towns—or parts of them— without destroying them in the process. Look," he explained as she frowned slightly, "in BayBridge, we've designed townhouses—some restored, some new—and apartments in renovated warehouses. Wherever possible, we've kept the past—the city's past—and made it livable, not only because it's a reminder of our beginnings, but also for variety. And we've designed them in so many shapes, sizes, styles, and price ranges they'll attract all kinds of residents, young couples, singles, families, retired people—the whole spectrum. The life of a place is in variety, not sameness."

He looked at his watch and signaled for the check. "The buildings will be low, joined by grass and brick paths. No towers, no high-rises, no concrete, no automobiles. They'll be parked on the periphery, screened by berms and trees and walls. The office buildings will be in a separate group and behind them a shopping mall with a community recreation center. The whole mall, including the central courtyard, will be on multiple levels to make it seem like a series of separate areas—something like small village squares. It's illusion but it works; even with a hundred shops it's scaled to people: intimate, warm, bright, open, with places to sit outside or in, places for kids to play...I can't tell you all at once; there's too much. But that's what we're trying to do in the whole plaza: keep each building and each area to a size and scope geared to people instead of the greater glory of engineers and architects and manufacturers of concrete and steel—"

He stopped. "Katherine, I'm sorry. I go on and on when I have a good audience."

His vitality and excitement had captured Katherine's imagination. "BayBridge is a small town," she said. "Isn't that it? A community. And if you make enough of them, they'll all be connected, like links in a chain, to make a new kind of city."

Ross's face lit in a smile. "Thank you. For understanding so completely and for expressing it more perfectly than I ever did."

Again, Katherine flushed. "I have to get back. Thank you for lunch, and telling me about your work; it was wonderful. The best antidote to Gil."

"Wait; I'll walk with you." He took her arm as they left. "How long are you going to work for this tyrant?"

"Until I can make a living some other way."

He thought back. "Once you said you were going to design jewelry."

"It didn't work. I wasn't ready. But I think I'm going to try again. Leslie knows a jewelry designer and she's going to ask him for the name of someone I might study with."

"Let me know how it goes." In Heath's doorway, they shook hands. "I'll call you soon; we'll have lunch again. And one night we'll go back to Victoria's for dinner."

She met his eyes. "I don't think so. But I'd enjoy lunch." Anticipating Gil's wrath, she said a quick goodbye and slipped through the door, almost running to the stairs. But, going down, she smiled at the memory of their laughter in the restaurant.

Another friend.

Leslie McAlister and Marc Landau left the theater while the actors were still taking curtain calls, to beat the crowd to the street. "I have a feast waiting in the oven," he announced in the taxi. "So tonight we go to my place."

Leslie grinned. "Gold dust in the salt shaker?"

"That was last month, to celebrate the success of my custom line. Tonight you will find salt. Do you think I can afford such gestures every time we are together?"

"It would depend on the woman."

"Ah." He gestured vaguely, his plump, manicured hand somehow sketching the difficulties of finding anyone who deserved from him more than an occasional lavish gift.

Looking at those pudgy fingers, Leslie marveled that they could be so delicate, not only at the worktable where he created the opulent jewelry that had made him famous and wealthy, but also in bed. An odd man, she thought dispassionately: soft and balding, but ruthless in business;

crude but sophisticated, callously promiscuous but occasionally sympathetic and sensitive. After two years of going out with him, sleeping with him, traveling with him, she still wasn't sure how much she liked him. But the older Leslie got, the fewer the men who were amusing and intelligent, and usually Marc was both. And, she thought as they took the elevator to his apartment, he could be helpful to Katherine.

"If not gold dust," she said, "how about a small favor for a friend?"

"Possibly."

"She's just moved here from Vancouver. She wants to design and make jewelry, but she needs to improve her technique and try out different materials. Can she work with you? She's already pretty good; it wouldn't be for long."

"You're asking me to reveal to a stranger the techniques I've spent years developing. Champagne?"

"Yes, thank you. Katherine isn't a stranger; she's my friend. And I'm not asking you to give away secrets, just help her learn to work with gold and silver and other materials—"

"Where will she get the money to buy them?"

"She's working at Heath's."

"My dear Leslie, if she's working when will she have the time? And how much can she be earning? Do you have any idea what gold and silver cost?"

"A lot. But that's not the message I'm getting." She put down her glass and looked at him narrowly. "It's just too much trouble, isn't it? The famous designer can't be bothered. She's my friend and I'm asking a favor, but there are a dozen goddamn reasons why you can't lift a finger to help. God, Marc, you are a bore. Never mind; I'll ask someone else. Is there more champagne?"

"There is always more champagne. And I am not a bore or you would not be here. As for your friend, I'll find someone to help her. I have no interest in coaching apprentices, but I know a man who takes small classes; I'll see if he has an opening. As for you, my dear, you seem to be turning into a charitable institution. First your brother—is he still at Heath's, by the way?"

"Still there. But I think he's avoiding me and I'm worried—"

"Spare me the details. And take care, Leslie, that you don't give too much of yourself to others; they suck you dry if you let them." He picked up the champagne bottle. "Now may we move on to the kitchen? We should inspect this elegant dinner I have personally prepared for you by standing in line at four exceedingly busy and exclusive delicatessens."

She laughed. "But you will help Katherine?"

"My God, I've said I would. Give me a day or two. In the meantime, here—and here—and here—" He pulled books from the shelf. "Tell her to read these. And leave me her telephone number before you go. Now, for the rest of the evening, you are to forget about good deeds. Except, of course, for those that belong in the bedroom. After dinner."

In a small room above a store on Geary Street, Katherine sat on a wooden stool at a workbench, cutting a leaf from a silver square. As she finished the stem, her saw blade, barely thicker than a hair, snapped apart, and she let out a sharp sigh before reaching for a new one. After a day of holding china and silver while Lister set a banquet scene, her arms ached and it was their trembling as she followed the pattern scored in the soft silver that had caused her to break four blades in one evening.

"It happens to all of us," her instructor said at her shoulder. "Keep the blade upright and hold the strokes steady. You'll be fine. You're almost through, you know."

Fitting a new blade to her saw, she nodded. This time her hand moved in a smoother rhythm, flowing with the softness of the silver, and in a moment the roughly shaped leaf lay before her. With a small file, she smoothed and also notched the edges, making the distinctive outline of a maple leaf. A drawer in her lap caught the silver dust and shavings. When the shape was complete, she clamped the leaf in a revolving vise and turned and tilted it while scoring it with an awl—one line down the center, shorter lines radiating out. When the leaf's veins were finished she removed it from the vise and placed it in a hollow in a block of wood, where she pounded it to a curved shape with a rawhide-covered hammer. And finally, she polished the leaf on a buffing wheel to a silver gleam.

The finished maple leaf shone in her palm, gracefully curved as if lifted by the wind. She touched it with her finger. It was no different from hundreds of others made by students in classes just like her own— yet it was different. Marc Landau had suggested starting from the beginning with a short course in metals and stones. That was why it was different: it was a beginning. Never again would this be a pleasant hobby to fill her extra time: she would be a designer, an artist, a professional. She carried a sketch pad now, wherever she went, to draw forms in nature or architecture that might be created in jewelry. Every night, after Jennifer and Todd were asleep, she worked at a small table in the corner of her living room, the only sound the scratching of her pencil as she doodled and drew and threw away and began again.

Craig watched her. She had had a snapshot enlarged and framed and it stood at the back of the table watching her: Craig in khakis and a plaid shirt, leaning against a tree at the top of Grouse Mountain. They had taken a picnic lunch, just the two of them—one of the few times they were ever alone. Craig had told her, as she was taking his picture, that Hank Aylmer had invited them to go with him when he next visited Eskimo villages to buy sculptures. A holiday, Craig said. It would be good to get away.

That was in May. One month before he disappeared.

Leaning against a tree—handsome, bearded, smiling—Craig watched Katherine bend over her sketches. He accused her of leaving Vancouver, of making a home with no place for him, of wanting to be a professional and manage on her own. "Well, what would you rather I did?" she asked his picture. "Sit in a corner and cry? Whine to your mother and father or the rest of your family—whom you never even told me about? What should I do?"

She waited, as if giving him a chance to respond. "Well," she said after a moment, and turned back to her work. A glint of light from the silver leaf caught her eye and she picked it up. The contentment of finishing it swept over her again, warming her as if she sat in a sunlit clearing. And if a shadow hovered nearby, which might dull the shine of her silver leaf, she did not look up to see if it was there.

CHAPTER 7

B Y the middle of October, Christmas materials had been delivered for Heath's windows and Lister and Katherine spent two days in the supply room, checking clothes and props against his master list. Katherine was unpacking linens for a children's bedroom scene when the telephone rang.

Lister took all the calls. This time he barked, "For you," and glared at Katherine as she took the receiver. He forbade personal telephone calls at work but, thinking of the children and Craig, Katherine ignored him. "Hello," she said, her voice low, her back to Lister.

"Derek Hayward, Katherine. We met at dinner—"

"I remember." She sat down. *Derek?*

"You're probably busy, so I won't keep you. Will you have dinner with me? Tomorrow night, if you can manage on such short notice."

"No," she said without thinking. "I'm sorry, but—"

"Next week, then. You name the night."

"No, I'm sorry but I . . . I don't go out to dinner."

There was a pause. "Then I should apologize; that didn't occur to me. Lunch, instead? Tomorrow? A business lunch."

"Business?" Katherine turned and saw Lister watching her. "I can't talk now and I can't imagine what—"

"Family business," Derek said. "Making you welcome. That's something more than one of us should do." His voice was like Ross's, warm and deep, and the words were casual, but they had an edge.

"Who—?" she began, then changed it. "How did you find me?"

He laughed shortly. "The family. Twice. Melanie told me she'd seen you at Heath's, and a day or two later Ross told Victoria he'd taken you to lunch, and Victoria told Tobias, who mentioned it to Melanie, who passed that along to me, also. Did you follow all that? It's one of the joys of a large family."

She would have laughed but he was not joking. "I've never known what that was like," she commented. He was silent. "I have to get back to work," she said. "I don't think lunch is a good idea. Usually I just bring something and eat here or across the street in the square."

"I'll meet you there," he said promptly. "And I'll bring lunch. Do you have a favorite bench?"

"I sit on the grass."

"Then I won't wear my best suit. Until tomorrow."

But he was wearing a suit when she saw him the next day, waiting at the soldier's memorial statue in the center of Union Square. "I might take off my tie," he said as they sat on the grass in a sunny corner between tall hedges. "But if I didn't wear a suit on a weekday I might forget who I am. And what are *you* wearing, after all?"

"I confess," she laughed. "A suit." He was handsomer than she remembered, with the same dark blond hair and deep-set eyes as Ross, but smoother and more polished. And there was another difference. He made her conscious of the way he looked at her.

"Lunch," he announced, and opened a woven straw hamper. "Of course I had very little time to plan it properly, but I think it deserves at least polite applause."

Katherine watched in astonishment as he took out a wooden box and unfolded it to a small table. Dipping into the hamper again and again like a beguiling magician, he drew out two china plates, heaped them with thin slices of rare roast beef, hearts of palm vinaigrette, and buttered rounds of rye bread, and balanced a silver knife and fork across each one. He poured a ruby-red Bordeaux into two crystal wine glasses and handed Katherine a linen napkin. "Of course I had very little time."

Katherine had expected sandwiches and potato chips in a paper bag. "You bought this just for today?"

"You said you wanted to eat on the grass; I bought a lunch for eating on the grass. But of course you're right; we should indeed use it again. In fact, from a strictly economic point of view, which I confess I had not considered, we can amortize the cost to reduce it to a rock-bottom ten dollars each by eating on the grass once a week for about thirty weeks. Can you arrange that? After all, we're right across the street from your office, or wherever it is you spend your time. Which reminds me, what is it you do over there?"

"Decorate windows." Six hundred dollars for a picnic lunch. She was appalled—and fascinated. "But that's not what you mean, is it? You're really asking what I'm doing in San Francisco."

He considered her. Of course that was what he meant, but he hadn't expected her to pick it up so quickly. She'd improved, he thought, since the night they'd met: the haggard look was gone and she no longer hunched over as if expecting a blow. But why the hell did she twist her hair in a bun and wear a suit that was too big and the wrong color for someone with pale skin and no makeup? With surprise he realized how good-looking she was. But she had no idea of what she might make of herself. Which meant Craig hadn't cared. Or hadn't looked. "I want to know all about you," he said. "Start with your job. And where you're living."

He listened as she talked, his face absorbed, and when he smiled at her imitation of Gil Lister, Katherine wondered how she could have thought of him as cold and aloof. Either she had been wrong or he was acting a part. But why would he do that? If he wanted something from her, all he had to do was ask. She liked him and she was having a good time; there was no reason not to be honest.

But their talk circled about, until Katherine looked at her watch. "I have to go in a few minutes. And I haven't told you why I came to San Francisco. I haven't even talked about Craig. And he's the reason you bought this incredible lunch."

Derek's eyebrows went up. Underestimated her again. Just because a woman is not glamorous, Victoria used to say when he was dating in high school, it does not mean she is simple. Katherine, without a jot of glamour, was not at all simple. "I bought the lunch to impress you," he said. "But of course I want to hear about Craig. I was about to ask if you plan to go back to Canada or stay here. And about his partner. Will he press charges?"

"I don't know. I just want Craig to come back; we can think about Carl then. Oh. That's what was worrying all of you at dinner. You thought I'd ask you to pay back what Craig took."

"Hardly." Derek smiled faintly. "I imagine we could scrape together that amount."

"Then what was it? Why didn't anyone want me?"

"*Are* you going back to Vancouver?"

"No! At least—not until I hear from Craig. What difference does it make?"

"Some of the family," he said casually, "think it might make a difference in the division of Victoria's estate."

"She's not dead."

"She's eighty-one. The question comes up—what Craig might get if he were here."

"You mean money."

He smiled again. "That would simplify it. Of course, money. But also, Victoria owns fifty percent of the Hayward Corporation."

Katherine began to understand what was involved. "Who inherits her fifty percent now?"

"As far as we know, Ross and I."

Money and control of the corporation, Katherine thought. Ross and Derek. "Ross wouldn't try to keep Craig away because of that."

Derek's face hardened, though his voice remained light. "Ross would do whatever is necessary to accumulate sufficient power and wealth to use the Hayward Corporation for his own purposes."

Katherine shivered at the knife-edged words spoken in his pleasant voice. I don't believe that, she thought. She looked across the square, at crowds waiting for streetlights to change. "Craig has been gone almost four months. If your family really is worried about what he might do, why isn't anyone trying to find him?"

"Claude hired an investigator."

She stared at him. "No one told me."

"There's been nothing to tell. He's found nothing."

"But I could give him information—"

"I'm sure he'll call you when he's ready."

"You still think I might have arranged this with Craig! Isn't that right? Your investigator doesn't trust—" She stopped. At the corner a man moved forward: bearded, with brown hair. He was talking to someone, his face partially turned from her, but the way he held his head, tilted a little—

She clambered to her feet. "Katherine!" Derek said. The light changed and the bearded man turned toward her to cross the street. Not Craig; not even like Craig. But as if her thoughts had brought him to the square, Katherine felt his presence so powerfully he might have been standing beside her in the warm afternoon sun. Derek's voice faded. She felt Craig's eyes on her, puzzled and reproachful, and she felt ashamed of her laughter and her pleasure in Derek's extravagant lunch. She was as bad as the rest of the Haywards, pushing Craig to the background, forgetting that he was in trouble, thinking only of the present.

Craig, she thought, missing him with the stab of pain that she thought had faded in the crowded weeks. She put out her hand, but no one was there. It's the sun, she thought dizzily. And the wine. And I was up so late last night, making sketches after my class. She closed her eyes against the glare.

Derek's hand, cool and hard, grasped hers. "Sit down. I'm sorry I upset you."

In the bright darkness behind her eyes, his voice sounded like Craig's. Everything reminded her of Craig. She opened her eyes. "You didn't upset me. I thought I saw Craig."

"You haven't finished your lunch."

"I can't. I'm sorry..." She took a step away from him. "Thank you— it was so impressive—I hope you can use the hamper again, and amortize the cost—"

"Wait a minute; I want to see you—"

"Goodbye, Derek." It was as if Craig were pushing her. Almost running, she crossed the street with the crowds, and pushed through the revolving doors that sent her into Heath's, and back to work.

Two nights later, after Jennifer and Todd were asleep, Tobias appeared like an apparition at Katherine's front door. "I know it seems rude," he said, ducking his head apologetically as he walked past her into the living room. "But one could call it a sign of intimacy. In the general sense"— he sat down and cheerfully began to inspect the room— "of closeness. To pay a visit without telephoning first." His inspection reached her face. "You don't agree?"

"Did Derek send you?" she asked.

Tobias looked bewildered. "Ordinarily I am not *sent* anywhere, by anyone, but even if I were, what in heaven's name would Derek have to do with it?"

"He didn't tell you we had lunch together?"

"Lunch," Tobias repeated.

"In Union Square."

He gazed at her blankly. "There is no restaurant in Union Square."

"On the grass. He brought a picnic lunch."

"*Derek?* On the grass? Not possible." Tobias sat erect on the edge of the couch, hands on his knees, and cogitated briefly. "I have learned over the years to believe many unbelievable things about Derek, but not this. What was he wearing?"

"A business suit. If he didn't tell you, why are you here?"

"Well." They looked at each other. He seemed so carefree, with blue eyes as bright and innocent as a child's, and an open smile above his little white beard. But now and then, unexpectedly, the blue eyes would turn sharp, not so innocent after all, and at others, when his smile dimmed, his face would sag in crepelike folds. He's seventy-five, Katherine remembered, but those creases in his face were from sadness as well as age. "Well," he repeated, and smiled like a friendly conspirator. Katherine found herself smiling back, liking him, even as she asked herself why another Hayward was suddenly paying attention to her. "I heard you were in the city. Ross told Victoria he'd taken you to lunch and—"

"Victoria told you," Katherine interrupted. "And you mentioned it to Melanie, who passed it along to Derek. But Melanie had already seen me working at Heath's and had told Ross, who then invited me to lunch. And I heard all that from Derek."

Tobias laughed delightedly. "'The babbling gossip of the air.' Shakespeare," he added helpfully. "You'd think he knew our family. I brought you a housewarming gift." He took a box from his coat pocket and gave it to Katherine, who looked at it nonplussed. "Open, open!" he cried, as eager as Jennifer and Todd, and Katherine unwrapped it to find a crystal and silver candy dish.

"How lovely," she said. "Thank you—"

Tobias was surveying the room again. A comedown, he thought, from the Vancouver home she and Ross had described. Overcrowded; brought too much furniture with her. Good quality, though a trifle shabby; his candy dish looked a bit out of place. But she'd made the room cheerful: light colors, an oil painting that looked like an original, a silk scarf knotted around a lampshade, making it glow like stained glass. Good sense of color and balance; she'd made the place look larger than it was. One oddity: a small table in a corner cluttered with pencils, buttons, string, sketch pads, construction paper, X-Acto knives, and empty, flattened toothpaste tubes. Tobias looked a question at Katherine.

"Homework," she said, adding almost defiantly, "I'm studying jewelry design."

"Ah." Tobias nodded. "But—toothpaste tubes?"

"For models. They're so soft I can cut and shape them the way I'd cut and shape silver and gold—if I had any. You haven't told me why you're here."

"To deliver my gift—which I'm pleased you like—and to talk. My dear, is there anything to drink in your house?"

"Oh." She was embarrassed. "I haven't had a chance to stock anything—"

She hasn't the money to stock anything, Tobias thought. "My favorite is ice water," he lied cheerfully. "Or coffee. If you wouldn't mind—?"

Following Katherine to the kitchen, he sat at the oak table, talking, while she made coffee. "I thought you should know something about us, since you're here—and you *are* here, aren't you? That is, permanently. Is that correct? You're not going back to Canada?"

Just like Derek. They all want to know when I'm leaving. "It depends on what Craig wants to do."

"Craig?"

"When he comes back." She met his eyes, daring him to challenge her.

"But until then," he prompted.

"This is where we live. The children are in school and I have a job. If you're trying to get rid of me—"

"No, no, what an odd thing to say; why would we want any such thing?"

"Because of the corporation, and his grandmother's estate."

"Where did you get that idea?"

"Derek said some of the family were concerned—"

Tobias began to laugh, his pointed beard dancing. "Katherine, dear Katherine. When Derek tells you someone in the family is worried about something, what do you think that means?"

She filled two mugs with coffee and carried them to the living room. "He told me what he meant."

"Yes, but with Derek, my dear, one looks under the words to pry out the unspoken ones. Now think; who is most worried about Hayward money and power?"

Katherine watched the steam rise from her coffee. She had liked Derek until he talked bitterly about Ross. She had liked Tobias until she heard the sharp glee in his voice as he talked about Derek. "Does your family always make accusations about one another?" she asked. "It's not very pleasant."

"Ah." Tobias, too, contemplated the steam. "Do you know how Hugh Hayward made his money?"

"Of course. Construction; the Hayward Corporation."

"Oh, my, no. The company was fairly modest until Curt took over— his son, you know, Derek and Ross's father—though Hugh had made the Hayward reputation for excellence. The real money came earlier, in the twenties, when Hugh smuggled liquor from Europe and Canada. Prohibition, my dear: good Scotch made many a millionaire in those dry days. No one in the family likes to recall it, but I find it amusing that our enterprising Hugh was slipping cases of Scotch past the eagle-eyed law, while he and Victoria danced at charity balls and had their pictures in the newspapers as fine young socialites who donated generously to good causes. 'Everyone is a moon and has a dark side which he never shows to anybody.'"

"'A dark side,'" Katherine repeated slowly. "Who wrote that?"

"Mark Twain. Fits the Hayward men like a glove. Hugh was only the first." He sighed and sipped his coffee. "I did enjoy Hugh. I still miss him, even after all this time. A huge man, devious, witty, handsome. How he adored Victoria. He would have handled that sailing mess differently, but he'd been dead three years, and Victoria had shut herself off, mourning him, and there was no real authority in the family. Is there more coffee?"

Katherine refilled his cup. Of course, she thought. He came to talk about Craig. "You mean the sailing accident," she said.

"Ah, well." Tobias looked around the room, nodding to himself. "It was a mess. Not that I ever heard the whole story, but I expect to know it some day. Professors of literature are experts at ferreting out long-buried tales. And as I am writing the family history, of course I must discover everything there is to know. Your husband, my dear, caused me untold problems, since no one would talk about him. These days of course everyone is talking about him because you're here, reminding us."

He sipped coffee. "Well. Of course Derek and Craig quarreled on the boat; actually, they came to blows. Ross says he doesn't know why, and Derek won't talk, and Craig, we now know, fled the scene, so I must wait. Now you, my dear, could learn more; no one has a better right to ask questions and demand answers." He looked at her with innocent blue eyes. "You could be my research assistant."

Katherine longed for Craig. He could tell her whether or not to trust this foolish-looking old man. She did want the truth; she wanted to learn as much as possible about Craig. But only to understand him better— and also herself: how she could live for ten years with a man and never suspect he was hiding in a maze of lies. But if she learned bits of Craig's past, why should she give them to Tobias or anyone else in a family she distrusted?

Tobias sighed and stood up. "I won't push you, my dear. But you and I could help each other and I'm quite reliable, you know. Well, of course you don't know that, but when you've been part of us for a while—"

"I'm not part of you," she said. "I don't want to be part of you. I'm waiting for Craig to come back and since none of you cares about him the way I do, just for himself, I don't need any of you."

"I think you might," he said gently. "Why don't you mull it over and I'll call in a week or so. Perhaps we could have lunch. Not in Union Square, however. My knees, you know...sitting on the grass..." He shook his head and walked to the door. "You've improved since that night at Victoria's. You're better-looking and I like your spirit. Craig would be proud of you."

She looked at him in surprise. He nodded, pleased with himself.

"Think about that." He opened the door and was gone, but suddenly his head appeared again, eyes bright blue and smiling. "We'd make quite a team, you know." And the door closed behind him.

"Just wait," Leslie said when Katherine told her about Tobias' visit and showed her the cases of wine, and boxes of cheese, nuts, and crackers, that had been delivered the next day. "Pretty soon there'll be another one. Looks like you've been discovered by the Haywards."

Katherine didn't want another one. She had enough on her mind. She had Gil Lister, day after day, and when she left him she came home to children who were cross and difficult to handle. At night she was restless, hungry for love-making and companionship. She went to her jewelry class twice a week, and Leslie came for dinner, or just to talk, at least once a week, but otherwise Katherine was very quiet, with plenty of time to think. Ross had called twice to see if she needed anything, but he had seemed distracted by problems at work, and something else— something personal—and when he did not mention another lunch, Katherine did not either. No more Haywards, she thought. Maybe later, when I figure out how to deal with them.

But Leslie had been right. A few days after Tobias' visit, Claude Fleming telephoned: not a Hayward but, as he had told her at Victoria's, almost one of the family. "The top of the Hyatt," he said when she agreed to meet him the next day after work. "Just across the square from Heath's."

He was waiting when she arrived: a tall man in his fifties with carefully brushed silver hair, observant eyes, and a well-exercised body set off in an expensive suit. When Katherine sat opposite him in the booth, he pointed to the crest of a distant hill where a salmon-colored, balconied apartment building stood alone against the golden sky of late afternoon. "Do you recognize it?" Katherine shook her head. "Pacific Heights. Victoria's. You were there for dinner."

The waitress brought wine for Katherine, Scotch for Claude, and a dish filled with toasted cereal and nuts. Claude slid it aside. "Execrable dish. The view, however, is fine. Are you settled in your apartment? And your job? And the children in school?"

Katherine gazed at him a moment. "Perhaps we should have a meeting of the whole family. I could answer all the questions just once and then find out what everyone wants from me."

His eyes narrowed. Then he smiled and lifted his glass. "To your new life. Evidently it will be a lively one."

Katherine's face was flushed. She wasn't used to talking that way, especially to polished and successful older men who made her feel like a child. She wished she hadn't come. She'd already said she didn't want any more of this strange family that had rejected her in June and now sought her out in October. They made her nervous and when she was with them she acted in ways that surprised everyone, including herself.

"—hope it is lively," Claude was saying, beckoning the waitress for another drink. "Everyone hopes so. As they hope to get to know you better."

"Why?" Katherine asked. "To find out why I moved here and if I'm lying about Craig? To keep tabs on me so they'll know, the minute he returns, how big a dent he might try to make in their bank accounts?"

He was taken aback. "Did Derek put that into your head? All we want is to help you. If Craig has abandoned you—"

"He hasn't!"

"Let us assume he has. It would not, after all, be the first time. After four months with no word or sign from him—"

"It's just as likely he had an accident," Katherine said stubbornly. "Or something happened that we haven't even thought of. I won't listen to you criticize him—any of you—you never liked Craig; you don't give him a chance."

"Some of us did," Claude said quietly.

"Not the whole family."

He smiled. "That's asking quite a lot of any family. But some of them adored him. He was in a peculiar position, you know: the first grandson. There were Victoria and Hugh, with their two sons, Jason and Curt—who were always in competition for one thing or another—and then Jason and Ann produced the first grandson, a year before Curt and his wife had Derek. Not that it was a contest, you understand, but Victoria adored Craig from the day he was born; so did Ann; and as Jennifer grew up, she joined the admiring female chorus. Hugh expected his grandson to be another version of himself—aggressive, dominating, confident; Jason wanted a son who was a legend like Hugh Hayward; and Victoria and Ann called Craig their golden boy: perfect, excelling in all things. I felt sorry for him; there was no way he could live up to any of those demands. Curt, who's retired now and living in Phoenix, never liked Craig; he thought he was coddled and weak. Derek followed his father's lead, but then Derek never could tolerate people on pedestals, especially a cousin only a year older than himself. Ross, far less competitive, was Craig's friend. I suppose it helped that Victoria loved Ross but never could like Derek and he never forgave her. Well—" He gestured with his hand. "Families. The best of them have their feuds. Ross escaped: went to college in New York, got married, found a job. In fact Curt arranged that; a friend of his in New York took Ross into his firm. Derek stayed here and was running the company long before Curt took early retirement. By now he's doubled its size—took some chances that could have been disasters but proved enormously profitable. A real gambler, is Derek. And no one interfered with him, not even Victoria, who's the major stockholder. He became the head of the family by default when Victoria withdrew from everything after Jennifer and Craig were killed—after we thought Craig was killed."

Katherine saw again the picture of the laughing girl. "What was Jennifer like?"

"Jennifer." He waved for another drink and looked inquiringly at Katherine, who shook her head. "Tobias called her sunlight and shadow. She was lovely, with a freshness that made one regret one's age. She danced through life, taking nothing very seriously, until the last few months of her life, when she became quite preoccupied. Tobias was here at Easter and thought her somber. I thought she was worried. Certainly Ann and Jason were. She was so changed: distant, stubborn . . . she'd been accepted at Radcliffe but then out of the blue said she wouldn't go. No one knew why."

After a pause, Katherine asked, "Why did Ross come back?"

"I think, to be near Victoria. He never explained it, though Derek tried his damndest to find out. But his return didn't change anything. He opened his own firm of architects, made a remarkable reputation entirely separate from the one Hugh and Curt and Derek had made at the Hayward Corporation, and he and Melanie built a house in Tiburon. There really was no family: Craig and Jennifer were gone, Jason and Ann had withdrawn to Maine, Derek and his father ran the company, Victoria was frantic with grief and then just got more and more crotchety. Nine years ago, when Tobias retired, she gave him an apartment on the second floor of her duplex. He and Ross were the only ones who got along with her. All of them went in separate ways, measuring their lives in different possessions."

The words caught Katherine's fancy. "What does that mean? Measuring—?"

"What we own, what we are, what we fight for. Derek, for instance, measures his life in money and power. Wives, perhaps, if you count the three he's had. And things: he accumulates everything from art to gadgets."

Katherine thought of a picnic hamper. "And Ross?" she asked.

"Accomplishments, I suppose. How much he can achieve in rebuilding the cities of America. No small dreams for Ross. In the meantime he makes good money—nothing near what Derek makes, but he's hardly worrying—and he cares about money, if for no other reason than his extremely extravagant Melanie, but I've never thought of him as measuring his days in dollars. Or power, though he must know it takes power to make his dreams a reality. Interesting man; isn't it because of him that you moved here?"

"Oh, no." She was dismayed. "I didn't even tell him." And I've only seen him once, she added silently. Six weeks ago. "How does Victoria measure her life?"

"Once it was the family: how firmly she kept it together. That stopped when Craig and Jennifer died. Well, not Craig—you know what I mean. For the last ten years, she's concentrated on making herself necessary. She's on governing boards of the opera, the symphony, the Museum of Art, and a couple of welfare organizations, and she's enormously influential because she really works. It was through her connections that the art museum got the Peruvian gold exhibit that opens this week. I recommend it: a brilliant show. Why *did* you move to San Francisco?"

"What?"

"I said—"

"No, I heard you. I grew up here."

"That's the only reason you moved from Vancouver?"

"I'm not after any Hayward money."

"I don't think you are." He looked amused. "I'll report that to the family. You're a pleasant young woman; you speak intelligently and listen well. In fact you've maneuvered me into talking about the family when I meant to talk about you. Admirable."

Katherine regarded him. "I don't believe anyone maneuvers Claude Fleming. You wanted me to know about the family."

He was signing the charge slip and his pen stopped momentarily. He smiled. "You'll do very well," he said, and finished writing.

"How do you think I measure my life?" Katherine asked.

Thoughtfully, he studied her. "By your independence," he said, and watched the swift changes in her face, from pleasure to confusion.

"And Craig?" she asked.

"Ah. Money, loving a select few, being admired, and successfully running from problems."

Katherine looked through the window, at the darkening sky. For the first time, she was not sure what to say in her husband's defense.

Leslie brought a bottle of wine and a birthday cake and they all helped set the table. "How old are you?" Todd asked.

"Ninety-nine," said Leslie. "But I'm told I don't look it. Some days I don't even feel it."

Katherine looked up. "What's wrong?"

"Nothing serious," Leslie said. "It's Friday. Lots of things seem wrong on Friday that are miraculously cured by having two free days. Shit, I forgot; you work tomorrow."

"Not this week. Gil told me he didn't need me. It's like a holiday."

"Gil? Being generous? Not in character. He must be up to something."

"How old *are* you?" Todd insisted.

"Thirty-six." Leslie tousled his hair. "Does that seem ancient?"

"Not as ancient as ninety-nine." He looked at his plate as they sat down. "Mom, what's this gunk?"

"Don't be insulting," Leslie answered. "Since it's my birthday, I got to choose the menu and it's ragout of beef."

Todd made a face. "It sounds awful. I'm going to McDonald's."

"You're staying right here," Katherine said. "And eating dinner with us. You haven't even tasted it."

"I don't like it and I won't eat it and I'm going to McDonald's and you can't stop me!"

"Hey," Leslie said with a quick look at Katherine's face. "You want to ruin my party?"

"Todd," said Katherine. "I left a box in Annie's apartment. Will you bring it in?"

He shrugged glumly. "Why not."

When he was gone, Leslie gave Katherine a questioning look. "He wasn't like this in Vancouver."

"I know. He's changed since we came here. He's disruptive at school and doesn't do his work—his teachers say he's acting out all his problems. I can't talk to him about it—"

"You don't talk to us about anything," Jennifer said. "You didn't even ask us if we wanted to leave Vancouver."

"Jennifer, that was a long time ago."

"Well, we haven't forgotten it. And we don't like anything about San Francisco or this apartment or school or your job or *anything*."

Katherine and Leslie exchanged a look. "I have an inspiration," Leslie said. "You two need a day at the Exploratorium. Next Saturday. At noon. Be ready."

"Exploratorium!" Todd cried, coming in with a large box in his arms. "No kidding? Mom promised to take us twice but she blew it both times."

"I had to work those days," Katherine said quietly.

"Todd, you're behaving like a pint-sized bastard," Leslie said. Taking advantage of his open-mouthed shock, she pointed to his plate. "Eat your dinner—which is terrific, by the way—and see if you can help me figure out my mystery."

. "Mystery?" Jennifer looked suspicious. "Are you making something up so we'll forget we're not happy?"

"No I'm not," Leslie said seriously. "I think we should talk about that. But this is my party and I don't want grouching to ruin it. If Todd blows out my candles with his huffing and puffing, I won't get my wish."

Todd and Jennifer smiled. "So what's the mystery?" Todd asked.

"We have at Heath's a new line of sweaters by a designer named Ralph Lauren; they're very popular, and selling fast. Also selling fast are Calvin Klein blouses, silk, costing two hundred fifty each."

Jennifer gasped. "*Each?* Is that the mystery? Why people pay that much?"

Leslie laughed. "Nope. This is it: more of those blouses and sweaters are gone from the departments than the clerks remember selling. How would you explain that?"

"Somebody stole them," Jennifer said promptly.

"That's what I thought, too. But the sales records in our computer say they've been sold."

"The clerks forgot," said Todd. "They had amnesia. Did you ask them if they fell down one day and were knocked out?"

"As a matter of fact, I didn't," Leslie answered. "I'll give it some thought."

"Something's wrong with the computer," Jennifer guessed.

"Computers don't make mistakes," Todd scoffed.

"Not ever?" Katherine asked. "What if a person makes a mistake in telling the computer what to do?"

"I've got it!" Todd cried. "It *is* the computer! A bunch of mice came into the computer when it was cold out and rubbed together to get warm and the rubbing made static electricity that erased part of the computer memory, so you're getting the wrong numbers!"

"Good thinking," laughed Leslie. "We'll look for mice on Monday morning."

"Leslie," Katherine said. "What's the real problem? It's more than blouses and sweaters."

Leslie sighed. "Nothing like a friend to see inside a person's head. You're right; there's more. There's my fellow vice-presidents. Four smug males waiting with tongues hanging out for me to make a mistake so they can kick me off their masculine turf. I don't know what the hell is happening with those blouses and sweaters, but if we're losing merchandise—which means money—they'll look to see who's fouled up store security, and that means me."

"You?" asked Todd. "Security?"

"It comes under Personnel. And I'm vice-president for Personnel and Payroll. See what I mean?"

Jennifer was watching Leslie with fascination. "Is the president a smug male who wants you off his turf, too?"

"He's better than the others," Leslie answered. "Though who knows," she added darkly, "what really lurks inside a big chief's head? All I want is to be left alone to do my job, and so far he's done that, but one good crisis could change everything..." She brooded for a moment, then briskly shook her head. "Enough of this. You're a terrific audience; you've cheered me up; and I love you all. But we are in danger of forgetting one of the most important parts of this evening. Didn't I see a cake in the kitchen? How can I swallow thirty-six years without chocolate cake to make it go down? And what about that huge box Todd staggered in with? Could that be for me?"

Katherine lit the candles on the cake while Leslie opened the box and lifted out a set of appliquéd throw pillows for her couch that the three of them had made. "You remembered!" she cried in delight. "And they're wonderful—just the kind I couldn't find anywhere." Todd and Jennifer beamed and launched into a lengthy explanation of the difficulties in appliqué.

"But it was fun," Jennifer said. "Even Todd liked it."

"I had this sword," Todd explained. "And I kept stabbing these monsters from caves that were about to gobble us up—"

"He means he was sewing," said Jennifer helpfully.

"Just don't tell the guys at school," said Todd. "They'd think I was really weird."

Katherine stepped back, as if she were watching a play. Her children and her friend sat at a folding table, festive with tablecloth and candles, in the center of the crowded living room. On a table in the corner, her models of bracelets, necklaces, and pendants glinted in the soft light. The grandfather clock boomed nine o'clock. Nothing in that room, none of the people, would have been there if not for her. Independence, Claude had said, sending a quick rush of pleasure through her. He'd been right, and her pleasure had been real. It would only be for a while, only until Craig returned, but still she savored it: she had done this alone. I'll always remember how it feels, she thought. Because I've never felt it before.

A few days later, Derek called. "I have tickets for a private opening tonight of a Peruvian art exhibit. I thought you'd enjoy it, especially the jewelry. It includes dinner—possibly grilled Peruvian goat—but if it's inedible, we can go somewhere else. Can I pick you up at Heath's?"

"Yes," she said without hesitation. Derek could tell her more about the Haywards and about Craig, she told herself, trying to explain her quick response. She thought of another explanation while filling out shipping forms to return last week's window scenery to the warehouse: she might find ideas for jewelry in the ancient gold work of Peruvian artisans. And besides, she decided as she helped Lister arrange witches and warlocks in a Halloween window, it will be good to get out, and Annie can stay with Jennifer and Todd. But, at the end of the day, meeting the skeptical grin of a jack o'lantern on her desk, she admitted that she had said yes because she wanted to see Derek again.

"I'm glad you're here," he said as she stepped into his car in front of Heath's and he pulled into the traffic on Geary Street. "I was afraid you'd turn me down."

The car was sleek and low-slung, and Katherine felt peculiar, sitting just inches above the street, watching other cars and pedestrians loom over her as Derek whipped through narrow spaces that made her flinch. She looked instead at his smooth profile and wondered how many women turned Derek down, or how often he really was afraid they would. "Why would I turn you down?" she asked.

"Another Hayward. I thought you might have had enough of us after being inundated for the past few weeks."

"Oh." She considered it. Did everyone in that family always know what the others were doing? "No. It's been very interesting."

"*Interesting?* Good Lord, wait until Tobias hears that." He turned into the Civic Center and found a parking place near the Museum of Art. "After meeting the Hayward clan, Katherine Fraser pronounces them interesting."

"I'm sorry," Katherine blushed, feeling slow and dull, and wondering how she was going to get through the evening.

"We'll survive." Derek walked around the car and opened her door. "You may even find that some of us are more interesting than others. Let's see what's going on inside."

He took her arm. Unexpectedly, she was filled with excitement. It had been so long since she went anywhere. It wasn't Derek, she told herself; it was getting away from the house, the children, the job, worrying over money, missing Craig, endlessly speculating about him, worrying about him. Her steps were light as she went into the building on Derek's arm.

But once inside, confronted with the crowd, Katherine's excitement drained away. Sleek men in black tie or dark business suits, and beautiful women in gala dresses, feathered, frilled, beaded, and bejeweled, took her measure when they saw her with Derek—and a hundred eyebrows went up, making her feel as dull as she had months earlier, beside the spotlight of Melanie's gleaming presence: as if she had crashed an exclusive party.

Unaware or indifferent, Derek made casual introductions, and Katherine shook hands and murmured greetings, wondering all the while why she hadn't been prepared. It would happen every time she tried to enter the Haywards' world. Derek might have warned her, but perhaps he had no idea how she felt, wearing a blue wool suit and white blouse, and a single strand of pearls Craig had given her for their tenth anniversary, while all around her stood women who outshone even the Peruvian gold in the museum's exhibit.

I won't go through it again, she thought; I'll leave. Derek won't mind; he belongs here and he'll hardly know I've gone. Yet she made no move to turn and walk out. Something held her and as she answered polite questions from Derek's friends, the thought came: *Craig ran. I won't.*

She pushed the words aside as if they burned her, and changed them. It's research. I'm finding out what jewlery wealthy women are wearing. One of these days I'll be designing for them.

"The jewelry is in the cases along the wall," Derek said. "Where would you like to start? The fourteenth century? I'm sorry about the crowd; private parties are never private unless you give them yourself. With luck, dinner will be quieter."

Dinner was quieter. The guests sat ten to a table and at first the conversation revolved around Derek. For the first time Katherine learned the full scope of the Hayward Corporation's activities in California and the West, from highways, bridges, and aqueducts to office complexes and industrial parks. She was stunned by the extent of the company under Derek's control. She had assumed it was like Craig's, constructing houses and office buildings and having a difficult time in the recession. In fact, the Hayward Corporation was only lightly touched by the economy. Offices and industrial parks had slowed, but the contracts for roads, bridges, and dams had been signed years before and there was plenty to keep the company busy. Remembering how Craig and Carl had been forced to lay off workers because there was not enough for them to do, and listening to the talk of Derek's huge projects and future plans, Katherine began to think he stood above everyone else, untouched by ordinary problems and fears.

And he seemed untouched by people as well. Men and women came up to him and spoke respectfully, often deferentially, some trying to curry favor, others sharing information. But Derek was the same to all of them. Self-contained, remote, caustic, with power coiled behind his polished social presence, he appeared impressive and inaccessible, unlike anyone Katherine had ever known. "Now," he said, dismissing the rest of the table by turning to her. "It's your turn. I want to know about your jewelry. You're taking classes?"

She answered briefly, reluctant to talk about her work. But he pressed her until she described some of her sketches.

"I'd like to see them," he said.

She shook her head. "I haven't found a style of my own yet."

"What do you think of that one?" He gestured casually at a woman across the room whose neck was encased in diamonds that flashed when she moved her head.

Katherine contemplated her. "She looks like a lighthouse, warning everyone away."

Derek's idle gaze swung to her as it had on their picnic. "You can be quite astonishing," he said. "And you aren't even aware of it."

She flushed and was silent, afraid to say something that was not astonishing. After a moment, he asked a question about Heath's and they talked easily for the rest of the evening. But Katherine was aware of his eyes on her, as intimate and absorbed as if they were alone. He had turned a dinner for three hundred people into a private evening.

She realized, as he drove her home, that he had not mentioned her clothes; he had not even seemed to notice them. Yet he dressed impeccably and fastidiously. So he must have noticed. I'll have to do something about that, she thought, if I see him again.

"I'll call you," Derek said as she unlocked the door of her building. Holding her hand, he kissed her forehead. "Thank you for coming. I enjoyed the Incas far more than I thought possible."

She smiled, watching him go back to his car, and was still smiling when she let herself into the apartment. Annie was waiting for her, a finger to her lips. Katherine's smile faded. "What is it? What's wrong?"

"Nothing, maybe," Annie whispered. "But I thought maybe you'd want to see this alone." She held out an envelope. "A letter from Canada."

Katherine's heart lurched. There was no return address and the postmark was blurred. No it wasn't; her eyes had filled with tears. She blinked them away and read the name of a town she'd never heard of, in Saskatchewan. What was Craig doing in—

Annie had gone to her own apartment; the living room was quiet. *Craig, Craig, Craig.* It was like a heartbeat as she tore open the envelope and pulled out a piece of paper. But there was nothing on it. Not a word of writing. Only, as she unfolded it, something that fluttered to the floor. She bent down to pick it up: five hundred dollars in crisp one-hundred-dollar bills.

CHAPTER 8

A TREMOR ran through Victoria's hand as she poured their tea. "And what will you do now?" she asked.

The money lay on the table between them, beside the silver tea service. Katherine's glance slid past it as she took the cup Victoria handed her. For three days the sheaf of bills had been the center of attention on her worktable. She had tried to explain to the children what it meant—that Craig was all right and knew where they were; that for some reason he couldn't come back to them yet, but he wanted to help them and so he sent the money. It wasn't very satisfactory but it was the best she could do. Then, Friday morning, while they were at breakfast, Victoria called, surprising her with an invitation to tea that afternoon, and on impulse she put the money in her purse. As soon as they sat down, she pulled it out and told Victoria what it was.

In the silence of the sunroom, Victoria sighed deeply, turning the five bills over and over, as if looking for a message. Katherine watched her. She sat erect, as serene and unapproachable as an empress in a knit suit of the finest burgundy wool, her white hair cut like a cap of small curls. Now and then she raised a thin manicured hand to the antique pendant she wore on a gold chain; except for that, her body was still. Even more than the women at the Peruvian exhibit, she made Katherine feel clumsy and poorly put together.

But Victoria's face was drawn and a vein in her neck was taut as she inspected the money. Katherine looked away, admiring the room where they sat. In the sunlit air, the white wicker furniture shone against dark green ficus trees, wisteria vines, and bushy, flowering plants. Everywhere were wondrous mementoes of Victoria's trips around the world—Mexican papier mâché birds, a bronze horse from Ceylon, Japanese ladies in jade, ebony masks from Africa. It was a lovely room, as beautiful and finely made as Victoria, but it had the hush of a place waiting for someone to bring it to life.

Victoria sighed again. "It could be from a friend."

"No." Katherine watched her place the money carefully on the table. "It's from Craig. We don't know anyone in that town, or" —she gave a small smile— "anyone anywhere who would send five hundred dollars anonymously. You don't seem surprised," she added. "Or pleased."

Victoria picked up the silver teapot and refilled their cups. "And what will you do now?" she asked, as if Katherine had not spoken.

"Wait," Katherine answered dispiritedly. No answers here, she thought. No help, either. "I've called the Vancouver police and they're working with police in Saskatchewan—"

"I'm talking about *you*," Victoria said. "Now that you know you're not a widow."

"I never believed I was a widow," Katherine shot back.

"Please," Victoria said coolly. "You need not shout."

Instinctively, Katherine replied, "I'm sorry." She was edgy. She had vowed never to come here again, but here she sat, as intimidated as the first time, and making things worse by snapping at Victoria. "I'm sorry," she repeated and said quietly, "I'll wait. For Craig to come back."

Victoria's hand went to her pendant. "Now that we know he is alive, you might say *we* are waiting too. After all this time. But Craig clearly has no intention of coming back to us. He has wiped us out of his life."

Katherine winced. *As he has wiped us out.* She looked at the table for reassurance. *No he hasn't. He sent us money.*

Victoria moved slightly in her chair. "I asked you here so we could get acquainted. I seem to be the last in my family to do so."

"You were angry, because of my rudeness. I'm sorry for the way I spoke that night."

"As you should be. You tend to jump at people, Katherine. And away from them. Quite erratic. You must learn to control yourself. And if you learned to sit straight, you would look like a woman who values herself, rather than a muskrat cowering in a storm."

Katherine smiled, but there was no answering smile on Victoria's face. Self-consciously, she straightened her spine, and pulled back her shoulders. Her head came up and her eyes met Victoria's.

"Much better. If you always learn so quickly, you will do very well. Now, then. It seems everyone else has had lunch with you, or afternoon cocktails, or—and we find this most odd—a picnic. What do you think of us?"

"I think you all want something from me," Katherine replied. "Different things."

"And what else?"

"You don't act much like a family."

Victoria poured more tea. "Have some cake, my dear; you look quite thin. In what way do we not act like a family?"

"You don't like one another very much."

Victoria laughed shortly. "That describes many families, Katherine. But some of us do like each other. Very much." Looking over her cup, she followed the silver gleam of an airplane crossing the city. "And of course you may be exaggerating. Perhaps you think we dislike one another because you dislike us."

"No—!" Why do they make every conversation a contest? she wondered, and switched to a neutral subject. "I saw the Peruvian exhibit at the Museum of Art; it was wonderful."

At last Victoria smiled. "Yes, isn't it? I couldn't be at the opening, but I heard about your appearance with Derek."

There are no neutral subjects with this family. "Derek told you?"

"Derek tells me nothing about himself. My friends told me about his companion. I could hardly fail to identify you."

"Did they wonder why he was with me?"

Victoria smiled again. "There was some curiosity—yes, Polk?"

"Mr. Derek Hayward, ma'am," said the butler. "On the telephone."

"He heard us talking about him. We should have said something libelous." Picking up the telephone, she grinned like a girl, surprising Katherine into laughter. "Yes," Victoria said into the receiver, gesturing to Katherine to eat some cake.

Katherine ate a small piece, then another, discovering how hungry she was. Soon Jennifer and Todd would be eating dinner with Annie. Then they would do their homework while Annie did hers across the hall, with her door open. Everything was all right; there was no need to rush home. Except that she was famished. Victoria could have asked her to dinner instead of late afternoon tea. Unless she didn't want Katherine Fraser at her table again until she had a chance to look her over and set some ground rules. *Sit up straight. Don't jump at people. Or away from them.*

"I didn't think so," Victoria was saying. "But you may be right."

Her voice changed when she spoke to Derek: it was cautious, even deferential. It should be the other way around, Katherine thought. But Derek was the head of the family, Claude had said. By default.

"Yes, she has," Victoria said. "But perhaps she would rather tell you herself. She's here now... certainly you may." She held the telephone across the table.

Katherine barely greeted him before he said, "You've heard from Craig?"

"He sent me some money."

"And what did he say?"

"Nothing."

"In the letter."

"There was no letter. There was nothing. Just the money."

"No letter. A money order?"

"No. Five one-hundred-dollar bills."

"Christ." Derek was silent. "Where was it mailed?"

"A small town in Saskatchewan. I've never heard of it."

"I suppose you've talked to the police there."

"I talked to the Vancouver police. They don't think they can trace cash, but they're sending Craig's picture to the Saskatchewan police to see if anyone saw him."

"How did he know where you are?"

"I don't know. I wish I did."

Again he was silent. "Not much. But it's a beginning." As if rousing himself, he added, "I was going to call you tonight. I'm spending tomorrow afternoon at some vineyards in Napa. Would you enjoy a private tour?"

"Vineyards?"

"I'm a partner in a few small ones. The harvest is over, but you can still see how the wine is made. Or is that something you've already done?"

"No, we haven't. I'd like very much to go. Could we bring Jennifer and Todd? They've never seen a field of grapevines."

There was a pause. "If you really think they'd enjoy it. I'd thought of dinner afterward, and it would be a late evening for them."

"Oh." Stupid, she thought. He's not the kind for family outings. "I'll have to let you know. Is that all right?"

"I'll call tonight," he said carelessly. "About eleven. Unless that's too late."

"No, that's fine." After she said goodbye, she looked up to meet Victoria's quizzical gaze.

"I gather Derek was not enthusiastic about entertaining your children."

"I should have refused. Weekends are the only time the three of us have together."

"But Derek is very attractive."

"Oh, no." Katherine felt herself tense. "I mean, of course he's attractive, but— I'm married; I'm not looking... I'm only looking for friends."

"*Craig let you down.*" Victoria's voice was fierce in the softly fading light. "He let all of us down. I remember"—the words became a reverie—"a long time ago, I used to count my family to make sure all was well. Especially when a storm came up at night, I would go through the names, and where each one was. Of course I seldom knew where they all were, but when I did, and when I knew they were all right, or at least safely inside somewhere, I was content."

Surprised, Katherine said, "That's what I always did when Craig was traveling or the children were spending the night with friends."

"Indeed. So Craig found another woman to worry about his safety in storms. Perhaps that made it easier for him to forget us. He knew how I counted my family to know if all was well. But he let us think he was dead, he let us mourn, *and he did not care.*"

As if Craig sat in the wicker chair across the room, Katherine saw him, very still, staring into space, an open newspaper on his lap. She had seen him that way often, especially in the evenings when she finished the dinner dishes and came into the living room to find him staring out the window at something she could not see. Now she knew he had been staring at the family he left behind. "He did care," she said to Victoria. "He wasn't very happy."

"Happy enough to stay where he was," Victoria scorned. "Happy enough to avoid the telephone, the telegraph, the mail...a plane to San Francisco."

"But not happy enough to talk to me." The words came slowly, but Katherine felt the pressure in them, tumbling out after years of being denied. "He never talked about his feelings. There were such silences ...such *spaces* between us. Once I told him he looked as if he were haunted and after that he closed up more than ever. Now I know why, but all those years I didn't; I only knew that I loved him and he wouldn't talk to me, he turned away, keeping all his secrets—"

Tears filled her eyes. "I've never admitted that to anyone, not even myself...that there were those cold spaces between us and I couldn't reach him—no, I'm not sure that's true. Maybe...maybe I didn't try hard enough." She frowned beneath Victoria's intent gaze. "Maybe I didn't. I don't know why. I kept waiting for him to change, to come to me and let me share whatever was bothering him...Maybe I should have pushed him more, to talk to me—of course I should have; it seems so obvious, now—but we had good things, too, and maybe I was afraid I'd ruin them...So the spaces got wider and Craig held on to his secrets...oh, if you knew how I hated his secrets—"

She was crying. Swiftly, Victoria came around the table to stand beside

her, touching her hair, then stroking it. Softly she kissed Katherine's
cheek. "My dear, we have so much to talk about. So many things I've
wanted to talk about for so long—"

"To Craig?" Katherine's tears dried and a soft contentment filled her,
feeling Victoria's hand on her hair and Victoria's cheek pressed to hers.
"You've missed talking to Craig—?"

"Oh, no," Victoria said quietly. "For fifteen years I've missed talking
to Jennifer."

Ross turned off the projector and switched on the overhead lights. The
men seated around the square table blinked in the sudden brightness and
fumbled for pencils and pens as he unrolled a large drawing and held it
down with a water pitcher and three glasses. When he began talking, his
voice was relaxed and conversational. An outsider would not have guessed
he was at the last stage of four years of planning, designing and negotiating
to get the biggest project of his career underway.

"I'm sorry to go over this again," he said. "Some of you have been
through it a number of times—"

"Go right ahead," interrupted one of the developers of BayBridge Plaza
seated in a row along the wall. "When you're spending three hundred
million bucks, you can't talk about it too much."

Ross smiled wryly as the rest of them laughed. That was what had
taken two of the last four years; everyone thought it couldn't be talked
about too much. Especially the people sitting around the table—representatives from the mayor's office, the Planning Commission, Zoning
Board, Citizens for Environmental Planning, the Community Neighborhood Association, the Department of Buildings, and half a dozen
other groups and agencies—who looked up at him now with satisfied
faces, prepared to give final blessing to a project that would transform
part of the landscape called South of Market. Picking up a pointer, Ross
wondered which of them would bring up the last-minute objections he'd
come to expect. He'd been through it before.

"I showed those slides of Quincy Market in Boston, Harborplace in
Baltimore, Society Hill in Philadelphia, and New York's South Street
Seaport Development, even though I've shown them before, because
they're our predecessors. Every time I think we're drowning in regulations
or confrontation, it's comforting to be reminded that others have gone
through this, and survived."

Another ripple of laughter ran around the table. "I'll go over it very
quickly..."

He began to talk, leaving out his own feelings: his excitement, four years earlier, when the developers had chosen him over all the architects they had interviewed to design the huge project; his frustration at the delays ("The pettiness of people goes up," Tobias had reminded him, "with the amount of money. They can't really imagine something that costs a million dollars, but watch them argue over a four-dollar versus a three-dollar light switch!"); the nights when he woke in a sweat over the leap he was taking by enlarging his staff from fifteen to eighty-five to handle the massive volume of work; the days and nights when he lost himself in the pure joy of creating the kind of urban development he had dreamed of since becoming an architect.

But none of that appeared in his factual description as he used his pointer to outline the forty acres where thirty-five buildings would be demolished, twenty-five restored, and twelve newly constructed, in addition to a mall of open shops, theaters, and eating places.

"With no building higher than eight stories," he said. "And open spaces connecting residential, office and retail clusters, BayBridge will have the atmosphere of a small town." He paused, remembering who had first called it that: Katherine, the day they had lunch together. "A link in the chain of small towns that makes up a city," he went on, still using her words. "While still being only a block from the commercial strip of Market Street, two blocks from the Civic Center, and within walking distance of bus lines and two BART stations. A setting, in other words, for people—"

"Yeh, but the people who're there," interrupted Ted Taylor, pushing up the glasses that kept slipping down his nose. He was the elected representative of the South of Market Neighborhood Association and for two years had been having the best time of his life, with the power to hold up a multi-million-dollar project just by raising an objection— sometimes just by raising a finger. He was sorry it was almost over; how often could ordinary guys like him force government officials and bankers and international businessmen to sit up and take notice? "What about the people? Lots of them still living there and running businesses—you're gonna kick 'em out to start construction in the spring?"

"We discussed this last month," Ross said patiently. "Twenty-eight commercial tenants and ninety-four residents are still in the area; all their leases had expired by last month but we gave them an extension of six months, to next April, and we're helping them relocate. When we set that up, you agreed. Do you have a problem with it now?"

"No," said Taylor dolefully.

One down, Ross thought. Now if the rest of them would say they have no problems . . .

"A few figures," he said, and pulled down a chart like a movie screen against the wall. "When complete, BayBridge will provide six hundred housing units with an estimated population of fifteen hundred people; it will provide twenty-five hundred jobs in one hundred forty retail establishments plus another two thousand in office and service jobs. The construction itself will provide one thousand jobs. Revenue from real estate taxes and sales taxes will increase as shown on this chart—"

He pulled down a second one. The city director of Planning nodded, to show he knew all that already. "Very satisfactory; one of the reasons we like it so much."

Two down, Ross thought, and told himself this was not the time to show impatience.

BayBridge had really started when the developers had begun to buy up the land. They had selected Ross Hayward Associates to draw up plans for the forty acres, then hired a consulting firm to evaluate those plans. When the consulting firm gave its approval, the developers bought the rest of the land, parcel by parcel, over a year and a half; arranged financing for the three-hundred-million-dollar project, started the rounds of government agencies for approval of every stage of the plaza, and began to line up major tenants for the shopping mall and office buildings.

Two years later, they signed a contract with Ross for detailed architectural plans of the whole complex. That was when Ross moved to another office building with space for the sixfold increase in his staff of architects, engineers, draftsmen, and computer operators.

The last step had been choosing a contractor. One of the developers, Brock Galvez—burly, aggressive, a man who had made vast wealth "by work and prayer," he said, "and the good fortune of buying a Mexican farm that turned out to be floating on a sea of oil"—fought hard to give the job to the Hayward Corporation, but the other developers balked. "It's Ross's family corporation; no way we're going to give the media a chance to smear us for making sweetheart deals."

Ross had stayed out of it. None of them had asked him if he wanted to work with his brother and when they chose another firm, and he seemed satisfied, they thought he was accepting the inevitable. It did not occur to them that he had no wish to work with Derek. And, though BayBridge was the major project of the year in San Francisco, Derek had never asked Ross for help in getting the job. It was all aboveboard.

But the haggling over approvals had dragged on, and at times he'd thought the project would never be built. "These are the final changes you asked us to make," Ross said, turning from the charts on the wall. Horsetrading, he added to himself, without bitterness. Everyone has fears; everyone wants a feeling of control. Local residents fear higher rents and taxes when we upgrade the area, so we add a community swimming pool in the lower level of the mall. The Landmarks Preservation Council is worried about proper restoration so we submit a description of all exterior materials and paint colors. Small businesses fret over losing customers to the mall, so the developers offer them space in the mall at reduced rents for the first five years. On and on, until, finally, everybody's had a hand in the trading.

"You asked for additional off-street parking," he said. Actually, they'd insisted on it as soon as Ross sought permission to close off one block of Eighth Street that would otherwise cut through BayBridge's largest park. Why is it, he wondered, that city streets are about as sacred as cathedrals and matrimony? It took seven months of negotiations until they got permission to close off the street, but in exchange they had to enlarge the parking deck. "This made room for fifty-five more cars," Ross said, pointing to the extended deck. "But it meant eliminating the snack bar at this end of the recreation area—"

"You took food out to make room for cars?" demanded an incredulous voice.

Noncommittally, Ross nodded. "I understand some vendors have applied for licenses for food carts to be placed around the mall and in the parks." They were making notes now, he saw. "In response to other requests, we've reduced air conditioning and heating energy requirements by adding solar energy reflecting glass on all south-facing windows. And in line with revised building codes relating to earthquakes, we've strengthened building number twenty-eight. As for other buildings—"

He talked on, keeping his feelings to himself, though he knew, with every step he took without arousing criticism, he was getting closer. Almost there, he told himself, elation growing beneath his relaxed voice. Almost there.

"What happened to the day care center?" asked a young man, looking up from furious note-taking. "In the recreation area—near the gymnasium—wasn't that where we planned it?"

"Shit shit shit," moaned a dark man across the table. "We've been *over* this. The government grant was cut! When we find the money, we'll put the day care center back."

"Who's trying to get another grant?" demanded the young man.

"I am," came a voice from the sidelines where the investors were sitting. "Someone in my office. We're working on it. You want to see what we're doing, come anytime."

"I'll do that," said the young man and made another note on his lined pad.

"Well, I like the whole thing." The chief assistant to the mayor stood and hitched up his pants. "Good concept, good feeling for people. Natural neighborhoods. Our office has approved it; I don't know why the hell we keep going around the mulberry bush; we all know what we're doing. Anybody got a comment on that?"

No one spoke. He asked about schedules and dates; the developers joined the discussion; Brock Galvez said, "We'll be out there within ninety days of sign-off of all the approvals." Ross let his elation soar. Done, he thought. Galvez was beaming. "No more than ninety days; we've waited long enough. We'll outdo Baltimore and Philadelphia and New York... we'll put this place on the map. Best goddamn set of plans I've ever seen."

They stood about, talking, as if reluctant to go their different ways. Ross stood with them, his tall figure relaxed as he joined their casual conversation, but inwardly, he was bursting with exultation. For the first time the kind of vast project he dreamed of would be built, remaking the landscape. And no one had put it better than the mayor's assistant who was just now shaking his hand and leaving the room. *Natural neighborhoods. A feeling for people.* For the first time, Ross thought. Not a dream on paper. A reality.

He debated going back to work for an hour or two, but he needed to talk. Too much excitement, he thought, steaming inside me; it isn't enough to have something wonderful happen—we have to share it to make it real.

He'd stop off at Mettler's, he decided; buy Melanie a present; take her to dinner. They'd celebrate and make promises and pretend they were at the beginning again, when they'd been able to talk and laugh and love.

On Post Street he parked in a No Parking zone and dashed into Mettler's rarefied, vaulted room. It occurred to him that he was only a few blocks from Heath's; he ought to go over and see Katherine. He hadn't called her for a long time; the weeks had slipped by while he pushed BayBridge through its obstacle course. He knew she was all right because everyone else had seen her and reported to Victoria who called Ross twice a week to give him all the news; Derek, of course, reported to no one, but evidently he'd taken Katherine to the Peruvian show. Ross felt a twist of irritation; why would she spend an evening with Derek?

It's her business, he told himself. Browsing along dignified glass and mahogany cases, Ross had other things on his mind. He wanted to get home to Melanie. The enormous success of his afternoon welled up, like a promise that everything would be all right. He saw a salesman watching him, gauging the proper time to approach. A pin, he thought; she likes them. And then dinner. Ernie's. The Blue Fox. L'Etoile. Whatever she wants. We'll talk about us, work out our differences, stop circling each other like suspicious strangers.

"It's Mr. Hayward, isn't it?" asked the salesman. "I helped you last time you were here. And what may I show you this afternoon?"

"The sapphire," said Ross. "Do you have it in silver? Or only in the gold?"

"We have a similar one in silver, and these as well—" The salesman drew out two trays but Ross was impatient.

"This one. I'm in a hurry, so if you'll write it up—"

"One moment, sir." The salesman sped to a spiral staircase leading to the balcony offices. "I need one of the blue boxes," he whispered to Herman Mettler's secretary. "For Mr. Hayward."

She tilted her head to the left. "In Herman's office."

Hurrying, he went to a cabinet in Mettler's office, found a box, and turned to go. "Miss McAlister!" he said, seeing Leslie perched on the desk. "Have you been here long?"

"Three minutes," said Leslie. "Marc is arguing with your boss about the cost of gold, or something equally mercenary. Which Mr. Hayward were you whispering about?"

"Ross Hayward."

"Point him out to me, would you?"

"You can watch me; I'll be writing up his sale."

From the balcony, Leslie gazed thoughtfully at the salesman's customer, remembering the light in Katherine's eyes when she described their lunch at The Compass Rose. No wonder, Leslie thought, seeing Ross's smile. Married, though. They always are. She watched him stride to the door. He's had good news or bad news and he's off to tell someone. With a peace offering in his hand.

"And what is so absorbing?" Marc Landau said at her shoulder. "Have you, even from this height, spotted a trifle you cannot do without?" He saw her looking at Ross's back in the doorway. "Or a man."

"A friend of a friend," Leslie said easily. "Are you finished?"

"Yes. Where would you like to go for a drink?"

"Someplace quiet. It's been a terrible day. Too many puzzles all at once."

Landau was silent as they drove to the top of Nob Hill. Finally, a little cautiously, he said, "Puzzles."

"Don't worry, Marc, I'm not going to burden you with my problems. Even if you were interested, they're confidential."

At that he looked at her. "Is Heath's in trouble?"

"I might be in trouble."

"But if it's confidential it involves Heath's." He parked in the curved driveway of the Mark Hopkins Hotel. "You can tell me all about it over a drink."

"You know, Marc," she said, putting her arm through his, "one of your most endearing qualities is your honesty: confidential news is more interesting than Leslie's problems. Let's talk about something else. Would you do another favor for me? Ask Herman to carry a few of Katherine's pieces next spring. She's taking two classes, but she needs encouragement. Just a few pieces, nothing major. Would you talk to him?"

They sat beside a window and Landau tapped the table with a silver matchbook. "Is there no end to the favors this young woman requires? Where is her pioneering spirit? Does being a woman entitle her to a smooth path to fame and fortune?"

Leslie gave him a long look. "You're not serious."

"No." He let out his breath and Leslie knew he had meant every word, but was not ready to quarrel with her.

"Katherine doesn't know I'm asking you. And I don't want her to know. I mean that, Marc. When Herman offers her space in his marble palace, he's not to tell her I had anything to do with it."

"You're assuming— All right. I'll talk to him, and swear him to secrecy. Is this your price for telling me about Heath's?"

"Oh, fuck it, Marc, what a rotten thing to say."

"It must be." He looked amused. "To get such a reaction. I'll help your little friend in any case. So you can tell me just because I ask."

Below them, the lights of San Francisco were coming on in the gathering dusk. Leslie watched them, drinking her wine and debating briefly with herself. "Nope. I'd like to but I can't." Because I can't trust you, she added silently. How pleasant if I could. How pleasant if you even tried to convince me I could. "Maybe some other time. Tell me about Herman. Did you sign a new contract with him?"

He gave in gracefully—another reason Leslie liked him—and talked about the spring line of jewelry he and Mettler had agreed upon that afternoon. Listening, she admired his neat balance of art and business, and the rest of the evening was as pleasant as Marc could make it when he tried. Then, because she was so tired and wanted to go home and worry quietly about meetings she'd heard the other vice-presidents had been having, excluding her, she ended the evening after dinner and once again he gave in gracefully.

Nice, she thought, when she was alone in the blue-and-white living room of her house overlooking the Marina. Having someone who makes no demands. Although—she turned off the lights, put on a record of dreamy piano music, and sat in a window seat to watch the ghostly shapes of sailboats swaying in the harbor—it would be nice to have someone who does more than make requests and give in gracefully. It would be nice to have someone who gives a damn.

The first time Katherine had dinner with Derek, on the Saturday they spent at his vineyards, she discovered he had ordered their meal when he made the reservation. "So you don't need a menu," he said. "In fact, you can't have one. It's all taken care of."

She protested. "I'd like to pay for my own dinner."

He smiled slightly. "But when I invite you to dinner I expect to pay. Do you see a way out of this dilemma?"

It had been a wonderful day, hot and dry, with a buzzing stillness in the vineyards that stretched between low hills beneath a canopy of cloudless sky. Leslie had taken Jennifer and Todd to the Exploratorium, and the whole day had been a special time pulled out of her everyday life, free of worry. She didn't want to ruin it by arguing over who would pay for dinner. So she met his smile with her own and said lightly, "But if I don't see the menu, how will I know what I'm missing?"

"You can take it for granted that you aren't missing a thing."

Since then, he had called twice a week, inviting her to dinner or a nightclub. Four times she had said yes, each time telling herself it was the last: she should spend her evenings with Jennifer and Todd, she ought to be working on her jewelry designs, she shouldn't be having a good time while Craig was missing. But she went, because Derek could make her light-hearted even after a day of Gil Lister's insults and dinner with her increasingly sulky children. She went, even if she didn't understand why he sought her out, because she was fascinated by his power and wealth, his charm and attentiveness, and the way he seemed to center them all on her, making her feel young and very special. And she went because she missed being with a man, and he was the only one who was calling.

The day before the excursion to the Napa vineyards, Leslie told Katherine she had seen Ross at Mettler's, buying one of Landau's sapphire-and-silver lapel pins. "Marvelous-looking man; too stern, but when he smiles it's a face to remember." She paused. "Why don't you call him?"

"Because he's busy with his own life," Katherine answered. "And what would I say? 'I'm fine, though you haven't asked in a long time; the children are fine, though you haven't asked; I've heard from Craig, though you haven't asked...' He probably knows how we are, from his family, and if he wanted to ask me he would. So there's no reason to call."

"I find reasons when I want to call someone," Leslie said.

"I've never called a man. And anyway, I'm married."

"What does that have to do with it?"

"Probably nothing." They laughed. "But I won't call, anyway."

So there was only Derek, introducing her to the nightlife of San Francisco. "A favorite of mine," he said one night when they went to the dimly lit Moroccan restaurant called Marrakech. They sat on a low sofa before a carved brass table and used chunks of bread to eat spiced shredded chicken, lamb with honey and almonds, and couscous with vegetables. After a tea girl washed their hands with rosewater, they sat over fruit and tea, talking in the languorous tones of those who have eaten too much and know they cannot stir for at least an hour.

Derek gave Katherine leisurely descriptions of the people in the restaurant whom he knew. One depended on a rich aunt to make up losses on the commodities exchange; one kept a mistress in Cancun; another wrote books for which her husband was famous as author and television personality. "And over there," Derek said, gesturing at a noisy group in the opposite corner, "are the seven dwarfs. One big happy banking family, mutually protective. They pay off irate husbands who catch Cousin Dopey in bed with their wives; they kick Cousin Sleepy under the table when he insults a hostess by snoring through the entree; they use Cousin Snoopy to spy on rival bankers; Cousin Doc tries to cure Droopy, who, as you may imagine from his name, has sexual problems—"

"There is no Droopy," Katherine laughed.

"True. Grumpy is the one with those problems, but Droopy is more descriptive. Now there's another group, at the table just beyond the dwarfs—" And he continued around the room, with caustic, intimate dissections that embarrassed Katherine but also intrigued her, because these were some of the city's top business and professional people, whose pictures she saw in newspaper society pages. "It's my job to meet them," he said when she asked how he knew so many. "And stroke them. They control everything we need—construction permits, zoning, structural requirements, highway funds, bank loans—the lifeblood of our company." He scanned the tables. "A dull lot, but we can't survive without them. Some of my favorite characters aren't here, but we'll find them at other places, on other nights—" He broke off, watching a couple cross the far end of the room to sit at a small table. "Idiotic," he murmured. "Here, of all places—"

Katherine followed his look. "Isn't that Melanie?" she asked.

"None other." His voice was dry.

"But who is she with?"

"A young—a very young—tennis pro from the Mill Valley Country Club. A tadpole on Melanie's well-baited hook. I think it's time for us to leave. Unless you want more tea—?"

"No. There's no room for another drop. And we've been here for hours."

"The only way to eat here is to make it an evening." His voice was preoccupied. "Ready?"

She stood and slipped into her jacket as he held it. "Isn't the wrong couple sneaking out before being seen?"

He turned his dark eyes on her with the intent look he always had when she impressed him. Smiling, he took her arm. "Possibly. I'll explain it sometime." He led the way between couches and ottomans to the exit. "On Friday," he said casually as they waited for the doorman to bring his car, "a friend of mine is having a party. Do you have something formal to wear?"

"No." It came out quickly, the dreamy languor of the evening gone in an instant. She could not afford new clothes. "Craig and I never went out very much. I didn't enjoy it."

"You love it," he said flatly. In the car, he drove slowly for once, past Japantown and then into Golden Gate Park—the long way back. "So Craig must have been the homebody."

"He worked hard," Katherine said defensively. "And he liked being home. Whenever he came back from a trip, he'd close the door behind him and say how wonderful it was to be there, safe and protected..." Her voice trailed away. They would kiss, while the children waited their turn, and Craig would tell them about his trip, and pull out little presents, tantalizingly, one at a time, so that it was like a long, drawn-out Christmas.

"Safe and protected," Derek repeated. "Like a womb." He turned off and stopped at the Chain of Lakes, brooding at the water in the misty light of lamps and a fragile moon. "Or Victoria's open arms. Or Ann's. After all these years, he was still looking for them."

"Fifteen years. You don't know anything about him."

"I know everything about him. Do you really think people change? However, I'm more interested in you. Did you—"

"Why? Why are you interested in me? Everywhere we go we meet beautiful women whom you know—some of them you've had affairs with—"

"Now how would you know that?"

"It's in your voice when you talk about them. You shape your words as if they're soft clay—as if you still feel her, whoever she is, under your hands."

"Good God." He shook his head. "Just when you seem most timid, you come out with something remarkable. How long are you going to hide under your cover? Cautious, careful, wearing dowdy clothes—"

"They're not dowdy!"

"By my standards they are. And you know what I mean; you do a full study of every woman in sight when we go out. Look, I have accounts at every store in town; take a day and fit yourself out properly."

"On your charge accounts? You can't be serious. You're not keeping me, Derek; no one is. I take care of myself. If you don't like the way I dress, you can go out with someone else."

"I do."

"Oh." Of course. All those other nights in the week.

"But I also expect to go out with you."

"Why?"

"Partly because I like women who are more complicated than they seem. The rest you'll have to figure out yourself."

After a moment, Katherine said, "Derek, I'd like to go home."

He started the car and drove out of the park, and within a few minutes pulled up before her building. Putting his hand on the back of her head, he kissed her lightly. "I'd like to help you escape from that prison Craig built. I don't think he kept the key." Reaching across her, he opened her door. "Think about some new clothes. You'll be more comfortable on Friday night."

"I'm not . . . free Friday night."

"Listen to me." Holding the door handle, he had his arm across her lap, pinning her in place. "I expect you to tell me the truth. If you don't want to be with me on Friday, say so. If you don't want to be with me at all, say so. But I will not tolerate your behaving like an adolescent who can't handle a simple relationship."

"This relationship," she retorted, "is no more simple than you are. It's easy for you to forget Craig—"

"Never easy," he murmured.

"—but I can't, and because of that I'm confused about a lot of things and none of them are simple. And I'd like you to remove your arm."

After a moment he sat back. "Free to go."

She pushed open the door and stepped out. "Marrakech was wonderful. Thank you."

"And Friday night?"

She looked at his narrow face, the hollows in his cheeks accentuated by the slanting streetlight, his mouth curved in a challenging smile. "How formal is it?"

"Black tie for the men; a little more flexible for the women."

Flexible. She had no money for a flexible formal dress. But as she was about to refuse, she stopped. Why shouldn't she go out with Derek? Everything about him was intriguing—even the cruel wit of his descriptions in the restaurant. And even if she was confused about Craig, missing him, worrying about him, bewildered by the money she was sure he'd sent—he had left her, after all, to fend for herself. Why shouldn't she allow herself the pleasure, and vanity, she got from Derek's attention?

But she needed a dress. I could ask Leslie, Katherine thought. Maybe I can find something on sale. And fix it up. I'll be home on Thanksgiving; I could do it then. Why not? I like being with Derek. And I don't have to live like a prisoner while I'm waiting for Craig.

It was only after she had agreed to Friday night, and was unlocking the door of her apartment, that she realized she had used Derek's description: living in a prison.

Thanksgiving. Rescued, Katherine thought, by Leslie and her brother. Derek had neatly passed over it when he invited her to a Friday-night party; Victoria and Tobias had left the week before on a museum expedition to Peru. Leslie had suggested a restaurant, which had horrified Jennifer and Todd. Thanksgiving meant home.

"Then I'll cook," Leslie said. "I should, now and then, or I'll forget how. And Bruce makes a wicked pumpkin pie. Wait till you taste it."

Bruce McAlister, ten years younger than his sister, had flaming hair as crinkly as steel wool, matching eyebrows that shot up and down in astonished arcs, and nonstop speech. If not for Bruce, Katherine thought, and the way he distracted Jennifer and Todd from memories of Canadian Thanksgivings, the evening could have been a disaster.

"It's bourbon that does it, I don't even measure, I just pour," he said when they all gasped at their first taste of his pumpkin pie. All through dinner, as they feasted on Leslie's stuffed turkey and Katherine's cranberry sauce and vegetables, he had entertained them with stories of his friends, who lived in an area called the Panhandle. "A few years ago, when we lived on unemployment and food stamps and love, it was a blast—good guitars, good grass, good women..."

"Bruce," Leslie warned.

"Shit, they know all this." His eyebrows shot up as he grinned at Jennifer and Todd. "Anyway things are different, it's depressing the way everybody's so straight all of a sudden, getting married, having kids, buying dishwashers, for Christ's sake, working steady... Even me," he added sadly.

Todd was transfixed by Bruce's jumping red eyebrows and gesticulating hands. "You work too?" he asked.

"I admit it with deep embarrassment, I do indeed work from eight thirty to five *five days a week* and I am grossly underpaid by that posh establishment called Heath's—"

"That's where Mom works!" Todd cried.

"And my sister as well, in fact she got me the job—who else would hire me with my background?—but *she* spends her days on the executive top floor while your mother and I slave away in the basement."

"I don't remember seeing you," Katherine said.

"You wouldn't, I never stir from the computer room; do you know that I can make a computer do anything except bake a pumpkin pie?"

And that was when he cut into his dessert and they all got their first taste of what Katherine would have sworn was a bottle of bourbon lightly flavored with pumpkin. "Bruce," Leslie laughed. "Where's the other one?"

"Alas my sis knows me too well; I do happen to have another one." Reaching under the table, he brought forth a box. "Unfortunately, you understand, this one has only vanilla, no bourbon, no brandy, just the stuff the poor Pilgrims had, and no wonder most of them never survived the winter."

They laughed and praised the second pie. We laughed most of the evening, Katherine thought later. Laughed and sang to Bruce's guitar playing and went home early, with smiles and leftover turkey, and even when we were alone again we didn't reminisce about Canadian Thanksgivings or our house in Vancouver. Thank God for Bruce McAlister; he got us through the day.

On Friday, Katherine asked Gil Lister if she could leave an hour early. He adjusted the ski jacket on a mannequin and zipped it closed before saying over his shoulder, "Kiddies sick?"

"No. I have something to do."

"Something personal."

"Yes. But, Gil, all the invoices are finished and last week's scenery will be ready to be shipped back by three o'clock—"

"Katherine, we've been receiving a number of personal telephone calls at work, haven't we? And we've been having lunches that lasted over an hour—"

"Only twice! And it's been more than a month since—"

"And a number of times in creating a window, you were not where I expected you to be. There is a *laxness*, Katherine, in your behavior. If this indicates dissatisfaction, if you would prefer to work elsewhere, we should part; I cannot work in an atmosphere of frowns and groans and hostility."

"I do not groan," Katherine said tightly. "And I frown less than you do. I try to be friendly, I don't think I'm hostile, but I would be more satisfied if you let me help design windows instead of treating me like an imbecile or a coat rack."

Lister's hands paused, then moved on, buckling a ski boot. He stood and bent the mannequin's knee. "Ski poles."

Katherine took a breath, then let it out without speaking, and handed him the poles. They finished the scene of a slalom race in silence. "Ah," Lister breathed, scanning the slope they had covered with styrofoam flakes marked by ski tracks behind the mannequins who were rounding flag-topped slalom posts. Without warning, he whipped about. "What would *you* do with it?"

"Bring it to life," she said bluntly. "It's dead." *I'll get another job; I don't have to take his insults.* "Use only two racers, with a third at the top, bending forward to start, and put spectators along the side, especially children and teenagers. Three-year-olds are skiing now, and Heath's has clothes for them. Put a digital time clock in that corner, and a finish line under it. A mountain background; I've seen one in the storeroom. And I'd have someone holding a trophy for the winner."

"Would you indeed."

His voice caught her up. What was the matter with her? How long might it take to get another job? "I'm sorry, Gil. The window is fine; it's simple and colorful. Do you want to put prices with them?"

"No." He was tapping his foot and studying the four racers. "I've never skied, you know; it looks quite exciting. Get downstairs and pack up last week's scenery. Don't seal the boxes; I want to check them. You may leave half an hour early if it is a matter of life and death."

"Thank you." She was trembling with fury. He'd let her apology lie there, unaccepted, unacknowledged. But it was my fault, she thought as she packed a box with plastic autumn leaves. I knew he'd be angry when I criticized him. Victoria was right; I jump at people. But then why does Derek say I'm timid?

I wish I knew what I really am.

Exactly half an hour early, she left work and rushed home. Leslie had found a dress for her and was coming at eight, just before Derek arrived, to pass judgment. Dinner with Jennifer and Todd was hurried; they were going back to school for a rehearsal of the Christmas choral concert and for once did not deluge her with complaints about school or fog or how often she was away from home. "You'll wait for Annie to pick you up after rehearsal," Katherine said as they were leaving.

"We really are old enough to walk home alone," said Jennifer. "But if it makes you happy, we'll wait."

"It makes me happy," Katherine smiled. "Have a good time."

"You too," Jennifer said. "Don't be home too late, though."

Wondering what that meant, Katherine told Leslie about it when she arrived. But Leslie was not listening. Head cocked critically, she was scrutinizing Katherine in her new dress. "Well, well," she said at last, softly. "Very well indeed."

The dress, found in the stockroom from last winter's Empire Room collection, reduced to one-eighth its original price, was of a timeless style and simplicity: a black cashmere sheath, as fine as silk, molding Katherine's slender figure, flared at the hem, long-sleeved, with a startlingly deep V-neck edged in tiny scallops. Two black silk cords wound twice around her waist, ending in long fringes reaching almost to the hem.

But as elegant as the dress was, Leslie knew the real attraction was Katherine herself: eyes bright, face flushed as she studied her reflection, unconsciously standing straighter because the dress demanded it. Leslie gazed at the delicate lines of her friend's face and figure, disguised until now by worry or sadness, or the slouch of her shoulders, or clothes that had become too big for her when she lost weight after Craig disappeared. "Wonderful," she murmured. "At least as a start. How about jewelry? You must have made a necklace in all those classes you've taken."

Katherine shook her head. "I'm not ready to go public."

"Well, then, the only thing left is makeup and your hair."

"No!" Katherine stepped back. "Not now, Leslie. This is enough." Enough change, she thought, astonished and a little disconcerted at the difference one dress could make. Putting up her hand, she blocked the reflection of her face and looked only at her graceful figure, almost as regal as Victoria's. Lowering her hand, she met her own eyes, pleased and shining, in the mirror. She looked like a young girl, about to step into the outside world, instead of a thirty-five-year-old working woman with two children. And a husband, she added swiftly. And a husband.

Leslie was watching her. "Enough change for one day," Katherine repeated. "It's only a party, after all; it's not so important."

Leslie opened her mouth to argue, then nodded casually. "Fine by me. But I did bring my own contribution—" She opened a white box she had brought with her. "Just for tonight."

"Oh, Leslie, I can't—!" Katherine began as Leslie took out her silver fox jacket and a black beaded evening bag.

"Yes you can, lady; don't argue. If I want to feel like a fairy godmother, the least you can do is let me feel like one. Someday you'll even let me finish the rest of you."

Katherine hugged her. "You make me sound like a piece of furniture—but thank you." Through the window, she saw Derek's car pull up.

"Thank you, Leslie, you're wonderful," she said, grabbing the jacket and evening bag, and was out of the building before Derek reached the door. It was one of her rules: he was not to step inside her apartment. She had seen his grandmother's; she had heard about his. She was ashamed of her own.

Norma Burton was celebrating her fourth divorce with a party for her closest friends. "How many does she have?" Katherine asked Derek. "Two or three hundred," he answered, appraising the crowd as he checked Katherine's jacket in the cloak room. "If she likes you for more than ten minutes, she counts you in. Generous if not discriminating, and very much a child. Let me look at you." He took Katherine's hand and contemplated her. "Do you know that you are a beautiful woman?"

She pulled her hand away. "No. I've never been beautiful. It would take more than a new dress..."

"Much more. Color in your face, the way you stand and hold your head, your eyes... Have you looked in a mirror?"

"Yes—"

"At your eyes?"

"Yes. Aren't we going to join the party?"

He took her hand again and pulled her to him, lifting her chin. "Your eyes are magnificent: enormous and bright—" He paused. "And now they look alarmed, as if you've come to a precipice. What might you be afraid of? Come." He tucked her hand beneath his arm and led her to the ballroom. "I'll introduce you to Norma's grab bag of friends; they are, after all, the evening's entertainment."

By the time dinner was over and dancing began, the faces and names had blurred, like drifting confetti. Everyone eyed Katherine with open curiosity, the glances moving from Derek's hand on her arm to her dress and then to her face. Everyone asked where she came from and, when she answered "Vancouver," how long she would be staying. Women maneuvered to see if she wore a wedding ring and, when they saw it, asked where her husband was. "On a business trip," she answered—so many times she began to believe it. Many of the guests asked familiarly about Derek's new apartment and one couple tried to talk about a shopping complex in Daly City they wanted him to bid on. "I'll be in my office on Monday," he said.

"Is your apartment new?" Katherine asked. "I didn't realize that, when you told me about it."

"About a year," he said. "I just finished putting it together. You'll see it once we get out of here."

She shivered. She felt small and light, cut off from familiar things, as if she had become one of the bits of confetti in the room. She danced with Derek and talked to his friends, but none of it seemed real. She did not feel drab and insecure as she had at the Peruvian exhibit, but each time she was thoroughly inspected by one of Derek's friends, she wasn't sure it was really Katherine Fraser inside the cashmere dress.

All evening, she felt Derek's closeness: his body guiding hers as they danced, his eyes watching her as she talked to others, his hand holding her arm when they walked across the room. "On a business trip," she said again and again in answer to questions, and she thought of Craig as she lied about him, as she moved smoothly with Derek to the music, as she said "Yes, of course," when Derek told her it was time to go.

At the cloak room, a huge man, triple-chinned and balding, with dimples and curly gray sideburns, greeted Derek. "I'm told this is Katherine Fraser," he said, and held out his hand. "Herman Mettler. I understand you're a jewelry designer."

Katherine saw in her mind a store she visited every chance she had, dreaming of her own jewelry in its mahogany-and-glass cases. "Mettler's," she breathed.

"The very one." His voice rumbled like a bass fiddle beneath the high notes of the party. "You're new in town? Looking for a store?"

"Yes, but how—?"

"One of my designers mentioned it. We're always looking for new work; it's possible we could find you a small space. Depending, of course, on what you have."

"Of course."

"Well, bring me your samples. A good selection; I don't make decisions on a handful and a promise. Make an appointment with my secretary; week after next. Derek, good to see you; hope you're well. Give my regards to Angela; lovely young woman. Mrs. Fraser, I'll see you soon, I suppose." And he was gone.

Dazed, Katherine put on the jacket Derek held. She thought of Craig again. What would he say if Mettler took her jewelry? Would he still call it her little hobby?

"Katherine," Derek said as they rode the elevator to the lobby.

"What? I'm sorry; I was thinking—"

"Don't put too much faith in Mettler. He's not always reliable."

"He didn't make any promises," she said. "So why would I put any faith in him?"

"You were building castles, little one, and you know it. Just remember what I said."

"I will. Who is Angela?"

"An ex-wife."

"Whose?"

"Mine. Herman is a little slow; we've been divorced for six months."

"He thought you were married? And at the party with me?"

Derek was silent. "Let me tell you about my apartment," he said at last. "One of Hayward Corporation's finest."

He described it as they drove: part of a complex of buildings, some still under construction, at the base of Telegraph Hill on Lombard Street, behind the restored warehouses and new buildings of Levi Plaza. When his company was given the contract, Derek bought the top floor for himself, working with the architect to make one huge apartment instead of the two in the original plans. "Of course it's big enough for a tribal rain dance," he said as he led Katherine on a quick tour of the rooms, stopping in the kitchen to take a bottle of champagne from the refrigerator. "But it has its nooks. For instance—"

He took her to a room enclosed on three sides with glass jalousies, furnished with tufted red velvet couches and armchairs, oriental rugs on a parquet floor, and brass lamps with fringed shades. It was an 1890s parlor—formal and overstuffed—but Derek had made it a joke by putting it in a starkly modern building. "Angela said it was decorated in early brothel," he said. "But she was only hoping."

"Why did you get a divorce?" Katherine asked. Her head was against the back of the couch, the light from a fringed lamp flickering through the bubbles in her glass. Derek had had three divorces, according to Claude. I've been married almost eleven years, she thought; and divorce never occurred to me.

"We were mistaken about each other," Derek answered. "What else ends a marriage? Angela thought she could reform me and I thought she was the only woman who didn't want anything from me. We were both wrong. She's very much like Norma: generous, impulsive, and a child. But you, my sweet Katherine, have become very much a woman."

He barely seemed to move, but his face was above hers, blocking the lighted lamp. He put her glass on the table and brushed her lips lightly with his. Then, sliding his arm beneath her shoulders, he kissed her with a demanding confidence that struck against her like a wave, pushing her back against the velvet couch.

Everything fell away. Her fears about Craig, her helpless rage at Lister, worries about the children, about money, about jewelry design, even the spark of jealousy she felt when Derek talked about women—all fell away. There was only Derek's body on hers, after months without anyone to hold her and make love to her. Katherine felt she was dissolving. His tongue against hers released all the longings she had held back for so long; her arms reached around him and her hips strained upward.

And then, through the roaring in her ears, she heard Craig's voice. The words were muffled, but Katherine knew they were the same ones he had said the first time they made love, when they held each other, laughing and already making plans, because they had been so lonely and now had someone to love.

She pulled away from Derek and sat up, wanting him so much that tears filled her eyes. But as she stood and walked the length of the room, she was not sure whether she was crying for him or for Craig. She kept her back to Derek until she could stop her tears. Then she turned around.

He was watching her, the bones of his face sharply shadowed in the light from the fringed lamp. "I gather my cousin joined us," he said ironically.

His cousin. It had been weeks since she thought of Craig and Derek as cousins. No two men could be more different.

Derek refilled their glasses. "Sit down and drink this. He can't see us, you know, and even if he could, you are allowed champagne every other Friday night, or rather Saturday morning, at precisely one fifteen A.M."

She gave a small laugh and came back to the couch. "I'm sorry."

"Don't apologize. You do too much of that. Has it occurred to you that he's not worth your fidelity?"

"No. That doesn't help, Derek. It's hard enough knowing how to behave without making up excuses. I don't know what happened to Craig, but he's my husband and I'd rather believe he is worth my fidelity."

He drained his glass and slowly refilled it. "Would you like to hear what happened the last time we sailed together, fifteen years ago?"

"Didn't Claude tell me? Last June?"

"The official version. He wasn't on the boat. I was."

"But you let him tell it."

"I always let Claude tell official stories. Do you want to hear mine?"

"You mean it's different from his. About Craig."

"All of us." He looked at her, waiting.

"Of course I want to hear it." Katherine spoke slowly, still shaking from the heat of her body and the memory of Craig's voice. Derek seemed untouched: cool and remote. "I've always wanted the truth," she said.

"The truth." He smiled faintly, then settled back on the couch. "We were sailing home across the bay," he began. His speech was flat, almost a monotone. "We'd been at a party in Sausalito, very dull, and when we left, Craig decided to sail home the long way, out past the Golden Gate Bridge and then in again, to the harbor. Since he'd appointed himself captain, there was no arguing; we went the long way. But when I told him I was in a hurry, he made a concession and put up the spinnaker; the wind was up and it gave us good speed.

"But then he changed his mind; he got worried about the currents and told us to put on lifejackets—Ross was in the cabin and Jennifer took one down to him—and then said we'd have to take down the spinnaker. I said I wanted it up and we argued about it. 'Too much sail,' he said. 'A strong wind could rip it to shreds.' Ross and Jennifer came up from the cabin in the middle of our mutual insults—got drenched by spray, I remember, because by then the boat was heeling and we were going at a good clip and water was breaking over the cockpit. It was the right way to sail—top speed and a roaring wind, spray flying, and waves slapping the boat—and I put my arm around Jennifer and said we liked living dangerously and no one was worried but the captain.

"Of course he couldn't take it: the boat was his turf; the only place he could feel superior to me. Besides, he was crazy about his sister—guarded her like a mother hen. He gripped the wheel and yelled at me to let go of Jennifer; he looked so wild that Ross stepped in, to distract him, and said *he'd* take down the spinnaker.

"Craig hardly heard him; he was so busy yelling—he told me if I didn't like the way he captained the ship, I could swim to shore, if I had the guts to try it in that water. Only an ass would have gone in willingly, but he made it a challenge to manhood, or some such thing, and I told him to shut up and get us home.

"Craig was twenty-two that summer, and I was twenty-one—a couple of kids who happened to be related but didn't like each other. We never needed an excuse to think up insults and that day was no different, except Jennifer was there. She always tried to calm Craig down, especially when he was attacking me, but she didn't have any luck that day, and she was probably frightened, too—the wind was so loud we had to shout; we were soaking wet; and Craig seemed to have trouble controlling the boat and his own temper. Jennifer started to cry and Craig went into a rage, blaming me for her tears, calling me a string of names he'd never used before—looking at Jennifer to make sure she heard—and then he began raving about the way I was managing a building we were constructing that summer, the Macklin Building. Craig spent a lot of time trying to convince the family he knew more than I did, making me out to be incompetent or crooked, or both. But that day he should have known better. He was having enough trouble keeping the boat under control but he had to try to impress his sister. When he sent Ross forward to take down the spinnaker, I went over to try to calm him down, but he'd worked himself up to such a pitch he thought I was telling him what to do, and he let out a roar and jumped me.

"Then everything happened at once. He'd left the wheel to get his hands on my throat and just as Jennifer was pulling on his arm, crying for him to stop, the boat changed direction—crossed the wind instead of going with it—because there was no one to hold it on course. The boom swung across and struck Jennifer on the side of the head. I barely saw it—I was trying to get out of Craig's grip—but I heard the thud and a second later I saw her tumble over the side.

"Craig screamed and dropped me. He lunged for the life preserver and marker pole and threw them into the water, yelling to Jennifer to grab hold, to fight. We were moving away from her, very fast, and the next minute Craig dove over the side, screaming her name. Ross was at the bow, taking down the spinnaker, and I grabbed the wheel, but I wasn't an experienced sailor and it took me almost ten minutes to get the boat turned around. Ross didn't know any more about sailing than I did— since then he's become an expert—so he stood at the side, calling Craig and Jennifer, trying to see them. It was getting dark.

"I headed for the light on the marker pole Craig had thrown in, and we finally saw the life preserver. Jennifer was propped in it, like a doll, staring at us. But she wasn't alive; I suppose we knew that long before we got to her. Ross started to retch, and then cry, and I told him to pull himself together and start calling Craig again; he had to be nearby.

"Ross called until he was hoarse, in between whimpering, 'My God, my God, both of them—' until I had to slap him to get him to pay attention. I told him to hold the boat and I went over the side and tied a rope around Jennifer and together we got her into the cockpit. I couldn't find a pulse.

"Ross called the Coast Guard. By then it was dark and while we waited for them, we got a searchlight from the cabin and swept the water with it, looking for Craig. But of course there was no sign of him. He was gone."

In the abrupt silence, Katherine sat shivering, so chilled by Derek's cold telling of the story her bones felt brittle. He had not moved; he had not raised his voice. His face had not changed. He might have been recounting a story about strangers. She clasped her hands, to keep them still. "Where was Craig while you were looking for him?"

Derek shrugged. "As Claude said, we assume he swam to shore. There were no other boats in the area and we weren't far from Lime Point. He was very strong and he could have made it. Obviously he did."

"Lime Point?" Katherine was trying to place the name.

"A small spit of land just below the north end of the Golden Gate Bridge. There's a lighthouse on it."

Todd walking toward a beach, and a lighthouse. "Can we go look, Mom?" "Not today; we're meeting the realtor, remember? We'll come back." "Lime Point," the fisherman said. "Great place. Out at the end, you feel like you're all alone in the middle of the water."

Katherine shivered. "Champagne," Derek said, filling her glass and handing it to her.

"Thank you." Her voice sounded distant in her ears. "Why did Jennifer drown, if she was wearing a lifejacket?"

"She wasn't. For some reason she didn't put it on when Craig told her to. But she probably didn't drown. We found later that when the boom struck her one of the cleats pierced her skull. It's likely she was dead before Craig got to her. My grandmother was vehement about not having an autopsy, and she pulled strings to prevent one. It didn't matter to the family; with both of them gone in one day, no one thought of anything but mourning."

"But... I don't understand. How did she get in the life preserver?"

"We assumed Craig put her there—discovered her dead in the water, got her to the life preserver—we never knew why—then was so exhausted he was carried away in the current and drowned. Obviously a faulty theory. But that was why everyone called him a hero. Jumped in without a lifejacket to save his sister."

"And then—swam away?"

"And then swam away."

"Why?"

"You'd have to ask him." She shivered again. "I'd better make you some coffee."

"No, don't. I'd like to go home. Please."

He nodded. "A good idea. It's been a long evening." His arm was around her waist as they walked to the door. "I have a place at Tahoe; if you'd like to get away we could go there for the weekend."

She shook her head. "Thank you, but you keep forgetting that I have two children. And I'd like some time alone. Could you give me a few days?"

"A few days." He rang for the elevator and they rode down in silence, and in silence drove to Katherine's apartment. "I'll call next week," he said as she opened her door. "You were an exciting woman tonight."

She shook her head again, not looking at him. She was worn out and would have liked some comfort; of all the things he might have said, that was the last one she wanted to hear.

All weekend, Katherine was haunted by Derek's story. During the days, she was with Todd and Jennifer, but at night, remembering it, even as he had told it in his cold, flat voice, she began to imagine it vividly. Yet the more real it seemed, the less she could understand it. Craig

enraged and losing control of himself? Craig physically attacking someone? Impossible. Craig never even raised his voice. When he was angry
he withdrew into himself, shutting everyone out. Then, some time later,
he'd begin talking again, smiling and even-tempered, and no one would
ever know what his thoughts had been, or how he'd resolved his anger.

And he hated physical violence; he would never lift his hand against
anyone.

But what if there were another Craig, who could become enraged,
throw insults and wild accusations, lose control of himself... and try to
strangle his cousin?

And embezzle... and desert his family.

Craig, which one are you?

The children slept, the lights of an occasional passing car swept across
the sofa bed where Katherine lay, while she relived Derek's story again
and again, trying to know who was the man she married.

How many of his silences had been caused by the memory of seeing
his sister die?

How many of his secrets had been about Derek, and furies he could
barely contain?

Why didn't you talk to me about them?

She went to the front window and looked out at the quiet street. The
first time Craig had talked to her was at the opening of an art exhibit in
Vancouver. Katherine was standing before a painting of a man sitting
hunched over at the counter of an all-night restaurant, when, beside her,
a stranger began talking about the vision of loneliness in that painting
and the others in the exhibit. His voice deep and warm, he talked about
the way Edward Hopper's people were painted within rectangles—windows, rooms, doors—to show how they felt trapped, cut off from the
world; and somehow Katherine had known he was talking about himself.
By that time they had exchanged names and were having dinner together.

He had seemed so calm and steady, his dark eyes somber, his full
beard making him look older than his twenty-six years, there had not
been a moment when Katherine had not loved and trusted him. Standing
in the window of her apartment in San Francisco, she remembered his
eyes, and his warm voice, and the way her skin felt when he held her—
the first time she had ever been touched by a man, the first time a man
had seen her naked, the first time a man had looked at her with desire.

"Craig," she whispered, aching for him. But then she thought how
long ago that had been. She had always believed they had so much love
but all those years, since he first spoke to her, Craig had carried that
terrible story inside him, and never let her share it.

If that really *was* the story.

The idea came suddenly. The truth, Derek had said with a faint smile. How did she know? Claude had told the official version; Derek had told his. But Derek himself had said he didn't like Craig. Why should she believe he was telling the truth?

The only one who could tell her was Ross. The last thing Katherine decided before falling asleep late Sunday night was that she would call him the next morning.

But those confused thoughts and questions about Craig had filled only a part of that hectic weekend. Long before, Katherine had promised Jennifer and Todd—to make up for her evenings out—that those two days would be theirs, to plan any way they wished. And so, just when she wanted to be quiet, the hours were crammed with excursions and chatter, hurtling on buses and cable cars from one part of the city to another, forcing herself, through the clamor of her own thoughts, to listen to her children.

"Look!" Todd demanded. It was Sunday afternoon, almost the end of the exhausting weekend, and they were walking through the Exploratorium, a cavernous museum of scientific exhibits made to be manipulated, examined, and played with as painless lessons in science and nature. Jennifer had rushed Katherine to some of her favorites: light bulbs that lit when she clapped her hands, a mirror that made her seem to float above the floor, a strobe light that left her shadow imprinted on a screen after the light had been turned off.

Then it was Todd's turn. "Look!" he demanded, pulling Katherine with him to a television screen. As he stood before it, his face appeared, transformed electronically into hundreds of different-sized squares that gave him one eye larger than the other, three sections of chin, a two-part nose, a jaw line stepping crazily up and down. "Terrific, huh?" He tilted his head, turned to look back over his shoulder, stuck out his tongue. "That's me. Terrific, isn't it?"

"Oh, Todd." Katherine knelt on the concrete floor and put her arms around him.

"Isn't it *terrific!*" he demanded, standing rigidly within her arms.

"Yes," she said. And it was. Because after weeks of sullen silence, Todd finally had found a way to tell her how he felt. "You're broken up into pieces, aren't you?" she said, still kneeling beside him. "Part of you in Vancouver and part of you here; part of you wanting Daddy home and another part mad at him for being gone. And I guess part of you being mad at me, too, for selling our house and dragging you here and then leaving you with Annie a lot of the time."

Todd stared at her. "How do you know all that?"

"You told me, by showing me the pieces on the screen. But, Todd, doesn't part of you love me, too?"

"Sure." But he did not move. Once he would have put his arms around her and kissed her. My son doesn't trust me any more, Katherine thought.

"Well," she said. "We'll have to talk about all those pieces. But for now—" She stood up and looked around. "What happened to Jennifer?"

They found her at the entrance to a separate room. "Wait till you see this," she said with a grin, and plunged in, giving no warning of what was inside.

Katherine felt like Alice in Wonderland: her familiar world disappeared as she seemed to shrink to the size of her children and they grew like giants above her. "I love it, I love it," Jennifer chanted, dancing about, and Todd, racing from one wall to the other, stopped briefly to kiss Katherine on her cheek. "It's the angles!" he shouted gleefully. "We learned about it in school. There aren't any right angles and the floor is slanted, and the ceiling is, too, and everything's crazy, so we look crazy."

Katherine did not understand, but it was more important that Todd had kissed her, and that once again the two of them had found a way to tell her how they felt. Later, at dinner, she said to them, "So you want to cut me down to size, is that it?"

Jennifer looked up cautiously from her soda. "We kind of joked about it. Did Todd tell you?"

"I didn't!" Todd said indignantly.

"You both did," Katherine said. "When you took me to that crazy room. Pretty smart, shrinking me down like that. But why can't we just talk, if you're unhappy? Do we have to go to the Exploratorium every time, so I can figure out what's bothering you?"

They exchanged a look. "It's just that we don't know what's going to happen," Jennifer said. "The other kids talk about Christmas and Easter and next summer, but we can't. We can't even talk about next week."

"Yes you can," Katherine said quietly. "We'll be here next week; we'll be here for lots of weeks."

"How do you know?" Todd demanded.

"Because—" She took an envelope from her purse and handed it to them. "This came in the mail yesterday."

Jennifer read the postmark, then slowly pulled out the piece of blank paper folded around five one-hundred-dollar bills. "The same as last time. There's no letter."

"No. But it was mailed in a town in Manitoba. I guess that means Daddy is moving around a lot and still doesn't want us to know where he is."

"Well, fuck him," Todd growled.

"Todd! Don't talk about your father that way! Do you hear me? You will not talk about him that way! We don't know why he's doing this. All we've heard is what other people say—we haven't heard his side. And until we do, we'll wait for him, and not forget how he took care of us for years and years, and" —her voice wavered— "trust him. Because we love him."

"We can get a bigger apartment with the money," said Jennifer. "I can have my own room."

"No. I'm sorry, Jennifer, but we're only going to use the money when you and Todd need clothes or special things for school, or to pay Annie. The rest we'll put in the bank."

"But he sent it for all of us."

Slowly Katherine nodded. "I know. It's not easy to explain." *He can't get off this easily. If he wants to support us, he has to let us share his life. When he's ready to do that, I'll be glad to take his money. Until then . . .* "We should try to make it on our own. We don't know that the money will keep coming. And I think it's important, while we're waiting for him, to try to build our own life."

Jennifer gave her mother one of the piercing looks that Katherine found so unnerving. "Is that why you go out with Derek Hayward all the time?"

"I don't go out all the time," Katherine began defensively, then caught herself. "I go out with Derek for companionship. He's a friend. Just as you're making friends at school. We all need friends. You should understand—" *Don't overdo it.* "You can understand that. Now how about telling me what the program will be for the Christmas concert?"

Deflected, because the chorus was a new experience and they were excited about it, they described again the Friday-night rehearsal, and by the time they left the restaurant, no one was complaining about not being able to plan for the future. Because, Katherine thought, we're making one every day.

But later, standing at the window while the children slept, going over and over Derek's story, aching for Craig, trying to imagine him lunging forward to get his hands around his cousin's throat, wondering about the secrets wrapped within his silences, Katherine clenched her fists in frustration.

Craig, which one are you?

The more she heard about him, the less she understood. And even when she decided to call Ross, and ask him about Derek's story, she wasn't sure how much she would know. Because as the weeks and months passed, Craig was becoming a different person. And so was she.

"What would you two think," she said casually to Jennifer and Todd at breakfast, "if I decided to do my hair a different way?"

Tilting their heads exactly as Craig did, they eyed her. "How?" Todd asked.

"I don't know. Leslie has some ideas. I thought I'd ask her."

"Will you look very different?" Todd asked.

"I don't think so. I'll have the same face."

"Then why do it?"

"To look my best when I try to sell my jewelry." She corrected herself, telling the truth. "Just—to look my best." It had nothing to do with business. It had to do with change.

"I think it might be all right," Jennifer said. "As long as we recognize you."

"If we don't," Todd said ominously, "we'll go off with some other mother who'll probably be an ogre in disguise, looking for human children to work in her basement, sweeping out the bones of people she's eaten, and the only way we can escape is to tie the bones together into a ladder and climb out—"

"Oh, *Todd!*" Jennifer said. She gathered up her books for school. "*Are* you going to change your hair?" she asked Katherine.

"If you and Todd don't mind."

"I guess we don't."

"Then I guess I will."

"About time!" Leslie exclaimed that evening. "Now—I just happen to have a list. Hairdresser, masseuse, manicurist, facial. What do you call the woman who gives the facial? Face-maker? She who saves face?"

Laughing, Katherine said, "Leslie, I was only thinking of a new hair style."

"Hair does not stand alone. Would you paint only one leg of a chair? Listen, lady, I have great plans for you. Here's a salon of experts, waiting to do your bidding—all of them conveniently at Heath's where you get an employee discount. I'll make an appointment for next Saturday at nine. Count on half a day. Yes?"

"Yes," Katherine said. And on Saturday she floated through the morning in the mirrored peach-and-silver rooms of Heath's salon—a hothouse fairy-land that banished the everyday world. For four hours she luxuriated in scented steam, creams and gels, soft sponges, brushes and puffs, and the caresses of skilled hands shaping her hair, filing her nails, massaging her muscles. Erasing, she thought a little sadly, the last traces of Vancouver.

"The very last," Leslie agreed that afternoon as they stood before Katherine's full-length mirror. Leslie was ecstatic. "A new woman. Was I right? I am always right about these things. Katherine, you're stunning. Not, I must say, the conventional beauty of the toothpaste ads. Different. Better. Much better. A new person."

"I'm not," Katherine protested, but she was uneasy at how different she looked in familiar surroundings. And when Jennifer and Todd came running in, and stopped dead in the doorway, their mouths open, her uneasiness deepened. "Hi," she said. "How was rehearsal?"

"OK." Jennifer stared at her mother. "You told us you'd have the same face."

"Hey," Leslie said. "You're not going to tell me that is not your mother's face."

"She looks like a princess," said Todd.

Katherine turned back to the mirror. She stood straight, her head high, as Victoria had instructed, the dark heavy hair she had imprisoned in a bun now closely framing her face, then falling in loose curls to her shoulders. Relaxing her hair had eased the tightness of her skin, and her face seemed fuller, her hazel eyes larger and wider apart, with a more pronounced upturn at the corners. Her high cheekbones and the faint shadows beneath them accentuated the warmth of her mouth. Derek had said she was a beautiful woman. Katherine looked in the mirror and knew he was right.

In a small voice, Jennifer asked, "Are you going to keep looking like that?"

"I think so," Katherine said. "Don't you think we might get used to it?"

"If Daddy could see you now," said Todd. "He'd come back right away." Katherine flushed. She hadn't thought of Craig. "Can we send a picture, Mom? To the place where the money was mailed? In Manitoba?"

"We don't have an address, silly," said Jennifer. She was watching Katherine.

He'd come back right away. Katherine glanced at her worktable, where a half-finished pendant lay. She thought of the checks she had written four days earlier, on the first of the month, signed Katherine Fraser, paid with money she had earned herself. She looked in the mirror at the reflection of a woman she did not yet know, still at the edge of discoveries.

I'm not sure I want him to see me now. The words sprang into her mind. *Because I'm not sure anymore whether I really want him back.*

CHAPTER 9

T HE letter was centered on Ross's desk. He skimmed it once more, then moved to the table along the wall where the scale model of BayBridge stood. Smiling to himself, he plucked out one building and replaced it with a modernized version. The last step. Ivan Macklin had written to say he had received Ross's check for canceling the lease and would be moving out. For the first time, the Macklin Building would be empty and Ross could get to work on it.

Part of BayBridge, he thought, sitting at his desk. But more important, vacant. Finally able to be inspected. He reached for a scratch pad and began scribbling notes for the engineers. Preoccupied, he heard his telephone ring twice before he remembered his secretary had taken the afternoon off for Christmas shopping. "Yes," he said, still writing. His hand stopped as he heard Katherine's voice.

"I called you last week," she said. "When you were out of town."

He waited. When had they last talked? Weeks ago. And he hadn't seen her since their lunch. Early September; he remembered the kids had just started school. Three months. In the silence, he became aware that she was waiting. He drew an embellished K on his scratch pad. "How are you?" he asked.

"All right. Fine. Jennifer and Todd are up and down, either happy with friends and school, or dragging around, blaming me for everything; we always seem to be arguing or making up. But otherwise we're... fine. Do you know about the money that's come? From Craig?"

"Yes." He'd kept up with her; he knew she was managing, even putting away most of the money that came in the mail. And he knew how she spent some of her evenings.

"I thought they'd tell you," Katherine said. "Did they say anything else?"

"No. How is your job?"

She hesitated, and he knew it was because of his distant politeness. "I guess it's getting better. Now and then Gil even asks for my suggestions. A couple of weeks ago he used my ideas to change a ski window after I'd gone home, and took credit for it when the president of the store liked it. Is that progress?"

"Of a sort," he said, smiling. "I understand you've seen Victoria a few times."

"Twice. For tea. It's wonderful, being with her; I always go home wanting more."

Ross felt a rush of pity at the wistfulness in her voice. "What about your jewelry?" he asked. "Weren't you going to try to sell some?"

"I've been studying..." He listened as she told him about her instructor, who was loaning her the tools and equipment she could not afford to buy. But he was thinking about her voice, lovelier than he remembered: low and clear, with a lilt that had not been there before. So she had changed, probably more than the others had told him. He recalled the frightened, bewildered woman he'd seen in Vancouver and at Victoria's dinner—how much he'd liked her and admired the spirit she'd shown even though her familiar life was crumbling around her.

But damn it, he thought, hearing her animation as she talked about meeting Herman Mettler, how the hell could she be sleeping with Derek? Of all the men she might have found to ward off loneliness while she waited for Craig, how could she choose a bastard who didn't know the meaning of sympathy or friendship?

And why was Derek interested in her? He never did anything without a reason and never paid attention to any but the most beautiful women. Yet gossips reported them all over town, from the Peruvian exhibit to Marrakech, where Melanie said she'd seen them when she was there with a group from her tennis club. So for some reason, he'd turned his charm on Katherine and she'd been taken in—not the first woman to think Derek Hayward was offering her the world. That was it, of course. Ross didn't know what his brother was up to, but he could understand how a lonely woman who thought she had few options could respond to a wealthy man whose options seemed limitless.

I might have helped her find some of her own, he thought. But too much had intervened: Melanie, his preoccupation with what was happening to their marriage, his work, and Katherine's place in the family as Craig's wife. Derek had no such concerns; Derek reached out and took whatever piqued his interest.

He became aware that Katherine had stopped talking. "You've made a good start," he said. "You can't do better than Mettler's."

"If he likes what I have. He didn't promise anything and I'm trying to keep my hopes down." She paused. "Ross, I want to ask you something. Last Friday, Derek told me the story of the sailing accident. There's so much I don't understand—that doesn't seem right—I wanted to ask you about it..."

Ross was silent. He didn't want to talk about the accident. He and Derek still had a score to settle from the events of that day, but they would do it between themselves, not by talking through Katherine. There was nothing he could tell her, anyway, that would make Craig a hero. It was better to remain silent.

In fact, there was nothing much at all he could do for her. She was building her own life; she'd made Derek a part of it; and Ross was in no position to interfere. Or compete, he reflected. "I think you should let Derek explain," he said at last. "I don't think I could add anything helpful." He felt a stab of regret, liking her, wishing there had been no obstacles between them. "I'm sorry," he added. "Maybe sometime—"

He looked up as one of his staff members appeared in the doorway, pointing to his watch. Ross nodded. "I'm sorry," he said again, to Katherine. "I'm late for a meeting. Good luck with Mettler; I'm sure I'll hear all about it from Victoria."

"Ross—?"

"I really am late. Goodbye, Katherine."

But he could not shake the memory of her voice. All through the meeting he heard the lilt of her first words and her bewilderment as she said his name the last time, sliding up in a question he had not allowed her to finish. Because I didn't want to talk about the accident, he thought, knowing that what he really meant was he hadn't wanted to talk about Derek and Katherine.

"We're putting together a schedule for the Macklin Building," he said to his senior staff. "I just got Macklin's lease cancellation; he'll be out in sixty days. That takes us to mid-February, which means if we get moving, we can begin work on it by spring or early summer. But we have to coordinate it with our schedules for the rest of BayBridge."

They knew he had owned the building for five years but hadn't been able to do anything with it because Ivan Macklin had insisted on a six-year lease before agreeing to sell. What he had never explained to them

was why he bought it: a single, rather ordinary building in a decaying
neighborhood where no one was talking about redevelopment; where the
first thoughts of BayBridge were more than twelve months in the future.
By now, with BayBridge a reality, his staff might consider him a wizard
for knowing where to buy, and when, and how to negotiate with the
developers to keep the building, leasing it to BayBridge Plaza. Well, let
them believe it, he thought humorously. Who wouldn't like his staff to
think he's got superhuman powers?

"We're responsible for the renovation, but the more we can use crews
as they arrive for BayBridge, the less expensive it will be. What I need
is a firm schedule. When can we have the building inspected? When
can we get final schematics for the arcade and the renovation of the upper
floors? How soon can we bring in a contractor? There's a problem—yes,
Donna?"

"Ross, I can't find an engineer's report on that building."

"That's what I was about to say. There isn't one."

"But didn't you get one before you bought it?"

"This building doesn't fit the regular pattern." He looked at them:
coworkers, friends, men and women he trusted. "I don't know what
happened to the engineer's report; it's missing. But I think there's a chance
the foundation is weak. It's only a guess, but if I'm right, it will have to
be strengthened, and that means we'll need plans for both repairs and
renovation."

"Well, we'll check the original plans," said Donna practically.

Ross shook his head. "That's part of the problem. I'm not sure the
building and the plans agree. If they don't, and if there are problems in
the foundation, I want them corrected as part of the renovation."

No one asked why Ross suspected a problem in the building. They
had a job to do; they trusted him; and they knew he trusted them. Donna
gathered up her notes. "OK; we need a foundation engineer to check the
support columns, and the soil they're in. Do you have some favorite
engineers, Ross?"

"I'll give you a couple of names. Now, can we work out a schedule
for the Macklin Building and what the rest of you are doing on Bay-
Bridge?"

They settled down to work. They were the original group Ross had
assembled when he opened his firm six years before and they were comfortable together, knowing one another's strengths and weaknesses. Like
a family, Ross thought as they left an hour later. But then, as he locked
the office door for the night, he contradicted himself. Ross Hayward
Associates was not like a family, because he had chosen its members to

balance and respect one another and work harmoniously as a group. Not like a family, he amended. Not, anyway, like mine.

Melanie was waiting in the living room when he came in. Her back was to the sliding glass doors that led to the deck and the starry ring of lights encircling the bay—that magnificent scene that made buyers flock to the Tiburon hills, thinking all their problems would fade away in an atmosphere of such beauty. But Ross knew they didn't. We carry our baggage with us, he thought—the accumulated grievances and tensions of years—and no scenery in the world can even begin to evaporate them.

Melanie was not looking at the view. She was dropping ice cubes into a martini, concentrating on how much liquid each cube splashed on the Bokhara rug. "You didn't call to say you'd be late. I've been waiting for an hour."

"I'm sorry. We had a meeting and I lost track of the time. Macklin's moving out, Melanie; I'll finally be able to get into the building." He watched her examine an ice cube and let it fall into her glass; a splash of gin landed on the toe of her alligator shoe. Stubbornly, calling himself a fool, he went on. "We talked about this, remember? The night I brought you the pin from Mettler's and we went to dinner—"

"The Wildings' party is tonight. I was going to it."

They stood a few feet apart in the blue-and-gold living room, but the space between them was immeasurable. "Why don't you go, then?" Ross asked.

"Because I'm ashamed to show my face! Everyone there knows about my party; how can I tell them I'm not having it after all?"

"Which party?"

"*Which* party! You know damn well which party! The one you canceled!"

"I didn't cancel the party. Only the garden and the ballroom."

"Only! Only! That was where I planned it! Where would you like me to put three hundred and fifty people? In our cozy living room? In your precious Macklin Building? It was going to be the party of the year— and if you had any sense you'd know that would help your business, too! I've been working on it for weeks—the decorations, the food, the invitations—and you decided, *without telling me*, you bastard—you didn't want it, so you made one telephone call and canceled everything I'd done. You humiliated me with the Fairmont and with my friends— these things never stay secret!—you had no right to treat me that way!"

Ross walked to the bar and poured a straight Scotch. "You're right. I apologize."

"You what?"

"I apologize. It was a cruel thing to do and I'm sorry."

"Then you'll call them back!"

"No." He downed his drink and poured another and walked toward Melanie. "I didn't apologize for canceling the Fairmont; I apologized for the way I did it. You've already given two parties this year at fifteen thousand dollars apiece. You've spent almost forty thousand dollars in the past six months on clothes and entertaining and trips. We can't afford your Fairmont party. Does it occur to you that I work for a living, that I do not enjoy an infinitely expanding income— *Come back here; I'm talking to you!*"

Ignoring Ross, Melanie went to the bar and filled her glass from the martini pitcher. Watching her, Ross realized suddenly she'd never worn that pin he'd brought from Mettler's. But they hadn't talked that night, either, as he'd hoped they would; Melanie had accepted the gift with a brief kiss and then talked nonstop all through dinner, amusingly, as she could when she tried; mainly about the children.

She was not trying to amuse him now; her face was stony as she dropped ice cubes into her drink, listening to him. "We're going to change a few things," he told her. "From now on you'll have two thousand dollars a month for household expenses. That includes your lipsticks and lace stockings and Godiva caramels. When you want to buy out Wilma's designer clothes or give parties, you'll have to come to me so we can share those decisions. Is that clear? I'm sick of writing checks for a greedy child who gives me nothing as a woman: no companionship, no sex, not even friendship—"

"You mean you'll write the checks if I earn them, is that it? You'll buy my services. What do I get for one screw? A pair of shoes? Does a blow job get me a matching purse? What do I have to do to give a party at the—"

"Be quiet!" he roared. "You don't have the faintest idea what I'm talking about. Do you know—I thought of going to Victoria this evening, to talk about my day, but I decided instead I'd come home to my wife and share with her the things that are hugely important to me. I thought I'd give it one more—"

"Then you're a fool."

"Oh, yes; that's quite true. But now that we both know that, I think it's time I stopped being one. Are you clear on how we're going to handle our finances from now on?"

"I will not come to you for permission to spend money."

"You will come to me for every major expenditure over your monthly budget."

With a scream, Melanie flung her glass at him. Ross jerked to the side and watched the glass shatter against an oil painting he had bought in New York the year they were married.

"When you calm down," he said, his voice like steel, "we will talk about money and anything else that needs settling."

"I don't want to talk to you!" she screamed. "You bastard, you're only doing this because Derek was helping me plan that party—"

"*Derek?*"

"You knew that!"

"No. I didn't. But Derek had nothing to do with—"

"You're lying. Why else would you cancel my party? You never did anything like that before!" Her voice rose higher. "You're always worse when your brother's involved; you're jealous of him because Curt always liked him better—poor little Ross, his daddy loved his brother best—you even ran away to New York to get away from him. And now you're making my life miserable because he's my friend. Everybody thinks you're so nice. My God, if they only knew!"

Very carefully, Ross put down his glass. "Melanie, listen to me. This has nothing to do with Derek. This is between us. I don't want to make your life miserable—I don't want to destroy anything—I want to find the way back to what we had a long time ago. There were so many wonderful things, especially in New York—"

"Well there aren't any more! There haven't been for a long time!" She was breathless. "I've been a perfect wife, I've done everything you wanted—I even moved here from New York when I didn't want to—I left all my friends and my mother and daddy—and you treat me like a child—you're cold and... heartless!" Her arms outstretched, she stepped like a tightrope walker around the broken glass. "I'll tell you what you can do. Draw me one of your fancy blueprints about how you're going to make it up to me for humiliating me in front of everyone. I'll look it over when I get back. See if I like it or not." In a few steps she was at the front door, yanking it open and slamming it shut behind her.

Ross stood in the silence of the living room, then slowly walked to the broken glass and bent to pick up the pieces. As he did so, a sound made him glance up. At the top of the stairs, in frozen stillness, sat his children, listening.

Thursday, December 10, was circled on Katherine's calendar. Eight A.M.: Mettler's. As the day approached, Jennifer and Todd grew as tense as their mother. "He'll think they're wonderful," Jennifer said, watching Katherine polish a pendant of blued steel, the closest she could come, on her budget, to silver.

Todd jumped on the couch and intoned in a deep voice, "My dear Mrs. Fraser, these are so good they will be whizzed to England and given to the queen, and when she sees them she'll jump on the Concorde and fly to San Francisco and parachute to our doorstep—if she can find it in the lousy fog—and say here's a million dollars, please give me enough jewelry for my family and friends and every single person in the, what's it called, House of Something—"

"Parliament," said Jennifer.

"No, House of Ordinary, something like that—"

Katherine burst out laughing. "Commons. Todd, you're wonderful, and I hope it all comes true."

"Am I wonderful, Mom?"

"Yes." She was concentrating on a curve in the steel.

"Then how come I never get any attention around here?"

"Oh, Lord." She put down the pendant. Swiveling on her stool, she held out her arms and Todd jumped down and came to her. "I'm sorry, sweetheart. There's so much to do before tomorrow morning."

"Yeh, I know." He looked at her closely. "Mom—if this guy likes them, and buys a whole bunch, and you make a bunch of money..."

"Yes?"

"You won't need Daddy anymore, will you?"

Holding Todd, Katherine's arms tensed. She looked to Jennifer, standing watchfully nearby, and Jennifer came to her rescue.

"That's really stupid, Todd. Do we only want Daddy back because he earns money or because we love him?"

"Because we love him, but—" Todd frowned, trying to recapture his train of thought. But Jennifer had confused him and, a little later, when they went to bed, he still had not puzzled it out.

But Katherine knew he would, and would bring it up again. Because he and Jennifer were beginning to recognize that there were many kinds of need. We'll talk about it, she thought—one of these days. When I know what to say. When I know what I feel about Craig.

He watched her. His picture stared at her over the jewelry samples and sketches she would take to Herman Mettler in the morning. Her chin in her hand, Katherine looked steadily back at him, recalling the small warm details of their life together. But when she tried to recapture her contentment, all the way back to the day Craig took her to their first apartment in Vancouver and made love to her on the floor while they waited for the furniture to be delivered, she could not do it. It was gone.

And she had no time to try to retrieve it. In spite of herself, her eyes slid from Craig's picture to her jewelry and sketches, and her thoughts moved ahead, to her appointment and what more she could do that night to make it a success.

"Ah, yes," rumbled Herman Mettler, arranging Katherine's four pieces like the points of a compass. They seemed small and insignificant beneath his splayed fingers on the polished emptiness of his desk. "Marc told me you were working in Tony's studio. A strong personality, Tony. Strong influence."

"Those are my own designs." Katherine handed him her sketches, bound in a folder. "So are these."

"No doubt, no doubt. But influence is like an aroma from a distant restaurant; you find yourself cooking onion soup for dinner without realizing that during the day you were inspired by inhaling its scent. However. Let's see what you have. Tony, after all, is better than onion soup."

Chuckling at his wit, he fanned the sketches like playing cards beside the finished pieces and gave them serious attention. Katherine sat rigidly, hands gripped in her lap. No one had seen her work but Jennifer and Todd. In Vancouver she had been fooled by her friends' uncritical praise into thinking she was better than she was. She would not let that happen again. So she kept her designs hidden, even from Leslie. Now, finding no clues in Mettler's impassive face, she looked around his balcony office. On the paneled walls, framed photographs of film and television stars were autographed, with gratitude, to Herman Mettler. "Friends," Mettler said. Startled, Katherine turned to find him watching her. "Women remember, when we help make them beautiful. Your work has promise; we'll start with a dozen."

Katherine's eyes widened. "A dozen pieces?"

"Bracelets, pins, necklaces. No earrings; I have enough to pierce every earlobe west of the Rockies." Chuckling, he fastened his gaze on Katherine until she realized he was waiting for her to join him in admiring his joke. She smiled. "Now." He settled back. "What I like I buy outright; no consignments. I'll buy the blued steel pendants today; the other two pieces don't interest me. How much are you asking?"

Katherine hesitated. "I haven't priced them."

"I assumed you hadn't. There's a skill to it; ask around." He pondered. "I'll charge seventy for the seagull; ninety for the snail—nice use of the carnelian, by the way; a center focus as well as an eye. One of the reasons I said you showed promise. My secretary will send you a check for sixty-four dollars—"

"Sixty-four?"

"Forty percent of the price I'll charge. Ordinarily, of course, my price would be a markup of what you charge me. Since you are uncertain what to charge, I've worked backwards. Any objection to that?"

"No. I just wondered."

"Well, then. I want ten more by the end of February, for our spring showing. We advertise heavily so your name will get around if you deserve it. Use color; some designers can handle black but nothing here tells me whether you can or not, so don't try. This sketch and this one are good; I'd try to ease the rose, however."

"Ease—?"

"Enlarge the opening in each petal. In other words, deflower it." This time he bellowed with laughter, and Katherine, knowing what was expected, smiled with him. Then he returned to business. "We do well with gold, silver, fine gems, cloisonné. Don't use enamel unless you have forms other than this."

Stung, Katherine said, "Tony liked that bird."

"Tony would. I don't like sculptured enamel. Private preferences, Mrs. Fraser. If you want me to make you famous, you'll indulge me. Or you can rely on Tony, who can't do a thing for you. Now pay attention." He swept together Katherine's sketches and samples and pushed them toward her. "You have promise. You have a certain amount of talent; how much I can't say yet and I doubt that you can either, until you've tackled a wider range of materials and styles. Continue to work with Tony if you want, but you would be better off away from his aroma."

"He lets me use his tools and equipment; I can't afford my own yet."

"Use him, then, but don't let his onion soup get into your designs. I'm not buying Tony; I'm buying you. You've shown some facility with blued steel and copper; stay with them if you like. Pity you can't afford gold, but if you do well with this order, we may be able to advance you something in February. When a jeweler does that, it's an act of gemerosity."

Shaking with laughter, he stood and held out his hand. Katherine took it and then found herself laughing with him. It was easier this time. She'd just made her first sale.

To celebrate, Leslie brought a bottle of wine to go with Katherine's meatballs. "A celebration," she reminded Todd as they finished desert. "So what's your problem?"

"Mom," said Todd glumly. "She's eight million miles away, thinking about jewelry."

Leslie regarded Katherine. "True. Good or bad thoughts?"

"Mostly worrying," Katherine said ruefully.

"Not surprising." Leslie watched Todd and Jennifer carry the dishes into the kitchen. "Mettler's forced you to the wall. Come out of your safe little corner, lady, and your happy dreams of success. Do your thing, deliver your goods and see if the fickle public buys or turns thumbs down. Scary."

Katherine gave a small laugh. "You're amazing. How do you know that's how I feel?"

"Because that's how I feel every day. Slightly different, but whenever I make a suggestion or decision it can be knocked down in three seconds by Heath's president or the executive committee. Enough three-second knockdowns and I'm out—slinking off to find another job. The big difference is that I'm anonymous, but you have to go public—how else can you make a name for yourself? Good reason to be scared. The dream of making it big . . ." Her attention veered off.

"What about you?" Katherine asked. "What are your worries?"

"Me? I? What makes you think I'm worried?"

"Is it Marc? Or something at the store? I tell you my problems; it's not fair to keep yours a secret."

"Well." Leslie spread her hands. "What a coincidence that you should ask." She pushed a crumb of cheesecake around her plate. "Remember the Ralph Lauren sweaters I told you about at my birthday party?"

"And Calvin Klein blouses. You're still trying to figure out what happened?"

"We're pretty sure we know what happened. They were stolen. And maybe other things, too; we don't know yet how much. We did a couple of spot inventories without advance notice, and, in lingerie, we can't account for a box of Simone bras. Twenty-four, at seventy-five bucks apiece."

Briefly, Katherine tried to imagine having enough money to pay seventy-five dollars for a brassiere. But then she concentrated on Leslie. "But if they were stolen, wouldn't they—?"

"They didn't show up as stolen. Look. We have a computer system that keeps track of all our merchandise, from the time we get a shipment in the receiving room to the time it's sold and paid for. Today, the computer says every Simone bra that we received has either been sold or is still on the shelves. If we hadn't individually counted every bra and sales slip in lingerie we wouldn't know twenty-four were missing. Don't you understand? *The computer's numbers all balanced.*"

After a moment, Katherine said. "The computer. You're worried about Bruce."

"One hundred percent." Leslie sighed. "And, of course, me. I got him hired to work in that department without divulging his unruly past. And now something is going on—maybe a computer operator making a bunch of simple mistakes, maybe something a lot bigger—and if my brother is involved, I'm involved. All those beetle-eyed vice-presidents, you know, watching for me to make a mistake."

In the silence, they heard Todd weaving a story about dishes that washed themselves or were set to self-destruct if they were not clean in five seconds. Leslie shook her head vigorously, like a pony tossing off a rainstorm. "I needed to talk and I feel better, for which I thank you, but we're supposed to be celebrating your triumph. So tell me—what are you going to make for His Highness Herman Mettler?"

It took Katherine only a minute to decide. She went to her worktable for her sketch pad. This time she felt confident enough to share her ideas.

"Much, much better!" Victoria exclaimed when she saw Katherine waiting in front of Podesta Baldocchi, framed by the shop's lush jungle of flowers and plants. "Forgive me for being late, my dear—but let me look at you! Katherine, you are quite lovely. I knew it. I am never wrong about women. Of course I am never wrong about men, either. Ah, and when you laugh you are really quite remarkable."

Laughing as much from happiness as at Victoria's firm judgments, Katherine turned on the crowded sidewalk and kissed her cheek. "Oh, my dear," Victoria murmured. She stopped and looked about, as if unsure of where she was. "How quickly we forget—and then become greedy again."

"You're thinking of Jennifer," Katherine said as they walked to Maiden Lane. She felt a flash of jealousy, but then it passed. Jennifer was dead and it was Katherine, wonderfully alive, whom Victoria had asked to go Christmas shopping, and even the gray drizzle of the afternoon could not dim the way she felt when Victoria admired her—as if she had found both the mother and grandmother she had never known.

"Some time we'll talk about Jennifer," Victoria said. "But not now. Now I am going to buy a new dress for Christmas dinner. Do you know it will be the first we've had at home in years?" They turned into Helga Howie. "Usually I am in Italy, or somewhere, but I thought, what a good idea, this year, for us all to be together. I hope I am not getting sentimental. At my age, it would look like senility. Renee, please," she said to a saleswoman and in a moment the designer appeared and greeted her as an old friend.

After Victoria introduced her, Katherine browsed among Helga's de-

signs and European imports while Victoria swiftly and decisively bought
three knit dresses. "Done," she said as they left. "I do not enjoy shopping.
Such a waste of energy. I refuse to do it."

"You just did," Katherine pointed out.

"But I did not enjoy it. The only civilized way to shop is to have
everything sent home. Why should I disrobe in a store when I have an
excellent dressing room of my own? However, I wanted you to meet
Renee. Someday you'll buy your clothes from her."

Katherine laughed. "Do you know that you spent two months of my
salary on those three dresses?"

Victoria paused. "Did I indeed? And yet you are not using the money
that . . . arrives each month on things for yourself?"

"No. Only for the children." She has trouble, Katherine thought,
using Craig's name.

"Well. I want you to help me with my shopping. The last few years
I've given money but this year I shall once again give gifts. More sentimentality, perhaps. And difficult. How do I know anymore what most
of them want?"

"How do *I* know?" Katherine asked. "I hardly know your family."

"Nonsense. You've spent time with all of us—a great deal of time
with Derek, I gather." They walked into Gump's and for the first time
Katherine discovered the heady joys of shopping with unlimited funds.
Victoria had been serious about wanting her help: she asked for advice
and most often took it, and Katherine chose what she liked, without
looking at price tags. For two glorious hours they delved into the world's
finest treasures, buying hand-carved lapis lazuli figures from Chile, Venetian opaline glass, Aynsley cobalt and gold china, suede jackets lined in
sable, and Hermes purses for Melanie and Ann. "Though God knows
why," said Victoria. "Ann won't use hers in the wilds of Maine and
Melanie . . . well, Ross keeps his own counsel but it's my guess their
marriage won't last out the year and if so, why am I buying that self-
centered woman this magnificent piece of leather? Well, it doesn't matter.
She can take it with her when she goes. We'll shop for the children on
another day; they aren't ready for Gump's. But I am ready for tea. Come;
I have a favorite place."

It was a short walk, across Union Square. "Now," Victoria said, seated
on a velvet couch at The Compass Rose. "Do you like it?"

"It's amazing," Katherine answered. She did not say she had been
there with Ross and that the room reminded her of his warmth three
months ago and how different he seemed just this week when he abruptly
ended their phone call. She did not even ask Victoria what she had meant
about Ross's marriage.

"You need this room," said Victoria, ordering Brie and fruit and tea for both of them. "You need a little eccentricity. Your taste at Gump's— impeccable, of course, or I would not have agreed with your choices. But, my dear, to be so proper—at your age—!"

"I don't understand. I thought—"

"You thought you were pleasing me." Victoria fell silent, her eyes on a far wall. "I want to tell you a story. Fifty-six years ago, in 1925, a young woman discovered that the money she and her husband were living on was made by smuggling liquor into the country."

"Prohibition..."

"Precisely. The young woman's husband was co-owner with his father of a small construction company, but he became obsessed with the thrill of defying the federal government. We will not discuss whether prohibition was good or bad; he was breaking the law and risking prison, and he continued to do so until Congress repealed prohibition. That was in 1933."

Katherine nodded. Hugh Hayward, she thought. Tobias had told her. But he said Victoria never talked about it.

"The husband's father had died in 1930, leaving the company in the husband's hands. In his passion for smuggling, he had ignored it. By the time of repeal, when he began to pay attention to it, the company was almost moribund. Then he was struck by a new passion: to rescue the company that bore his father's name. It was not a simple task. The country was in a depression and construction companies were dying no matter how hard anyone tried to save them." Victoria drank her tea and gazed through the great doorway that looked into the busy hotel lobby. "By 1934, when it seemed he could not revive the company, he went into his own depression in the midst of the national depression. Day after day, he sat in his room, looking through the window at the world passing by. You should have seen him, Katherine—tall and wonderfully hand- some, with a smile that strangers turned to as if it were a beacon. When Ross smiles he looks exactly like him. He had broad shoulders and when he walked into a room he took ownership of it just by being Hugh Hayward. I'll show you pictures of him, but they can't tell you how beautiful he was because you had to be with him to feel his magnetism. Then, to see him hunched in a chair, staring out the window, his fingers picking at his pants on his thigh—picking, all day long—and his mouth moving as if he were talking, but making no sound... It was so terrible I had to get away. I had to get out of that house."

Katherine let her tea grow cold, afraid to break Victoria's reverie.

"In the fall of 1934, I went to the office of the Hayward Corporation and sat down in Hugh's chair. I had no idea what to do, but I knew that a construction company had to have something to build. So I called on the men who had shared Hugh's smuggling adventures and told them I would build them new houses. They laughed at me and patted me on the head. Never let a man pat you on the head, my dear; it means he is about to put you on a leash or kick you out. However, Hugh's friends were great fools. They had written letters about their business and sexual activities—can you imagine? *They wrote them down!* And Hugh kept them. And I found them. In his dresser, under his boating socks. Naturally, his friends preferred that the letters not become public, so they ceased patting me on the head and the Hayward Corporation, under my direction, with the help of two fine men who had started it with Hugh's father, built some very expensive houses in Tiburon and Sausalito and Berkeley—oh, but land was cheap, then!—and I tucked the letters into the safe."

Victoria signaled for more tea. "And more fruit," she told the waiter. "Katherine? More Brie?"

Katherine shook her head. "Please go on."

Victoria smiled. "We also had help, indirectly, from money the government was spending. When schools and highways, and even post offices, were built by the WPA, people in the neighborhoods began to think about enlarging or repairing their homes. We could give credit because we had all that smuggling money. Once, we renovated an apartment building in Oakland. We stripped banisters and oak floors, rearranged walls and restored broken moldings, even replaced stained glass doors and windows. It took a year and a half. We finished on March 21, 1938."

The waiter put a plate of grapes and pears before them, and poured fresh tea. "You are wondering how I remember the date. I remember because on that morning Hugh woke up, dressed himself, and went to work, as if on a normal day. Four years had passed and he knew it, but his depression was gone, so he went to his office and sat down in his chair and began running his company."

Katherine studied Victoria's expressionless face. "But it wasn't his company. You'd made it yours."

"It was Hugh's company. There was only one office and it was his, one desk and it was his. He thanked me for what I had done and sent me home to take care of our sons."

"But they weren't—how old were they?"

"Curt was twenty and Jason nineteen."

Their eyes met and they began to laugh. "But it isn't funny," Katherine said. "It's sad."

"Certainly. But you see, Hugh was a genius and I knew it. I had kept the company alive, but he made it one of the largest and most influential in the state. And besides the monstrous projects that multiplied after the war—roads, bridges, dams, shopping centers—he carried the idea of restoration much farther than I ever dreamed. And if he took credit for thinking of it in the first place, what difference did it make, since he did it so brilliantly? You see, Katherine, all Hugh took from me was a small company. I never would have succeeded as he did."

They were silent. Around them, conversations rose and fell, cultivated murmurs and the clink of silver spoons. "He took more than a company," Katherine protested. "He took your *place*. It was important to you."

"True."

"And you missed it when it was gone."

"Oh, my, yes."

Katherine was thinking. "Would you tell me," she said hesitantly, "what Jennifer was going to study in college?"

"Ah." Victoria's eyes were bright. "I knew you would understand. Didn't I say I was always right about women? And men, of course. Jennifer wanted to be an engineer."

"And work in the Hayward Corporation?"

"In fact, we often talked about my financing her own company."

To finish what you began. You wanted Jennifer to live the life Hugh took away from you. So you could live it through her.

Victoria sighed. "It's late, and we haven't talked about you. We must make definite plans for you, now that you have an order from Mettler. You'll come to tea so we can talk quietly." She signed the check, slipped her arms into her fur jacket, and kissed Katherine on both cheeks. And they walked down the carpeted stairs and through the lobby as clusters of people made way for Victoria's imperious figure and determined stride.

Late that night, Derek called. Katherine had not seen or heard from him in the two weeks since he told her the story of the sailing accident. "I understand you and my grandmother bought out Gump's this afternoon."

She smiled to herself. "Aren't you the one who made a comment about the joys of a large family?"

"I am. But a grapevine is often valuable. Did I wake you?"

"No, why?"

"You sound subdued and it's after midnight."

"I'm working on a new design."

"And?"

"I shouldn't be so glad to hear from you."

"Victoria told me you'd been transformed," he said. "But evidently you still say what you think."

Katherine picked up a pencil and began to shade in the bracelet she was drawing.

"Are you still there?" he asked.

"Yes, of course."

"I am looking at a stack of invitations for parties between now and New Year's Eve. Most of them will be dull. A few will be interesting if you're with me. Are you free between now and the New Year?"

"Derek, it's only the middle of December."

"What does that have to do with it?"

"I don't know what I'll be doing. I have to spend time with my children; I have to work at night—oh, you don't know that; I have an order from Herman Mettler—"

"He told me."

"*He* told you?"

"I was in his store the other day and he mentioned it. Katherine, I have before me invitations to two cocktail parties, three dinners, and a New Year's carnival. I will accept them if you will be with me. The dates are—"

Automatically, as he listed them, she jotted them down beside the drawing of the bracelet. "Derek, that order from Mettler is very important to me."

"Of course it is." Smoothly his voice changed, as if he had moved closer. "And I should be congratulating you. How many pieces?"

"Twelve."

"A good start. When will they be in the store?"

"Spring, he said. If he likes them."

"He knows what he's getting, from your samples. I wouldn't worry. Can you be in front of Heath's at five thirty on Tuesday? Cocktails and dinner in Portola Valley and it's over an hour's drive at that time of day."

His voice was like a long ocean wave, sweeping everything before it. Katherine drew a box around the dates he had read to her, looked away from Craig's picture, and said she could.

She had only the black dress. She skipped lunch the next day to search through a vintage clothing store she had seen advertised, and took home a high-necked lace blouse, an exquisite velvet and silk patchwork vest, missing some buttons, a white tunic, loosely woven of gossamer wool, a belt of hammered bronze medallions, a cranberry-red fringed shawl, and a filmy silk scarf, long and trailing, in blues and pinks. In Heath's junior department she found a deep green velvet skirt that came just to her ankles. And on Tuesday, after work, she changed in Heath's washroom into the velvet skirt and lace blouse and the patchwork vest, newly fitted with mother-of-pearl buttons.

Combing her hair in front of the mirror, Katherine thought of her children, who depended on her; the jewelry she was making, that would someday earn her living; Victoria, who loved her; Derek, who would spin her through December's festivities—and when she walked from the store, her head was high not only because of her clothes and hair and makeup, but also because she was beginning to believe in herself.

Her pleasure was reflected in Derek's face as she stepped into his car. "Victoria understated it," he said, taking her hand, but a cacophony of angry horns and shouts from other cars forced him to pay attention to driving. At the first stoplight he looked at her fully. "Stunning. You've learned to be dramatic. If you'd looked like this ten years ago my poor cousin would have been too intimidated even to come close, much less propose. And if by chance he did make it, you'd have looked past him for something better."

Katherine's face clouded as Derek turned away, shifting gears to move with the traffic. She smoothed her velvet skirt, the excitement she had felt all day crumbling beneath his casual contempt. "Derek—take me home," she said tightly. "I'm sorry, but I don't want to go, after all."

He drove on without speaking, then swung the car to the curb and stopped. "Because I spoke unkindly of my cousin?"

"Because you spoke with contempt—of my husband."

Surprise flashed across his face, then was gone. "I've never disguised the fact that Craig and I were not friends. You like to romanticize the idea of a family, but you can't seriously imagine that sharing a last name automatically brings love. Should I pretend that Craig and I were intimate, loving, filled with respect and admiration and mutuality of interests, when none of that was true? Or should I tell you openly that we never liked each other, and that now, knowing he ran off fifteen years ago, and last summer deserted you and your children, I am less likely than ever to think well of him? Which would you have me say?"

"Neither," she said almost inaudibly.

"No. Neither would please you. But neither would it please you to go home now. Let me suggest" —putting his hand beneath her chin, he leaned over to kiss her lightly— "that I promise not to speak of Craig again; that we go to this affair in Portola; and if you feel uncomfortable, with me or with anyone who asks about Craig, we will leave on the instant. Is that acceptable?"

A weight lifted. If he made no demands on her and did not force her to choose between loyalty to Craig and going out with him, she could relax. "Yes," she said. "Thank you."

He kept his promise that night and a few nights later at a dinner party in a penthouse on Russian Hill when, for the first time, Katherine was completely at ease in a glittering crowd. No longer were eyebrows raised when Derek introduced her; instead there were admiring appraisals. "Vancouver," someone said at dinner. "I was there once. Pleasant. Though not quite *cosmopolitan*, you know. Perhaps it was the lack of our charming hilltop houses."

"We do have some," Katherine said seriously. "Every city has people who need to be looked up to."

After a tiny pause, there was a shout of laughter from everyone but the critic of Vancouver. Katherine was flushed and Derek contemplated her thoughtfully as the other guests began to vie for her attention. By the time dinner had ended and they were dancing, Katherine felt swept up, as if the long slow wave of Derek's voice had become a heavy surf, drowning her everyday problems. Nothing seemed unmanageable. Even Craig's shadow was obscured by the brilliance around her and her increasing confidence. She floated on the swell of voices and laughter, the gleam of candles and diamonds and admiration, Derek's absorbed look, his hand on her arm and his dark blond presence, smooth and remote. She floated timelessly, and nothing seemed impossible.

Two days before Christmas, she was brought back to earth at a buffet supper in Mill Valley.

When they had eaten, a magician entertained the fifty guests with sleights of hand and fortune-telling. Moving about the room, he reached Katherine. "You have seen much sadness," he boomed portentously. "You will also see joy. You will hold gold and silver in your hands and a man will come from far away to fall at your feet and beg you to love him and let him live with you."

The others laughed and applauded but Katherine sat frozen. It doesn't mean anything, she told herself. He could have said that to anyone; no one takes these things seriously. But still it was uncanny. She looked at Derek, who smiled slightly. "He is less a magician," he murmured, "than you are an enchantress." Instinctively, Katherine drew back. "God damn it," he exclaimed. "Must you feel guilty every time—?" He stopped and took her hand, kissing it lightly. "We'll talk later."

It was as if his lips had brushed her whole body, arousing her with a touch. But the magician had brought Craig back, pulling her in the direction of her memories, and she forced herself to sit unmoving, almost not breathing, until the rush of desire subsided. And when they left, Craig went with them; she could barely say goodnight to Derek, because Craig was in the way, hurrying her inside. She closed the door and huddled on the couch. *What will I do if he falls at my feet and begs me to love him and let him live with me?*

They had always made their own Christmas presents. Craig liked to shop, but Jennifer and Todd made presents in school, and Katherine made jewelry or designed and knit sweaters. This year, when they had to make gifts because they couldn't afford to buy them, Jennifer and Todd grumbled as they set up a tree that was half as big, Todd complained, as the ones they'd had in Vancouver.

"This room is half the size of the one we had in Vancouver," Katherine said mildly. "And it would be pleasant if you stopped making a fuss about everything." She opened the box of ornaments they had brought from Canada. "You act as if you'd buy me a mink coat if things had been different."

"Well, maybe I would," said Todd defiantly. "Or something like it. Daddy always bought you fancy things."

Oh, yes, Katherine thought. A shearling coat one year, a cashmere robe another, an antique sterling silver and enamel dresser set another. "I don't need fancy things," she told Todd. "Just us, being together."

Scowling, Todd hung ornaments on the small tree. "I wish Dad was here!" he burst out. *"Why isn't he here?"*

Katherine put her arms around him. "I wish I knew." She thought of all their other Christmases, when Craig sang lusty carols, put up a huge tree in the living room, and wreaths on all the doors, and hung six-foot stockings at the fireplace. Christmas was a time, he said, when everyone could be a child and celebrate having a family—the most precious of all their possessions. It was a time for love.

"I waited for him all day," said Jennifer. With careful precision she hung the last smiling angel on the top of the tree. "I kept thinking, *Now he'll walk in the door.*"

"Me too." Todd sat on the couch, glumly picking at a scab on his arm. "Every time I heard somebody outside I thought it was Dad." His eyes filled with tears. "Don't people always come home at Christmas? I mean—isn't that the whole idea?"

Jennifer plopped down beside him. "We shouldn't even have Christmas. It's a fake, without a Daddy."

"It's a fake to have Christmas *Eve*," Todd said, "when you don't make cookies and things with your mother 'cause she's gone."

"At work," Katherine said defensively. "I had no choice; I explained that to you; I tried to get the day off, but I couldn't."

"So Todd and I had to do everything," Jennifer said to the ceiling, asking for sympathy. "Except, Annie helped us make cookies. And we're going to read the story ourselves." She pulled a book from beneath a cushion. "Surprised?" She looked a challenge at Katherine. "Did you think we'd forget?" Without waiting for an answer, she opened it to the first page and loudly began to read. "'Marley was dead, to begin with. There was no doubt whatever about that.'"

But after two pages, she burst into tears, "I can't do it!" She threw the book across the room. "I hate it and I'm never going to read it again!"

Katherine bent to pick up the book and smoothed the creased pages. A *Christmas Carol* by Charles Dickens. Every year Craig had read it aloud on Christmas Eve. Then they would eat dinner and open their presents.

"We had a tradition," Jennifer sobbed. "And now we don't anymore."

"Not now," Katherine agreed quietly. "We don't have it right now." She sat with them on the couch. "But we can't stop our life from changing. It started to change the day Daddy didn't come home, and it will keep on until he's with us again. And we're going to change, too, because everybody changes; we can't stop that, either, because we're alive. If we didn't keep busy and happy with new friends and new experiences it would be as if we'd died."

"What if we change too much?" Jennifer asked.

"We'll still be us. When Daddy comes back, we'll keep some of the new things we've done and we'll drop others, but we'll still be the same people. Does that make sense?" They looked at her dubiously. "Well, think about it. But in the meantime, we can't sit around crying and complaining all the time. If we do, we'll be as wrinkled as prunes, and then how would Daddy recognize us?"

Todd perked up. "Prunes!" A smile broke through the gloom. "Daddy would come to the door and say 'Who is this? I thought Katherine Fraser and Jennifer Fraser and Todd Fraser live here but who is this?' And I'd say, 'I'm Todd.' And he'd say, 'Oh, no, Todd is four feet nine inches tall and he looks like a boy. In fact he looks like me.' And I'd say, 'I'm Todd the talking prune. Eleven inches tall because I cried all my juices out.' And Daddy would say—"

"Oh, shut up!" Jennifer shouted. "Who cares about your stupid stories? Daddy isn't coming home ever again and I wish you'd turn into a prune and disappear into the garbage can, 'cause it's nothing to joke about!"

"Jennifer!" Katherine made her voice firm and unhesitating. "Your father will come back as soon as he can and in the meantime I expect you to behave yourself and help Todd instead of jumping all over him. Now, I want to open my Christmas presents and watch you open yours and then we're going to Victoria's for dinner. And whatever happens in the future I don't want to hear you yell at your brother or me again because we're doing the best we can. Is that clear?"

Her mouth open, Jennifer stared at her. "You never talked like that before."

"I'm trying to keep things together around here," Katherine said bluntly. "And I'd like a little help instead of having to fight every step of the way. You're not the only ones who are unhappy, you know."

"We don't go to parties all the time," Jennifer said.

"No, but—" *Must you feel guilty every time?* Derek had asked. "You're right; you don't and I've gone to a few. But we're all going to one tonight, and I'll bet we find a stack of presents waiting for us. Now do we open these presents? Or do we wait until tomorrow?"

"NO!" yelled Todd and lunged toward the small pile beneath the tree.

More slowly, Jennifer followed. But by the time she and Todd unwrapped the zippered sweaters Katherine had knit them on her lunch hours, she was almost smiling. Katherine exclaimed in delight over the carved wooden candlesticks Jennifer had made in shop, varnished to a shining butternut finish, and the clay paperweight model of the Golden Gate Bridge that Todd had made and painted a bilious orange. By then, they were friends again.

Leslie and Bruce had joined forces to fill a box with Dungeons & Dragons books for Todd and Jennifer. Todd lay on his stomach and plunged into them. "This is for you," Jennifer said and watched as Katherine opened a large box and sat in stunned silence. "For New Year's Eve," the card said. "Compliments of Heath's, Leslie and Bruce. Have a ball."

"Oh," Jennifer sighed in a long breath as Katherine held up the dress— a billowing white taffeta skirt and a black lace top, the collar a high lace ruffle, the sleeves ending in lace ruffles two inches long. "More parties," Jennifer said, but she could not resist the dress. "It's so beautiful! Will you save it, so I can wear it someday?"

"Of course," Katherine said. "But you'll have your own wonderful dresses by then." She held the dress and imagined herself wearing it, dancing in it. Folding it carefully in its box, she thought, New Year's Eve. With Derek.

She caught herself. A new year. Promises and resolutions. Without Craig.

"We'd better go!" she cried, springing to her feet. "The whole family is going to be there and Victoria does not like people to be late to her parties!"

They hurried. Jennifer and Todd were thinking of a stack of presents, but Katherine, with thoughts of a new year, was reflecting that she had lied to her children. How could anything ever be the same again? If Craig came home tonight, or tomorrow, or the next day, how could they pick up their lives and behave as if they were the same people? They couldn't; of course they couldn't. She'd lied, to herself as well as Jennifer and Todd.

She felt a moment of panic. *We've gone too far.* They couldn't find their way back; they would all have to begin again. Her stomach was churning as it had when everything was coming to a close in Vancouver; all this time she'd thought they could pick up the pieces of that other life and put them together again, but now that had come to a close, too. She could only go forward. It felt, Katherine thought, as if she were lost again, looking for guideposts and a helping hand.

But on the bus she told herself it wasn't the same. She was learning to find her own guideposts. And for a helping hand—if she wanted, she had more than one waiting for her. At a family Christmas dinner at Victoria's.

Victoria answered the door, wearing a full-length gown of silver-blue Italian silk velvet, and greeting Katherine with an embrace so warm that everyone was reminded of her carefully correct one only six months earlier. Coming up behind her, Derek took Katherine's hand with a familiarity both exciting and disconcerting. Todd and Jennifer were gone in an instant, taken by Carrie and Jon to see their new Lionel train, set up in the study, leaving Katherine, as before, to face the rest of the family.

There were greetings and kisses. "Oh, my, oh, my," said Tobias, kissing her on both cheeks. "'A lovely lady, garmented in light from her own beauty.' Shelley, my dear, and you are a poet's dream. May I bring you champagne?"

But Derek was ahead of him. He brought Katherine a brimming glass and a plate of oysters and celeriac. "Are you occupied with Tobias or can we finish a conversation we began the other night?"

"Derek," said Tobias gravely. "I am overcome by your subtlety. But I am leaving; I must search for a book."

"The tiniest bit rude," Katherine said lightly. "Or do I exaggerate?" She saw Ross watching her with a frown. But Derek's hand was on her arm.

"Only a trifle. Shall we finish that conversation?"

Melanie was standing by herself, near the piano. When Katherine looked at her, their eyes met.

"Derek," Victoria said, coming up to them. "Will you help Tobias search the library? He seems to have lost Dickens."

"Dickens?" Katherine repeated. Derek shrugged, briefly tightened his hand on her arm, and left.

"A family custom we are reviving tonight," said Victoria. "When Craig and Jennifer and Ross and Derek were growing up, we would begin Christmas Eve in the afternoon, reading Dickens' *Christmas Carol*—is something wrong, Katherine?"

"No." *I shouldn't be surprised. His roots are in this family.* "Craig always read that to Jennifer and Todd at Christmas."

"So he didn't entirely forget us." After a moment, Victoria beckoned to Ross. "Craig kept up our Christmas readings."

"Did he act out the parts?" Ross asked Katherine.

"All of them. He was very good."

"So is Tobias," said Ross.

"Tobias is memorable," Victoria said. "He'll read it after dinner, for anyone who wishes to listen. If you would like..."

"Perhaps I will."

Victoria nodded and moved away. Ross was searching Katherine's face. "You look wonderful," he said. "I'm glad you're doing so well." He put out his open hand, as if asking forgiveness.

Melanie appeared at his side. "Claude is looking for you," she told Ross. He hesitated, then apologized to Katherine, and left. Melanie and Katherine faced each other. This time, there was no bright flare; this time Katherine could hold her own. And Melanie did not look well. Beneath heavy makeup her face was drawn and her eyes heavy, and her full-length orange dress looked garish beside Katherine's black one. But she smiled so gaily that Katherine found herself smiling back. "How you look," Melanie murmured. "Amazing. I might not have recognized you." Katherine had to strain to hear her voice. "Is it the fog? Or sexual variety? I understand either one improves the complexion, though in your case so much is improved you must be having a great deal of variety."

Katherine's smile disappeared. Her head felt constricted. *What have they been saying about me, among themselves?* Across the room, a movement caught her eye. Victoria had raised her hand to her hair, and as

Katherine looked her way, she winked. Katherine was dumbfounded. Serene and regal in her tapestried palace, Victoria winked. Katherine's head cleared; she smiled gratefully and turned back to Melanie. "I had help from generous friends," she said pleasantly. "Instead of ambushes from insecure women."

"Why you little bitch." Melanie's smile became rigid. "If you think you can talk that way just because Derek has been squiring you around, keeping tabs on you so he'll know where your husband is—"

"What?"

"Oh, come. Come now. You can't think he's been seeing you for your charm and wit. Derek? Who can have any woman he wants? I know Derek so well—if you didn't have a wandering husband who needs careful handling if he wanders back, Derek would have trouble remembering your name."

Katherine drained her glass of champagne. "Perhaps Derek takes me out because I provide relief from relatives who know him so well. Excuse me," she added icily and crossed the room to refill her glass.

"What did you do to Melanie?" Derek asked. He took Katherine's arm with a possessiveness that ran along her skin like warm fingers. She saw Melanie watching, and Ross, too, and pulled away. "And what are you afraid of?" he added.

"Not knowing the truth. Derek, why do you—?" She stopped. This was not the time to ask him. "Where are the children? Have they been banished?"

"I'm afraid not. Victoria and Tobias plan to turn them loose on that Everest of gifts beneath the tree. Shall we find a quiet corner away from flying Erector sets?"

"I'd rather stay; I enjoy watching them."

"Criticized and judged," he murmured. "We wouldn't have stayed away long in any case. I want to watch you open your presents."

She looked alarmed. "Why? Derek, we didn't bring anything elaborate."

"Then we shall send you home," he said lightly. "I like what you've done with your scarf."

She had draped it around her neck, the fringed ends hanging down her back, altering the look of the black cashmere dress. "I'm glad," she said. "I was afraid black would be too somber. No one else is wearing it."

"No one else looks like you. What did you say to Melanie?"

"It isn't important."

"If I ask about it, it is important."

"Then I'd better practice my answers. Thank you, Tobias," she said as Tobias appeared behind her and kissed her cheek.

"Meaning, you thank me for my kiss?" asked Tobias. "Or for diverting you so that you need not answer Derek?"

"You, at least," said Derek, "are never at a loss. How dull that must be, Tobias. Katherine, we sit together at dinner. I'll see you then." He went off and Katherine saw him silhouetted against the window with Melanie.

She closed her eyes briefly. In half an hour, the family had entangled her in its web. "I've been talking to Ross," said Tobias. "'We boil at different degrees.'"

"Who does?" Katherine asked.

"Ralph Waldo Emerson, since he wrote it, but I meant that if I were as angry as I think Ross is, I would boil over. But Ross controls himself. Now what, we ask, is Ross angry about?"

"I don't think it's my business."

"It is, however, mine, as I am the family biographer. Have you heard rumors of an impending divorce?"

Katherine remembered what Victoria had said. "No," she answered.

"How badly you lie, Katherine." Tobias sighed. "Did you know that William Congreve wrote, 'Tho marriage makes man and wife one flesh, it leaves 'em still two fools'?"

She laughed. "No. But he's probably right. Sometimes."

"More often than not. I am across the table from you at dinner. Will we be able to talk?"

"Why wouldn't we?"

"Derek might monopolize you. Well, well, look at that; he came after all."

Katherine followed his gaze. Jason and Ann were coming in from the vestibule and close behind them a tall, handsome man, lean and darkly tanned, an older, silver-haired Ross and Derek, who ignored everyone to come directly to Katherine. "Curt Hayward," he introduced himself. "My son has told me about you. So have others." Holding her hands, he stood back to look at her. "Lovely. You have brought consternation and pleasure to this family. I understand Craig sends you money but keeps his whereabouts a secret."

He resembled Derek more than Ross: sleek and polished, aloof, smoothly charming.

"He is in Canada," Katherine said.

"A large country. Ah, here is Jason. We'll talk later, Katherine. I want you to know how pleased I am, for both of you, that Derek had the inestimable good sense to step in where he perceived a vacuum. Jason, a merry Christmas to you."

Shocked, Katherine raised a hand to call him back, but Ann was hugging her, telling her how glad she was to see her. Katherine barely heard her. *He thinks Derek and I are sleeping together. Do they all think that?*

Jason and Curt shook hands; brothers who barely resembled each other. In a whisper, Ann confided, "They've seen each other only three times in fifteen years. They never were close, you know. Brothers, of course, but not friends. That was their father's fault: Hugh always preferred Curt. Jason never forgave him for that. Fathers shouldn't favor older sons, don't you agree? It leaves scars that never heal."

Involuntarily, Katherine looked from Ross to Derek just as Victoria, standing beside the tree, clapped her hands. "We shall distribute the gifts. Polk, please bring in the children." She looked doubtfully at the vast array of packages. "Derek, will you organize them? Tobias and Ross will help. I shall watch."

The next hour was a flurry of wrapping paper, ribbons and shouts of glee. The gifts for the children ranged from books and clothing to Erector sets and skis and, for Jennifer and Todd, a present that struck them momentarily dumb: a complete home computer with a video screen, disc drives for recording, games and school programs, and its own printer. Jennifer read the card aloud. "From Derek."

"It's too much," Katherine said to him. "We can't accept..." Her voice trailed away. If he had told her in advance, she would have refused it, but now, as Todd and Jennifer looked at her with faces like two bright suns, she could not take it away.

"Mom!" They scrambled to their feet and rushed to her. "Come look at it! We can play games and do math and write papers for school and do puzzles—"

"How about a thank you?" Katherine said.

"Yeh, but who to? The card says Derek. Who's Derek?"

"Why, sweetheart," Melanie said in tender amazement. "You mean you haven't met your mother's very good friend Derek? He's standing right next to you."

Katherine's face was hot. "You met last June. When we were here the first time."

Todd looked up at Derek. "You're who Mom goes out with at night? And you bought us the computer?"

Derek held out his hand. "How do you do? Yes, I bought it."

"Maybe we shouldn't take it," said Jennifer reluctantly. "It's an awful

big present from somebody who doesn't even come in the house when
he takes Mother out."

"Jennifer!" Katherine exclaimed.

"Well said." Derek smiled faintly. "I shall come inside, most properly,
from now on. With your permission."

"Don't ask me!" Jennifer protested. "I don't have anything to do with
it!"

"Maybe you could help us with the computer," Todd said. "Learn
how to program it and stuff."

"No." Derek's face was expressionless and for the first time it occurred
to Katherine that she had never heard him laugh. "But if you have trouble
with the instruction book, I'll give you the name of someone in my
company who can help."

Rebuffed, Todd stepped back. Then his face lit up. "Bruce! He runs
the whole computer at Heath's! I'll ask him!"

"Todd," Katherine said.

"Oh. Yeh. Thanks a lot. We really—thanks a lot."

"Thank you," Jennifer said politely. "If you'd like to use it sometime,
please do."

"Now," Victoria said. "The children have had their turn and I am
anxious to see what Katherine has brought me." She unwrapped the small
round package and held up a jar, tied with a red bow, labeled "Preserved
Ginger." "My dear," she said after a moment. "Did you make this?"

Katherine nodded, unable to speak. She had known her preserves and
jams and jellies would be outshone, but there was nothing else she could
afford for the whole family. She had thought of making jewelry, but
rejected it. Not until she was established with Mettler's, or somewhere
else. And when she had arrayed the colorful jars on her coffee table at
home and tied them with gaily colored ribbons, they looked so bright
and festive she thought they would be all right.

But when Victoria held one in her hand and Katherine saw how tiny
and plain it looked, she knew with a sinking heart that this family would
find her gifts stingily small. She'd been dreaming when she thought she
might fit in with people who had enough money to buy anything they
wanted.

But Victoria came to Katherine, laid a gentle hand along her cheek,
and kissed her. "How did you know preserved ginger is my favorite?" She
spoke loudly enough for all of them to hear. "Others have bought it for
me but no one ever took the trouble to make it. And Tobias recently
found a superb recipe for chicken with preserved ginger. You will come
to dinner and the three of us will be quite gluttonous and share it with

no one. Thank you so much, my dear. Now please open your gift."

Katherine would rather have waited, but Tobias took her hand and led her to a stack of boxes. "But which one?" she asked.

"All!" he announced, his face bright with anticipation. "From all of us—Victoria, Ross, Ann, Jason, and me. Open, open, open!"

Not Derek, Katherine thought. Not Melanie. Self-consciously, she knelt and opened the first box. Lying before her, in symmetrical order, was a complete set of American and Swedish files for use on metals—oval, square taper, knife edge, lozenge, cant, pippin, barette, and crochet—in different lengths and seven degrees of fineness. Beside them lay a set of handles. Almost fearfully, Katherine touched the gleaming rows.

"They won't break, you know!" said Tobias, almost dancing in delight. "And now the other boxes!"

She could guess what they contained. Quickly she pulled off all the wrappings until she was surrounded by open boxes of pliers, dapping die blocks, chasing tools, sanding materials, a saw and set of blades, and two small motorized wheels for buffing and polishing. She stood up, then, in the midst of a collection of jeweler's tools she had not been able to buy for herself, and looked at the family—*my family*—with a face so radiant that Derek drew in his breath and Victoria and Tobias came to put their arms around her.

"You haven't opened my gift," said Derek, handing her a narrow box. Katherine unwrapped it and took out a strip of gold, one inch wide by ten inches long. Wonderingly, she met his watchful eyes. "Mettler likes gold," he said casually.

"Gold—!" Melanie exclaimed. "Why, that must have cost—"

"I'd guess about a thousand," said Curt approvingly.

"Vulgar commentaries have no place at Christmas," Victoria declared. "Or any time. Derek? Will you move the gift-giving along?"

"But I haven't thanked you," Katherine said. She held the cool strip of gold, and stood beside the shining tools on the carpet. "You've given me the freedom to work. I don't have to borrow; I can work in my own home, in the daytime or at night; I can try different techniques and styles because I have the tools for them. Do you know what this means to me?" Tears filled her eyes. "It's as if you've given me a life. The tools to shape a life. I can't really say it—"

"You've said it quite well," Melanie commented sweetly. She was standing beside Derek. "You like your freedom. I wonder if we ever heard the real story of why Craig disappeared."

In the shocked silence, Tobias was the first to recover. Drawing himself up, he roared, "'Farewell, farewell, you old rhinoceros! I'll stare at something less prepocerous!'"

The four children, huddled around the computer, burst into laughter. Jason, Ann, and Curt laughed with them. Victoria's lips twitched, Ross chuckled, then grew quiet, and Derek smiled, watching Katherine. But she had turned away, embarrassed, because she had laughed and then seen the helpless fury in Melanie's eyes. The children rocked back and forth, repeating "prepocerous rhinoceros!" until Victoria, holding her lips tight, signaled the butler to help them carry their gifts to the library.

"We owe Katherine an apology," she said, but Katherine vigorously shook her head. "Then we shall finish with the gifts and go in to dinner. Ross, I thought you and Derek were managing this. Where have you been while Tobias clowned?"

"Applauding him," said Ross quietly, and knelt to distribute the remaining gifts.

Christmas was the one time Victoria allowed the children to eat with the adults. Everyone sat at the long table decorated with berries and chrysanthemums twined among white candles in crystal holders, and ate goose and duck, fresh cranberries with orange rind, and the largest *bûche de Noël* Katherine had ever seen. When coffee was served, the children and Tobias slipped out, to the library. Soon after Victoria and Katherine followed. By the light of a dancing fire, Tobias was reading A *Christmas Carol*, abridging it since they had begun so late. Standing, squatting, hopping, and prancing about the room, he acted all the parts in a dozen different voices. Glancing at her children, Katherine saw tears streaming down their rapt faces, and her own tears well up as memories of Craig's voice mingled with Tobias', reading those same words at their small family celebrations in Vancouver. *You had no right to leave*, she told him fiercely. She moved back into the shadows to let her tears come, and saw Ross sitting quietly near the door. An hour later, when Tobias ended with Tiny Tim's "God bless us, everyone!" she looked again, but he was gone.

"Melanie has many virtues," Derek said on the telephone. "But common sense, perception and discretion are not among them. Craig has nothing to do with my wanting to be with you."

"Nothing?"

"Even if it were true, what difference would it make? When we met, you were intriguing; now I find you irresistible. And you are too intelligent to take Melanie seriously. We have plans to see the New Year in together. Nine o'clock?"

"Yes."

A month before, in his apartment, she had known she wanted him, and she knew it when he walked through her door on New Year's Eve, reminding Jennifer that he was coming for her mother in a proper manner, nodding when Todd told him something about the computer, but never taking his eyes off Katherine. She watched him watching her, as if they were playing a game: Katherine telling him with her eyes that she wanted him, and Derek's eyes appraising and caressing the exquisite vision in black and white, lace and taffeta, and the strong yet delicate lines of her face that at last, freed of despair and a sense of inferiority, glowed with an arresting beauty. He took a long breath. "I think I will not make love to you in front of your children," he murmured, and swept her out the door.

They kissed in his car. Katherine felt the rush of her body's demands before they pulled apart and Derek started the car. She rested her head against the back of the seat as they sped up steep Christmas-wrapped streets to a white mansion ablaze with candles and technicolor lights.

The three floors had been transformed into a carnival. Crowds of guests tried their skill at sharpshooting and baseball-pitching booths, darts, bowling, and fishing in a tub for sterling silver dolphins; others watched a striptease show in a tent on the third floor, acrobats in another tent, and, in a third, trained dogs doing mathematical calculations and barking rhythmically to Christmas carols played on a trumpet by a foot-tapping clown.

"Slightly overdone," Derek commented dryly. "But they were afraid of being anonymous among the rich."

"They've made everyone else anonymous," Katherine said, as they made their way through the rooms.

"Good God, Derek!" exclaimed a thin, mustached young man. "How have you discovered this beauty before me? I thought I was always a step ahead of you."

"No one is ever ahead of Derek," said a dark, burly man. He bent over Katherine's hand. "Brock Galvez. A pleasure. Derek—" They shook hands. "Have you been upstairs? Some madman has taught dogs to bark 'The First Noël.'"

Derek looked at Katherine. "Shall we avoid them? Or would you like to go up there and work our way down?"

"After the dogs," Katherine said. "Perhaps one can only go up."

Galvez laughed. "What would you prefer?" Derek asked.

"Whatever you like." Swaying toward him, her eyes meeting his, Katherine was strung as tight as a fine wire. The sensuous play of taffeta and lace against her skin, the open admiration on all sides, the deafening chatter and music, left her open to the wild fantasies of the carnival and the dreamlike evening. There were no responsibilities, no restrictions— and no Craig. She was alone with Derek.

At midnight they toasted the New Year, kissing lightly, and ate dinner with some of Derek's friends who were in the state legislature. At one thirty, when they left, Katherine discovered that a crowd was coming with them to Derek's apartment. "Tired of the dogs," said a redhead. "You can't have a romantic New Year's Eve with a bunch of dogs barking Christmas carols. Pretty fucking unromantic, in fact."

They all settled themselves in the leather and chrome and glass of Derek's living room. The doors to the Victorian room were closed. "Katherine," said a woman whose long black braids were wrapped about her throat like a scarf. "Could I have a gin and tonic?"

Katherine looked for Derek but he was in the den, putting on a tape of music. So she became his hostess, moving through the rooms, showing guests to the bathrooms, and helping them fix their drinks. When the telephone rang she started to answer it, but stopped. After all, it wasn't her house. But by three thirty, when Derek had smoothly urged the last guest out, she felt almost as if she did live there.

"Well done," he said. "You were magnificent."

She raised her head higher. "Was that a test?"

"Not after the first five minutes. Come with me."

He opened the doors to the Victorian room and she followed him to the red velvet couch. "Derek," she said, "do you turn everything into a drama?"

"Only for those who can play it out. Do you want a drink?"

"No."

She leaned toward him, then paused, fearful of the surge of her passion, but Derek held her, his mouth on hers, forcing her back against the arm of the couch. Katherine opened her mouth and kissed him, her arms tightening around his shoulders as his hand covered her breast.

But she felt suddenly that she could not breathe, and pulled her mouth free. "Wait," she whispered. "I don't—"

"Oh, yes you do. You want this, you've missed it, and you've known all evening you would lie under me tonight. My God you were superb— it's not often I'm taken by surprise but you—" He kissed her again, his tongue possessing her mouth. "My exquisite creature," he murmured.

Like a pause in a storm, Katherine's passion was arrested in its flight.

Derek's words echoed starkly. My creature. My possession. No, she thought. But the fantastic carnival still throbbed within her, and when Derek slid down the zipper on her blouse and it lay like a black lace cloud about her waist, her thoughts fled; she knew only that for six months she had been starving, and now held in her arms a feast.

Slipping off her camisole, Derek held her breasts in his hands and bent over them, his tongue playing slowly on one nipple and then the other. Katherine gave a low sigh as the long surf that was like his voice swept through her.

"My God," he said, and something in his voice told her he did not usually wait so long for a woman.

"Why—?" she murmured but he was leading her to the bedroom, and the question drifted away. He lay her on the bed and bent over her, his mouth opening hers, his tongue deep against hers, as he pulled off her skirt. The sounds from outside grew faint, carried away like pebbles in the windstorm that roared in Katherine's ears.

And then, cutting through it, the telephone rang. Derek did not move. "Derek," she said against his mouth.

"Ignore it."

"No, wait." She struggled to sit up. She had heard the telephone earlier and ignored it. Now it shattered the last spell of the carnival and stilled the roaring in her ears. "Please answer it."

"I will not answer it; are you mad?"

"Then I will."

Expressionless, he contemplated her.

"I should have answered it earlier. I left this number with Annie. Something may be wrong at home."

Without a word, he reached down to the lower shelf of the nightstand and handed her the telephone. She picked it up at the start of another ring. "Yes?" the word was a whisper. She cleared her throat. "Yes?"

"Mommy!" Jennifer cried. The words reverberated through Katherine's head. "Come home in a hurry! Daddy's here!"

CHAPTER 10

PAST all the revelers weaving homeward, Derek drove in silence, his face a mask. Occasionally, disconcertingly, he chuckled.

He had begun in his bedroom, when Jennifer's piercing voice reached him. In one swift motion he was off the bed and across the room, chuckling, then laughing aloud. "Did it again, by God! Fifteen years and he's still cutting me off, that son of a bitch. Still doing it, as if he never left. It's almost comforting, knowing how little the world changes. Come on; I'm sure you're in a hurry to get back to hearth and home."

She was pulling on her skirt. "You don't have to take me." His laughter and his words clanged against the guilt swelling inside her, making her feel sick. She wanted to be alone. "I'll get a cab."

"You'll go in my car."

They drove in silence, his low car flying along the Embarcadero to Market Street and then across town, cutting off other drivers, barely slowing at red lights, until they reached the Sunset, where Katherine's neighbors had long since gone to sleep and the only light that burned was hers. Braking sharply at her building, he smiled thinly. "Give him my regards."

Katherine opened the car door, but a sudden reluctance held her back. "Thank you for—" It was lame and feeble; there was nothing she could say. "The party," she finished, and began to step out.

He stopped her by lifting her hand to his lips. "Katherine, you were magnificent. At the party, at my home, with me." She shuddered. "And I wish you joy with your husband."

"I don't know..." she said, and stepped onto the sidewalk. As soon as she closed the door, Derek slammed the car into gear and tore away, leaving her to meet Craig.

But when she walked in, she was met with silence. No one saw her come in; no one greeted her. The room was empty. No, not empty; Jennifer and Todd were curled up on the couch, asleep. As if a vise had been released, Katherine's thoughts flew in all directions. *Where is he?* She crossed the room to look into the kitchen. Empty. She felt a premonitory chill. The bedroom. A husband would wait for his wife in bed. Her skirt rustled in the silence as she took three long steps and jerked open the door. But the two beds, neatly made, were empty.

"Jennifer," Katherine whispered, kneeling beside the couch. "Jennifer."

"Mommy!" Jennifer sat bolt upright and looked about the room, squinting in the light. "Where's Daddy?"

"He's not here. Jennifer, are you sure he was? You didn't have a dream that seemed so real—?"

"He *is* here! He is! He's been here since midnight! Todd and I were waiting for the New Year and Daddy came and we called you. We called and *called* but nobody answered, and Daddy said he had to leave but finally you answered and he said we should go to sleep 'cause it was so late and he'd sit with us and wait for you. He can't be gone! He said he'd wait! *Why did it take you so long to get here?*"

"I was on the other side of town."

Todd woke, rubbing his eyes. "Dad?"

"He left!" Jennifer cried. "Without even telling us!" She clenched her fist and looked narrowly at Katherine. "Daddy doesn't like Derek, does he?"

They're going to blame it on me. "Did he say that?" Katherine asked.

"No—but he said he was lonely—he called us in Vancouver in *October* and the phone was disconnected and he asked somebody to get our address from the post office and that's how he knew where to send the money. But then he asked where you were and we said a New Year's party with Derek, and Todd said you went out with Derek all the time, and when you answered the phone at Derek's house that was when Daddy said we should go to sleep." Her eyes met her mother's with a woman's knowing look. "So he could leave. Just like he did before."

"Don't imagine things," Katherine said sharply. "Just tell me what happened. He came here at midnight?"

"He knocked on the door," Todd answered. "So I looked through the window like you said to when we're alone, after Annie goes across the hall. And there he was! Just the same as ever!"

"Thinner," Jennifer said. She screwed up her face. "He promised he'd wait for you!"

"He hugged us and hugged us," said Todd. "And he looked in the kitchen and the bedroom and everywhere. He opened all the closets and drawers and he asked where his big desk was—"

"He asked if we sold it!" Jennifer said loudly. "What does he think we are, anyway? We told him it was waiting for him in Vancouver, in storage, 'cause there's no room for it here."

"And then?" Katherine asked. She was sitting on the hassock, head bowed, arms around her knees. Her children's voices drifted to her as if from far away; she tried to picture them with their father, but instead she saw a stranger poking through her house.

"He looked all over your worktable," Todd went on. "And picked up his picture and looked at it and then, real careful, put it back and said he knew you wouldn't forget. And then we all sat on the couch and he gave us our Christmas presents. Only—"

"Only what?" Katherine asked.

Todd opened a box and took out an Icelandic sweater. He held it against his shoulders. "It doesn't fit."

"It's too small," said Jennifer scornfully. "So's mine." She dangled another sweater by a sleeve, trying to turn disappointment into anger. "Doesn't he know we've grown up? He didn't think about that! He just pretended everything was exactly the same as when he left!"

"He didn't know," Katherine said. Clasping the soft wool sweaters between her hands, she buried her face in them, tears burning her eyes. "But he tried."

"He said Christmas was awful." Todd's voice was somber. "Awful lonesome, and he missed our house and he missed us..."

"What else did he say?"

"He told us about Alaska—he's working there—he didn't say doing what. Maybe the pipeline. Or something else. He wasn't real definite."

"Not about anything." Jennifer looked at her mother again with that same woman's look: a child growing up too quickly. "He was hard to talk to. It was like he had all these secrets and the more we asked, the more he closed up. He kept changing the subject the way you do when you don't want to talk about something. He'd ask about school and stuff. Or you. Mainly you."

"What about me?"

"Everything—"

"Boy, was he surprised!" Todd broke in. "We were talking about Christmas and we showed him the computer and your jewelry tools and we

told him about Carrie and Jon's train and the Atari games in the library
and he kept saying, but who? Who? Like an owl." He laughed, then
hiccupped, and his eyes filled with tears. "Mom, he looked so sad."

He crawled into Katherine's lap, crushing the two sweaters, and she
held him tightly in her arms. "Jennifer," she said. "What did you tell
him?"

"He didn't know we knew the Haywards. He didn't even know we
knew about them being his family. You know that story about the man
who slept for twenty years—Rip Van Winkle—and then woke up and
didn't understand why everything was different? Daddy didn't understand
either. He looked all confused and he kept shaking his head. We told
him how we sold the house and moved here, and Leslie helped you get
this job at Heath's, and about your jewelry order that's going to make
you famous, and Todd said you looked all different, like a princess, and
started talking about dinner at Great-Grandmother's—"

"And Daddy said, in a loud voice, 'WHO?'" interrupted Todd. "And
I said Great-Grandmother Victoria, of course—"

"And Daddy shook his head real hard and we said that was what she
told us to call her, and she is our great-grandmother, isn't she? And Todd
told about Tobias and the prepocerous rhinoceros and—"

"And Derek."

"Sure. Everybody. Then when you answered the phone at Derek's house,
Daddy said something real quiet, we couldn't hear it, and he said we should
go to sleep while he waited for you. I didn't want to go to sleep, Mommy,
but I was awful tired. And it took you so long to get here."

"He brought you a present, too," said Todd, picking up a small box
from the floor. "Oh, here's a letter. I didn't see it before."

Slowly, Katherine opened the box. Wrapped in cotton lay an ivory
bracelet, delicately carved with flocks of birds. Inscribed on the inside
were the words "I love you."

"Oh, beautiful," Jennifer breathed.

"Well, you shall wear it," said Katherine. "Since your sweater didn't
fit. Here. Try it on."

"Too big." Jennifer turned it on her narrow wrist.

"No, it's perfect; it's not supposed to be tight. You keep it, for special
occasions."

Jennifer looked at her shrewdly. "When will you wear it?"

"Someday. I'm busy making my own jewelry right now, remember?"

Todd had opened the envelope. "It says 'Dearest Todd and Jennifer,'
but I can't read it." He handed it to Jennifer.

"'I'm sorry,'" Jennifer read. "'I can't—can't wait for—'" She shook her head. "It's hard to read." She gave it to Katherine. "You can read it. It's probably really for you, anyway."

"Dearest Todd and Jennifer," Katherine read aloud, making out Craig's hurried scrawl.

> "I'm sorry I can't wait for your mother after all; it's late and I have to leave. But I promise someday we'll all be together again, for good, the way we used to be. Remember what I told you: sometimes things happen to us that we can't help, and then we have to go away. I love you and I love your mother and I didn't want to go away but I had to. Please believe me. Maybe I can make you understand when I come back—as soon as I get everything straightened out. That's what I'm trying to do now. Tell your mother that, she'll believe it because she believes in me and she loves me and as long as I know she's waiting for me, I know I can work everything out and we'll be happy again. I'll see you as soon as I can get back. Take care of your mother, tell her ~~Derek~~ I love her. And I love you, and miss you all. Dad."

•   •   •

Craig's letter lay on the worktable for a week, while Katherine tried to make out the words he had crossed out. The first was "Derek." The others had been marked out so heavily the paper was torn. *Take care of your mother, tell her Derek*—what? Tell her Derek does not like her husband? Derek already told her. Tell her Derek will want to take her to bed? She knows that—and she wanted it, too. Tell her Derek holds the power in the family? She knows it. Tell her Derek has a streak of cruelty? She knows it. Tell her Derek quarreled with Craig on a sailboat fifteen years ago? She knows it; she knows it; she knows it. *Tell your mother*—what?

Each night, after Jennifer and Todd were in bed, she stared at the letter until she could no longer sit still; then, asking Annie to keep her door open for a while, she walked the short distance to the ocean. Beneath the steady beat and whoosh of breaking and receding waves, her fury grew. *He was still keeping secrets from her.* The blackened space in his letter was just like the spaces in their marriage.

But he did say he'd be back, she told herself, and help us understand what happened. He'll tell us what he's been through, what he's been thinking—

How can he, if he couldn't even face me, or write down what was in his mind?

He might have been able to, a small voice responded cuttingly, if you hadn't been with Derek.

I don't know that for sure, she thought angrily. I don't know why he left. I don't know why he crossed out what he started to write.

Her tears mingled with the salty mist from the ocean. How could she ever know what he was thinking if he kept shutting her out? I'll never know who he is, she thought despairingly, if he keeps running away. *Tell your mother—*

Damn it, tell me yourself!

There was no one she could talk to. Victoria and Tobias were in Italy for a month; Leslie knew the family only through Katherine's eyes; Ross didn't seem to have time to talk to her; and Derek—how could she ask Derek what he thought Craig might have written? Besides, Derek had not called.

"So call him," Leslie said a week after New Year's Eve. "Times have changed, you know; we no longer languish beside the telephone, faint and frail, waiting for our master's voice."

Katherine shook her head. She was twisting a soft piece of wire around her wrist, imagining it in gold. "I don't want to call him. I'm not proud of myself. I don't think I like either of us very much right now."

Leslie sat back on the couch. "Don't you think you're making too much of it? You only wanted a simple screw, not something that— OK, I'm sorry, don't look at me as if I'd suggested roast thumbs for dinner. You don't mind not seeing him? Or having him around?"

"No."

"My, my," Leslie drawled with a grin. "What a change from the early days."

Katherine took off the wire bracelet, and laid it gently beside a sketch of a matching ring. "Sometimes I think so...and sometimes I don't. Last summer I was terrified at having to make my way without Craig. In some ways I still am, because I don't understand myself. What kind of woman lives with a man for ten years and doesn't see through him? I feel like a blank slate, starting from scratch. Not even a name. Fraser isn't Craig's name, so it isn't mine either."

"You've used it for ten years; it's yours. And about seeing through a man— I don't know. We see what we want to see. You knew he had secrets, but you liked what you had with him, so you didn't push. I don't think you'd be that way if you met him now. You're more demanding. Not so anxious to be protected. If you hadn't changed, you'd be calling Derek."

Katherine laughed slightly and picked up the strip of gold. "Do you think his gold would make a good substitute?"

"You could try. I know a lot of men who love it more than sex."

They laughed, but in fact it was Derek's gold that Katherine thought most about in the next two weeks. She had been afraid that Jennifer and Todd would slip back to their early sullenness after Craig left a second time, but instead they were strangely cheerful and, after Christmas vacation, very busy at school. When Katherine talked to them about Craig, they answered politely, but she saw they were uncomfortable with what they had discovered: their father was alive and had come to see them; he said he loved them and loved their mother; he sent them money. But he would not stay with them.

Awed by the immensity of those facts, which they could not understand, they pushed them out of sight. "Vancouver is gone," said Todd one day. "A fleet of a hundred dolphins came along and swallowed it up. Once in a while, when they burp, a piece of our old house might come up, but Vancouver is *gone*."

"You know it's still there, Todd," Katherine said gently.

"Not for us," he insisted, and she let it go. In a way he was right; Vancouver didn't exist for them. There would be time enough to resuscitate it if they ever were to go back. Right now, it was more important to Katherine that the three of them were busy and looking ahead, instead of back.

Every day she carried books to read on the bus and on her lunch hour: art books and books on design, architecture, folk art, and archaeology. At night and on the weekends, she was at her worktable until twelve or one o'clock, and by the third week of January, she had finished her sketches and models. The day she made her first cut in the gold strip Derek had given her, Leslie came to watch.

"An important moment; I didn't want to miss it. If you don't mind an audience." Bent over her work, Katherine shook her head. Leslie looked about, a puzzled expression on her face. "Something's changed."

"I did some rearranging," Katherine said, concentrating on the lines she was scoring in the gold. "I needed more room."

"I should say," murmured Leslie. Shelves now filled the wall above the worktable, stacked with boxes holding Katherine's new tools. Other tools hung from hooks or were spread on her worktable and a new folding card table nearby. Empty Heath's shoeboxes on the floor beneath the worktable held wires, string, solder, and other supplies. Craig's picture was gone.

"It's in the children's room," Katherine said as Leslie eyed the spot on the worktable where it had stood since August. She bent to her work again, scoring lines in the soft gold where she would make cuts.

Leslie watched in silence. When Katherine picked up one of her new saws and fastened a blade in it, she said, "It *is* a substitute for Derek, isn't it? And maybe for Craig? The way you handle that gold—"

Katherine laughed. "No, it's not a substitute. But if you don't have love, you ought to have work you love to do."

"I read that somewhere," said Leslie. "That the two things we can't do without are love and work. I wish to hell I wasn't battling all the time at Heath's. Since love does not cast a rosy glow over me and Marc, or me and anybody, I could use a fun job. That's all I ask; at least for a while, it would be plenty."

"I wish you had one," Katherine said, and then concentrated on making the cuts in her piece of gold. But later, after Leslie was gone, the words still echoed in the room. Love and work. She gazed at her collection of shining tools, her sketch pads and the materials she had gathered, waiting to take shape under her fingers. Craig was in the background; Derek was gone. I have my work, she thought. And at least for a while—she smiled to herself—it's plenty.

Heath's profits were down for the six months ending in mid-January. Even the post-Christmas shopping spurt had not changed the percentages; profits were below what they should be. Someone had to be at fault, and at the Tuesday morning executive meeting, fingers were pointed at Leslie McAlister, vice-president for Personnel and Payroll.

"The computer and I have become one," she said wearily to Marc on Friday night, collapsing beside him in a booth in a lounge high above Union Square. "I pushed that crew to buy it; now I do nothing but defend it."

"Why bother?" he asked.

Looking through the window, she said wryly, "You could have chosen a place where the view wouldn't have included Heath's."

"Look beyond it."

"You mean literally."

He shrugged. "You could get a job anywhere. If they attack you for your pet project, why waste your time on them?"

"Because we took inventory yesterday and got some crazy numbers, and one explanation might be that my pet project fouled up."

He looked at her with the shrewdness that sat so strangely on his plump face. "Pet project or pet programer?"

"Both." She sighed. "Bruce scares me sometimes; he's so damned laid back I'm not sure what he'd think is a joke. Like feeding false information into the computer."

"What false information?"

"That theft is only one and a half percent—" She stopped abruptly. "I don't see a drink before me. Has everyone gone on strike?"

"I'm sorry. Your usual?" She nodded and he ordered for both of them. "My dear Leslie, you can talk to me."

"It's confidential. You know that."

"Then let me guess. The computer says theft is one and a half percent. Considerably below industry average. Most stores would cheer at such news. Why, then, is Leslie McAlister worried? Because she thinks someone is giving the computer false information so that it pumps out a false figure. And if someone is going to all that trouble, the correct figure must be higher." Taking out a pencil, he began figuring on his paper napkin. "Retail stores..." he murmured. "Average theft... Heath's annual volume approximately one hundred million dollars... an additional loss of..." He eyed Leslie. "I'd guess that what worries Leslie McAlister is that someone is robbing Heath's of approximately a million dollars in merchandise and fixing her pet project so the numbers balance and it doesn't show up. How close am I?"

She put out her hands and let them fall. "On the button."

He nodded with satisfaction. "And you propose to investigate a million-dollar loss and keep it confidential?"

"I don't propose; I hope, and I try. Marc, it's my job; anything that happens from now on is going to be dumped on my doorstep. One of my fellow executives even reminded me today that I got my brother a job as a programer. Any way you look at it, or any way *they* look at it, I'm responsible."

"Not for computers, for God's sake. No one even understands them, much less willingly takes responsibility for them. Blame the devil. The tides. Sunspots. The Lord. Who probably doesn't understand them either, but at least is big enough to shoulder the blame for them."

She laughed. "Thank you, Marc. You do put things in perspective. And yes, though you haven't asked, I would like another vodka martini. Well."

"Well?" He gave the order to the waiter as Leslie bent to look more closely through the window. "What attracts your attention so far below?"

"A sports car that looks familiar. And a woman getting into it. I think I know that coat."

"What woman?"

"It's not important." She turned back to him and thoughtfully ran her finger around the edge of the glass the waiter put before her. "Just that

I didn't know they were seeing each other again. They had a—misunderstanding on New Year's Eve and I thought she'd have told me if they'd cleared it up. Maybe I'm just feeling left out; things happening without my knowing it." As she took a drink, she saw his quick frown. "I gather I'm talking about myself too much. Sorry. Your turn."

"No. I have no intention of spending the evening with a nervous woman. I want you at your best or not at all. So tell me—you aren't really frightened of those idiots at Heath's."

"You're damn right I am; I'm scared stiff. Marc, can't you understand that those idiots, as you call them, control my future?"

"You should never allow anyone to control your future. Go elsewhere."

"I don't want to go elsewhere. I want to stay at Heath's. It's been my whole life for ten years; I've built a small power base there and I won't throw it away or let anyone take it from me." She looked at her hands. "As for allowing others to control my future—you're right: I don't like it. But it goes with the way I make my living and I can deal with it. It might be different if we were talking about my private life."

"My dear Leslie, are you asking me to marry you?"

"God forbid." She laughed. "I don't want to marry you, Marc, any more than you want to marry me. But I've been thinking—" She sipped her drink and said carefully, "My life doesn't seem to have much...shape. Or meaning. Other than making Heath's bigger and better, of course. I need something more."

"A hobby? Leslie, if you're thinking of making jewelry—"

"No; good Lord, no. I'm thinking of making a baby."

"I beg your pardon?"

"Don't look so shocked. Women often think about having babies. It's easy when they're married; harder when they're not. I've been thinking about this a long time, trying to figure out what I need, and I've decided what I need is to be responsible for someone else. The way I live—most of the time I'm thinking about me. It's a little...narrow. Maybe it's being with Katherine and her kids; whatever it is, I want more than what I have now."

He nodded. "I see that. And why are you telling me?"

"Because I'm not so young. I have to decide pretty soon and there aren't many men I like well enough to ask. Marc, if I decide to have a child, would you be the father?"

He looked at her, momentarily paralyzed. "I thought I was beyond surprises." She waited. "With what strings attached?" he asked.

"Not one. My child, my little family, my income, my cherishing. I'm talking about a seed, not a contract."

"You understand, it would change everything. I would not adjust my schedule to fit an infant's. It would be impossible to continue what we have now."

"Of course."

"Well, then," he said amiably. "If you're serious about attaching no strings, and if you put that in writing, I would consider it."

"Fair enough." She put her hand on his. "Let's talk about something else. Make me laugh and forget profits and computers and my advanced age. Tell me about the jewelry business."

"It prospers. No matter how bad the economy, there are always people who make money, and spend it, especially on jewelry. Mettler tells me he can't keep enough twenty-thousand-dollar watches in stock. He sold two necklaces at a quarter million each within a week of showing them. There are those who worry about groceries and those who worry about satisfying the greed of wives, mistresses, and lovers. Fortunately, I deal with the second group."

"The rich are always with us."

"Thank God. You need them as much as I. How else would Heath's survive?"

"It wouldn't. Marc, what is the matter with the waiters tonight?"

"The waiters are the same as ever, but you are impatient. And since when do you have more than two drinks before dinner?"

"Only when I need them. I've worked every night this week and after the inventory yesterday I stayed until three in the morning, getting preliminary reports—"

"My God, why didn't you tell me? You shouldn't be in a restaurant at all. Come. We're going home."

"Whose home?"

"Mine. I will provide a massage and a sauna, champagne to clear the head, and then dinner. And bed. If you feel like it."

She looked at him curiously. "You know, Marc, for a selfish bastard, you can be exceedingly thoughtful."

"My foolish, beautiful Leslie," he said, standing up. "Why else are you here? How many men understand that even bright, aggressive women are worth a little thoughtfulness? You yourself said there aren't many like me. I agree." And he held her coat so they could leave.

Derek drove with his customary speed, slowing only when he turned into a short curved street. As he stopped the car before a stucco house in a manicured yard, Katherine heard the pounding of ocean surf. "Sea

Cliff," he said, opening her door. "The four of us grew up a block from here."

Inside the house, enormous rooms looked out on a steel-gray ocean below a fading sunset. Among the guests Katherine recognized familiar faces, but as soon as they greeted their hostess, Derek steered her through the house to a table in a deep bay window. "We need some privacy. I have to show myself at one of these Mardi Gras dinners every year, but that doesn't mean we can't find some quiet. And it won't be easy to talk later, at the race track."

"Talk about what?"

"Why you're here with me," he said. "After deciding not to see me again." A waitress brought an open bottle of Fumé Blanc and two glasses. Derek poured, and sat back, watching Katherine smooth the surprise from her face. Learning fast, he thought. Another few months and she could hold her own with any of them: as beautiful and carefully dressed, her emotions as controlled, her wit as sharp. And something even more interesting: a seeming vulnerability that made others want to help her. Clever woman. Assuming she planned to give that impression.

"And why *am* I here," Katherine asked. "If I'd decided not to see you again?"

"Because you're infatuated; because you've been starved for a long time and you know I can satisfy you; because I bring you excitement and introductions to people who are important to your profession."

She contemplated him over her wine glass: a different man from the one she had hungered for on New Year's Eve—harder, the flashes of cruelty closer to the surface, but his charm undiminished, his magnetism so powerful that she realized with dismay she still was attracted to him. "Is that all?" she asked.

He smiled. "As for why I am here, though you have not asked, it comes from wanting you. And because I expected you to call after our New Year celebration and it interested me that you did not."

"You left out something," Katherine said. "You want to hurt Craig by sleeping with his wife."

The waitress paused in passing their table, hoping to hear more. But Derek waited, patient and amused, until reluctantly she moved on. "A curious idea," he said. "I wouldn't have expected it from you. Did you get it from someone else?"

Katherine's voice became as cool as Victoria's. "I'm learning not to depend on others. It was something you said, when Jennifer called."

"That Craig had come between us. I thought it an accurate description. Craig often did that when we were children: he would smile slyly—others said sweetly—and say, to Victoria or Ann or anyone in authority, how wonderful it would be if he had—whatever it was. He never whined or complained, he almost never asked outright. He just let it be known that shy, innocent Craig would be so happy *if*... When it didn't work, he simply walked away. Or ran. That's his style: to run from confrontation or crisis. By now you ought to recognize it a mile away. Yes," he said, seamlessly changing his tone of voice as a waiter approached.

"The buffet is in the dining room, but if you prefer, I can prepare some plates for you."

"Katherine?"

"Whatever you like." She looked at the ocean. She was ashamed, as if Derek's scorn had been for her as much as for Craig, and it made her feel stifled, closed in, wanting to run away. And she knew, as if Craig were telling her, that this was how he felt when he couldn't face whatever was happening. Craig hated it when people analyzed him. He held his thoughts close and despised people who told him they could have guessed what he'd do because they knew his style. Craig, she thought, would despise Derek.

Evidently he did. And evidently it was mutual.

"Now listen to me," Derek said when the waiter had left. "I don't lie to women. I want you. Not because you're Craig's wife or because Ross was the one who brought you here—"

"Ross?"

His eyes became hooded. "It has nothing to do with Ross. Or anyone else. I find you enchanting and elusive; if you knew me better, you would know that those are the qualities I cannot resist in a woman. It's as simple as that. I told you: I do not lie to women."

You're lying to me, Katherine thought. But at the same moment she knew that it didn't matter. She lied, too, every time she pretended she was free. She wasn't free; she was tied to Craig, dogged by his presence and the loose ends dangling from their marriage. Earlier, when Derek called to ask her to the Mardi Gras celebrations, all she could think of was that it had been three weeks and she wanted to see him. Now, looking at his lean face and dark blond hair and unrevealing eyes, she remembered the precision of his hands holding her breasts and knew her body hungered for him, even though she did not like him as much as before. But none of it mattered. She was not free to sleep with him. "I think we should be friends," she said evenly.

His eyes flickered. "Friends," he repeated.

She nodded. "Not lovers." And as soon as she said the words, in spite of her hunger she felt a burden lift from her.

Derek raised his wine glass. "In that case," he said with a remote smile that meant he was already moving to other thoughts. "To friendship." And he touched her glass lightly with his.

The jewelry gleamed in the lamplight—necklaces, lapel pins, a linked bracelet. Nine pieces, ready to be delivered. In the quiet room, where the only sounds were the rain against the window and the muffled tapping of her hammer, Katherine sat in a circle of contentment, making a tenth piece. Beneath her fingers, the pliable gold seemed alive, shaping itself through her thoughts, as if it were part of her.

She had never worked with gold and as she curved its sensual gleam into a bracelet she felt the exhilaration of working with what jewelers called the king of metals. For centuries it had beckoned toward exploration and conquest; in Katherine's living room, it meant something else. Professionals used gold.

She had dipped into her savings to buy silver, so the gold would last longer, but not even worries about money could invade her contentment. She was shaping beautiful things to be sold in one of the finest shops in the city; in the other room her children slept after the three of them had spent the evening reading and laughing together; she saw Leslie frequently, and once or twice a week Derek took her to dinner or a party. That, she acknowledged, was not always easy. He was charming and cool and made no demands, but, though her mind knew what it wanted, her body still wanted Derek and sometimes she thought it would be easier simply to stop seeing him. But that would mean giving up the gilded evenings he offered. She wondered whether Derek and his evenings were inseparable. Probably. When she got over one, she would no longer need the other.

The golden bracelet lay with its matching necklace of thin gold textured discs in a cotton-lined box. Eight other pieces lay in separate boxes. Katherine stood beside her worktable, studying them, listening to the rain. She knew they were good; tomorrow Mettler would tell her what he thought. Tomorrow, she repeated; tomorrow.

The rain was still falling the next morning, blowing in long sheets across the pavement. Katherine heard it behind her as she entered the store, and then it was gone. In Herman Mettler's office, the only storms were those he made himself.

"They're very good," Mettler said, turning Katherine's jewelry in his splayed fingers as if he were inspecting fruit for rotten spots. "Very good technique. Excellent technique. More than Tony has taught you—individual touches here and there—very good—very good technique."

"Thank you." Katherine shifted in her chair.

"I place great emphasis on technique," Mettler said, putting his palms together beneath his chin as if he were praying. "The best design in the world can be ruined by poor technique."

She nodded, twisted inside so tightly she thought she would snap, waiting for him to talk about design.

"However, the reverse is also true. The best technique in the world cannot disguise weak design."

Katherine sat on the edge of her chair, her back straight.

His hands still praying, Mettler looked down at the boxes of jewelry, jumbled from his handling. "These pieces, now. Excellent technique. Very impressive. But the design, I fear, leaves something to be desired." He paused and gave her the same cool inspection he had given her jewelry. "Frankly, I'm surprised that a woman as attractive as you would be so cautious. Beautiful women can afford to take chances other women cannot. So why do you bring me safe designs similar to those I see in other fine stores?" He leaned back in his chair. "Customers only buy technique when they pay a high price for design. Am I making myself clear? These are nice pieces, pleasant pieces, superbly made. I have no doubt that I can sell them, and I intend to, but in the cases in the rear, not those up front. Our customers expect uniqueness at Mettler's. They are willing to pay for it. I see nothing here that is remotely unique."

Furious, Katherine bit her lip to keep quiet. He could have softened his criticism. But suddenly Victoria's voice came to her. *You need a little eccentricity. To be so proper... at your age...*

Mettler was waiting. Hastily, she said, "I was worried that you might not buy anything too different, from someone new..."

"No, no, no; what nonsense. You've studied our display cases? Then you know how much we value the avant garde. The excellent avant garde, of course; we are not interested in the merely sensational. Your designs are neither. They are simply—rather ordinary. In any case—" Shooting his cuff to look at his watch, he became brisk. "As I said, I intend to sell these. And you brought prices. Good." Reading from her list, he jotted figures on his notepad. "One hundred for the bracelet... not much for your labor there. I'll have to charge five hundred; my competitors would run me out of town if I charged less. And you want fifty for the..." He talked to himself for a while. "All right. Your total is fine; twelve hundred for the ten pieces. And I can take another dozen, even if they're like these. There is always a market for the tried and true. I need them by June, for our fall collection. Thank you, Mrs. Fraser. I'm sure we'll work well together."

"But—"

Mettler's secretary appeared in the doorway, invisibly sent for. Katherine stood up. Twelve more, four months from now. Not enough to quit her job; not enough to make a name for herself. All her dreams were sliding away. But Mettler, looking again at his watch, would not know that. She held out her hand, surprising him into shaking it. "Thank you," she said, her voice strong. "I'll get them to you as early as possible."

And downstairs, lingering beside the glass cases at the front of the store, she vowed to herself that that was where her next twelve pieces would be displayed. Somehow, she thought as she left to face Lister's sarcastic wrath for being late—next time, I'll find a way to make Herman Mettler sit up and take notice.

Victoria and Tobias had been back from Italy only a few days when they called, separately, to invite Katherine to dinner the following week. It was a blustery night, the beginning of March, and when she arrived the butler led her to the library, where she found them in front of the fire, with Ross.

"My dear!" Victoria exclaimed, rising to kiss her, and Ross turned, as startled as Katherine. In the flickering light, she had thought at first it was Derek; then, in a swift comparison she was barely aware of, she saw that the cheekbones were not as sharp, the shadowed hollows not as deep, the mouth, even unsmiling, wider and a little fuller. His face was gentler than Derek's but not soft; in fact, as Katherine sat between Victoria and Tobias, she thought he looked as severe as he had in Vancouver, when he was forcing her to accept the truth about Craig.

He stood and greeted her formally and brought up Craig's New Year visit. "Victoria and Tobias told me about it. He still won't give you a chance."

Tears sprang to Katherine's eyes. He was the only one who saw exactly why she had been so hurt and angry.

He asked about her children. "Jon and Carrie enjoyed seeing them at Christmas."

"We might get them together some time," Katherine said.

"We might." They were silent. Victoria and Tobias watched with interest. Ross asked about Katherine's jeweler's tools and she asked about BayBridge and then silence fell once more. "I was just leaving," Ross said at last. "I'm expected at home. I only stopped by to greet the returning travelers. I'm sorry—" He paused. "I'm sorry we've seen so little of each other."

"So am I," Katherine responded, puzzled by the strain in his voice.

"But I know how busy you are. And I've been busy, too..."

He nodded. "So I've heard." Their eyes met. Then, turning abruptly, he bent over Victoria and kissed her. "Lunch on Friday. Don't forget. Katherine... it was good to see you. Tobias, I'd like to ask you about some books I'm thinking of buying." Tobias shrugged in silent apology to Katherine and left the room with Ross.

Victoria raised her eyebrows. "Ross isn't usually so abrupt. But he's concerned about you, you know."

"I doubt it," said Katherine.

"Oh, yes." Victoria handed her a glass of sherry. "We all are."

Katherine was puzzled. "Why? You can't know anything about Mettler yet."

"Mettler? What about him? No, wait; Tobias will want to hear it, too. What we are worried about is you and Derek."

"*Derek?*"

"Well, my dear, it's been four months. People talk when a beautiful woman is seen about town with Derek for one month, much less four. They talk to me, anyway, and to Tobias, and we were discussing that when Ross came in."

"But what difference does it make if I go out with Derek?"

"None, as long as you don't fall in love with him." Katherine was silent. "Are you in love with him?"

"No. And I don't expect to be. I have a husband, you know."

"When was that ever a guarantee—? In any event, you haven't seen your husband for almost nine months. It's natural that you would be attracted to other men. But it should not be Derek."

Katherine drank her sherry and looked at the flames in the fireplace. "A strange way to talk about your grandson."

"I am saying he's not good for you. Is it strange for me to tell my granddaughter that?"

A rush of love swept over Katherine. *My granddaughter.* "Thank you," she said. "You make me feel as if I belong."

"But of course you belong," said Tobias cheerfully, taking his seat and pouring more sherry into their glasses. "Though we were slow to see it at first. How have you been while we romped through Italy?"

"Something is wrong about Mettler," Victoria said, and while the butler set the table beside them Katherine described what had happened the week before.

"A pox upon him!" Tobias thundered.

"What you must do, Katherine," Victoria pronounced as they sat at the table, "is choose one style and one material—gold would be ex-

cellent—which will give you an identity with customers. I've been thinking about your career, my dear, and I've decided you should take advantage
of your charmingly old-fashioned quality which I find so endearing."

"Old-fashioned?" Katherine asked.

"My dear, I may be as old as the century but I am aware that, today,
when a woman says she will not fall in love with someone because she
has a husband, that may safely be called old-fashioned. I find it charming.
Most people would, at least privately, because they long for what seems
to have been a simpler past. If you pattern your designs, for example,
on my antique jewelry, women will buy them."

"No men?" asked Tobias mildly.

"Some; but women wear most of the jewelry, Tobias, you know that.
You yourself wear none."

"Who buys most of it?"

"Ah." Victoria sat back to allow the butler to remove her soup plate.
"So you think jewelry is aimed at males. That might be. Male fantasies?"

"'Hopes and fears and twilight fantasies—'" Tobias quoted.

Katherine was struck by the words. "Who wrote that?" she asked.

"Shelley." Tobias smiled, grateful for an audience. "From *Adonais*.
Would you like to hear more of it?" Without waiting, he quoted, "'Desires
and adorations... Splendors and Glooms, and glimmering Incarnations
of hopes and fears, and twilight Fantasies; And Sorrow, with her family
of Sighs—'"

"Yes," said Victoria abruptly, her keen eyes on Katherine's somber
ones. "But I thought we were talking about Katherine's career. Katherine,
before you do anything else, you must speak to the other important
jewelers in town. Herman Mettler may think he's the only one, but I
myself often shop at Xavier's and Laykin Et Cie. I'll call first and tell
them you're coming. Take your sketches. A pity you have no more
finished pieces; it's possible no one would agree with Mettler. Especially
if he made such a point of your technique." Without warning, she struck
the table. "Bastard! To praise your technique and then call you ordinary!
I remember when he was peddling fake pearls during the depression. I
shall buy nothing more from him. In fact, I shall write him a letter. If
he thinks he can speak that way to my granddaughter—"

"No, please. Don't do that." Katherine looked troubled. "I have to
make my own way. Craig forced me to do it, but now I really want to."
She smiled. "You did say I needed to be eccentric. And my pieces really
weren't unusual. I mean, I thought they were beautiful, but I wasn't
trying to be different—"

"You don't need to be different," Victoria declared. "You must only
be yourself, no one else."

"How about a younger, successful Victoria?" asked Tobias, and the room was silent except for the whisper of the fire.

"I am not trying to force Katherine into anything," Victoria said at last. "She does not have to be successful for my sake. But" —she looked at Katherine through half-closed eyes— "you want a place to belong, yet you insist on going your own way."

"Finding my own way," Katherine corrected quietly. "I need a place to belong, I need your help, or, at least, your concern and interest and—"

"Love?" suggested Tobias helpfully.

"Love," Katherine echoed. "It makes me feel wonderful when you swear at Mettler, but I don't want you to swear at him in person. I need to win him over myself, with my work. Otherwise, I'll never know whether I'm any good or not."

"Even if you fail," Tobias prompted.

"Of course. I'm sorry," she said to Victoria. "I know you want me to succeed. But I have to know."

After a moment, Victoria took her hand. "Be sure to tell me when Mettler puts your pieces on display. I shall be the first to buy one."

For a month, rumors had drifted through Heath's. Business was bad or the chain was about to be sold or somebody on the fifth floor was playing a hell of an April Fool's joke. Whatever it was, an outside accounting firm had been hired to examine the sales records of all departments, and inventories were being ordered in different departments without warning.

When an inventory of the design department was called, Gil Lister went into a frenzy. "Do the windows!" he ordered Katherine the minute the store closed. "Everything! Merchandise, props, every fucking champagne bottle in the wedding scene! By God, they want an inventory, I'll give them one they'll never forget!"

In the strange, cavelike windows, screened from the street, Katherine stood in the center of a gala wedding reception, with memories of her own wedding flooding over her. She could feel Craig's arm around her waist as they stood in the judge's living room; she could see Leslie and the judge's wife: their witnesses. In the corner a Raggedy Ann doll stared at the ceiling. Craig had said there was no one he wanted, and so they had begun their new family in a strange living room with only Leslie as Katherine's link with her past.

In the curtained window, Katherine walked around the vacantly smiling mannequins, jotting down department and style numbers of dresses, men's cutaways, shoes, purses and gloves, glasses and bottles of champagne, trays of polyethylene hors d'oeuvres, silk and paper flowers. Long ago she and Craig had given parties, though never very many, and after a while they stopped altogether. Katherine had loved every part of them, planning, cooking, and cleaning for days in advance, grateful to Craig for letting her do it even though he was uncomfortable with groups of people and always breathed a sigh of relief when the last guest was ushered out.

She'd always been grateful to Craig, Katherine realized, standing in the window beside the bride and groom. First because he loved her and married her, and then, over the years, for giving her a home, for taking care of her, for being a loving father to Jennifer and Todd, for building a beautiful house and encouraging her to buy whatever she wanted to make it perfect. She gazed at the mindlessly grinning groom. She had even been grateful for her orgasms. When I had them, she thought; usually I didn't. In the last two years, when Craig had been so rushed and preoccupied, there had been almost none.

But he hadn't known that. He would have been hurt if she'd told him she wasn't satisfied. The groom leered at her, and suddenly the thought came to Katherine—No, he wouldn't. He wouldn't have been hurt at all. He'd have found some way to make it seem my fault. *He would have run from it.*

It was as if she'd turned a corner and come upon a familiar view from a different angle. "I have to stop this," she said aloud. "I'm beginning to sound like Derek." She hurried through the other window displays, scribbling numbers on her lined paper. With a final look around, she went back into the store and walked through the aisles, so eerily empty, her footsteps echoing as she went down the stairs to the basement.

The display storeroom was empty. "Gil?" Katherine called. When there was no answer she put her clipboard on his desk and stood uncertainly, wanting to go home but afraid to leave anything undone. There was no new paperwork on her desk, but along one wall was a row of merchandise cartons packed with materials they'd removed from the windows the day before, when they created the wedding scenes. Perhaps he expected her to check them. They should have been sent back to the warehouse that morning, but the driver had been sick and though Lister had been offered a replacement, he had refused, saying he'd wait for the regular man.

I'd better do them, Katherine thought, or he'll sneer at me for being in a hurry to leave.

The dresses and shorts were neatly folded, layered with tennis rackets and hiking gear, and Katherine went through them rapidly, marking them on her master list. But halfway into the second box, she came upon a plastic bag with six Perry Ellis cardigans that had not been used in the window displays. Damn, she thought. If somebody's got new things from the receiving room mixed up with ours, it could take hours to straighten out.

Methodically, she began emptying all the cartons. In the next four, she found merchandise that had not come from window displays or the display storeroom: Francesca of Damon dresses, Anne Klein blouses, ten boxes of Hermes silk scarves. She was about to begin the fifth carton when Lister walked in. He stopped short, a doughnut halfway to his mouth. "What the fuck are you doing?" he screamed. "Who told you to do that? Get away from there!"

Katherine sprang to her feet. "I'm sorry, Gil; I didn't know if they'd been done and I thought—"

"You thought! You thought! You're not supposed to think! You're supposed to do what I tell you and I told you to do the windows!"

"I did the windows! I didn't have anything else to do and—"

"And you didn't wait for my orders! How many times have I told you never to do anything unless I order it? Well? A hundred? A thousand? Ten thousand? But you've never liked that, have you, all ga-ga'd up with your new haircut, and looking down your nose like the queen of Sheba— you and your high and mighty ideas about art and design and window decorating—but I'm the one in charge here, whatever you may think, and your sucking around a certain person on the fifth floor won't help you a—"

"That - is - enough!" Shedding all her caution, Katherine strode across the room. Lister, a gleam of alarm in his eyes, scuttled backwards until he was against his desk. "Leslie is my friend," Katherine said deliberately. "But I've never used that in my work here and you know it. I've taken your insults and rudeness and offensive jokes and I've never told anyone about them. I've never told anyone how many window ideas you steal from other stores. I've never told anyone how many of *my* ideas you've used and claimed credit for. Because I needed this job—" My God, she thought; I still need this job. But it was too late; the resentments of the past months were a torrent that drowned out everything else.

"You are a mean, vulgar little man, always trying to prove how important you are by crushing someone. It's usually me, because I'm the closest, but you've made life miserable for everyone who's ever worked with you. You have no artistic sense; you don't even have the tiny bit of talent that nasty people need to make others tolerate them. You have a minuscule imagination and an inflated ability to copy from others and nothing else—"

"That's enough, that's enough, that's enough!" Lister pushed himself off the desk as if it were a diving board and scampered to the other side where he sat in his high-backed leather chair, glaring at Katherine. "Not another word! I knew you would go too far! And now you've done it; you've done it; you've gone too far! You were foisted on me and you've spent half your time on personal telephone calls and lunches—"

"That is a lie."

"Don't call me a liar! I knew from the first day you were a social climber and a troublemaker and a fraud and now you have the gall to criticize my artistic ability, which has *won prizes*—"

"The last one was for a window I designed."

He began to sputter. "You think you can hide behind McAlister— you think you know so much—you're an unreliable, stubborn, insubordinate bitch, and I want you out of here! This minute! I want you gone!"

Katherine opened her mouth but no words came. Frantically she tried to think of something to say, but all she could think of was pleading, and she could not bring herself to do it.

"Did you hear me? I want you gone!" he screeched as Katherine looked at him numbly. "Are you deaf?"

"You're firing me."

"Dear God, I have finally gotten through to her. Yes, yes, and yes. You are fired. Dismissed. Terminated. I have wasted enough energy on you; you are untrainable. Get out! Did you hear me? Out! Out! Out!"

The last thing Katherine heard as she walked blindly down the corridor was Gil's high voice, following her with furious syllables.

"*I want you gone!*"

CHAPTER 11

BY seven o'clock in the morning, the line stretched from the front door of the building down Mission Street and around the corner. The people in front of Katherine and behind her knew each other and as the line inched forward she listened as they compared experiences with the state unemployment system. It's only a bad dream, she tried to tell herself; but the hours passed, the morning fog gave way to sunlight and a mocking blue sky, her feet hurt, and by noon, when she had learned the names of all the people around her, she admitted it was real. She was out of work and almost out of money and she was standing in line to ask the state of California for help.

It had taken her a week to decide. The first thing she had done, the day after Lister's screech followed her out of Heath's, was call Leslie and tell her she had been fired. And Leslie had been furious. But also, distracted.

"Shit, that little fart... But, Katherine, you've gotten along with him up to now. Why all of a sudden—?"

"I don't know; I can't even remember how it started. He was screaming at me for something—worse than his usual, I guess—and I blew up and told him off. And he fired me. I suppose he's just been waiting for me to give him a chance to do it. He said he knew one day I'd go too far; he even accused me of trying to use my friendship with you."

"Did he."

"Leslie? What's wrong?"

"My job and my evasive brother. But let's talk about your—"

"No, wait." Katherine heard the note of alarm in Leslie's voice. "Why is he evasive?"

"How do I know? He's always trying to be cute, but this is something else. Every time I try to talk to him about his work, he scampers away. Literally."

"As if he's up to something."

"That's it. Katherine, I'm sorry about Gil; what do you want me to do? I'll give you a reference—and call some people in other stores—"

"What about Heath's? Aren't there any other jobs open? I'd do anything, Leslie."

"There isn't a thing. Damn, we just filled a job in accounting."

"Well, I don't know bookkeeping anyway."

"Listen, can I call you back? I'm up to my eyebrows in problems over here; if you can give me a day or two—"

"Leslie," Katherine said. "You don't think Bruce is a criminal."

"I'd rather not. But when I look at the evidence—"

"Real evidence? Solid? He can't be a criminal, Leslie; Jennifer and Todd are crazy about him."

Leslie laughed. "We'll put them on the witness stand. No, it's not solid. But it's pretty damning."

"But if you believe in him . . . You did believe in him, didn't you? When you hired him?"

"And even after. Until this business started."

"But why should that change your mind? You must have had good reasons for trusting him; were you wrong or did he change?"

There was a pause. "Neither. He just got evasive."

"But Bruce is like that a lot of the time, isn't he?"

After another pause, Leslie said, "He is indeed."

"Well, if you know that, and if you don't think you were wrong when you hired him, I think you shouldn't worry about him."

"Be the loyal and trusting big sister?"

"What's wrong with loyalty and trust?"

Again they were silent, both of them thinking about what Katherine had said. "Nothing's wrong," Leslie said at last. "Except my head. You're wonderful and I should have talked to you weeks ago. Now listen, lady, we have to find you a job."

"Let me try on my own; you've got enough on your mind. I'll take you up on the reference, though. I won't get anything from Gil."

"Nothing you'd want to use. I'll make some phone calls, Katherine, and get back to you in a few days. Let me know if you find something."

And so, feeling as if she were back in Vancouver, Katherine began reading want ads.

"Inventory clerk," she told Tobias on the telephone a few nights later. "The only office skill I've learned. I applied at a company in Oakland; they'll let me know tomorrow."

"Long hours and low pay," he said. "When will you work on your jewelry?"

"At night. I did it before."

"Yes indeed. And if you fail again that would be your excuse."

"Tobias!"

"'God loves to help him who strives to help himself.'"

"Oh, Tobias, don't quote things at me. If that's why you called—"

"No, no, my dear. I merely point out that as early as 500 B.C. Aeschylus was saying that we have a duty to help ourselves. Now tell me: when have you ever put a total effort into your work?"

"You might remember that I have to earn a living."

"I haven't forgotten it. Victoria and I have been discussing a fund for you and the children while you complete the order for Mettler; it would pay your bills and buy whatever materials you need. We would deposit it directly in—"

"Tobias."

"My dear?"

"I wish I could—" The temptation was so strong Katherine could almost taste the freedom he offered. But how much freedom did she have if she was always dependent on others, always being grateful? Leslie had found her a job, the Haywards had given her tools, Derek had given her gold. When was she going to stop taking handouts? "—but I can't. I appreciate it, I love you for offering, but I can't do it."

But Tobias' challenge to put all her efforts into her work stayed with her. He was right, of course; she never had. Other things had always come first. But how else did anyone succeed, except by working full-time, overtime, whatever was necessary?

I could give it a few months, she thought. And that was how she found herself in the unemployment line.

It still stretched behind her as she reached the building after waiting six hours. And then she discovered it was only the beginning.

"Fill out the form on top," a harried young woman recited, handing Katherine a packet. "Turn it in to any one of us for orientation. Next?"

When Katherine returned the filled-out form, another harried young woman skimmed it. "Looks OK," she said. "Earned more than nine hundred dollars in the last fifty-two weeks... name and address of last employer... you didn't quit; you were fired... well, here's what you should know." She rattled off four regulations requiring Katherine to look for work and to report any income during the time she was receiving unemployment. "Any questions, read the booklet in that packet you got. It's all there. Now you'll need an appointment in two weeks..." She turned the pages of a calendar.

"*Two weeks?*" Katherine repeated.

"This goes to Sacramento," the young woman said, writing Katherine's name on a folder. "Computer there checks your salary information and to see if you were fired because of misconduct. Takes a couple of weeks, so we'll give you an appointment—"

"Misconduct." *Unreliable*, Lister had said. *Insubordinate*. "What kind of misconduct?"

"I don't know; they have a list."

"If that was the reason... if someone is fired for misconduct—"

"Not eligible," said the young woman. "Usually. Might depend on the circumstances. Let's give you an appointment. April 27. Two weeks from today. They'll figure your eligibility then, and how much you get. You ought to start getting checks a couple of weeks after that."

A month from now, Katherine thought, writing down the date. If someone doesn't decide I've been guilty of misconduct.

And that was when the lure of Craig's money—all of it—became too strong to ignore.

"Well, why not?" agreed Tobias, cutting another piece of chocolate cake and lifting it precariously to his plate. "If he didn't want you to use it, he wouldn't be sending it."

"But I didn't want to use it for myself, until we were together. It isn't *money* I want to share with him."

"Yes. Perfectly sensible. But now?"

"Now I'll use it until I know I can earn my living in jewelry... or get another job."

He tilted his head quizzically. He had invited himself to Sunday dinner, bringing steaks and artichokes, and Katherine had made dessert. It was raining and the two of them sat at the kitchen table while Jennifer and Todd watched a television program in the living room. A regular family, Katherine thought. And in a way it was, because she could not think of any other man she would rather be with at that moment than Tobias, smiling at her, his white beard wagging. "And why will you use it now?" he asked.

"Because I owe it to Jennifer and Todd. They were terrified when I told them I'd lost my job; I could just see them thinking: first Dad, then Mom; who's left to take care of us? I had no right to talk to Gil that way as long as I'm responsible for them. Do you know, I don't even have medical insurance now? It went with my job. I have to buy some tomorrow morning and I can't afford it without Craig's money. Don't you see? I had no right to put us in this position." She shifted uncomfortably in her chair. "I think about Craig all the time. He must have felt this way when he began taking money from his company. There we were, the three of us, depending on him to bring home a big check every couple of weeks—so somehow he had to bring it home. I never realized how vulnerable people are when others are dependent on them." She gave a small laugh and got up to refill their coffee cups. "I don't much like it."

"Being responsible for Jennifer and Todd?"

"Being vulnerable."

"The same thing. Wonderful cake; should I have a third piece? No." Sadly he pushed away his plate. "I can still hear—after seventy years!—my first-grade classmates laughing at my waddle in the gymnasium. Even after I thinned out, their laughter stayed with me and all my life it has forced me to refuse third helpings of chocolate cake. How the past does haunt us! Yes, of course Craig hated vulnerability. He hated being responsible for making Victoria and his parents happy by living up to their expectations: triumphant long-distance runner, all-A student, dutiful son and grandson... Well! Who wouldn't hate it? The only one he seemed happy to be responsible for was Jennifer, because she wanted only affection and companionship and gave as much as she got. Except for Ross, I think she was Craig's only friend. You should have seen those two race a sailboat! Ross sometimes went along, watching and taking lessons, and he said they were the greatest team on the water. But all of that was certainly a mixed blessing."

Katherine watched Tobias' face change as he thought back. His beard had stopped fluttering and the lines around his mouth had deepened. "Why?" she asked.

"Because when Jennifer took up with Derek it wasn't only Ann and Jason who were upset; Craig was nearly out of his mind. What a stew they all made!"

"Jennifer and Derek?"

Tobias gave her a quick look. "That's right, you didn't know. But you should; it's part of our history. The one you were going to help me research, remember?"

"What does that mean—Jennifer took up with Derek?"

"Do you know, I'm really not sure. I was living in Boston and everything came to me secondhand. Victoria said that Ann said a seventeen-year-old girl should go out with boys her own age, but Derek was only twenty-one, so it was probably Derek, not his age, she was unhappy about. Even then, you see, Derek was a . . . forceful person. He certainly could terrify me when he fixed me with one of those looks I could feel in my toes. But then I grew my beard, and it seemed to give me a magic power to resist both his scorn and his charm. Or perhaps it was staying away for four years. The next time I came back was for Jennifer's funeral. She, poor child, had no magic powers. Victoria says she adored Derek. Actually, I think I'll have one more small piece of cake . . . Will you join me?"

"What? Oh. No thank you. Did Derek adore her?"

"I doubt it, but I wasn't privy to his thoughts or emotions, nor was anyone else. And if Jennifer was, she told no one. But, according to Victoria, her schoolwork had slipped badly and two or three months before graduation Jason and Ann forbade her to see Derek again. Always a mistake, I think. In years of teaching, I've learned that direct orders often cause mysterious chemical changes in youngsters that make them totally deaf in the presence of adults. Which is exactly what happened to Jennifer. She went right on seeing Derek, pretending to be with her girl friends at night and on weekends. Of course Jason and Ann found out and went to Curt, who told Derek he thought they should break it off. So Derek became deaf. It never fails."

"Derek refused—"

"Ignored them all. Girls right and left calling him up—handsome fellow, whatever you think of him—but he wanted Jennifer. And she was a lovely little thing, so alive and laughing. I've often wondered whether that quarrel on the boat between Derek and Craig was about Jennifer. Ross says he didn't hear it and Derek becomes deaf when I ask him."

"It was about a building they were working on."

"Is that so? Did Derek tell you that?" She nodded. "Well, I shall ask you to tell me all about it. Still, a researcher looks for the story beneath the story. I think there was more to it. Don't you?"

"I don't know. The more I hear about your family, the less I know."

"Or like?"

Her chin in her hand, she studied his face. A small chocolate crumb was caught in his white beard. She reached over to remove it. "I like you," she said.

·   ·   ·

"Close the door," Leslie told Bruce as he came in. She pushed a button on her intercom. "No calls, please." Taking a file folder from her desk drawer, she held it out to him. "Can you explain this?"

"Golly gosh gee, sis," he said, taking it from her. "What's so serious you can't even give your loving bro a kiss?" But, flipping through the papers in the folder, he scowled. "How the hell did you get this?"

"Is it yours?"

"Sure but it was in my desk—how the hell—?"

"What's inside it?"

"Is this an inquisition, sis—do I get a lawyer or what?"

"Don't be funny, Bruce. What are those papers?"

"Notes I made, I told you I had an idea—remember?—about how somebody could use the computer to rip off the store and I was going to write a program to see how it might be done, and these are my notes for it, to see if maybe for instance you could steal hot-selling stuff and change figures in the computer for just that stuff without leaving a record—are you following me?—I am of course a genius for thinking of it—"

"You are a goddamn fool. Are you saying you don't know we've suspected that something like that has been going on for months?"

Stunned into rare silence, Bruce stared at his sister. "Those spot inventories!" he cried at last. "Somebody is doing it? Ripping off the store?"

"Keep your voice down, damn it. Don't you understand what it means that a blueprint for stealing was found in your desk?"

"Now wait—sis, I swear in thirty extinct languages I did not know about any stealing going on and I didn't write a program to do it; I only made notes for a program—and I told you I was going to do it—*last summer!*"

She looked at him steadily. "I don't believe you."

"For Christ's sake, my own sis—!"

"Look: you asked me to get you a job in Data Processing and then you told me you were investigating the new system—and God help me, I encouraged you—to see if it could be used to rip off the store; to close any loopholes, *you said.* In less than a year, profits are down; an audit of sales records gives figures that don't match the computer sales figures; you just said you had the idea of changing figures without leaving a record; and handwritten notes for doing it are found in your desk. Why should I believe you?"

"Search me, it sounds pretty devilish—how about the fact that your brother tells you on his honor it ain't so? Damn it, sis, listen, I have to my great shock discovered that after my wild youth I really like working— *I like working here,* I wouldn't steal a fucking pair of socks because I don't want to get fired, and even if I did why why *why* would I leave the damn notes in my desk for someone to find?"

"I don't know." Leslie sighed, watching his agitated pacing. "Why were you trying to write your own program?"

"Sis, what is the matter with you, *I wanted to see if it could be done*, then I could write a program to *prevent* it!"

"You didn't write one that could be used?"

"Sis! I swear on the great goddess Mary Jane I didn't—"

"Well, who else could do it?"

"Only a few people in Data—" He cocked his head, thinking, then hitched up his pants. "Time for a little detective work."

"No. Bruce, I'm sorry, but I'm going to put you on temporary leave of absence. And it has to be without pay."

"What the hell—!"

"Listen to me. You are in trouble around here. Your boss took these notes to my boss and by now everyone thinks you're part of some theft ring. So for a while you're out."

"Hey, now—"

"*No arguments!* I'm doing the best I can, but I've got my own problems and I can't take much more from you. You disguise your fantastic brain under a lot of bullshit, you drive me crazy, and I want you out of here while I do what I can to protect both of us. Why don't you go to San Francisco State, take some computer courses, maybe get a degree?"

"I know more than they do."

"Probably true. Then take other courses. Or find another job. Just keep out of trouble."

"If I'm in so much trouble, how come the police aren't hauling me off in handcuffs?"

"Because we're keeping it quiet while we try to solve it. And I'm counting on you not to talk. That's part of the deal. You don't come back if I find out you've been talking."

"Why would I talk, I'd be arrested, Christ, my first decent job and this has to happen, shows what you get for being a good boy."

"What you get for being a good boy is a sister who will help you and keep your job waiting for you. Go on now, I have work to do. Take care of yourself. Come to dinner on Sunday."

He pushed out his lower lip and squinted at her. His shoulders drooped. "You're the boss, sis, see you Sunday."

Leslie watched him drag himself through the door. The first time, she thought, that I've violated a direct order from the president of the store. And an executive committee already trying to break my contract and kick me out. I think I need a lawyer. I think Bruce and I both need a lawyer. She debated. Katherine, she thought. Katherine knows one of the top lawyers in the city. He's practically a member of the Hayward family. She turned and picked up the telephone.

Crumpled papers filled the wastebasket; the worktable was piled with notes, crossed-out drawings, string, and bent and broken wire. Nothing was finished. Nothing, Katherine thought in frustration, was even begun. In the three weeks since Tobias challenged her to work full-time, she had not created one design good enough to turn into a piece of jewelry. She was blocked. Trying to think of curves and whorls and angles, of gold and silver and precious stones, she relived instead the cumulative shocks of Mettler's cool response, Lister's fury, and the sense of defeat that descended on her the first time she used Craig's money and knew she hadn't come so far after all: she still wasn't making it on her own.

When Derek called, she was grateful for a reason to get up from her worktable. "Friday night," he said. "I have to make an appearance at a benefit at Ghirardelli Square. We don't have to stay long; there's a new jazz trio at—"

"Derek, I'm sorry, but I'm busy Friday night."

"Busy?"

Annoyed, she said, "I do have a life when I'm not with you."

"I apologize," he said smoothly. "But there are times when I expect you to be available. Friday night is one of them."

"I'm sorry; I can't change my plans."

I expect you to be available. Meaning, she owed him something in return for his tolerating her abstinence. But abstinence was a problem for both of them; he wasn't the only one who wanted to go to bed. Katherine had thought it would get easier once she made up her mind, but it didn't: the more courteous and distant he was, the more her hungers gnawed her.

But whenever she wavered, something would happen to remind her of the other side of Derek: his cutting comments and contempt for others; his cold assumption that in some way she was his possession and owed him her availability in exchange for his tolerance and letting her into his glamorous life where she could meet the women who might someday buy her jewelry. And there was Tobias' story about Jennifer. Katherine had been trying to bring it up since she heard it, but lately Derek had refused to talk about the accident at all, abruptly changing the subject whenever she mentioned it.

She was pulled too many ways by Derek, and it was a relief to refuse him for Friday night, even if it meant missing a benefit where she probably would see many of the women she was beginning to know by name. But, as it happened, she spent that evening at Ghirardelli Square, after all. "I didn't plan this," Leslie said as they arrived and saw the mass of people in front of them. "But with things as they are, when my president tells me to represent the store, I can't refuse."

As they struggled through the crowd to an elevator and then to the doorway of the Mandarin, Katherine thought she had never seen the place so crowded. Once a chocolate and spice factory and a woolen mill, the red brick buildings had been renovated years before to a delightfully quirky ten-story maze of boutiques, theaters, and restaurants built around open squares, with small stairways and sudden corridors that made it seem endless and endlessly inventive. Always a tourist attraction, when it became the site of the May benefit for the Family Welfare League, its normal population was instantly quadrupled.

But the crowds and the noise receded as Katherine and Leslie were led through the Mandarin, past softly lit rose brick walls and silk tapestries to a table overlooking the bay. "Almost as private as a Chinese tomb," Leslie said with satisfaction.

Katherine, happy to be with Leslie, was happy even with the crowd; its electric vitality helped her forget that she had been feeling sorry for herself for much of the past month. "It's wonderful to be here. In fact, it's funny, but I would have been here anyway; Derek asked me to come with him. I don't suppose I'll see him in this crowd."

A waiter poured their wine and in the lull Leslie asked, a little too casually, "Did you talk to your friend?"

"He said he'd meet us here. I didn't tell him very much."

"Thank you. Isn't it odd: Heath's has a dozen lawyers, but when I need one for myself I come to you for help."

"I think Claude is supposed to be very good."

"Good? He's one of the best. Very posh firm, very solid."

"But if you knew that, why didn't you call him?"

"I'm small potatoes compared to his other clients."

Katherine shook her head, watching the waiter arrange skewers of marinated meat on a small tabletop stove. "If you're fighting Heath's executive board to keep your job, that's not small potatoes."

"The point is, he'd rather have Heath's as his client than Leslie McAlister."

"He didn't refuse when I asked him to meet you."

Leslie lifted her glass. "To better times. I've seen him at parties, you know. Tall, handsome, silver hair, blue eyes. He collects nubile maidens."

"He what?"

"He's one of those fiftyish bachelors who won't look at anyone but young lovelies in their twenties. To the collective despair of those of us who are single and approaching forty."

"I didn't know that about him."

"Not important. It's my neck I care about, not his sex life."

There was a quaver in her voice that Katherine had never heard before. Ever since she drove to San Francisco in her rented truck, Leslie's positive, forceful presence had encouraged and cheered her; she had been the friend Katherine could cling to and the successful woman she could look up to because she had everything Katherine did not have: beauty, confidence, independence, a future she was sure of. But now a tremor ran through Leslie's voice and Katherine recognized the same uncertainty that had trailed through her own voice for months. "Tell me about it," she urged, and realized they had traded places: she was the one offering support.

"The pack is closing in," Leslie said, trying to keep her voice light. "And I've probably given them the last excuse they need to kick me out—though they haven't discovered it yet."

"What did you do?"

"It's what I didn't do. In the last few days so many arrows started pointing at Bruce for manipulating our inventory programs that his big sister was ordered to fire him on the spot. Hello."

She was looking at Claude, who had materialized in the dim light beside their table.

Katherine stood and kissed his cheek, feeling like a magician who conjures people from thin air. She barely knew Claude; she had not seen him in months; but because Leslie asked, it had been easy to make a telephone call. For the first time since Craig disappeared, Katherine was helping someone else instead of worrying about herself. She smiled quietly. She hadn't realized what a burden she'd been to herself until she forgot herself for a few minutes.

Claude was looking from her to Leslie and she saw the two of them through his eyes: red-haired Leslie, green-eyed, sophisticated, her beauty as polished as a fine gem despite faint curved lines, like parentheses, on either side of her mouth and a jaw that jutted slightly, especially when she talked about Heath's; and Katherine, dark-haired, hazel-eyed, her head high, wearing a soft wine-colored dress from a designer resale shop—in almost no way resembling the woman Claude had seen in June at Victoria's and in October when he bought her a drink and tried to find out what she was up to. She smiled again and said, "I'm so glad you're here. This is Leslie McAlister. Claude Fleming. Have you eaten? We haven't ordered yet."

"I haven't eaten." Claude shook hands with Leslie as he sat down. "I heard the last few words. You were ordered to fire your brother from his job. I gather you didn't."

Leslie's eyebrows shot up—exactly like Bruce's, Katherine thought. "Why do you gather that?"

"Katherine told me you need a lawyer because you think an effort is being made to oust you from a job for which you have a three-year contract. Those trying to oust you must think you've given them a reason. Such as disobeying an order. Did you fire your brother?"

"No. I couldn't do it. He's never had such a good job and he was doing so well—I've never seen him so happy with himself. He'd tried everything else—drugs and as much booze as he could drown himself in and bumming around Europe and Asia, but nothing made him content with himself. Until he discovered computers."

"Predictability," said Claude. "Logical, reliable, programable. Correctible. Much better than drugs and booze."

Leslie looked at him with interest. "That's impressive, to understand that about a kid in his twenties."

He chuckled. "I know something about people in their twenties."

"Oh, yes," Leslie said coldly. She tilted the wine bottle. "We need another. Or would you rather we just talked about my problem so you can leave? I'm sure you have other plans for the evening."

"I have no other plans." He stopped a passing waiter and ordered another bottle. "You care for your brother very much."

"True. He's related to me."

"Simple family obligation? It sounded to me like love."

She turned the stem of her wine glass in her fingers. "Well, it is. Bruce is very special to me. We had a family once, but as soon as we got to voting age our parents and cousins and uncles scattered around the planet, doing this and that. Bruce, like a fool, went looking for them. The ones he found were very busy, so finally he came back, looking like he'd met up with a gang and lost. Not that our busy family beat him up; they just ignored him to a pulp. So he came to me and it happened to be a . . . difficult time in my personal life and I wasn't at all busy. I gave him a bed to sleep in and an ear to listen to him and a kiss when he started crying. We took to each other."

"You're older than he."

"Oh, yes." Leslie gave a short laugh. "Ten years older than his twenty-six."

Claude nodded. "And you gave him a home."

"No. He has his place; I have mine. What I give him is a door that's always open, and someone to hang on to when he needs it. We give those to each other."

Quietly, Claude repeated. "A door that's always open. Not easy to find. What did you do," he asked, "if you didn't fire him?"

"Put him on temporary leave of absence without pay. I didn't tell him I was supposed to fire him; I just told him to get out until he heard from me again."

"That's all you told him?"

"I told him to come to dinner on Sunday."

They laughed together. Katherine wondered if she had become invisible. "I'm very hungry," she said mildly. Without hesitation, Claude centered himself between the two women and made himself their host, conferring with them on the menu, beckoning a waiter, and, all through the meal, punctiliously including both Katherine and Leslie in his conversation. It was so pleasant that Katherine was sorry when they were finished and Leslie said she had to leave. "I've been assigned to accept an award for Heath's, for being the top donor of the past year. I think a most boring ceremony awaits me. If you two would like to wait here..."

"No," Katherine said.

Claude pushed back his chair. "We haven't finished the business part of the evening. Unless you've changed your mind about retaining me as your attorney."

"I would be delighted to retain you as my attorney."

"Then we still have a great deal to discuss. Perhaps after your ceremony? There's a club not far from here..."

Walking from the restaurant and down the stairway, Katherine decided not to go with them. She shouldn't, anyway; she wasn't involved in their discussion. Suddenly she felt depressed, and it deepened as they merged with the crowd. Everyone was part of a couple. The whole world was a huge Noah's ark. She'd been part of a couple, too, but the other half had run off—evidently because she wasn't good enough for him to ask her help in solving his problems and keeping their marriage together. Keeping their family together.

I'll go home and cry, she thought. I haven't done that for a long time.

"My, my," Leslie said as they reached the ground floor. "That's a flashy lady Derek found to take your place tonight."

Katherine followed her look in time to see Melanie put her arm through Derek's and whisper in his ear.

Claude made a sound between a cough and a snort. But his voice was level. "I suppose Ross was too busy with his new plaza. Good of Derek to accompany his sister-in-law."

"The protective family lawyer," said Katherine, as much to her own surprise as to Claude's. "Leslie, we should get to your ceremony."

But Derek had seen her and with a quick word to Melanie, who turned a frozen face to Katherine, he made his way toward them through the crowd. "Claude," he said as they shook hands. Leslie forced him to shake hers by holding it out and waiting. "Leslie... Katherine..." He glanced from one to the other as if trying to decide which one was Claude's companion. "A pleasant surprise."

"An understatement," Leslie murmured, the words almost lost in the noise of the crowd.

Claude heard. He smiled and took her arm. "The sooner you get that award, the sooner we can escape these crowds. Katherine?" He offered her his other arm.

Katherine was looking at Derek, her thoughts racing.

Derek and Melanie.

Derek and Katherine.

Derek and Jennifer.

"Katherine?" Claude repeated.

"If you could wait," Derek said to her.

She nodded. "Do you mind, Leslie? I'll catch up."

"Lovely dinner," Leslie said, kissing her cheek. "Thank you."

"It was your dinner. I should be thanking you."

"You know what I mean. See you soon."

Katherine watched them disappear in the throng, then turned back to Derek. "Was there something special you wanted?"

"Don't talk to me that way." He put his arm around her waist and began to lead her toward a nearby coffee house.

"Derek, you can't—Melanie is—" She looked, but Melanie was gone. "Where is she?"

"I assume she's gone home or found other friends. I told her I wanted to talk to you. She's very understanding."

That is a joke, Katherine thought as Derek moved ahead to talk to the hostess. Somehow, in the crowded room, an empty table appeared. He held her chair. "Was there something special *you* wanted?"

"Yes. I want to ask you—"

"Wait." He ordered cappuccino for both of them and sat back. "You look very lovely. How curious, that we are together here after all. As soon as we drink our coffee, which will give us time to adjust to our sudden good fortune, I shall introduce you to some friends upstairs who can be very useful to you." He contemplated her. "What *is* the matter?"

"I was wondering... about Melanie—"

"Here you are now," the waitress said gaily. She set mugs of the foaming coffee before them, with spoons and paper napkins.

"Melanie," Derek said flatly. "What would you want to know about Melanie?"

"Not only Melanie. Jennifer, too. Jennifer and Melanie—and me. I wondered why—when there are so many women in the world—you've gotten involved with the three who are closest to your brother and your cousin."

Not a muscle moved in his face or his body as he looked at Katherine through the steam curling up from their coffees. Then she saw the taut vein in his neck. "You've gone somewhat beyond your territory, my dear," he said at last. His voice was light, almost pleasant. "You know very little about us, or, indeed, about anything, you've been Craig's sheltered little weed for so long. You seem to think that because you've learned to look like a flower you understand the garden. You have neither the knowledge nor the authority to speak about the things of the world. They are far beyond your comprehension." He drank from his mug. "I've been patient with you; the smallest reward you could give me would be to understand that it is better to remain silent than to demonstrate that you are a fool."

His light voice, almost a monotone, was a thin blade, cutting through the noise and laughter at the crowded tables, sliding coldly into Katherine. Her breath came faster. She remembered the desire that had eaten at her for so long and wondered at it. Surely it had been for someone else. "It doesn't help to call me a fool. That won't change the fact that you've been using me. You have been, haven't you, Derek? Because I'm married to Craig and fifteen years hasn't been long enough for you to stop hating him. And you don't like Ross either. I don't know why, but it doesn't matter. And Melanie is married to Ross. And Jennifer was Craig's favorite."

"Katherine." His face and voice had not changed, but the muscles in his neck were quivering ropes. "You are in a singularly poor position to talk about being used. For months you have used me as your guide into a world that otherwise would have been completely closed to you. You have used me for lessons in behavior and for satisfying your insatiable need for praise; as an escort to replace the husband who discarded you, and for sexual titillation without a sexual liaison. You're a good match for your husband; both of you run from responsibility."

Katherine's face burned. "You mean my responsibility was to pay for your services with sex."

He let out a long breath, relaxing the explosive pressure behind his rigid muscles. "This will stop. Now. I am not ready to end our curious affair—"

"But I am." Breathing rapidly, Katherine leaned forward. "I couldn't go on now. Because even though I did use you—you're right, of course; you've given me a great deal—but did I really take anything from you that you didn't want to give? You never said a specific coin was necessary to pay for what you did for me." Feeling ashamed, she held her head high. "How could I go on after this?"

"Are you asking for advice? Listen to me. You have grandiose ideas about making something of yourself, but you are no one in this city; you have nothing. The best thing for you is to go back to Vancouver, get some simple job that you can keep for more than a few months, and wait for your pathetic husband to crawl back into your lap, where he belongs and where you probably like him best."

Katherine looked at him in disbelief. "Is that a threat?"

"I never threaten." He picked up his mug and showed a flicker of surprise as he found it empty. "But if you were not a fool you would have learned something about power by now—in our family and in this city. That, too, was offered for your use; you had a choice between your husband's cowardice and the terms I might have offered if you'd been willing to be what I wanted. But you were afraid of that and threw it away."

"I didn't—" A wave of revulsion made her choke. She fumbled blindly in her purse to take out a five-dollar bill and put it on the table. "This is for my coffee." She stood, looking at him as if he were a small figure in a painting. "I won't try to pay for the food and drinks you've bought me since October; I paid for them in the last few minutes by listening to you insult me. I don't know anything about your kind of power because I don't care about it. I want a family, not a battlefield, and I wanted companionship from you, not a contest. If you do have power, that only proves to me that a man can be handsome and charming and powerful, and still, underneath, crude and vulgar. And that kind of man I don't want to see again."

She took a step back as his face darkened with fury, then turned, forcing her way through the crowd. Unexpectedly, violently, she began to tremble, and she let herself be carried along with the brightly colored mass of people to an arch across the square, and through it, to the street. It was quieter there, almost peaceful. It's all right, she said to herself. It's all right. Everything is all right.

And as a cab came to a stop in response to her raised arm, she knew that, in fact, everything *was* all right. Once before, after she decided she would not sleep with Derek, she'd felt as if a burden had been lifted from her. Now another was gone. She did not want him; she did not need him. She was free.

CHAPTER 12

ROSS swiveled his chair to look through the window behind him. His gaze took in the steady stream of traffic on the Embarcadero, and beyond it the city's bustling piers, stretching like thin fingers into the choppy, deep blue bay. Two years earlier, when he was expanding his company to work on BayBridge Plaza, he had moved into this building, a former icehouse converted to bright office suites with interior brick walls and tall windows reaching exposed-beam ceilings. He had furnished his own office in rosewood and leather, with patterned American Indian rugs on the floor. No outside sounds breached the thick walls, and in the silence Ross let himself daydream about Paris.

"Work with me," Jacques had urged earlier, on the telephone. In college he and Ross had shared an apartment; since then, across the thousands of miles between them, they had shared ideas about work, wives, their countries, and those thoughts often expressed more easily with someone far away. Now Jacques Duvain, believer in the new and modern, was in the midst of renovating a forty-room Parisian townhouse built in 1605, converting it to four apartments of ten rooms each. "You always preach to me—'Keep the past; as much as possible, keep the past.' Here is the past and I am being paid to keep it. Work with me on the Place des Vosges; be my consultant."

"I know nothing about renovating seventeenth-century French townhouses," Ross had said.

"And I," Jacques promptly replied, "know little of new American renovation techniques. We will learn from each other. Besides, is this not a perfect way to pry my friend from his American drafting table to visit with me?"

Place des Vosges. Ross pictured in his mind the magnificent square of brick and plaster townhouses surrounding a park, once the Paris residences of the royal court, lately—having survived almost four hundred years of use and misuse—being bought by investors for renovation as condominiums, shops, and restaurants. On his last trip to Paris, two years earlier, Ross had been given a tour of the square by Jacques, and he remembered still the elegant dimensions of the rooms, the grandeur of curving stairways, carved moldings and ceilings, and the intimacy of private courtyards hidden in the center of each of the houses.

He had wanted to go back, but work on BayBridge intervened. Over the two years, Jacques had sent him progress reports that in many ways matched the progress of BayBridge; now he was ready to make his detailed plans, and he wanted Ross to join him.

But I have two major projects already, Ross thought, brooding at the view from his window. BayBridge, which is just taking shape, and my marriage, which is losing whatever shape it had.

"Mrs. Hayward is here," his secretary said over the intercom. "Should I call the others to tell them the meeting will be late?"

Her words were carefully chosen. Ross knew, from past experience, they meant there was a storm on Melanie's face that probably could not be dealt with in the five minutes before his scheduled meeting. "Yes, do that," he said. "I'll let you know when we can get started. And tell Mrs. Hayward—"

But Melanie was already there, closing his office door as she walked in. With her ebony hair and tanned skin, wearing a white silk blouse and red suit cut geometrically to make her shoulders broader and her hips narrower, she looked like a drawing in a fashion magazine—even, Ross thought, to the cold, faintly defiant look with which she swept his office, just as models sweep the audience as they glide down the runway.

Melanie glided across the office to drop her purse and gloves on his desk. "I was shopping and had some extra time, so I decided to stop by and talk."

Flattering, he thought. But probably not true; she came expressly to talk, since we don't talk at home. Which means there's a crisis. He went to a credenza near a leather couch and chairs grouped beside the high windows. "Coffee?"

"You could offer me a martini."

"If I had it. The best I can do is coffee."

She shrugged and sat on the edge of the couch, drumming her fingernails on the glass coffee table. "Wilma tells me your Mr. Macklin is getting a divorce."

"He's not mine. I don't even know him well enough to be interested in his affairs." Ross handed her a cup and carried his own around the table to sit beside her. "Do you?"

"I'm interested in divorce."

"So you've told me. Wilma's stock in trade." He was playing for time; he knew she had not meant Wilma's gossip. "Was there something special you stopped by to talk about?"

With an exasperated clatter Melanie set her cup on the glass table. "Do you have to be difficult? Couldn't you once, just one goddamn time, be understanding? I'm not talking about Wilma; I'm talking about me. *I* am interested in divorce because *I* want a divorce. I've—"

"Just a minute. Wait." They had always stopped short of this point. "We've never talked about this; we never even talked about finding a way to—"

"What difference does it make? I've found somebody who's better for me than you, somebody who really cares about *me*, about what *I* want and how *I* feel and what's good for *me*. So I want a divorce. Right away."

"Someone else?" He hadn't heard any gossip; he'd never thought of that. "Who is it?"

"It doesn't matter. All that matters is that I've found someone who really cares about *me*, who pays attention to me and satisfies me—"

"Can you control your teenage tantrum?" Ross asked bitingly. "And use a few words besides *I* and *me*?"

"Damn you," she spat. "That's what you do every time. You *treat* me like a teenager—a baby—you make me feel *little*."

Instinctively Ross put out a hand. "I know. Melanie, I'm sorry; I know I—"

"I don't want your fucking apologies; it's too late for that! Don't you understand? I'm sick and tired of feeling like I'm not smart enough or grown up enough for you. I'm as grown up as you are, and I want somebody who'll treat me like that, somebody who knows how grown up I am—"

"Who is he?"

"Somebody special."

"*God damn it*, who the hell is he?"

"You can swear at me all you want; I'm not afraid of you. It's somebody wonderful who's going to take care of me and buy me presents and bring me breakfast in bed—"

"Melanie. I asked you who he is."

At the low steel of his voice, she took a quick look at his face. "Guy Walker."

"Guy Walker?"

"He's a very famous champion tennis player. He gives lessons at the club, but when he's on tour he wins trophies. He's going to marry me."

The words struck an odd chord. "What about you?" he asked. "Are you going to marry him?"

"Don't try to make me look silly. Of course I'm going to marry him."

It registered then. Ross sucked in his breath, feeling as if he had been punched in the stomach. He'd known how far apart they had moved; even Carrie and Jon knew it, watching, listening, moving through the house with delicate footsteps, as if afraid of making a noise that would bring the whole structure tumbling down. Already tumbled, Ross thought; the evidence had been there for a long time—the spaces, the quarrels that came up like thunderstorms and were as quickly spent, their silences, the way their eyes never quite met.

But he'd willfully ignored the signs, assuming that however bad it was, they would work it out; assuming that because it was familiar and pre-dictable, it would be easier to repair than to destroy.

Wrong. All the assumptions: wrong. Panic welled up, and he turned from Melanie, staring out the window. He remembered the day he'd moved here and first looked at this view. He was beginning BayBridge and was boundlessly confident: sure of his wife, his home, his profession. Idiot, he thought. Secure, satisfied—blind.

I miss knowing the boundaries of my days. Where had he heard that? In a moment it came to him: Katherine, at The Compass Rose. *I miss being sure of what will happen tomorrow and the day after. I miss knowing the boundaries of my days. None of it was true, nothing was certain, but it was so comforting to think it was...."*

I knew as little as she did, Ross thought.

"Are you listening?" Melanie demanded.

Frowning, he turned back to her. "I was thinking of something else."

"Something else! Something more important than your children?"

"What about the children?"

"I'm keeping them. How many times do I have to repeat it? They'll stay with me and you'll move out. I'm keeping the house. I don't want Carrie and Jon changing schools and doing all those upsetting things that make children hate divorce. We'll stay in our own house and everything will be the same for them."

"Except that their father will be gone."

"Well, yes. But the really important things won't change—their house and school and friends. And me of course. And they'll have Guy. Don't worry about them Ross; they'll be fine."

She said it with such earnestness, mixed with defiance, that Ross felt a flash of pity. But then he thought: what if she's right? What if they would be fine without him? His panic grew; spreading through him, cold and heavy.

Melanie was still talking. "—and visitation rights, because I suppose they'll want to see you, once in a while. Our lawyers can settle that—"

Visitation rights? A schedule for telling your kids you love them? How do lawyers work that out? He felt sick—and then the coldness inside him froze all feeling. Facing Melanie, he felt nothing. "We'll settle it now, between us. I'll want them every weekend, one night a week for dinner, and at school holidays. Thanksgiving, Christmas, spring vacation, long weekends, and of course all summer—"

"Are you crazy? They can't always be running off to stay with you! How can we make a new family if we're not together at Thanksgiving and Christmas? You can have them—my lawyer said if you made a fuss you could have them every other weekend—if you really want them that often—and a week in the summer . . . well, maybe two weeks, but no more because of camp. And you'll pay for camp; that's on a list—my lawyer has it—things you'll take care of, alimony and child support and the dentist and all those things. Ask my lawyer; he'll show it to you; here's his card. See him tomorrow, Ross, or get your own lawyer to call him; don't wait, because Guy's impatient—"

"To get his little family started."

She shot him a look. "Don't use that tone of voice with me."

"You've forfeited the right to tell me what tone to use." What emotions had broken through that cold barrier to make his hands tremble? Anger? Pain? He stood and walked to his desk, his back to Melanie. "You'd better leave."

"Well, I guess I've said what I had to say." There was a pause. "Did you think you'd come home tonight?"

"I hadn't thought about it."

"Well, you'd better not try. I've had the locks changed."

He whipped around. "Change them back. Or give me a new key. That is my house and I haven't moved out."

"I'll do what I want! It's in both our names!"

"Until I move out, I have the right to enter that house and use it and I advise you not to try to stop me. Give me the key." She wavered. "I won't rape you," he said, his voice grating.

She flushed. "I didn't think you would. I just don't want you around! But if you'll call first—"

"I'll be damned if I will; *that is my house*. Give me the key!" When she still hesitated, he said evenly, "I don't think you'd want your friends to hear that your husband called the Tiburon police to witness him breaking into his own house."

"God damn you to hell," she said, and held out a key.

He crossed the room to take it, clenching it to hide the trembling of his hands. "I'll pack when Carrie and Jon aren't home. Probably tomorrow while they're at school." *To go where?* He held open the door. "One more thing. I'm not leaving them. I intend to be with them far more often than you and your lawyer think." *Where? Doing what?* "You'll have to organize your new family around my schedule. Remember that. I'll make you spend the next five years in court if you try to keep those children from me."

"You bastard. You just want to ruin my marriage to Guy the way you ruined ours." She ducked, as if expecting a blow, and scurried out.

Ross watched her stumble and catch herself. Tripped, he thought, by the wreck of our marriage. He wondered if she was right: that he could have prevented the destruction if he'd been different—better, kinder, more patient...

"—the meeting?" his secretary was asking.

He rubbed the back of his neck. "I had a reason for scheduling it today. Do you remember what it was?"

"We couldn't get everyone together for at least another two weeks."

He nodded, prodding his thoughts like a shepherd herding reluctant sheep. "We'd better have it then. But give me half an hour. I have to pick up some pieces, and put myself together."

Across the bay from San Francisco, the houses in the Berkeley Hills climb so steeply they look over the roofs of those below, offering a vista stretching as far south as San Jose. The house Ross rented stepped down from the front entrance hall, past two airy bedrooms to a long living-dining room and a square cedar deck screened by trees and bushes but still giving a clear view of the Golden Gate and San Francisco–Oakland Bay bridges, the San Francisco skyline, and the softly rounded hills of Tiburon where, only five miles away, his wife entertained her tennis-playing lover.

Carrie and Jon sniffed suspiciously the first time they explored his new home. "It doesn't look *anything* like our house," Carrie declared. "Was this the best you could find?"

"What's wrong with it?" Ross asked mildly, hiding the panic that still gripped him when he let down his guard—*What if they refuse to come here? Lawyers can forge agreements but who can make my children want to be with me?* "I thought it felt like a home."

Slowly, Carrie turned in place, her head tilted, considering the heavy, worn furniture in half a dozen different fabrics and colors, with soft cushions that retained the shape of the last person to sit in them. No interior decorator had ever set foot in these rooms; the professor's family had simply collected furniture over the years, never throwing anything out; and Ross knew, seeing it through Carrie's critical gaze—exactly like Melanie's—that no place was more unlike the perfectly modulated velvet and silk rooms of his Tiburon home.

But, unlike Melanie, who would have scornfully dismissed it, Carrie began to smile. "It's not bad," she conceded. "It's kind of friendly. Of course," she added hastily, not wanting to betray her mother. "It's not as beautiful as home. But it's... *comfortable*. Like you could jump on the furniture."

"Dad!" shouted Jon from the deck. "They've got a jacuzzi!"

"*We've* got a jacuzzi," Ross said as he and Carrie joined him. "Thanks to the professor."

"But it's his, isn't it? You didn't buy it."

"Until he gets back, a year from now, it's ours."

"Yours," muttered Jon, becoming very busy with the controls. "We're only visitors."

"Jon." Ross sat on the edge of the round tub and turned his son to face him. "This is your house as much as mine. You'll be spending a lot of time here; we'll all be here, together."

"But we don't *live* here." Jon turned red, then blurted, "Dad, we were wondering if maybe you'd come back."

A deep ache filled Ross's lungs. "I can't do that, Jon. When a marriage dies, there's no way to bring it back to life."

"Why did it have to die?" Carrie demanded. "It used to be fine. Didn't it?"

"We thought so. But then something made us go in different directions. We started having separate ideas and thoughts, even separate feelings and dreams about the future. As if—" He paused. "If each of you tied the end of a cord around your waist, and began to walk away from each other, the cord would stretch tighter and tighter, and if you kept on walking it couldn't take the stress. It would fray and then snap. That's what happened to our marriage."

Carrie chewed the end of a blond curl. "You could tie a knot in the cord."

"Some people try." Ross put an arm around her shoulders. "And sometimes it works. But you have to move closer together to do it. And if you've been too far apart, with too many different thoughts, the chances are you'd start straining against the cord again and the knot wouldn't hold."

"You shouldn't pull apart in the first place," Jon muttered.

"You're right." Ross drew his son to him and he and his children leaned against each other. "I don't know why we did. When we were married, and the two of you were born, I thought my life had a shape, like a house I'd designed, with rooms for the people I loved and the work I loved, and places for friends and holidays and sailing... I was so excited with my imaginary house, because everyone and everything that was dear to me was in it. And I think your mother felt the same way."

"You're not sure?" Carrie asked.

"I'm pretty sure she was at first. Later—I don't know exactly when— she began worrying about all the things she might be missing. But I think for the first few years she was happy. I know I was." The three of them were silent, holding each other. "But then we went in different directions and the cord between us snapped. And we've gone too far to mend it; you mustn't wait for that to happen. The only good thing left from our marriage is you, and how much we love you."

"Love," snorted Jon.

Ross tightened his arms around them. "That's what we've got. We're held together by cords, too, the strongest I've ever seen. And if we spend lots of time together, they'll never get frayed; they'll never come close to snapping. I promise that."

Carrie turned and flung both arms around his neck. Ross tried to keep his voice firm. "That's why this is your home, too," he said. "You'll have a key for when you're staying here, and you can be here whenever you want."

Jon shook his head. "Mother said—" He stopped.

"What did she say?"

"Never mind."

"You started to tell me."

"Never mind."

"I'd like to know, Jon."

"It's not important."

"It might be."

Stubbornly, Jon shook his head and Ross sighed, seeing his son begin to build a wall between two houses, two families, two loyalties. "Maybe someday you'll tell me. In the meantime, *I'm* going to call this our home, and I hope one of these days you will, too." He looked over Jon's head, past the pines in his yard, at the distant silhouette of Mount Tamalpais rising above the misty Tiburon hills. The air was fragrant with roses and narcissus; the flamboyant beauty of cymbidiums and flowering plum covered the bushes beside the deck. A stairway led to a lower garden where a neglected hedge of thorny raspberry bushes grew. Deep foghorns blasted through the Saturday morning quiet; a dog barked; someone was practicing piano scales. Our home, Ross thought. And tears filled his eyes.

His days became fragmented, like shards of a broken bowl. In his office he worked with the BayBridge contractor, going over the final plans, and with his staff on proposals for new projects. In his lawyer's office, meeting with Melanie's lawyer, he laboriously negotiated downward her demand for ten thousand dollars a month alimony and child support, worked out a schedule for visiting his children, and arranged to have his huge collection of books and recordings packed and shipped from Tiburon to Berkeley, leaving Melanie the house and everything else in it.

At night he sat in his new living room, with piles of work he had brought home and lists of people and companies to whom his secretary would send change-of-address cards. But he spent most of the time trying to think logically.

What the hell was wrong with him? He hadn't had a real marriage in years; he didn't miss the glossy magazine atmosphere of the home Melanie had made—in fact, he'd never liked it—and he didn't miss Melanie. So what was he mourning?

Twelve years ago, he'd married a beautiful, ebony-haired debutante who had enthralled him with her carefree gaiety in the dark days after Jennifer and Craig had died. By the time Carrie and Jon were born, the carefree debutante had become a restless wife; and after they moved to San Francisco it seemed the only way a Tiburon housewife, as she called herself, could allay her fears of missing out on life was by spending large sums of money, even though the things she bought always seemed to lose their desirability once they were hers. Soon Melanie's beautiful lips had tightened at the corners in perpetual disappointment and dissatisfaction, at least when she was with her husband.

All this Ross had known and lived with, finding more satisfaction in his work as he got less from his marriage. Melanie would not listen when he tried to talk about the gulf between them, and after a while he let it go; it was easier not to try. They'd do it later.

It had not occurred to him to leave her. Why not? he wondered now, gazing absently around his new living room.

Because they were married. Because they had two children. Because his life was devoted to restoring, not destroying. Because he'd thought if they could work out the biggest problems, an imperfect marriage was probably better than none.

"But it's over," he said aloud. "And it should have been, long ago." He listened to himself and understood why he had spoken out loud: to force himself to face the truth about the woman his wife had become and his own failure to do anything but drift through the years, preferring that to change.

More and more often he thought of Katherine. She must have the same kind of mourning for a marriage, and even something like the shame Ross felt at his ignorance about Melanie; she had had to face her own, about Craig. He wondered if she carried on silent dialogues, as he did, trying to understand, and to calm the turmoil within.

I could call her, he thought, and find out. But he did not. She had Derek—that was lasting a long time. He didn't understand how a woman as bright and proud as she was hadn't yet seen through his brother, but he wouldn't seek her out to find the answer—at least not now. It was the wrong time: there was too much he was wrestling with already. He knew he wanted to see her, but until he understood what had happened to him, and why, and where he was going, he'd stay away.

The more he thought about it, the blacker his mood became. He took to sailing at night, having to drive to Tiburon Harbor for his boat because he hadn't yet found a slip close to Berkeley. The drive made his mood even worse and once on the water he brooded at the dark waves lapping his boat, the brilliant white stars above, and the gold lights below, embracing the bay.

He was a superb sailor. Tobias had called it his obsession, when, after Jennifer was killed, he grimly took lessons and crewed for others in races or on long trips. For a year, there had been no pleasure in it; he fought the boats as if they were enemies. But as he became technically skilled he discovered that each boat had its own characteristics—almost its own personality—and if he worked with it he could use the wind and the currents instead of being their victim. Then sailing lost its horrors and he understood Craig's passion for its freedom and power: the joy of skimming silently between sky and water, part of the earth yet flying, controlling yet bending to the wind.

But after the separation from Melanie, Ross sailed simply to be alone and to wear himself out. One night he sailed for the practical purpose of moving his boat, at last, to a slip in the Emeryville marina, just south of Berkeley. But mostly he sailed to get away from everything on land.

Still, it wasn't enough; he needed something else. He was too wound up with doubts about himself, too angry without a specific target, too lonely, with a feeling of isolation that neither his friends nor Victoria nor Tobias could ease. He thought he would explode from the energy trapped inside him if he could not find a way to work it off. And that was when he discovered gardening.

In Sea Cliff, when he was growing up, there had always been gardeners, almost invisible except when Ross and Craig and Derek needed gardenias or camelias for the girls they took to dances. Now, trying it whimsically, then more seriously, he was amazed at how satisfying it was. It gave him a sense of accomplishment and wore him out even more than the easy sailing the bay had offered in the two weeks since he moved from Tiburon. With the vigor of a convert, he dug and hoed and chopped. At first he killed as many flowers as weeds, but soon, after a week of studying a garden encyclopedia propped up at the breakfast table, he began to tell them apart and even felt confident enough to plant two rows of radishes and red peppers. Leaning on his hoe one morning before leaving for the office, he surveyed his territory and gave a short, satisfied nod. He might have made a mess of his marriage, but he sure as hell could keep a garden in order.

On June 16 it was one year since Craig had kissed Katherine goodbye and driven off in a taxicab, waving to her through the rear window. Todd had drawn a fierce X with a red Magic Marker beneath the date on the kitchen calendar and he and Jennifer shot nervous glances at it whenever they walked past. By the time the day arrived, they had worked themselves to a pitch of anticipation, anxious and quick-tempered from the minute they leaped out of bed, spilling their cereal at breakfast and snapping at Katherine when she suggested they try not to walk through it.

"Now hold on a minute," she said calmly, though their anxiety had proven contagious and she was as jumpy as they. Already keyed up about delivering her new jewelry to Herman Mettler on Friday, she also had begun to wonder, like Jennifer and Todd, if Craig would choose June 16 to return. One year, she thought, remembering back to Vancouver and the long nights when the porch light had blazed while she waited, curled up on the couch. Her memory sped forward—dinner at the Haywards', the trip to San Francisco in a rented truck, their first dismayed look at this apartment, the strength of her friendship with Leslie, Gil

Lister's daily insults, lunch with Ross, Derek's fantastic box lunch, the Exploratorium with Jennifer and Todd, her first sale to Mettler, her love for Victoria... A long, crowded year. A long way, Katherine knew, from the fears of those first dark nights. And as she thought that, a new idea came to her: if June 16 was the anniversary of Craig's disappearing, it was also the anniversary of her beginning to find herself.

He left and I came out, she thought whimsically, then pushed the thought away. "Maybe it would be better," she suggested to Jennifer and Todd, "if we didn't think about today being different from any other day."

"It's an anniversary!" Todd protested. "People celebrate anniversaries— everybody knows that!"

"It seems different to us," said Jennifer reprovingly. "It's like a birthday. You're the same age all year, but your birthday is still different from other days. *Daddy* would understand that."

Katherine felt a flash of impatience. "I understand that, too. But I don't think a birthday is very much like the anniversary of a man deserting his family."

"*Mother!*"

Todd jumped up and stomped in a circle on the spilled Rice Krispies. "You *said* we didn't know why he went away and we had to wait till we heard his story."

"That's still true." Her chin in her hands, Katherine gazed at the pulverized cereal. "I shouldn't have said what I did, at least not quite that way. But it doesn't help to lie about what happened. Your father did leave us a year ago, without a word—we even thought he might be dead, remember?—and it took us a long time to get ourselves put together. I think we should take credit for what we did and not forget how hard it was, how unhappy we were, the trouble you had in school, the problems I had with my job... Even if we don't know why he disappeared, I think we ought to remember that he did just... leave us."

"So you can stay mad at him?" Jennifer asked shrewdly.

"So someday we can find out the truth," Katherine said steadily. "Whether he really had to leave or not."

It was the first time she had said it aloud. Jennifer's eyes narrowed. "You shouldn't talk that way about Daddy. He tried to come back on New Year's Eve but you were too busy with Derek to get here in time so he left. He thought you didn't want him. It was your fault he went away; he probably knew you were going to bed with Derek—"

"Jennifer!"

"Well, everybody does, don't they? When they're out late and go to somebody's apartment? I used to wake up when you came home and look at my clock and see how late it was and the kids at school always talk about it so what else were you doing? Daddy knew. That's why he left; he felt awful and he went away again." Stonily she looked at Katherine. *"What did you do to make him go away the first time?"*

Stunned, Katherine stared at her. Once, they had asked what *they* had done to make their father leave. "What did *I* do?"

"Well, you and Mr. Doerner lied that Daddy stole money, so we figured you made that up so you could pretend it wasn't your fault he left—you did something that got him mad—because why else would he go away from us unless you made him—?"

"Stop it, Jennifer! This instant! You don't know what you're talking about!"

Jennifer burst into tears. "I know I don't! But you never tell us anything!"

"Mom," Todd blurted, looking from Jennifer to Katherine. "Should I sweep up the cereal?"

Katherine's eyes met Jennifer's and unexpectedly a small laugh escaped them both. "In a minute," Katherine said. "First, we'd better talk."

She contemplated them across the breakfast table, her bright, beautiful children who had to pick their way through the minefields of adult behavior. Children ought to be happy and carefree, Katherine thought, but how can they be, if they're caught in our complicated lives?

"I didn't lie. It does seem that Daddy took money from the company; I told you, I'm waiting to hear what he says about it. But that's separate from everything else. I didn't want him to leave; we didn't fight; he wasn't angry at me. We loved each other, and we were happy. All of us." As vividly as if she were in Vancouver, Katherine saw the slanting afternoon sunlight bringing her living room to life—the flowered furniture, the patina of Craig's oak desk, the gleam of black Eskimo sculptures—and Craig's smile when he held her close, telling her he loved her. "We were happy," she repeated and her voice broke on the words. It hadn't seemed so real for months.

"What about Derek?" Jennifer asked, her voice subdued.

"Derek was exciting," Katherine answered truthfully. "I told you about those enormous houses we went to, with fancy food and bright lights and people wearing beautiful clothes. All those parties, where no one was poor and no one ever seemed worried about anything... Going out with Derek was like being in a fairy tale."

"I guess that was wonderful," Jennifer said.

"A lot of the time it was. But Derek turned out to be not so wonderful, and after a while I didn't want to be with him anymore. You know that, because I told you when I stopped seeing him, almost two months ago."

Wordlessly, Jennifer scrutinized her. "No," Katherine said. "I didn't go to bed with him. I thought about it, but I didn't."

"You thought about it?"

"Everybody does," Katherine replied, using Jennifer's words. "It's one of the important things men and women do together. But every woman doesn't do it with every man and I didn't do it with Derek."

Jennifer's eyes were bright with relief and gratitude. "Now," Katherine said, looking for a change of subject. "Could you give me some help this morning? I'm trying something new for my last piece for Mr. Mettler and I'd like your opinion, and some help in polishing. And I thought tonight we'd have dinner at the Hippo; I could use a good hamburger. How about you?"

"Me too!" Todd grinned.

"Jennifer?"

Shamefaced, Jennifer looked at her lap. "You're so nice. But I wasn't nice to you."

"Not very," Katherine agreed. "But you were unhappy, and you tried to spread it around. Remember what we decided at the Exploratorium? Don't keep things bottled up; let's talk about them."

"Dad kept things bottled up, didn't he?" said Todd, making a discovery. "Maybe if you'd asked him to talk about them—"

"I did," Katherine replied shortly. "Now I'm going to work. After you sweep the floor, come on in."

Filled with sudden resentment, she sat on the stool at her worktable. Please go away, she begged Craig silently. Stop creeping into all our conversations; let us get on with the things we have to do. But then she added quickly, I'm sorry; I didn't mean it. Of course we should talk about you. Jennifer and Todd need you and I know you're still part of our lives. But you make it very hard for us.

She picked up a piece of polished lucite and closed her hand around its cool surface. The tightness inside her began to ease. This was where she was happiest. The frustrating weeks of April, when she could not draw a sketch or begin a piece of jewelry, had ended, astonishingly, almost as soon as she walked away from Derek in Ghirardelli Square, seven weeks ago. It was as if in escaping from the web of his charm and cruelty, the dominance of his power and sexual magnetism, she suddenly discovered herself. By freeing herself of needing Derek, she had freed her own energy and inventiveness, and since that night, her imagination had soared. Images came to her: bold shapes and vivid colors, exotic combinations and fantastic designs too complicated for jewelry, but containing some single idea that she could use—and those were the ones she put on paper. Sketches flowed from her pencil as fast as her hand could move, followed by watercolor paintings of the best of them and, finally, models of the twelve she chose for the collection she would take to Mettler.

The hours and days had passed in silent absorption, in the same circle of contentment Katherine had felt when she made her first gold bracelet. She was satisfied to be alone. Now and then she thought of Derek, but only fleetingly and always with relief that it was over. Leslie stopped by occasionally, to share a quick supper or cup of coffee, but she always left, with an indulgent laugh and a kiss, when Katherine's attention wandered to her worktable. At dinner one night Victoria and Tobias told Katherine that Ross and Melanie had separated, but she felt only casual interest and a flicker of regret that she and Ross had never become friends. She was caught up in the excitement of her work; it tugged at her demandingly, making everything else seem distant and faint. And so she spent most of her time alone or with Jennifer and Todd in their small apartment until eleven pieces of jewelry lay nestled in individual boxes and the twelfth, almost finished, was in her hand: a necklace of clear lucite ovals alternating with small, irregularly shaped chunks of lucite in deep shades of burnt orange, like small pieces of the setting sun.

"Sensuous and aloof," Mettler said admiringly soon after Katherine arrived on Friday morning. Leaning far back in his chair, he let the necklace slip slowly through his fingers and glanced across his desk at the boxes lined up in front of Katherine.

He had reached for them when she first came in, but after shaking hands, she had moved away and sat down even before he invited her to. Gone were the days when Katherine would give over her jewelry or sketches to be viewed at the whim of someone else while she clenched her hands and waited for criticism. She had learned from watching Derek manage encounters so that they included only the subjects he wanted, and lasted only as long as he wanted. She had learned from Derek how to withhold something—a comment, a smile, a handshake, a piece of information—until the time when it could be used to control.

She had never put his tricks into practice until Herman Mettler reached for her jewelry boxes. Smiling, she shook her head. "I'd rather show them to you," she said softly and casually rested her arm along the gleaming surface of his desk, the sleeve of her suit jacket pulled back just enough to reveal two bracelets on her wrist.

Mettler frowned with sudden concentration. "I'd like to see those."

"Of course." Removing them slowly, making him wait, she laid the two bracelets in the palm of his hand. He picked up one of them—strands of ivory beads twisted with strands of red and dove-gray stones in different sizes and shapes, fastened with a silver clasp like a small palette embedded with three red stones. "Bone, carnelian, and gray agate," Katherine said as Mettler examined the strands. "The clasp is silver, set with carnelian. It could be gold, if a customer wished, though in that case I would replace the gray agate with black onyx." He gave her a piercing look and she returned it calmly, one hand clenched so tightly in her lap it was numb. He turned back and picked up the other bracelet, a smoothly curved band. "Gold," Katherine said, though of course he knew it. "Bisected by a strip of onyx marble."

Mettler slipped the bracelets over the upraised fingers of his hands, and examined them. "Why did you wear them together?"

"To get your attention."

He began to smile. They both knew the bracelets—one flamboyant, the other exquisitely restrained—should not be worn together. "You succeeded. What else did you bring me?"

"Do you have any other questions about these?"

He sighed—amused, annoyed, curious—and let her run the interview. "Not at the moment."

"You'll want the price list." Katherine slid a blue folder across the desk. "You'll find photographs and descriptions of each piece. Now, for the necklaces..." Opening one of the boxes, she took out the strand of clear lucite alternating with burnt orange, slipped it over her head so he could see it against her black turtleneck sweater, then removed it and handed it to him.

He slipped it through his fingers. "Brilliantly simple. And a different medium from the others. Have you mastered them all?"

"Not precious stones; I won't be working with them. I like semiprecious stones, glass, gold, and silver. And lucite now and then, for relaxation."

"Indeed. Relaxation."

Katherine had stopped trembling. Bringing out her other pieces one at a time, she described them in a voice that grew increasingly confident as she saw Mettler lower his eyes like a poker player to hide their gleam of excitement. But he gave in to emotion when Katherine held up her last piece: a necklace of gold segments, roughly shaped, hammered to an antique finish and fastened together with short double strands of tiny, geometric, bezel-set stones in amber, blue, and deep green.

"Magnificent!" he burst out, almost snatching the necklace from her. He turned it in his hands, murmuring to himself. "Totally new, yet almost ancient. Modern, but echoing of the past. Katherine." He looked up and for the first time his voice was without pomposity. "I salute you. An extraordinary collection, free of the commonplace, free of other influences. Excellent throughout."

Katherine flushed, her heart pounding. She had sometimes been alarmed by the flights of her imagination, but she had trusted them, and, combining them with the techniques she had mastered in Tony's studio, had done what she dreamed of: created pieces that were completely new and beautiful.

"We'll feature you, of course," Mettler was saying. "In the showcases at the front of the store. A full frontal attack," he added, chuckling with satisfaction. "We can't market you to a specific clientele, since you fit in no narrow category, but we'll make that a virtue and introduce you as a designer for all our customers—the same way we handle Marc Landau and Angela Cummings and Paloma Picasso. And the publicity—! My God, I can get stories on these designs wherever I want. Spectacular photos, and your own story, of course: human interest. Divorced, are you? Beautiful woman, children—you do have children?— they help. Struggling night and day to support your young children with the work of your hands—and such work! Such talent! We'll get you in *Vogue, Cosmo, Savvy*—different markets—and I'll take full-page ads... 'Jewelry by Katherine Fraser—exclusive at Mettler's.'"

Katherine looked up sharply from the torrent of his praise and heady plans. "We never discussed that."

"True. But obviously you understand it is to your benefit to be connected with one store where you are well-treated, where customers know they will always find your work, where your newest pieces will get immediate exposure. I'll have a contract drawn up and of course you'll want to read it; if you want a lawyer to look it over, let me recommend—"

"Just a minute, please." Katherine tried to imagine how Derek would regain control of a conversation after he had lost it. "I'm afraid this is a little too fast for me. We haven't discussed the price list I gave you."

"Katherine. I am offering you a showplace. I won't quibble over prices and you won't try to rob me. After all, I know what the market will bear. We'll get along, never fear. But I want you exclusively. The same thing you want: security."

"I just don't know." It might be all right, but it bothered her. It's like a marriage, she thought wryly; locked into one person, whatever happens... And Mettler was pressing her—all business, no jokes—which probably meant he knew others would want her, too. Would it increase her value, or decrease it, to sell only through one store? I've never had to cope with success, she thought, and said, "I can't decide this minute.

I never even thought of an exclusive contract; I wasn't that far along. If you won't wait for me to get some advice, perhaps I should go somewhere else."

"My dear Katherine," said Mettler hastily. "You shock me. I never give ultimatums. But if you reflect a bit, you'll see that it is to your advantage. In fact, I can't imagine why you would refuse. Unless" —he frowned at a sudden thought— "is it possible these are not actually your own designs? I would have to be privy to that information. Tell me, Katherine, is all this truly yours? It is quite amazing, you know, for someone to create highly original designs only a few months after making a collection that was quite ordinary. A transformation, you might say. I could not, of course, advertise the line as Katherine Fraser's if you used other—Katherine!"

Shaking with shock and outrage, Katherine was sweeping the jewelry across his desk, letting it fall over the edge into her purse. "I cannot believe," she said icily, "you would jeopardize a business relationship you were so anxious to make exclusive. It's a strange way to do business and I don't want to have anything to do with it. I'll find someone else to carry my jewelry. My... grandmother, whom I think you know, Victoria Hayward, says she frequently shops at Laykin Et Cie and Xavier's; it will be interesting to see what they think of my designs. *My* designs, Herman; Katherine Fraser originals. I'm sorry we wasted so much time this morning; it won't happen again."

"Now Katherine, just a minute. Just a minute." Mettler walked around the desk, holding his splayed fingers in a small gesture of apology. "I regret seeming to impugn your integrity. But *my* integrity is on the line in every display case in my store and I must guard it religiously. If I say an item is an original, my customers believe me. Marc Landau is an original; unscrupulous manufacturers copy him—he expects it, in spite of the fact that jewelry designs are copyrighted—but Marc Landau copies no one; that is why his pieces command exorbitant prices. I am not interested in jewelry copied with minor variations from Marc Landau or Elsa Peretti or—as inevitably will happen—Katherine Fraser; I am interested only in originals. My customers trust me; I must be able to trust my designers. But come now; we mustn't get too excited."

Pulling up an armchair, he sat close to Katherine. "Your work is superb. If you say it is yours, I accept that. I will not press you for an exclusive contract, but in the long run, you will do better with me if you have one. I'm making myself clear?"

"Yes."

"Good. Now, I am buying these pieces, but I want at least a dozen more before I introduce you to the world. I'll wait until fall and feature you then. Is that acceptable?"

"Yes."

"Then we will shake hands. We have just begun the career of Katherine Fraser, jewelry designer *extraordinaire.*"

Holding back the excitement rushing through her, Katherine shook his hand. She would have to sort everything out, ask Claude what he thought about exclusive contracts, and Victoria and Tobias, too. But there was time for that. For the moment, even as she and Mettler talked about the pieces she would make for September, she savored his words. Katherine Fraser. Jewelry designer. *Extraordinaire.*

"Katherine and I are celebrating at dinner," Leslie said, pouring coffee for Claude and herself. "Which gives us all day, but not the evening."

"We'll be done by evening," he responded, settling back on the blue suede of Leslie's couch. "I'd invite myself, but I gather it will be just the two of you."

"Just the two of us." She sat beside him. "We miss each other when we don't get together often."

"I like that," he said. He was admiring her, thinking she was like a summer flower: white jeans, yellow shirt, bright red hair against the blue couch. "And I envy it. How many men can say, without embarrassment, that they miss each other when they're not together often enough?"

"Maybe they don't miss each other."

"I think they do. But it doesn't sound manly. Whatever that means."

Leslie sliced coffee cake. "I made this. First time in years. Oddest thing." But what was truly odd, she knew, was that after six weeks of dinners with Claude, drives in the country and weekends at Tahoe, she was feeling domestic urges she hadn't felt since she was a romantic twenty, wondering which of a dozen handsome up-and-coming professionals she would marry. "Bruce!" she exclaimed as the front door opened, and she leaped up to hug her brother.

Claude looked at the two flaming, curly heads close together, and at the slice of spiraled coffee cake on his plate, and heard in his mind Leslie's warm voice, talking about her friendship with Katherine. My God, he thought, I'm in love with her. Tough, aggressive, beautiful, but with a sharp jaw, and an unladylike vocabulary—and thirty-seven this fall. A long way from fantasy. He laughed silently as he became aware of the relief surging through him: never again to have to keep up with a twenty-year-old.

"Welcome home," Leslie said, her cheek against Bruce's. "I missed you. This is Claude Fleming—my brother Bruce McAlister. Have some cake and coffee. How was the vacation?"

"Not vacation, sis, a sincere attempt to be a wild youth again with my cohorts in Los Angeles—only it failed. I kept thinking about Heath's and the bastard who stole my notes and ripped off the store—so here I am, ready to solve your whodunit, clear my name, and go back to work and by the way, when it's all finished, I want to be the new head of Data Processing."

Hiding a smile, Claude said, "It sounds like you think someone framed you."

"Bright fellow, got it in one." Bruce took a piece of cake. "Sis warned me not to talk; sounds like she talked to you."

"Claude is my lawyer," Leslie said coolly. "Yours, too, if things get rough, so be polite."

"I'm a gentleman, sis, you know that. Why a lawyer?"

"Because everything pointed to Data Processing or store security—or both—and either one meant me. Rumors were flying and I was on the verge of being forced out—until Claude threatened to sue everyone including the mannequins if they broke my contract. Then my president piped up that he really believes in me, and nothing would be done until we have a storewide inventory after the June sale. So I'm being left alone. At least until July."

"Most important," Claude put in, "the thefts have stopped."

"Since when?" Bruce demanded.

"Since the day someone brought your notes to Leslie."

"Ah ha! You see, when they aimed the finger at me they had to stop their evil doings... what's wrong, sis?"

"You don't seem to understand. The thefts stopped at the same time you stopped working there."

Bruce gaped at her, his eyebrows moving as if on a spring. He looked from Claude to Leslie. "What half-assed son of a bitch would believe that?"

"My fellow vice-presidents," Leslie said, thinking: And I nearly did, until Katherine talked to me about things like loyalty and trust.

"Christ, sis," Bruce sputtered. "I did good work there, doesn't my record count, how can they look at everything I've done for them and think—"

"Cut it out," Claude snapped. "Everything points to you, and running off to Los Angeles didn't help. What are you going to do about it?"

"Tough lawyer, sis." Bruce sighed deeply. "Well, I see it's up to me. I have figured out that the villain is Dick Volpe, my boss, head of the de-

partment, and I'm the only one who can check it by going through his programs because I cracked his password one day when I was bored—"

"Password?" Claude asked.

"We each have our own, like a code, that lets us work on our own
programs; you can type all day and get nothing on the screen if you don't
know the password—supposed to keep out spies and such—"

"But you figured out Volpe's."

"I'm smarter than your average spy; so sis, how's about you give me
your master key and I'll take a look around my old office." He held out
his hand.

"Bruce, you're out of your mind. I can't give keys to nonemployees.
I can't even *take* you into Data Processing."

Claude coughed. "If you'll excuse me... back in a minute."

After a bewildered pause, Leslie burst out laughing. "You know where
it is." As he went upstairs, she stood. "OK, let's go. Seems Claude trusts
you and thinks you ought to take a look around but he doesn't want to
know we're violating company policy. He'll wait for us here. Come on,
damn it! How long do you think he can stay in the bathroom?"

"Forty seconds, if he pees normally. How come he knew where it
was?"

"He's been there before."

"How often?"

"Often enough to keep a spare shaver in the cabinet. Are you being
protective, Bruce?"

"Hell, no, I'm being approving—best choice in a long time—tough
and cool and think of all that free legal advice." He kissed her loudly.
"Good for you, sis."

"Hey," she protested. "Nothing's settled."

"Good vibes, though. OK, all is well; let's go solve this thing."

With no children to keep him company in the morning, Ross began
arriving at the office earlier each day. He liked the cool morning quiet
of the streets as he drove down the hill from his house, everything hushed
and still, like a painting about to burst into life. Only the joggers were
out, their shoes slapping the pavement. As they passed, Ross returned
their exuberant greetings with a wave of his hand, sharing with them that
private moment suspended in sunlight above the fog that obliterated the
Golden Gate Bridge and the skyline of San Francisco. Others slept, but
they savored the morning.

Driving down the hill, Ross followed the boundary of the university campus with its smooth, sloping lawns and earth-tone buildings. Above it all rose the slender Campanile Tower, a white beacon visible for miles. In the afternoons, when Ross reversed the trip and the tower came into view, it beckoned, telling him he was almost home.

Amazing how we adjust, he thought, parking his car and taking the stairs to his office. A year ago I wouldn't have believed I could do it. A year ago, he realized, he had been in Vancouver, meeting Katherine Fraser. Her life had been crumbling; his had been under control. He wondered if she'd commemorated the year: not an anniversary, but a milestone of sorts. She might even have heard from Craig. Maybe he should call her, to find out. No; what difference would it make? If Craig showed up, they'd all hear about it. From Derek.

Sitting at his desk, he looked out the window at the Embarcadero. Few cars; empty sidewalks. Down the street, the stepped red brick buildings of Levi Plaza still slept; behind them, in his apartment on Lombard Street, Derek presumably slept. In Tiburon, Carrie and Jon were probably awake, perhaps making breakfast, since the cook didn't arrive until seven-thirty. Across town, Katherine might be awake by now, especially if Jennifer and Todd—

Damn it, why did he keep thinking of Katherine? Turning from the window he pulled out his Monday morning agenda. He probably wanted sympathy and thought she would understand him well enough to provide it. But he'd find sympathy elsewhere: on Sunday he and Tobias would be cooking a sumptuous farewell dinner for Victoria before she left for France. Considering how those two felt about Melanie, he'd find sympathy to spare.

He concentrated on his work until the members of his staff arrived and he gathered up his papers and strode down the hall to the conference room. It looked as if a tornado had blown through. Papers, charts, computer printouts, blueprints, sketches, pencils, and notepads covered the oval table and draped to the floor; a few lay on the rolling table in the corner where an automatic coffee maker sputtered and gurgled as its carafe filled to the top. Twenty men and women stood about, chatting, holding styrofoam cups as they waited for the coffee. "Breakfast," one of them announced, handing a box of Danish pastries to Ross. "I figured you'd be hungry, since you get here at the crack of dawn."

"I am," Ross said. "Thanks, Will." He sat in the center of one side of the table and waited until the others were seated. "Let's start with the latest crises on BayBridge. Who goes first?"

"I'd better," said one of them. "You won't believe this, but when the crews began gutting the Number Three warehouse yesterday they found a structural column fifteen feet from the southwest corner—a goddamn column through all ten floors, in the goddamn middle of what's going to be a goddamn living room!"

"*Christ*," someone whispered. "How the hell—?" someone else began. The rest sat in stunned silence.

Feeling his anger build, Ross got up to refill his cup, moving slowly and deliberately, keeping his face calm. He was supposed to be the steadying influence around there. But it wasn't always easy. You design a massive project, he thought; you put your best people on it; you get the approval of half a hundred committees, agencies, and everyone else who's interested; you get written up in the newspaper as innovative, bold, brilliant—and then you spend the next year or two putting out fires that no one could have foreseen.

He returned to his chair. "If it's a structural column," he said quietly, "I'd guess it was added during construction, fifty years ago. Probably the warehouse began settling while they were working on it and they stuck in a support column and then forgot it. No one bothered to redraw the plans to show what they'd done. Any ideas on how to get around a concrete column in the middle of a living room?"

They began to bounce suggestions around the table as Ross listened.

"Make the living room smaller and hide it in the wall."

"A twelve-foot room on that corner, with that view? You want your biggest room there!"

"So make it longer. What's wrong with a twelve- by twenty-foot living room? If you take five feet from the east bedroom—"

"You just eliminated the east bedroom's closet."

"Shit."

After a while, Ross said, "How about going up?" They looked at him. "Multi-story apartments. If you can't have a modern loft, build a Victorian house. Two rooms wide, two or three stories high. Spiral staircases if we don't have room for conventional ones..."

They caught the idea, liked it, enthusiastically began embellishing it. Ross scheduled a meeting for later that week to work on final drawings. "Any more crises?"

No one spoke. No more fires, he thought. Until tomorrow. "I have one item before we go to other projects. Donna, I just got a copy of the engineering report on the Macklin Building. You've seen it?"

"Of course, Ross. I ordered it."

"You ordered it. And it says the northeast corner has settled two inches." She nodded again. "Damn it, I knew that already. You would have, too, if you'd gone to look at it. I don't need a consultant to tell me what I can see from the cracking pattern on the walls." He was aware of the surprise on the faces around the table; he wasn't being the steadying influence they expected. But he was worried and didn't hide it. "The question isn't *if* it's settling; it's *why*; and if there's something wrong with the foundation, what should we do about it? Is that building in danger of collapse? Should we halt the renovation work until it's fixed? That's what I asked you to find out last December; what the hell are you waiting for? Where's the foundation engineer's report?"

"It hasn't been done," Donna said defensively. "You said there was only one company you wanted to use, in Los Angeles, and they have more work than they know what to do with. I gave you a memo on this, Ross; it looks like they won't get to us until July. I did look at the building, and I tried to get the engineers here earlier, but they can't do it. If you want, I'll call someone else."

"No, I remember now. I know you don't let things slide, Donna, and I know you wouldn't work on a building without inspecting it. I apologize." He looked around the table, at faces that were sympathetic, even solicitous, and he knew they were telling themselves he was tense because he and his wife had split and he was living alone, spending weekends with his kids . . . he needed understanding in this difficult time.

And probably they were right, he thought later, as he went back to his office; there was a lot going on at once. "Derek Hayward called," his secretary said. "He'll be a few minutes late." Ross nodded. Something else going on: why had his brother, who had never set foot in his office, made an appointment for this morning?

"Good job," Derek said, looking around the renovated office as they shook hands. "How are you? Melanie is telling her friends you are devastated, callous, and obstreperous."

Ross chuckled. "What does that mean?"

"No one knows. Probably not even Melanie. It may, however, have something to do with money."

"It may indeed." They smiled together and Ross felt a moment's regret that they were not close. They looked close, he knew; a stranger would have noted the physical likeness, the easy way they sat in their chairs, the smile they exchanged, the quick, almost intuitive way they sometimes communicated. Like good friends, Ross thought. But we aren't. We're only brothers. And there is nothing either of us likes about the other.

He made a fresh pot of coffee and they sat on the leather couch. Derek deliberated a moment, then asked amiably, "Who's controlling the BayBridge contracts?"

"A number of people."

"But you're pulling the strings."

"I'm not even trying to pull the strings. Your spy is giving you false information, Derek."

"I don't need spies; I know everybody in this business." The brief amiability was gone; his voice was metallic. "And from what I hear, the Hayward Corporation is getting the contract for a four-million-dollar parking lot and deck. Four million out of a three-hundred-million-dollar project."

"That's not public knowledge."

"I heard it."

Ross was silent, wondering who was feeding Derek information. Someone in the contractor's office, or one of the developers.

Derek sat back. "It's true, then."

"As far as I know."

"You son of a bitch. Where did you learn to play like the big boys? You made yourself a nice little reputation since you moved here—you can't imagine how many people think they'll please me by praising my little brother to the skies—but you never played for stakes like these. And it went to your head. One of the biggest projects this city ever had, and you couldn't risk competition. *I should have been the contractor on that project.* But you kept me out of it."

"You're wrong. I wanted you in."

"Bullshit. You had the developers eating out of your hand; all you had to do was point in my direction."

The first time in our lives, Ross thought, that I had any influence over something Derek wanted. "They chose the contractor on their own. I wanted you in as a subcontractor, to build the shopping mall. But I only made suggestions, none of the final decisions. You know everything else; you know that, too."

"You're lying."

"God damn it—!" Ross took a breath. "Use your common sense. Most of them never backed a project like this before. They didn't know how long it would take, or how much they'd have to spend, before we could begin. The day we got commitments for federal money they bought champagne; five years later, when we were still waiting for final approvals from federal and city agencies and community groups, and they'd spent twenty million dollars on land, feasibility studies, schematics, all the rest, *and we still hadn't dug the first hole,* they were too cautious even to buy beer. All of them were on edge, swearing this was going to be the cleanest project since cave dwellings; they didn't want any hitches. So how do you think they felt about giving a seventy-million-dollar contract for the mall to a corporation owned by the architect's family, with the architect on its board of directors?"

Derek's mouth was a thin line. "Who the hell do you think you're talking to? I know developers; I was handling them while you were still kissing professors' asses in college. Nobody's clean, little brother. And all this fucking piety about the family corporation...you might show some piety about getting your family a chunk of your three-hundred-million-dollar baby. Why didn't you call me at the beginning? We could have set up a front company to funnel contracts through, and a fund to pay off the bush-league politicians in Sacramento—"

"Why didn't you call me and suggest it?"

"Call you? Ask favors from you?"

"What are you here for now?" Ross asked evenly. There was a pause. "It doesn't matter. I wouldn't have done it; I don't work that way. But it wasn't—"

"Don't give me that choirboy bullshit—!"

"Derek." Ross's voice was low but it cut through the room. "We're in my territory, not yours."

There was another silence, long enough for Ross to reflect that it had been more years than he could remember since he and his brother had argued. In the past, when Derek charged like a bull, accusing or attacking, Ross had retreated—once as far as New York—reluctant to confront him, revolted by his tactics. But something had changed. BayBridge, he thought; giving me a sense of what I can achieve. And Melanie; forcing me to be alone, and find out who I really am. He leaned against the wall, contemplating his brother's rigid face. "The decisions on contractors for BayBridge were never up to me. The developers made it their game, their baby—not yours, not mine. And they decided to award the Hayward Corporation the contract for the parking lot and deck; nothing else. They didn't ask me; they told me. Whatever you heard, that's the way it was."

Derek was silent, the muscle beside his eye pulsing in the smooth mask of his face. "What about Brock Galvez? Didn't he have anything to say to your brave band of developers?"

"A lot. He even suggested setting up a front company to funnel contracts through. He did his best. How much did you pay him? No, never mind; it doesn't matter." A wave of revulsion swept through Ross and he turned to the windows, his back to his brother, watching the noon crowds gather with their lunches on the grassy knolls and benches of Levi Plaza. Galvez could buy and sell the Haywards; if Derek had bought him, it wouldn't have been with money, but services—drugs, sex, insider information—and Ross didn't want to know about them.

"If we're going to talk about payment," said Derek softly, "how much did you pay for advance information on BayBridge before you bought the Macklin Building?"

Ross turned. "I didn't know about BayBridge when I bought it."

"Didn't know," Derek mocked. "The way I heard it, you bought it in 1976 and didn't do a damn thing with it; even let Macklin keep his office space. And one year later developers begin buying land just behind it for a three-hundred-million-dollar development. Amazing coincidence—or someone selling information." He waited, but Ross made no answer. "Why else would you buy it?" he demanded.

His brother was worried, Ross thought, about the Macklin Building. But he wasn't ready to talk to him about it. "I'll tell you someday. As for Galvez, he did his best for you; I suppose he'll go on trying. But he's not a fool; when he's outvoted he backs off and goes with the majority. And they're not about to bend."

Derek nodded thoughtfully and turned to leave. Cutting his losses, Ross thought. He seldom made mistakes as serious as this—counting on one developer without gathering information on the others—but when he did, he didn't waste energy; like Galvez, he knew when to back off. Besides, after swallowing the bitter pill of coming to his brother to ask for help, he wouldn't stay a minute past the time he knew he had failed.

But at the door, Ross held him back, asking, before he could hold back the words, "How is Katherine?"

Imperceptibly, Derek's face changed, as if a thin cloud had passed over the sun. "Quite well."

Ross waited. "And her jewelry? Is she selling through Mettler?"

"Yes."

"Enough to make a living?"

There was a brief pause. "With an allowance."

Their eyes met. It had not occurred to Ross that she was taking money from Derek.

"You should call her," Derek said pleasantly. "Now that you live alone. She's extraordinarily accommodating."

Ross drew in a sharp breath. "You crude bastard."

"My, my, such sensitivity." Derek smiled in cold amusement. "It must come from being cuckolded by a younger man. Don't bother to see me out; I can find my way." He strode through the reception room, and then was gone, his diminishing footsteps echoing on the wood floor of the corridor.

Ross was gripping the edge of his office door so tightly it left a ridge on his palm when he went back to his desk. Because no matter how much he thought he had changed, his brother still had the power to infuriate and frustrate him. Derek might have lost the round on Bay-Bridge, but it was Ross who felt battered, even sullied, by the encounter.

Sitting at his desk, contemplating the paperwork demanding his attention, it was a long time before his muscles loosened and he could begin to relax. Because he knew it wasn't only Derek who was the source of his frustration. It was also Katherine, and as Ross turned to the piles of paper on his desk, he wished to hell he could forget her and concentrate on more important things.

When Katherine arrived, Victoria was supervising the packing of a dozen suitcases and garment bags. Dresses, skirts, and blouses lay everywhere in the white-and-gold bedroom like exhausted figures that had flung themselves on the wide bed and the silk loveseat and chaise to catch their breath. "Just look at it," said Tobias, quoting wickedly.

> *"Dresses to sit in, and stand in and walk in;*
> *Dresses to dance in and flirt in and talk in—*
> *Dresses in which to do nothing at all.*

Dear Victoria, do you or do you not have full closets awaiting you in France?"

"Most likely," she said. "Though when one has not been there for a year, one cannot be sure of anything. Lily, may I have those?" The maid handed her two knit suits. "St. John and Castleberry," she mused. "So very much alike. Why did I buy them both?"

"To support the knitting industry," Tobias hazarded.

"I know nothing about the knitting industry, Tobias; as you are well aware, I must have had a reason, though I cannot imagine what it was. This is quite wasteful; Katherine, they're your size; please take one."

"I'd love to," Katherine said easily. "Thank you." Once, she would have refused, instinctively, even rudely, thinking every offer of help was a criticism of Craig or of her own helplessness. But now, more confident of herself, she admired the superb cut of the two pale-blue skirts and cardigan jackets, and the silk blouse hanging beneath each one, and kissed Victoria's cheek. "I shall look quite elegant, thanks to you."

"You always look quite elegant. But of course clothes do help. I have several other—"

"Victoria," Tobias warned.

She gazed at him. "I do not flirt," she said. "Where did you find that ridiculous poem?"

"In a book of forgotten poets. It amused Katherine; I saw her smile. We haven't seen you for a while, my dear. What have you been doing?"

"Working, and borrowing money," Katherine said ruefully. "I didn't want to, but I was afraid of using the household money for buying gold and silver."

"Well done," Tobias declared. "Much better to borrow than use your own. Which bank?"

"The Bank of America."

"Very solid."

"But I used Mettler's order as collateral. If he doesn't buy the whole collection—"

"Katherine, you are better than you think you are. Always. If you remember that, you will age less rapidly."

"Never worry about a loan, Katherine," Victoria said peremptorily. "Until time to pay it back. What is this?" She took a long dress from a pile on the bed. "Satin. Why is it here? I would never wear a satin dress in Menton. The rest of the Riviera, perhaps, but I keep the villa in Menton precisely because it is unpretentious. And where is my black sweater with the pockets? Lily, this is not well organized. Come with me."

As they disappeared into the dressing room, Tobias said cheerfully, "She has twenty sweaters in the bureau to the left of her bedroom door in Menton. After this summer, she will no doubt have thirty. Are you feeling melancholy, my dear?"

"About the loan? No—"

"I was not thinking of the loan."

Katherine gave a little laugh. "It's not fair that you can read my mind, Tobias; I can't read yours."

"Of course you can. Why do I think you might be melancholy?"

"You think I'd like to go to the unpretentious south of France and stay in my own villa and take side trips to Paris and the wine country and the Alps."

"And wouldn't you?"

"Yes."

"Quite right. I would be profoundly worried about you if you didn't. What are you going to do about it?"

"Nothing, Tobias; what can I do? I'll feel better when Victoria has left for her villa. I have plenty of work to keep me busy, and you'll be here to cheer me up; I won't brood all summer, if that's what you mean."

"Of course you won't brood; you're not the type. I was simply wondering why you don't go to the south of France."

"I cannot afford to go to the south of France."

"True. But Victoria does not demand rent from her guests, and three airline tickets could be called an advance birthday present—your birthday is in August, is it not?"

"Three airline—? To France? To stay with Victoria? But she's never said a word about it."

"Ah, but she has. To me. Since Christmas, she has fretted over how to ask you to join her in Menton. Why do you think she is going in July when her usual time is April and May? She waited until Todd and Jennifer were out of school. But still we kept debating how to ask you. Victoria is not timid, as you no doubt have noticed, but after your severe refusal last March of her offer to help your jewelry career, she tiptoes around you, wanting to give, but afraid to try. You are so fierce in your rejections, my dear. But just now you graciously accepted a knit suit and it occurred to me that you might accept a trip to France if I explained it carefully, which I have just done. Now, my dear, quickly, before you have time to think of obstacles: would you like to go to France with Victoria?"

"Of course I'd like it—I'd love it. I've never been there, I've never been anywhere in Europe. But how can we? I haven't made arrangements—"

"No obstacles allowed! Of course we should have asked you earlier, but each time we talked about it, we put it off. Two old people afraid of being turned down. But it's not complicated; you don't need much time. Let me think. Passports. Are they current?"

Katherine shook her head. "We never traveled. And we didn't need them to move here..."

"Oh, dear, oh, dear. Well, we have friends in the government offices; we'll manage. What else? Your jewelry. You can work on designs in France and make the pieces when you return. You could stay quite a while and still accomplish that. Three weeks? Four? The children, of course, are out of school, and you said you would not be sending them to camp."

She nodded.

"Yes?" Tobias asked.

"Yes, I'm not sending them to camp." They laughed.

"And you told us some time ago you are no longer seeing Derek, so unless you have returned to him or found someone else—?"

"No."

"Then there is not even a romance to keep you in the city."

"Not even that," Katherine said. "There's really nothing to keep me in the city." *Except Craig.* The words were dark against Tobias' bright confidence. *If he comes looking for us, he'll find another empty house.* But excitement was running through her like quicksilver, and thinking of Craig only reminded her of the times, long ago, when she wanted to plan trips to Europe and Craig refused. He preferred trips in Canada, he said, though when she asked why, he gave no specific reasons. Now, suddenly, she understood why. He didn't have a passport. He couldn't get one without a birth certificate... and there was no birth certificate for Craig Fraser. I suppose he could have had one forged, Katherine thought. But perhaps he thought enough of his life was forged already. She felt a rush of pity for him. He wasn't free to travel about the world, and he couldn't explain that to me without telling the truth about himself. So there was one more secret, one more space between us...

"Nothing to keep you here," Tobias was echoing with a gleeful smile and Katherine felt her excitement return as Victoria, who had been listening, came out of the dressing room, her arms filled with clothes, saying, "Of course, Katherine, you will want your blue jeans and your own casual things, but I have far too many sweaters and shirts and all of them are perfect for you—" She stopped as Katherine and Tobias burst into renewed laughter. "As part of your birthday present," she went on calmly. "I cannot imagine why you two should find that hilarious. Katherine, it will take a day or two for you to get passports, but after that, how soon can you come? You will fly to Nice; the limousine will meet you, and you and I will take a separate shopping trip to Paris. Did Tobias say four weeks?"

"Yes," Katherine breathed. "But I'm not sure—"

"Four weeks sounds quite satisfactory. Can you be ready to leave in a week? July fifth. My dear" —Victoria laid her hand on Katherine's cheek— "forgive me if I seem a trifle autocratic; I am so very happy that you will let me give you this. It has been so long since there were young voices at the villa... We think we become self-sufficient and tough, but we never stop longing to share the things we love. Without it, we're only half-alive. How wonderful that you are coming!" She coughed and impatiently wiped her eyes. "Well, then" —briskly she turned back to the piles of clothes on the bed— "it's settled. Tobias will arrange for passports and three tickets for July fifth. Unless, of course, you have a serious objection—?"

"'Take the good the gods provide thee,'" murmured Tobias urgently. "Dryden. Wise man. Valuable advice."

"Of course," said Katherine softly. "After all, she only seemed to be a trifle autocratic." Their eyes met in a smile. Then her excitement was too much to contain and jumping up, she put her arms around Victoria. "Thank you. Thank you. Oh, it sounds so *pale*—how can I tell you—?"

"Quite sufficient, dear Katherine. As long as you are pleased."

"I love you," Katherine said. "And now I'm going home because I can't wait to tell Jennifer and Todd. Or may I help you pack?"

"Lily is here. And Tobias helps by telling me I need nothing, which reduces the amount I pack. I'll call you tomorrow morning before I leave." Victoria kissed her on both cheeks. "Tell your children to practice their French. Oh, my dear, what fun we are going to have!"

Katherine was smiling as she left the building, her voice dancing with such delight when she said goodbye to the doorman that his face creased in an answering grin. It was still there a few minutes later when he opened the door to let Ross in. "Happiest young lady I ever saw, just left Mrs. Hayward," he said, shutting the grille on the elevator and starting the stately ride to Victoria's floor.

Ross had seen her, walking down the steep pitch of Washington Street. Her distinctive beauty drew glances from passersby, but it was the brightness of her face that had struck him, and the eagerness of her step. At a stoplight, she had crossed in front of him, her eyes looking to the distance. A happy woman, he thought: joyously anticipating, hurrying—probably because someone is waiting.

"You just missed Katherine," Victoria said, kissing him. "You'll have sherry with us, won't you? Tobias thinks it is sustenance for packing."

"Otherwise I grow faint from your exertions," said Tobias. He handed Ross a glass. "Derek was here earlier, to wish Victoria a good trip, and Ann and Jason called, from Maine. It is astonishing how the solicitude over Victoria's well-being has increased in the past year."

"Has it?" Ross asked. "I didn't know."

"Do you know why?"

He reflected. "Craig, of course. The chance that he might come back. Odd, how he hovers over the family."

"Disruptive," said Tobias sagely. "Thoughts of him bring thoughts of emotional and financial disruptions."

Ross pictured the Craig of his youth: brown eyes watching for approval as he busied himself with model airplanes, wood carvings, and intricate matchstick houses, or sailed his boat on the bay, dreaming of the skyscrapers he would build, and the trips he would someday take to Europe and Asia, as far as he could go. Disruptive? Only Derek had found him disruptive in those days.

"Derek mentioned BayBridge Plaza," said Tobias very casually. "He seems to think we're being frozen out. Where would he get that idea?"

"He got it from me. Don't be cagey, Tobias. Derek told you he came to see me."

"So he did. I thought I should hear your side of the story before forming an opinion."

"The Hayward Corporation will have a small part of BayBridge. The rest will be built by other subcontractors. The developers are afraid of the appearance of a conflict of interest. That's all there is to it." Ross began to pace from one end of the bedroom to the other. "I didn't think, Tobias, I'd have to make excuses to you. There's never been any reason for you to doubt my honesty. Or my family loyalty." His strides grew longer. "Of all the places where I hope to find acceptance this is the one I count on most; I don't expect to walk in at the end of a hellish week and be grilled about my relationship with my brother."

"Whoa, whoa, now, dear friend." Tobias looked keenly at Ross. "I was speaking of the corporation, not you and Derek. However, this is not the time. You seem tired—"

"—seem!"

"And fuming. Would you care to dump your problems—as the young people say?"

Ross gave an apologetic laugh. "I'm sorry, Tobias. You didn't deserve that. Do you really want to hear about my week?"

"Does it have more plot than Victoria's discussion of what she will pack—which I have listened to all day?"

They laughed. "Well, then." Sitting on a hassock, his elbows on his knees, Ross described his staff meetings on crises at BayBridge, and his session with Derek. "And at least a dozen times this week I started a letter to Jacques Duvain, telling him I can't be his consultant in Paris."

"Started?" Tobias asked. "Not finished?"

"Not yet. For some reason I keep putting it off. I'll do it tomorrow. But I haven't finished with my week. Friday evening I picked up Carrie and Jon. Do you know what it feels like, Tobias, to knock at a front door that was mine for years?"

"You said Melanie gave you the new key."

"I won't use it unless I have to. I don't live there anymore, so I knock."

"Correct but depressing." Tobias poured more sherry. "And how did the three of you get on?"

"Acrimoniously. We squabble over little things—trying to get used to everything, I suppose. This afternoon, when I was driving them home, Carrie said, 'Mother goes around singing about Guy what's-his-name, and you have a house with a jacuzzi; we're the only ones who are unhappy, and what's fair about that?'"

"What indeed?" asked Tobias. "How did you answer?"

"I told them life wasn't fair." Ross began to pace again. "On my way over here, I bought a stack of books on divorced fathers. Do you think they'll help?"

"They'll show you you're not alone. That should help."

Quietly, Victoria had come up behind them. She put a hand on Ross's hair. "Poor boy. So many pressures on you."

Tobias glanced up sharply at the note in her voice. No one knew Victoria as well as he; no one else, hearing her sympathize with her grandson, would have been aware that her thoughts were racing ahead with plans. "Yes," he agreed. "A difficult time for Ross."

Victoria smiled at him with a glint of conspiracy, then as if suddenly inspired, exclaimed, "Ross! I have a grand idea!"

Ross looked up. "You mustn't worry about me; I'll be all right. You're supposed to be thinking about France, and taking a rest from all your boards of directors."

"I am thinking about France! How clever of you to understand. *You* shall come to France! You have work to do in Paris—"

"I'm turning that down."

"Please do not interrupt. You just told Tobias you put off writing your letter. Why? Because you want to go. *Voilà!* You shall go. Do your consulting in Paris and when you are finished come to Menton. You haven't been there in far too many years. We will have a visit. Are you listening?"

"I'm listening. Carrie and Jon are spending July with me."

There was barely a pause. "Bring them. The Riviera is very healthy for children. And their fathers. Your staff can handle your new plaza for a while. You haven't had a vacation since Melanie began refusing to go away with you; I am offering you one, with a chance to do the work you wish to do. There are other reasons—"

"Stop," Ross laughed. His head was up, his body felt lighter and more buoyant than it had in weeks. "You don't need any more reasons. You've convinced me. I don't know why I never thought of going; it's exactly what I need." He stood and hugged Victoria, kissing her boisterously. As he turned, he saw the glance she and Tobias exchanged. "What is it? What don't I know?"

"How happy you've made me," Victoria said smoothly. "How much I look forward to seeing you in Menton. How sorry Tobias is that he is not going. Oh, my," she added with a tremulous sigh. "What fun we are going to have!"

CHAPTER 13

HUGH Hayward had dreamed of a villa near Nice since spending several months there during the First World War. Not yet mobbed by tourists, it had a leisurely pace, vivid beauty and year-round golden warmth that he remembered for the next thirty years. The depression and another war intervened before he could return, this time with Victoria, to explore the region of Provence from Marseille to Nice until they found the Villa Serein. At the time, in the spring of 1948, it hardly matched its name, being far from serene as it huddled, empty and desolate, behind tangled weeds. Its stucco walls were flaked, its windows broken, the roof pocked with holes, and all its doors had been used during the war for firewood.

But the villa stood near the top of a hill overlooking Menton and its harbor, long a favorite of European royalty, and its rooms were large and solid. Besides, so soon after the Second World War, properties on the Côte d'Azur were bargains, especially those in disrepair. Before returning to America, Hugh bought six, and some years later sold five of them at a handsome profit.

There never was any question of selling Villa Serein. Once the weeds were gone, the trees tamed, and the rooms newly whitewashed, Victoria had fallen in love with it and undertook its renovation with the experience and enthusiasm that had been pent-up since she had run the Hayward Corporation.

After Derek and Ross were born, the villa was enlarged to fourteen rooms with a terrace in front and a garden with a small pond at the rear.

255

Over the years it was refurbished many times, and when Katherine and the children arrived, they found square, low-ceilinged rooms, bright and inviting, filled with plump furniture in the sun-filled colors of Pissarro and Matisse, painters who had lived in Provence and whose paintings, bought by Hugh when he was a soldier, hung on the walls of the villa as well as in Victoria's apartment in San Francisco.

"*Magnifique*," pronounced Todd. "*Merveilleux. Beau.*" Having nearly exhausted his French vocabulary, he added a final, "*Merci.*"

Victoria laughed. "Well done."

Jennifer, remembering instructions from Katherine, said, "It's very good of you to have us here."

"It is a pleasure," Victoria responded. "I want you to have a wonderful time, so we shall begin by going over your choices..."

There was swimming in the Olympic-size pool in Menton, tennis lessons in town and sailing lessons at the harbor, badminton and croquet, which Victoria had imported from England, the villa's own library, with French and English books, down the hall from their bedrooms ("Our own rooms," Todd said, jabbing Jennifer with his elbow), and a garden filled with vegetables to pick for lunch and dinner.

To help them choose, the next morning Victoria gave them a supply of francs to pay for lessons or to go shopping in town. And finally she introduced them to the gardener, and Sylvie and Charles, the couple who cooked and managed the villa, and who would watch over them for the next few days. "Because your mother and I are going shopping in Paris," she announced.

"We just got here," objected Todd, "and you're already leaving."

"We will be away for three days," said Victoria calmly. "I am confident you will cope quite well."

Katherine let her thoughts drift while Victoria took charge. How pleasant, she thought, to let someone else take over for a while.

It was a little space of time in a fantastic place like none she had ever known. Tropical palm trees along the harbor; cypresses and ancient, gnarled olive trees on the steep hills, shading flat-roofed villas covered with climbing roses; the narrow dusty-pink houses of Menton stopping just short of the harbor's edge, beyond which huge, gleaming yachts and sixty-foot sailboats rocked gently in the soft breeze. A little bit of time in a place so beautiful and warm, the sun heavy and golden, the air spicy and sensuous, it was impossible to believe anyone could frown or worry or weep. Far from familiar routines and problems; far from everyday thoughts; far from memories.

Far from Craig.

He wasn't there, Katherine realized. And the next morning, when she and Victoria flew to Paris, it was still true. His shadow had not followed her. Crossing an ocean to a different world, she had broken away from him. For a while.

The next morning, as the plane climbed rapidly above the white crescent of Nice, Victoria said, "I waited for you, so we could go shopping together. One of the few joys of being old is introducing the young to new pleasures. It would take you months of wandering to discover the best places by yourself, while I can show them to you in three days. So unfortunate, the tourists who have no one to direct them."

"Perhaps they enjoy wandering," Katherine suggested.

"Nonsense. Without a plan? I cannot imagine it."

Katherine smiled. "You always have reasons for what you do. What is your reason for bringing me to Paris?"

"I told you," Victoria said coolly. "A shopping expedition."

Katherine felt a clang of warning—*she's hiding something*—but it faded as she watched the mountain ranges of central France give way to dairy farms and wheat fields and then, suddenly, Paris: the soaring, echoing concrete of the Charles de Gaulle Airport, and then the crowds and noise of the city—the sidewalks jammed, traffic nearly immobilized, and outdoor cafés crammed with small tables, each a center of vigorous discussion. Even the noble lobby of the Hotel Meurice was a shifting mass of people carrying on rapid high-pitched conversations.

"Now," said Victoria with a sigh in the silence of their suite as the maid hung their clothes in the wardrobe and Katherine, striving not to gape, took stock of the lavish adjoining rooms. "We shall go shopping. We lunch at two at Maxim's with Henri Flambeau. An old friend," she said at Katherine's questioning look, "who, it so happens, owns a number of fine jewelry shops. You must always expand your circle of acquaintances, my dear. Especially in France. Nothing makes an American designer more desirable than being desired by the French."

Katherine laughed. "Thank you; I'd like very much to meet him." That was Victoria's surprise, she thought; her reason for the trip to Paris. A rush of gratitude and love swept through her, mingling with the excitement of being in Paris, and when they left the hotel and walked in the sunlight past the great gardens of the Tuileries, it was as if every fairy tale she knew had come to life, and she was the heroine of all of them. Her feet began skipping into little dance steps and she had trouble matching her pace to Victoria's dignified stroll.

On the Rue Cambon, Victoria stopped at the House of Chanel. "Why don't you go ahead?" she suggested a little too brightly. "You shouldn't be burdened with my dawdling. I'll tell you how to get to Maxim's, to meet me for lunch."

"No," Katherine said swiftly. "I'd rather you showed me your favorite places."

"Well." Victoria put her hand on Katherine's arm. "Of course you must not say that just to please me."

"I want to be with you."

"Well," she said again, and beamed. "What a lovely day. So often it is too hot in Paris in July. We'll browse for a moment in Chanel and then go on."

Victoria's Paris was almost entirely contained within a triangle with Napoleon's column in the Place Vendôme in the center. Here were the narrow streets and wide boulevards dedicated to culture and consumption: the world's most elegant stores, with discreet entrances and displays, alongside the national library and the Opéra, with its domes, columns, and extravagant stonework. "The Opéra is open to the public now," Victoria said in passing. "Most impressive. We shall visit it if we have time." And when they passed the Bibliothèque Nationale, "The dome of the library reading room is quite astonishing. We shall visit it if we have time." And, "Madeleine: one of my favorite theaters: we shall visit it if we have time. But the plan for today is to visit shops."

Katherine wanted to linger everywhere, in buildings and at intersections where carefully planned vistas stretched down long streets, but she stayed with Victoria and got a succinct lesson in European designers, and the best places to shop. She wished Leslie were there; with her flair and income she could have used Victoria's guidance far better than Katherine, and taken back to America enough clothes for a decade. Or, Katherine amended, remembering Leslie's closet, at least a year.

At Maxim's, Henri Flambeau was waiting. He watched the two women walk toward him in the sunlight—of equal height and slenderness and a certain way of holding their heads that made passersby look twice—one old, with sharp bones, her skin finely scored, her beauty fragile, fading, like a painting seen in the failing light of dusk; the other young, her loveliness arresting in its opposites: a face delicately shaped yet strong, a complexion pale but flushed, magnificent eyes, knowledgeable but as wide and eager as a young girl's. Such different kinds of beauty, Henri mused, and—as he saw them exchange a smile—how they love each other.

"Tell Henri about your jewelry," Victoria commanded as soon as they were seated.

Self-conscious, Katherine was brief, but he was attentive, at first to her beauty, then to the designs he asked her to sketch as she talked. "Ah," he said, studying them and nodding noncommittally, until Victoria demanded, "Are you interested or not? This is not a game, Henri."

He spread his hands. "Of course not; Madame Fraser is most serious in her profession. But she understands that I do not commit myself until I see her work. The designs are interesting."

"Interesting!" Victoria raised her eyebrows. "So cautious—and you a Frenchman."

"The French are the most cautious of all people," he replied. "It is the Americans who like to think we are reckless. Madame Fraser, when you wish to sell in Paris, please let me see before anyone else what you are making."

Smoothly then he changed the subject, asking them if they had seen the Beaubourg, a modern museum of outrageous architecture built inside-out with exposed pipes, structural beams, and escalators running up the outside of the building. "The entire Marais has been rediscovered," he said. "All those grand mansions that had been used as factories are being restored as homes and apartments. Imagine: after two centuries of neglect, it is once again acceptable—indeed, chic—to live on the Right Bank."

"Someone told me," said Victoria thoughtfully, "of a royal square in the Marais being completely redone. The oldest in Paris...what *is* its name..."

"Place des Vosges," said Henri. "You have not seen it? But it is quite extraordinary; in all the tourist books, in fact. If you have time for a visit—"

"We'll make time," Victoria declared. "Perhaps this afternoon. Katherine? Would you have an objection?"

A little bewildered by how suddenly they had time, Katherine shook her head. "Whatever you would like."

And that was how it happened that Katherine and Victoria were standing before Number 21 Place des Vosges at four thirty in the afternoon, just as Ross Hayward emerged from a nearby archway and looked up from the photographs he was studying into Katherine's wide, uncomprehending eyes.

They stared in silence. "Well, Ross," Victoria said with mild surprise. "I thought the name of this place sounded familiar when Henri mentioned it. Is it the project your friend Jacques asked you to work on?"

Awareness grew in Ross's eyes as he looked from her to Katherine. "You know perfectly well it is," he said, kissing Victoria on one cheek and then the other. Slowly he shook his head. "Couldn't you have told me the truth, instead of going through that play-acting?"

"One should never take chances," she said calmly.

What truth? Katherine asked herself. Ross was watching her and she met his gaze, waiting for him to explain. She had not seen him since those few minutes in March, when she had arrived at Victoria's and he had left almost immediately. Now she was struck by his looks. Carrying a suit jacket, his shirt open at the neck, his skin bronzed and his hair lightened by the sun, he was more relaxed than she remembered: tall, with an athletic stride, his face strong and expressive, his deep-set eyes studying her with curiosity and a promise of warmth. "You didn't know I'd be here—and was invited to Menton?"

"No." Katherine understood then. Turning to Victoria, she said, "You should have told me."

"*Should?* Indeed not." Victoria tilted her chin. "Since when must I report to my grandchildren? Tobias told you I've wanted to bring you to France for months—I thought it would help you break your relationship with Derek, though you did manage to do that on your own" —Ross's head snapped toward Katherine, brows drawn together, and she realized he had not known about it— "and I wanted to share with you a place I love. But I had to wait until your children were out of school. I asked *you*," she told Ross, "because you were in despair over your children and pressures at work and Lord knows what else; you desperately needed to get away and anyone who cared a fig for you would have helped you; it would have been peculiar if I had not."

Imperiously, she eyed the two of them, daring them to respond, but, wisely, they were silent. "In addition," she said tartly, "I expect harmony in my family and I've waited quite long enough for the two of you to become friends on your own. If you cannot do that—for whatever reason— you certainly can tolerate each other during the few days you will be together at the villa. Now." She took a breath. "I am finding it quite tiresome to stand here. Is no one going to take a frail old woman in off the street and buy her a glass of wine?"

Katherine and Ross glanced at each other, exchanging a smile. Sighing, Ross took his grandmother's arm. "The privileges of age are often abused. Come this way; it's just a few steps."

Katherine lagged behind. She was uncomfortable; her dancing delight at being in Paris had faded. Henri wasn't the reason for their visit; she'd been brought here so she and Ross could "run into" each other. It didn't help that Ross had known no more than she; Katherine felt used, not trusted to share in a decision.

I've been treated that way before. By my husband.

Silently she joined Ross and Victoria at Ma Bourgogne, a small café under an arcade in one of the buildings of the Place des Vosges. They sat in rattan chairs at a round table and, as Katherine watched Victoria and Ross chat about Paris, she felt like an outsider. Ross kept glancing at her but she could not participate in their gossip and talk about a city they both knew well and she knew nothing about. She wished she were alone.

The waiter brought a bottle of Bordeaux and filled their glasses. Ross and Victoria talked on. Katherine sat back in her chair, sipping the mellow wine, contemplating the aloof elegance of the mansions on all sides of the grassy square, speculating about the people who lived behind their tall, many-paned windows, dreaming about living in such a place herself someday.

"Katherine?" Victoria said.

She started. "I'm sorry. I didn't hear you."

"Dinner, my dear. We decided on Tour d'Argent. Too many tourists, but I want to watch your face when you see it the first time. And it will be my dinner: I shall treat you both, to compensate for not confiding in you."

She began to tell Ross about their lunch with Henri. Half-listening, Katherine wondered what Victoria expected to happen. Were they supposed to fall in love—or just become instant friends? Her carefree sense of adventure had disappeared; she didn't know how she was expected to behave. "Nine o'clock, then," Victoria said at last, gathering her purse and gloves and rising as the waiter held her chair.

Swiftly, Ross came to hold Katherine's chair. He had sensed her discomfort, and knew she'd rather he weren't there. "Only dinner," he said, his voice low. "Then I won't interfere with any more of your trip."

She looked at him, silenced by surprise and embarrassment.

"It's important to Victoria," he added, leaving out the fact that he was looking forward to the evening. He had thought about Katherine so long, and stayed away from her for so long, that discovering her in Paris seemed almost magical—even if it were no wizard but his grandmother who had brought her there. But he would not tell her that; she was uncomfortable, whether from Victoria's secrecy or because she didn't want Ross intruding on her holiday, and he had no wish to add to her discomfort. "The Tour d'Argent is spectacular," he said. "Enough to make up for even unwelcome dinner companions."

Victoria took Katherine off so quickly she had no chance to respond and there was no chance that evening, either. First Victoria insisted on absolute silence as they were led to their table so she could watch Katherine's delight in the view. For a few moments the three of them gazed without speaking at the barely rippling water of the Seine, reflecting the darkening sky, and the brightly lit Notre Dame cathedral looming from its thickly wooded island, so close it seemed they could touch its square towers and needle-like spire.

"Lovely," Victoria sighed. "I never saw it with Hugh. I wish I had." She turned to Katherine. "There is a famous story about this restaurant—"

The story was lengthy, about a visiting chef and a foreign dignitary, and Katherine tried to follow it while studying the shapes and shadows of Notre Dame and the other ancient buildings on the two islands in the Seine that had been the original city of Paris. She felt Ross watching her, and wondered what he was thinking, and wished she were having the uncomplicated holiday she'd expected.

But suddenly Ross and Victoria became charming companions, as if apologizing for leaving her out that afternoon, entertaining her all through dinner with a colorful history of the kings and queens of France and the dueling, lusting, sniping, gossiping courts that revolved around them in the palaces of Paris. They took turns telling stories, from books they had read, from theater-going in Paris and evenings with Parisian friends, all for Katherine, who was content to listen and laugh with them. By midnight, when the waiter presented Victoria with a bill that made even her worldly eyebrows rise, the evening seemed as friendly and uncomplicated as Katherine could wish.

"Thank you," said Ross, kissing Victoria as they waited for a taxi, "for a most pleasant evening. I haven't told so many stories since I was in college."

"And these were probably far less bawdy," Victoria smiled. "It was a pleasure, dear Ross. I had a delightful time."

At the Meurice, Ross walked with them into the lobby and took Katherine's hand. "I hope your trip is everything you want it to be. You have the best companion in the world. And the villa is a perfect retreat."

"Such formality," said Victoria with a trace of anxiety. "You'll see us in Menton in less than a week."

"I'm not sure." He looked at Katherine's slender hand, still enclosed in his. Nothing she had said all evening indicated she wanted to see him again. "There's more to do here than I'd expected. And my children will be here soon and I thought I might introduce them to Paris. We'll come if we can," he said quickly, as Victoria opened her mouth to reproach him. "I'll let you know, one way or another." Briefly he tightened his hand on Katherine's. "Have a wonderful time. If there's anything I can do for you before you leave Paris, please let me know."

"In my day," Victoria snorted as she and Katherine walked into the elevator, "a gentleman would have offered to buy us a lavish breakfast in the morning." She lapsed into silence. "It would have been pleasant if Ross had done that."

Yes, Katherine thought, surprising herself, as they reached their floor. It would have been very pleasant.

The Place des Vosges is a green park surrounded by thirty-six tall brick and plaster townhouses, or *hôtels*, of dusty pink to deep red, with wrought-iron balconies and round windows in steeply pitched slate roofs. White stone arches lead through each *hôtel* to a private courtyard. Four hundred years ago the park was the scene of royal tournaments and festivals; two hundred years ago the mansions were abandoned for new residences across the Seine, on the Left Bank; in the 1960s they were rediscovered and slowly reclaimed from the factory owners who had boarded up windows, bolted heavy machinery to the rich parquet floors, torn out ornately carved doors, and dumped trash in the inner courtyards.

When Ross first saw it, a few *hôtels* had been bought and were beginning to be restored. When he returned fifteen years later as Jacques Duvain's consultant in restoring one of the *hôtels*, the Place had become a lively blend of new and old. Some of the buildings were still in disrepair, but many had been renovated, hiding, behind identical exteriors, private homes, apartments, schools, restaurants, a synagogue, and a number of fine, small shops.

The second floor of Number 9 Place des Vosges was owned by the Architecture Society, and through Jacques, who was a member, Ross had been given his own quiet corner with a desk, drawing table, and two armchairs for as long as he was in Paris. On the day after his dinner with Victoria and Katherine, he sat at the desk, trying to work. *In my day,* he had heard Victoria scoff as he left them, *a gentleman would have invited us to breakfast.* He had considered it, then decided against it, but still, throughout the day, he thought about Katherine, heard Victoria casually say she had broken with Derek, pictured her as she had looked at the Tour d'Argent—poised, yet eager and curious, making no attempt to seem worldly. She was without pretense, willing to admit there was much she did not know, yet firmly determined to be independent. And in that contradiction, she was both strong and vulnerable. In the past year, Ross thought, she had been different each time he saw her, changing from Craig's protected wife to the elusive woman he had dined with last night. And he realized he knew nothing about her.

But competing with those thoughts was a busy day. He and Jacques worked on various plans for putting an elevator in the four-story *hôtel;* they spent an hour with specialists in matching segments of broken moldings on the fifteen-foot-high ceilings and restoring the parquet floors to their original luster; they met for another hour with the contractor, discussing ways to install modern plumbing and wiring in plaster walls that had withstood wars and revolutions but often crumbled at the bite of an electric drill. Since he had arrived, Ross had studied, read, learned, from early morning until late each night; he had inspected other buildings marked for restoration; he had given advice. He was having a wonderful time. And even when distracted by Katherine's sudden appearance, he was absorbed by the special fascination of bringing into the twentieth century a building constructed in 1605.

"Yes, yes," Jacques admitted when they met for lunch at La Chope des Vosges, at one corner of the Place. "Certainly it is fascinating. And yet—" He paused as they heaped their plates from the hors d'oeuvres buffet near the entrance and found a table. "This elevator—weeks I have spent on this elevator! And now I am trying your idea of hiding it behind the staircase, but of course we must not disturb the sweep of its curve—impossible!"

"I'm working on that."

"I delight to hear it. I also am working on your other suggestion—that we put it at the front of the entrance hall. But you say I may not use the cloakroom. A perfect space! A perfect size!"

"Well, we may have to use it. But it means moving a wall on the third floor."

"Precisely the problem! Why all this effort and cost? It is cheaper to tear down and begin fresh!"

"Not always."

"I concede that. But consider: buildings are made for specific times and people, with specific customs and idiosyncrasies. No one builds for people who will not be born for four hundred years."

"Jacques, working on this *hôtel,* you'd still erase it if you could?"

"Whoosh it out. Begin fresh. An odd debate, is it not? The Americans are the best at tearing down, even buildings only thirty or forty years old. Occasionally they are wrong, but most often I agree. Begin fresh. No clutter of old ideas, no rubble from other generations, no messy traditions, no—"

"Variety," Ross finished helpfully. "Or contrast or history or excitement."

"Well—" Jacques shrugged. "So you say. But what we lose we replace with what is truly ours. Look at us, you and me. Did we not start all fresh? Of course people are not the same as buildings, but what do you think? Was it not better that you and I left wives who were not congenial so we could begin again and improve our situations? Should we not seek perfection? We change; we require new marriages and new buildings. The old no longer satisfies. Who would pay ten million francs for a *hôtel* of four floors with no elevator? Who will tolerate a marriage that is all uphill?" He grinned. "That is not bad."

"Not bad," Ross agreed, then said, "I have two children who are part of my old marriage. Would you have me throw them out . . . give them up?"

"No, no; that is different. You would regret it; so would they. Allow me to speak from experience. My wife and I own an art gallery together. We are good partners, yes?—but ferociously bad at living together. So we kept what was good: we are together often, we dine, we laugh, we shake hands and go to someone else for love. One must leap to new adventures; one does not look back, even if occasionally one regrets losing something along the way. You comprehend? Here is the check; is it my turn to pay?"

"No, mine." Ross pulled out his wallet and smiled. "You're the real consultant, Jacques. We disagree, but without you I'd have no ancient building to study, and you also offer me the bonus of your curious philosophy. I don't give you half as much."

"Not so. You bring me friendship and American technology. As for ancient buildings, it is not your fault America has nothing from the sixteenth century on which you can practice."

"Only wigwams," Ross said and they were chuckling as they walked through the shadowed arcade into the sunlight. Shading his eyes, Ross turned toward the *hôtel* and for the second time in two days found himself face to face with Katherine.

He stopped short. His grandmother's idea—or hers? Then he saw her eyes, self-conscious, determined, a little wary, as if she had steeled herself to be here and feared he might turn his back on her. Ross took her hand. "Welcome back." He looked around. "Are you alone?"

"Yes." She glanced inquiringly at Jacques, who hovered at Ross's shoulder.

"Jacques Duvain," said Ross, piqued by the intense admiration that lit Jacques' face. "Katherine Fraser."

Jacques lifted Katherine's hand and brushed it with his lips. "How pleased I am to greet you." He smiled broadly and, through him, Ross saw Katherine as if for the first time, separated from the familiar back-

ground of San Francisco, with no husband shadowing her, no grandmother as chaperone, no Derek. In a low-necked sleeveless blue dress
with a white jacket over her shoulders, she stood alone, tentatively, as if
on a threshold: a young woman of unusual beauty, hesitating before
opening a door to the unknown. Ross understood why Jacques was intrigued. "I have heard you are visiting," Jacques went on innocently,
with barely a sidelong glance at Ross. "I do not wish to intrude, but if
at some time you desire a guide who has lived here always..." A movement from Ross caught his eye. "Of course my friend Ross knows Paris
almost as well as I. So I leave you" —again, he touched Katherine's
hand with his lips— "but I hope to see you again..." He looked at Ross
and grinned. "I spoke of starting fresh. I did not realize my admirable
friend was far ahead of me. Perhaps dinner one night, the three of us,
if it becomes possible—?"

He drifted off. Silence filled the space left by his chatter. "Why don't
we walk?" Ross suggested. "You didn't get to see the whole square yesterday." Katherine nodded. She was nervous and he wondered again
about his grandmother as they strolled through sunlight and shadow. On
one side was the green park with its fountains and benches, on the other
the stately old *hôtels*. They paused to look through a shop window at a
craftsman restoring a clavichord. "What time are you meeting Victoria?"
Ross asked.

"I'm not." Katherine watched the man's quick fingers. "She went back
to Menton this morning."

He turned sharply. "Was she ill?"

"No." Katherine met his eyes and smiled. "She thought she was being
cool and crafty."

Ross chuckled and then Katherine laughed with him. "Well," he said
as they walked on. "Maybe she was. Here you are."

Katherine stopped, her face deeply flushed. "I act on my own," she
said. Her nervousness gave way to anger; her large eyes were clear and
unwavering. "I'm not a puppet to be manipulated; I make my own decisions."

Ross cursed himself. "I'm sorry; I didn't mean that. I thought you
didn't want me to share your time in Paris, and it was so clear that
Victoria wanted—"

"Of course it was; she even admitted it. But she left without making
any suggestions, without even a hint. She knows I wouldn't have come
to you just because it was something she would have liked, especially
after yesterday."

Ross looked at her averted eyes. "Why did you come?" he asked quietly.

"Because I wanted to." For the first time, her voice wavered. "Because I wanted to see you."

The words struck him with their simplicity. Just as simply, he responded, "I'm glad to see you." In a moment they walked on. "How did Victoria explain her sudden departure?" he asked.

They were passing a sculpture gallery and Katherine paused to look through the window. "She said she'd give me a chance to explore on my own." She smiled, almost to herself. "In a way, she was telling the truth, because yesterday she knew she was holding me back. But whatever her reasons, she gave me our hotel suite and two days in Paris, and that was wonderful. *She's* wonderful, and I'm grateful, and I love her."

"Yes," Ross said. "That's something we share." His eyes had the same tenderness Katherine had seen in Vancouver, the first time she heard him speak of Victoria. "When did she leave?" he asked.

"After breakfast."

"And left you *no* instructions for touring Paris? That doesn't sound like my grandmother."

Katherine laughed. "She left me names of her favorite restaurants and the finest buildings, the places to go for the finest views, small boutiques for the finest of—"

"Everything," he finished and they laughed together. Ross put his hand on Katherine's arm and led her into a restaurant filled with flowers. "Have you followed all her instructions?"

"I'm afraid I forgot most of them. I bought a map; I walked; I took the *Métro*..." She hesitated. "And I took a bus tour."

"A bus—!" He caught himself. "And what did you see?"

"A great many buildings and statues that all looked alike after ten minutes."

He smiled. "That happens on most bus tours. And then?"

"I came to find you."

How natural she made it sound. "Why?" he asked.

"I was thinking about you. I never really knew whether you liked me or not, and it bothered me, and this seemed a good place to find out, but I knew you'd never call me; I knew I had to come to you."

A strange lightness was spreading through Ross. "Why is this a good place?"

"Because it isn't San Francisco. I couldn't have done it there." The waiter brought a carafe of wine and filled their glasses and Katherine raised hers, looking through it at the colorful flowers surrounding them. Seen through the pale gold wine, the petals were elongated and curved, oddly changed. "I feel as if I've broken away from everything I knew, everything I've ever done. Whatever I look at is new. Even ordinary things like groceries and street signs and price tags are exotic and mysterious. So it seems all right to behave differently. In fact, I feel that I ought to, since everything around me is different." She gave a small laugh. "It sounds so foolish."

"No." Ross sat back, stretching his long legs. "When I work with Jacques on the building he's renovating—it's around the corner; I'll show it to you later—we stand in front of fireplaces more than three and a half centuries old, large enough for three men to stand comfortably, and we walk on parquet floors that were laid long before the Pilgrims came to America. It's not easy for me to hold on to twentieth-century thoughts when I stand there; nothing seems quite real."

Katherine's eyes were bright. "Yes. That's exactly it."

"But you didn't think I'd understand. Since I might not like you."

She flushed, then challenged him. "Do you?"

"Yes," he said easily. The waiter reappeared, dividing the remaining wine evenly between their glasses. "We can talk about it, if you'd like. At dinner. Will you have dinner with me? And tomorrow, if you'll let me, I'd like to show you my Paris. It's quite different from Victoria's, but I think you'll enjoy it. If you have no other plans, of course. And if it would please you . . ."

For the first time, Katherine's smile was relaxed. "It would please me very much," she said.

Dinner was at Chez Philippe, small, casual, crowded, with vociferous conversations bouncing off the stone walls, beamed ceiling and red tile floor. Ross had reserved a table in a quiet corner. "It's not always so noisy," he said as they were brought a bottle of country wine. "But it's a neighborhood place and when it's crowded it's like one big family gathering. Are you disappointed?"

"No," Katherine said, surprised. "Why would I be?"

"It's a long way from Tour d'Argent or Taillevent or L'Archestrate. I should have told you I'm not fond of spectacular restaurants. It doesn't matter how special the food, I can't enjoy it when it takes second place to mirrors and silks and black-tie waiters who whip silver covers off the plates like penguin magicians."

Katherine was smiling, but, uncomfortably, she remembered how impressed she had been when Derek took her to San Francisco's most glittering restaurants. And it was true that she had expected one of the places Victoria or Derek would have chosen, and had dressed for it. And pale yellow silk seemed excessive in the simple room.

"You look wonderful," Ross said, watching her look at the other women. "And not out of place. Chez Philippe prides itself on individualism. Is that a Parisian dress?"

"Yes; is it really all right? I found a wonderful shop yesterday; one of the designers Victoria introduced me to told me about it, a place called Miss Griffes—" Ross nodded, and she said, "You've heard of it?"

"Melanie heard of it. Designer clothes that had been used on mannequins in store displays—isn't that it?—sold for next to nothing. Melanie never went there; she said she didn't like used clothes."

"Victoria told me you'd separated."

"Yes," he said shortly. "So you liked Miss Griffes?"

"Liked it? I went into a trance. I didn't even count dollars; I just spent francs. I haven't spent so much on myself since—for more than a year."

"It's about time you did. You're very lovely, Katherine." Her color rose and she looked again around the room as Ross contemplated her. Her beauty was softer and less vivid than Melanie's, her gestures less sharp, her dress, though exquisitely cut, simpler than one Melanie would have chosen. But perhaps because of that she seemed steadier than Melanie, more steadfast, more—

Damn it, he cursed silently. Why the hell am I comparing her to Melanie? They have nothing to do with each other.

"I'll order, shall I?" he asked as the waiter approached. "The food is Basque and you might find it unfamiliar."

"I might," she agreed. "Since I don't even know what it is."

He laughed. "It's from the Pyrenees, a cross between Gascon France and northern Spain. Do you like roast quail?"

"I have no idea."

"We'll share, then." He ordered it, then added, "And *cassoulet*. With a Pomerol or a Saint-Emilion. I leave the choice to you; the best year of the two." He sat back. "If you dislike any of it, we'll order something else. But I think you'll find it worth giving up the showplaces."

"I wish you'd stop expecting me to be disappointed," Katherine said mildly. "I like it here. I don't need showplaces; that was exactly what I didn't like about the bus tour. Everything I saw was magnificent, but it was the public face of the city. I kept wanting to see the hidden part, to make discoveries—"

"—to turn a corner and find real people—"

"—doing the laundry or making dinner—"

"—or eating together in a neighborhood restaurant."

They were laughing. As the waiter brought glasses and the Pomerol,

Ross put his hand on Katherine's. "You have my promise," he said, "that for the next two days, you will see only the hidden side of Paris."

He kept his word, beginning at seven thirty the next morning. "Victoria would be appalled at the hour," he grinned when he met Katherine in the Meurice lobby. "But she would approve of my buying your breakfast."

"I don't think this is quite what she had in mind," Katherine commented as they stood at the bar of a small café while having their croissants and coffee. But she laughed as she said it, because the morning was sunlit and cool, the croissants hot and buttery, and she was as eager as Ross to begin—not to sit in a restaurant at the mercy of a waiter's deliberate pace, but to hurry into the city that awaited them.

There are so many cities called Paris that no one can count them, for no two people view it the same way and no one views it with indifference. Brilliantly beautiful, deafeningly noisy, jammed with people and traffic, stunning in its vistas, grubby in its corners, infinitely varied and experimental in food, couture, culture, churches and erotica, it is a city that prides itself on being at once a vast museum and a vibrant, living part of the modern world.

Ross's Paris embraced it all, but especially the hidden *arrondissements* behind the city's grandeur: narrow, twisting streets where generations of families have lived and loved, worshiped, worked, died, and been buried. Over the years, in trips with his parents and then alone or with Melanie, he had explored those labyrinthine neighborhoods, each centered on a church and a small square or park, listening to conversations in the bistros, making friends, reading French history and literature, and studying the architecture that religion and everyday life had inspired.

These were the streets he and Katherine walked, while he told her their legends and histories. It was as if he were peeling off layers of the past, revealing the quirks and dreams of centuries. "The owners found eighteenth-century torture instruments in the lower cellar," he said as they stopped before the massive double doors of a renovated building. "If you can picture it—revolutionaries suspended over vats of boiling oil, while, three floors up, in the kitchen, the cook measures olive oil for the salad dressing. An eerie symmetry: death and life, killing and creating..."

Katherine gazed at the carving of the Greek goddess of justice above the door. "I wonder if every family has a cellar it would like to forget."

A smile lit Ross's eyes. It was a thought he'd had often when restoring old buildings, but he had never talked about it with anyone. "People, too," he said. "We have our cellars inside us—things in our past we try to bury and ignore."

The words hung in the air. Repeating them silently, Ross thought of the one person they best described. He scrutinized Katherine, trying to think of her as Craig's wife. But Craig was remote; absent. Nothing seemed real but Paris.

Katherine looked past him. His words had tugged at her, but the pull of the present was stronger. Just as she had at Victoria's villa, she felt cut off from everything that had happened before. At least for a while, it had been left behind. She met Ross's eyes. "I'm sure we all do," she said easily.

Slowly, he let out his breath and together they turned and walked on. In the Rue de la Bucherie they came to a wall that Ross said had been part of the Faculty of Medicine five hundred years earlier. "Only monks practiced medicine then," he mused. "They prescribed eating earthworms in white wine to cure jaundice, droppings of mice for bladder stones and the blood of a hare for gallstones." He glanced at Katherine. "In a classic case of discrimination, women weren't permitted medical care."

"Fortunate women," she murmured, and they laughed as they moved on. A few blocks farther, Ross touched Katherine's arm.

"Here's the other side of the story of torture in the cellar." He ran his hand over a dark stone embedded in the corner of a new building. "Buried treasure. When the old building was condemned, and wreckers ripped open the wall, a torrent of *louis d'or* gold pieces poured out—over three thousand twenty-two-carat gold coins—and the will of a man who'd disappeared in 1757, bequeathing it all to his daughter. Eventually eighty or so descendants of the daughter were found, and they divided up the fortune."

"The other side of the story," Katherine repeated slowly. "Torture and treasure, balancing each other. Symmetry. Is that what you look for in your work?"

Ross felt the rush of joy that came with having someone to share his thoughts. "In my work and for myself. To be able to juggle things so that, even if I go off half-cocked over something, eventually I can come back to a balanced center. That's probably why I love Paris, because it exists by its own balancing act: some of the bloodiest history of all time alongside a reverence for life; memorials to hermits next to monuments to the family; the wildest post-modernism a few feet from the most lovingly preserved works of ancient times. All those wonderful contradictions that add up to symmetry."

The idea intrigued Katherine. He had described not only architecture, but jewelry design as well. They strolled on and she thought about it, exhilarated by having a new way of thinking about familiar things. "Ross," she said impulsively. "I'm having a wonderful time."

His eyes swung to her, almost stunned with surprise. "I'm glad," he said. "There's so much more I want you to see..." And as they walked on, Katherine wondered what had surprised him: that she was having a good time, or that she had told him she was.

They walked all that day, the hours passing for Katherine in a reverie of the past intertwined with the bustle of a modern city. She and Ross convinced sextons to show them through ancient churches, and concierges to let them look into renovated apartment buildings with their inner courtyards and formal gardens; they stopped at kiosks where Ross translated the colorful posters plastered on all sides, announcing everything from operas to protest marches; they dawdled at open bookstalls on the Left Bank of the Seine where neither could resist buying ("Just a few," Katherine kept vowing, "I'm getting heavier by the minute"); they paused beside sidewalk artists and musicians; after lunch in a small bistro they climbed steep steps to the plateau at the top of Montmartre where Paris disappeared in the crooked streets of a small village of dilapidated studios of earnest young painters and sculptors. And they walked along the quays beside the Seine in the soft, silver light of early evening that lay like a delicate veil over the river and its arched stone bridges, and the people, lingering before going home.

For two days they traversed the city, on foot, by bus, or on the *Métro*, with its wide, brightly lit corridors lined with huge paintings and enlivened by young musicians sitting cross-legged, playing guitars or saxophones or flutes. But most of the time they walked and Ross talked, and as he did, Katherine's eyes kept returning to his face. The harshness she had often seen there was gone. Except at their first lunch, when he had told her about BayBridge, she had never seen him look so relaxed, his deep voice warm and animated, with a boyish delight in sharing what he knew. But what struck her most were his hands when he ran them over ancient stones and grillework: warm and sensual as if the material were alive. Mine must look like that, she thought, remembering the feel of warm gold as she shaped and worked it, and she knew they both felt they could touch the hidden life of stone and metal through their fingertips. But Ross had something more, she thought enviously; he also touched the work of others, as if he clasped hands, over the ages, with builders long dead but living still in the structures they left behind.

"It's a way of staying close to my grandfather," Ross said, startling Katherine by seeming to respond to her thoughts. They were standing in a small courtyard tucked away on the Rue Jacob, facing two houses, one restored and inhabited, the other empty and crumbling with the ravages of three hundred years. Ross ran his hand over one of the two stone lions guarding the restored house. "Every time I bring a building to life, I'm keeping him alive. In fact," he added half-humorously, "I can hear him criticizing me or approving the kind of restoration I'm doing, as if we're still having the long conversations we had when he was alive. It's almost as if we're working together."

"I wish I'd known him," Katherine said.

"He would have loved you." Ross opened the gate and they left the courtyard. "You would have reminded him of Victoria."

Katherine flushed with pleasure, and was silent, treasuring his words as they walked together toward Rue Bonaparte and Ross pointed out details on houses and shops that he admired. Watching his long fingers trace fanciful wrought-iron gates and stone figures from mythology or the Bible, Katherine wanted to put her hand on his, to share his sensual touch on the material and his connection with the past. Instead, she shared them by talking with him and watching the movements of his hands, his mobile face, and the sights he pointed out, liking him more and more for his concentration and depth of feeling. We share that, too, she thought, remembering her own absorption in her work, until she realized that in Ross's concentration there were times when he seemed to forget she was there. Which is more important to him, she wondered—the past or the present?

Which is more important to me? The thought sprang out, but no sooner was it there than she pushed it back. She was thinking about Ross; later, she'd think about herself.

When they went to their separate hotels to change for dinner, Katherine lay in her marble tub, soaking muscles that had carried her through countless Parisian miles. The next morning, she would fly back to Menton. She thought about the past three days, and about Ross Hayward— who avoided fancy restaurants but was expert in fine cuisine and wines; who moved easily in international social and professional circles but sought out the hidden streets of Paris; who built the most modern urban developments while preserving buildings from the past; who had a family but avoided talking about it; who was handsome and successful but who almost never spoke about himself; who had given her two of the most companionable days she had ever known after months of being cool and distant in San Francisco. And she knew she did not understand him at all.

"One last hidden part of Paris," he said as, that evening, they walked through the kitchen of Allard and were shown a table. "One of my favorites."

The waiter knew Ross, jovially calling him *Monsieur le Président* as he did all his favorite customers, and conducting a vigorous debate with him over their after-dinner drink. "Of course it doesn't matter," Ross confided to Katherine. "They bring Calvados whatever one orders, because that's what they consider proper. But debate comes first; one must honor tradition."

The past and the present, Katherine thought. "Is that most important to you?" she asked. "Tradition? The things of the past?"

"They endure," he said.

"But they don't. They crumble."

"You were in St. Julien le Pauvre today. Built in 587."

"But—what does that mean? That you trust stone because sometimes it endures?"

"It's a better bet than paper. Better than metal, clay, wood...Or love," he added lightly. "Or marriage." The waiter brought their Calvados and poured from the bottle into two snifters, addressing Katherine as *Madame la Présidente* and complimenting them on what a *harmonieux* couple they made.

Swirling the brandy in his glass, Ross said, "You deserve an answer. The things of the past are important to me for the same reason I became an architect; because I need to feel there's a continuous line holding us together, all the generations and ages. We aren't in a void, spinning out our lives and then disappearing; we're part of something that stretches behind us and ahead of us, that gives meaning to our lives and everything we create. We all want to leave something behind; that means we need to believe others will see what we've made, touch it, bring it to life. In a way, that's what keeps us alive."

He smiled and took Katherine's hand. "I didn't mean to lecture. At the moment I'm very much enjoying the present. Which reminds me. I'm meeting Carrie and Jon at the airport tomorrow. It's occurred to me" —his voice grew casual— "that they'd probably enjoy the country more than the city. And Todd and Jennifer's companionship. Would you mind if we join you tomorrow—when you fly to Menton?"

CHAPTER 14

ROSS had telephoned ahead, so Victoria was prepared for the invasion when the limousine arrived from the airport in Nice, and few would have guessed, from her unruffled smile and calm kisses, that she had not planned from the beginning to spend the month of July with four children under the age of twelve. But Ross, feeling responsible, whispered as he greeted her, "They won't bother you; I'll keep them on a leash, never out of my sight."

"Oh, but you mustn't," she said in alarm. "You'd have no time for yourself."

Or to be with Katherine, he thought, which was what she really meant. Amused, he watched her welcome the children. Stubborn, tenacious, trying to manage her family's lives, so she could live through them. And clever, he reflected; she knew Katherine and I would get along. "We'll make time for everything," he promised, bringing a smile to Victoria's face as she watched them go to their rooms to unpack.

The children were in a wing of four rooms and a playroom, with its own courtyard, that Hugh and Victoria had added to the villa, anticipating noisy visits from grandchildren. Craig, Jennifer, Derek, and Ross had stayed there every summer, and as they grew older the playroom grew with them: rocking horses and Tinker Toys replaced by motorized Erector sets, model airplanes, and, finally, drafting tables, a television set and stereo, and a cabinet filled with chess, backgammon, Scrabble, Chinese Checkers, and Monopoly.

From the doorway, Ross shook his head wonderingly. "She hasn't changed a thing," he told Katherine as they walked into the room. "The last time I was here was 1966; the four of us came for a couple of weeks when school ended. The next month Jennifer was killed and Victoria closed the whole wing. But" —gently he touched a chessman and a model of the Wright Brothers' first plane— "she didn't change a thing."

Katherine picked up a small open box with a strand of black pearls coiled inside. "Jennifer's," Ross said. "She left it behind when we went home."

"She forgot it?" Katherine asked.

"She didn't want it. Which rooms are yours? Did Victoria ever tell you she has a scheme for assigning suites to visitors?"

"No." He had cut her off. Too personal, Katherine thought. They walked out of the playroom and turned a corner into a wide corridor. One side was entirely of glass, looking through horizontal wooden slats into the villa's flower gardens and, beyond, the badminton court, croquet lawn, and vegetable gardens. In the mornings, the slats were closed to keep out the sun. On the other side of the corridor, doorways led to three suites, each with sliding glass doors opening on to the terrace that overlooked the pink-beige roofs of Menton, the crowded harbor and the azure Mediterranean. Wooden slats formed a canopy over the terrace, and were tilted after lunch to shade the house from the blazing afternoon sun. "Here is mine," said Katherine, turning into a bedroom and sitting room in sage green and ivory: a cool oasis amid the blinding colors of the Riviera. "And what was Victoria's scheme in choosing it for me?"

Ross sat on the arm of a chair and looked about the two spacious rooms. "When we were growing up, the villa was always full of guests— writers, painters, diplomats, businessmen—coming and going, all summer long. Mostly we didn't pay much attention, but those who were given this suite we watched, because Victoria made it clear they were her favorites. What we didn't know was whether she put them here because they were special, or whether they became special by staying here. Finally we decided the rooms were magic and each of us, I guess, dreamed of the day Victoria would ask *us* to stay in them." He smiled. "Of course it never occurred to her; why should it? We had a whole wing to ourselves. And she had her special people. Not many—Victoria doesn't love easily or casually—but a few every summer, enough to make me remember these rooms. Do you know what her plans are for dinner tonight?"

"No." He'd done it again, she thought; offered a glimpse of himself, then skidded away to something else.

"Because, I thought we might take a drive after dinner," he went on.

"Monte Carlo is a few miles down the road; worth seeing once and then avoided. Unless you had enough sightseeing in—?"

"Dad," said Jon, charging in. "Carrie says I have to unpack. We're gonna be here all month; why do I have to unpack this minute? Why do I have to unpack anyway? I can find everything in my suitcase. Carrie's only dumping on me because she's mad at Jennifer."

"Why is she mad at Jennifer?" Katherine asked.

Jon looked up dubiously, not sure how to behave with Katherine. She was butting in on their vacation, but his dad seemed to like her, so he and Carrie had talked it over and decided it would be smart to be careful. "Just 'cause she and Todd were here all week," he said, "they act like they live here and we don't belong."

Seeing Katherine's dismay, Ross said quickly, "I think this requires some diplomacy. Do you mind if I handle it?"

She shook her head and watched the two of them leave the room. *Did she mind!* For a year she'd been forced to settle every squabble and soothe every anxiety by herself. Now she stood in the perfect silence of her room, content to let Ross deal with her children. And that, she thought, makes this a real vacation.

Sheltered from the gusting north winds, in an almost tropical climate, lush palm trees grow in Menton; citrus orchards yield oranges, tangerines, grapefruits, kumquats, and lemons year round, and pine, olive, and cypress trees grow thickly on the hills beyond the town, hiding the villas tucked among them. A short drive away, the world's wealthy gamble all night, and tan by day; a two-hour drive away, skiers find snow all year long in the Alps. Aloof from them all, the villas of Menton, reached by paths and steep staircases, guard their privacy and ignore the tourists below.

At Villa Serein, Victoria attempted to impose her benevolent rule. "I have a complete list," she told Ross and Katherine, "of the music and art festivals between Menton and Aix-en-Provence—a fine day's trip— plus the museums and churches and Roman ruins you will want to see. Hugh and I loved poking through them; Katherine, you must take your sketch pad; you'll find extraordinary formations. As for the children—" She spread a sheaf of papers on the table.

"I've arranged private sailing and rock-climbing excursions, and swimming and diving lessons in Menton's pool. In addition, I've spoken to a friend in Monaco who has tennis courts and his own coach; the children are welcome there any time. And of course, there are movie theaters, the library in the villa, and the games in the playroom. I presume they are appropriate." She looked up. "If not, I will buy whatever..." Her voice faltered as she saw Ross shaking his head. "What is it?"

"You know what it is; we've been through this before. You cannot organize every hour of everyone's day. I need time with Carrie and Jon; I have to return to Paris for a few days; I want some time with you and with Katherine; I'd like some time alone. I think it would be best if we work out our own schedules and then try to put them together."

"It would not be best," Victoria said tartly. "I become exceedingly nervous when I don't know what is happening under my own roof. But I understand about the children; I should have realized. You and Katherine could take them sailing, in place of some of their sailing lessons; I'll arrange that—"

"I don't want you to arrange it," he said. "You've been arranging since you took Katherine to Paris."

"And what was wrong with that?" she demanded. "You had a fine time—!"

"Couldn't we decide this together?" Katherine asked. "Everything you've thought of is wonderful, but it doesn't leave me any time either; I have to design at least a dozen new pieces of jewelry. And you didn't say what you're going to do. Couldn't we discuss it? Ross?"

"A good idea. We'll have a conference."

"Would that make you less nervous?" Katherine asked Victoria.

"Most likely," she said. "Often I think I'm most nervous when I don't get my way."

Ross laughed. "Often I think so too. Well, let's see what we can organize."

Uphill of the villa, with a view of the terrace where the adults were talking, Jennifer, Todd, Carrie, and Jon sat cross-legged in the shade of a cypress tree, eating oranges and playing Scrabble. It was a morose game. Jennifer and Todd thought Carrie and Jon had been foisted on them, cutting into the exclusive attention they got from their great-grandmother while their mother was in Paris; and Carrie and Jon, remembering their mother's biting comments, thought Katherine and her children were intruders and troublemakers. But Ross had practically ordered them all to get along, saying he expected a peaceful vacation and they could be peaceful separately or together, but they had to understand that sailing and rock-climbing and tennis weren't for one person at a time. Either they did them as a group, or not at all. It was up to them.

So they were a group, playing a glum but determined game of Scrabble. They watched Todd ponder his letters, then place three tiles on the board.

"B-U-X," he spelled aloud, adding in a rush, "That's fourteen points and it's doubled so I get—"

"There's no such word," Jennifer said indignantly.

"There is too." He looked sideways at the others and began to giggle. "It means lots of money."

A smothered laugh burst from Jon, and in spite of themselves Carrie and Jennifer laughed, too. "Not bad," Carrie conceded.

"Then I can have it?" Todd asked. "Twenty-eight points?"

"No," they all said in unison.

"Nuts." He pondered, found another place to make "bull," then watched sternly as Jennifer took her turn and made "filial." "*That's* not a word, either."

"It is too. Just because you never heard of it—"

"It is a word," said Carrie.

"Meaning what?" Todd demanded.

"Being a son or daughter."

"Oh. Well, it isn't a word for everybody."

"It *is* for everybody!" Jennifer said impatiently. "When you have a mother and father you're a—"

"I don't have a father. Neither do you."

"That is the stupidest thing I ever heard!" Furious, Jennifer shoved aside her letters. "We do have a father. He just isn't here right now."

"If he isn't here we don't have him."

"Hey," scowled Jon. "My dad doesn't live with us but we still have him."

"That's not the same," Todd retorted. "You know where your dad is, even when you're not with him. That's a lot better than with my dad—"

"It isn't better, it's worse, 'cause I know he's there and it's crazy that he's not living with us—I mean, you know he's just across the bay, you can sort of see where he lives—but he's not with you when you want him and that's *crazy*..."

"It's better than not even knowing if your dad is alive or not!"

"How do you know!"

"Oh, stop it!" Jennifer cried. "The worst thing of all is never seeing your father and we haven't seen ours in months and months—"

"Yes, but then you get used to it," said Carrie. "I mean, with our dad we're always saying goodbye. We spend a weekend with him or have dinner or something and then he takes us home and he never comes in, he stays outside and we say goodbye. Every time I turn around I have to say goodbye!"

"You say hello, too," Todd countered.

"Yes, but I'm always thinking about later, how I'm going to have to say goodbye all over again. It's awful and I start to cry because I never get used to it."

"Well I'd rather cry," said Jennifer flatly, "than not have a father at all."

"You said we did have a father!" Todd yelled.

"Not close by, like Carrie and Jon. We have a father somewhere, and he sends us money, but we never talk to him or go places with him like they do... they see their dad every day!"

"Only here," said Carrie. "Not at home." Her eyes filled with tears. "And if you want to know what's really the worst of all, it's looking out your window and watching your father drive away. Seeing the *back* of his *car*."

"You think *that's* bad," Todd declared. "Try thinking you'll never see your father again."

Silence fell. Orange peels lay on the wild grass; a bee circled over them, buzzing loudly before disappearing into the bushes nearby. "This is silly," Jennifer said in a small voice. "We all have things that are bad. I don't want to have a *contest* about them."

"I don't either," said Carrie. "Nobody would win."

Todd was staring glumly at the Scrabble board. Suddenly he raised both hands and furiously rubbed his head, making his hair stand on end, as if he were vehemently washing it clean. He looked at them challengingly. "I'd win," he said. "If anybody would let me use 'bux.'"

There was a startled pause, then a shaky laugh from Jennifer, and then they all were laughing, louder and louder, unable to stop, their screeches echoing off the cliffs and reaching the adults below, who smiled at the sound. Gradually, the laughter slowed and faded away. They wiped their eyes and smiled at each other—and were friends.

The days fell into a rhythm that turned out, not surprisingly, to be similar to Victoria's plans. Most mornings, Katherine worked on her jewelry designs; Ross was with his children; Jennifer and Todd entertained themselves, or were with Katherine when she wasn't working, or were invited to join Victoria in the garden, where the three of them had a glorious time picking their way through vegetables and flowers and pulling a weed here and there while the gardener stood by in silent agony, waiting for the moment when he could reclaim his private kingdom.

In the afternoons, everyone went in different directions. Victoria read in her sitting room; the children went off on whichever excursion or lesson she had scheduled for that day; and Ross and Katherine explored the countryside.

They had begun the first night, after dinner. Ross had rented a car and they drove along the coast to Monte Carlo. "Not impressed?" he inquired when Katherine stood silently before the marble and bronze, gilt and crystal of the palace-like Casino and Hotel de Paris, glaringly lit against the black Mediterranean night.

"Very impressed," she answered. All around them, between the Casino and the hotel, a constantly shifting stream of people paraded in glittering evening dress, tuxedoes, capes, and feathered hairpieces that nodded like the palm trees above. "It's a little like a bakery," she added thoughtfully.

It pulled him up short. Once more he surveyed the chandeliers, curliqued balconies, and decorations of plaster caryatids and exaggerated flowers. "A bakery?"

"At Christmas. Puff pastry, meringues, and layer cakes. Iced, sprinkled, tinted, decorated, absolutely gorgeous, and festive, because they're overdone and unreal. And they look so expensive."

"And they are." Amused, Ross surveyed the crowd as he and Katherine walked through the rooms of the Casino where bored gamblers sat at the tables or wandered in the smoky air, peering over shoulders or stopping to exchange a tidbit of gossip. Ross pointed to a croupier spinning the roulette wheel. "The chef?"

"Or a spun sugar Santa Claus," Katherine responded and they were laughing as they walked back to the car.

The next day at breakfast, Ross casually mentioned the hill town of Saint-Paul, an easy drive from Menton, a pleasant way to spend an afternoon. His afternoon was free; was Katherine's?

Katherine looked inquiringly at Victoria. "Certainly you should go," Victoria said promptly. "Nothing else is scheduled. Stay for dinner, if you wish."

"I'd like to be back for dinner," Katherine said.

They left after lunch and spent the afternoon in the old village that clung to the top of a craggy peak, surrounded by the stone wall built a thousand years earlier to protect it from invading armies. "I used to come here when I was in high school," Ross recalled. "Usually alone. My grandfather was the only one who found it as fascinating as I did, but even he had enough after a while. I never tired of it." His voice echoed off the stone arches above the narrow, climbing streets. "I made up stories about the people who lived here, the battles they fought, the games they played..."

"And you were the hero," Katherine said.

His eyebrows rose. "How would you know that?"

"I made up my own stories. I didn't have a wonderful stone village on the top of a hill—I only had Golden Gate Park—but I had battles and games and imaginary friends, and a family... I can't picture you being alone, with your family around you."

"I was alone when I wanted to be; I escaped from them and came up here. I had a place like it in San Francisco, not as remote, but private enough to suit me. Special places," Ross added thoughtfully. "I loved being alone." He laughed shortly. "I seem to have lost that, as an adult. I've had to learn it all over again."

"Did you?" Katherine looked at him curiously. It was the first time he had volunteered something about himself. "You've always seemed to me so self-sufficient and sure of yourself; I thought there was something wrong with me because I had such a terrible time getting used to being alone."

"Probably something wrong with you if it came naturally." Ross told her about the first time Carrie and Jon had come to his house in Berkeley. "Jon still refuses to call it ours. And that reminds me that they'll leave and I'll be alone and I'm still not used to it."

"I know," Katherine said in a low voice. "I used to talk to myself—"

"Did you? I wondered about that. Especially when I found myself doing it."

"—and then I'd be embarrassed and turn on the radio."

"I didn't think of the radio. I ordered myself to get used to the silence."

"And did you?"

"No."

They had walked beyond the town, and in a few minutes reached the Maeght Fondation, where they strolled through the art museum and its sun-washed sculpture gardens, pointing out the pieces they liked best, agreeing, they discovered, far more often than not. Later, they returned to Saint-Paul, for wine and cheese at La Colombe d'Or—"Also a museum," Ross said as Katherine admired the colorful Léger mural in the courtyard where they sat. "Wait until you see the paintings inside. It all began when the owner, Monsieur Roux, allowed his poorest customers, who were also his friends, to pay for dinner with their paintings when they had no money. The customers were named Picasso, Braque, Miró, Matisse, Dufy—among others."

"A wise man," Katherine said. Mischievously, she asked, "Which would he have said endures best? Friendship or stone?"

"Appetite," Ross replied instantly. "It's his livelihood." They shared a smile in the shadows lengthening across flower-filled stone urns and glossy dark ivy cascading over the walls behind them. "I thought we might drive to San Remo tomorrow," he said. "Just over the Italian border. The drive along the corniche is supposed to be worth seeing."

Victoria confirmed it at dinner. "Magnificent. The most wonderful palms at Bordighera, and flower gardens covering the slopes beside the road..." Her voice became soft. "Hugh always bought me flowers. He couldn't stop; he admitted it was like a disease—but a most benign one. Every time he saw a flower vendor he'd stop the car and buy a bunch of everything. By the end of the day people would see our car heaped with flowers and stop *us* to buy. When I'd tell them my husband had bought them for me, the tourists would say, 'Where will you put them all?' but the French would nod wisely and say, '*Folie ou amour.*' Madness or love." She laughed softly. "*Folie ou amour.* But they knew it was *amour.* Well, then." She looked contentedly at Ross and Katherine. "San Remo. I most certainly recommend it."

After San Remo, each morning at breakfast Ross would casually mention another town, or one of the modern art museums strung along the Riviera, or a drive through the Alps. Occasionally, gingerly, Victoria would make a suggestion from the store of her memories, but usually she smiled quietly as Katherine and Ross pored over maps, making plans. On weekends, when the children had no activities, they took the four of them along, but the rest of the time they went alone, each day roaming a little farther, taking different turns in the roads that twisted through the hills to explore a château or a garden with a thousand tropical plants growing on cliffs and in underground caves, or a ruined olive mill with ancient wooden sprocketed wheels and grinding stones in stone troughs.

Everywhere were the scents of Provence: herbs, olive oil, tomatoes and garlic, orange and rosemary, fruit trees and lavender, baguettes fresh from the oven. One morning Ross brought a round-handled basket to the breakfast table and that day they left the villa before lunch, carrying the basket that Victoria's cook had filled with a Niçoise onion tart, cheeses and fruit, and a bottle of Provence rosé wine.

Two hours later they opened it beside a stream in an Alpine meadow, sitting beneath a tall pine on a carpet of silken wild grass. The stream was bright with hundreds of tiny waterfalls spilling over rocks and boulders in its rush down the mountain; the air was clear and warm. "I feel so lazy," Katherine said, lying on the grass. Above her, the rough branches and dark needles of the tree were silhouetted against a deep blue sky. "And not at all ashamed."

Ross handed her a cluster of grapes. "Why should you be ashamed?"

"Because I'm not doing anything."

He settled back against the tree and looked down at her. "You're relaxing. Contemplating nature. Enjoying sun and shade. Giving great pleasure to your companion. Busy enough for a summer day. You can't mean you've never taken a holiday before."

"No, of course I have. But I don't think I ever let myself feel really lazy. Part of me was always thinking ahead, making lists of all the things I should be doing, planning schedules... there were so many *shoulds* in my life..."

"And now?"

"Mostly questions." Katherine sat up, crosslegged. "They all begin, 'Can I—?'" She looked at Ross. "Isn't that odd? I thought I had more restrictions now, because I'm responsible for the three of us. But somehow I don't. I have fewer."

"Because you've proved what you can do."

Katherine shook her head. "I haven't proved anything yet. But I'm finding out."

Still not sure of herself, Ross thought. But, after all, how could she be? She'd only had a year. And a good part of that must have been spent getting used to being alone. He watched her gather pine needles into a fragrant bundle in her palm, and wondered when she would begin to take her accomplishments for granted, as well as her beauty and all the other changes of the past year. When she's convinced her life is settled, he thought. Until then, who can blame her for being uncertain and a little tentative?

Without warning, Ross thought of Derek. How uncertain had she been with him? Contemplating Katherine's pensive face, asking himself the question, Ross couldn't make sense of it: the more he learned about her, the more impossible it seemed that she had been one of Derek's conquests. He started to ask her about it, then stopped himself. What would he say? *Who are you, really, that you could embrace my brother?* If I want to understand her, he thought, I'll do it by understanding who she is with me, not who she might have been with Derek. I owe her that much.

But still, he could not prevent the thought from slipping through: *Someday I may have to ask her.*

"Tell me about your life in New York," Katherine said, when she looked up and found Ross watching her.

She was, as he had discovered, a good listener. Ross told her about his apartment on the West Side with its glimpse of the Hudson River between two other buildings; his friendship with Jacques Duvain; his work on urban redevelopment projects in Boston and Philadelphia that had gained national attention. "By then Victoria was calling once or twice a week, asking me to come back, not to the company—she knew I didn't want that—but to start my own firm. She said she needed me, for friendship, companionship, the family; and I knew I needed her for the same things. Besides, I was confident enough to think I was ready for my own firm. She clinched it by offering to recommend me to her friends and fellow board members—"

Katherine laughed. "She did the same for me, with jewelry store owners."

"One of her most lovable qualities is her consistency. You turned her down?"

"It was important to me that I do it on my own."

"Because you were just beginning. But I'd had those years in New York, and enough success behind me, to take her up on it. Some of my best commissions came through her contacts, and most of them came back for second homes or office buildings. My favorite is a real estate tycoon whose house I designed in Mill Valley. The second job I did for him was a shopping center he named after himself. He was so proud, he said he never wanted to leave it, so he had a mausoleum built for him and his family beneath the main store."

"Cash registers instead of gravestones," said Katherine wryly.

Ross laughed. "We never put it that way, but that's perfect." He lay the empty wine bottle in the basket. "We'd better get started if we want to be back for dinner. Although we don't really have to, you know..."

"I want to." Katherine stood up, brushing off her jeans. "It's a good time to be with the children, and I think it's important to Victoria."

Ross picked a fragment of pine cone from her hair. "It's also important to Victoria that we have time together." She looked quickly at him and he smiled into her clear eyes. "She's a very wise lady."

Katherine returned his smile but did not answer. He had talked about everything, she thought, except his wife, whom he had met and married in New York. She wondered about it through dinner, and afterward, on the terrace, while she and Ross played Chinese Checkers with the children under Victoria's critical eye, but she thought mostly about Ross and his grandparents. He had moved back to San Francisco because Victoria needed him, and because he missed her. The year before, in Vancouver, almost his first words had been that he was there because his grandmother had sent him. And he felt he was still connected to his grandfather. *A continuous line—holding us all together, all the generations and ages.* Katherine had never known anyone who moved comfortably across the generations, who knew where he fit within them, and it seemed to her that Ross's world was infinitely larger than hers, with more places to belong.

But her world was growing, she thought; it was expanding, stretching ahead with more possibilities, more people to consider, so much more to think about...

"Ha!" cried Jon, using his marble to leap over four others to reach the colored triangle that was his goal. "First one in."

"Not for long," Ross responded with a wicked gleam and jumped over six marbles to his own goal. "Katherine? Are you with us?"

"Oh. Yes. Let me see..."

"Dad," said Jon as Katherine surveyed the board. "There's a party this weekend at the Casino in Monte Carlo. We've been invited."

Ross raised his eyebrows. "They don't allow youngsters in the Casino."

"One of the kids' fathers rented a private room and they're putting in roulette and blackjack and everything. Really neat. It starts at eight o'—"

"Hold on," Ross said. Jennifer, Todd and Carrie watched him, almost holding their breath. "This party is for nine- and ten-year-olds?"

"Well... most of the kids are like sixteen and seventeen but they asked us 'cause we're good on the diving team. So can you drive us?"

"No. I don't want you at the Casino, even in a private room, especially with an older crowd."

"Dad—!"

"I doubt that you'd even be allowed in, but we're not going to find out. You have plenty of things to keep you busy; gambling isn't one of them."

"But, Dad—!"

"No, Jon. That's final. It's no place for any of you. You're not going."

"Jee-sus," muttered Jon.

"I told you," Carrie said. "I knew he'd say no."

At the obvious relief in her voice, Ross and Katherine exchanged an amused glance. "About the diving—" Ross began.

"Maybe I'll just go home," Jon muttered. "If you won't let me do what I want, maybe I won't stay. Or visit you anymore on weekends, either."

"Jon!" said Katherine sharply. Ross was frowning, his mouth tight, and for the first time she saw in practice the power of his children.

"Jon," she said again. Jennifer, recognizing the tone in her mother's voice, became so nervous she dropped one of her glass marbles and as it rang on the flagstone terrace, she and Todd scrambled down to look for it. Katherine waited until Jon looked at her. "Blackmail," she said softly, "is a nasty means of persuasion. And when it uses love as a weapon it is disgusting. Do you understand that?"

Ross had turned, his eyes fastened on Katherine. Victoria, too, was watching her, uncharacteristically silent.

"Do you?" Katherine repeated.

"No," Jon muttered.

"It means it is disgusting when you threaten to withhold love from people who love you and need your love."

"I didn't—!"

"Yes, you did. You said if you didn't get your way you'd walk out. And your family would be left behind, missing you. Don't play hard-to-get, Jon; it hurts the rest of us, and it hurts you. Is any party worth all that?"

After a moment, Jon mumbled, "I don't want to go home anyway."

"That's not the point," Katherine said gently.

"She means apologize," Carrie whispered loudly.

Ross put his arm around Jon's shoulders. "Why don't we talk about this later? Katherine's right, you know: if you threaten to go home every time I say something you don't like, we'll have a hard time getting along. You'll end up like a yo-yo, back and forth so fast we can't keep track of you..."

Below the table, Jennifer and Todd began to giggle, mostly in relief at the easing of tension. "Can we get some cake from the kitchen?" Jennifer asked, standing up now that the air was clearing.

"A fine idea," Victoria said crisply. "And Sylvie made more lemonade; help yourself."

"Come on," urged Todd when Jon still sat in his chair.

"I'm sorry, Dad," Jon said. "I didn't mean it."

Ross tightened his arm around his son's shoulders. "Good thing," he said casually. "This place wouldn't be the same without you. Go on, now; get yourself some cake."

As the four of them walked into the living room, Carrie's piercing whisper could be heard on the terrace. "Wow, did Katherine ever tell you off!"

"She's gotten real tough since Dad left," said Todd. "She used to kind of be careful, but now sometimes she just lays it on us. I don't know..." His voice diminished as they went through the swinging doors into the kitchen. "Mostly she's great, but she sure is different."

Ross took Katherine's hand. "Thank you. For caring, and for giving me a chance to catch my breath. I live with that damned fear every day, wondering when they'll decide they have better things to do than stay with me..."

"I don't think they will," Katherine said. She wanted to lift her hand and smooth the lines between his eyebrows; instead, she said quietly, "I've watched them follow you around; they're crazy about you and they need you. I think they're testing their weapons. Jennifer and Todd do it, too, only with different ones. I just hope Jon doesn't pull that one too often."

He chuckled. "Now that he knows he has Jennifer and Todd's tough mother to contend with, I doubt he'll ever do it again. Thank you," he repeated, his voice low, and later, when he went to talk with Jon, his step was light.

The children's diving team was scheduled to practice the next day from morning until late afternoon, and Ross and Katherine took advantage of the day, leaving before breakfast for Aix-en-Provence and its international music festival. Ross took an inland road that was, at that hour, almost empty, and they drove in silence amid the green-and-gold splendor of the countryside. The air was soft and caressing; the sun spilled like honey over orange and olive groves that parted suddenly to reveal small stone villages with steep rust-colored roofs and flocks of pale brown sheep watched over by a single shepherd, hands clasped behind his back, his staff sticking out as if he, too, had a tail.

Aix was filled with the music of the festival, and it was market day, with stands crowded together in the Place de Verdun beneath a rainbow of parasols. Ross bought a bouquet of carnations and pinned one to the collar of Katherine's cotton shirt and when they turned to walk on, their hands touched and their fingers twined together. They strolled through the market and the quiet side streets, along worn stone walks shaded by enormous plane trees, and then to a concert in the courtyard of the archbishop's palace, and when they sat down Katherine took another carnation from the bouquet and pinned it to the lapel of Ross's sport jacket. In the afternoon, blue shadows lay across the town, and fountains in the courtyards reflected the sunset. And much later, on the drive back along the Mediterranean, the brilliant lights of the Riviera blocked out all signs of the small towns, the orange and olive groves, and the single shepherd with his flock.

Everyone was asleep when they reached the villa. At the door to her rooms, Katherine sighed, resting her head against the wall. The spicy scent of carnations was all about them, and the pungency of the almond paste *calissons* they had brought back for Victoria and the children. "We brought the day home with us," she said, and laughed softly. "Such a perfect day."

His face was shadowed in the dim corridor. "More than any I've ever known." He held her face between his hands. "Thank you."

Katherine shook her head. "I'm the one who should thank you. For all the perfect days." She stepped back, into the doorway, wanting more than his hands; refusing to admit it. "Goodnight, Ross."

"Goodnight, Katherine." He lingered a moment, wanting her, knowing she wanted him. Not yet, he thought. We have time. "Is tomorrow the diving competition?"

"Tomorrow morning."

"I'll pick you up at the breakfast table."

She laughed and watched him walk down the corridor and turn into his own rooms.

They had avoided the populous vacation areas and the next morning for the first time they encountered the impenetrable crowds of the Riviera's high summer season. "July," Ross murmured as they descended the steep stairway from Victoria's villa and found themselves surrounded. "Don't fight it; don't even try to walk; they'll carry you."

The crowd was cheerful and noisy, exchanging shouted itineraries and names of restaurants. Everywhere, strangers held out their cameras to other strangers, asking them please to take their pictures. A large round man with a Polaroid snapped a picture of Katherine and kept pace with Ross as the image developed. *"Bella, bella,"* he said. *"Uomo fortunato."* Amid a torrent of Italian he handed Ross the photograph, nodded amiably and turned to walk on.

"Grazie," said Ross, and he and Katherine looked at it together. Katherine's eyes widened. *Is that really me—that woman laughing in the sunlight? She looks so happy. I didn't know she was so happy.* She felt vaguely uneasy—as if everything was speeding up and she was not sure she was in control.

But then they reached the pool, and she saw Jennifer and Todd standing near the diving board, lean and tanned, chattering excitedly with a swimsuited group that included Carrie and Jon. We're all happy, she thought, and nothing is out of control. With another glance at the picture, she asked Ross, "Did you understand what he was saying when he took it?"

"Most of it." Ross pulled two chairs together near the edge of the pool. "He looked at you and said you were beautiful. And then he told me I was a fortunate man." The crowd milled about them but there was a small space of silence around their chairs. He tucked the photograph in his pocket and took Katherine's hand in his as they turned to watch their children's diving skills. "And of course he was absolutely right."

The shapes and colors of the Riviera glowed in the sketches spread on the drawing table Victoria had bought for Katherine's sitting room. There were fish and birds, exotic cactus flowers, the scalloped edges of the orange overlapping roof tiles of Provence, the symmetrical arches of Roman bridges, the swirl of water rushing over stones in a mountain stream.

Katherine had redrawn the sketches she liked best, then, on each, tried different variations of the basic shape until she had one that was bold, simple, striking: uniquely hers. When she was satisfied, she colored it with oil pastels—a cross between colored chalk and crayons, with subtler shades and a permanent finish.

She had been holding a blue-black oil pastel in her fingers for half an hour, wondering if the soaring bird she had drawn, with wings outspread, should be a perched bird with wings folded back. A simple problem, but she could not resolve it because her thoughts kept returning to Ross. Finally she threw down the colored stick and raised her head to gaze through the glass doors at the sailboats swaying in the harbor. "Ridiculous," she said aloud. "I'll finish it tomorrow."

She walked down the corridor to Victoria's room and knocked on the closed door.

"Yes," said Victoria. "Ah, Katherine, how lovely; come in. I thought you would have left by now."

"We put it off for half an hour. Ross had some telephone calls to make before he goes to Paris tomorrow."

"How nice. For us, I mean. A quiet time together." Lying on a silk chaise beside the open doors to her terrace, she tilted her head, inspecting Katherine's madras shirt and khaki jeans, her dark hair held by a gold band, her hazel eyes flecked with blue in the Mediterranean light. "You look delightful: a week in the sun has put color in your face. Where do you go today?"

"Ross said the Turini Forest and Vesubie Valley. Does that sound right? My pronunciation..."

"Is improving. Ross is invariably sensible. You will have a memorable afternoon."

"And it's been two weeks in the sun."

"I beg your pardon?"

"We've been here almost two weeks for the sun to put color in my face."

"When time goes too quickly, Katherine, I make a practice of ignoring it. What else has Ross planned? Has he mentioned the folk festival at Nice?"

"We're taking the children when he gets back from Paris. And we want you to come along."

"No, my dear, how pleasant that you thought of it, but no; I shall stay here and wait for you to tell me about it."

Katherine sat on the edge of the chaise. "You haven't gone anywhere with us, except to dinner, twice. After Paris, I don't want to accuse you of being obvious, but—"

"Katherine. I am never obvious. I may occasionally become careless and tip my hand, but I am not obvious. My dear, I do not go with you because I no longer enjoy all-day excursions, or even half-day ones. I'm too tired."

Worried, Katherine asked, "Is something wrong? You always seem to have so much energy."

"The only thing wrong is my age. As for my energy, I have plenty, so long as I know when to rest and preserve it." She grimaced. "It's dreadfully tiresome; I get so annoyed at my body. Until recently, I could force it along and think I'd fooled it into renewing itself. But it was going its own way, wearing out, and then one day I could no longer ignore it. I'm eighty-two, my dear, and I no longer can romp through the Vesubie Valley. And if I cannot romp, I refuse to go at all."

"Are you sure you're all right?" Katherine pressed. "You haven't even gone out with your own friends since we arrived."

"Oh, that has nothing to do with me; they're not here. Most of them scatter to their other homes in July and August."

Katherine remembered something Tobias had said. "You came in July because of us. So you missed all your friends."

"I have you; I have Ross. Who is more important to me? And if I know where you are *and what you are doing*, I may be lying here like a piece of crumpled tissue paper, but I can imagine myself with you. I remember all the places, you know, so clearly. And it gets easier to pretend, the older I am."

"I'm sorry," Katherine said. "I didn't realize... So much has been happening and I've been selfish, only thinking of myself instead of spending time with you."

"But you must be selfish! Don't you understand, the more you do, the more pleasure you have, the more successful you are, the more of everything *I* have. I did think *that* was obvious! Now, my dear" —she patted Katherine's hand— "be off and have a wonderful day. If you're too late for dinner, I will entertain the various offspring, but I'll expect a full report tomorrow. Every detail."

Katherine bent to kiss her forehead. "Every one."

"I hope not," Ross laughed when Katherine repeated the conversation as they drove through a mountain valley. "It's a bad precedent."

"Why? If it's all she has—"

"Did she say that?"

"Not exactly, but—"

"All she said was she wants to be part of our lives because it makes her feel less old and limited. Katherine, Victoria is the majority stockholder in the Hayward Corporation and she sits on four other boards of directors, helping manage and raise funds for some of the most powerful institutions in San Francisco. That's hardly a picture of a helpless little old lady lying like a crumpled piece of tissue paper while the busy world passes her by."

Involuntarily, Katherine smiled. "Hardly." Her face grew thoughtful. "But she wasn't really lying."

He shook his head. "Bending the truth. She's intelligent and wily enough to know that the one thing her wealth can't do is slow down the years, so she uses whatever means she has to hold on to parts of the world she can no longer experience directly. Like the Vesubie. It's all right, you know; it's a benign form of tyranny."

Katherine looked at him. "That's not kind."

"It's accurate," he said simply. "She's using our love for her to make us feel responsible, to keep her at the center of our lives, even though she knows that's impossible—ultimately we'll have to pass her by. But she tries. And I admire her persistence, and love her deeply, but I have no intention of telling her everything that fills my time. And if you do, and I see you whip out a pencil to take notes to report to her" —Katherine began to laugh— "I'll probably become silent and quite possibly immobile. Whereas, if you agree with me, I will take your hand, so, and hold it while I get us through the Brevera Valley."

He took his eyes from the road for a split second, to share her smile, then, holding her hand firmly in his, he drove slowly along the narrow road that looped back and forth as it climbed through the mountains. The scenery grew wilder and they were silent, awed by the maze of deep, shadowed gorges separated by sunlit meadows. Twisted trees clung to the rocky slopes, while in the meadows pines grew amid boulders that crashed from above each spring when melting snows set off avalanches. The air turned cool and Katherine pulled on her sweater. As the atmosphere thinned, the farthest craggy mountains came into sharp relief. And then they drove into the Turini Forest—dim, cool, dense with huge trees and twisted undergrowth.

Ross kept going on the zigzagging road until they rounded a curve and came upon the tiny village of La Bollene-Vesubie, where he pulled the car to a stop. "The backpacks are in the trunk. From here on, we hike."

From the village, the trail climbed rapidly through forests and meadows, leaving the last vestiges of civilization behind. The air was chilly but as they climbed, they were almost too warm in their sweaters. Once

Katherine leaped from one boulder to another, weightless; when she landed lightly, bending her knees to cushion her fall, Ross held out his hand and she took it, sharing with a smile the joy of their isolation. They hiked for an hour, pushing through bushes, jumping across streams, following a trail that sometimes disappeared among rock outcroppings or underbrush, and reappeared farther on. They barely spoke, except to point out, now and then, a soaring bird haloed in gold against the blue sky, tangled skeins of brilliant wildflowers weaving about gray boulders with orange, gray, and black lichen covering their north sides, wide pastures smooth as velvet, the flick of an animal on the trail, and over everything the crystalline air and vast silence, broken only by the piercing songs of birds.

The sun moved higher, warming the sheltered valley. They stuffed their sweaters in their backpacks, moving on into a landscape less rugged, trees and bushes shimmering in the dazzling sun, until at last Ross said, "I don't know about you, but I'm famished. If you see a good spot—"

"There!" Katherine exclaimed, pointing as they came to the crest of a small ridge. "Just waiting for us."

They clambered down the slope to a grassy nook protected on three sides by high rock formations. Nearby, a stream widened into a clear blue-green pool before narrowing again and disappearing among the trees. "The old swimming hole," Ross murmured. He looked at Katherine, eyebrows raised. "What do you think?"

"I think it will be freezing and we ought to try it."

He laughed. "You're wonderful." Dropping his backpack on the soft grass, he seemed not to notice the flush on her face and the brightness of her eyes. "Right away, don't you think? Better to do it before we eat."

Katherine set her backpack next to his. "I'll beat you in. Unless you feel it's a man's job to test the waters."

"It's a man's job to know when to let the woman go first."

Laughing, she disappeared behind a cluster of pine and chestnut trees. But as soon as she pulled off her shirt and khaki pants and felt the sun burning on her bare skin, she was swept with a dizzying surge of desire and anticipation, and reached out to steady herself against a tree. The rough bark was solid, deeply textured, and she clung to it, aware of Ross, close by, as if she could feel him as sharply as she felt the bark of the tree. I didn't know, she thought. I didn't know how much I wanted him. But deep in this valley, cut off from distractions and carefully constructed reasons, protected in the sunlit niche from the cool air beyond the rock walls, she knew that all their days together had led to this one, and that Ross knew it too.

The dizziness was gone. Katherine left her clothes on a rock and, in silk underpants and brassiere, slipped from the cluster of trees to the wild grass bordering the pool. She did not see Ross, but rather than give herself a chance to think twice, she took a breath and made a shallow dive into the clear water.

She gasped in the shock of the icy cold. Every cringing muscle seemed to curl into a tight defensive knot. "Once," she gasped aloud. "Once across, then out." In a strong crawl, kicking hard, she cut through the mirror images of trees that seemed to grow down from the surface, and reached the other side, where she grasped a low-hanging branch, pulled herself out of the water and, shivering in the shade, turned to look for Ross.

Across the pool, the water broke into a long wake. Katherine heard his shout as the cold struck him, and she watched him swim toward her with powerful strokes, bursting through the water to grab the same branch she had used. "I'll race you back," he panted.

"I thought I'd walk around," she said through chattering teeth.

"Sensible. No risk of losing."

"Oh—!" Without warning, she dove back in and kicked away from the shore, leaving Ross in a fury of droplets.

"Unfair!" he yelled, and followed, within a moment pulling even with her. Her lips were blue, he saw, but her body was strong and sinuous in the frigid water. They swam together until he gave a final spurt and finished half a length ahead of her.

"You're wonderful," he said again as they staggered from the water. Exulting, they laughed through numb lips. "Do we have any towels?" She shook her head. "Damn. Poor planning. Sit here; I'll see what I can find."

She leaned against a warm rock. The molten sun dried her almost instantly, but her skin was still covered with small bumps from the cold that seemed to have soaked into her bones. Staring vacantly at the deceptive, sun-sparkled pool, she thought of nothing at all, but there was an image in her mind, like a photograph, of the two of them, swimming side by side with matched strokes.

"One towel," Ross said, returning. "Wrapped around the wine. Not very big, but enough to share." He looked down at her. His muscles quivered from the cold that pervaded him, but he stood still, gazing at her. "My God," he breathed. "You are so lovely."

Katherine's thought stirred and she saw herself as he did: half-lying on the grass in transparent wet underclothes. Brushing her dripping hair from her eyes, she made a move to stand up. "No," Ross said and, kneeling, he began to dry her hair with the towel.

"The sun..." Katherine murmured. "It will dry—"

"I know." Holding the towel, his hand moved rhythmically, caressing her hair in long strokes and then her neck and shoulders. She was beginning to feel warm again. From Ross's own drenched hair, a drop of water fell like an icicle on her breast and she flinched. He laughed shakily. "Dangerous..." With a swift motion he ran the towel over his hair, then, bending down, put his lips to the spot on her breast. For a long moment they stayed that way, barely breathing, engulfed in sunlight, their flesh beginning to glow, as if, at last, the sun ran through their veins.

"Katherine," Ross murmured. "My God, how many times I've said your name to myself...dearest, lovely Katherine." He pulled off her wet brassiere and pants and Katherine put her hands on his soaked cotton underpants and pushed them off. They lay on the fragrant grass, bodies burning hot, cool where their wet clothes had been, and Ross slid his arm beneath Katherine's shoulders and brought his open mouth down to hers.

They held the kiss, prolonging it, letting their desire grow, letting it flow through them, like the sun. Katherine's arms kept Ross close. "I thought of this," she said, her lips against his, "before I went in the water. I wanted you—"

"I thought of this in Paris," he said. And then, lying on her softness and delicate strength, he felt her legs part for him and he thrust into her, into the darkness of her body while sunlight spun in brilliant wheels behind his closed eyes and Katherine whispered his name in the clear mountain air.

There was so much to say they chose silence, lips meeting in small kisses as they lay quietly, Katherine's head on his shoulder, one of Ross's legs lying across hers, its heaviness as pleasurable as their caresses. Ross moved his palm slowly up the curve of her hip to her breasts, brushing the nipples, and then to her throat and face, as if sketching the lines and textures of her body; and Katherine lightly slid her hand along his back to his shoulders and muscled arms, and stopped with her fingertips in the blond hair of his chest. She raised herself on one elbow, looking down into his dark eyes. "I feel so greedy," she said, embarrassed.

"Not greedy," he said, and smiled at her, the sun running through his veins. "Alive, marvelous, part of me..." He kissed the fullness of her breasts, taking her taut nipples into the warmth of his mouth.

A long sigh came from deep within Katherine, freeing the last of the hungers and fears she had restrained for so long. Everything was all right; everything was wonderfully right between them. She was filled with a joy that was like the sun, warming her after she had been so cold, and the joy sang within her as Ross's mouth moved from her breasts to her stomach. "You taste like pine trees," he murmured, his mouth on her soft skin. "And wild clover and mountain streams." A heavy languor held her still, while his touch swept through her in widening ripples; he was everywhere a part of her, surrounding her, and she felt herself press against the earth, melting, open, waiting, as his hands parted her thighs and his tongue whispered against her.

The touch, sharp and soft, leaped through Katherine's body; a low moan escaped her and she dissolved into feeling as his tongue moved lightly, exploring, pushing inside her—*alive, marvelous, part of me*— until she felt herself draw together, like a flower curling to hold within its petals the golden liquid of the sun. She drew together to one blazing point until it was too great to be contained and with a cry, her body arching, Katherine felt it burst, spinning through her veins, then slowly fading away.

They lay together, and kissed. For a moment Katherine drowsed in the sun, and then they murmured together about dressing, eating, hiking back—but instead they looked at each other through half-closed eyes in the brightness and let their bodies waken in a long embrace. "If I could take you onto me," Ross said. "And hold you there..."

"Yes," Katherine said. "Yes." And when his hands went to her hips, she moved on top of him.

His arms enfolded her so tightly her breasts were crushed against his chest, her face buried in the curve of his neck and shoulder. Stirring, she raised her head so her lips could make tiny kisses along his neck. "Your skin is so warm," she murmured. "Hard and smooth and warm— and I can kiss your heartbeat here—" She kissed the hollow of his throat and then his mouth, open and as demanding as hers.

He lifted her and Katherine sat astride him, lowering herself upon him, feeling him slide upward, filling her. She smiled down on him, his dark blond hair still damp, his deep-set, dark eyes as warm as the sun, his lips curving on her name.

"...lovely, magnificent woman," he murmured. His hands held her breasts, his palms against her erect nipples as their bodies found a rhythm as perfect as the one they had found in the water. Katherine bent over Ross again, her dark hair falling in a curtain about their faces as their mouths met and clung and they moved together, faster, merged in a haze of sunlight and pure feeling, faster still, climbing, to the narrow peak of a mountain against a clear sky, until, together, they leaped free and, trembling, came gradually to earth.

Night falls quickly in the mountains, the sky flaming to crimson, orange, and amber, fading to violet, smoky-gray, and then black, blotting out everything but the ghostly outlines of snow-covered peaks. Driving through the valley, Ross and Katherine watched the sunset fling its brilliance across the sky and then retreat, leaving them in a darkness broken only by the brightness of their headlights.

At the small crossroads town of Sospel, they stopped for a late dinner and lingered over coffee on the terrace of a hotel overlooking a cobblestone square. Hands clasped, chairs touching, they watched the play of light and water from a fountain covered in a mosaic of brightly colored pebbles. Relaxed, sated, filled with a soft, glowing happiness, Katherine rested her head against the back of her chair and gazed at the black sky, so close above them, crowded with brilliant clusters of stars, and the pale frozen lace of the Milky Way. We're always outdoors, she thought idly, remembering how everything with Derek had been inside: restaurants, hotel ballrooms, night clubs, private homes. But she and Ross were almost always outside—everything open, fresh, limitless. She started to tell him, but stopped. They'd never talked about Derek. Long ago, Victoria had said Ross was concerned about her, because of Derek. We'll have to talk about him, she thought. And they'd never talked about the reasons she'd been unsure whether Ross liked her or not. And they'd never talked about—

"We have to talk," Ross said when they were in the car again, descending on the corniche to Menton. "So many things we've been avoiding. At least, I have."

Katherine laughed softly. "I was just thinking of all the things I want to talk to you about. But not tonight. Tomorrow."

"Tomorrow I'll be in Paris."

"Oh." She had forgotten. "But you'll be back."

"In three or four days." The road made a few final twists, then straightened, and the car raced forward. "I'd rather not go at all," he said, his hands relaxed on the wheel as they sped faster, passing other cars. "It's the wrong time. If I'd known, when Jacques and I made our plans—" He paused. "Why don't you come with me? You'd have the days to yourself and I'll cancel my dinner meetings—why not?" he asked as she shook her head.

"Because we have things to think about. And it might be a good idea for us to be apart for a little while."

"Before we talk?"

"I don't know. Yes. Before we talk."

They fell silent, preoccupied with their own thoughts. Suddenly Katherine began to laugh. "What?" Ross asked.

"Victoria. Remember? She gave me strict instructions to tell her every detail of our day." Simultaneously they pictured their bodies twined together on the grass. "And you said it would be a bad precedent—"

"And I didn't want you taking notes," he finished, his laughter joining hers.

At the villa, they parted at her door. "I'll be gone before you're up," he said, and the next morning, when she woke, she found a spray of carnations and roses on her drafting table, with a note written across her sketch pad.

> Thank you for the most wonderful of days. I'm taking you with me, because from now on you'll always be inside me. One more thing for us to talk about when I get back. Soon. Ross.

"Well," said Victoria, searching her face when she came in to breakfast. "You found the scenery satisfactory."

"Magnificent." *I'm taking you with me.* But he was still here—as if he had become part of *her*—and Katherine was uncomfortable. Too much, too fast, she thought, and remembered feeling, just a few days earlier, that events might be out of control. She wondered what Victoria had seen in her face, and knew she was not ready to talk about Ross. Pouring juice and coffee at the sideboard, she asked, "Where are the children?"

"I believe in the playroom. Two of them grumbling, two being sympathetic." Katherine looked puzzled. "When Ross said goodbye early this morning, he told Carrie and Jon to call their mother. They were supposed to do it once a week and they missed last week. They say they have nothing to tell her—though they're always busy every minute of the day—and for some reason Jennifer and Todd understand this perfectly. So they sympathize while the other two grumble. Does this make sense to you? When my children were young they would have had no difficulty calling me; they told me everything."

Katherine smiled. "Did they really?"

"Well, probably not. Probably I was better off that they didn't. And I suppose children would never become independent if they didn't have secrets. But from you, my dear, I want to hear about everything that gave you that radiant look. Come, sit down, sit down, I want to hear it all, from the beginning. Where did you leave the car—La Bollene or St. Martin? And where did you hike? Sit down, my dear, drink your coffee, eat something, and tell me all about it."

"I will. But if you don't mind, I'd like to check on the grumbling, first. I'll be right back."

Walking down the wide corridor to the children's wing, she shivered, as if a chill breeze had found its way through a crack in the wall. Melanie, San Francisco, the outside world. Craig. For three weeks they had barely existed, invisible in the glare of the Mediterranean sun, the unfamiliar landscape, the force of Ross's presence.

Now the chill breeze brushed her and she almost turned back. But then she heard Carrie's voice and caught a quick glimpse, in the playroom, of Jennifer and Todd on the couch, watching gravely as Carrie spoke on the telephone with Jon beside her. Katherine stepped back, not wanting to make them self-conscious. She wavered between going and staying, then stayed. She would just listen for a minute; just to make sure everything was all right.

"Nothing much," Carrie was saying. "We go swimming and there's Scrabble and stuff in the playroom and that's all." She listened, tapping her foot. "Well I suppose we're bored. I don't know." She listened again. "No, she's nice. She lets us do lots of things and she jokes with us and she's funny... she drives the gardener crazy by picking vegetables he thinks aren't ripe, or flowers that aren't—what? Oh. Well, I can't help it if you don't care about the gardener. Here. Jon wants to say hello."

Scowling, she thrust the phone at Jon. "Hi, Mom, we're fine. What? I don't know. I don't think I'm bored. We do things all the time with Jennifer and Todd and—Carrie, cut it out! What are you doing?"

"Hitting your head, stupid! Oh, never mind."

"Wasn't I supposed to tell Mom they're here?"

"I don't know. I just thought maybe we wouldn't."

Jon frowned at the telephone, then said into it, "Sorry, Mom, Carrie was beating on me. What? Jennifer and Todd Fraser, you know them." He looked at Carrie and rolled his eyes. "We didn't *know* they'd be here, so how could we tell you? Sure she's here; they all came together. We don't see her a lot though 'cause she works every morning and then in the afternoon she and Dad go places. How do *I* know where? They don't tell us. I guess every day; we do our own stuff; we don't watch them. I don't *know* what time they get back. Usually for dinner. Mom, I gotta go. There's another diving contest and we have to practice. No, I can't get Dad to the phone; he's in Paris. He left this morning. I don't know. Carrie, when will Dad be back?"

"Three or four days."

"Three or four days. I don't know; Carrie, what's Dad's hotel?"

"L'Hotel on the Rue des Beaux Arts. The same one he was in before. You know all that."

"Yeh, but— Mom? L'Hotel. The same one he was in before. OK? Gotta go; talk to you soon. 'Bye."

Melanie hung up the telephone and stared, unseeing, at the lights of San Francisco.

Across the room, Derek took ice cubes from the refrigerator behind the bar. "I didn't get all of that, but I gather Victoria has imported someone to entertain Ross."

"Katherine Fraser," she said, still looking out the window.

He stood still. "Ross and Katherine? How clever of Victoria."

Melanie turned. His face was smooth, but his eyes were dark with fury, and she felt a stab of jealousy. "Does that bother you? Katherine and your brother? I must say, it didn't take long; we only split in May." She watched his expressionless face. "Jon says they're having quite a time, every afternoon and night. . . sending the kids off to play tennis or whatever so they can be alone. He leaves me stuck with this house while he plays on the Riviera. . . and he certainly isn't spending time with his children, which was the reason, *he said*, he wanted them in France for the month. I should demand them back; they both say they're bored; they don't have a mother *or* a father."

Derek was looking off in the distance, the muscle beside his eye jumping erratically. He put back the ice cube tray. "It's after eleven. If you want to get to this party we'd better go. When is your tennis champion due back?"

"Tomorrow."

"And what are you going to do with him?"

"Marry him, I suppose."

"Why?"

"Because I love him."

"Bullshit."

Standing at the vestibule mirror, Melanie smoothed her hair with nervous fingers. "Because he's young and makes me feel young."

"That's not all. What else?"

"Damn you, Derek." She took a silk shawl from the closet. "I'm afraid of being alone."

He nodded. "I wish you well."

"No you don't. You don't really care anything about me. You used to make love to me—you *pursued* me—and lately you won't. Even though I ask you. I *never* ask! *Anybody!* But I ask you, and you turn me down!"

"Katherine said I wanted you because you were Ross's wife."

"*Katherine* said! What does that bitch know about any of us?"

"Considerably more than you do." He opened the door, his thoughts cold and bitter. Derek understood himself well enough to know when someone saw through him. Ordinarily he was indifferent to what others said, but on the rare occasions when someone got past his barriers and reached the Derek Hayward he took care to hide from the world, he reacted with fury. It had been bad enough when Katherine did it in April; now, knowing she was with Ross, imagining them talking about him, he felt his insides twist with rage and knew he had to be careful until he calmed down. Abruptly, he said, "Are you ready?"

Melanie swung upon him. "Are you in love with her?"

"No."

She persisted. "Were you, when you were going out with her?"

"No. And what difference does it make?"

"I don't know," she said. They walked to his car. "I'd just feel better if you weren't."

He made no answer and after a moment, unable to endure silence, Melanie began to talk of something else. She talked all the way across the Golden Gate Bridge into San Francisco and to the top of Nob Hill where Derek parked on the steep street in front of Herman Mettler's townhouse.

It was a very large party, the kind Mettler gave every summer when business was slow. Assuming everyone else was bored, too, he provided various entertainments: a choice selection of pornographic films in the basement projection room; an orchestra playing dance tunes in the living room that took up most of the first floor; and Polynesian hors d'oeuvres served by circulating waitresses in grass skirts. Upstairs, a glass case held a sampling from Mettler's fall line of jewelry.

"Of course she doesn't do your kind of thing," Mettler said to Marc Landau as their gaze fastened on a gold necklace labeled "Katherine Fraser." "But she's got quite a talent, no doubt about it. Might even rival you someday, Marc. Make her own mark." He chuckled. "Especially if her work keeps changing as incredibly as it has so far."

"No one rivals Marc Landau," Leslie said slyly. "He's told me so himself. But that necklace is spectacular, isn't it?" She turned as someone called her name. "Excuse me; I'm going to mingle."

Landau studied the necklace. "Her work changed?"

"Like day and night. Her first batch was nice, well-made, the kind you see at Williams and Baylor, or Corfert's. The second...well, you see it. Inventive, bold, unique...fascinating use of materials. The first time she kept to safe channels; the next she broke free. Astonishing. And you know, I nearly ruined it. I was so surprised I made the almost fatal mistake of asking her whether they were really hers. Ah, Derek." He interrupted himself. "Good to see you."

They shook hands. "Have you been accusing someone of stealing designs?" Derek asked.

"God forbid! I only asked. Your friend Katherine Fraser; she didn't tell you? She seemed angry enough to tell the world, just because I made an innocent comment when she brought in *totally* different work and refused to consider an exclusive contract. What a high horse she got on! It made *me* hoarse—apologizing. I'd let on how impressed I was, so she knew she could go elsewhere, and she almost walked out on me. Hard to believe she didn't regale you with the whole story, Derek."

"She didn't because she didn't see me," Derek said, thoughtfully contemplating Katherine's necklace. "The last time we saw each other was sometime in April."

"Lovers' quarrels," said Mettler whimsically. But his curiosity was like a persistent itch. "I'm sure you'll patch it up...or has it gone too far?"

Seemingly absorbed in the necklace, Derek said softly, "Herman, I never talk about young women's problems."

After a pause, Mettler asked, "Problems?"

Landau frowned. "Leslie said she was settled and doing well."

"Problems about her work?" Mettler asked Derek.

"No. Personal. I wouldn't worry, Herman; chances are they won't affect you at all."

In the midst of the party's gaiety, a small, dark silence fell among the three men.

"*Chances are,*" Mettler repeated. "Shouldn't I be the judge of that?"

Derek shrugged.

"God damn it, Derek, I asked a civil question. I'm investing in this woman and if she has problems that might affect her work, *I want to know about it!*"

"There's no cause for hysteria, Herman; I only know some isolated facts. Nothing more."

"Facts! Facts! What the fuck are you talking about? Marc, if you don't mind... Derek, in private—" Taking Derek's arm, he led him to a corner away from the crowd. "Now, what the hell is going on?"

Derek drank half his Scotch. "I haven't the faintest idea whether something is 'going on,' as you put it. Katherine is a troubled young woman, with more than her share of problems. Her husband is an embezzler who disappeared over a year ago after admitting to his partner that he'd stolen from the company for years. Less than two months after he disappeared, Katherine sold their house at a loss and fled Canada; soon after she arrived here she started receiving money every month from her husband. And last New Year's Eve he came to see her. We've asked her to tell us where he is, so we could help him, but she insists she doesn't know. More likely she's afraid to trust anyone."

Mettler passed his hand over his face. He had heard parts of that story—though nothing of embezzling—but coming from Derek it sounded far different. "Are you saying..." He cleared his throat. "She might be involved in her husband's embezzling? She might be a thief?"

Derek shook his head. "Doubtful."

"You're not sure?"

"One has only her word. She seems honest."

"But you're not sure. And if she's a thief, she could be stealing other things. Like jewelry designs."

Derek smiled thinly. "That's quite a leap, Herman. I wouldn't accuse her of any such thing."

After a moment, Mettler blurted, "She married into your family!" Derek was silent. "That's why you're so cautious! Protecting your family!"

"Pull yourself together," Derek said coldly. "You're going off the deep end. I don't know how this came up; you have nothing to worry about."

"I have plenty to worry about! You know how much my customers pay for the assurance that they're buying originals! Jewelry designs are copyrighted, damn it; my customers know that; they didn't get rich by being naive! Do you know what they'd do to me if they thought they were investing in copies or—my God—stolen designs? They'd find someone else to trust! Then where would I be? God damn it, if I'd known—!"

"Has Marc wandered off?" Leslie asked, pushing through the guests to reach them. "I thought he was with you. Good heavens, Herman, has someone died?"

Mettler looked at her blankly. "Marc went off. I don't know where he is."

"Thanks," she said dryly. "I'll find him. And do let me know if it was someone important who died."

She found Landau fending off a short man with heavy jowls who wanted him to design a necklace for his wife. "Must go," Landau said in relief as Leslie came up. "Drop me a note with a sketch; never do business at parties. He won't write," he muttered to Leslie as they made their way across the room. "Because he can't. Inherited all his money, plays a pathetic game of golf and never learned to write. That's all I know about him. Except that his wife likes emeralds. Are we eating dinner here or will you come home with me?"

"Here, if you don't mind."

"Leslie."

"Yes?"

"When were you last in my home?"

"April twenty-ninth."

An eyebrow went up. "Extraordinary memory. Or something happened to fix the date in your mind. And to keep you from my bed for nearly three months. Who is he?"

"You don't know him."

"Even so, I assume he has a name."

"Claude Fleming."

Landau studied a manicured fingernail. "You're right; I don't know him. But I know his firm. Shall we eat?" In a walled garden, a buffet held ice sculptures of birds, weeping as they melted above hot and cold kabobs and hollowed pineapples heaped with fruits. "You're moving up," Landau said as they filled their plates. "From a humble jeweler to a partner in one of the stuffiest law firms in the country. Isn't that a rather old-fashioned way for a woman to get ahead these days?"

"Don't overdo it, Marc," Leslie said, walking ahead of him to a table. "If you're nasty, I might think you really care what I do."

"Or is it that he is willing to father this mythical child you once prattled about? That sentimental tale of longing for single motherhood. Have you been looking all this time, while I continued to escort you, for someone who longs for fatherhood?"

"I'll be damned," she said. "You do care. Marc, you're as jealous as a teenager."

"Don't talk nonsense. I'm saying I don't allow anyone to take advantage of me."

"That's what you were saying? You could have fooled me." She pushed her plate away and stood up. "I'm sorry, Marc; I wanted to stay friends. You're the only son of a bitch I know who sometimes has a heart of gold. But I wouldn't want you to feel taken advantage of, and whatever you may think I don't want you to be unhappy. If I'd known you cared a hoot in hell about me—well, I don't know—Claude might not have made such an instant impression. We'll never know, will we? But damn you anyway, Marc, for sleeping with me for years and keeping all your feelings to yourself. God, I'm so tired of cool, clever people. No, don't get up; I can find my way out; you stay and enjoy the party. Cheer up our host; he looked like Derek gave him a dose of poison. Goodbye, Marc; thank you for a pleasant few years."

She strode through the living room to the foyer. Shouldn't have gotten upset, she thought. But she felt light with relief. For three months she'd been unable to break it off—still unsure enough of Claude, and her own feelings for him, to cut loose entirely from someone as reliable as Marc. But now it had happened almost by itself and she gave a small skip as she went outside, stood for a minute, debating, then walked briskly two blocks to the Mark Hopkins to catch a cab.

She got home early, spent an hour on paperwork, and had it organized when she arrived at Claude's office the next morning. "Here it is," she said, handing him her typed notes. "All but the last chapter. I don't suppose Bruce is here yet?"

"Bruce is here. Crisis inspires him to rise early. Can I get you coffee?"

"Yes." She sighed with pleasure. Everything was coming together; everything would be all right. She hadn't felt so well protected in years.

"Morning, sis," said Bruce from the floor where he sat yoga-style. "I'm meditating if you want to try—"

"Bruce, could we go over this once more?"

"You're nervous," he said accusingly.

"There's a lot at stake. I don't want to be wrong."

"We're not wrong! I know everything—well, almost everything—"

"Bruce." Claude sat on the arm of Leslie's chair. "Go through it again."

With a glance at the two of them, Bruce sighed. "Right. Here goes. You want to steal merchandise from a store—not just a sweater or a purse, but maybe a million bucks worth a year—what do you do? First you write a special computer program that lists each week's high-priced stuff that's selling fast—it's on sale or specially advertised or whatever. Then you give the list to somebody who goes through the store lifting the stuff, a dozen sweaters, maybe, or two dozen scarves or a couple of five-hundred-dollar jackets... not enough to be noticed when things are selling fast. He'd have to do it after store hours—"

"Night watchman," Leslie interrupted.

"Or security guard, whatever. At the same time another part of this special computer program changes the inventory record for the store— *showing the stuff as sold!* Got that? If you used the regular program to do this you'd leave a record, but this special program bypasses all the controls we put in and doesn't leave a trace of tampering! Clever bastard, but I was almost on to him, when he found my notes and stole them—"

"That's what the special program does?" Claude asked. "The one you found, but won't tell me how?"

"Damn it, you know where I—oh. Right, all the king's horses couldn't drag out of me how I got into the office to find it, right, that's what it does, without leaving a clue. But I confess I'm stumped on how they got it past the sensors and television cameras and out of the store. Janitors, using trash cans? Carpenters? Painters, with paint cans?"

"Leslie and I have an idea," said Claude. "We have to call Katherine to check it."

"Katherine in France?"

"Yes. But first I have some questions. This special program took an expert, is that right?" Vigorously, Bruce nodded. "How do we know it wasn't you?"

Bruce sprang from his meditative position. "Because we know who really did it! My boss, Dick Volpe—the one who framed me by stealing my notes—I told you all this!"

"Grow up, Bruce," Claude snorted. "Who'll believe you?"

"Fuck you, Fleming! I thought *you* believed me! If you think I'll let you marry my sister if you call me a—"

"Bruce!" Leslie cried. "No one's said anything about marriage!"

"Stick to the subject," Claude ordered, but the corners of his mouth twitched as he tried not to smile. "What's your defense when someone accuses you of lying about your former boss?"

"Oh—that's what you're doing?—working on my defense? A lousy defense lawyer, scaring the shit out of me...I told you, Volpe and I are the only ones who know enough to get past the controls on these programs, and Volpe has his own way of writing arrays—you don't know what that means, but never mind—we always knew which programs he wrote because of his style—wait, I'll show you—"

"Just explain it," said Claude. "Is it like different styles of painting or writing books?"

Bruce nodded.

"Different handwriting?"

"Not quite, but close."

"Could computer experts identify one person's style?"

"Yes, damn it! That's what I'm saying!"

"And yours is different from Volpe's?"

"Every which way."

"We can go with that," said Claude. "I'm satisfied. Leslie, are you?"

She nodded. "I apologize for my brother's wild fancies."

He met her eyes. "I didn't hear any wild fancies."

In the silence, Bruce cried, "Well? Are we calling Mademoiselle Katherine in her French hideaway?"

"Leslie is," said Claude. "But only a question, Leslie. Not a word about Bruce's theory."

"Why not? Claude, she's my friend and she knows what I've gone through—"

"I want to finish it first. Make sure we have the whole scenario, and that we're right. Leslie, I'm thinking of what is best for you. And Bruce."

"You're thinking of getting a conviction," she said.

"Which will keep your job and perhaps make Bruce head of Data Processing if that's what he wants. Damn it, Leslie, Heath's hasn't hired me; I don't care if they're robbed to their foundation. All I care about is you."

Leslie remembered coming home one night and curling up in her window seat, thinking how lovely it would be to have someone who gave a damn. "A convincing argument," she said with a small laugh, and picked up the telephone. Claude lifted the receiver on the extension at the other end of his office as she dialed the number Katherine had left her of Victoria's villa in Menton.

"Hi," she said casually, when Katherine came to the telephone. "I called to say hello and—"

"Leslie! Good heavens...a voice from the outside world! How are you? Have you gotten my letters?"

"All of them, and they're wonderful. But, Katherine, this is really a business call. The social one comes later. I'm in a meeting and I need to know why Gil fired you."

"Gil? Of all the people I never think about—"

"I know, but it's important or I wouldn't ask. Could you tell me what happened? It was the night you took inventory, wasn't it?"

"I did a wedding scene in the window," Katherine said, thinking back. "When I finished I went back downstairs...Gil wasn't there but he'd been in such a terrible mood I was afraid to leave if there was still counting to do. There were some cartons on the floor—display materials from the windows we'd taken down that week. They hadn't gone back to the warehouse, because the regular driver was sick and Gil refused a substitute, so I thought I'd better count them. About then he came back and started screaming at me."

"While you were going through the cartons?"

"I'd gone through two or three; it was taking longer because there was new merchandise mixed in with the display materials..." Leslie and Claude exchanged a triumphant glance, as Katherine's voice faded. "Leslie?" she said. "I thought at the time the receiving room had made a mistake, and then later I was so shaken up by Gil that I forgot it, but..."

"Katherine, I'm sorry," Leslie said hastily. "I know what you're thinking but I can't talk about it now. Not yet; pretty soon. I'll call you as soon as I can; is that all right?"

"Of course, but—"

"I'm sorry—so much is happening—goodbye, Katherine, I promise I'll call you back."

She and Claude hung up simultaneously. "Well?" Bruce cried, squirming in frustration. "Well, damn it?"

"Very well," said Claude with a smile seen in courtrooms when he was closing in on a trail of evidence.

"Window display cartons," Leslie told Bruce. "The stuff was packed in them just before they were sent back to the warehouse—past the sensors, past the guards and television cameras—and nobody asking any questions because those boxes were *supposed* to go out of the store. Katherine found them because they were there longer than usual; the regular driver was sick and Gil refused—" She looked at Claude. "Gil refused a substitute. And fired Katherine when he saw her going through them."

Claude nodded. "I would imagine either he or Volpe was the leader. They needed two others: someone to take the merchandise from the departments to the basement storeroom, and the driver. A wonderfully simple scheme."

"So that's all?" Bruce demanded. "You don't need anything else?"

"We need to have a chat with Gil Lister. And then, if all goes well, Heath's president. And then, Leslie, you can call Katherine back, and tell her your news."

Katherine and Victoria were on the terrace when Leslie's second call came. "Be prepared for a spectacular story," she said abruptly as soon as she heard Katherine's voice. Rapidly, she outlined what they had found. "And then we went to the little man himself, sitting in his high-backed leather throne in his little kingdom, and he collapsed like a punctured souffle. My only regret was that you weren't there to savor it."

"And then?" Katherine asked.

"We told the story to the executive committee, and Bruce explained the computer program—without a single vulgarity, by the way, which proves he can do it, and I got a huzzah from my president and grudging grunts from the others. The whole thing went beautifully. Bruce behaved, and Claude was perfect—cool and smooth and devastating. Very impressive."

"Only professionally impressive?"

"Oh, hell. You mean you can hear it in my voice?"

"What I hear is that a lot seems to have happened while I've been away. I'd like to hear more."

"I'll tell you all about it when you get back. Mainly I wanted you to know that I'm in the clear and so is Bruce. They did a nifty job of framing him—Lister let slip that they thought he was the type who'd run from problems, which would incriminate him even more—and it almost worked: it almost convinced his own sister. But in the end Bruce was the one who did them in. What do you think of that?"

"I think you're right: it's spectacular. Now tell me more about you and Claude."

"When you get back. It's only a few more days, isn't it?"

"Five." The word jolted Katherine. Five days. Ross would be back from Paris in two days, and three days after that she and Jennifer and Todd would leave. Even while she said goodbye to Leslie, those words repeated themselves. *Five days. And then we'll be part of the world again.*

"Sad news?" Victoria asked when Katherine rejoined her on the terrace. The dinner plates had been removed and crystal bowls of strawberries with orange zest and Curaçao were at their places. Below, the tall masts in the harbor swayed against a russet sunset, and through an open window the two women could hear the children giggling as they invented dire predicaments for their characters in Dungeons & Dragons.

"No," said Katherine. "Good news." She told Victoria the story, from the time Gil Lister fired her to Leslie's description of the executive board meeting that morning. "And there's more. She and Claude seem to have become very close."

"But isn't she your age? Claude likes young, wide-eyed maidens."

"That's what we thought. But perhaps he's changed?"

"If so, she must be a remarkable young woman."

"She is. I hope Claude knows it. I want her to be happy and she's been wishing for a family a long time."

"Ah." From a fluted silver dish, Victoria spooned a small mound of whipped cream and set it floating on her coffee. "I noticed a postcard for you in today's mail."

Katherine burst out laughing. "Yes. From Ross. Now what could have made you think of that?"

"I can't imagine," said Victoria calmly. "You know how an old woman's thoughts skip about. Is he busy?"

"Busy and happily watching walls being torn out. And collecting postcards for all the children. The one he sent was a picture of a place we had dinner the night before we came here."

"Postcards for the children," Victoria said ruminatively. "When Craig was a boy, he collected postcards. I remember the first time we took him to Tahoe, he insisted someone had drained the lake because it looked so much smaller than its picture on postcards we'd sent. Hugh roared about the difference between reality and pictures but that only terrified the poor child, so finally they went out in the boat and spent the day motoring around the circumference of the lake. Hugh never sent any postcards after that. I'm not sure what Craig learned from it all."

Craig. Katherine looked at the harbor, lit now by floodlights: a tangle of masts and ropes, and sails wrapped in bright canvas shrouds. All that month she'd barely thought of him; no one had spoken his name; his shadow had not followed her. But now it was here. What was he doing now? she wondered. What was he afraid of now?

"If Ross buys postcards for the children," Victoria was saying, "he should tell them they're not the real thing. Do you miss him?"

"Yes," said Katherine quietly. She had been avoiding Victoria's questions, but now, in the chill of Craig's shadow, she wanted to talk.

"And you think about him?"

"Yes." She smiled. "Enough to interfere with my work."

"And what is it you think about?"

"Nothing specific. Just—about him."

"What you do with him, or what you would like to do with him?"

"Are you asking me if we're sleeping together?"

"No, no, no, I would not ask that! It may be modern to discuss such matters, but in that respect I am most emphatically not modern. That is no one's business but your own, and his. I meant, do you think of him as a husband?"

"No." Agitated, Katherine stood, and went to the low stone wall bordering the terrace, holding her face up to the faint breeze. "I don't think of him as a husband because I already have a husband—"

"Whom you should divorce."

"—who is also my children's father... What? What did you say?"

"I said you should divorce Craig. Why should that surprise you? He deserted you thirteen months ago and except for some money and one visit, from which he ran away again, you haven't heard a word from him. Do you really call yourself married?"

"I don't understand. In the past, you've always defended him."

"So I have. In some circumstances I still might. But I also have you to think of now. And it has become obvious to me that you cannot think clearly about Ross, or indeed any man, or make an unobstructed future for yourself, until you are free of this shadow that follows you about, clouding your view."

"I can't do that."

"Of course you can; it is not at all difficult; Derek has done it three times. I've asked Claude about it—of course he is the perfect person to help you: discreet, almost a member of the family—and he explained it to me. In the first place, it is not 'divorce' any longer, but 'dissolution,' and all you need do, since you cannot find Craig to serve him the papers in person, is place a legal notice in the Vancouver newspapers, for one month, that you are petitioning for dissolution. If he does not respond in that time, you will go to court, accompanied by Claude, declare that your differences with your husband are irreconcilable, and the judge then issues the order. Claude says it takes about three minutes. And in six months it becomes final."

"Very simple," Katherine said. "But that isn't what I meant. I can't divorce Craig because he isn't here."

"I have explained that he doesn't have to be here—"

"Victoria, you know what I mean."

"Yes. Of course." Victoria laced her fingers together. "I suppose I was trying to prevent you from talking to me about fidelity. It does not seem applicable."

Something was nagging at the back of Katherine's mind. Something Leslie had said. She sat on the stone wall, staring through the swaying masts at a boat coming toward the harbor, running with the wind. Running. Bruce. Someone thought Bruce would run. *They thought he was the type who'd run from problems, which would incriminate him even more.* Someone framed Bruce for a crime because he seemed like the type who would run away.

They did a nifty job of framing him . . . it almost worked . . . it almost convinced his own sister.

The boat had come into the harbor; Katherine could see the small figures of the crew pulling down the main sail and furling the jib. Dizzily she gripped the rough stone. "Katherine," Victoria said sharply. "What is it? Come here, before you fall."

But Katherine was thinking back, a long way back, remembering some-

one shouting at Carl Doerner. It was at her party for Leslie, that Friday
night when Craig didn't come home. Someone had shouted...

*Pretty free with accusations, Doerner! You're known for that, aren't
you? Especially false ones—*

*Listen you bastard, that was two years ago. And when I found out I
was wrong, I paid the costs and it was over.*

"Katherine!" Victoria commanded.

Obediently, Katherine returned to the table, but she did not sit down.
"Would you mind if I go out for a while?" she asked. Her voice was very
soft, as if she were afraid of breaking something. "I'd like to take a walk.
There are some things I have to think about."

"Of course, my dear, if you're all right. If I said too much, I apologize—"

"No. It was nothing you said." Bending down, she kissed Victoria's
soft cheek. "I love you. I won't go far."

But she had already gone a long way, all the way back to Vancouver,
to the day Craig left. The day he ran away. Not necessarily because he'd
committed a crime but—perhaps—because he'd been framed for one.

But Carl said Craig had confessed. Katherine remembered his shaggy
presence in her living room as he held out an envelope with what he
said was proof. And then later she'd found all those bills, past-due notices,
sheets of scribbled numbers...

But still... Why hadn't it occurred to her that he might have been
framed? For ten years she had known him as a good man; he'd been
good to them and she loved him. *Why was I so ready to believe my
husband was guilty?*

Because he wasn't there. Because he ran.

Why would he run, if he was innocent?

Maybe because he didn't know what to do, and had no one to talk to
about it.

I was there, she reflected angrily; he could have talked to me. Whose
fault was it that he was better at keeping secrets than sharing?

His. But maybe I didn't make him feel I really wanted to know them.
What was it Leslie had once said? *You liked the life you had with him,
so you didn't push.* I tried to get him to talk, but after a while I stopped,
and let him have his secrets. If I'd asked more questions, maybe he would
have told me about the Haywards, and about our overspending—and
maybe other secrets that I haven't even thought of.

Walking along the harbor, a silent figure among crowds of vacationers,
Katherine knew it was not an excuse for running. There was no excuse
for Craig's deserting them. But if he thought he couldn't talk to her about

what happened—whether he was framed or really did steal—didn't she have something to do with that?

Can you be married for ten years without sharing some responsibility for what happens?

If I'd been different—would Craig have run?

CHAPTER 15

SOMEHOW Victoria saw to it that everyone was occupied and out of Katherine's way from early the next morning until well after dinner. "I don't know what is bothering your mother," Katherine heard her answer Jennifer's question. "But if she needs a quiet time to think, we can help by leaving her alone."

They all left her alone. She took the car that Ross had left for her to use and drove into the hills behind Menton, where ancient "eagles' nest" villages clung to the rocky peaks. In Eze Village, she stopped and sat for hours beside an old stone house hundreds of feet above the sea. Below, on the coastal corniche, cars rolled like tiny marbles on a narrow strip between the beach and wooded hills. Behind the houses of Eze, the cactus gardens were in full bloom. But for Katherine, the magic and dreamlike isolation were gone. All the questions that had haunted her before had found her here; she hadn't escaped them after all—she'd only pushed them aside for a brief time.

She remembered thinking, in Sospel, that she and Ross ought to talk about Derek—but it was Craig they really had to talk about. And when she'd been uncomfortable, at breakfast with Victoria, thinking Ross was becoming a part of her—it was Craig she was uncomfortable about, still with her, shadowing her, part of her life. And it was Craig she had to deal with, no matter how important Ross had become.

"What time do you expect Ross tomorrow?" Victoria asked after dinner.

"He said sometime in the morning."

Victoria nodded and returned to her book and in a moment Katherine returned to hers. They were sitting opposite each other in deep, soft armchairs, and now and then they glanced up and smiled, happy with each other. But Katherine was restless and just before midnight, when Victoria kissed her goodnight and went to bed, she went to her own rooms. The housekeeper had turned down the bed and left small lamps on, casting a soft glow over the sage green and ivory furnishings. Unbuttoning her shirt, Kathering walked from the sitting room to the bedroom and back, thinking of Jennifer and Todd asleep in their own rooms just off the playroom. She pictured the three-room apartment awaiting them in San Francisco and thought ruefully that they'd have to get used to it all over again, as they had the year before.

She paced restlessly, then, pulling on a robe, went back along the corridor to the darkened living room where she had left her book. As she reached for it, a key turned in the front door and Ross walked in, a suitcase in one hand, a bunch of packages in the other, dangling like balloons from a loop of string.

"Hitched a ride," he said, as casually as if he had not been gone at all. He dropped the suitcase and packages and strode across the room to take Katherine in his arms. "I missed you. I woke up missing you and went to sleep missing you. Did you get my postcard?"

"Yes—"

"I wrote twenty. The other nineteen are in my suitcase. I didn't want you to think I was overdoing it." And as she laughed, he kissed her.

Enfolded in his arms, Katherine held him in her own, her lips opening with his in a long breathless kiss and then small, murmuring ones. Their arms seemed like a charmed circle, she thought, with no secrets or doubts. Ross untied her robe and pushed it open. The buttons of his sport jacket had left faint impressions on the smooth skin of her breast and stomach and he kissed each one, lingeringly, before Katherine took his hand— not thinking, not planning, dizzily wanting him—and they walked down the corridor to her rooms.

But once inside, when he had shut the door, they moved apart. Katherine saw the somberness of his dark eyes, intent on her face. "All the way back from Paris," he said, "I wanted you. And I knew we'd have to wait. We have too much to talk about."

No charmed circle after all, Katherine thought. She nodded. "I spent hours yesterday at Eze Village, wondering where we'd begin."

"Could we begin with some food? I flew down with a friend who was in a hurry to leave, so we didn't take time for dinner."

"Of course," Katherine said. And added softly, "Thank you," knowing he would understand that she was grateful to him for giving her something to do, giving them both something to do, until their bodies cooled and they could talk. And then she thought how rare it was to find someone she could trust to understand her. We can tell each other the truth, she reflected. Remembering Craig, nothing seemed more important.

In the lower half of an olive-wood cabinet in her sitting room was a small refrigerator. Katherine knelt in front of it. "I'm not sure what's here. We may have to go to the kitchen."

"My wants are simple," said Ross beside her, then laughed— "and what could be simpler than this?" —as he pulled out three kinds of cheese, sliced Westphalian ham, locally grown clementines and dates, and a crusty loaf of French bread. He piled everything on a platter and from the upper shelves of the cabinet chose a bottle of Côtes du Rhone, and they carried it all to the terrace, returning to the cabinet for plates and wine glasses, cheese knives and napkins. "Who could resist a woman who provides such a midnight snack?" he murmured.

"Her name is Sylvie," said Katherine. "She's run the villa for Victoria for fifteen years, and seems content, but she might consider an offer if you wanted to make one."

He chuckled and kissed the top of her head, then sat beside her at the round cypress table. "I don't think I'll steal Sylvie from my grandmother. Though if she has a sister, I could use her in Berkeley; I'm ashamed of how little I know about keeping house. How do women know these things? Their mothers can't possibly prepare them for every crisis that crops up."

"I think they got the message a few thousand years ago," Katherine said dryly, "that if they didn't pay close attention and learn on the job, they'd be *out* of a job."

"You mean out of a marriage."

"Probably. But it's mainly attention and practice. You'll learn very quickly."

"Of course. I've already begun."

"And how are you getting along?"

"Carrie gives me advice." They laughed, and then were silent.

The soft air was fragrant with roses and pines, and an elusive breeze brought whispers of the sea. The terrace was deeply shadowed, lit only by the glow from the sitting room and bedroom, and when Ross leaned forward to fill Katherine's glass, her face filled his vision—pale, faintly flushed, with dark hollows: as fine as a delicate etching. "You are so lovely," he murmured, then let out his breath in a long sigh. "Do you know, the whole time we've been together, with everything we've talked about, we've managed to avoid talking about Craig—and Derek."

"We talked about us," Katherine replied. "About our feelings. As if no one else were real." She looked at him gravely. "What do you want to know?"

"I want to know you. What you were before I met you, what you were with Craig, what you were with Derek." He paused. When he spoke again it was as if the words were wrenched from him. "I have no right to ask about Derek. But from what I do know about you, it makes no sense... that you stayed with him as long as you did." He waited, but Katherine said nothing. "I know what he offered you, and I know how much you needed it. But I don't understand how it lasted, why the glamour didn't fade when you got to know him, how he uses people—"

"He didn't use me."

"Derek uses everyone; he sets up power plays and maneuvers people through them. He always has, even in our family."

"Jennifer," Katherine murmured. "Melanie. Myself."

"What? What does that mean?"

"Once I asked Derek why he pursued women who were close to you and Craig."

"How did you know about Jennifer? What made you think he was ever involved with Melanie?"

"Tobias told me about Jennifer. I saw him with Melanie one night, and guessed."

As if struck, Ross sat back in his chair. Phrases, looks, small details from his marriage ran through his mind and he knew it could be true. He'd never suspected, because Melanie talked about Derek so much— too much, one would have thought, for a woman burdened with the guilt of an affair. But why should he assume that Melanie had any guilt?

A flash of rage tore through him, then, surprisingly, faded, and he realized how little importance Melanie had for him now—even when his brother was involved. Once, that might have crushed him; now, sitting beside Katherine, he found his thoughts moving beyond Melanie and Derek to something even more surprising. "You said that to Derek and he took it? I've seen him destroy reputations for less."

"I didn't stay to give him a chance."

"But you'd stayed a long time."

"Ross, you said you understood what he offered me: glamour, excitement, a chance to be with people who controlled events instead of being jostled by them... And you must know how charming he can be, and how clever. I needed all of that; I enjoyed myself with him." Seeing his dark frown, she sighed. "You want to know if I slept with him." When he was silent, she said slowly, "You think I did."

Ross refilled their glasses. "I told you I have no right to ask. But I spent a lot of time in Paris thinking about you, about being in love with you and wanting more than picnics and swimming holes. So I had two choices. I could say the past is unimportant, that you and I begin from our time in Paris; or I could say it's more important than ever that I understand the past, because it means understanding you. I decided I had to understand. That was why I came back early. I couldn't wait."

His words were like heartbeats beneath Katherine's thoughts. *In love with you.* "I didn't sleep with Derek." But then she knew that wasn't enough. If we don't have the truth, she thought, we don't have anything. Taking a deep breath, she said, "But I wanted to."

Quickly, looking beyond him, at the harbor, she said, "Craig had been gone for almost seven months. Derek was the only man I was seeing, and he hadn't pressured me. I suppose he thought he wouldn't have to. Instead he took me into his world and made me feel beautiful and desirable, instead of like a housewife who'd been deserted. And there was something else." She gave a small, embarrassed laugh. "He had none of Craig's virtues. He wasn't gentle or kind or loving or anxious to please... I never knew exactly what he expected of me. He was like the dark side of my husband and somehow that was so exciting—I felt like a child, sneaking cookies from the cupboard. And I think Derek knew that; he encouraged that feeling of something forbidden..." Again she paused. "I didn't love him, but he was hard to resist. Then, last New Year's Eve, he invited a crowd back to his place after a party and I became his hostess. It was as if all my fantasies had become real. By the time everyone left, there was only one thing I didn't have, and hadn't had for months. But then... Jennifer called. Telling me to come home. Craig was there."

She turned, Ross's eyes were shadowed. He sat still, saying nothing, his face hard and unyielding.

"Why can't you understand?" she burst out. Springing from her chair she walked the length of the terrace. "What is it about Derek that makes you pull away? Both of you—he's just the same—you can't talk about each other... you become cold and distant..."

Ross stared fixedly at the distant lights of Menton. It was so quiet they heard the scurrying of a small animal through the wild grass below the terrace wall. "I do understand." He spoke without turning. "I'm sorry I didn't make that clear. I'm sorry I seemed cold." His voice was gentle, with a thread of sadness. "I've never talked to you about Derek; I've never told you how he dominated us, all the years we were growing up... Katherine, please sit with me."

Slowly, Katherine came back to her chair, and Ross went on. "Derek always seemed so sure of himself, like a pile driver, even when he was wrong. He had a way of taunting us that made us feel we'd bungled something. . . and the damnable thing about his power was that we'd feel that way even when we knew we'd done it well. He can still do that to me—at least momentarily, until I catch myself. The only ones he didn't do it to were my grandparents, but when Hugh died and Derek and Curt took over the company, there was no stopping him." He brooded at the dark shapes of olive trees, barely visible against the starlit sky. "Melanie always held Derek up to me as the kind of man I should be, who'd protect her, coddle her, give her what she wanted." He laughed shortly. "I didn't take that well. I knew she was wrong—Derek wouldn't protect or coddle anyone unless it served his own purposes—but I didn't try to tell her that; instead I found a way to punish her for idolizing him. When she'd come running to me, bubbling with excitement over a party she'd dreamed up, or taking a trip to the Caymans—something she'd spent days or weeks thinking about—I'd cut her off with a few words. Her excitement would disappear and the life would fade from her face, and I'd hate what I'd done. But with you" —he turned to Katherine— "I didn't mean to pull away. I never want to pull away from you. I don't know what the hell got into me."

"You didn't want to know that I'd had any pleasure with Derek." Katherine's voice was muffled and she cleared her throat. "I didn't finish. After New Year's, the spell—I suppose it was a spell—was broken. I still went out with him once or twice a week, but finally I broke it off. In April."

"April? I saw him in June. He said he was giving you money."

"He never gave me money! Once he told me to buy clothes and charge them to him and I refused. I never took a penny from him! Why would he tell you I did?"

"To wound, I suppose; to cause pain; he'd failed to get something he wanted and he was lashing out—"

"He thought he'd hurt you by lying about me?"

"He was right."

"Even last June you cared what he said about me?" .

"Even then."

"But how did he know?"

Ross shrugged slightly. "He knew I'd cared about you since I met you in Vancouver. And Derek always has been able to identify the vulnerable spot in people."

"But you didn't ask me about what he said."

"I should have. I was swamped with my own affairs. That's probably why Victoria didn't tell me you'd broken off with him. She was waiting for a time when I was less preoccupied, more receptive." He thought a moment. "New Year's Eve... Victoria told me you didn't see Craig."

"He was gone. Jennifer told him I was with Derek, and he left before I got there."

"Oh, Christ! Poor Craig. Whatever he'd done, whatever he came back for, to find his wife with the person he hates most in the world..." Katherine winced. Startled, Ross realized that, for the first time, he was thinking about Craig as if he were alive, and part of their lives. He glanced at Katherine and saw her watching him. "I told you I didn't call you because I was swamped. But there was another reason. I wasn't sure how to think about you—my cousin's wife—how much I could risk getting close to you. But it wasn't a real issue. I haven't had a cousin in sixteen years. It's strange," he mused. "I was in your house in Vancouver; I saw those photographs you brought the first night you came to Victoria's; and you and Jennifer and Todd are part of us now... but Craig had no reality for me. I mourned him too long, accepted him as dead for too long, to feel that he was alive. There were only memories that had no connection with me or anything I did or thought."

"He's alive for me," Katherine said. Restlessly, she walked to the stone wall, then back to the table, repeating Ross's words to herself. *No connection with me...* She'd felt that, too, the past few weeks. But not any longer. "He's alive and... everywhere. No matter what I do, he follows me. The same as before. Everything is the same. I still don't know what he was really like; sometimes I think the more I hear, the less I know. Because I don't know what to believe. Ross," she said abruptly, "tell me about the sailing accident. I've heard Claude's version, and then Derek told me his, but I never knew whether to believe it or not. I've wanted to ask you, but in the past few weeks..."

"You didn't think about Craig. Neither did I. Katherine, do you know, I'm still hungry?"

"You've been talking instead of eating."

"Then I'll make up for lost time." He heaped his plate with cheese and dates and bread. "Is there anything left in that bottle?"

She filled their glasses and nibbled on dates while he ate. "Is all this to avoid answering my question?"

"All this is to provide the narrator with sustenance. It's not an easy story. Do you want to tell me how Derek told it?"

"No. I just want you to tell me."

"Well, then." Hitching his chair closer to the table, he took a few more bites, then once again forgot the food. "The four of us were sailing home from Sausalito, across the bay. It was July—my God, sixteen years ago this month—a cool, clear evening and Craig decided to take a longer way back, making a loop through the Golden Gate. He was in charge; he always was, on the water—the best sailor I've ever seen. I think it was the only time he was really happy, absolutely confident, cut loose from people making demands on him. In those days I was more interested in swimming and tennis, and Derek had just bought his own speedboat, so Craig was in charge when he took us sailing. That day, when Derek wanted more speed, he said we could put up the spinnaker. Have you ever sailed under a spinnaker?"

"I've never sailed."

"You've—" Stunned, he said, "That never occurred to me. We'll correct that when we get back."

"Ross, please tell me what happened."

"Well, with a spinnaker and a good wind, you skim the water, weightless, flying, but with the waves at eye level. The most fantastic feeling . . . Jennifer was ecstatic; she threw her head back, laughing into the wind. That's the picture I carry in my mind: her hair blowing, her face bright and laughing, her arms wide when she burst out 'I love all of you so much.' We . . . loved her, too. So much."

After a moment, he went on quietly. "When we were more than halfway home, Craig asked me to go below for a winch handle, and Derek called down to bring him a bottle of Scotch from his pack. Then Jennifer came down, saying Craig had ordered lifejackets for everyone; the currents are tricky near the Golden Gate and the wind was coming up. 'Derek is so unpleasant when he drinks too much,' she said. 'Could you . . . forget to bring up the bottle?' She was trying to be cool and sophisticated, but she couldn't quite make it; she was young and impressionable, full of life and love, one of the dearest people I've ever known." He drew in his breath. "Incredible, how grief stays fresh. I said I'd forget to bring the bottle and she kissed me. It was the last time Jennifer ever kissed me.

"When we came up from the cabin, Craig and Derek were arguing about the spinnaker; Craig said it should come down; it could get ripped apart in a strong wind. And by then the wind was very high: wild and sometimes gusting, with a kind of whistle—sometimes we had to shout to be heard—and the boat was heeling, with spray coming in the cockpit. Derek put his arms around Jennifer and told Craig—his voice cut through the wind—they liked living dangerously; the only one who was afraid was the captain.

"Craig's face, when he saw Derek holding Jennifer . . . I'd never seen him look like that: enraged but terrified, his mouth working as if all the words were trying to rush out at once. He screamed at Derek, 'Get your goddamn hands off—!' and started toward them but he couldn't let go of the wheel. He had to stay there, shouting to Jennifer to move away, and to Derek to take his hands off her. Neither of them moved; they stood still, staring at him. Everything had changed, in just a few minutes, from laughter and exhilaration to something terrifying. I was scared to death, because *Craig* was scared—I didn't know of what, which was even more frightening—and he didn't look as if he could control himself or the boat. I had to do something, so I yanked Jennifer away and asked Craig if I should take down the spinnaker.

"The sound, roaring in our ears—you have no idea what it was like: wind and spray breaking over us, Derek and Craig yelling at each other— it all mixed together into a nightmare. Craig couldn't stop: he shouted at Derek that he was the captain and if Derek didn't like it he could swim to shore, if he had the guts to try it—he found a dozen ways to doubt Derek's courage and skill—and then he told me to go forward and take down the spinnaker. But Jennifer grabbed my arm, begging me to stay and stop Derek, because he'd begun taunting Craig in that way of his that always drove us mad. I didn't know what to do first—comfort Jennifer, who was starting to cry, or slug Derek, or tell Craig to ignore him, or go forward and take down the spinnaker—and then I remember thinking that it didn't matter what I did; something was going to happen and *there was no escape.*

"We were crammed in that sailboat, flying over the water in a roaring wind, heeling at a crazy angle, soaking wet from waves washing over the cockpit, and Derek stood there, absolutely still, his voice like a knife, calling Craig the little golden puppet, his grandmother's toy... well, a string of brutal insults. Jennifer was crying and when Craig saw that he got so livid I thought he'd burst. He roared out—making sure Jennifer heard—that Derek was a liar and a crook—he'd cut corners to save money on a building we were putting up, and bribed an inspector to OK the job. I hadn't worked on that building and I asked what the hell he was talking about and Derek, like ice, said 'Golden boy changed the specs on the Macklin Building to be Grandma's hero—even bribed the inspector—but now he's scared and shifting the blame. Running away,' he said. 'As usual.' And then, out of the blue—the damndest thing— Craig laughed. I've never known why. He said he cared about the Hay- ward reputation more than Derek, and he was going to tell the family and the city officials what Derek had done. He was still laughing when he told me again to take down the spinnaker.

"I got about halfway forward when I felt the boat change course. I turned around to see what the hell Craig had done and saw him with his hands on Derek's throat. Jennifer was pulling at his arm. And then everything happened at once. The boat had changed course because no one was at the wheel, and the wind pushed the mainsail to the other side. The boom swung across and slammed against Jennifer's head. There was blood—like a rose, bursting into bloom just beside her eye—and then she stumbled and fell overboard. She never made a sound. She just fell. But Craig and I screamed—my God, I still dream about this—the blood and the two of us screaming—'JENNIFER!'—and Craig lunging at the life preserver and marker pole to throw them over the side. Jennifer was floating face down; the water was choppy all around her. It looked so cold—it hadn't looked that cold all day—and we were moving away from her. With that wind and all the sail we had, we were going so damned fast... I raced to the spinnaker and hauled it down. Slashed my hands on the ropes and never knew it until I saw the blood when I ran along the deck back to the cockpit.

"Derek was at the wheel, cursing because he couldn't get the boat to respond; it wasn't like his speedboat. He told me Craig had jumped in after Jennifer. I grabbed the wheel from him; I didn't know much more than he did, but with the spinnaker down we'd slowed, and I managed to turn us around. Then I told him to take the wheel again and I took down the mainsail and started the motor."

"But Derek said—"

Ross turned, suddenly aware of her. "Derek stood by the cabin, looking at the water, and never moved a muscle or said a word while I turned the boat. I remember thinking he was figuring out how all this would affect him, because that's how Derek looked at everything, but I didn't have enough energy even to be angry: I was dizzy and sick and trying to get back to Jennifer and Craig. It took me ten minutes—ten minutes, when today I can do it in three!—and that was too long. It was too late. We got back to the marker pole and Jennifer...

"She was...tucked into the opening of the life preserver...like a doll...her eyes were staring...The wind was a steady screech, and Jennifer was staring at us, not seeing us... And I was crying. I couldn't stop. I stood at the wheel, crying."

Katherine felt her own tears well up, and she closed her eyes.

"I shouted to Craig, but there was no answer. I thought he'd be close by, waiting for us after he put Jennifer in the life preserver, but I couldn't see him or hear him. It was almost dark and I was still crying. I told Derek we had to get Jennifer. It was the only time in our lives I gave orders and Derek followed them. He went in the water and tied a rope around her; and we got her into the boat and put a blanket over her. Derek tried to find a pulse but he couldn't. That was all, really. We shouted for Craig and Derek called the Coast Guard on the radio and I kept the boat close to the marker pole while we waited for them, shouting for Craig. Our voices seemed so small in the darkness, with just the circle of our spotlight moving over the black water, and in the distance the lights of San Francisco and the lighted bridges strung across the bay— so damned beautiful, but I kept thinking, 'Jennifer can't see it'—and we kept shouting Craig's name into the wind... But, my God, we sounded so infinitely small. The night swallowed our voices. I don't know if Craig heard us. He never answered."

Katherine was crying, her muscles tensed, as if she stood beside Ross on the boat, calling to Craig. Ross put his arm around her. "That night we were all at Victoria's. I suppose we talked about what happened, but I kept hearing Craig's voice. In a room full of people, all I heard was Craig shouting Jennifer's name, and I kept seeing Jennifer's eyes."

His voice became dry. "The next morning, I went to see my father in his office. I hadn't slept, but at least I was thinking again, and I had to know what Derek and Craig had been talking about. My father had been with me all night, of course, but I hadn't said anything about a fight on the boat and it took him by surprise. Not for long; he never takes more than a few seconds to recover from surprise. Derek is like that, too. I asked him to have the Macklin Building checked, and just then, Derek came in and heard me, took a quick look at our father, sitting behind his desk like a judge, and said to him, 'Craig changed the specs; I didn't tell you at the time because it wasn't serious, and I took care of it.' I asked him what he did, and he said he'd strengthened the footings and there wasn't anything to worry about.

"My father asked him if he was sure he'd corrected the problem. Those were his words. And Derek said it was all taken care of. They were very smooth, except that the nerve next to Derek's eye was jumping. I thought they were lying, but I didn't have any evidence to back me up. My father gave me hell for doubting my brother, suggested I was distraught over the accident, and offered me a trip to Europe, after the funeral. I took it.

"Probably I shouldn't have. But I was exhausted and sick of all of them; I just wanted to get the hell out of there. When you're twenty years old, it's hard to accept the fact that your father might be a liar or dishonest; especially if you're already having trouble coping with nightmares about seeing your two cousins die in the same afternoon. So I went to Paris.

"In the fall I went back to school and when I graduated my father asked a friend in New York to hire me as a junior architect. It occurred to me today, for the first time, that he wanted to keep me away from the Hayward Corporation."

"So you wouldn't ask questions?"

"So I wouldn't snoop and discover that Derek hadn't repaired anything, and my father knew it. And there was another reason, I suppose, why they wanted me out of the way: to make sure that Derek would take over the company." He reached for the wine and poured what was left in their glasses. "If they'd asked, I would have told them I never wanted to take over the company. But I did worry about that building, and finally managed to buy it and get it vacated. It was inspected this week; I got the report yesterday in Paris."

After a moment, Katherine asked, "What didn't Derek repair?"

"The footings that supported the building. We hired a foundations engineer to check them and the first thing he found was a column...damn, I'm sorry, I didn't mean to get into this."

"Tell me," she said. "I want to hear it."

Ross smiled at her. Nice words, he thought. "He found a column that hadn't been sunk deep enough and then, under it, a footing that was cracked because it hadn't been reinforced with enough steel. We assume that if it's true of one, it's true of all of them, which means the building is in danger. Do you remember the accident at a Hyatt Hotel in Kansas City, when people were dancing on a skyway and it collapsed? The reports say it was the same problem: shortcuts in construction that made it unsafe. In other words, someone deviated from the original specifications to save time and money."

"And that's what happened in the Macklin Building?"

"We think...What the hell, that's what it had to be. The footings are substandard, which means the specs were changed, which means, I suppose, an inspector had to be bribed to approve them."

"Was it Craig?"

The name echoed on the terrace. "I don't think so," Ross said slowly. "I always had trouble believing Craig would knowingly do anything to jeopardize a building's integrity; he was absolutely straight in construction. He thought of money last. I always felt I could trust Craig with any building I designed."

Trust Craig. Katherine rested her head against Ross's arm, feeling drained. A faint glow made her look to their left. "Sunrise," she said wonderingly. The sky brightened: a wash of pale pink and apricot spread above them, and then the sun burned through, turning the cypress and olive trees to burnished red-gold. "So beautiful," Katherine murmured. "But everything followed us here, after all."

She left the circle of Ross's arm and perched on the stone wall, gazing down the hill at the sand-colored buildings of Menton, growing brighter as the sun rose. Ross watched her, the downcast curve of her neck, the tremble of her lips. "Divorce him," he said bluntly. She swung around. "Katherine, somewhere in all the talk tonight, I told you I love you. Did you hear it, or did it get lost in the conversation?"

"I heard it," she answered. "And... I'm grateful—"

"Grateful!"

"I mean... oh, damn, how can I say this? Ross, it doesn't change anything. I can't say, 'Ross loves me, so I'll divorce Craig...' I can't just walk away from him."

"He walked away from you."

"Is that why I should do it? Whatever he does, I do in return?"

"It's hardly the same. You have a reason; he had none. And you've given him more than a year to come back."

"But there's so much I don't know. He's in trouble but I don't even know what kind, or how it happened." She told Ross about Leslie's call, and Carl Doerner's quarrel at her party in Vancouver.

He looked at her in disbelief. "You can't be serious. Because a kid at Heath's was framed and a year ago some people quarreled... Katherine, they have nothing to do with Craig!"

"How do you know? Isn't it a possibility? You just said you don't believe he altered those specifications—he was absolutely straight, you said, you trusted him. Why would he have been any different in his company? If he was framed, and he ran because he thought no one would believe him, he was right, wasn't he? Everyone, including his wife, believed he was guilty. And now you say I should divorce him."

"You don't want to divorce him?"

Katherine slumped, her energy deflated. "Sometimes I've wished I could. No, that's not right. Sometimes I've wished he would just be gone. Really gone. Not—"

"Clinging."

"Yes, that's how it feels. But I've never thought about divorcing him. How could I? What would I tell Jennifer and Todd? I got tired of waiting for Daddy? I'm cutting him from us, even though he's sending us money and probably trying to find his way back to us? Is that what I should say?"

He did not answer. "Ross, I can't leave Craig because I owe him something after he loved me and took care of me for ten years. I don't see how I can erase that because he did something I don't understand."

Steadfast, Ross thought, remembering their dinner in Paris, when he had found himself comparing Katherine to Melanie. Steadier; more steadfast.

"And something else," Katherine said. She came back to him, putting out a hand to smooth his hair. She hardly knew what she was doing, but she felt she had to touch him to make him understand, and then he had pulled her to him and she was on his lap, her arms around his neck, her face against his, crying quietly. "Don't you see—I can't make a future with you, I can't even think of one, until I finish with the past. Everything is dangling. I don't have any answers, I don't know how much I'm responsible for, *I don't understand what happened and who I am now.* Ross, don't you see? When you said you loved me, you said your choices were to wipe out the past or to understand it. You decided you had to understand it. So do I. I can't make a future until I understand the past, and finish it."

Ross pushed back her hair and kissed her closed eyes, her cheek, her lips, tasting her tears. He tried to think what it would be like if he and Melanie had not gone through a final confrontation, wound things up through their lawyers, signed documents—finished their marriage. "Yes," he said. "Of course I understand. But I don't know how you're going to do it."

"Craig and I will do it. Together. When he comes back."

"And how long will you wait for that?"

"I don't know."

The piercing trill of a bird broke the silence. Within the house, a door opened; water ran in the kitchen; the fresh smell of coffee reached them. The day had begun.

CHAPTER 16

SAN Francisco was cool and airy after the Riviera's molten heat and, his first evening back, Ross walked from his office to the top of Telegraph Hill to reacquaint himself with his city. It spread below in soft pastels and the fresh green of eucalyptus trees, tinged with pale gold from the slanting rays of the setting sun. Sighting down the hill, past the roof gardens and sun decks of the houses covering its slope, Ross saw the city as a canvas, always changing, always waiting to be changed. He picked out the site of BayBridge Plaza, where he had spent the morning inspecting work begun while he was in France, and other neighborhoods around the city he and his staff planned to work on in the future.

Restore and renovate, he reflected. Our days are spent remaking and rebuilding. And when necessary, destroying. When nothing can be saved, we tear down.

He wondered which one Katherine would decide to do.

His memory held the image of her beauty in the coral glow of the sunrise over Menton, and the troubled look in her eyes. She had to finish her marriage, she said, and understand it. But what if understanding gave her a reason to try to rebuild it? Steadfast, he reminded himself. And loyal.

Walking back down the hill, Ross thought about Craig. Why the hell hadn't someone found him? The money came every month, and even though it was always mailed in a different town, some enterprising investigator should have figured out a way to trace it. Claude had hired one, long ago, but after four months he'd had nothing to report. No one had anything to report. But Craig had a profession; he had habits, and contacts—why the hell hadn't someone put all those together and found him?

Maybe because no one cared enough anymore. Doerner's loss must have been covered by insurance, and not enough money was involved to keep police on it full time for fourteen months.

But I care, he thought. More than the police, more than Doerner, even more than the tax people. Because I want Katherine to be free.

I can't make a future with you until I understand the past.

Find him, then. Help Katherine put an end to her past, or rebuild it. Either way, it's better for both of us than not knowing.

I could call Carl Doerner; get the names of people Craig worked with. Maybe someone knew something, but didn't want to help the police find him. Maybe that someone would help Craig's cousin.

Ross considered it. He had three meetings tomorrow; he could be in Vancouver the next day. But that was when Katherine and Victoria would be home from France. But he'd only be gone a day or two. And impatience was pounding inside him. He had to do something; Katherine would understand that. He thought of her, in the Vesubie Valley, leaning over him, his hands holding her breasts, the sun beating down—

He went back to his office to call Carl Doerner.

He found him at home. "My name is Ross Hayward," he began. "I'm trying to locate my cousin, Craig Fraser—"

"Aren't we all," Doerner said flatly.

"—and I'd appreciate it if you'd give me some information."

"After fourteen months? There isn't anything I can tell you that I haven't told every policeman in Canada and the States. I'd love to find the son of a bitch—you know how I trusted him and he let me down? —if you want to try, lots of luck. You'll need it."

"I grew up with him," Ross said. "I knew him pretty well at one time. I might be able to figure out his thinking if I knew what he was working on when he disappeared."

"Skipped."

Ross was beginning to dislike him. "What was he working on?"

"The police have that information. Look, I'm about to eat my dinner—"

"I'd like the names of contractors he worked with in other cities."

"The police have that, too. I gave them a list a year ago."

Evasive and unhelpful, Ross noted, and wondered why. "I thought you might have remembered some other information," he said. "If we find my cousin, or even hear word of him, my family is thinking of repaying the money he took."

There was a pause. "What does finding him have to do with repaying it?"

"We'd want him to share in the repayment."

After another moment, Doerner said, "There was one thing. Nothing definite, just peculiar. I told the police about it—they checked it out and said it wasn't anything—but I still wonder."

Ross waited.

"I think something was going on in Calgary. Craig was there an awful lot in the last two years—the whole time he was stealing from me. He *said* he was making contacts, getting new clients—but he did it on his own time. I called around after he skipped, to see if he was working for a competitor."

"And?"

"Couldn't find one. But there's no doubt in my mind he was. Obviously he needed a lot of money, and untrustworthy once, untrustworthy twice, I always say."

"Profound," Ross murmured. Aloud, he said, "Do you know of a contractor he might have gone to?"

Carefully, Doerner replied, "There was a Len Oxton we worked with once or twice. But I told you, the police have a list."

"I remember," Ross said. "Thanks."

He was about to hang up when Doerner's voice, a little anxious, burst from the receiver. "What are you going to do next?"

Gently, Ross touched a picture of Katherine he had taken in Saint-Paul, smiling in a field of flowers. "I'm going to Calgary," he said.

Two days later, catching his first glimpse of Calgary from his plane, he thought it looked like a steel island floating on the wheat fields of Alberta, where the Bow and Elbow rivers met. It was bigger than he had expected, even though he knew that oil and gas had made it the fastest growing town in Canada for years. "About six hundred thousand," said the man beside him when he asked its population. "And growing, eh?"

A habit of Canadians: to end their sentences with a little explosion of air. Ross wondered if Craig had picked it up. He wondered what he would do if he found him.

Bring him back to Katherine and hope she doesn't decide to rebuild.

Last month, he recalled, I was arguing with Jacques, saying it was better to restore than to destroy.

When possible, he amended. There are times when it's not. It depends on where you're standing.

From a telephone in the airport, he called Len Oxton. "Police talked to me, eh?" said Oxton. "Couldn't tell them much; I liked Fraser but I never worked with him and wouldn't have the faintest where he might be. Noah Johnson, now, he might; I think he and Fraser worked on a bank building a few years back."

Noah Johnson was a man of few words. "Fraser, eh? Knew his stuff, easy to work with, kept to himself. Never got friendly. Bob Vessen knew him better."

Bob Vessen liked to talk. "Fine fellow, Craig; low-key, good ideas, loved to use glass. We put up an office building with a combined greenhouse and cafeteria; sensational in the winters. Craig carved me a little horse once—now there was something else he really knew: sculpture, especially Eskimo. But if you're asking me where he might have gotten to, that I couldn't say. He wasn't much for giving away feelings or private thoughts. Hold on, though; he did seem friendly with Danny Nielsen... Nielsen Builders, you know. Danny might have an idea."

And so, late that afternoon, Ross found Danny Nielsen. And Danny took him to Elissa.

Elissa Nielsen, Craig's mistress for almost two years, before he disappeared.

"Of course I never told the police anything," Danny said as they drove from his office to the outskirts of the city. "Crocodiles couldn't have dragged it out of me. All they wanted was to make Craig look bad, like a real bona-fide criminal, you know; they didn't want to clutter their minds with the possibility that he wasn't guilty or maybe had serious reasons for doing what he did. It was easier to think he was just an ordinary crook."

Hardly ordinary, Ross thought in disbelief as Danny drove him toward yet another of Craig's lives. San Francisco, Vancouver, and now Calgary. Had Katherine suspected? Of course not; she would have told him.

"You think he wasn't guilty?" he asked as he watched the city speed by. New construction was everywhere, cross-hatched girders reaching to the blue-white prairie sky. Enough to keep Craig busy for years. But of course that wasn't why he came here.

"No," said Danny. "I don't think Craig was guilty. But I don't like to think about it. We cost him plenty, you know. Here we are."

The house was a small cottage with four rooms and a screened porch. A tricycle lay on its side in the front yard; on the coffee table in the living room was a wooden carving of a large sleepy-eyed turtle with a gleeful little boy astride it. "My sister," said Danny. "Elissa Nielsen; Ross Hayward."

"Well," she said and put out her hand. "I've heard so much about you I'm glad to see you're real."

She was as tall as Ross, large-boned, with long, light brown hair and wide-spaced blue eyes—clear, honest, appraising. Not quite pretty, she had such an open look, ready to be friends, that Ross, holding her hand, found himself liking her, wanting her to like him, even though, driving there, he had been blaming her for all of Katherine's problems. "Heard about me?" he asked.

"Craig told me all about you," she answered. "How about a drink? We're having chicken for dinner; did Danny tell you?"

"I didn't," said Danny. "And I'm not staying. You two have plenty to talk about. Ross, call me later and I'll drive you back to your hotel. I'm glad you found us; I always thought Craig was the best guy in the world. See you later."

When he was gone, Ross said, "I'll take you out to dinner."

"No," said Elissa. "Thanks, but no. It's quiet here and anyway I've already cooked the chicken. What will you drink? I have Scotch, left from Craig's last visit—but it's better when it ages, isn't it?—and sherry."

"Sherry, thanks."

"Keeping a clear head, I see. Danny said you're looking for Craig."

"He thinks you know where he is."

"He's wrong. I don't know where Craig is; I haven't seen him or heard from him since a year ago June. He called to tell me he was going to Toronto and he'd try to fit in a couple of days with me on the way back. I haven't heard from him since. All I've heard is about him. The police talked to Danny in July; they said he was an embezzler. I never believed that." She handed him a glass. "To your good health. And welcome to Calgary."

"But he disappeared," Ross said. "You didn't see him again. If he hadn't committed a crime, why was he gone?"

"Well. You wouldn't understand, but if you're a woman and your guy is married and has a family and all, you expect it. I mean, you know that one day he's going to choose his family over you. His wife will get suspicious or he'll run out of excuses or he'll just get tired of running back and forth—and he'll stop coming around. So you prepare yourself. It doesn't really work; it still breaks your heart when it happens; but at least you think you know what's going on."

"Did it break your heart?"

"Of course it did. I love him."

She said it so naturally that Ross felt a stab of pity. "Why didn't the police find you?"

"Because Craig always registered at a motel in town before he came here. In case he got telephone calls, you know. I mean, his kids could have been sick... some emergency... When the police checked, they found the registrations. And my neighbors, and people in the shops around here, knew him under another name." At Ross's exasperated sigh, she became defensive. "He had to; he was protecting his family. Anyway, he thought he had to, and I understood, and that's how everyone knew him. And when he stopped coming around, well, they just thought we broke up. It happens, you know."

Ross walked about the small living room, crowded with memorabilia: dolls and stuffed animals from amusement parks, glass paperweights embedded with the names of Canadian cities, a bowl filled with restaurant matchbooks, pictures of Elissa and Craig, some with a young boy grinning happily between them. Ross looked at her.

"He's not Craig's."

I hope not, he thought, and moved on, stopping in front of a calendar from Vancouver Construction. "Last year's," he murmured.

Elissa gave an embarrassed laugh. "I should take it down. But if I throw that out, what about all the other things Craig brought me? I mean, where do you stop, if you're trying to forget someone? Every time he came here he brought a paperweight or a carving or... Well, anyway. Did Katherine throw out the things he brought her and the kids?"

Startled, Ross said, "Do you know her?"

"Katherine? Good Lord, no. Craig would have died if I'd even come near Vancouver. But I heard so much about her I might as well know her. I mean, she's sort of like a relative you hear about but never meet. So I talk about her like that. More sherry?"

"Thank you." Ross saw her hand shake as she poured. "What did Craig tell you about Katherine?"

"What didn't he, would be more like it. He didn't tell me he'd leave her, if that's what you're asking. That was the last thing on his mind. He was crazy about her." She saw Ross look again at the photographs around the room. "You don't understand."

"No," Ross replied. "I don't."

She sat on the couch and motioned to the space beside her. "Don't you want to sit down?"

Sitting with her, Ross felt her warmth, the comfort of her strong body and calm gaze. Remembering Craig, he began to understand what had drawn him here.

"You knew Craig," Elissa said. "So you know he wasn't really happy unless somebody needed him. Not demanding things of him—he hated it when people told him what he ought to do or how he ought to behave— but just needing to be taken care of. It made him feel good to take care of people who were in trouble. That was me when he met me: I was in trouble and I sure needed to be taken care of."

She took a sip of sherry. "Do you want some crackers or pretzels or something?"

"No, thank you."

"Well, when we met, I was three months pregnant and no one was around to be the father. Isn't that the damndest luck? First my little boy's father and now Craig. Good thing I'm not superstitious. This guy, the father, was working on an oil rig and he got transferred and said he'd send for me when he got settled, but he never did. I have a feeling he was a little scared by the idea of fatherhood. I tend to take up with men who scare easily; I wonder why that is. Excuse me."

She left the room and was back in a minute. "Turned on the oven. Whenever you start getting hungry, let me know. I met Craig when Danny took me drinking with them one night. I was pretty down and Craig tried to make me feel better and I ended up telling him all my problems. I'd been sick with some kind of anemia—pernicious anemia, does that sound right?—and I'd lost my job and there I was pregnant with no man around. Little did I know I was practically seducing Craig; he couldn't resist a sob story like that. The next night he showed up on my doorstep with a couple of steaks and two pints of cherry vanilla ice cream and some bottles of Scotch and wine. He said in my condition I needed protein and good cheer and he was providing them. He provided them for almost two years."

In the silence, Ross asked, "How old are you?"

"Twenty-nine."

"And where is your little boy?"

"I sent him to a friend's house for the night. He's just about gotten over missing Craig; he didn't need to hear any of this." She looked somberly at Ross. "What you have to understand is that Craig didn't come here because he liked a roll in the hay with someone who wasn't his wife. He came here because he needed me as much as I needed him. I'm not criticizing Katherine; she sounds like somebody I could be friends with. But Craig said she thought he was perfect and if he told her the truth about himself—*any* of the truth, way back to the sailing accident... oh, sure," she said as Ross's eyebrows shot up, "he told me about that. He couldn't tell Katherine because he was sure she'd stop believing in him, stop loving him, if she knew that he caused his sister's death and ran away and let his whole family think he was drowned. And he said he was going to be blamed for some building that wasn't built right—I never understood all of that, but he said he couldn't fight his son-of-a-

bitch cousin Derek, and Derek's father, to prove he wasn't the one who
did whatever Derek did. He was so full of hate for Derek you wouldn't
believe it. There was something else—something he couldn't even tell
me, it hurt so much—but most of it he talked about over and over. He
had to; he said he'd never told anyone and he could hardly stand it."

"He had a wife who loved him," Ross said. "He could have told her."

"Didn't you hear what I said? He couldn't tell her because he loved
her."

"So he shut her out."

"Is that how she felt? Well, I can see how she might. But Craig didn't
think of that. He was just scared of telling her."

"Why wasn't he scared of telling you?"

"Because he didn't love me," Elissa said simply. "He needed me to
talk to; he was comfortable with me; he was *happy*. But he didn't love
me. He loved Katherine and he couldn't risk disappointing her." In a
moment she stood and said briskly, "I think I should put the chicken in
the oven. About fifteen minutes until dinner. Is that all right?"

"Yes." Preoccupied with his thoughts, Ross absently followed her into
the kitchen, perching on one of the stools at the linoleum-covered breakfast counter.

"Craig used to do that," said Elissa, putting a covered dish in the oven.
"Sat there drinking Scotch and talking away while I cooked the food he
brought. He always brought food; he always acted like he had plenty of
money. Do you know, I can tell you what every room in his house in
West Vancouver looks like? I used to dream about how it would be to
live there."

"Did you ever tell Craig that?"

"Of course not. It would have made him feel bad and then he couldn't
talk about it anymore. What I was best at with Craig was listening. He
never thought of me envying his house because..."

"Because he never thought of you."

"That's not true! He thought of us all the time! When my boy was
born and this anemia thing of mine came back, he took care of us. He
bought us things—he paid the mortgage on this house!—and never
refused me anything. And it seemed we were always needing something.
He didn't steal because of us, did he? Do you think it was my fault? I've
thought and thought about it and I don't believe he stole at all. He wasn't
the kind. He was so good to us..."

"Danny, too," she said, putting pickles and olives on a plate. "He and
a friend had saved money to start their own business and Craig loaned
them the rest, without even being asked. He heard them talking about

borrowing money and said he'd take care of it. He liked doing things for
people."

"He liked showing people how much he could do for them."

"It's the same thing, isn't it? He didn't even tell Danny when to repay
the money, but Danny started anyway; he'd made two or three payments
when Craig disappeared. It's too bad he always ran when things got
difficult—and I know it wasn't right that he spent money on us instead
of his family—but he acted like he had plenty, and when he'd say he
couldn't tell Katherine things, and smile that sad little smile of his... Well,
I loved him, and wanted to make him feel good about himself. Oh,
damn, damn, damn—Ross, I keep wondering where he is, and if he's
all right, and what I did wrong to make him disappear. Everywhere I go,
he's sort of there... but not really... and *I miss him.*"

Standing beside Elissa in her kitchen, with his arms around her, Ross
silently cursed his cousin, who twice had found wonderful women, and
had hurt them both.

And I'm at a dead end, he thought. Which Craig would I look for
from here—Craig Fraser or the one Elissa's neighbors knew?

All I've found is another shadow.

Their three rooms looked even smaller than Katherine had anticipated,
and Jennifer and Todd wandered through them reminding her how great
it had been to have separate rooms. "We're getting too old to be in the
same room," Todd declared after dinner. "Especially Jennifer. Girls need
privacy for intimate matters."

Katherine laughed. "Who told you that?"

"Carrie. And Jon told me I need my own space, too."

"They're right; we all need privacy. I sleep in the living room, remember? But we can't afford a bigger apartment yet."

"When can we?"

"Pretty soon, maybe. If I get my new jewelry made this month, and
Mettler's customers buy it... I guess then we could look for a place with
lots of room."

"And rooms," Todd grinned.

"That too." Katherine began to sort the mail they had picked up from
the post office that afternoon. "Here's something from school for you
and Jennifer."

"Is that all? No letters?"

"You have to write letters to get letters."

"I would, if I knew where to write."

"Oh." Katherine put her arm around Todd and held him close. "I'm sorry, sweetheart. I guess I gave up expecting a letter from Daddy a long time ago."

"So did I, I guess," said Todd. "I was just asking. I'll be out in front with Jennifer, OK? Mom? Is that OK?"

"What? Oh, yes, fine. Just don't wander off; it's getting close to your bedtime." Katherine looked back at the letter she had just opened with *Mettler's* embossed at the top. "Dear Mrs. Fraser," she read.

> When we discussed your jewelry, I hoped we were
> beginning a profitable relationship. However, the recession
> has forced me to change my plans; like all prudent retailers,
> I must reduce my inventory; and since I cannot alter
> my relationship with trusted, long-standing suppliers, I
> must reluctantly withdraw my verbal offer to you of last June.
> I am returning your jewelry by special messenger. Please
> do not think unkindly of me; some day we may yet
> work together. With all best wishes for a successful
> career, I am—

He can't do this. Katherine crumpled the letter in her hand. *I was so sure I'd made a start... He can't... Of course he can; it's his store.* She hurled the letter across the room. *Bastard.* He was lying; the economy hadn't changed in two months. Anyway, Leslie had told her that Marc said people like Mettler held their customers even in bad times.

Her thoughts racing, she held her head in her hands. He decided he didn't like my work after all. It wasn't what he wanted... it wasn't as unusual or as good as he thought at first...

That's not true!

She jumped up and went to the kitchen and with furious energy began washing the dinner dishes. "It's not true," she repeated aloud. She remembered Mettler's face when he saw her pieces; they *are* good, she thought fiercely. I know they're good.

But he knows more about jewelry than you do, a small voice said. Maybe he had reasons... She shook her head. I know how much I've changed; I know what I can do. Whatever happened while I was in France, I know my work is good.

Then she thought: I shouldn't have gone to France. Maybe, if I'd been here, I could have found out why he did this, and turned it around.

But then, I wouldn't have had a month with Ross.

The telephone rang and, answering it, she heard his voice, distant, with static on the line. "I tried to call you this afternoon," he said.

"We went grocery shopping and to the post office. Are you out of town? You sound so far away."

"I am. I have a lot to tell you. I just got back from dinner with—"

"Ross, will you be away long?"

"I'll be back tomorrow. What's wrong, Katherine?"

"Nothing—"

"Something is; I can hear it in your voice."

"Nothing that can't wait until tomorrow. Where did you say you are?"

"I want to know what's bothering you."

She gazed at her soapy hand on the telephone receiver. "Herman Mettler canceled my order."

"Canceled—! Why?"

"The recession, he says. I think it must be something else, but I can't imagine..." Her voice broke.

"Katherine, he can't arbitrarily cancel it. You have a contract."

"Only verbal, as he carefully said in his letter. I never insisted on a written contract."

"And you didn't ask Claude about it? Or any lawyer?"

"I was going to; I just didn't think it was urgent. He was so excited, talking about where he'd advertise my work, and display it, it never occurred to me there was anything to worry about. And then Victoria invited us to France and I just forgot about it. But I wouldn't have worked all month on new designs if I didn't think we had an agreement."

"That son of a bitch—what the hell got into him? My God, for you to come back to that...Katherine, dearest Katherine...damn it, I should be there, to help you."

Dearest Katherine. "I'd rather just have your arms around me."

His warm laughter seemed to fill the room. "Tomorrow. As soon as I can get a flight."

"Ross, I haven't let you talk at all. You had something to tell me. Dinner with someone. Did you tell me where you are?"

He laughed again. "No. I'll tell you about it when I get back. You have enough to think about right now. Katherine, could you have Jennifer and Todd looked after this weekend? I want to be with you. We'll have lots of family weekends; this time I want you to myself."

"Yes," she said. "I'd love it. I'll see what I can do."

"Try Victoria," he suggested. "They all had a good time together in France; she and Tobias can't spoil them too badly in one weekend."

Her despair began to lift, and the next morning she went to Victoria and Tobias. She found them at breakfast in the sunroom. "Ah, Katherine," said Tobias, kissing her on both cheeks. "'Journeys end in lovers meeting.' I understand yours did. Sit down, have coffee with us, and tell me everything."

Katherine flushed and glanced at Victoria. "It seems there's nothing left for me to tell."

Victoria was unruffled. "I gave Tobias no details, since you gave me none. I did mention your wonderfully expressive face, which was radiant most of our time in France." She looked closely at Katherine. "And now it is not. What is it, my dear?"

Briefly, Katherine told them about Mettler's letter. Tobias began to sputter. "But—but—but—"

"Wretch!" Victoria exclaimed. "Viper!" She cast about. "Reptile!"

A laugh broke from Katherine. "Much more creative than I." She leaned over to kiss Victoria. "All I thought of was bastard."

"Of course," Victoria replied. "But it is not sufficient."

"'When angry count four,'" Tobias quoted through clenched teeth. "'When very angry, swear.' Mark Twain." He sighed. "I cannot swear in the presence of women. My mother would be proud, having drilled that into me, but it is terribly frustrating. Why did he do this? We don't really think it is the economy, do we?"

"No," said Katherine. "Something made him change his mind about my jewelry. Maybe he decided it wasn't good enough for him after all—"

"Poppycock!" snapped Victoria. "I shall call him this instant! He has lost my business forever...and my friends'—!"

"My dear—" cautioned Tobias, his eyes on Katherine's face. "By all means stop buying from him, but beyond that...perhaps we should ask Katherine what she would like."

"Katherine!" Victoria glared at him. "Katherine would not stop me!"

"I think I would," Katherine said hesitantly. "At least for a while. I think I should talk to him, and then—keep going. I believe in my work more than I did before—I want to believe in it—I want to believe in myself. But I'm still finding out what I can do on my own. If I give in to a setback—"

"Setback!" Victoria exclaimed. "Treachery! I shall speak to him—I shall not allow that scoundrel a moment's peace of mind."

Tobias sighed deeply and loudly. Victoria frowned. "Well," she said. "You think it should be Katherine's decision." He nodded solemnly. "Katherine?" Victoria asked. "You are sure of yourself?"

"Mostly," Katherine said. "You see...even if he gave in, to keep you as a customer, he wouldn't be very happy with me. He might put my pieces in a display case at the back of the shop, and forget them, and I wouldn't be much better off. You can't force him to be enthusiastic, however angry you are."

"Wise Katherine," said Tobias softly.

His praise was as warm to Katherine as Victoria's indignation. "I'll see if I can find out the truth," she said. "And then I'll go to some smaller shops. Maybe I shouldn't have tried to start at the top."

"No, no, no!" Victoria punctuated each word with her fist on the table. "Always the top, never anything but the top! I will remain silent, since you and Tobias are so sure that is best for you, but you must not temper your ambitions; you must not let that donkey defeat you! Where is Ross?" she added abruptly. "I called and his secretary said he was out of town."

"He'll be back sometime today," Katherine said.

"Where did he go?"

"I don't know; he said he'd tell me when he got back." Katherine hesitated, then asked them about the weekend. "I can't leave Jennifer and Todd alone, even with Annie across the hall."

"Alone!" Tobias exclaimed. "Of course they must come here; we'll have a delightful time...they can alphabetize my file cards on the Hayward family tree."

"No," said Victoria firmly. "They might never come again. But of course we'll take them, Katherine; they'll brighten our weekend. And a pleasant diversion is just what you need." She put her hand on Katherine's cheek. "I wish I could go with you to Mettler." She grinned like a small girl. "Give him hell, my dear."

Walking down the steep hill, past lush purple and pink gardens cooled by silver-blue ice plants, Katherine repeated it to herself—*Give him hell, my dear*—smiling, to keep from knotting up inside. And so she was smiling as she walked into Mettler's and climbed the spiral staircase to the balcony.

It seemed the secretary did not know what had happened. "How nice to see you, Mrs. Fraser," she said. "He's not busy; I'll let him know you're here."

"Don't bother," Katherine said, and swiftly reached the closed door, swung it open and walked into Herman Mettler's office.

He was reading a brochure on the French Riviera and looked up, frowning. "Mrs. Fraser!" His face went through a series of rapid transformations. "An unexpected pleasure! What can I do for you? I am at your service, though only briefly; some customers are due to arrive at any moment... and due customers are better than don't, are they not?" A brief chuckle came and went. "So."

Katherine stood near his desk. "I found your letter yesterday, when I returned from France."

"France!" He waved the brochure. "I leave this weekend for Monte Carlo; I cannot resist the gambling. As a recent traveler, you must tell me what else I can do there."

I'd love to, Katherine thought with grim humor, but aloud she said, "I'd rather you tell me what your letter means."

"It means what it says! Dear lady, times are bad! Unemployment is up, interest rates are up, bankruptcies are up. Sales are down. The future is uncertain. What more can I say?"

"Monte Carlo is very expensive."

"Well, but, one must get away for one's health!" He coughed. "Mrs. Fraser, I thought my letter was clear. If you have nothing else to ask me—"

"Of course I have; I'm asking for the truth." Katherine moved closer to his desk. In a slim blue linen dress belted in white that she had found at the discount designer shop in Paris, and wearing a broad-brimmed white straw hat, she stood over him. "The last time I was here, you called me Katherine and talked about advertising my work in *Vogue*. Two months later you cancel my order and call me Mrs. Fraser. Something happened in between and it wasn't the economy. I want to know what it was."

"Mrs. Fraser, I am a busy man," he said, and pushed back his chair. "I can't waste my time—"

"You've wasted my time," Katherine retorted, gazing coldly at him from beneath the brim of her hat. "I spent the month of July working on designs you'd contracted for—"

"We never had a contract!"

"We had a verbal agreement between professionals, but you behaved badly, without good faith—"

"I always act in good faith! And if you knew what was good for you, you would not insult Herman Mettler!"

"What is good for me is selling my jewelry. I spent valuable time working on designs you requested and now I'm forced to spend more time visiting your competitors—"

"You won't get far! They know about you, too!"

Bewildered, Katherine stared at him. His gaze dropped. "What do they know?" she asked.

After a moment, he shrugged. "What the hell, Mrs. Fraser, there's a cloud over you."

Katherine's chest tightened. "A cloud," she repeated.

"You don't have to pretend with me. I know about your husband; I know he's on the run; I know you ran away, too—sold your house at a loss and got out of Canada." He sighed. "It's just too much, Mrs. Fraser. You know how demanding our customers are—how jealous of the uniqueness of their possessions. I can't take a chance on designers with questionable backgrounds; I can't risk buying jewelry that might be . . . copied."

"You mean stolen," Katherine said, keeping her voice steady. "But you have no reason to think that of me. If you're worried because someone told you these stories, why didn't you ask me—?"

"I did! I asked you about the authenticity of your designs!"

"And I answered you."

"Not to my satisfaction."

"You were satisfied at the time."

"Mrs. Fraser, listen to me. The truly wealthy live in a very small world. They meet at the same parties, dinners, weddings—no matter what country they're in. And their memories! My God, they remember the dress each woman wore at a dinner party nine years earlier . . . they even remember who her husband was then. So of course they remember jewelry. And would they come back to Mettler's if they paid three thousand or three hundred thousand for a necklace and then saw it on someone else?" He sighed again. "There is no malice in my heart; you are an attractive young woman, but I must protect my business and myself. I will not take a chance when the shadow over you is so dark. And now, Mrs. Fraser, I have customers due . . ." He held open the door. "Good of you to come in; I do wish you well. I hope you and your husband work out your problems so you can go back to Canada."

Katherine gazed at him. "You're a coward, Herman."

"True," he agreed. "But even if I took risks, Mrs. Fraser, it would be for someone more important than you. Now will you please go?"

Numbly, Katherine walked through the outer office and down the stairs to the main floor. The store sparkled with gems and gold and silver, but she saw it dimly, as if a shadow obscured her view.

There is no escape from Craig.

The boat gleamed a pale white in the dense fog, the roar of its engine bouncing back at them as Ross steered through the harbor. Seven o'clock in the morning and they were the only ones out, avoiding the traffic jam of weekend sailors. They moved past the ghostly shapes of other boats, out of the harbor, and then there was only fog and a small clear space around them. Ross slowed the engine. "It's all yours," he said to Katherine. "Keep a straight course while I get the sails up."

"I can't see a straight course," she said, trying to sound casual. "I can barely see the land behind us."

He put his arm around her. "You have the compass. But the fog isn't so bad. Look." He pointed and, straining her eyes, she saw a faint shape in the distance. "Treasure Island," he said. "I've been out on days when you couldn't see it until you were practically part of it. Watch the compass and keep us west northwest, heading for the island. It's a big target. Hard to miss."

"I'd rather miss it," Katherine said.

He chuckled. "I think we will; I'll take over before we're even close. You'll do fine; I trust you." He kissed her lightly and moved away from the wheel. Katherine took his place, watching him jump easily from the cockpit to the deck before she turned to check the compass heading and the faint shape of the island. Relax, she told herself. Everything will be fine. She shivered and zipped up her jacket against the damp fog. But it wasn't only the fog. She was nervous—about sailing, about telling Ross what Mettler had said, and about Ross's odd reluctance to talk about his trip.

"You have enough on your mind," he'd said when he called the night before, soon after he got home. Then he suggested ways to spend the weekend: driving to Big Sur, staying at his house, or on his boat. "We can sail up the coast on Saturday, and come back on Sunday. The weather's fine and even though you might think living on a boat is a bit primitive, I think you'll enjoy it."

As nervous as she was, Katherine knew what sailing meant to him. "I think I'll enjoy it, too," she replied.

And as she steered the boat, looking alternately at the misty outline of Treasure Island and then at Ross, bracing his feet to pull on the mainsail halyard and then turning the winch to raise the huge sail to its full height, she found her nervousness fading. The wheel was solid beneath her hands; the compass told her she was on course. She surveyed the gangway leading down to the cabin, the benches with blue cushions on three sides of the cockpit, the side decks with thin steel railings shining dully in the fog, the bright aluminum mast where Ross stood, tying the halyard—and began to relax. Ross had shown it all to her before they cast off, naming and explaining everything, moving lithely and confidently around ropes and railings and jutting obstacles that seemed to leap out just in time to trip Katherine. She had been tense and anxious, and he had said gently, "We sold Craig's boat after the accident. This one is quite different."

"If you've never sailed—" Katherine began.

"—all sailboats seem alike," he finished. "But try to remember that this is mine. It was new when I bought it and its only history is the one I make for it. The one you and I make," he amended.

You and I. As Ross stood at the mast, looking up at the tall sail that had billowed into a white curve, Katherine watched his face—absorbed, serene, content. The wind blew his dark blond hair, his lean body was as taut and graceful as the sail. It was as if he had become a part of his boat, and she wished she could share that with him.

"—the motor!" he shouted.

"What?"

"Turn off the motor!" He pointed to the key and she reached down and turned it. Instantly, the engine stopped, and silence, like a clear glass bell, enclosed them. Ross grinned. "I always wait for this," he said in a conversational voice. "So quiet you can feel it."

Katherine felt it. The only sounds were the whisper of wind in the mainsail and the soft slapping of waves. "I'm going to put up the jib," Ross said. "I could use some help. Lock the wheel when I tell you; then come up here and pull on this rope."

He went forward and fastened the jib to the slanting cable at the bow. "Ready," he said. Katherine locked the wheel, climbed to the deck and pulled hand over hand on the rope. When she realized she was pulling the jib up the cable, where it caught the wind and snapped into its own curve, she felt a surge of exultation. The rope scraped against her palms, she pulled harder against the force of the wind in the sail, and then Ross took over, winching the sail tighter and fastening down the rope. With both sails in place the boat was picking up speed. "Four knots," Ross said. "Do you want to keep the wheel?"

"Yes."

He put his arm around her and they smiled at each other. "Head northwest until we're past Treasure Island; then we'll go around Alcatraz, straight to the Golden Gate Bridge." He sat on the bench behind her. "I'll watch your technique."

Katherine laughed. They floated in the fog, completely alone. Nothing on land seemed real. Herman Mettler receded to a character in a play; Craig to a figure in a painting. Even Ross's evasiveness about his trip seemed unimportant in the vast silence of that shrouded world. All that mattered was her happiness at being with him, cut off from land.

Ross took the wheel when they were beneath the bridge, keeping to the center of the channel until they had passed the headlands. And then they were in the ocean, turning to follow the coast. Within minutes the fog began to come apart, as if torn into large pieces. They sailed through the ragged openings, long tendrils of mist swirling about the boat, and then, suddenly, the sun burst through, flooding them with gold. Katherine gasped with the beauty of it and Ross reached out to her. She stood within his arms, facing forward as he held the wheel, his lips in her hair. "Thank you," he said. "For sharing this with me."

The waves were tipped with gold beneath a cloudless sky; the boat skimmed through the water, alone in the sun-filled, sea-scented air. Katherine turned within the circle of his arms and kissed him. "Thank you for letting me be a part of it."

His lips smiled beneath hers. "You're a part of everything I do. Haven't I told you that? But there is a problem, at the moment, of seeing where I'm going..."

"Oh, that." Laughing softly, she ducked under his arms. "What can I do? Tie a rope or untie one or hook something...? How can I learn if you don't give me assignments?"

He took her hand. "There is a moment of perfection in sailing, when the wind and water are in harmony with the boat. A wise sailor never interferes with that. We'll have a lesson some other time. When you're ready for lunch, you'll find sandwiches and beer in the refrigerator; until then, there's nothing to do but relax. And talk. Do you want to tell me what happened with Mettler?"

"Later. Do you mind?"

"Of course not." He pulled off his jacket. "Would you toss this in the cabin?" He watched her take off her own and lean into the gangway to drop them on one of the bunks. "Katherine." She turned to him. "Do you see a time when everything is in harmony for us?"

"Now," she said swiftly. "If we can just be together, one day at a time..." She searched for other words, but at last said only, "It's perfect. Now." And that was the closest they came that weekend to talking about the forces that drove their lives on land. Katherine refused to let Mettler interfere with their serenity, and whenever Ross thought of Elissa he put her aside. She'd been there for the two years Craig knew her and the year since he had disappeared; there was plenty of time for Katherine to hear about her.

They ate lunch in the cockpit, their voices mingling with the wind and waves and the calls of curious, swooping gulls. All afternoon they followed the cliffs that came to the water's edge, taking turns at the wheel.

Occasionally they passed a small beach, or rocks with sea lions sunning themselves. As the sun dropped lower, a fiery streak of orange blazed across the water and the breeze quickened. Katherine threw back her head, her skin red-gold in the brightness, the cool air caressing her throat. She heard Ross pull in his breath and at the same moment she felt unsteady with the heavy pull of wanting him. She put out a hand to support herself. "Are you all right?" he asked.

"I'm fine." She smiled at him. "I was just thinking how much I'd like to make love to you."

A slow smile lit his face. He held out his arm and Katherine moved inside it. "We'll dock at Drake's Bay," he murmured, holding her against him. "There's a cove I remember from years ago..."

It was dusk by the time they dropped anchor and stowed the sails. They worked together, Ross giving instructions, Katherine memorizing each step, and as they moved about the boat the shared tasks were another kind of love-making.

In the cabin, Katherine lit kerosene lamps and pulled shut the blue-and-red curtains on the small windows above the bunks, while Ross prepared dinner by transferring food from the refrigerator to the oven. Together they set the table between the bunks with a checked cloth and pottery dishes, and Ross poured wine and served a platter of tiny crabmeat cakes and stuffed mushrooms. He touched Katherine's glass with his. "To primitive living."

She laughed. "If the Pilgrims had lived this primitively, you couldn't have dragged them off the *Mayflower*."

"And none of us would be here," Ross said, taking their dinner from the oven. He handed her a plate. "Chicken breast with Dijon sauce, wild rice, and glazed baby carrots. I warn you; I did it all myself, without Carrie's help or advice. If it's inedible, we go over the side and catch whatever we can find."

Katherine shook her head. "It's wonderful. You'll spoil me."

"I hope so."

The small cabin was snugly enclosed within its curtained windows, softly lit by flickering lamps reflected on mahogany paneling. As they finished their coffee, Ross said, "Do you want music? Our primitive home has a radio..."

"No," Katherine said. "I want the silence."

He held her face between his hands and kissed her eyes, the tip of her nose, the corners of her mouth, the small hollow of her throat, holding his lips against the pulse that beat there. Katherine's arms tightened around him, then she pulled away, laughing into his eyes. "Close quarters. There's the table, but..."

"You've discovered the primitive part," he said. "You have to get rid of the dinner dishes before you can make love."

They piled the dishes in the sink, lowered the table and extended the double bunk over it. "Better," Katherine said and they undressed each other and lay on the bed, their mouths meeting, tongues exploring as their hands explored their bodies, sliding slowly along warm hollows, the hardness of muscle, the softness of hair.

"Dearest Katherine, I love you," Ross said, his mouth on her breast. He murmured "I love you" on each nipple, taking them lightly into his mouth. His hands slid beneath her hips and Katherine turned so that he barely had to move to lie on her and enter her; effortlessly, they flowed together and the sharing of the day became the sharing of their bodies, until Ross heard Katherine cry out beneath his mouth and in another moment, clasped in her smooth, throbbing warmth, he let himself go, his cry meeting hers.

They lay still, their lips touching, until Katherine said lazily, "Is the boat moving?"

"Rocking."

"Not floating away?"

"No. Don't worry; we won't go anywhere."

"I wish we would. So far nothing could follow us."

"Someday."

His voice was so low Katherine was not sure she heard it. "What?"

He raised himself on one elbow and looked at her in the soft light. "You're going to make a wonderful sailor."

After a moment, she said, "And then?"

"Then, with a good set of sails, there won't be any place we can't go."

She smiled faintly. "A lovely dream."

"Katherine. Tell me you love me."

She touched his lips with her finger. "I'm afraid to. I'm almost afraid to think it. I was so settled; I never thought of myself as falling in love again. It's as if, when I think about you, I become someone else—I move farther away from the person I was. And I get frightened: who am I now, and what do I want and how can I dream of you and long for you and still feel bound somehow to Craig...? And," she added, trying to speak lightly. "I haven't loved—I mean, fallen in love—for ten years. I've forgotten what it's like to be pulled out of myself, toward another person. I like it—I think—but it's confusing. It's all so new—and so *enormous*—"

Ross leaned over her. "Thank you." He kissed her slowly, lingeringly. "As long as that's true, the words can wait."

Katherine ran her finger down his throat, to his chest. "I love the way you feel." Her fingertips brushed the skin of his hard, flat stomach and the softness of his groin. "Your body is so wonderful—you move on the boat like a lion, smooth and graceful, never looking at your feet..."

"That's to show off. Sometimes I take a flying leap that way. And if we're going to talk about wonderful bodies—"

"We're not going to talk," Katherine said. Sliding out from under him, she kissed his lips, then followed with her mouth the path her fingers had taken, down his throat to the blond curls of his chest, his narrow waist, the smooth skin of his stomach and groin. She held her lips to that soft hollow; her hands slid up his thighs, and she felt his fingers encircle her breasts as she ran the tip of her tongue along warm flesh and clustered hairs and then took him into her, deep into her throat, so that he filled her once again. A low moan broke from him and she exulted in arousing him, giving him pleasure, even as she lost herself in the sensuality of enclosing him in her mouth, feeling with her tongue the solid smoothness and ridges, the hot, throbbing life of his penis. Her hands held his buttocks, pulling him against her, pulling him to the back of her throat where small murmuring sounds rippled, like the pleasure spreading through her. Then, abruptly, Ross pulled away. Sliding down on the bed, he entered her, fiercely, insistently—one body, not two, with blinding streaks of passion joining them like jagged lightning, raising them higher and higher until they stopped, balanced on the thin edge of pure feeling, and then fell, through a dark echoing tunnel, to lie motionless, gazing at each other with small, wondering smiles.

"I never realized how long I've gone without love," Ross said at last. "More than a year... Married, but alone."

"Both of us," Katherine said. "In different ways... Ross," she said drowsily. She touched her lips to his. "I love you."

He cradled her in his arm, their faces together, and they slept.

They woke twined about each other in a tangle of sheets. "Playing hard to get," grumbled Ross. "One minute you say you love me; the next you set up an obstacle course."

"Love conquers obstacles," Katherine said, her eyes bright, and together they pushed the sheets off the bed. She lay back, her slender body open and waiting for him to lie on her and begin the day with love. "But is there an obstacle to breakfast?" she asked a little later. "And sailing again?"

"I knew you'd make a good sailor," Ross said resignedly. "All they're interested in is sailing and food."

"When tempted," Katherine pointed out. "I make time for other things."

But they waited for breakfast until they had motored away from the fog that was a regular feature of Drake's Bay and had put up the sails. Then, heading south, at ease in the sunny cockpit, they divided oranges and rolls and coffee, and watched shifting shadows on the cliffs along the coast and wheeling sea gulls, gray and white against the deepening blue sky. All day they sailed in a haze of lazy talk and timeless, contented silence.

It shattered when they were in the channel that led to the Golden Gate Bridge. Leaving the emptiness of the ocean, they were suddenly surrounded by boats: dozens of white sails bobbing and circling about them. Taking the clearest path, Ross steered under the northern end of the bridge. Katherine idly watched them draw near a group of rocks thrusting like spires near a spit of land with a lighthouse, and a tiny beach beyond. Unaccountably, she began to feel anxious. A memory tugged; she turned questioningly to Ross and found him watching her. "Lime Point," he said quietly.

The weekend was over; they were home.

Carrie found Melanie on the deck, her eyes protected from the sun by a mask. "Mommy," she said.

"Yes, sweetie."

"I need two more cards for the country club."

Melanie raised the mask an inch and squinted at her daughter. "Have you and Jon lost yours?"

"No—"

"Well, then?"

"I need them for Jennifer and Todd."

Melanie sat up and replaced the mask with dark sunglasses. "Who?"

"You know who I mean! Jennifer and Todd Fraser!"

"Why should you get cards for Jennifer and Todd Fraser?"

"Because they don't belong to a club and there's all of August before school starts and we want to be with them. We're friends."

Melanie contemplated her daughter. "They're not our kind, Carrie. They'd be uncomfortable at the club."

"Oh, Mother!"

"Don't 'Oh, Mother' me. These things are complicated and children don't understand them. Someday you will."

"I don't see why," said Carrie.

"That's what I mean. You're not ready to understand."

"So can I have two more cards?"

"Carrie, what did I just say?"

"I don't know, because I didn't understand it."

"Oh, my God." Melanie walked to a table where tall glasses and a pitcher stood on a tray.

"Can I have some, too?" Carrie asked.

"It's gin and tonic; you aren't ready for that, either. Carrie, the club doesn't like strangers coming in."

"Lots of people bring friends from out of town."

"Your friends aren't from out of town."

"They live in San Francisco; the club is in Mill Valley."

Melanie drained half a glass and refilled it. "Why are you asking me? Let your father get them in on his membership."

"He resigned from the club when you made him resign from our house."

"That's not funny," Melanie snapped. "I suppose this was his idea, for you to bring those children."

"It's my idea! Mine and Jon's! We can't help it if you don't like Katherine—"

"*Katherine?*"

Carrie stamped her foot. "She said to call her that. We're friends! And I don't see why you care if Daddy likes her; you like Guy, don't you? He's always in your bed so you must like him—"

"Carrie!"

"Well, isn't he? When your door is closed? But it's OK; everybody's parents do it; we don't care except why get mad at us just because you're mad at Daddy or whoever? Can't you just leave us alone? You like us to leave you alone and we don't get in your way; I mean, we mostly do what you tell us and we don't bug you when you've got problems—all the kids have mixed-up parents—so you could let us do what we want with our friends—it doesn't have anything to do with you anyway—and *I want two more cards for the club!*"

Her drink halfway to her mouth, Melanie stared at her daughter. When did she get so fiery? she wondered. And how does she know so much? She used to be soft and cuddly, telling me I was her pretty mommy, with her little arms around my neck. What happened to her?

"*Well?*" Carrie demanded.

"Does their mother know how long a drive it is?"

"They don't have a car. The club has a van that picks people up at Union Square. You know that. Mother, *please.*"

"Well, that's the first time I've heard that word today." Melanie shrugged. "I'll call the manager; I don't suppose they'll mind two more kids. Just make sure your friends behave themselves. They probably aren't used to private country clubs."

Carrie bit back a reply. "Thank you," she said. "It's very nice of you. I'll bring you the phone."

"How come you aren't with your father this weekend?" Melanie asked when she returned.

"He went sailing with Katherine. We're going to his house next weekend. Here; do it now. I want to call Jennifer and tell her we can go swimming tomorrow."

"All *right*," Melanie said. But when she lay back on the chaise, she wondered, as she did so often these days, why everything seemed so difficult when she'd been sure that from now on she would live happily ever after.

The sketchbook was crammed with drawings from the Riviera; the portfolio contained a dozen designs ready to be worked in gold and silver; a felt-lined box held the twelve pieces of jewelry Mettler had returned. Beside them was a pad of paper with a list of jewelry-store owners.

Katherine had called two of them. Both said they had heard of her interesting work; both said they were not taking on any new people just then. "The economy," they said. "You understand how it is..."

Katherine understood. She sat on the stool at her worktable, chin in hand, absently rearranging the jewelry she had made for Mettler. It gleamed dully in the gray light filtering through morning fog: very expensive, highly original, vibrant in its perfect balance of shape, texture and color. But she couldn't sell it.

So, in spite of Victoria's declaration that only the top would do, she had to move down from the top, and go to smaller, less prestigious shops. But not with these pieces. She needed what Mettler would call nice, ordinary ones.

For two weeks she worked from breakfast to midnight. She saw Ross for a few late dinners, Tobias and Victoria only once. Leslie was out of town for the opening of a new branch of Heath's, and, miraculously, Jennifer and Todd were occupied. The friendship with Ross's children had endured past the trip to France and somehow Carrie and Jon had gotten country club privileges for them. Each morning at eight o'clock, a club van picked them up in Union Square; each afternoon it returned them there. They took a bus home, arriving happily worn out and bubbling with their adventures. That left Katherine free, and, using sketches from the Riviera, she spent two weeks in concentrated energy, making up another collection. At the end of that time she had ten pieces, ready to be sold.

Traveling from one of San Francisco's shops to another, her samples tucked in a slim shoulder bag, Katherine avoided the glittering displays at Mettler's and Laykin Et Cie, Saks Fifth Avenue and Xavier's, and the half-dozen other exclusive shops she had once dreamed of. She kept her eyes firmly on small stores that specialized in mass-produced jewelry but also offered their customers a small selection of original pieces. By the time another week was up, she had visited nine of them. Three had bought her pieces, and ordered more.

Not quite a triumph, she thought, getting off the bus at her corner at the end of the week. In a way, she'd gone backward: she was no farther than she'd been eight months earlier, when Mettler first bought from her. And this time she'd sold to stores less prestigious than his.

But a little over a year ago, in Vancouver, she had given up. Katherine remembered the feeling of defeat that had swept over her when the last envelope came in the mail, containing her sketches and a letter of rejection. She'd been convinced she was no good; she'd had fun with a hobby but hadn't been a professional.

All that was behind her. Now she had a profession, and she'd begun to earn her living at it. Not at the top, but still—three good stores; three written contracts. She might not have escaped Craig, but she'd gone around him. I can make my way, she told herself, walking home with a light step. Three jewelers believe in me; and Ross, and Tobias, and Victoria. And so do I.

CHAPTER 17

ROSS called while they were at breakfast. "Happy birthday," he said. "I'm making sure we still have a dinner date for tonight."

"Of course," she said. "How could I forget?"

"I can't imagine, but the way you've been working I thought it possible. I planned, if this meets with your approval, to include Jennifer and Todd, so they can share their mother's birthday dinner. Then we'll drop them off at home and go to my house for dessert."

"Dessert," Katherine said and began to laugh.

"Often the best part of the meal, but it must be savored very slowly. You sound happy. Did you sell to another store yesterday? I'm sorry I didn't call; my meeting went on until all hours."

"It was a good day. I'll tell you about it tonight."

"Six thirty?"

"We'll be ready."

"We?" said Jennifer, and Katherine told them about dinner.

"But what about today?" Todd asked. "Aren't just the three of us going to celebrate?"

"Of course we are," Katherine said, dropping her plans to work. "What would you like to do?"

They spent the day riding rented bicycles through Golden Gate Park and picnicking on the island in Stow Lake. "It's nice when it's the three of us," Jennifer said as they walked home. "Most of the time you're working or out with Ross, and we're with Carrie and Jon—it hasn't been just our family for a long time."

Our family, Katherine thought. Just the three of us. How naturally

353

Jennifer had said it. "You're right," she replied quietly. "It's very nice; it's been a lovely birthday."

Her thoughts were moving ahead to the rest of her birthday—dinner with Ross, an evening with Ross—as she unlocked the door. "What's that smell?" Jennifer asked, sniffing.

"Perfume?" Katherine guessed. "No, flowers." The scent pervaded the apartment.

Annie opened the door across the hall. "They came while you were gone. I put them in the—"

"Hey!" Todd shouted and staggered in from the kitchen, almost hidden behind a vase of white roses. A small envelope stuck out from between his fingers.

"Golly," Jennifer breathed. She began counting. "Thirty-six. That's how old you are. Are they from Ross? Or . . ." She saw Katherine's face. "*Oh.*"

Katherine was reading the familiar handwriting. "Happy birthday, sweetheart. With love." And he had signed it as he always did, with his initial.

"It's Daddy, isn't it?" Jennifer asked in a small voice.

Katherine nodded.

"What does he say?" Todd asked. "Like—to us?"

"Nothing, silly," Jennifer said when Katherine was silent. "It's not our birthday, after all."

"Well, but still—"

The doorbell rang and Todd ran to peer through the window. "It's Ross," he said, and opened the door.

Ross looked from Katherine's stunned face to the mass of white roses and the card in her hand. Anger welled up in him as he understood what had happened, but he kept his voice calm as he said to Jennifer and Todd, "There's a surprise for you in my car. Do you want to get it now?"

"Sure," Jennifer said. "And you want us to stay there."

"I'd appreciate it. While your mother and I talk. Then we'll go to dinner. Is that all right?"

"Sure," Jennifer said again. "I just wish I understood all this."

"So do I," said Ross. "Off you go now."

Todd, strangely quiet, followed Jennifer. Ross took the roses into the kitchen, out of sight; then he came back and sat beside Katherine and took her in his arms. She buried her face against his shoulder and burst into tears. "Damn him," she sobbed, her voice muffled. "Damn him for his hide-and-seek games and . . . *hanging on.* Damn him for not being honest with me. Damn him for *being.*"

Ross held her until her sobs quieted. At least she's angry, he thought.

It's about time. He considered telling her about Elissa, as he did every time they were together. But again it seemed the wrong time to force her to face another shock about her husband.

"Katherine," he said firmly. "I have brought you a birthday present; I made arrangements for dinner. If you're too distracted, we can skip dessert at my house, but you should be able to handle the rest of the evening. And I want to hear about your triumphs with jewelers this week."

Katherine raised her face to his. "How did you know I had triumphs?"

"Because you deserve them. Are you going to change for dinner? I'd like to be festive."

"Yes . . . I'm sorry; we just got home before you—"

"I was early. Go ahead and change; I'll wait." He picked up a book. "Are you reading this? I've been meaning to buy it. I'll read; you take your time. We have a seven thirty reservation at Fisherman's Wharf."

"Oh, Jennifer and Todd will be thrilled." At the door to the bathroom, she turned back. "What did you get me for my birthday?"

He laughed. Recovering fast, he thought. "Do you want it now or later?"

"Now, please."

He handed her a paper bag he had left inside the front door. Katherine pulled out a silver-wrapped box: a shoebox, she saw, when the elegant paper was removed. Giving him a puzzled glance, she lifted the lid and took out one shoe, then its mate: handsewn leather with white rubber soles, and leather thongs laced through brass eyelets all around and tied in a bow at the instep. A card was propped in one of them: "Steady feet and a steadfast heart—I love you." "Deck shoes!" Katherine cried, and burst into delighted laughter. "For the boat!"

"Safer than those tennis shoes you wore," he said. "You aren't disappointed? I thought of perfume and silk and other luxuries, but you'll be spending so much time with me on the boat and if you want to move around without worrying about slipping—"

"Oh, Ross, I love you," Katherine said and, holding a shoe in each hand, put her arms around him. "No one has ever given me deck shoes for my birthday; no one has ever given me shoes. Thank you, thank you—" She kissed him and he thought how natural those words sounded in this small apartment that she had made for herself and her children. She tilted her head. "I'll wear them to dinner with my yellow silk from Paris, shall I? And set a new style?"

"Why not? It might be just the thing for Fisherman's Wharf."

"Don't tempt me," she said, laughing again as she disappeared into the bathroom. And by the time she was toweling dry after a quick shower, thinking back over the past week, it seemed to Katherine that she had everything: work, Ross, her children, the love of Tobias and Victoria, the friendship of Leslie. She opened the door a crack to let out the steam and was struck with the pervasive scent of white roses.

No, she thought. Not everything. I have it all—except my freedom.

"He's out on bail," said Leslie, helping herself to more pasta as she answered Katherine's question about Gil Lister. "Working in a warehouse in Oakland."

"A warehouse?" Katherine asked.

"I think he tells the robots which merchandise to pull down from which shelves. Or maybe the robots tell him. One of these days he'll go on trial and we'll all be called as witnesses, but until then I don't pay much attention to him."

"Will he go to jail?" Todd asked.

"I hope so," Leslie said cheerfully. "He's the one who fired your mother, you know. We wish only discomfort for him."

Katherine handed the platter to Bruce. "And what about you?"

"Head of Data Processing," he said promptly. "As of today, September first, a memorable date. My sis has more clout than ever, so my well-deserved promotion came through—of course, as I predicted, I am doing an admirable job, in fact, offers are pouring in for my unique services from far and wide."

"You're not going away, are you?" asked Todd.

"Ah, afraid of losing your private instructor."

"No," Todd said. "Well, partly. But mostly, I'd miss you."

Bruce's eyebrows danced up and down. "Well, now, that's mutual. No, I'm not going, at least not yet—my sis needs my protection until she makes up her mind to get married."

"Bruce," Leslie sighed.

"And anyway the truth is I don't want to go anywhere—I don't want to leave my family."

"Your family?" asked Jennifer. "Who do you have besides Leslie?"

"No one. Leslie is all I need. A family is one person who loves you and cares who you are and makes your private world a rich and boundless garden. Of course the more the merrier, but if you've only got one be thankful. Does anyone mind if I finish the spaghetti?"

"I do," said Todd, and they divided it. "Our family's weirder than yours," he said, slurping in dangling strands. "There's Mom and Jennifer and me, and there's Dad, who's gone, unless you count last New Year's and last week when he sent about a hundred roses for Mom's birthday that smelled up the whole house, and then there's Victoria and Tobias who are kind of funny, but fun, and Carrie and Jon who are great, and Derek who nobody likes, and then there's Ross who Mom is in love with and is probably going to divorce Dad and marry."

Seeing that Katherine was speechless, Leslie said casually, "When?"

"What?" asked Todd.

"When is your mother going to divorce your father and marry Ross?"

"How do we know?" he said indignantly. "Nobody tells us these things!"

"Then how do you know she's going to do it at all?"

There was a pause. "Carrie and Jon say that's what all the parents in their school do."

"Most of them," Jennifer put in.

"Well, most of them. But anyway."

"What I think," Leslie said thoughtfully, "is that your mother isn't about to do that."

"Why?" asked Jennifer.

All of them, even Katherine, looked at Leslie, waiting for her answer. Hell, she thought. Look who's a guru; I can't even answer my own questions about me. "Because," she said wisely, "when you're in the middle of a tornado, you sit quietly and wait for things to settle down so you don't get clobbered."

"Tornado," mused Bruce. "Tornado, tornado—why, sis, what a clever thing to say."

"There isn't a tornado," Todd declared, but doubtfully, since Bruce had approved it.

"A tornado," Leslie stated, "is turbulence sending things flying in all directions. Your dad is in Canada or Alaska or somewhere; you're in San Francisco, in the Sunset; your great-grandmother and Tobias live on Pacific Heights and you never even knew you *had* a great-grandmother until a year ago—"

"But—" Todd began.

"Don't interrupt; I'm just getting started. You go to a country club in Mill Valley, across the bay; you've just come back from France, across the ocean; your mother worked at Heath's and then had a contract with a scoundrel named Mettler and now has contracts with three other stores; Carrie and Jon live with their mother in Tiburon and spend most weekends with their father in the Berkeley hills; Ross and your mother seem to have become very good friends while they were in France—maybe they even fell in love—but she's still married to your dad . . . good Lord, are things going in all directions or aren't they? A wise person makes no predictions. Everything could change tomorrow or next week or not until next year. The best thing to do is sit tight, don't worry, and remember to duck when unidentified flying objects come your way."

Katherine had been smiling, then, as Leslie went on, she grew thought-ful. Everything could change, she repeated silently. Remember to duck. *Someone is going to get hurt, no matter what happens.*

Jennifer and Todd were giggling. "Sis," said Bruce, "you are a genius. I am proud to be your family."

"I'm proud to have you." She gave him a long, prodding look.

"Oh, right," he said, remembering. He turned to Jennifer and Todd. "You want to talk about mothers and fathers and turbulence? I can tell you a thing or three about all that—and I can do it while beating you at underhand-overhand Frisbie."

"You cannot," said Todd.

"I can indeed and I say it so confidently that I declare the loser will buy ice cream cones—do we go to the park or don't we?"

In a minute they were gone. "Planned in advance?" Katherine asked Leslie.

"Of course. Isn't he impressive? I told him I wanted a private talk with you and he managed it like a pro. He is a pro. The best thing that ever happened to Heath's Data Processing department."

"You're the best thing around here, today. Thank you, Leslie. Every time I think I'm getting better at handling whatever comes up, something new comes up."

"It certainly does. Are you going to tell me about it?"

"I wrote to you and last week I told you on the telephone—"

"Yes, but not how you felt. Not the inside Katherine. If I hadn't been out of town I'd know everything by now. Are you in love with him? Well, I see you are. Was Todd right about divorce and so forth?"

"No."

"You're not going to divorce Craig?"

"No. And you haven't told me anything about you and Claude."

"My loose-lipped brother did it for me."

"It's true, then? You are going to marry him?"

"It sounds like college, doesn't it? Comparing our love lives. All we need is a dormitory and a box of candy. Am I going to marry Claude? Sometimes. My mind changes itself, depending on the day of the week. I assume Todd exaggerated the number of birthday roses that arrived from Canada."

"You're changing the subject."

"Not anymore than you did. Anyway, we're both talking about hus-bands, aren't we? One potential; one absential."

Katherine laughed. "You sound like Tobias."

"I couldn't; I don't read poetry. Katherine, are you in love with Craig?"

"With Craig?"

"Your husband. Remember?"

"I don't think so. I mean, of course I remember, but I don't think I'm in love with him anymore. I'm not the same person I was; I don't suppose he is, either. Whoever he is. Craig Fraser. Craig Hayward. I've learned more about him in the past year than in all the years we were married."

"*Were* married?"

"Living together; we're still married."

"And he's been gone almost fifteen months. Katherine, what the hell are you waiting for? You just celebrated—or deplored—your thirty-sixth birthday. When you get to those numbers you stop dallying and make quick decisions. Haven't you noticed how the years slip through your fingers? You barely grab one and it's gone."

"What about you? When are you getting married?"

"I told you, my mind changes each—"

"And what about a baby? You were thinking of having one."

"I haven't decided yet."

They broke into laughter. "OK," Leslie conceded. "I may not be the one to give advice on quick decisions. But what *are* you waiting for?"

Katherine's laughter dropped away. "Less turbulence," she said.

"Less—? Oh. My tale of a tornado. That was only to divert your kids; it wasn't serious."

"It was to me; I do feel as if we've been tossed around by a storm. We're still being tossed—when those roses came, that's how I felt. And if you recall, you said we should sit tight and remember to duck. It was good advice. A tornado is no place to make a decision."

"So you're not going to do anything."

"I'm going to work, spend time with Jennifer and Todd, wait for Craig..."

"Without Ross?"

Katherine shook her head. "I can't stop seeing him. I love him... and I haven't felt this way in so long—as if I have the most wonderful secret that's always there, with me, whatever I'm doing... It makes everything more complicated, to love him, but it makes everything so wonderful... I can't push him away."

"That sounds like a decision, lady."

"Half of one. He thinks I should divorce Craig."

"Sensible man. Katherine, what are you worried about? Someone getting hurt? Someone always gets hurt. Even when you least expect it. Let me tell you about Marc; he wormed Claude's name out of me..."

Curled up in a corner of the couch, Leslie told Katherine the story. "Now you tell me," she said at the end of it. "Did I owe Marc anything after all those years when he spent money on me, squired me all over town and a good part of Europe, and was a most pleasant companion in bed?"

"Hardly a marriage," Katherine said dryly. "He didn't support you; you didn't have two children and a home you'd made; you never made a commitment to spend the rest of your life together."

"True. So you owe Craig undying loyalty and I owe Marc nothing?"

"I don't know what anyone 'owes' anyone," Katherine said, feeling frustrated. "It's what we *feel* that's important."

"And you don't feel that you want to be free?"

Katherine looked at her in silence. Finally, she asked, "Why can't you make up your mind about Claude?"

"Because I'm not sure I trust my feelings, and that means I'm not sure what's best for both of—oh, well." She grinned at Katherine. "I see what you mean. All right, I shouldn't push you. But, Katherine—"

"Yes?"

"Think of yourself first. I know you have to pay attention to your kids and all those other people around you, but you owe it to yourself to take care of yourself. You're the only one you can really trust to do that."

After a moment, Katherine said, "In a good marriage, or a good friendship, people take care of each other."

"There aren't many good marriages or friendships. When women think of themselves last, which they usually do, men and kids think of them last, too."

With a glint in her eye, Katherine said, "Were you thinking of yourself first when you didn't fire Bruce?"

"Well, but sometimes... Oh, hell," Leslie admitted ruefully. "Love messes it up. You start wanting to protect someone, or help, or just *do for*..."

"And doesn't Claude want to help you, and do things for you?"

"He does. I'm not used to it yet. Maybe I don't trust it. After all, you thought Craig wanted to protect and do for you... Damn, I'm sorry, Katherine."

"It's all right. It's true. But he did take care of me for a long time, and I still don't know what forced him to stop doing it. And even if I was wrong about him, does that mean I shouldn't trust anyone else?"

"No, of course not."

"Then why not try trusting Claude?"

"When you put it like that—damned if I know. But that's enough of Claude; I want to talk about you."

"No, it's enough about me, too. Tell me about Heath's."

"All right; if you tell me about France. Your letters were wonderful, but I want more. All the details. What is it?" she asked when Katherine began to laugh.

"You sound like Victoria."

"Well, whatever that means, tell me what you think I should hear. Bruce promised to make the game and the ice cream last at least a couple of hours. God, lady, I missed you—I haven't had a good talk since you went away."

Ross had talked about BayBridge so often that Katherine thought she had a clear picture of it in her mind. But, on Saturday morning when she stood with him and saw its length and breadth, with twenty-five buildings gutted but still standing, and construction equipment scattered about like huge yellow insects beside excavations and newly poured foundations, she was stunned. "I had no idea. I remember saying it sounded as if you wanted to build small towns... but I never thought I'd see one coming to life, all at once."

"It's not ideal," Ross said. "I wanted a larger park, and wider walkways between the townhouses, but that would have meant fewer units to sell, and the developers balked. Next time, if I can get more control, we'll have more air and light, lower buildings, more parks and fountains—" He caught himself. "Why don't you gag me, or better still, kiss me, when I start lecturing?"

"Because I like listening."

"Dad!" Jon shouted. "What's this?"

Ross looked and saw nothing. "Where are you?"

"Here!" Four grinning faces peered from behind what looked like a miniature oil rig on a yellow flatbed truck. Drills like huge corkscrews, and long flexible pipes, were strapped to its sides.

"Come down from there," Ross ordered. "That's not a playground."

They clambered down. "But what is it?"

"A drilling rig. The foundation engineers use it to drill holes for pumping concrete around building supports."

"This building?" Todd asked. Contemplating the Macklin Building, Ross nodded. "What for? Doesn't it have concrete under it already?"

"I think it needs more," Ross said. "I can't vouch for its safety in case of a tremor."

"Tremor," Carrie said. "Earthquake?"

"When it's big enough it's called an earthquake."

Todd ran his hand over one of the drills. "It digs down like a corkscrew?"

"Exactly. Then one of these pipes is fed through the hole—"

"Like a snake," said Jon.

"Right. And the concrete is pumped through the pipe, under tremendous pressure. It's like an injection, forcing concrete around the footings under the columns that hold up the building, making them bigger and stronger."

Jennifer and Carrie stood nearby. "Even in an earthquake?" Carrie asked.

"In most earthquakes."

"Then why wasn't it done that way the first time?"

Ross paused. "We don't know. But it has to be done now, before it's an office building again, or we'll always have it hanging over our heads, like a sword about to fall."

In a dramatic voice, Todd intoned, "The surgeons are ready to vaccinate the Macklin Building. Will it work? Or will it still come tumbling down, cutting off our heads like a sword?"

"Does it cost a lot to do?" Carrie asked.

"Yes," Ross replied.

"How much?"

"About a quarter of a million dollars."

Todd whistled.

Katherine was watching Ross. "Who pays for it?" she asked.

"I do," he answered. "It's my building."

"But you weren't the one—" She stopped as he shook his head in warning. "Wouldn't it cost less to tear it down?" she asked instead.

"No. It's almost always cheaper to repair a building. Let me show you what we're doing."

He led them through a rough opening in the building. "New front door," he said, then described the arcade that would cut through the building from Mission Street to the shopping mall on the other side: "An atrium going through all ten floors to the roof, with a glass dome on top. The workmen had opened it up through the second floor when we stopped the work. We'll start again after the concrete is pumped in."

Todd and Jon walked over to a forest of beams shoring up the ceiling and, tilting back their heads, looked through the jagged hole above them. "If you cut out the middle of the floor, what keeps the rest of it from collapsing?"

"These." Ross pointed to the temporary beams.

"On every floor?"

He nodded.

"Forever?"

Smiling, he said, "Only until the atrium is built. Look, here's how it works." He squatted down and in loose sand on the floor drew a quick sketch of the building. The four children squatted beside him as he described the problems he and his staff faced, making them sound like puzzles and challenging the children to find solutions. He was enjoying his audience, Katherine saw, and his seriousness as he considered their guesses, and offered his own ideas, held them like a magnet. She looked from one rapt face to another. *I wish Jennifer and Todd had a father.*

"So the atrium helps support all ten floors," Ross finished. "And then we take away the temporary beams." He stood, stretching the kinks from his muscles. Leaning casually toward Katherine, he whispered, "I love you." Then he said aloud, "I'm cooking dinner tonight. And I have a couple of scale models of this building at home, if you want to take them apart and put them together your own way."

They walked outside and as the children ran ahead to the car, Katherine asked hesitantly, "Ross, shouldn't Derek pay for the work? At least part of it?"

"None of it. I haven't even told him I'm having it done."

"But—why not? If you think he was the one who didn't build it properly—"

Their steps slowed as they approached the car, and they lowered their voices. At the same moment, their eyes met and Ross felt a rush of love and gratitude. "I'm glad you're here," he said. Automatically, their hands met, their fingers interlocked—and then they saw the children look their way and quickly pulled apart.

"I'll tell you why I haven't told Derek," Ross went on. "If I asked him to share the cost, he'd smile and say he didn't know what I was talking about. I can't prove anything and he'd figure out in a few seconds that I've kept quiet because I don't want it to become public knowledge that the Hayward Corporation was involved in bribing an inspector and putting up a substandard building." He laughed shortly. "Derek's legacy. It's going to be all I can do to handle the cost, but I don't see that I have a choice. Victoria is eighty-two years old; I'd do a lot more than spend some money to keep a scandal from ruining however many years she has left."

Katherine was silent.

They reached the car and Ross opened the door for her. "Does that sound irrational?" he asked.

"No," she said. "It sounds loving."

By the middle of September, they had settled into a pattern, spending three or four evenings a week together, alone or with the children. One night, after dinner at Ross's house, the four children were leafing through Katherine's sketchbook, reliving the month in France through her drawings. "Could I have this one?" Carrie asked, lingering over a vivid watercolor of the cactus gardens at Eze Village.

"Of course," Katherine said.

"Me too?" asked Jon, holding up a charcoal sketch of a Roman olive mill.

Katherine's face was bright with pleasure as she took both pictures and wrote on them, "With my love, Katherine."

"I'll hang it up," Carrie said, holding it at arm's length, admiring it. "Of course not at home," she added with a shrug. "You know. But—"

"Here," said Jon. "At Dad's house."

"Whose house?" Katherine asked.

"Our house," Jon grinned. "I meant our house."

Ross met Katherine's eyes with such love she caught her breath in wonder. "Thank you," he said quietly, "for making us a family." And looking at the six of them at the table, Katherine thought she had never been so happy.

Some nights they took the children to outdoor concerts in Stern Grove, or for an evening sail, but mostly the two of them were alone, on the boat, going to the theater, driving to the wine country, making love. Katherine remembered when Derek's whirlwind had seemed magical; but she knew now that this was the real magic: the love that grew slowly, steadily, beating within her, inseparable from the beating of her heart. And Ross found it impossible to get through a day without talking to her on the telephone or sending her a flower, a note, a newspaper clipping that had amused him, a magazine article he wanted to share.

Occasionally he called to ask her to lunch, but Katherine was reluctant to take time off during the day. With Jennifer and Todd back in school, she was concentrating on making and selling as many pieces of jewelry as she could, because she was afraid Mettler's story would reach other shops, and no one would do business with her.

"It won't happen," Leslie assured her. "Only a few shops specialize in copyrighted originals. You don't have to worry."

Still, each morning, as soon as Katherine sat down and began to sketch and shape bracelets and bar pins, pendants, and earrings, Mettler's voice would echo in her mind, reciting the evidence that inescapably linked her to Craig.

"Divorce him," Victoria said at dinner. "Then you can sell through the top stores. How else will you make a reputation? You must divorce him. Cake, my dear?"

"Yes, thank you. Divorcing him wouldn't help. I'd still be known as the woman who was his wife when he was charged with embezzling; who fled Canada, according to Mettler; who gets money from him every month—"

"But it might help you be yourself," said Tobias, cutting an oversize piece of cake and transferring it to his plate. "Help you get away from the past and look ahead. 'In the deserts of the heart, let the healing fountain start.'"

The words struck Katherine and she was silent, repeating them to herself. "I don't know," she said finally. "It seems that the happier I am, the harder it is to... drop him. Because I don't believe he's happy; and if he had to run away because he was framed—"

"He could have stayed," Tobias said. "He could have fought."

Victoria shook her head. "We never forced him to learn that."

"Then I don't think," Katherine said gently, "that you're the ones to tell me to divorce him."

But the urgings from everyone stayed with her. And so did her memories, appearing unexpectedly, bringing back the best parts of Craig and their marriage as well as his brooding silences, the spaces that kept them apart. Derek's exasperated voice stayed with her, too: *Must you always feel guilty?* And Mettler's accusing voice, tying her to Craig. And Ross's, deep and warm: *Dearest Katherine, I love you.*

"I can't make the decision for you," he said as they lay in bed the night after her dinner with Victoria and Tobias. They had eaten on the deck of his house, and made love on the wide chaise beneath the stars, and then, in the white light of a full moon, slipped naked into the jacuzzi, letting the jets of hot water massage their muscles into almost total collapse before they climbed out and ran through the chill air into the warmth of Ross's bed.

"How can anyone make a decision after that?" Katherine asked languidly, her head on his shoulder. She didn't want to move. "I have no energy for decisions."

"Did you know," Ross murmured, "that Todd asked me today if I'm trying to make him and Jennifer forget Craig?"

Her lethargy vanished. "What did you tell him?"

"That I wanted them to remember their father, and their love for him, but that was separate from the fact that he isn't here and we have no expectation that he will be here again; that I love him and Jennifer and would like to take care of them; and that I am deeply in love with you and would very much like to marry you."

Katherine lay still. "Todd didn't tell me any of that."

"I asked him not to. A man ought to do his own proposing."

She laughed slightly. "Was that a proposal?"

"No." He pulled away to look at her. "You'll recognize it when it comes. I'm waiting for you to make up your mind about Craig. With him or without him."

"With him," Katherine said. "I can't do it without him. Not yet, anyway. Can't I make you see that I want to do this decently, that I want to end our marriage as equals? We began that way; I want to end that way."

Ross thought of Elissa, and Katherine's loyalty, and his own responsibility. I should tell her, he reflected; she should know all of it. But she'd been hurt enough by Craig's lies and pretenses. Knowing about Elissa would change nothing; she already has plenty of reasons to divorce him. "Treating him as an equal is more than he's done for you," he said at last.

"Maybe that's why I want to do it." Turning up her face, Katherine kissed Ross with small, leisurely kisses. "I love you. I might even propose to you someday. But not now. Not yet." After a moment, she sighed. "What I have to do now is go home."

"It's early."

"What time is it?"

"A little after midnight."

"How much after?"

He laughed reluctantly. "About an hour and a half after. All right. Get dressed, my lovely one; I'll drive you back."

Later, in the car, he said, "I hope you noticed that I didn't say I would drive you home. Home is wherever the two of us are together. Do you believe that?"

"Yes," she said simply. And they drove across the bridge and into the city in silence, content with each other, and in silence kissed goodnight in front of her door.

But it's not enough, Ross thought, making the return trip. Contentment isn't enough. Even love isn't enough. We have to build something together and we can't do that when we date like teenagers, jumping apart when our children find us close together, making love almost furtively, driving home at one thirty in the morning so the children won't know we've been in bed.

At home, pulling off his clothes for the second time that night, looking at the empty bed, wanting Katherine there, her eyes dark with passion, her body opening to his, he thought how ridiculous they were. The children knew exactly what they were doing. One of these days, the sooner the better, they'd all sit down together and have an honest—The telephone rang and he lunged for it. Katherine had found something wrong at home—

"Yes," he said loudly. "What happened?"

"Ross?" said a familiar voice. "Can I talk to you? It's Craig."

Part IV

CHAPTER 18

THE years fell away. Craig's voice had not changed and for a moment Ross felt as if they were boys again and he had called to make plans for the day, saying, "Ross? Can I talk to you?"

"Sure," he said casually, as if they truly were in the long-ago time, but his body was as tight as a clenched fist as he struggled to think clearly through the numbing shock of hearing a voice when for so long there had been only a shadow. "Of course we can talk. Do you want to come here, or meet somewhere?"

"No, I meant now. On the phone."

"Craig, after sixteen years we ought to be able to talk face to face."

"I'm not in San Francisco."

"Where are you?"

"It doesn't matter. Ross, I need help and there isn't anyone else I can call. If you won't talk to me on the phone—"

"Of course I will; whatever you want. Are you all right?"

"Fine." Craig laughed. "How does that sound? I'm fine. I've lost everything, but I'm fine."

Ran away from everything, Ross corrected him silently. But he was aware of changes in Craig's voice that he had not heard at first: it was deeper and stronger than he remembered. "What kind of help do you want?"

"I need advice. And money. I wouldn't ask—I never thought I'd be able to come to you again, after leaving you...with Jenny..." He stopped. "I can't talk about it. I've tried to write to you, or call, so goddamn

369

many times, but I couldn't—and I still can't. Someday I will; I swear it; but this is more important... Ross, I've got to have my wife and kids back. I want to start over again. The mess with Carl got out of hand; I could have straightened it out—we'd had misunderstandings before—but I panicked. And then there's—"

"You mean you didn't—?"

"Katherine." Craig went on without pausing. "I need to explain to her—make up for..." His voice faded.

"Craig?" Ross said loudly.

"Sorry. I get stuck on telling Katherine. I don't know how the hell I can explain... It was bad enough last year, when I left, but now..."

Stiffly, Ross said, "She's your wife."

"That doesn't guarantee anything; that was part of the problem. I have to think of the right way to tell her, otherwise she won't... Ross, can you loan me some money? There's a high-powered lawyer in Vancouver, but he wants a retainer. Can you do it?"

"Of course. How much do you need?"

"I don't know. Probably five thousand to start. But I may need a lot more."

"I'll try to get you whatever you need. Craig—"

"I was crazy to run; I know that. I could have worked everything out, found a way to keep the whole mess from Katherine—"

"Keep it from her? You should have told her!"

"You wouldn't say that if you knew her. But you see her now and then, don't you? Do you know if she got the roses I sent on her birthday?"

"She got them..."

"The kids told me she works at Heath's but she can't be earning much—my God, have you seen that apartment? She ought to be able to do better, with the money I send. That's one thing: as hard as it's going to be to work everything out, at least she knows I helped support her all this time."

Ross paced as far as the telephone cord would stretch, then back the other way. *Call her; come back; she wants to talk to you.*

No, stay away.

Steadfast Katherine. What would happen when she heard the plea in Craig's voice and took pity on his aloneness, and saw her children greet him and call him Dad?

"Ross, are you listening? I've got to know how things are before I call her. Is she still seeing that bastard? When I came last December, to take her back to Canada, the kids told me she was with him, *at his place...* they said she saw a lot of him. Christ, I thought I'd gotten away from the son of a bitch—that he'd never get his knife into me again—and then almost the first thing I hear is my kids talking about him... I won't go through that again; I don't want to come back and find out she's with him. Or someone else."

Ross was silent.

"Well? *Is she still seeing him?* Damn it, he'll chew her up, destroy her; she's so naive... she doesn't understand..."

"She broke off with him," Ross said.

Craig sighed. "I thought she would. Katherine's too smart not to see through him. She probably didn't spend much time with him anyway. After all, she's not a young girl who could be taken in, hypnotized... So is that it? She hasn't got anyone? Or is there someone else?" He paused. "I'm asking you, Ross. Is my wife waiting for me or has she found someone else?"

Poor Craig, Ross thought involuntarily. He hasn't changed. He can't take the risk of calling his wife without making sure of what he'll find.

"Ross, did you hear me? It's a simple question, Or is it? Are you trying to protect someone?"

"No—"

"Then what the hell is going on?" He waited. "Damn it, Ross, *I'm asking for help!* I counted on you; we were friends once. At least I thought we were... What's going on with Katherine? Who are you covering for?"

"Craig, she's been waiting for you—"

"*Who is it?* You're a lousy liar, Ross; something's going on and you're lying about it. *This is my wife we're talking about*... and you and I used to be honest with each other. I wouldn't be so surprised if it was that bastard—I'd expect him to lie to me, make me squirm, keep me in the dark... but you! For Christ's sake, you're no better than he is. When did you start acting like your brother?"

"You damn fool," Ross exploded. "Katherine and I are in love with each other. I want to marry her, but she won't divorce you. She has a kind of loyalty you couldn't begin to comprehend, and she won't marry me or even live with me until she understands why you left her, until she finishes with the past, finishes her marriage—"

"She said that?"

"Damn it, do you think I'm making this up? She wants to finish her marriage with you, but only face to face, as equals—that was how she put it—which is a hell of a lot more than she ever got from you—" A small click broke through his torrent of words. "Craig? CRAIG!" he shouted, but there was no answer, only dead silence from the telephone in his hand.

Ross flung himself from the house and strode through the darkened hills, going over the conversation in his mind, cursing his clumsiness. He'd bungled it. With Craig in his grasp, he had let him go.

Toward dawn he was home again, thinking of Katherine, repeating the conversation over and over in a bitter rehearsal for when she would arrive. She'd be there in a few hours to spend the afternoon with him; a time they had planned lightheartedly in bed the night before: Friday, the end of the week, a chance to spend a few daylight hours without the children. "And this time," Katherine had said, "I'll pick you up; Leslie loaned me her car while she and Claude are in New York. I'll be there about noon."

Waiting for her, Ross prowled from room to room and was outside, on the deck, his back to the house, when he heard her footsteps. "Hi," she said softly, coming up behind him. "What requires such deep thought you can't—" He turned and she saw his eyes. "Ross, what is it? What's happened?"

He put out his hands and took hers. "Craig called me last night."

The sunlight lurched. Everything around them, from their clasped hands to the great bridge below, snapped out of place, then slowly settled back. The world grew still. A solitary bee dived into the silence, its buzz a deafening roar. Gently, Katherine pulled her hands away and walked across the deck. "When is he coming back?"

"I don't know. Perhaps not at all."

"Not at all!" She swung around. "He must be! Why else did he call? Why *did* he call? Why didn't he call me?"

"He wanted to know if you were still seeing Derek."

"He could have asked me...Oh. He couldn't take the chance...?"

"He wanted my help. And I made a mess of it."

"But you told him to come back."

There was a pause. "No," Ross said.

"You didn't— Ross, you know I must see him!"

"*I was afraid!* Can you understand that? Of course I know you have to see him, but when I heard his voice, I thought of what might happen when you were all together again, the Fraser family—"

"But...what about embezzling? Being framed? What did he say?"

"We didn't get to that."

"Ross!"

"Damn it, I tried to ask him but he kept changing the subject—"

"You didn't ask him about embezzling and you decided not to tell him to come back."

"I didn't decide anything. That was the problem. Katherine, I've gone over it so many times I can repeat the whole thing. If you'll just sit down..."

Slowly, she came back to him. In the fragrant sunlight, they sat apart from each other and Ross repeated the conversation.

When he finished, Katherine was looking past him, shaking her head, her hands gripped together. "How could you tell him about us? That was for me to do!"

"I know; I hadn't intended—"

"You had no right to tell him! I was going to—"

"I know that! I hadn't intended to tell him anything!"

"Then why did you? Oh, Ross—to have him so close and then to make him run away—!"

"Katherine, no one makes Craig run away; he does it by himself."

"But you knew that; you've always known that. Of all people, you should have known how to talk to him."

"Right. I should have known." Slowly, he said, "He goaded me. But I might have told him anyway. I remember thinking, at one point, that you might not do it yourself."

"You knew I was just waiting until he got here—"

"That's what you said. Maybe I didn't believe it."

"Didn't—!"

"Katherine. Look at yourself. Your husband deserted you more than a year ago; you love me and you're loved by me. But you still cling to someone who's betrayed you—"

"You think I should pay him back. Has it occurred to you that the only thing left of my marriage is knowing that I haven't destroyed anything, that I haven't been the one to cut him off from his wife and children?"

"He doesn't deserve them!"

"That's not the point! I'm not thinking of Craig; I'm thinking of myself— what kind of person I am. Do I run away as he did? Or do I wait for him—"

"So you can be better than he is."

"Well, why not? What's wrong with trying to be better than someone who's hurt you? Are we only supposed to be loyal when it's reciprocated?"

"It's not a bad idea." Ross studied his hands. "I started to ask you— when I said you should look at yourself—what if it's not loyalty at all?"

"What are you talking about?"

"I'm talking about a woman who's so afraid of marriage she hides behind an absent husband rather than risk another failure."

"That is ridiculous!"

"Just think about it for a minute. I'm going to get us something to drink." He disappeared into the house and returned with a pitcher and two glasses. "Iced tea. With home-grown mint." He filled the glasses. "What do you think?"

"About the tea?"

"Katherine."

"I'm not hiding behind Craig. Maybe I am afraid—a little. Everything's happened so fast, I'm not sure where I am—how far I've come. I still don't know how well I can do on my own; I don't know if I can support the three of us by myself; I don't know how strong I am without a man. Maybe that's why I'm not sure I want to trust love yet. But I'm not hiding behind Craig; you're wrong about that. I *owe* him something."

"Whatever it is, you've paid it."

"It's not that simple. I have to think of Jennifer and Todd; of what's best for them."

"A stable family is best for them." He stopped abruptly. "Are you saying you *might* go back to him? To have a stable family? God damn it, he deserted you!"

"*I know that!* And I haven't thought, for a long time, that I'd go back to him. I told you I was just waiting... I told you I still don't understand what happened to us. We loved each other and had a life together and were happy—I think we were happy—and then everything collapsed ...*and I don't know why!* And until I do, I'm not going to start another marriage."

Katherine's eyes were hurt and angry. "I told you all that—I thought you understood—but then, when he finally called, you drove him away! Ross, do you know what you've done? I had a chance to talk to him, to ask him so many questions... but now I'm still where I was before—wondering, imagining, waiting, *not knowing.* And I don't know how long it will take him to try again, to get up his courage, the way he did after Jennifer and Todd told him about Derek." She began to tremble. "I don't know what he's thinking; I can't even imagine what it will be like to see him again if—when—he does call again; I don't know what we'll say to each other or how I'll feel or how I'll tell him..." The glass of tea, wet with condensed moisture, slipped from her shaking hand and shattered on the deck. Katherine burst into tears. "I'm sorry, I'm sorry, I just don't know how everything is going to end... I don't know what's really best for the children... and I worry about Craig... he's all alone and I have you, and Jennifer and Todd, and Victoria and Tobias... I have a family and he has no one and he knows it now, because you told him about us... Ross, you think all you have to do is remind me that he deserted us, but it isn't that simple..."

After a moment, she wiped her cheeks with the back of her hand and sat up straight. "I'd better get a rag and clean up this mess."

"Sit still. I'll take care of it later." Ross had not moved, though his arms ached to hold her; he sat apart from her, his anger growing as she wept. "He isn't worth your tears. He doesn't know the meaning of love or loyalty or steadfastness—"

"Don't, Ross. You hardly know him anymore, or anything about him. I don't find it admirable when you attack him—"

"Admirable—! Good God, he kept another woman for two years while you were married! Was that admirable? That was why he needed so much money he had to steal it!"

"That's not true! I don't know where you heard it, but it isn't true! Craig would never . . . he told me he never wanted . . . *I would have known!*"

Ross looked at her in silence.

"All right, I didn't know everything about him, but I would have known that! Two years?" she cried wildly. "You expect me to believe . . . *two years?* He couldn't have; he was always home." She fell silent, then, looking at her hands, asked, "Where did he—where was he supposed to have someone else?"

"In Calgary."

"He spent a lot of time there, on business. And he always left me the number of his motel." A thought struck her. "Did he tell you . . . he didn't *tell* you this!"

"Of course not. Craig never admits anything unless he's forced to. I discovered it by accident."

"Well, whoever told you was lying."

"Katherine, listen to me. I went looking for him; I wanted to find him so you and I could be alone, without his damned shadow following us all the time. What I found—"

And so, starkly, he told her about Elissa, leaving nothing out.

At first Katherine kept shaking her head, murmuring, "No, no, no," beneath his words. Then she was silent, her eyes closed. Another Craig. Even another name. Another space separating them. But something else was bothering her . . . something Ross had said . . . And then she had it. "August. That trip you took—you called me from there, the day I got back from France."

"And I didn't tell you about it," Ross said, before she could. "I meant to, but you'd just found Mettler's letter canceling your order, and you had enough to worry about—"

"But that was August; this is the middle of September. When were you going to tell me?"

"Look, you've had a lot on your mind—"

"Ross, Craig had secrets; we don't! I want to know the truth about the world I live in!"

"All at once? I was waiting until things calmed down; I thought it would be best if you didn't have to tackle everything at the same time."

Katherine shook her head. "You decided to look for Craig without telling me, and then you decided not to tell me about Elissa—you even decided to tell Craig about us—all on your own. Don't I have anything to say about decisions that involve me?"

He gestured helplessly. "Of course you do. You're wrong about my deciding to tell Craig about us—that was an accident. But the rest, about looking for him, and finding Elissa—you're right; I did those on my own and I suppose I should have told you. But it was done from love—"

"Ross, I've spent all these months trying to find out who I am, what kind of a woman I can be on my own, without being shielded, as if I were in some kind of cocoon... I've been through that with Craig!"

"So you never want protection again, is that it? You think it's some kind of a weakness. If you weren't still tied in knots over Craig and his secrets, you'd know better. It isn't all or nothing—"

"All right; maybe that's true. Maybe I am exaggerating because I'm afraid of going backwards, but—"

"And you're lucky," he went on, "when you find someone who cares enough about you to try to shield you. How many people spend their lives looking for that? How many people—men or women—find someone to protect them from pain?"

"I don't know what that means anymore." Katherine twisted her hands together.

"It means—at least this time—that I kept putting off telling you what I'd done because I didn't think it would change the way you feel about Craig; it would just make you more unhappy to discover another hidden piece of his life, another lie—"

"But I have to know all the pieces! All the lies! And you know that!" Katherine looked beyond him, at the skyline of the city across the bay, and the towns extending down the peninsula, fading into mist. "How do I know how many other lies there are? Can't you see—*I lived with him for ten years and I was blind to all those lies! How can I understand myself until I understand him?* And you let him go! I'm sorry, I keep coming back to that, but that's the worst of all... he was so close! And I don't know when he'll be that close again... when I can break free and move ahead..."

Tears streamed down her face. She made no attempt to wipe them away, but sat still, looking past Ross and past the city, as if she could not bear to look at anything nearby. Watching her, Ross hurt inside with love, and anger at Craig, and frustration. "You understand more about him now than you ever did. Katherine, you've changed so much—what difference does it make what you were with him, now that you've found out what you can be without him?"

"I'm still finding out," she said doggedly. "You always make things sound so simple, when they aren't."

"I know they're not simple. But one of these days you may have to decide it's enough anyway."

Katherine turned to him. "You mean if he doesn't come back. But he's tried twice; I can't believe he won't try again."

"And in the meantime he's always with us." Ross gave a short, bitter laugh. "I had the wrong sword over our heads: it's not the Macklin Building; it's your husband. We can't make any plans; we can't think about the future. We argue when we should be enjoying each other, sharing the kind of love we've never had before..." He stood and paced the length of the deck, furiously kicking aside some small stones near the edge. "We can't even go back, can we? It used to be that he was in the background; now he's between us."

"Yes." Katherine's voice was almost inaudible. "He's so far away, but he's...here. And then I look at you and I can't even think straight anymore..."

From the opposite end of the deck, Ross said flatly, "I make it harder, don't I? I can't help you; I can't tell you what to do; I can't even try to protect you from pain because we don't agree on what that means. I only confuse the issue." When she was silent, he said slowly, "It might be better if I got out of your way. You'd be able to concentrate on thinking about your husband and your marriage. Maybe you'd even decide you do know all you need to know—about him, and yourself, and us."

Katherine gazed at him, her heart pounding.

"And maybe I could use some time, too," he went on carefully. "To think about how I feel about sharing you. If I'm making too many decisions on my own, I ought to know it and do something about it."

Katherine breathed deeply to slow the pounding of her heart. *Not to see Ross. To wake up in the morning and not be able to think, "Today I'll see him; today we'll talk; tonight we'll make love..."* Not to see Ross. She swallowed hard, feeling her heart beat in her throat. *But—to be alone for a while, with no wild swings of emotion, with no pressure to decide, to act, to choose, to do...* "Yes," she said, forcing it out. "I think it would be a good idea."

His breath escaped in a small burst; he had been holding it. "Whatever you think is best." Swiftly, he went to her and took her hands between his. "I love you. I'll do whatever you want—" He turned her hands and kissed one palm, and then the other, her skin cool and soft beneath his lips, rippling with the tremor that ran through her.

I don't want to leave you; I want to be close to you... "No," she murmured.

He stood, bringing her with him, enfolding her in his arms. But she remained motionless, her arms at her side instead of embracing him, as if already she had begun to withdraw. In a moment of panic Ross wondered what the hell he'd done. To be without Katherine; to go through the days without her smile, without seeing her eyes light up in response to something he said, without feeling her beneath him... What the hell had he done? And what would he do if she did find Craig and began to rediscover, with the children, the bonds that had held them for ten years?

It won't happen. They've gone too far. We've gone too far.

Katherine moved within the circle of his arms and immediately he dropped them. He would not force her to stay. "Whatever I can do to help you—" he said.

Tremulously, she smiled. Teardrops glistened in her dark eyelashes. "I think I'll just be alone for a while... and think about the three of us... and everything that's happened..." She reached out, touching his face with her fingertips. "I love you, Ross." Then she turned and walked quickly across the deck and through the glass doors into the living room. In another moment Ross heard her open the front door, and close it firmly behind her.

Elissa saw the taxi driver peer at the address, then stop at her front gate. Not Craig, she thought; he'd tell the driver which house. She saw a woman step out and pay the driver and she knew, even before she saw her face, that it was Katherine.

Hell, she thought, feeling her stomach grab, there's nothing to be scared of. She held the door open, watching the prairie wind lift eddies of dust and carry them along the street like tops. She saw Katherine turn and give an appraising glance at the house—I know it's not his type, Elissa told her silently; and he didn't want me to paint the door red, but I did it anyway, when I decided he was gone for good—then Katherine was walking toward her. She was more beautiful than Elissa had thought; her pictures didn't do her justice. "I'm Katherine Fraser," she said, holding out her hand.

"I know," said Elissa. "I've seen your picture. I'm Elissa Nielsen."

Gravely, they shook hands. "Please come in." She led the way. "I wondered if Ross would tell you about me."

"He only told me yesterday." Katherine gave a swift glance at the living room.

"Why don't you take a good look around?" Elissa asked. "I won't be insulted. You want to know where Craig lived part-time; I would, if I was you. Ross only told you yesterday? He took his time."

"He didn't want me to be hurt," said Katherine. Turning, she met Elissa's eyes. They looked away at the same time and then fell silent.

Elissa fidgeted with a candy dish as Katherine picked up the carved wooden turtle and ran her finger over the small boy on its back. "He's not Craig's," Elissa said. "I guess Ross must have told you. And that Craig helped me when I was pregnant? Without Craig...well, without Craig, I just don't know."

Katherine walked about the crowded room, seeing small touches identical to those she remembered in their Vancouver house. She felt disoriented, as if the two houses had merged and she'd gotten lost among objects that were strange but somehow hers. "Would you like something?" Elissa asked. "Tea or coffee? There's sherry and Scotch, but I thought, before lunch, you know."

"Coffee would be fine." She followed Elissa into the kitchen. "Is it true that you haven't seen Craig since June—a year ago June?"

"True. Haven't seen him or heard from him." She ran water into the percolator, gazing out the window until it ran over, splashing her dress. "Damn, damn, damn. I guess I'm a bit nervous." Carefully, she plugged in the pot. "Ross is in love with you."

"Did he tell you that?"

"No, but it's all over him, like measles. Well, prettier than measles." Involuntarily, they smiled at each other. "It's nice, to see a man in love. I just wondered if you're in love with him."

"Why?" Katherine asked.

Elissa hesitated, then shrugged. "No special reason. Do you take cream? Or sugar?"

"Just black, thank you." She watched as Elissa put mugs on a tray, arranged doughnuts on a plate, dropped one, made an exasperated sound and threw it away. "Let me help," Katherine said. Gently she took the package from Elissa's hand and put out the rest of the doughnuts. "Where shall we sit?"

"In the living room; there isn't anywhere else. Craig wanted to build a nook off the kitchen—a breakfast room, you know—he'd drawn the plans for it, but then...he didn't come back."

Katherine heard the tears behind the simple words, and she knew that

Elissa still missed Craig, still longed for him and waited for him. And that was why she had asked if Katherine was in love with Ross; she wanted to know if Craig would be free when he came back. "I'll carry the tray," Katherine said, and this time she led the way to the living room. There were things she wanted to know, too.

"Did Craig really steal from his company?" she asked bluntly as they sat down

Surprised, Elissa said, "You don't know?"

"Only what his partner told me."

Elissa considered it. "I don't think he did."

"But you don't know."

"He didn't tell me. He told me most everything else. But I don't believe he's a thief. I don't think he took a damn thing."

You don't want to feel responsible for his needing money, Katherine thought, remembering what Ross had said. "Then why did he disappear?" she asked.

Elissa looked at her directly. "I guess you ought to be able to answer that better than me."

"I didn't know who he really was. I didn't know about you. How could I know why he left?"

"You must have known *something*. If I lived with a man for ten years I'd sure know a hell of a lot about him."

Yes, you would. And I didn't.

The questions that had haunted Katherine before rushed back with Elissa's words. Why hadn't she known more? Why hadn't she asked questions about Craig's past, and their house, their bills, their finances? Why hadn't she forced herself into his silences?

Maybe because I didn't really want to. Or didn't want to enough. Maybe it was more pleasant not knowing. Not worrying. Like a little girl.

The silence was stretching out. "Tell me about Craig," Katherine said. "You know him better than I do."

"That's true," Elissa responded frankly. "He was pretty relaxed and easy around here. Like somebody who's been locked into a suit and a tie all day, very proper, and then he comes home and puts on an old T-shirt and jeans—and kind of slurps his soup?"

"Locked in," Katherine echoed.

"Well, it was more like he felt *burdened*. He said you needed somebody to look up to, who'd protect you from things that were ugly or scary, and he couldn't always do that. Though I must say you look a lot more able to take care of yourself than he made you out. I might have guessed he was exaggerating. Anyway, he said when you two met, you were so innocent all you wanted was love. You didn't ask how much money he made or anything about the future—or the past either, for that matter; you didn't ask a lot of questions about his so-called orphan childhood; you were just happy to love him and have him love you. He was pretty impressed with that except he thought it made you awful vulnerable. But it was a powerful force on him; it was why you were the only woman he was in love with."

She was so matter-of-fact that Katherine was embarrassed. "He didn't love me enough to be honest with me."

"He loved you too much to be honest with you. Can I ask you something?"

"Of course."

"Were you a virgin when you met him?"

"Yes."

"Well that explains part of it. He always talked about you as if you were a virgin in everything—not just sex, but getting along in the world."

"But that's nonsense," Katherine said. "I'd been to college; I had a job; I had friends..."

"Not to hear him tell it. He kept saying all the things he'd taught you, the kind of life he gave you. I had this crazy idea that he sort of thought of you like his sister—you know, kind of frozen at her age? So, he had to believe he was first in everything, I guess: not just your bed. But then he was always afraid he'd make a mistake and you'd be disappointed in him and stop loving him."

"A mistake in what?"

"How he behaved. Acting like his family, showing his anger."

"But he wasn't an angry person. The times he did get angry, he usually controlled it and it passed."

"It didn't pass. It dug in deeper. He said all the men in his family were like that. He remembered his grandfather, Hugh, roaring at him about something real silly, like picture postcards, I think, and then there was Derek—the all-time champion of anger. And Craig was like them but at the same time he was afraid of angry people. Scared to death of Hugh and Derek, and Derek's father—Curt—and even himself. He was scared of being angry."

Restlessly, Elissa stood and moved about the room. "Do you know, I could tell you the story of every Hayward all the way back to Hugh's grandfather? I know every piece of jewelry Hugh bought Victoria; I know the color of the dress Jennifer wore when she graduated high school; I know...oh, damn, I'm sorry...I didn't mean to hurt you."

"It's all right. I was just thinking—he told you the things he missed, the people he loved and couldn't forget. After fifteen years."

"He didn't love all of them, you know; and they didn't all love each other. He told me about Derek's girls and how Jennifer cried—"

"Derek's girls? Jennifer?"

"That was the last time they were in Menton. They had their own apartment, sort of, with bedrooms around a kind of playroom, and there was a garden with a wall, and a door in the wall, and Derek would sneak girls into his bedroom. Didn't Ross tell you? He knew about it. Jennifer didn't, until one night she found out and ran into the garden, sobbing, and no one could get her to stop, not even Craig. And the next day, when they went home, she left behind a necklace Derek had bought her in Monte Carlo. She didn't like it anyway, Craig said; it was black. Death around her neck, Jennifer called it. So she left it there. Derek was furious—he'd paid a lot for it—but *he* wouldn't take it home, so it stayed there. That was only about a week before she died. Scary, isn't it?"

Katherine recalled a black necklace, coiled in a jeweler's box, in the playroom of the villa. Everything is a circle, she thought, coming around to its beginning. And when Craig comes back, the circle will be complete.

Elissa talked on, quoting Craig, showing Katherine a shelf of his wood carvings in her bedroom, and his plans for the breakfast room. She made lunch, still talking about Craig; they ate in the living room, talking about Craig, and after lunch Elissa brought out a photo album of the two of them. They had made a marriage, Katherine realized, and in the small, cluttered room, listening to the love in Elissa's voice, she understood why Craig had not been able to give it up.

Finally, she said, "I have to leave soon; my plane is at five. But I want to ask you something." She paused. "I'm grateful for everything you've told me, and I believe you when you say you haven't seen Craig, but I think you must have heard from him. I think he needed you too much to cut himself off—the way he did me."

Elissa's eyes filled with tears. "Thank you for saying that. I thought you'd hate me and think I was trying to ruin your marriage; I didn't think you'd understand. But I needed him, too, you know. I still need him—he was my friend and my son and my brother and my lover and my husband—I'm sorry, but he was—all at the same time and I miss him...oh, hell and damnation." She wiped her eyes. "Anyway, I swear I haven't heard from him. I kept thinking I would; there'd been times before when a few weeks would go by and he couldn't get here, so I kept thinking he'd show up and everything would be back to where it was—but it never happened. I'm still waiting. Silly, maybe, but that's how I am. Are you?"

"Am I what?"

"Still waiting."

"Of course."

"To live with him?"

"I don't know. I don't think we can live together again."

"But you're still waiting. Even though you haven't heard anything either."

"Well, yes we did—" Katherine stopped at the look on Elissa's face. She was terrified. She had talked on and on, filling the hours, giving Katherine no chance to say she had heard from Craig. And now, seeing that terrified look, Katherine couldn't bring herself to tell Elissa that Craig had called Ross, wanting his wife back. "He sent me roses," she said. "On my birthday."

Elissa's face cleared. "White ones, I'll bet. Craig told me you liked white roses."

"Did he," Katherine said dryly. "Didn't he ever talk about anything but his family—his two families?"

"He talked a lot about Eskimos. Didn't he talk to you about them? He loved the kind of life they led: harsh, uncomplicated, close-knit. That was how he saw it. He and Hank used to talk about Eskimos all the time."

"Hank?"

"Hank Aylmer. He travels to Eskimo villages in Alaska and Canada and buys soapstone sculptures to sell in the States. You met him; Craig told me you did."

Katherine stared at her. "I'd forgotten," she said slowly. Hank Aylmer. A long time ago, Craig had said Hank Aylmer had invited them to go with him on a buying trip to Eskimo villages. Scattered all over, he'd said; a real sightseeing vacation. Scattered all over. Hank Aylmer traveling from village to village, from one province to another—*mailing money to Craig's family from a different post office every month.* "Where is he?" she asked. "Hank. Where is he?"

"Home, last I heard," Elissa replied. "But he doesn't know anything about Craig; I've asked him."

"Home? Where?"

"Calgary," said Elissa. "The other side of town. Do you want to call him?"

"Yes!" Excitement was stirring in Katherine. Of course Hank knew where Craig was. If he hadn't told Elissa, it was because Craig had asked him not to. But he would tell Katherine; he would tell Craig's wife. "If I can use your phone..."

"Here's his number. I'll be in the kitchen if you need me."

"Thank you," Katherine said, and dialed, tightening her grip on the receiver when he answered.

"Hank Aylmer here."

"This is Katherine Fraser, Hank. We met a few years ago, if you remember. My husband introduced us. Craig Fraser."

There was no response.

"Hank?"

"Right here. Katherine Fraser, did you say?"

"Hank, don't pretend with me. You remember the name and tribe of every Eskimo from Alaska to Hudson Bay; you remember me, too."

A rumbling laugh came over the wires. "Right, then, I do. And your two little ones—Jennifer and Todd, right?—how are they?"

"Fine. They'd like to see their father."

"Well, now. Well, now. Sometimes we lose track of friends, Katherine. I haven't seen Craig for an age."

"Where is he, Hank?"

"Can't say. I know he left Vancouver some time back—"

"Fifteen months ago."

"Right, then, it was that long ago. But I can't say where he is now, you know. I don't keep track of him."

"You see him every month. He gives you money and you mail it to me, always from a different town."

"Well, now, that's...very imaginative. I wish I could help you, Katherine, but I can't."

"Hank, I want to see him. I want to talk to him. Would you tell him that?"

"Katherine, you're jumping to all sorts of conclusions."

"All right, don't answer. Just listen. Tell him I got the roses he sent for my birthday; thank him for me. Tell him I want him to come to San Francisco. He knows where I live; tell him I'm waiting for him. Are you listening?"

"Right, but you mustn't get your hopes up, Katherine."

"Just listen. Tell him the three of us are waiting. Just the three of us. Remember that, Hank; it's very important. Tell him it's just me and the children. No one else."

"You mean you're not bedded down with anybody, is that it?"

She sighed. "That's it. You'll tell him?"

"I didn't say that. I was just clarifying what you said."

"And I want him to come to San Francisco! Will you tell him that? Please, Hank; if he won't tell me how to come to him, he'll have to come to me."

"Right."

"You'll tell him that?"

"If I see him, I'll tell him."

"When?"

"Katherine, if I see him, I'll give him all your messages. That I promise. More than that I cannot do. Right?"

"Right," Katherine said.

"Goodbye, then, and give my regards to those fine children."

"I will." She hung up the telephone, staring into space.

Elissa came to the doorway. "He didn't know anything?"

"He wouldn't say. I left a message with him."

"For Craig to call you?"

"For him to come to San Francisco. I have to see him."

Elissa reached out her hand. "If he shows up . . . and you decide not to get together again . . ."

"I'll tell him you're waiting." They looked at each other for a long moment.

"I wish we could be friends," Elissa said.

Katherine gave a small smile. "I think we are, don't you?" Moving swiftly across the room, she laid her cheek briefly against Elissa's, then turned and went to the front door. "Thank you," she said, and later, flying home, she silently thanked Elissa again—for making her acquainted, after ten years of marriage, with her own husband.

Once again the days and evenings were spent at her worktable. More confident with each piece, Katherine worked more quickly than ever before, and when an idea came to her and she began to sketch it, she knew immediately whether it belonged with the jewelry she was selling now, or whether it was so striking and distinctive that it had to be put aside in a separate folder, kept on a shelf above her table, marked "Henri Flambeau."

"I'll never sell to the top people here," she told Victoria at dinner a week after she had seen Elissa. "They won't take a chance on me. And the small stores I'm selling to now won't buy my so-called 'far-out' designs. So when I have enough of them, I'll see what I can do in Paris."

"You don't need Paris," Victoria said tartly. "I intended Henri to offer you a second country; your first reputation should be made here."

"Not with Herman Mettler talking about me."

"He won't do it forever; he's too indolent and self-centered to pay attention to anyone else for very long."

"But I haven't got forever; I'm barely making enough money now, and

I promised Jennifer and Todd we'd look for a larger apartment. And I'd like to take a trip, just the three of us, over Thanksgiving."

"To avoid a family dinner," Victoria declared. "Why are you so foolish? Why can't you and Ross be together while you resolve your dilemma?"

"We're not ready," Katherine said.

"Nonsense! Love isn't like a roast turkey that is or is not ready. It simply *is*, and you must let it guide you. Why don't I call Ross now? He can join us for dessert."

"No," Katherine said. But she was smiling, thinking someday she'd tell Ross Victoria had compared them to roast turkey.

There was no word from Craig, nor from Hank Aylmer. Ross did not call and she did not call him. Reluctantly, Victoria honored her request and did not invite them to dinner on the same nights, so there was no place they might run into each other. Without him, Katherine's days seemed choppy: everything that happened was cut short because it could not be shared with him—a newspaper item, one of Todd's wild fantasies, a special piece of jewelry. She would feel a surge of longing, and then frustration over his allowing Craig to slip away, and then impatience because Craig had not called—until the space around her worktable was crowded with feelings and images and voices, clamoring to be heard.

But all the time, her hands were steady, adding to her collection of jewelry, boxed, priced, and lined up on a shelf. As an experiment, she had made two belt buckles of randomly shaped silver cut out in delicate patterns like lace and scattered petals. To display them, she bought a strip of dark blue velvet and another of wine-colored silk and made two wide belts by gathering the ends into the two halves of her buckles. She wore one of them—for good luck, she told herself—the day she went to the bank, to talk about her loan.

She had pushed it out of her mind, but when September was almost gone and she added up her bills, and what she thought she could get for her new jewelry, the numbers did not balance. They hardly ever do, she reflected wryly. But if I extend my loan for twelve months, the payments will be smaller. Then we can go somewhere at Thanksgiving.

At the bank, she filled out the application and gave it to a loan officer, waiting for more of the probing personal questions she had answered when she first applied for the loan. But this time it was different. The officer scanned the application, typed rapidly on his computer keyboard and in a few seconds read aloud her name and address from the screen. "Loan made in June," he went on. "Payments made on time in July, August, and September. And the loan recently guaranteed..." He read silently. "Well, Mrs. Fraser, I see no problem; we'll begin with October fourth, next Monday, for twelve months. We'll have a new agreement for you to sign in a few minutes; the computer does it, you know; wonders of technology, aren't they?" He turned back to the terminal and began typing.

"Just a minute," Katherine said. "I think there's a mistake. No one guaranteed this loan; that's why I brought the contracts I have with three jewelry stores—"

"Guaranteed by Ross Hayward, according to our records, Mrs. Fraser, on September twenty-fifth. Just three days ago, in fact. So of course, there is no impediment to the extension." He returned to his typing.

Katherine opened her mouth, then closed it. Ross knew she would refuse money, so he found another way to help her. Clever, she thought; no one with any sense would reject a guarantee on a loan.

As soon as she was home, she called him at his office. "I was just at the bank," she said, rushing through her words to get past the jolt of longing she felt at the sound of his voice, and his surprise and delight when he heard hers. "I found out you'd guaranteed my loan. It was wonderful of you. Thank you."

"You're welcome," he replied. "How are you? Victoria says you're working very hard."

"I am. That's what she tells me about you."

"Then she's right both times. Have you sold to any new stores?"

"No; I'm still working on the collection for Henri. Are the engineers working on the Macklin Building?"

"They had to put it off for two or three weeks."

"Oh. That's too bad." There was a silence. "I went to Calgary," Katherine said abruptly. "I spent the day with Elissa."

"Did you! That must have been difficult."

"It was easier than I expected. She's a very easy person to be with. And she told me so many things I never knew...."

"You liked her."

"Yes. And I understood why Craig went to her. She loves him so, and she's still waiting—"

"Even after you told her about Craig's call?"

"I didn't tell her," Katherine said ruefully. "I couldn't; it would have made her so unhappy, and it wouldn't change anything for her, at least not now, before Craig and I... have had a chance..." Her voice faltered. "To talk."

There was a long silence as they both recalled her anger at Ross for not telling her about Elissa. "Well," Ross mused aloud. "That sounds like something I once said."

"I should have told her," Katherine said faintly.

"Probably. But you cared about her feelings. She's lucky to have such a friend."

Don't rub it in, Katherine told him silently. After a moment, she said, "I guess I'd like to think about that."

"Good." His voice was warm.

"I wanted to tell you something else. I talked to a friend of Craig's, the man who's been mailing the money each month—"

"He said he had?"

"No. But he didn't deny it, either. I'm sure he's in touch with Craig and I left a message, asking Craig to come here."

"To come back to you?"

"I said I had to talk to him. I'd hoped to hear from him by now, but it may take Hank a while to reach him. If he does. But I think he'll be here soon."

"Do you know what you'll say to him?"

"I'm thinking about it."

"Good," he said once more.

"Ross, I haven't told Victoria and Tobias about Elissa."

"Of course not."

Katherine heard the door open; Jennifer and Todd, home from school. "I'd better go," she said. "Thank you again. I'm grateful for your help."

"I was glad to do it. Take care of yourself, Katherine."

Hanging up, she turned to see two grouchy faces. "What's wrong with you?" she asked.

"Nothing," said Todd, and went to the refrigerator.

"Jennifer?" Katherine asked.

"They announced the Father's Dinner today; it's in two weeks."

"Father's Dinner?"

Todd slammed the refrigerator door. "Some dumb teacher thought it up; they didn't have it last year. You're supposed to bring your father and there's this big dinner in the gym and then some of the fathers and their kids put on a show."

"It's to honor fathers," Jennifer added. "Whatever that means."

"We thought we'd borrow Ross," said Todd off-handedly as he cut a chunk of cheese. "But he hasn't been around lately, has he?"

"No," answered Katherine. "Do you want crackers with that?"

"Sure. Where is he?"

"Where he always is. He's pretty busy..."

"Yeh."

Katherine took down a new box of crackers and handed it to Todd. "Sometimes people stop seeing each other for a while. They're still friends; it's just that they aren't together all the time."

"Or ever," Jennifer said. "Did you have a fight?"

"We had a disagreement. And then we decided we were... getting in each other's way when we needed to think about some important things."

"Like what?" Todd asked.

"Like whether we should be together so much when I'm waiting for your dad to come back."

Todd screwed up his eyes, then blurted, "Do you love Ross more than Dad?"

Katherine's throat tightened. I should have expected that, she thought. "I love them in different ways," she said at last. "And I love you in another way. And Victoria and Tobias in another—"

"Then why can't you be with Ross while you're thinking about waiting for Dad?"

"Because I get distracted," Katherine said a little frantically. "It's hard to explain..."

Todd shook his head glumly. "It's a crock." He tilted his head at Katherine. "How come you can't find a man who'll stay with you?"

"*Todd!*" cried Jennifer. "That's mean!"

"It sure is," Katherine said, feeling bruised. How much do you excuse, she wondered, because they're young and bewildered and don't have much control over their lives? Not much. I get bewildered, too, and I didn't have much control when Craig decided to leave. "It was a low blow and I think I deserve an apology."

Todd scowled. "Well, I'm sorry. It was just that I was wishing we had a father."

"You're not the only one," said Katherine.

"How about Uncle Tobias?" Jennifer giggled. "We could borrow him."

"I think you'd have a wonderful time," Katherine replied.

"Seriously?"

"Seriously. He's never been a father; it would be a new experience for him."

"I want him!" Todd shouted. "He's better than Ross!" He glanced at Katherine's expressionless face. "I mean, nobody else will have a father *anything* like him."

"Can I call him?" Jennifer asked.

"Why not?" said Katherine. "And then I'd like some help in the kitchen. We're having guests for dinner."

"How will they taste?" Todd asked, trying to make Katherine smile.

She did, and gave him a hug. "Tough but sweet. It's Leslie and Claude."

They laughed. And as Jennifer went to the telephone, and Todd finished the cheese and crackers, Katherine gave a small, private sigh. Another crisis bypassed—at least for a time.

Jennifer stood beside Claude, waiting, while he opened the bottle of Spanish sherry he had brought and filled three glasses. He looked at her grave face. "Would you and Todd like some?"

"No thank you. I hope it doesn't hurt your feelings, but we think it tastes awful."

He smiled. "No hurt feelings. Did you want to ask me something?"

"Todd and I would like to borrow you to be our father, just for one night."

A stunned look settled on Claude's face. Across the room, Katherine looked puzzled; Leslie alert and curious. "Was this planned with someone?" Claude asked.

"Just us," Jennifer said. "We need a father for the Father's Dinner at school, and our own father is gone, and we can't ask Ross because he and Mother get in each other's way when they think about important things so he doesn't come around anymore, and I did ask Uncle Tobias but he has to be at an alumni dinner that night. And you're here."

"So I am," Claude agreed. Jennifer and Todd stood side by side, watching him. "I'd be honored to be your father. But I've never been one and I'm not sure I can do it in a way that will please you."

"Just stay around for a while," muttered Todd.

"Longer than one evening?" Claude asked.

"No," said Jennifer. "That will do. Two weeks from tomorrow—that's a Wednesday night, is that all right?" He nodded. "Could you be here at five thirty? Then we could walk to school together. We should be finished by eight o'clock, so if you have more important things to do that night you can still do them."

"That will be the most important thing I have to do that night," said Claude. "Am I supposed to perform? Sing or dance?"

"Do you sing or dance ordinarily?" asked Jennifer.

"No. Definitely no."

"Then you don't have to. Just be with us."

"It will be a pleasure. Now, if you'll excuse me—" He carried the tray of sherry glasses to Katherine and Leslie, who had been whispering and now watched him with small, soft smiles.

"You're amazing," Leslie murmured as he sat beside her on the couch. "Where did you learn to talk to children?"

"I don't talk to children. I talk to people. Leslie, did you and Katherine plan that?"

"Damn it, of course not. You know I'm not that devious."

"What does that mean?" Katherine asked.

Leslie held her glass by its stem. "Katherine, will you drink to our momentous decision to marry?"

A smile lit Katherine's face. "How wonderful! Of course I will. To all the joys you'll have together." After they drank, she said, "But I still don't understand—"

"You see, we've been having a dialogue. I want a child. Claude, being fifty, doesn't think—"

"Fifty-one."

"Almost fifty-one, doesn't think he is at an optimum age to become a father. So when we walk in your front door and almost immediately he is asked to be a father, even for one night, he is naturally, or unnaturally, suspicious. I, on the other hand, think it's wonderful. Dress rehearsal."

"What's wrong with fifty-one?" Katherine asked Claude.

"I'm set in my ways, I've never had to take infants into consideration when I schedule my days and nights, I've long since forgotten what the anxieties of childhood are like, and I'll be sixty-one when this child wants to play baseball. What kind of a father is that?"

"A little slow at running bases," Katherine said. "But if you learn how to throw a fast one—and lawyers occasionally do, don't they?—the rest won't matter." Claude chuckled. "What's more," she went on, "you just said you don't talk to children; you talk to people. If you want to know about children's anxieties just think about people's anxieties; they aren't much different."

"Faultless reasoning," he said admiringly. "Do you think Leslie will be happy as a homebody?"

Katherine looked at her. "You'd give up your job?"

"How do I know?" Leslie asked crossly. "Claude thinks I can be president of Heath's if I fight for it. Maybe I don't want to fight. Or maybe I do, but not right now. Maybe I want to be domestic for a while. Maybe I'll decide to do both, like a four-armed wizard. Do I have to decide this very minute?"

"No," Claude said. "And I'm sorry if I was pushing." He put his hand on the back of Leslie's head, caressing her red curls and the nape of her neck. "I adore this woman," he told Katherine. "I want to give her vacations in Italy and moonlight cruises in Scandinavia and balloon flights over the Himalayas, but all she wants, at least right now, is a child. I have a suspicion she really wants two, but so far I've managed to refrain from asking. Well, dear Leslie, I think we should have a child and see how we like it. If things don't work out, we'll give him or her to Jennifer and Todd."

"You'll what?" cried Jennifer from across the room.

Leslie kissed him. "I'm marrying a clown. Things will work out. We can always come to Katherine for words of wisdom."

Katherine jumped up. "I forgot about the wild rice," she said and went to the kitchen.

Leslie followed. "What's wrong?"

"Nothing." She turned down the flame a fraction. "You two looked so happy. And settled."

"And you're not. What happened with Ross? Can't I go to New York for a few days without you getting into trouble?"

Katherine laughed slightly. "We decided to stay away from each other for now. Jennifer and Todd act like it was a divorce."

"They're fond of Ross."

"I know. He's very good with them."

"So what are you going to do about him?"

"Nothing. Until I do something about Craig."

"Like divorce him?"

"Maybe."

"The alternative is to go back to him."

"I know."

"Listen, lady, you wouldn't do that."

"I don't think so."

"What do you *want*, Katherine?"

"I think I want Ross. I'm still trying to work it out; I don't understand it all, yet. I can't even talk about it, Leslie. Let's talk about something else."

Leslie paused. "OK." Something cheerful, she thought. "I was going to ask you anyway. Where did you get that belt? Did you make it?"

Katherine looked at her waist. "Yes. I'd forgotten I had it on. I wore it for good luck."

"Did it work?"

"Yes."

"Can you make me one?"

"You mean for good luck?"

"I mean because it's sensational and I want one."

"I'll give you one now. Burgundy silk or blue velvet, whichever you want; you can put in any fabric, to change the look."

"How many do you have?"

"Two."

"How fast can you make them?"

"I don't know. I didn't keep track. Why?"

"Because I want to sell them at Heath's. Can you make me a dozen?"

"I can make as many as you want. You really think you can sell them?"

"Damn right; in fine jewelry or the Empire Room. I might even design my wedding dress around one."

"When?" Katherine asked. "Leslie, I'm sorry; I got sidetracked and never asked when it would be."

"You would have been told; you're part of it. Christmas, we think. By then, you'll have your problems solved and you and Ross can be best man and best lady. Will you?"

Katherine lit the candles on the table and turned down the lights. "I'd love to be part of your wedding. I can't speak for Ross. Can I ask a favor?"

"Name it."

"I'd like to make your wedding rings."

"That's a favor? I was going to beg you on bended knee to fit us into your schedule! Why is it a favor?"

"Because I can pretend," Katherine said. "I always do, when I make my best pieces; I pretend I'll be the one who wears them, for some special event."

"Then I have a suggestion." Leslie put her arm around Katherine. "Make two sets. You can pretend twice as hard, and you'll have an extra pair—in case a special event should come along."

Katherine laughed. "I just might. Now let's get the children and their borrowed father to the table. We'll have a family dinner."

CHAPTER 19

On Friday, the first of October, at 9:34 in the morning, an earthquake sent shock waves rumbling across San Francisco and the surrounding area. Centered beneath the bay and registering 4.7 on the Richter scale, it was not considered severe, especially by those who remembered a more damaging one fifteen years earlier, but it was strong enough to shift furniture, knock groceries off shelves, cause doors to open and shut, and slosh coffee out of thousands of cups. In a warehouse at BayBridge Plaza, Ross was perched on a sawhorse, going over blueprints with the construction manager, when he felt the shock. The sawhorse jolted beneath him and he fell. "Ross!" someone yelled. "Look out!" Instinctively he rolled to the side as a stack of lumber toppled and crashed, grazing his arm, covering him with a cloud of dust.

For ten seconds the ground shook. Buildings creaked and a brown haze of plaster dust and wood shavings filled the air. Then walkie-talkies began to chatter as workers reported to each other from one end of the construction site to the other. "OK in Number One..." "Pile of bricks down in Number Two..." "Bag of Oreo cookies crushed in Number Ten—" Ross chuckled as he stood and brushed himself off; then he froze. "Couple guys hurt in the Macklin Building! Get some help over here!"

He dashed through the building, jumping over piles of lumber, bypassing the construction elevator to take the stairs. Outside, the dusty haze blurred buildings and equipment and workers hunting for tools that had fallen and bounced away amid scattered lumber and bricks. Ross ran past them to the Macklin Building, where a cluster of workmen stood just inside the door, arguing loudly among themselves. The floor was littered with debris below a gaping hole in a corner of the ceiling. "Let me through," Ross ordered, shoving the men aside.

"Who the hell do you think you are?" one of them demanded.

"I own the building; now stop that damned shouting and somebody tell me what happened."

"Ceiling fell," a voice said caustically. "Couple guys underneath got hit."

A man was lying on the floor. Ross knelt beside him. His eyes were open; so was his mouth. "Shit," he muttered. "The fucking ceiling..."

"He ain't the worst," someone said. "It's Bud—"

Ross followed his pointing finger and saw a pile of shattered concrete, with a man's leg jutting from it. Christ, he thought. Not dead; please God, not dead. "Has he moved?"

The men nodded. "We pulled some of the shit off, but we can't get at him. But he moved and he said something..."

"He did not!" a voice yelled. "He ain't said a—"

"Somebody called the fire department?" Ross demanded.

"Yeh, sure," a heavy-set man said. They heard the wail of a siren. "Fast work," he joked nervously. He pulled a flask from his back pocket and knelt beside Ross. "Medicine for my friend," he said.

The man had pulled himself part way up and sat slumped against the wall. He saw the flask and reached for it. He was all right, Ross thought. But the other man's leg had not moved.

Another, closer siren was heard; the undulating sound pierced through the building, then stopped as if cut with a knife. Two fire trucks pulled up, then an ambulance. In a few minutes the space was crowded with firemen and paramedics. "Cutters!" one called and they began cutting through the twisted steel bars that had reinforced the concrete ceiling.

"A hoist, damn it, you can't lift that concrete!"

"You want a rope?"

"Damn right I want a rope! Over that beam—"

"Have to get something under the concrete to lift it—"

"A sling."

"Right; and the hooks in the truck..."

"Tie the fucking rope to the hooks! You think we got all day?"

Ross and the workmen slid the makeshift sling beneath the largest slab of concrete as the firemen made a hoist with a block and tackle attached to an overhead beam. "Everybody keep that slab from swinging sideways when we pull the rope," the fire chief ordered. "Got that?"

"Do it," Ross said, gritting his teeth, and with the workmen he strained to steady the slab as it stirred and began to move.

"Little more! Little more!" grunted the fire chief. He and his men pulled on the hoist. "More! Keep it up—!" And slowly the slab rose a few inches above the still form lying beneath. "Grab him!" yelled the chief, as Ross and one of the workers already were shoving aside small pieces of concrete and then easing the man from beneath the hanging slab.

"OK," Ross gasped and the slab crashed back into place as the hoist was released. Two paramedics lay the limp figure on a stretcher and as they inserted an intravenous tube into the vein on one of his hands Ross grabbed the other to find a pulse. He found it, strong and steady, and closed his eyes in relief, counting for a full minute. "OK," he said again, and stood up. "No, wait a minute." He turned to the workman with the flask. "How come you were in here? All the work in this building had been stopped."

"Came to get some wire we'd left." The man rubbed his head. "Just for a minute. That's when it hit."

Just for a minute, Ross thought. So much for precautions. He took a notepad from the inside pocket of his jacket. "Can you give me that man's name and address? And phone number; his family has to be notified."

"Sure. He all right?"

"Looks like," said one of the paramedics. He held the intravenous flask while the other strapped the man to the stretcher. "Small pieces kept the big one from crushing him. Lucky guy," he added as they lifted the stretcher and carried it to the fire department ambulance.

Ross squatted beside the other workman. "Names and addresses," he said. "For both of you."

"My cousin's a lawyer," the workman said. "I gotta call him."

"Names," Ross said again, and he was writing them as the construction manager came. Ross gave him the paper. "Greg, would you make this call?"

"Right." He stood there, looking with Ross at the gaping hole in the ceiling. "If somebody fucked up—" he muttered.

"Is that what you think?"

"Tell you the truth: I don't know. I thought your engineer did an OK design for the temporary support beams—he said a herd of elephants could do a polka on it and tell you the truth: I thought so too. 'Course we weren't figuring on a quake, but still and all, I wouldn't of thought that little bit of shaking would make this much mess. Shit, now we'll have lawyers all over the place."

"Probably," Ross said. "How about making that call?"

"Sure. Be right back."

Ross stood amid the debris. His throat was dry. He'd thought he could repair the building and keep its history a secret, but now it would all come out. Because he knew there was too much damage for a minor earthquake: it had to be more. It had to be what he had worried about from the moment he read the engineer's report: some of the support columns had settled just enough to cause the ceiling to break apart. And because the temporary supports weren't designed to hold the entire weight of the ceiling, when it pulled away from the columns, they collapsed and a chunk of the ceiling came crashing down.

And two workmen were in the way.

If they sued BayBridge, there would be an investigation. One earthquake, one investigation, and out into the open would come a sixteen-year cover-up by his father and brother of illegally changing specifications and bribing an inspector—and a two-month cover-up by Ross Hayward after he had the building inspected in July and could no longer say he only suspected problems.

The Hayward Corporation could survive it; Ross Hayward Associates might not. If he had to pay damages to those two workmen he could be wiped out. And Victoria would be forced to watch a dream splinter in scandal.

Unless they could settle out of court.

With the force of a physical pain, Ross wanted Katherine beside him. I wouldn't keep it from her, he thought; I'd share it; I'd ask for her help. I'll have to tell her that.

Except that he wasn't telling her anything these days. He was waiting for her to make up her mind about her husband.

So this one he'd have to handle by himself. And in fact, the solution was really very simple. All it took was money.

Katherine had asked if Derek was going to help pay for the repair of the footings. Ross had said no. But now everything had changed. Now, after sixteen years, Derek and their father were going to share the responsibility for the Macklin Building.

He went outside, to see if any other buildings had been damaged. And it was then that television came to BayBridge.

All that hectic Friday reporters raced about the bay area, gathering earthquake stories for the evening news and a later special report. "Thank God it was in the morning," they told each other. "Nothing worse than late-afternoon disasters; no time to get them on the air."

By the time Ross got back to the Macklin Building, Greg Thorpe, the construction manager, was looking with loathing at two cameras and the microphones thrust in his face. He waved in relief. "Ross Hayward," he told the reporters. "Architect for BayBridge, and he owns the Macklin Building."

They switched to Ross: reporters from two different television stations, flanked by bored men in shirtsleeves holding mini-cameras on their shoulders. Shooting questions, the reporters kept an eye on their watches; they had a quota of earthquake stories and the Macklin Building wasn't really news: no one had died. They wouldn't even have come if BayBridge weren't so important.

"The beams," one of them began. "They were temporary?"

"While we cut the atrium," Ross said. "We had to—"

"Yes, sir, what I meant was, were they safe?"

"Of course." Quickly, without letting them interrupt, he described the shoring up of the ceiling. "I wouldn't have allowed work to start in there if I didn't think it was safe. No one should allow workmen in a building that isn't secure."

"You're defending your engineer, then, and saying it was only the earthquake, is that right?"

"We'll be reviewing the plans, but I have no doubt the earthquake caused the damage."

"Thank you, sir. You don't mind if we do a few interior shots—?"

Ross saw the televised story, cut to thirty seconds, while sitting in Victoria's library. "Today's earthquake also caused injuries to two workmen in the Macklin Building," the reporter said, "part of the BayBridge Plaza development south of Market."

The camera panned across the BayBridge site to the Macklin Building, then moved inside, pausing at the hole in the ceiling and the debris on the floor. Greg Thorpe appeared glumly on the screen. "We followed the plans on the temporary beams," he said. "Though I did think at the time I would have made them stronger."

Ross shot up in his chair. "Liar," he said.

"But that wasn't up to me," Thorpe added. "It was the engineer on Mr. Hayward's staff."

"Ross Hayward Associates," the reporter's voice said as Ross appeared on the screen, "are architects for BayBridge Plaza and the renovation of the Macklin Building."

Watching himself, Ross thought he looked disheveled and faintly guilty. "No one should allow workmen in a building that isn't secure," he said. "We'll be reviewing the plans—"

The reporter replaced him on the screen. "The Department of Inspectional Services had no immediate comment. In other earthquake news—"

"Son of a bitch!" Ross exploded as Tobias snapped off the set. "That wasn't what I meant and he knew it."

"Have some more Scotch," said Tobias. "You could use it."

"I could use a new construction manager. If I carry any weight around there, the contractor's going to fire Greg tomorrow morning. But Scotch will do for now. Thanks."

"Ross," Victoria said anxiously. "You're not really worried about this, are you? It will be forgotten in all the other earthquake news. There were far worse incidents than yours."

Ross kissed Victoria's cheek. "I'm concerned about it, but you shouldn't be. I'll take care of it. I won't stay for dinner, though; I'm going back to the office for a while."

"Mr. Hayward," the butler said from the doorway. "There's a telephone call for you."

Ross thought of reporters. "I'm not here."

"It's Mrs. Fraser," said the butler.

"Take it in here," Victoria said quickly. "We'll be in the dining room."

Ross grabbed the telephone. "I saw the television report," Katherine said. "I was worried about you. I called your house, and your office... Why didn't anyone mention the work on the footings?"

"It hasn't started." Listening to her low voice, he wanted her so desperately his words seemed to stumble. "They'd rescheduled it for next week."

"Then it might not come up at all. But—if people are looking for reasons, do you have to say your engineer was at fault so no one looks any further and maybe gets to the footings?"

She'd seen it all, Ross thought; the whole of his dilemma. Protect Victoria and the company by keeping the footings out of the story; or point to them to get his own company off the hook for the design of the temporary beams. "We may be able to blame the earthquake by itself. Especially since there was damage in the whole area."

"The reporter made you seem responsible."

"He was looking for a good story and he distorted what I said. Victoria thinks it's too small a disaster to be remembered. She may be right."

"But she doesn't know about the footings. Ross, is there any way I can help you?"

"You can come to me. Help me get through this mess and whatever it leads to. I need you. I love you, I want you with me, I want you part of me."

He heard her long sigh. "I'd come now. But it would be the way we were before."

"That's not good enough. I said *part of me.*"

"I haven't heard from Craig or Hank. I'm still waiting."

"And calling me up."

"I was worried about you. I can't just turn off my feelings—"

"Katherine, there has to be a time when you make up your mind, in spite of Craig. You can't wait indefinitely."

"No . . ."

"Well, when is it? When will you say it's been long enough?"

"I don't know. That's one of the things I'm thinking about. Ross, please trust me. I have to do this. If you don't want me to call you anymore, I won't."

"Of course I want you to call me. I reach for the phone a dozen times a day to call *you*. Whenever something happens, good or bad, I turn around to tell you—and you're not there."

"But you don't call."

"No. Because I'd begin pushing you about timetables and decisions, the way I just did. And then you'd tell me this is something you have to do, the way you just did. And I understand that. Katherine, you're a remarkable woman; you've made a new life with pride and dignity from the rubble your husband left behind; you hold up your head and face whatever comes instead of hiding or running away; you're honest with yourself. I don't want to try to force you to see things as I'd like you to see them. I don't want to stand in your way and prevent you from finishing what you've begun. Does that make sense to you?"

"Yes," Katherine said softly. "Do you know, the more you tell me what you want for me, the more I miss you?"

"I hope so," he said, and she heard the smile in his voice.

When they said goodbye, nothing had changed, Katherine was no closer to coming to him than she had been before, but Ross was still smiling when he stopped in the dining room to say goodnight to Victoria and Tobias, and her words—*I miss you*—stayed with him as he went back to the office to organize his strategy on the Macklin Building.

"Sit down," said Derek, gesturing toward a chair while continuing to talk on the telephone. Ross chose one of the couches at the other end of the office, leafing through a copy of *International Architect* while waiting for his brother's conversation to wind to its leisurely end. The office was in glass and chrome and burgundy leather: desk, chairs, and conference table at one end, and simulated living room at the other. Track lighting illuminated blown-up photographs of bridges, shopping malls, aqueducts, office buildings, and expressways built by the Hayward

Corporation since its founding in 1918. In a corner, almost hidden by a massive Ficus tree, was a photograph of the Macklin Building.

"Well, what a pleasure," Derek said, swiveling his chair to face Ross. "You don't often pay us a visit. Haven't seen you since you went to Paris, in fact. Place des Vosges, wasn't it?"

Ross closed the magazine. "And Menton."

"So I heard. Melanie said the youngsters had a fine time."

"We all had a fine time."

"And did Katherine finally learn to order from French menus? They always used to intimidate her."

"Katherine learns whatever she puts her mind to," Ross said evenly. "She's not easily intimidated. I came to talk about the earthquake damage in the Macklin Building."

Derek's faint smile did not change. "I heard about it. We had some damage, too: displacement of a roadbed in Daly City; nothing serious. Well? What is it you want to talk about?"

"Two workmen were injured by falling concrete. I had a letter this morning from their lawyer; they're going to sue my firm, and me, for negligence. Five million dollars."

"Insane. Are they permanently disabled?"

"I haven't talked to their doctors. I doubt it and their lawyer isn't claiming it—yet. He mentioned time lost from work, medical bills, rehabilitation therapy, psychological trauma, pain and suffering to the family, and one or two others. It's all in the letter; I brought you a copy, since you're an interested party."

Derek shook his head. "Nothing to do with it." He was no longer smiling. "I haven't much time; is there anything else you wanted to tell me?"

"You know there is." From his briefcase, Ross brought out photographs he had taken on Friday and printed in the office darkroom Saturday morning. He laid them on the coffee table one at a time. "The south side of the Macklin Building, showing settling cracks in the wall... the first-floor interior where the wall and ceiling separated; also the collapsed ceiling... basement floor showing the amount of column settling. And this is the report of the foundation engineers who tested the soil and inspected the footings in July. You can keep it. But don't take the time to read it now; you already know what it says."

Expressionless, Derek gazed at him. He had not glanced at the photographs. "I have no idea what it says. Nor any interest in it."

Ross closed his briefcase. "I've contracted to stabilize the foundation by pumping concrete under and around the column footings; it should be done by mid-October. I'm paying for it. And I'll pay for repair of the earthquake damage. But I'm going to try to settle the suit out of court, and whatever that costs, you're going to pay half. Or you and Dad, if you can get it from him."

"What the hell are you babbling about?" Derek's voice was contemptuous but Ross noted he was not demanding that he leave. "I'm going to pay? Like hell I am. You can clean up your own shit."

"It's yours, too, and you'll help clean it up. Those columns wouldn't have settled if you'd built them the way they were originally designed."

Derek shoved back his chair and strode the length of the office to pick up the photographs. He leafed through them. A corner of his mouth twitched, then he forced it still. "Would you care to explain what these have to do with me? You're demanding that I hand over a couple of million—for what? To help you pay off a pair of cretins who see dollar signs because their fucking lawyer says they can hold you hostage? Why in hell would I touch that with a ten-foot pole? Brotherly love?"

Ross stood, and their eyes were level. "To keep it out of court."

"What the hell do I care whether it goes to court? What do you care? Let it go; you'll win. There was an earthquake, dozens of buildings were damaged, a few people were killed, a few more were hurt. So what? That's what people expect. There's a mob of lawyers out there giving dumb workmen visions of sugarplums, and engineers and architects are going to go down like tenpins, unless they're smart. So get yourself a sharp lawyer—not Claude; he's too straight—and if you're still worried, find an inspector whose wife wants a vacation in St. Croix and buy them one. He'll swear to the design of your temporary support beams and he won't look any further; he'll say it was the earthquake. Christ, why do I have to explain all this? It's mother's milk in this business."

"That's not the way I work. Who got the vacation when you changed the specs on the Macklin Building?"

Derek flung the photographs on the table. "Listen, you sanctimonious ass, the Hayward Corporation wasn't built by prayer; I doubt your little firm was either. But I don't ask where you put your dollars; and it's none of your business where I put mine. You look after yourself, little brother, and don't worry about the family corporation. The value of your stock is just fine."

"Until city inspectors start looking at damaged buildings where there are lawsuits. What's mother's milk for city officials, for God's sake? They're primed to look for fraud, and sixteen years doesn't mean a thing if they find it; there's no way the Hayward Corporation could come out of that clean. That means you and Dad. Hugh had died two years earlier; the two of you were in charge. And it won't be as easy to brush off the city as it was to get rid of me when I asked you about it."

"We told you there was nothing to worry about. We believed that."

"You lied. Both of you."

"Don't call me a liar!" Derek lashed out, but his eyes were focused inward; he was weighing his options. Of course they had to keep it out of court; no one had more to lose than Derek Hayward, who was liable because he'd built the damn building, and also could be cut out of his grandmother's will, if she found out. But Derek knew Ross was worried about Victoria for a different reason; like a fucking white knight he wanted to shield her from the whole mess. Which was why he wanted to keep it out of court as much as Derek did, perhaps even more. Good enough, Derek concluded, and almost casually called Ross's bluff. "It was Craig's little game; we had nothing to do with it. If you want to pay off those workmen, go ahead. But you're on your own. I'd let it go to court."

"Craig had nothing to do with changing those specs."

"Is that a revelation from on high? Craig floating down on a sunbeam to whisper sweetly in your ear?"

"No, damn it, it came from you: that pack of lies you told Katherine about the sailing accident. The sanitized version of your fight with Craig— that he didn't like the way you managed the Macklin Building. Why didn't you tell her you accused Craig of being a crook? Why didn't you tell her the story you and Dad made up the next day for my benefit? For months you'd been trying to make her see Craig through your eyes and hate him the way you do. There was your big chance to completely blacken him, and you passed it up. You never pass up a chance like that; why did you do it then? Because you couldn't take the chance she'd tell Victoria. Or me."

"Horseshit. That's one of Katherine's fairy tales. I told her Craig lost his temper when I showed him up in front of Jennifer."

"That's a lie."

"I told you—don't call me a liar! Are you so besotted you don't know she makes up stories as she goes along? She lies when it suits her, to get what she wants, and now she wants to get back at me by twisting what I told her about her spineless husband. She must regret her passion more than I realized—those worshipful eyes, her extraordinary body, offering itself—"

Rage exploded in Ross; the room spun in red streaks. "You son of a bitch!" He grabbed Derek's jacket, jerking him toward him, but Derek wrenched free and backed away, his face taut, his breath coming in hoarse gasps.

"Don't touch me—God damn you—if you come near me—!"

Ross caught himself. Breathing hard, he flexed his fingers. *Don't hit him; don't let him make you react.*

His voice still hoarse, Derek said, "Everyone lies. Craig made up a whole new life, all lies. And even before that, the two of you, all those years we were growing up, turning Victoria against me with lies... so you never had to fight for anything..." His eyes darkened as he stopped himself. "Fairy tales," he said, his voice rasping. "Like the one you brought me today. I don't believe in fairy tales."

Deliberately he turned his back and walked to his desk. Ross stood where he was, his thoughts racing. *Turning Victoria against me... you never had to fight for anything.* The room had stopped spinning; the red streaks of his rage were gone. His muscles loosened and he felt the lightness that came when he cut the motor on his boat and silence descended. He looked at Derek's rigid figure: the tight, narrow face and contemptuous smile that hid a maelstrom of anger, competitiveness, and fear.

Fairy tales, he thought, hearing again the fury in his brother's voice as he had said it. But it was Derek's life, he realized, that was the fairy tale: an intricate web of wishes and fabrications to get attention, love, admiration, deference from his father and grandparents, clients, business associates, women, even—though Ross had never suspected it—his cousin and his brother.

Ross looked back through the years, as far back as he could remember. Derek had perfected his skill at manipulating people by practicing on his family, forcing Ross and Craig to feel they were competing with him— and losing. And so from the time he was a boy, Ross had feared and envied his brother, longing to have his compelling power and magnetism, even, sometimes, his single-minded ruthlessness that seemed to sweep all obstacles aside. But at the same time his fierce dislike of Derek had grown and he had tried to keep a distance between them—even refusing to consider working in the family company because that would have meant working with Derek. But there could never be enough distance, even when he moved to New York. All his life, Ross had been tied to his brother by the strongest bonds of envy and hatred.

Now, for the first time, he saw that Derek's magnetism was desperation, that the brother he had feared and envied was a chameleon furiously plotting, lying, changing colors to snare and impress others. With a shock he realized how much Derek was like Craig. No wonder they hated each other; they understood each other too well.

"Well?" Derek demanded. Usually he used silence as a weapon, making others so nervous they would say anything to break it. But Ross had outwaited him. "Well?" he repeated.

Ross picked up his briefcase. "I think we've finished for today. I have work to do." He saw uncertainty flicker in his brother's eyes. He had never seen that before, and he knew that Derek was fighting to regain his balance: to recover from that brief moment of letting down his guard, and to recapture control of their conversation. But Ross would not let him. For once he had called Derek's bluff, and he was the one who was leaving.

Derek watched him cross the room and open the office door. "What the hell are you going to do?" he burst out.

From the doorway, Ross looked at him thoughtfully, without answering.

"You're not going to let it go to court!"

"I'm not sure. I have to make some plans. You'll hear from me." He opened the door. "Good luck with repairing your displaced roadway. It's always best to have a straight path, isn't it?"

He strode down the corridor. As he reached the elevator, the image of his boat returned: pushing away from the dock with no constraints or ties. Whatever he needed to do, however he had to do it, he had left the bonds of competitiveness and envy behind. Derek could no longer touch him; he was free.

Victoria handed the portfolio of Picasso lithographs to Katherine. They sat together on the silk couch in the library; a low fire burned in the fireplace though the evening was mild. "A wonderful collection," she said. "Hugh and I bought them in Paris so long ago I can't remember. I'll miss looking at them each day."

"So why donate them now?" Tobias asked as he poked a log and laid a new one upon it. "Put them in your will. The museum can wait."

"Board members are expected to make donations to set an example. Besides, I want to be able to see people enjoying them."

Katherine looked up from a picture of a bull and a young woman that would have been called obscene if anyone but Picasso had drawn it. "Why are you doing this now?" she asked.

"Because I'm getting old and the years vanish and there's so much I still want to do. I've promised our nineteenth-century collection to the Palace of the Legion of Honor and the rest to the Museum of Modern Art and I want to space it out so I can see them all mounted, and hear experts pontificate about the Hayward collection and my generosity."

"I mean, why do you talk about dying? It makes me think I'm about to lose you."

"Dear Katherine, I'm shockingly healthy; I don't intend to die for years. Although worrying about you and Ross makes me feel very old."

"That's blackmail," Katherine said.

"The older you get, my dear, the more weapons you are willing to use to get what you want."

"Actually," Tobias put in. "We are most worried right now about Ross. Mournfully, he quoted, "'. . . the shriveled, hopping, loud and trouble-some insects of the hour.' Certain injured workmen, that is, and their lawyers."

"The ones in the Macklin Building?" Katherine asked. "What about them?"

"They are suing Ross," said Victoria bitterly. "For five million dollars."

Katherine drew a sharp breath. "Has he said how he'll fight it?"

Tobias gave Katherine a keen look. "If it goes to court, which it may not, he'll say the support beams were strong enough and anchored prop-erly, and the damage was caused by the earthquake. Is there any other explanation?"

Five million dollars, Katherine thought. And no one to help him. She put the portfolio of lithographs on the table and stared into the fire. *What do I do now? Ross wants to protect Victoria . . . but I want to protect Ross. Or at least do whatever I can to help him.*

Which means telling Victoria and Tobias, because they're the ones who can do something for him.

And, after all, why shouldn't they know? Victoria is a pretty tough lady. Ross told me that himself, in France. *It's not accurate to think of her as a helpless little old lady who lies like a crumpled piece of tissue paper while the busy world passes her by.* But still he thinks she needs to be shielded.

He thought I did, too, when he found Elissa.

But he underestimated us. We're stronger than he thinks. And families should be told, when one of them is threatened; they shouldn't be pre-vented from helping each other.

But who am I, to make that decision? Maybe Ross had other reasons for keeping quiet; how do I know what I might be starting? For the first time in months Katherine felt uncomfortable, almost like an outsider again, involved in events she shouldn't know about, telling a story she had no right to tell, violating a confidence without any idea what train of events she might be setting in motion.

I don't know what to do!

"Well, my dear," said Tobias mildly. "Is there a way we can help you solve whatever dilemma keeps you in silent dialogue with yourself?"

Katherine started. "I'm sorry. I was being rude."

"No, no. Something is troubling you and you are not sure whether you should tell us. Of course we think you should, because we love you. But you must do whatever you think best for all of us. Your whole family."

The weight of the dilemma slipped from Katherine; she began to smile. *Your whole family.* She wasn't an outsider; she hadn't been for a long time. *I'm sorry, Ross. I hope you'll understand. I love you; I want to help you; and I want Victoria and Tobias to be able to help you, too.*

"There is another defense," she said at last. "But Ross won't use it."

"Yes?" Tobias was alert.

"And that is—?" Victoria demanded.

"The building was weak," Katherine said, choosing her words carefully. "The support columns, or the footings under them, weren't as strong or as deep as they should have been. Ross suspected it and when he had the building checked in July he found he was right. But the repair work kept being delayed, and then the earthquake came. The problem wasn't the design of the temporary beams; it was in the building itself."

"*That's* why he bought it!" exclaimed Tobias. "He suspected—"

"Just one moment!" Victoria raised a peremptory hand. "Katherine, are you suggesting the Macklin Building is substandard? It was built by the Hayward Corporation!"

"I know. The specifications were altered to cut costs."

"But the building inspectors...?" Tobias asked.

"Ross thinks they must have been bribed."

"Rubbish," declared Victoria. "Curt or Jason would have known about it."

Katherine nodded.

"Curt," Victoria said, her voice blank.

Katherine nodded again.

They were silent, locked in their own thoughts. The butler appeared in the doorway and announced dinner. Victoria roused herself and as they moved into the dining room, she put her hand on Katherine's arm. "This has been difficult for you. Ross told you he thought he could keep it a secret?"

"He was going to have the building repaired as part of the renovation. He didn't want you to face a scandal—"

"—in my declining years," Victoria finished, scoffing. "Of course I am not nearly as delicate as my grandson thinks; how fortunate that you knew that. But my dear Katherine, what a dilemma—keeping Ross's

secret or telling me! Thank you, my dear, for choosing me. I promise
you will not be sorry. But of course now that you know I will not faint
upon the spot, you must tell us everything, wherever it leads. We want
to know it all."

As Katherine smiled gratefully, Tobias asked, "How long has he known,
or suspected?"

There was a pause before Katherine replied, "He's suspected, for sixteen
years."

"Sixteen—!" Victoria exclaimed. "And told none of us! He should be
ashamed of himself!"

"No, that's not fair. He couldn't tell you then, because—"

"The sailing accident," Tobias broke in. "That's when he began to
suspect? You told me Craig and Derek quarreled about the Macklin
Building."

"Good God in Heaven!" Victoria burst out. She whipped open her
napkin and laid it across her lap. "Was I the only one who knew nothing?"

"I know no more than that," soothed Tobias. "Katherine. Please."

"Craig accused Derek of altering the specifications on the footings in
the Macklin Building; Derek came back and said *Craig* had done it, and
bribed an inspector to approve the work."

"But more likely it was Derek." Spearing a wedge of mango, Tobias
had a gleam of discovery in his eye. "Always was impatient—and thinks
he's above the law."

Victoria toyed with her food. "And of course Curt knew about it. He
and Derek always worked closely in those days; I remember how confident
I felt; Hugh was dead but my son and my grandson were there... My
son and my grandson!" she repeated contemptuously.

Her face was drawn, her eyes looking to the distance. "Hugh always
insisted on safety. Our reputation, he said; the lives of the people who
trusted our buildings... He never violated that trust. He was scrupulous
in following city regulations, earthquake safety codes—he even helped
write some of them! And now... my son and my grandson... cutting
corners... bribery... Dishonorable! Despicable! Playing on the desperation or greed of others... Damnation!" she burst out. "An old woman
should be able to relax; she should be able to trust her heirs to protect
her name and the company she and her husband built from nothing and
made famous and respected...!"

"This old woman," Tobias said pointedly, "insists on being chairman
of the board of the Hayward Corporation."

She looked at him imperiously. "I am the majority stockholder in the
corporation."

"Then perhaps you are not ready to relax."

"Ah." She gave a small laugh. "You have a point." The butler offered a silver platter of veal and tiny potato puffs to each of them. Serving herself, Victoria frowned thoughtfully, then said, "Of course the suit against Ross cannot go to trial. It is intolerable to contemplate others poking through our affairs. So we must settle it out of court, which will require... Tobias, Ross said the workmen were injured but not crippled. What is a realistic sum their lawyer would be likely to accept?"

"Perhaps a quarter of a million."

"And it is Derek's responsibility. Do we agree on that? Katherine? Didn't you bring us this information so we could bring pressure to bear on Derek?"

"Not only to settle the suit," said Tobias quickly, "but also to pay for the repair of the building."

Uncomfortably, Katherine said, "I'm not sure what I expected. I just thought you should know, so Ross wouldn't be alone."

"Ah." Victoria sighed with satisfaction. "Then we must decide what to do. Obviously Derek must assume the responsibility for various expenditures. Can he be blackmailed?"

"Good heavens!" Tobias exclaimed. "After seventy-five years, to find I still do not know my own sister..."

"Surprise keeps us young," Victoria said. "It's the glue that holds people together." She smiled at him with such tenderness that Katherine felt a spurt of envy. After years of separate lives, how lucky they were, she thought, to find companionship and love.

"'He is as deaf to angels as an oak,'" Tobias quoted. "How do you reach a man who loves no one, who has more money than anyone needs, and who finds morality boring? His only enduring passion is power. Might we threaten that?"

"Derek runs the Hayward Corporation admirably," Victoria said. "He makes a great deal of money for all of us."

"Yes, yes, very practical. But—"

"In fact," she declared suddenly, "if I'd paid more attention to what he and Curt were doing, all along, none of this might have happened. I've been complacent; quite satisfied to let them run the company—"

"Come, come!" Tobias exclaimed. "You cannot blame yourself. We all are responsible; none of the board members, myself included, asked enough questions. Now we will. Derek's leadership has threatened us with a scandal, possibly a large cash outlay, serious damage to our name, perhaps the ruin of Ross's reputation. I must say, when Derek does something, the repercussions are not small. And I have another thought.

How do we know where else Derek has taken it upon himself to cut costs? What other surprises might be in store for us? Perhaps our Derek needs his wings clipped."

"Perhaps he needs an overseer," suggested Victoria.

"Ah." Tobias cogitated. "It would be better if we had proof. Katherine says he accused Craig, and Craig is not here to refute that."

Katherine had been watching the two of them. Now, hesitantly, she said, "Wouldn't building inspectors have forms to sign, approving the jobs they inspect?"

"Indeed!" Tobias tipped back his chair, his beard wagging vigorously. "On file at City Hall. Indeed." Then he frowned. "Why wouldn't Ross have dug them up to convince Derek to pay?"

"He wasn't going to ask him," Katherine said. "He didn't want to stir anything up, since he thought the repair would be part of the renovation." Tobias shook his head. "Stubborn."

"We shall deal with that," Victoria said calmly. "Tobias, dear, would you call Claude and Ross and arrange a conference? The time has come for the chairman of the board to make some decisions."

Leslie called on the weekend. "I have no problems left. Tell me yours. Unless you've solved each and every one—?"

"Hardly," laughed Katherine. "But I have no new ones to offer."

"Then we'll share glad tidings instead. I got your grandma's Halloween invite today; it sounds like one of those parties people will talk about for years. What are you wearing?"

"I don't know. I don't much like costume parties."

"It's not costume and you'll like it. Claude says she and Hugh used to give one every year and those who weren't invited committed suicide, went into mourning, or slunk away in humiliation. Since we are among the favored throng, all we have to do is look magnificent."

"Leslie, where can I get a magnificent dress at a less than magnificent price?"

"Have you tried Val's?"

"Not lately. Their prices have tripled."

"Well, I have some hot information. The prices were tripled by a new manager who took one look at those designer seconds and went gung ho for profits. He has been booted. His replacement is at this very moment marking everything down. Get there early Monday, before the mob scene. I'm off; dinner with Claude. Oh. No word from Craig, I take it."

"No. You'd be one of the first to know."

"I hope so. See you soon."

No word from Craig. Katherine had been so sure he would call within a few days of her trip to Calgary that she had sat by the telephone, jumping every time it rang, just as she had a year and a half earlier, in Vancouver. But the silence was unbroken. Back where we started, she thought.

No, not the start, she corrected herself. Because she knew, from Ross, that Craig wanted to come back. Whether he stole the money or was framed, he wanted to come back and make amends for leaving her.

Well, jibed an inner voice; isn't that nice of him?

Her thoughts argued with each other: all the voices of those who had urged her to make up her mind, to do something, to divorce Craig, to cut herself off from the past. So what if parts of it were still dangling; so what if her marriage was unfinished; so what if—?

What's the hurry?

Why were they all rushing her? Craig had been gone a little over a year. She and Ross had been together less than four months—and for the last three weeks they'd been apart.

If I want to take some time to think about all this—sort out who I am and where I'm going—what's wrong with that? Why is everyone rushing me?

"Mom?" said Todd. "Could we get started? You said you'd help us, and all this stuff is due on Monday."

"Right away," Katherine said. "Give me a minute to clean up."

She found the two of them waiting for her at the kitchen table, surrounded by bits and pieces of clay models they had volunteered to make for a school diorama on space exploration.

"Actually, we volunteered because we knew you'd help us," Jennifer confessed as they watched their mother's skillful fingers fashion a clay model of Voyager II. "We didn't think you'd mind too much."

"I don't mind at all," Katherine said. "I'm having a wonderful time."

"Really?" Jennifer asked. "How come I don't think it's so much fun?"

"Because for you it's a school assignment. For me it's like going back to mud pies and childhood."

"Oh." Jennifer thought about it. "I don't want to be a child again. Why do you?"

Katherine kept herself from smiling. "I had less to worry about in those days."

"We have a *lot* to worry about," said Todd. Looking intently at his slightly deformed model of the Columbia space shuttle, he added, "Carrie and Jon brought Ross to the club yesterday; he went swimming with us and bought us lemonade."

Katherine's heart skipped. "I hope you thanked him."

"He asked how you are."

"And what did you say?"

"That you miss him."

"Todd!"

"He said he missed you, too," said Jennifer.

"So do Carrie and Jon," added Todd. "They wanted to know where you were. They like you."

"They got used to all of us being together," Jennifer explained.

"The same way we did," said Todd.

"I like Ross," Jennifer commented.

"Me, too," Todd chimed in. "He's nice to be with."

They were tossing the conversation back and forth like a beach ball. "Have you two rehearsed this?" Katherine asked.

"We talked about it," Jennifer admitted. "We told Ross about the computer program we're writing."

Katherine pictured the three of them talking together and felt jealous of her children. "The one for math?" she asked.

"No." Todd looked at Jennifer. "The one to see if you'd marry Ross or get together with Dad again."

The clay model slipped and she grabbed it. "What are you talking about?"

"We made a formula. Dad equals X, and Ross equals Y, and the number of months Dad is away equals N, and the times you ask us about Carrie and Jon when you really want to hear about Ross, equals R, but we haven't got an answer yet—"

"I'm not surprised." Katherine went to the sink and rinsed off her hands. "Why don't you finish up? I guess I'm getting a little old for a whole afternoon of clay modeling."

"You said you were having a wonderful time," Jennifer reminded her. "Mud pies and all that."

"I was just reminded that I'm a long way from mud pies and all that." Standing at the sink Katherine studied them. "What do you think I should do?" she asked abruptly.

Taken aback, they stared at her. "I'd like Dad home again," Todd said finally. "The way everything was."

"I guess I would, too," said Jennifer slowly. "Except I don't think things would be the same. Ever again."

"Sure they would," Todd said. "Oh, you mean our house? We'd build another one. That's easy."

"No." Jennifer met her mother's eyes. "I don't think Mother and Daddy feel the same way about things anymore. Neither do we."

"So?" Todd demanded. "We're older."

Furiously, Jennifer dashed a piece of clay against the wall. "I don't trust him anymore!" she cried and burst into tears.

Katherine swept her into her arms and held her tight. "Jennifer," she whispered. "Dear Jennifer—"

"I'm sorry!" Jennifer sobbed. "I'm an awful person to say that! I shouldn't even think it—!"

"You're not awful. If someone makes you unhappy, it's natural to worry that he might do it again. It doesn't mean you're awful. It just means you're worried about what's going to happen; you're not sure of the future. And once upon a time you thought you *were* sure." Katherine pulled back from Jennifer and said seriously, "That's what childhood really is: a time when you think you're sure of tomorrow. And I guess, in that way, you aren't a child anymore."

None of us is, Katherine thought later, sitting at her worktable. We all grew up when Craig left us. And Jennifer is right: nothing can ever be the same again.

She bent to her work, concentrating on linking together the segments of an amethyst bracelet. By now she was making jewelry for four small stores, and belts for Heath's. She was earning almost enough to rent a larger apartment, though not yet enough to take time each day to make enough jewelry to send Henri—and also other designs that crowded her imagination: wrist watches, pen and pencil sets, desk sets, even candlesticks and napkin rings. Her fingers itched to make them all. She might still feel trapped by Craig, but in the evenings, after her other work was done, when her pencil flew across empty expanses of paper, she was free of everything, soaring in a world of her own making, without limits or bounds. Someday she would make them all. Now she could not afford the time, or the materials.

But—Victoria was giving a party. She ran her fingers over the square white parchment envelope addressed in gothic lettering, and reread the invitation inside.

"'So hallow'd and gracious is the time,'" it quoted from Shakespeare, and Katherine smiled at the evidence of Tobias' hand. "All Hallows Eve...a time for celebrating dreams...for dining and dancing in the Fairmont Ballroom and Garden, Saturday, October 30, at 9:30 P.M."

For Victoria's party, she thought, she might make some jewelry for herself. Eventually she could sell it, perhaps in Paris. She'd never made herself a special piece. And if she found a magnificent dress...why not?

The telephone rang and, thinking of jewelry, she answered it. "My dear," Victoria said. "I'm calling to invite you—"

"The invitation came in the mail," Katherine said, "and of course I'll come; how could I stay away from your party?"

"Party? Oh, yes: All Hallows. Tobias' secretary sent those out; we have been occupied with other matters. Katherine, there is a time for parties and there is a time for business. I am calling about business. There will be a special meeting of the board of directors of the Hayward Corporation, next Thursday. I would like you to be there."

"But... I'm not a member. I know nothing about it. Why would I... why would you want me there?"

"Because you are part of us. Because if it were not for you, and the information you brought us the other day, there would be no meeting. Because I want you beside me. I have not forgotten the frivolity of the All Hallows ball. We will have that, too. But this is more important. And it could be extremely important to you. Please, Katherine. Ten thirty, Thursday morning, the twenty-eighth. And please don't be late."

Hanging up, Katherine stared into space. Ross would be there. And Derek. And the shadow of Craig. And Katherine Fraser—still finding out exactly where she fit in with all of them, for now and the future.

CHAPTER 20

IT was the first time since Christmas that they were all together. Jason and Ann flew in from Maine, and Curt from Palm Springs; Ross walked the mile from his office near Telegraph Hill to the Hayward Corporation's offices in Embarcadero Center where, on the thirtieth floor, Derek strolled the hundred paces from his office to the conference room; Tobias and Victoria were driven in a limousine from Pacific Heights, stopping in the financial district to pick up Claude; Katherine took a bus from her apartment.

They were there because Victoria had summoned them as directors and shareholders of the Hayward Corporation. Refusing to give a reason, or an advance agenda, she had simply demanded their presence. And so they came, greeting each other with questions as they poured coffee from the large pot on the slate-covered sideboard ("Enough for all day," Derek muttered to his father) and took their seats at the long rosewood conference table where each place was furnished with a pad of paper, newly sharpened pencils, and a water glass.

Ross poured a cup of coffee and took it to Katherine, who was sitting in a corner of the room. When she thanked him, he shook his head. "I'm the one to thank you. I wanted to call you, but it seemed better to wait until today. I was wrong about Victoria, and you knew it; you did what I should have done long ago."

"I'm glad it's all right," she replied. The coffee cup trembled in her hand as she fought back the longing for him that pulsed through her. "I thought you might be angry. And I didn't know what I might be starting— with the family."

415

"You started quite a bit. But I wasn't angry; how could I be angry with you? You took the burden from me. What I really feel is a strong desire to hold you in my arms." He saw the startled look in her eyes, and smiled. "I see I'm not the only one."

Tobias came up and almost apologetically suggested Ross sit down. "Claude and Victoria will be here any minute," he said. Ross touched Katherine's hand briefly, then took his place at the table, where the others were all talking at once.

"...heard from Craig," Ann suggested tentatively. "Why else would she call us?"

Brusquely, Jason growled, "Probably called his grandmother so she'd smooth his way back to the company. But he's wrong if he thinks I can just forget, as if he'd never run away..."

"I doubt he'll want to come back," said Curt. "Derek runs the company and Craig would know there's no place for him. Though Victoria may try to force us to take him...Or she's simply rewriting her will."

Simply! thought Derek.

Ann twisted her hands. "I don't like the way any of you are talking. We have to welcome him back—"

"Welcome," Curt snorted. "What has he done to deserve a welcome from any of us?"

"He doesn't have to do anything," Ann replied with spirit. "You don't have to earn your way into your own family."

"You have to earn your way everywhere," said Derek contemptuously. He was tense, every nerve taut and ready—to react, retreat, attack, plan. He didn't know what was happening—a rare and infuriating situation— and so he had to be prepared to respond to whatever was proposed: to buy Craig off before he had a chance to dilute Derek's power in the company; to handle the Macklin problem if Ross had gone running to Victoria with the story; to counter any rearrangement of Victoria's will that could inhibit his total control of the company once she was dead.

His eyes met Tobias'. "If only I were a playwright," said Tobias with relish. "What I could do with all of you!"

"Tobias," Ross said. "That doesn't calm the atmosphere."

"True," said Tobias penitently, and fell silent, but the atmosphere was no calmer. Katherine felt it, sharp with speculation and apprehension, as if hundreds of tiny knives were flashing beneath the fluorescent lights that reflected on paneled walls and the rich rosewood table. It touched her, too, in her chair in a corner, away from the table, as everyone shot covert glances at her while hazarding suppositions about Craig. Across the table, Ross watched her and when their eyes met she stirred restlessly with vivid memories of their times together. Derek sat a few feet away, and she was aware of his glances, not only because Ross was there, but because his wariness was unnerving. She had not seen him in months and he reminded her of a tightrope walker—thinner than she remembered, withdrawn into himself, rigidly controlled as he scribbled on his pad of paper.

Victoria walked in, followed by Claude, and stood at the head of the table. Wearing a black silk suit with an ivory blouse, and a bar pin of silver filigree with coral that Katherine had made her, she stood regally erect, her eyes piercing and unsmiling, resting briefly on each of them.

Stiffly formal, as if giving advance warning of the bombshell she was about to throw, she said, "The special meeting of the board of directors of the Hayward Corporation is called to order. Tobias will take the minutes. I have called this meeting because I have recently gained information which is dangerous, disgraceful, and repugnant. It demands immediate action. Our agenda is to deal with this information, which affects the reputation of the corporation, its liability for past misdeeds" —Derek's mouth tightened— "and its future shape and direction."

"Future shape and direction?" Curt queried. "Not in one meeting, without advance notice so we can prepare suggestions."

"Perhaps," said Victoria distinctly. "I was not understood. I gained this information only recently. It is intolerable. And as long as I am alive and own fifty percent of this corporation, when I find something intolerable, it will be changed. Immediately."

No one spoke. Standing perfectly straight, hands clasped loosely before her, she was imperious and formidable. Katherine loved her and was in awe of her. She looked at the others: Ann and Jason puzzled, Curt suspicious, Derek withdrawn, Ross, Tobias, and Claude watchful—they know, Katherine thought; they know what this is about.

"Claude?" Victoria said. "If you please." She sat in the wing chair at the head of the table, her head high, observing all of them.

Claude was seated at the other end of the table. "Sixteen years ago," he began in his resonant courtroom voice that reminded Katherine of the first time she had heard him, at dinner in Victoria's apartment, "the Hayward Corporation built the Macklin Building on Mission Street. There were delays due to a strike, and to make up for lost time and money, the specifications were altered in such a way that the building was constructed in violation of city codes."

"What's that?" Jason said. "Nothing like that ever—"

"Highly unlikely," Curt rumbled. "Claude, I'd like to know to whom you've been talking—"

"Over the years," Claude continued, "the building settled, causing cracks but no immediate danger, until the earthquake of October first, when part of the second floor collapsed, injuring two workmen. Together, they are suing for five million dollars." He raised his voice as Curt and Jason exploded with questions. "They are suing Ross, who bought the building some years ago, and his company, which designed its renovation. However, an investigation—and there will be one if this goes to trial—will reveal that the floor collapsed because of excessive settling of the foundation, which occurred because the Hayward Corporation, under Curt's presidency, with Derek as construction manager, knowingly and illegally put up a substandard building."

"You lying bastard," said Curt tightly.

Jason pounded the table. "Why the hell wasn't I told this?"

"Jason," said Ann. "It was 1966."

"God damn it, I know what year it was. But when did this happen? Before or after the sailing accident? Before or after we left for Maine?"

Derek seemed to pay no attention. He jotted an occasional note on his pad, but otherwise sat absolutely still.

Curt shoved back his chair and hunched his shoulders, facing Claude. "You won't be able to practice law in a stable of shit when I get through with you. I know a conspiracy when I see one; Derek warned me something was going on—"

"Curt!" Victoria flared. "How dare you speak like that in front of me? Sit still and behave yourself! I will accept an apology."

After the briefest of pauses, Curt said suavely, "I apologize. I forgot myself." He pulled his chair to the table, cursing whatever weakness in him made him feel, at sixty-four, like a schoolboy when his mother scolded him.

"It is curious, however," said Derek lightly, turning to a fresh sheet of paper, "that someone has fabricated this story at this time." He glanced up. "When Ross is being sued. Could that someone be his little friend and companion—trying to make sure we all contribute when the hat is passed—so she spreads a pack of lies that would virtually force us to pay and be silent?"

"You rotten son of a bitch!" Claude roared—calm, careful, unemotional Claude—violently shoving back his chair, beating Ross to it by a fraction of a second, shocking everyone into momentary paralysis.

In that small pause, Tobias sent his voice like a trumpet down the table. "'Envy's a coal come hissing hot from hell!'"

Nervous laughter erupted around the table. Victoria, who had briefly closed her eyes, fastened her gaze on Derek as she said, "Thank you, dear Tobias. And my dear attorney. Now may we continue?"

A mistake, Derek acknowledged. Unsure where Claude was heading, he'd thought he could force him to admit the danger to the corporation if they publicized the Macklin Building. He hadn't known that Claude, like Victoria, had been mesmerized by that woman. Fuck her. Every time he thought he knew what she could do, he discovered he'd under-estimated her again.

Claude had sat down, reluctantly passing up his first and probably only chance to feel his fist ram Derek's mouth. "I don't waste my time on a pack of lies," he said shortly. "The history of that building is no longer a secret."

Derek's pencil tapped his pad of paper, making small specks, like a storm of insects. His head had begun to pound from the frustration of not knowing what was happening, and he went on the attack, to retrieve what he could. "This has nothing to do with personalities," he told Victoria, as if they were alone in the room. "My first concern is the corporation. From what I've heard, Ross's engineer was incompetent in his renovation design and then had the misfortune to have it tested by an earthquake. Bad luck, but not ours; it wasn't our project or our en-gineer. We can't risk the corporation's reputation by accepting respon-sibility for the incompetence of others."

Jason glared at him. "*Whose* incompetence? What about yours and" —he shot a glance at Curt— "my brother's, sixteen years ago, that nobody bothered to tell me about?"

Derek's pencil skidded across the sheet of paper. "God damn it, you were vice-president; you hadn't run away yet to the backwoods of Maine. Weren't you paying attention to business? Were you blind? *Or are they lying?*"

"You and Curt," Jason muttered, his face dark with embarrassment and anger. "You worked together; shut me out."

"We filled a vacuum, Uncle," said Derek smoothly, feeling his power return as Jason's slipped. "You weren't paying attention."

"I was working on other projects! And I was worried about my daughter, sneaking out at night, after her mother and I ordered her to stay away from you!"

Derek gazed at him, his mouth twisted in a tight smile.

Claude's courtroom voice sliced between them. "I have a statement to read that will clarify matters and speed our proceedings." He picked up a sheet of paper. "This past week I located and interviewed a former city inspector. This is his statement, dated October 11, and signed Frank Beecher."

Derek's head jerked up, the tiny nerve beside his eye beginning to flicker.

"'On July 11 and 12, 1966,'" Claude read,

"Working for the city of San Francisco, I inspected the foundation columns and footings of the Macklin Building being constructed by the Hayward Corporation on Mission Street in San Francisco. I signed four reports saying they met the engineering specifications and plans already approved by the city and the state Seismic Commission. But the fact is, based on my experience, I thought the columns weren't sunk deep enough in that particular soil, and the amount of steel reinforcing in the footings didn't seem adequate. I checked the specs, and the columns and footings met them, so I thought the specs might have been changed after the city approved them. I talked this over with the construction manager, Derek Hayward. He suggested I approve the work in exchange for ten thousand dollars cash, and I did. That was my only contact with the Macklin Building."

No one moved. Jason's face was dark with fury. "Is that public knowledge—what he wrote?"

"Not yet," Claude replied.

"Then how did you know enough to look for this guy?"

"Katherine gave us the background—"

"*Katherine?*" said Derek. "So I had the right woman but the wrong man." His twisted smile flickered again, but Katherine heard a change in his voice; he was losing control. "It was her husband she was protecting, not Ross. How disappointing for Ross to discover she's still turning loyal somersaults for her runaway."

"Derek—!" Victoria began icily.

But Derek could not stop. "*None of you can believe that tripe!* Christ, only a lawyer could read it with a straight face. A child could see through it. Who the hell is Frank Beecher? A piece of fiction dreamed up by Craig and his faithful little woman, with Claude's help, to ruin me and bring their golden boy back in a blaze of glory. *Craig* was the one who altered the specs on the Macklin Building and paid off that beer-bellied liar to approve the whole thing; *that's* what we've known for sixteen years!"

A stunned silence settled on the room. No one moved. But in that moment, as in an earthquake, the power and alignments of the Hayward family shifted, and everyone felt it.

Victoria sighed. "Katherine," she said, without turning, "please sit beside me."

Katherine brought her chair to the table. Victoria's regal posture had not wavered, but her eyes had filled with tears, and her hand shook as she sipped from her glass of water. She reached for Katherine's hand and held it tightly. "Now," she announced, keeping her voice cool and steady, "I shall talk about the future structure of the Hayward Corporation."

The stillness in the room was as heavy as the morning fog. Katherine saw Derek and Curt exchange a glance, then look away, staring into space, waiting. "Hugh and his father built it," Victoria said. "Hugh made its reputation for excellence. And Derek, for the most part, has managed it brilliantly, built it to its present size, and increased the wealth of all of us."

She drank again from her glass. "Once, for a few years, I ran the Hayward Corporation. Ever since then, I have felt quite proprietary about it. And when Hugh died and left half his stock to me, it was his way of telling me that *the company and the family were mine to care for.*"

She contemplated them. "I waited almost fifty years to put my mark on this company. Even after Hugh died, I waited. Curt took over; when Jennifer died I lost interest... then Curt retired and Derek took his place... and things were going well..." Her voice had wandered into the past and she caught herself. "But now I'm getting old. I cannot leave to chance, or even to tomorrow, the affairs of a company and a family I love."

She put down her glass, her hand steady. "Everyone has always assumed Derek would have full control after I die, that I would divide my shares between him and Ross, and, since Curt gave Derek some of his shares when he retired, and also votes with him on all issues, Derek would have a clear majority. However, nothing is obvious any longer." She paused. Prolonging the drama, Katherine thought; just like Tobias. "Because of what we have discovered, I have decided on a complete reorganization of the company."

Curt grunted, as if he had been hit in the stomach. "Talked into it," he muttered.

"*I* decided!" Victoria blazed. "Is that clear? This is *my* decision, which I have worked out with our corporate attorney over the past two weeks. He will describe it to you. I want no questions or comments until he is finished. Is *that* clear?" Her breathing was rapid and she clung to Katherine's hand, but still she sat erect. "I expect silence and attention; I am tired of hearing you wrangle like children and I am disgusted by obscenities that demonstrate nothing more than infantilism and limited vocabularies." She paused. "Claude? If you please."

Claude unfolded a chart and pinned it to an easel beside him. "The

Hayward Corporation will be reorganized as the parent company of three subsidiaries: Hayward Construction, Hayward Development, and Hayward Associates. Victoria is transferring eighty-two percent of her stock in the Hayward Corporation to Ross, and eighteen percent to Derek. Added to the stock they already have, Ross will own fifty-one percent of the Hayward Corporation, and Derek twenty-nine percent. Curt will still have ten percent, and Jason and Ann, five percent each."

A rustle, like an autumn wind, moved through the room, but no one spoke.

"The Hayward Corporation will own fifty-one percent of each of the three subsidiaries. The remaining stock will be divided as follows:

"Derek will own forty-nine percent of Hayward Construction. He remains president and will continue to lead the company in large-scale construction, as in the past.

"Ross and Derek will divide equally forty-nine percent of the stock in Hayward Development, an entirely new company which will concentrate on major urban redevelopment projects.

"Ross will bring in his architectural firm, Ross Hayward Associates, as one of the subsidiaries, and will own forty-nine percent of it.

"I have corporate and tax details worked out in these booklets, which I'll give all of you later."

"He got everything," Curt seethed.

"Not at all," Derek said tightly, understanding more quickly than his father how masterfully it had been done. *Damn them. God damn their clever hides.* His thoughts twisted and turned, looking for a way out through the pounding in his head. The walls were closing in. He flung himself from his chair and left the room.

Claude barely paused. "Put simply, Ross has majority ownership and control of the parent company, the Hayward Corporation, which, in turn, controls three subsidiaries. I might add that all the shareholders in the Hayward Corporation will realize substantial financial gains by this reorganization."

But Ross has control, Katherine thought, understanding the rage in Derek's face. They took away the only thing that really means anything to him: his power. He'll make more money than before; he can build his bridges and highways and aqueducts; he'll still be pursued as a wealthy, charming bachelor. Outwardly his life won't change. Except that his brother is now at the center of power.

But—Ross hadn't wanted this. He hadn't wanted to be a part of the Hayward Corporation.

Katherine remembered the look between Victoria and Tobias. *Perhaps Derek needs his wings clipped.* They had talked Ross into it. Because there was no one else. And in fact, wasn't it what Ross had always wanted? A wealthy corporation, with the resources to build as he dreamed, to remake large landscapes, changing the look of cities...

"It won't work," said Curt, clipping his words. "I won't let you remake this company overnight, and I won't let you give it to Ross. He doesn't have the experience to run the whole show. The idea of a development subsidiary isn't bad, and if you want to merge Ross's firm with ours, I'd go along with that. But not with the rest of this scheme the three of you have cooked up." Coolly, he pushed back his chair. "That so-called statement of Beecher's doesn't mean a damn thing. You wouldn't let this go to trial; too much damage to the corporation. If I know Claude, he's already working on an out-of-court settlement, and of course, we'll contribute to that if Ross needs help in paying it. As for the rest, you've gone too far. I'm voting against it. And you need a unanimous vote of the shareholders for this kind of reorganization. Claude will remind you of that, in case you've forgotten the bylaws."

Victoria gazed down the table. "You were such a pleasant child, Curt. Hugh and I had twelve years of enjoyment from you before you grew hard and quite unlovable. Now I have discovered that you lied to Ross after the sailing accident, telling him there were no problems with the Macklin Building; you kept it from all of us, all these years; and you and Derek tried to shift the blame to Craig. You have been irresponsible and corrupt and I am ashamed of you, as my son and an officer of this corporation. Look at me when I speak to you! And listen carefully because what I am about to tell you is in your interest." She looked at Derek's empty chair. "Will someone find Derek and bring him back?"

Tobias slipped out and a moment later returned. "He'll be—"

Derek came in, his face remote, his eyes shadowed, and took his seat.

"First," Victoria said. "Derek and Curt will pay the cost of settling the suit against Ross. You were quite right, Curt; we intend to keep it out of court. You will pay whatever is required to do that. In addition," she said calmly, "you will vote for the reorganization of the corporation. The vote will be unanimous. If it is not, I will strip Derek of the presidency of the Hayward Corporation and appoint Ross in his place, and I will sign over to Ross my fifty-percent ownership in the corporation. Derek will then have no place in the company at all. Do you wish to have me clarify any of that or do you understand it?"

Derek sat without moving. His mind raced one last time around the walls that had closed in, then came to a stop. There was no way out. At least, not that he could see. Next year, perhaps, or the year after. Or in five years. But not yet.

Curt gave Victoria a long look. "Do you know," he observed, "you are a formidable woman. I always wondered why my father stayed with you. Now I understand."

"I am not flattered," she said, and turned away from him.

"Is it going to be unanimous?" asked Ann.

"Of course," Jason said, "And not a bad idea, either."

"Is that so?" she retorted. "Tell me this. Where in this plan is a place for Craig?"

Softly, Tobias quoted, "'Your shadow at evening rising to meet you.'"

"I'm so weary of all this," murmured Victoria.

Katherine felt the coldness of her hand. "You should lie down."

"I will, as soon as we vote. Too much emotion; quite exhausting. Ann," she said, raising her voice, "the board of directors will discuss Craig's place in the Hayward Corporation. I will no longer be a member, and I will not try to influence anyone on it. However, there is also my personal estate. That has troubled me deeply. My love for Craig was intact for many years, but I have learned too much about him, and too much time has passed. He has forfeited it all."

"No—!" Ann began, but Victoria stopped her with an upraised hand. How strange, Katherine thought, that these two women, who had done the most to burden Craig with demands that he perform, excel, live up to the image of their golden boy, had grown so far apart in their thoughts of him. "He has forfeited it all," Victoria repeated. "His wife and children—oh, how absurd to call her 'his wife'! Katherine has made her own place in this family, and a larger one in my heart, and she and Jennifer and Todd have a major place in my will. What you and Jason decide to do with your stock is your affair, but of course you have too little to make any difference in the structure of the new company."

"You're shutting him out!" Ann cried. "Katherine, you could convince—"

"She cannot," Victoria said impatiently. "Why must I keep repeating myself? I make my own decisions. I want this company to be exactly as Claude described it. And I want it voted on. Must I make the motion myself?"

"I move," said Derek flatly—for the second time that day causing a stunned silence at the table— "that the reorganization of the Hayward Corporation as described be accepted unanimously."

"Second," said Claude quickly.

Victoria stood. "All those in favor, please raise your hand."

The hands went up: Ross, Claude, Tobias, Jason, Ann, Derek. Victoria raised her own. She looked at Curt. Slowly, his hand went up.

Victoria sighed. "The motion is carried." Turning, she said, "Ann, if I could speak to you a moment?"

Derek pushed his chair away from the table. The walls hadn't closed in completely after all; the possibilities were enormous. Managed properly, the corporation could be transformed: rich, versatile, powerful, international. When they combined the base he'd established in construction with what he had to admit was Ross's architectural genius, plus the vast market for urban development... *that* would be a company to fight for. I'll work my ass off to help him build it up, and then I'll find a way to take it over. He looked up, and met Ross's eyes.

Gathering his papers together, Ross stood and tilted his head toward the corner of the room, telling Derek to join him there. The son of a bitch, he thought. Cutting his losses, probably planning already how to take the company from me. We'll fight every step of the way. Briefly, he recalled their last meeting, when Derek's fear had cracked his composure. If it hadn't been for that, Ross reflected, I wouldn't have accepted Victoria's offer. But now that the company was his, and he had the chance to do what he'd always wanted, the way he'd always wanted, he knew it would be worth even the battles with Derek that loomed ahead. And he could use Derek; he was damned good; he just had to be controlled.

In the corner of the room where two armchairs stood beside the coffee maker on the sideboard, Ross poured a cup of coffee, and waited. There wasn't anything he would worry about in the months ahead, not even the battles with his brother, if Katherine were with him. He'd enjoy winning them all the more if she could share the victories.

He glanced at her, but she was listening to Victoria and Ann. I'll see her at the ball, he remembered. By then I'll be able to tell her about the first session between the president of the Hayward Corporation and the president of Hayward Construction. The first time in our lives I'm controlling our direction. We have a lot of adjustments to make.

At that moment, Derek rose and walked slowly over to join him. "You wanted to see me," he said smoothly, and, pulling out the armchairs, they sat down and began to talk: two businessmen in a neutral corner, discussing the future.

"—want you to understand," Victoria was saying to Ann. "We've needed something new for a long time. A company. A family." Her glance lingered on her grandsons. "Maybe they'll learn to get along with each other. Or at least fight constructively. And now it's done. I won't have anything more to do with the company; I'd only be in the way." She stepped back. "Ross will sit at Hugh's desk and make his dreams and mine come true. And now, Katherine, you too must be part of it—"

Katherine smiled and shook her head. "You've just organized a new company. Isn't that enough for one day?"

"Well, we can talk about it tomorrow. Oh, I forgot to mention . . . Ross! If you and Derek are defining the activities of the subsidiaries, you should include Claude, for tax purposes—"

"That had occurred to us," Ross said gently. "Do you want to join us?"

"No." She laughed ruefully. "An old woman has trouble letting go. The finality of it . . . like giving away the art collections of a lifetime. Relinquishing one thing after another; dying one step at a time. Oh, if I could be seventy again! Go on, go on with your talk. Katherine will help me to the car. After all, you're in charge now; why aren't you presiding over the meeting?"

She went to the two of them. "Derek, I'm pleased that you stayed. I was afraid you would resign in a pique and that would have been unfortunate."

Expressionless, he bowed his head slightly. Victoria put her hand on Ross's shoulder and he stood and walked with her to the door. "Dear Ross," she said. "You are like Hugh in so many ways. Take care of what he built. Take care of what we made together." He held her close and kissed her. "Bless you," she whispered, and, on Katherine's arm, nodding to the rest of her family, Victoria left the board room of the Hayward Corporation for the last time.

CHAPTER 21

ON Saturday afternoon, Victoria called to ask Katherine to be the hostess for her All Hallows party that night. "I've organized it all; it only needs someone to make sure everything is running smoothly. Tobias will be there, of course, but he does get lost in his quotations."

"But you'll be there," Katherine had protested. "It's your party!"

"Naturally I'll be there; I wouldn't miss it. I intend to sit on a gilded throne, graciously accepting greetings, allowing my guests to touch my hem, and sending you forth as my other self. Can you be there early, to check on the table settings?"

"Yes, but—"

"Don't be alarmed, Katherine; there won't be much to do. And if you need help, Tobias and I will be there. And Ross."

When they had said goodbye, Katherine shook her head at Victoria's stratagems to team Ross and Katherine as replacements for Hugh and Victoria. The two of us, she thought, and our four children, starting a new Hayward dynasty. She's forgotten Craig.

Or she hadn't forgotten; she was simply ignoring obstacles, trying by sheer force of will to make events go the way she wanted. Katherine was never sure, with Victoria, how much was pretense and how much was real. Maybe it didn't matter, if in the end she got her way, as she had at the board meeting.

"Mom, we're going," Todd said. "We're helping Annie make hamburgers for dinner."

She hugged them. "Have a good time."

"You have a good time," Jennifer said. "Will Ross be there?"

"Of course. His mother is giving the party."

"Tell him hello for us."

"All right."

Todd said brightly, "You can even kiss him hello for us."

"All right."

"You can even invite him to dinner," Jennifer said. "We'll make hamburgers."

"We'll see. You could make hamburgers for Leslie and Claude some time."

"Sure." Jennifer and Todd looked at each other. "But we promised him dinner that day he went swimming with us."

"You didn't tell me that."

"We like him." Todd said. "That's all. And it's fun going places together. We just like him, and we thought—after what we said before—about Dad—you might not understand. That's all."

"Understand what?" Katherine asked.

"That you need sex and companionship," Todd blurted. "Carrie told us. They really hate the guy their mother has—his *name's* Guy, which is weird—and we really like Ross, so we figure if you have to have somebody... Well, anyway, that's what we meant."

"Thank you," Katherine said.

"And have a wonderful time tonight," Jennifer said. "And don't rush home. Be as late as you want."

"Thank you," Katherine said again.

Now I have permission from everyone, she thought, taking her new dress from the closet. At least for sex and companionship.

"You're not dressed!" Leslie said, swooping in half an hour later. "I came to help; Claude's picking us up in a few minutes. He told me about the board meeting; I'd like to bow down before Victoria and kiss her feet. My God, is this your new dress? You'll be the star of the party. Turn around; let me zip you up."

They stood in front of Katherine's mirror. "Look at you," Leslie said quietly.

Katherine was all in gold: the dress a strapless silk sheath in antique gold, with a lace overblouse, pale gold and long-sleeved. Her dark hair, tumbling to her shoulders, was a deep burnished brown against the fragile gold lace and her pale skin glowed softly, barely touched with color.

She had removed the button that fastened the blouse at her waist and replaced it with a miniature gold seahorse with an opaline eye and a slender coiled tail nestling a fleck of abalone shell. But it was the necklace and matching bracelet that Leslie reached for with shining eyes.

"Incredible. They're art, not just jewelry. Why the hell you're wasting your time at those little shops..."

"You know why."

"Your belts are selling at Heath's. I'll have to talk to our jewelry manager again." They heard the doorbell. "Claude—come to take his ladies to the ball. Can I try on the necklace first?"

"Go ahead." Katherine went to the door and when she and Claude came in they found Leslie sighing at her reflection. Her dress was wine taffeta leaving one shoulder bare; around her throat flowed the slender, curved gold segments of Katherine's necklace, held together with small clusters of tiny bezel-set gems—teardrops, triangles, and circles—in amber, pale blue, deep green, and black. Leslie sighed again. "It belongs in a palace—seventeenth-century Italy or France—on a woman wearing a crown or at least a tiara."

In a low voice, Claude asked Katherine, "Is it for sale?"

"No." She smiled. "This was my present to myself. But I could make a similar one."

"I'll buy it."

"Sight unseen?"

"Of course; I trust you."

"It's very expensive."

"I don't doubt it. I want it, whatever it costs. My wedding gift to my bride. I congratulate you, Katherine; it's brilliant." He stood beside Leslie. "You belong in a palace. But not tonight. Victoria asked Katherine to be early; we should leave."

"I'm ready. Katherine, Tobias would say 'A thing of beauty is a joy forever,' and he'd be right. My God, your jewelry has me quoting poetry. Here; take it back before I break into song."

By the time they reached the Fairmont, Katherine was thinking only of the party. It would be her first social event since the whirling months with Derek, and she wasn't even sure what Victoria expected her to do as a hostess. Check the tables, she thought, and whatever else it takes to make four hundred guests happy. A cinch, as Leslie would say. Just a little gathering, like the one I gave for her in Vancouver.

She stopped short in the middle of the ornate lobby, marble-pillared, floral-carpeted, velvet-upholstered, remembering the softness of the summer night as she stood on the terrace of her home in Vancouver, telling Leslie it was too bad she couldn't stay over, to see Craig. I was waiting for him then, she thought. I'm waiting for him now. Two different parties. She glanced in a mirror. Two different women.

"Katherine," Leslie called. "Didn't you want to be early?"

"Yes," she said. She might still be waiting for him, but nothing else was left from that other party. Go away, she told his shadow. I have so many other things to think about right now.

She walked with Leslie and Claude along what seemed to be endless corridors to the glass doors that led to the ballroom. Only the bartenders were there, but in the adjacent dining room waiters and waitresses were setting wine glasses on forty round tables set with ivory damask cloths, white and gold china, floating candlewicks, and centerpieces of russet and white chrysanthemums in woven baskets. Clusters of Norfolk pines stood like miniature forests along the walls, in the corners, and below the stand where an orchestra was tuning up. Chandeliers glowed with amber lights. The Fairmont dining room had been transformed to a New England autumn forest.

"Tobias," Claude said, surveying the scene. "He misses Boston in the fall so he's recreated it in San Francisco."

A large man in a tuxedo approached, looking inquiringly from Katherine to Leslie. "Mrs. Fraser? I'm Arvin Wallace, assistant caterer. Mrs. Hayward said I was to discuss any problems with you."

"We'll be in the garden," Leslie said.

Traitor, Katherine thought. "Is there a problem?" she asked Wallace.

"The caviar mousse, madame. The chef used Beluga instead of the American Golden that Mrs. Hayward ordered."

Katherine looked at him blankly. Beluga instead of American Golden. When a woman puts on a new gown and the most elegant of jewelry, she does not anticipate a lesson in subspecies of caviar. "Have you tasted it?" she asked.

He looked offended. "But of course, madame. How else would I know which caviar had been used?"

"You could have asked," Katherine said mildly. "How did it taste?"

"Excellent, of course," he said. "It is, of course, the finest caviar one can buy."

"Then what is the problem?" Katherine asked.

"But, madame, surely it is clear... Mrs. Hayward originally asked for Beluga, but we thought it was unavailable and therefore the price we quoted for the dinner did not include it. I thought of course madame would see that immediately."

Snob, Katherine thought. He's worried because he's going to be stuck with the extra cost. Well, he's not going to make himself feel better by making me feel inexperienced, even if I am inexperienced. She raised her chin and calmly scrutinized him until his eyes flickered. "Mr. Wallace, at this moment, is the most important consideration cost or excellence?"

"Madame, there is no question—"

"Good. It seems inappropriate, then, to raise the issue of cost two hours before dinner. I am confident the mousse will be as excellent as you claim, and tomorrow we will study the matter. I will, of course, discuss this with Mrs. Hayward."

He lowered his eyes. "Of course, madame." He turned to go.

"Mr. Wallace, about the centerpieces—"

He looked up and Katherine saw the flash in his eyes. "The centerpieces, madame? Did Mrs. Hayward—?"

"Mrs. Hayward didn't mention them. But they're skimpy. And the two colors aren't bright enough against the ivory cloths. I would guess that some flowers are missing."

He looked at her with grudging respect. "Yes, madame. By mistake the florist sent red dahlias instead of yellow asters. Quite gauche; I left them out."

"Let me see them."

He sighed, left her, and was back in a moment with a handful of ruby-red dahlias with yellow centers like tiny suns.

Katherine arranged four of them among the chrysanthemums in one of the woven baskets. The centerpiece sprang to life, brightening the entire table. Silently she looked at Wallace.

"It does seem pleasant," he said.

"Please take care of the other tables. Four to a basket; five if you have enough. Is there anything else?"

"No, madame." He hesitated. "Thank you."

Flushed with success, Katherine wandered about the dining room, admiring the tables. She pointed out to a waitress a place setting that lacked a wine glass; she straightened a centerpiece that was perfectly straight; she spoke to the orchestra leader about his selections and asked him to include the Autumn section of Vivaldi's *Four Seasons*. By then the beautiful room seemed hers and she walked toward the ballroom feeling sure of herself, in charge, a hostess—until she saw the first guests arriving, and quailed. I can't do this alone, she thought, and went to find Leslie and Claude. "You have to stand there with me," she pleaded. "I can't possibly greet four hundred strangers without support. Why isn't Victoria here?"

"She makes a grand entrance at ten," said Claude. "Come along; I'll fill you in on personalities."

He stood at her shoulder, with Leslie beside him, and whispered capsule descriptions of approaching guests. "Just came back from Majorca..." "And how was Majorca?" Katherine asked, smiling, as she shook hands. "Owns a pool with flamingoes..." "Are the flamingoes flourishing?" Katherine asked, smiling. She was beginning to have a good time. "Mounts stuffed elks in his hunting lodge," Claude whispered. "*Whole* elks?" Katherine asked in astonishment. The guests looked bewildered as she and Claude and Leslie burst out laughing. "I'm sorry," Katherine said to the dignified man standing in front of her. "How nice to see you; I've heard so much about your elks."

When Ross came, Claude whispered, "In love with a brilliant jewelry designer," and so she was smiling when she put out her hand to him. He held it tightly. "Is Victoria ill?" Katherine shook her head. "Claude says she'll make a grand entrance at ten."

"And she asked you to do her chores?"

"Yes."

"But we'll have time—" He hesitated, then, as others came in behind him, said, "Later," spoke briefly to Claude and Leslie, and went on.

Finally, Claude said, "That's most of them. Come; I'm parched. The three of us have earned champagne."

By ten o'clock, four hundred guests in tuxedoes and lustrous gowns strolled in the ballroom and garden. Waiters and waitresses circulated with mirrored trays of champagne and hors d'oeuvres; the orchestra played show tunes; and in a pause between numbers, Victoria appeared in the doorway, in ivory velvet edged in silk. On Tobias' arm, she walked to a high-backed chair on a small platform between the garden and the ballroom, where she could observe everyone.

A few feet from her, on the other side of the glass, was the garden, a luxuriant oasis of towering palms like thickly feathered umbrellas, raised circular beds of flowers separated by grass and walkways, an illuminated fountain, lampposts topped with softly lit spheres, and six-foot Bird-of-Paradise bushes covered with brilliant blue and orange flowers like birds in flight. As guests came to greet her, Victoria saw Katherine at the far end of the garden, standing with Leslie and Claude, Marc Landau and his newest companion, and a group of board members of the San Francisco Symphony. They stood beside one of the Bird-of-Paradise bushes, but, in Victoria's eyes, Katherine outshone the flowers and more than held her own with the women around her.

It was a different crowd from the ones Katherine had met with Derek. This was Victoria's elite: the wealthy benefactors of the city's museums, concerts, ballet, theater, colleges, and universities. Many of them had several homes in or near the world's great cities; most of them represented wealth that had been transmitted through the generations; all of them gave away more than most people earn in a lifetime. Katherine stood among them, smiling, chatting, listening, learning.

"Look at her," Victoria said to Tobias. "Would you guess she grew up over a grocery store?"

"I would guess," he mused, "that she is terrified and exhilarated in equal measure."

"Nonsense. Well, perhaps so. But how well she carries it off!" She saw Katherine break into laughter, her face glowing. "How full of life she is! Tobias, I do love her so."

"Yes, quite right," he agreed, thinking how extraordinary was the train of events that began with the cowardice of Craig and led to the love between two women who needed each other.

"Where is Ross?" Victoria demanded. "I don't see him anywhere."

Tobias chuckled. "Whatever made you think of him?"

"Katherine made me think of him, as you well know. Well, would you bring her to me, Tobias? I haven't greeted her and I want to look at her jewelry; several people have mentioned it. Please, my dear."

Tobias wended his way through the crowd, nodding and smiling at the sleek, successful guests who treated him with respect because he was Victoria's brother and had written a number of scholarly books, but who also thought him amusingly eccentric because he had been content as a professor, unconcerned with what they called serious money.

I am serious about books, Tobias mused, and as greedy about acquiring them as others are about acquiring money. He chuckled. Perhaps they would admire me more if they knew I was as covetous in my way as they are in theirs.

At that moment he found Ross beside him. "Can you share your joke?" Ross asked.

"No, dear boy; it was on me, so I keep it to myself. Have you seen Katherine?"

Ross looked at the group beside the Bird-of-Paradise bush. "Yes. Would you introduce me to her? If we pretend we're just beginning, with no past to deal with, I could ask her to dance."

"Ask her anyway. Tell her you're doing it not for yourself, but to please Victoria." Ross laughed. "It *would* please Victoria," Tobias said. Almost to himself, he quoted, "'However long we were loved, it was not long enough.'"

Ross came to a full stop. "Say that again."

Tobias repeated it. "You should always listen to the wisdom of poets, Ross. And of old men. There is never enough time. Damn it, boy, ask her to dance!"

"Have you a poem that explains loyalty and betrayal?" Ross asked quietly. "And a fear of repeating the past? And a shadow that darkens everything it touches? Of course I'll ask her to dance. But after that..." He shrugged slightly. For the past hour, as he moved among the guests, finding old friends, making new acquaintances, fending off commiserations and probing inquiries on his separation from Melanie, he continually found himself near Katherine. How it happened he was not sure, but wherever he turned, her vivid loveliness was not far away, surrounded by broad-shouldered tuxedoes and glittering gowns and jewels. She was a slender, golden flame, swaying slightly in the currents of the crowd, drawing others to her, as he was drawn, to stand close to her glow and the lilt of her voice and laughter.

As he and Tobias walked toward her, the thought suddenly came to him: She doesn't need any of us. She's come this far without Craig, without me, without Victoria. She's done it all herself. She can go as far as she wants, by herself. He felt the emptiness of loss. He'd thought he was protecting her when he kept Elissa a secret, but that had only shown her one more step she could take on her own; she could do without him.

But then Katherine looked his way and he saw the swift succession of joy, love, and caution in her clear hazel eyes, and he thought it might be all right after all. She didn't depend on him to survive and make her way in the world, any more than he depended on her, but if she needed his love to be a whole person, as much as he needed hers, that would be more than enough on which to build a life.

"May I introduce Ross Hayward?" Tobias was saying. "Ross, this is Katherine Fraser; I think you two should get acquainted. But first" —he tugged lightly on Katherine's arm— "Victoria demands your presence. If I can spirit you away, just for a moment..."

"Tobias," Katherine said as they walked into the ballroom. "Was that a private joke?"

"Ross wants to start from the beginning," he explained cheerfully. "A good idea. When he asks you to dance, tell him you'll accept not for yourself but because it will please Victoria."

Katherine looked at him closely. "That sounds like something you'd tell Ross to say to me."

"Great heavens!" Tobias expostulated. "Am I condemned to live my entire life with intelligent women who see through me? Victoria, here is your granddaughter. I leave her to you. I go in search of gullible guests."

The pitch of conversation had reached a level that almost drowned out the orchestra, and Katherine had to lean close to Victoria to hear her. "The dahlias are perfect," she said, kissing her cheek. "Wally tried to tell me they were his idea, but I know better. You seem to have put him properly in his place. He is the worst kind of snob: a small-minded and very dull man who looks down on others because he moves among people who happen to have money. Salespeople at certain exclusive shops are the same; I avoid them."

"I should tell you," Katherine said. "The caviar—" Quickly she explained it. "I don't know how much more it costs—"

Victoria waved it away. "They'll make it up; it's their mistake. They knew they'd have to; Wally tried to intimidate you because you weren't arrogant enough to impress him. You handled it perfectly, my dear; I'm sorry I missed seeing you do it. Have you seen Ross?"

Katherine nodded.

"Will you dance with him?"

"Of course."

"Excellent. Let me look at your jewelry. My friends are asking me where you bought it." Katherine took off her bracelet, a smaller version of the necklace. "Ah, my dear, the feel of it, almost as if it breathes. Have you ever done anything like it? No, of course you haven't. Neither has anyone else. Do you know, Katherine, I almost *covet* it."

Katherine laughed and kissed her again. "It's yours."

"No, no. But if you would make me something like it..."

"You know I will."

A trumpet call from the orchestra announced dinner and the crowd surged toward the dining room. From Victoria's platform, Katherine had a full view of the mosaic of richly colored gowns interspersed with black and white tuxedoes—patterns forming and dissolving, shifting, flowing, thinning out until the last of the guests had gone through the doors and she and Victoria were alone. "I should have brought my sketch pad," she murmured.

"You'll remember," Victoria said serenely. "You have an artist's eye." As they walked to the dining room, she said, "Katherine, dear, when you make my necklace and bracelet, will you also make the seahorse? Such simplicity; almost Florentine. How did you learn that?"

"I don't know."

"It just comes to you? How exciting that must be. And satisfying."

"And demanding," Katherine said. "I can forget whatever else is happening—at least while I'm concentrating on it."

Victoria nodded. "I think of you working at your table, the way I once worked at Hugh's desk. It gives me such enormous pleasure to think of you at work."

In the center of the dining room, Ross sat at a table with seven people Katherine did not know. Two chairs were empty. "For us," Victoria said, and as Ross held the one beside him, she took it.

A burly man with masses of waving hair and a mustache to match held the other chair for Katherine. Ross introduced him. "Brock Galvez— Victoria Hayward—Katherine Fraser. Brock is one of the developers of BayBridge Plaza, Katherine; he talks about it almost as much as I do."

"More," Galvez declared. "My wife Brenda here, she gets upset; says a mistress she could handle; BayBridge has her stumped."

In the general laughter, as waiters served the caviar mousse, he said to Katherine, "We've met. New Year's Eve, wasn't it? Some crazy shindig with dogs barking Christmas carols. You were with Derek. Haven't seen him tonight. He out of town?"

"I don't know," Katherine replied. "He's been very busy lately."

"Good man, Derek; knows how to run a construction team. He built us a helluva—excuse the expression—office building down Cupertino way. Doesn't have the—how would you say it—*vision* of Ross, but I had a drink last night with Curt—known him for years—and he says they're all getting together in a new company. Quite a team, that'll be. Where'd you find that necklace?"

"I made it."

"*Made it?*"

"I design and make jewelry."

"I'll be damned. Can you make me one? And" —he peered at her waist— "don't mean to be impertinent but could I see that thingamajig?"

Katherine unpinned the seahorse and handed it to him. Brenda Galvez asked to see it, and it was passed from hand to hand. Ross watched, a thoughtful expression on his face, and when a woman across the table said, "I'd love to buy one for my daughter," he held a quick whispered conversation with Victoria. "Who carries them?" the woman asked.

"It's one of a kind," Katherine answered. "And I don't sell these to—" Ross raised his hand slightly, and, puzzled, she broke off.

"Well, one of a kind is what I prefer," the woman across the table was saying. "It's unbearable to see just everyone wearing something I've spent a fortune on to be different. Do I order from you?"

As a slow, wicked smile spread across Victoria's face, Ross said casually, "You'll find the Fraser collection at Xavier's in about a month."

Speechless, Katherine stared at him. Victoria looked at her with dancing eyes. "Try the caviar mousse," she urged. "It is quite the best I've had in a long time."

But as superb as the mousse was, and the watercress soup and fillet of duck in Calvados that followed, and the dessert of Crème Brûlée and lacy almond tuiles, Katherine barely tasted any of it. Xavier's? What was Ross talking about?

Cognac and port were offered as the orchestra in the ballroom struck up a waltz. Gradually, the dining room emptied. Brock Galvez asked Katherine to dance. Marc Landau followed; then a string of men she did not know, all animated, flattering, light on their feet, successful in business—and none of them Ross. An hour passed, then two. Katherine went to sit with Victoria. A few minutes later Ross joined them. "Will you dance with me? For no one's pleasure but my own. And, I hope, yours."

She gave a low laugh, so intimate his hands felt the curve of her body even before he held her on the dance floor. "I want to carry you off," he said, "and hold you and tell you I love you and let no one come near to distract us, until you say we're so much a part of each other you can't imagine a life without me."

"Ross, please don't—"

"Katherine, your jewelry," interrupted a tall woman Katherine did not know. "Xavier's? In November?"

"I don't think—"

"Well, even December . . . as long as it's in time for Christmas." The woman and her partner spun away.

"—handsome necklace," said the president of the Bank of California, pausing in the dance with his wife.

An electronic flash went off as a photographer captured Katherine in Ross's arms, chatting with the president of the Bank of California. Within the next half hour, photographers from the *Chronicle* and the *Examiner* circled the room to give their readers a pictorial report of Victoria Hayward's All Hallows Eve celebration, while society reporters eavesdropped and scribbled notes.

Victoria watched with a wide smile, and Katherine said, "Ross, what is that all about? It's not true . . ."

"Not yet. But what do you think will happen when these people call Xavier's next week asking about the Fraser jewelry collection?"

"They'll be told there is no such thing."

"My dear love," he smiled. "More likely, the astute people at Xavier's will be delighted to take the names of the callers, to notify them when the collection is available, and when they have a list of potential customers, they will call you."

Katherine shook her head. "Only in fairy tales."

"Business isn't so different from fairy tales; they both have obstacles, rewards, coincidences, fairy godmothers and godfathers, winners and losers..."

"But fairy tales have happy endings."

"I'm working on that."

They danced in silence. "You had your own happy ending," Katherine said. "I meant to congratulate you after the board meeting."

"Not an ending," he said. "A beginning. With a long and very bumpy road ahead. If I were smarter, I'd be scared."

She tilted her head and studied him. "But you're not. You're excited; you can't wait to get started."

He kissed the top of her head. "Do you know what it means to me when you understand me, without explanations?"

Tobias materialized beside them. "Katherine, my dear, I have again been commanded to deliver you to Victoria. She wants to say goodnight."

"Goodnight?" Katherine asked. "But it's only—" She looked at her watch in disbelief. "Three o'clock?"

"So it seems. And the two of us are ready for bed."

Victoria was fastening a cape at her throat when they found her at the cloakroom. "A highly satisfactory evening," she said. "You did very well, Katherine. Now kiss me goodnight and go back to your dancing."

"I think I should go home, too. There's no such thing as sleeping late on a sofa bed in our living room."

"Stay awhile," Ross said. "I'll take you home whenever you're ready."

"Very sensible," Victoria commented. "My dear," she added to Katherine, "promise me something. Don't make any sudden decisions about your jewelry. Take your time."

"All right," Katherine said.

"Promise me."

"I promise."

"And you'll tell me what happens."

"I promise that, too."

"Excellent. Goodnight, my dears. I'll talk to you tomorrow."

The music was soft and slow and they glided in a gentle, swaying rhythm. Katherine touched the smooth cloth of Ross's sleeve. "Do you know, I've never seen you in a tuxedo? You look exceedingly handsome."

"And you are wonderfully beautiful," he said quietly. "You haven't responded to what I said earlier."

"You mean about becoming a part of you. Ross, I already am—as much as I can be. I miss you and I want you, and I find myself reaching out to share with you—"

"Katherine—!"

"—but you said you wanted to let me finish what I began. That was why you weren't calling me, you said. And then tonight—to tell me you want me to be part of you..."

"It's not consistent."

"Or fair."

"It would be easier to be consistent and fair if I could stop worrying about what you might do when Craig comes back."

"Has it occurred to you that you worry about that more than I do?"

He thought about it. "No. I don't think you know how you'll react to him any more than I do when he starts playing on your memories and sympathies, and his needs and your kids... Katherine, we don't have to be so far apart; if we love each other we can find a way—"

"Ross, please. I'm trying to do what's right."

It struck him like a blow. *Trying to do what's right.* If she thought she knew what that was, how could he tell her she was wrong?

He repeated it as he drove her home. *Trying to do what's right.* In fairy tales, Ross thought, that was always rewarded; happy endings, Katherine had said. They walked to her front door and he held her for a moment, as he had when they were dancing. "I hope, whatever happens, it is what you want," he told her, and waited until she had closed the door behind her before he went back to his car, and drove home.

Monday morning's newspapers were strewn about Victoria's chaise as she sat on her sun porch, clipping the society pages. "Most satisfactory," she said, almost purring, as Katherine came in. "Especially the photograph of you and Ross talking to that bank president..." She kissed Katherine soundly, then looked closely at her. "Something has happened. Come, come, what is it?"

Katherine's eyes sparkled. "I had a telephone call this morning. From Herman Mettler."

"Ah." Victoria grinned. "He's read the papers. I'll bet it spoiled his breakfast, to read about Katherine Fraser and see her picture as she moved in the highest society among people who will buy her jewelry. But he gets no sympathy from me; he does not deserve it. What did he say?"

"He called me Katherine—"

"Cozy," Victoria observed scornfully.

"And wanted to buy back the jewelry he'd returned, and any more I had. He also said my husband had nothing to do with our business dealings."

Victoria laughed delightedly. "And what did you tell him?"

"That I couldn't decide right away."

"Quite right." Victoria nodded vigorously. "How pleasant it is when people get what they deserve! You did well."

"I followed your advice."

"It was good advice; therefore, you did well."

Katherine smiled. Restlessly, she walked to the windows, looking down at Lafayette Park, the sun glistening off its dark green leaves and the white uniforms of nurses pushing buggies and strollers. She considered telling Victoria about the rest of the conversation with Mettler; that he had let slip that it was Derek who had given him the idea Katherine Fraser might be a thief. But what good would it do? Victoria knew what Derek was like, and she had already punished him, in the board meeting, by stripping him of most of his power and putting him beneath Ross's authority. There was nothing more anyone could do to Derek. It doesn't matter anymore, Katherine thought. It's over. I can't even be angry. I've gotten past him.

Turning from the window, she asked Victoria, "Why did you tell me not to make any quick decisions about my jewelry?"

"Ross told you why. To give Xavier's a chance to get requests from customers."

"Victoria, do you and Ross tell each other everything?"

"Certainly not. There are many things a grandmother and a grandson do not share. But others we do. He would make you very happy, Katherine. I am not trying to force you; I am simply saying he would make you happy. And he needs you; the next years are not going to be easy for him, putting together that company I forced him into. You could help him; you would be good for each other."

"And Craig?" Katherine asked.

"Craig is a fool!" Victoria exploded. "And Ross is a romantic. How can you even hesitate in choosing between them?"

Katherine laughed ruefully. "It's so easy for you to forget I'm married to one of them."

"Not anymore, you foolish girl. Craig ended it, long ago. You are the only one who clings to it."

Katherine had not told her about Craig's telephone call; neither, she realized, had Ross. I don't want to repeat it now, she thought, and said only, "Then it's my foolishness. May I ask you about something else?"

Victoria looked up, her eyebrows raised.

"Why did you give that party last night?"

"Hugh and I gave one every year. It was our tradition. Besides, I wanted to watch you take my place."

"That was my initiation?"

"An odd way of putting it, my dear."

"And if I had failed?"

"If I thought you would fail, there would have been no party. I knew you would not."

"But you don't know what will happen with Craig."

"For sixteen years I thought Craig was dead; for the past year and a half I haven't had any idea what would happen with him. But I trust you. Whatever you decide—whether you are with Ross or Craig or someone else—or alone—I trust you. When I die, Katherine, I am leaving you this apartment, complete with Tobias, if he outlives me; he must be able to live upstairs as long as he wishes. But the rest will be yours, and more than enough money to end your worries. No, don't say anything now; I won't change my mind. Just listen."

She held out her hand and Katherine took it. "Sometime in the future, when I am no longer here—will you keep all of them together? Even when they wrangle and compete and run off to Maine or God knows where ... keep them in touch, keep them feeling like a family. For the children, you know, to give them a haven. The world spins so wildly, we're thrown apart, we lose one another—unless we have a solid core to hold on to. No one knows that better than you, my tenacious Katherine; you don't let go easily or lightly."

She touched Katherine's cheek. "When Craig and Jennifer died— were gone—I thought I'd stopped caring. But you've made me believe we can be a family again. It is maddening!" she burst out, "that I won't live another fifty years and see the four children marry and have children of their own ... see what becomes of the Haywards. It's like being forced to leave a movie in the middle. I can't even convince myself I'll be sitting somewhere, watching all of you after I die—"

"You couldn't bear that," Katherine said. "Watching us without being able to comment or organize our affairs ..."

"Good Lord, you're right; I would go mad. So I must arrange as much as possible while I'm here. Promise me you'll do this, Katherine. There is no one else I can ask. Keep a family for the children, and their children. Don't let everyone get trampled by private needs, and then scattered like dust ..."

Katherine put her arms around her, aware of her own youth, the firmness of her skin, the vigorous pulsing of her blood. She kissed the cool parchment of Victoria's cheek. "I'll do my best," she said, then gave a small laugh. "And even if you aren't sitting somewhere, watching us, you'll always be inside me, telling me what I should do."

"Of course," Victoria said serenely. "I'm counting on that."

• • •

It was nearly five o'clock when Ross's prediction came true and the manager of Xavier's telephoned Katherine. "I have been inundated with requests for jewelry by Katherine Fraser," he said. "I do have the right Katherine Fraser? Victoria Hayward gave me this number."

"You called her?" Katherine asked.

"Just a few minutes ago. She wondered why it had taken me so long."

"She couldn't have said that."

"We've known each other many years and she said exactly that. Mrs. Fraser, my customers have excellent taste, and all the cities of the world in which to shop. If they are impressed with your jewelry, I want to see it, everything you have, including designs or sketches. Unfortunately, I'm busy tomorrow, but can you come in on Wednesday? Christmas isn't far off, and we should begin as soon as possible."

Excitement was rushing through Katherine, warm and heady, like red wine; she could barely sit still. "Wednesday is fine. In the morning?"

"Ten o'clock, if that's convenient."

"That's fine." Any time was fine, Katherine thought, hanging up; whatever time he wanted. She phoned Victoria and told her; Victoria called Tobias to the telephone and Katherine repeated her news; at dinner she told Jennifer and Todd and because she was so excited she did not try to dampen their fantastic plans for castles in the sky.

All evening her excitement raced at its high pitch. She tried to calm down by sorting her jewelry and sketches, but when the thought came to her that she was finally escaping Craig's shadow, she became so restless she could not sit still. She called Leslie, but even talking to her was not enough, and at last Katherine admitted to herself that it was Ross she most wanted to share her excitement. Without thinking further about it, she dialed his number, and then listened to the empty ringing of his telephone. She called again and again, and at midnight was trying once more when the doorbell rang. It can't be Ross, she thought; he said he wouldn't even call. But still, her heart was pounding as she ran to open it—and saw Craig, standing on the doorstep.

CHAPTER 22

T HEY did not touch. Craig's hand made a small movement toward her, then dropped back, and he stayed in the doorway, waiting, until Katherine stepped aside and he walked in.

"You're so beautiful," he said wonderingly. "And the way you stand... I remember, Jennifer and Todd told me you were different, that night I was here."

His eyes were hungry and restless, fastening on Katherine's face, darting about the small room, then back to her face and slender figure in the white velvet robe Ross had brought her when he came back to Menton from Paris, then down, down, lingering on her bare feet. Katherine watched him, her mind in a turmoil. *I waited so long, and now I don't feel ready...* "But I didn't think you'd be this different," Craig said, and smiled—the gentle smile that brought everything back to Katherine, almost as if he had never been gone.

"Would it be too much trouble to make some coffee?" he asked. "I feel like I've been traveling for weeks."

"Of course," Katherine said. Her voice seemed to come from a stranger. "I mean, of course it's not too much trouble. We can sit in the kitchen."

The oak table was the one they had used for ten years. Craig sat down and pulled his chair forward exactly as he always had and watched Katherine make coffee as he always had. And when she brought the mugs and a plate of coffee cake to the table, and sat with him, he looked just the same, his beard full and brown, his eyes eager, his smile tentative, waiting for approval and love.

443

"Thank you," he said and sipped the hot coffee as he always had.

Dizzily, Katherine looked away. *This is my husband.* She was sitting in the kitchen, drinking coffee with her husband, and nothing had changed.

Everything has changed. Remember that.

"Katherine," Craig said. "I love you. You've got to believe me: I love you." He leaned forward. "I've never stopped thinking of you, needing you... Even when I couldn't find a way to come back, you were always the center of my life; I never stopped loving you and wanting you."

Katherine looked at him across the table. *This is my husband.* All the feelings of being married were rushing back—love, companionship, the comfort of familiarity—but tangled with them was the feeling that this was a stranger. Which is he? Katherine thought with a surge of panic. I don't know who he is, or how to talk to him.

"I've said that to you every night for the last sixteen months," Craig was saying. "Told you I love you, talked to you, told you what I was thinking... Katherine, I'm sorry for what I did to you; I'm sorry for the mess I made of things, for letting you down... Christ, all I ever wanted was to take care of you. But I'll make it up to you, I promise. Just give me a chance. I know how much I destroyed, but I want to—"

"Why did you leave?" Katherine asked.

"Why did I—? *You don't know?*"

She shook her head.

"But you must. Hank sent me the newspaper stories; he told me reporters were badgering you and the police were in and out of our house... and I can't believe Carl didn't come looking for me, that hypocritical bastard, full of thunder and lightning and sanctimonious talk of trusting me... Didn't he? Didn't he tell you what happened?"

"He told me you'd embezzled seventy-five thousand dollars from the company over two years, and admitted it when he confronted you, and you told him you were going to Toronto to borrow money to pay him back."

He was watching her steadily. "Clear and concise. And you still don't know why I left?"

Puzzled, Katherine realized she had been wrong about him: he *had* changed. Tanned and lean, his hands calloused, wearing slacks, a white shirt open at the neck, and a corduroy sport jacket, he was handsomer than she remembered, and more assured. When had Craig ever talked so directly, especially when it was about something unpleasant? "Craig," she burst out. "Did you really steal it?"

"My God," he said staring at her. "You didn't believe him?"

"*Did you steal it?*"

"Yes. And Carl had proof." Almost sadly, he said, "I didn't think you'd have so much faith..."

"I know," Katherine said shortly. "And I did believe it at first, when you didn't come back. But then something happened this summer... it's a long story. But it made me think you might have been framed."

He looked stunned. "Framed. I never thought of that. Did you ask Carl?"

"I didn't want to ask Carl. I wanted to ask you. I wanted to believe in you."

"Why?" he asked bluntly. "I'd left you."

Katherine looked at him in astonishment. She had never heard Craig talk like that. "I loved you," she said.

"*Loved.*"

"And you still haven't told me why you left us."

"I thought it was obvious." He drained his mug. "Is there more coffee?" Katherine refilled it and, without being asked, made another pot. He watched her as she stood at the counter. "It all came crashing down. Carl screamed at me that I'd betrayed him and he'd see me in jail and make sure everyone knew what an ungrateful bastard I was. I thought a trial would mean an investigation and they'd dig up my past, and you'd hate me, if you didn't already, for stealing... There was no good ending to it! Do you know how many hundreds of letters I've written to you, trying to explain all this?"

"I didn't get any letters," said Katherine.

"I never mailed them. Hell, I never finished them. How do you tell someone you love that you deserted her because everything was crushing you and you felt trapped and helpless? That morning I left I didn't even realize what I was doing until I told the cab driver to stop at the bank on the way to the airport. That was when I knew. I told him to go on, I deposited the money for you, and then I walked—two or three hours, I think—until I hitched a ride with a truck driver."

"*Two or three hours...!*"

He shrugged. "You're right; I had time to change my mind. But how could I? The more I walked, the more I thought about it, the more everything closed in, crushing me. I couldn't tell you I'd stolen; I couldn't tell you about my past; I couldn't ask anyone for help. I couldn't do anything but run. And once I'd started I had to keep on, keep moving, because when I stopped, I couldn't stand the loneliness and I'd turn around to come back to you, and it would all come back—all the things I couldn't tell you, crushing me, so I couldn't breathe... Katherine, if

I could make you understand... whenever I tried to come back *I couldn't breathe*. I had to keep running..."

His voice stopped. Katherine was silent, feeling his panic.

"But I got past that," he said. "Because I had to see you. Katherine, I want you to come back to Canada with me. I'll get the money to settle with Carl and we'll start again, make a home...I know you sold the house; we'll build a new one, a better one, and start all—"

"Craig, wait..."

"You can't be surprised. Why do you think I came back? Why do you think I called Ross? Ross did tell you I called, didn't he?"

"Yes."

"I told him I love you. And want you back. Did he tell you that?"

"Yes."

"Well." His voice became flat. "He told me he's in love with you. I'm not surprised...and it's natural that you'd look for help and affection. I know it's been a rough time for you; you have nothing to be ashamed of. And Ross is as decent as they come and trustworthy...at least, I always thought so." He paused. "What are you thinking?"

"What about your family?" Katherine asked. "If you go back to Canada."

"You're my family! You and Jennifer and Todd!"

"And Victoria and Tobias, Ann and Jason, Derek and—"

"Not Derek, God damn it; he's no part of me and never will be!"

Katherine shrank from the fury in his voice and instinctively put her finger to her lips. "Todd and Jennifer—"

"Sorry." He stood up. "I'd like to take a look at them. You don't mind—?"

"Of course not."

Katherine watched him cross the living room and inch open the bedroom door. She felt a stab of pity at the stiffness of his back as he stood in the doorway; then, very gently, he closed the door and came back to her. "They look wonderful."

"They are wonderful. They felt betrayed when you disappeared on New Year's Eve."

Embarrassment and anger swept over his face. "You were with Derek. I couldn't handle that. All I could think of was that if I'd told you about him you would have been warned."

Katherine frowned. "What are you talking about? You never told me about any of them. You lied about being an orphan; you kept yourself locked inside your secrets. For ten years... *What was so terrible that you couldn't tell me about them?*"

"Something...a long time ago. I thought about telling you but after a while it wasn't important. I didn't have to talk about them, Katherine—

Possessions

I didn't even think about them—as long as I had you. It never occurred to me you'd meet them. You can't imagine how strange it is to hear you talk about Victoria, Tobias, my parents—it's all wrong; you never were supposed to know about them." Slowly, he shook his head. "I put so many years and miles between us. How did you find them?"

"Ross found me." Katherine brought the fresh pot of coffee to the table. "It was Jennifer, wasn't it? The terrible thing, a long time ago. On the sailboat. When she died."

He jerked back, as if stung. "Who told you about that?"

"Derek. And Ross. But I want to hear it from you."

He cupped the mug in his hands, looking at the trembling surface of the coffee. "I didn't know they'd talk about it." The room was silent. The building slept; the street slept. There were only the two of them, facing each other across the oak table—until Craig began to talk, slowly at first, then faster as the story poured out.

"We were sailing home, across the bay. We'd been invited to some damn party in Sausalito and Jenny asked Ross and Derek to sail across with us. It was a dull party with nothing to do but drink, and by the time we left I felt rotten. We all needed to clear our heads and it was so peaceful on the water I wanted to stay out as long as possible, so I decided to sail past the Golden Gate Bridge and then in again, to the harbor. But Derek decided he was in a hurry, and he harped on it, so I put up the spinnaker. Derek usually got what he wanted, one way or another. Jenny loved it. She put her head back and laughed into the wind; she opened her arms and said 'I love all of you so much.' She was so lovely and happy. Oh, God..."

He was looking past Katherine, at the dark window. "Near the Gate the currents were strong and the wind started to pick up, so I told Jenny and Derek to put on lifejackets, and sent Jenny down to the cabin to tell Ross. I shouldn't have; it left us alone. Usually I made sure Derek and I were never alone. We fought all the time—mostly over power, I suppose, but there were other things, too. Love, attention, money...I was a year older but we were both first sons and Derek made it a war: enemies and rivals from the start. And he could always get to me—make me lose control—so I tried to keep others between us. But that day, for some reason, Jenny stayed below with Ross for a few minutes, and I said something about the wind, and taking down the spinnaker, and Derek called me a coward, said I was afraid to sail at anything more than a crawl...said if I didn't have my mama and grandma around I couldn't even shit by myself. Crude bastard, when he wanted to be...smooth when he wanted..."

He contemplated the coffee pot. "Do you have any Scotch?"

Katherine shook her head. "Only wine."

"Well, then, if I could—?" She brought a bottle to the table and a corkscrew, and pulled out the cork. "That always used to be my job, remember? Thanks." He filled the glass she gave him. "I told Derek to shut up—the spinnaker had to come down. It was too much sail for that wind; a bad gust could rip it apart, might even overturn us. That was when Ross and Jenny came up from the cabin. Derek reached out and pulled Jenny to him...put his arms around her...standing sideways so I could see...Ross couldn't...his hand on her breast...Christ, I can't make that go away!—I still see it, at night, when I'm trying to sleep...his thin fingers curled over Jenny's breast, his cold eyes, daring me...'Jennifer and I like living dangerously,' he said. 'The only one who's afraid is the captain.'

"It made me sick—it was the first time I knew for sure there was something between them. I yelled at Derek—because I couldn't let go of the wheel—to get his goddamn hands off Jenny and I yelled at Jenny to get the hell away from him. It looked like she was trying, but he held her—she looked like a scared little bird caught in a trap—

"God knows what my face looked like; it scared the hell out of Ross. He yanked Jenny away and asked me if he should go forward and take down the spinnaker and I think I said yes, but I was yelling at Derek— I couldn't stop—telling him to get below or get off the boat; he could swim to shore for all I cared, if he had the guts to try it in that water...

"Derek came back at me in that voice he used on all of us, high and light, like fingernails on a blackboard, calling me a puppet, a doll, Grandma's toy...who could only get it up when Grandma stroked it...The wind was roaring, we were all drenched from the waves and spray breaking over the cockpit, and that bastard stood there like a goddamn soldier, absolutely straight, his voice like a knife, talking, talking, and I was shouting back and Jenny started to cry. 'Don't,' she said. 'I love you both; don't fight.'

"I went crazy, I guess. First seeing Derek hold her, and his voice, cutting into me, and then hearing Jenny say *she loved us both*—I had to stop her, make her despise him, see what he really was under that fake charm...so I screamed at him—so Jenny would be sure to hear—that he was a crook; he'd changed the specs on a building we were putting up after the city had approved them; he'd violated a pack of laws and was a rotten crook who didn't give a shit if he built a dangerous building. His face was like stone. I'd seen the changed specs that week and couldn't figure out how they'd gotten past an inspector, so I made a wild guess and accused him of bribing the inspector on the job.

"When Ross asked what the hell I was talking about, Derek turned it around—he could recover and attack faster than anyone I ever knew—and in that damned scraping voice he said: 'Golden boy changed the specs on the Macklin Building to be Grandma's hero—even bribed the inspector—but now he's scared and shifting the blame. Running away, as usual.' That was when I knew I was right, and I laughed. I remember how good that felt, to laugh in Derek's face because he'd given himself away. I told him I cared more about our reputation than he did and I was going to my father and his and get him kicked out of the company before he got us into real trouble.

"That was when I told Ross to go forward and take down the spinnaker—while I was laughing at Derek. And while Ross did that . . . while Jenny huddled in a corner, and spray and waves washed over us and the wind roared . . . Derek came up to me, close to me, and told me—so goddamned soft and friendly—that Jenny was in love with him and . . . pregnant . . . by him . . . *pregnant by Derek* . . ."

Katherine drew in her breath sharply, but Craig did not hear. ". . . and they hadn't decided what they were going to do, but if I got in his way, he'd tell the family . . . and anybody else who might be interested . . .

"I broke apart inside. I saw Derek's eyes watching me and I had to close them—crush him—so I went for his throat and got my hands around his neck. I could feel Jenny pulling on my arm, and I was sick, thinking, *Derek's child, Derek inside you, Derek's child*, and I exploded—'You whore, Jenny! You damned whore; damn you, damn you—!' and then suddenly she was gone. Everything was gone . . .

"I didn't see it, but I felt it: when I left the wheel, the boat changed course and jibed, and the boom swung across and slammed into Jenny. I heard it, a terrible thud, and saw her stumble—blood, a starburst of blood, next to her eye—and then she went over. She didn't make a sound. She just . . . fell. I dropped Derek and got to the life preserver and the marker pole and threw them to Jenny—she was face down and I screamed at her to grab the preserver—JENNY! JENNY! JENNY!—I still hear that scream inside me. I screamed it when I dove in and swam to her—and when I held her head out of the water and saw her eyes, staring at me, not seeing me, not seeing the sky . . . not seeing ever again . . . Because she was dead."

He was crying. "The boat was gone. There was no one but Jenny and me and the water—choppy and dark, so cold—and an awful silence.

"I got Jenny to the life preserver and tucked her into it so her face was out of the water and I stayed with her. It was so cold, but I had to talk to her . . . I was crying and treading water and telling her I was sorry. I had to make her understand that I didn't mean what I said, I'd been crazy because I hated Derek and he'd used her the way he used everyone... I kept saying, 'Please, Jenny, forgive me—please, *please*—'"

Tears ran down his face and caught like raindrops in his beard. "I saw the boat, coming back, and I heard Ross calling me, and I thought how it would be getting into the boat with him and Derek, taking Jenny home, her eyes staring through everyone... and I couldn't do it. I'd destroyed everything and I couldn't go back to them. If I hadn't jumped Derek, Jenny wouldn't have been killed. My parents and my grandmother had asked me to watch over her when she started going out with Derek. They said, 'Craig, stop her; she listens to you.' And I failed. I didn't try hard enough to stop her because I couldn't let myself believe it was serious. I let everyone down, and then I killed Jenny. I hated Derek so much I let him become more important to me than Jenny. And Jenny died.

"And even when I was asking her to forgive me, I was still sick and furious because Derek had been inside her. And once—only once—I thought, 'It's good that Derek's baby is dead.' I couldn't face myself after that—or anyone else—so when Ross called, I swam away. I didn't know which direction I was going; I didn't care. I thought eventually I'd just go under. But instead, after a while, I don't know how long, I came to a spit of land with a flashing light..."

"Lime Point," Katherine murmured, and Craig's head shot up. He had forgotten her, forgotten where he was, and he squinted through his tears as he looked closely at her.

"You're crying," he said. "For Jenny?"

"And for you," Katherine said. She was crying for all of them—for Jenny and Craig, for Ross, calling into the darkness, even for Derek, gnawed inside, all his life, by jealousy. Bit by bit, she recalled the pieces of all the stories she had heard, and as she put them together, she felt another rush of pity, stronger than before, for Craig.

"I'm sorry for breaking down," he said. "I've never told the whole thing." He wiped his face with his handkerchief. "How did you know about Lime Point?"

"Ross and Derek told me. When they learned you were alive—"

"When was that?"

"Not until last year, when I came here the first time. Then they thought you must have made it to Lime Point. Everyone told me how strong you were. Ann said she had your trophies from college. For running."

He nodded. "She was always so proud of those."

"And you left them behind. With everything else. You made yourself into another person...?"

He shrugged. "It's not hard, you know. A social security card, a driver's license, a job... anyone can get them. And Vancouver was big enough; I could be anonymous."

"I didn't mean that," Katherine said. "I was thinking of *inside...*"

"It takes longer." He shrugged again. "You shed bits of yourself, and it hurts, but you do it. You begin to live a different kind of life and after a while you think of yourself as a different person. If you do it enough, you wake up one day and you know you can't go back to your other life. It's too late."

Katherine stared at him. *Which one of us is he talking about?*

The bottle was empty. Katherine had made another pot of coffee and absently Craig filled both mugs, glancing at the clock as if they were a normal couple wondering if there was time for one more cup before leaving for work. "My God, it's two thirty. I'm keeping you up."

It was so absurd that they looked at each other and laughed, a soft laugh: the first they had shared. Memories rushed in on Katherine, overwhelming her with images, words, laughter, hope... the brilliant light of nostalgic love that burned away the bad times, leaving only the good ones.

She forced herself to stand up and walk away from the table, away from that warm spell. "If you'd told me all this... years ago..."

"Why? For a while I wanted to, but then I realized that I wanted even more to get away from it, not to be forced to think about Craig Hayward ever again. Why should I tell you about him when I was happy as Craig Fraser? We were both happy; we had a full life together; how would a long confession have helped us?"

"It would have let me share part of your life."

"A part I hated and wanted to forget."

"But you never forgot it! You just kept it from me. And then you kept our finances, and other things—"

"You hardly made a point of asking," he said coldly. "You enjoyed the way we lived without asking if we really had the money to pay for it, or where it came from—"

"I know." Katherine's face was burning. "I've thought about that. You're right; I should have asked; I should have known what was happening. But that was what you wanted, Craig; someone who wouldn't question your decisions; someone who wouldn't ask questions at all."

He shook his head. "*You* wanted someone who wouldn't burden you with answers."

They were silent. "Well," he said with a short laugh. "An impasse."

"It always was," Katherine responded. "But I should have insisted. I've learned that. Then we would have been two grown-up people instead of a husband shielding a little-girl wife."

Craig leaned back in his chair and gazed at her. Then he smiled, almost wistfully. "Do you know, Katherine, I'm not sure it would have made a damn bit of difference what you did or how you behaved. I don't think I could have told you. I never was able to show my weaknesses to people I love."

Slowly, Katherine walked back to the table and stood beside him. Almost fearfully, she put out her hand and touched his. "That's the first time you ever told me a simple truth about yourself," she said.

"But it's not true anymore." He grasped her hand. "I've had sixteen months to think about it; I know what I did to you, to both of us, and I won't let it happen again. I've changed, Katherine; everything will be different now." He stood and faced her, still holding her hand. "We have a lot invested in each other: ten years, ten wonderful years, and the children—we can't just throw it all away."

"But that's what you did when you left." Confused by the tenderness she felt, Katherine eased her hand away and stepped back until she was standing against the counter. "You turned your back on all of us."

He shook his head. "I did the best I could. It was a lousy solution, but I never really turned my back. I sent you money; I tried to come to you in December. And I thought about us—how we could both change, and start again . . . Katherine, listen to me. I love you. There was a time when we had so much together, we did so much for each other—you haven't forgotten that."

"No," she replied. Studying his face, she thought he *had* changed. He was stronger, more open and direct, without having lost the gentleness she had loved. And he looked so much like Todd she found herself wanting to comfort him.

"I'm asking for another chance," he said. "For the children, for the years and energy we've invested in each other, for the good things we did for each other. We can build something together that we could have had from the beginning, if I hadn't been such a fool, and if you'd been more involved . . ."

Katherine was dizzy under the hammer blows of his reasons. And the question came to her—why not? He'd learned, he'd changed, he was her husband, he was Jennifer's and Todd's father—and surely this tenderness she felt was more than pity . . . wasn't it just as likely a revival of memories, and a renewal of the love she had felt, or the first step back to it?

Watching her intently, Craig said again, "Another chance. To make up to you and the children for what I did—"

"Craig," Katherine said faintly. "Give me a minute to catch my breath. You're piling everything on—"

"I'm fighting for my life!" he said. "Can't you see that?"

"No," she answered as another memory returned. "I thought I did. I believed you. But—all this talk about change—even now you aren't being honest with me."

"What does that mean? After I went through that whole story—tore myself apart over it—told you about everything—"

"Except Elissa."

He stiffened. His shoulders drew together; his face became smooth and blank, as if he were a deaf person pushing through a crowded street. Finally he said, "What are you talking about?"

"Craig!" Katherine cried. *"Don't run away!"*

Another minute went by. Stiffly, he shook his head, looking past her. "I don't know what you're talking about."

"Oh, Craig." She moved in front of him to force him to look at her, but he turned his head. They stood that way as the silent moments passed, Craig's features rigid and stubbornly defensive. Poor, frightened Craig, Katherine thought. And with that, the same feeling swept through her that had lifted and carried her along when she left Derek in Ghirardelli Square. She was free.

She knew all the stories, now; all the evasions. She knew she had played a part in them, but she also knew that she had learned enough, grown up enough, to leave that passive child-wife behind forever. But Craig still created his evasions, weaving them into a screen of lies and silences that shut out reality whenever he could not face it. And he would never change.

"I spent a day with Elissa, in Calgary," she told him. Drooping with fatigue, she did not even try to soften it. "I liked her; we liked each other. She's still in love with you. Your carving of the turtle with the little boy is still on the table in front of the couch. All the mementoes of your times together are still there. Her little boy had a hard time when you left. He missed you. Probably as much as Todd and Jennifer did."

Craig's shoulders slumped. He sat down again, turning his coffee mug around in his hands. "She promised me she'd never call you."

"She kept her promise. She never called any of us. Ross found her."

Dully, Craig echoed her words. "'Ross found her. She never called any of us. *Any of us.*'" His head came up; he looked at her accusingly. "You've lined up with them."

"This isn't a war," Katherine shot back. "They're my family. And yours, if you'd let them be."

He shook his head. "I can't be part of them."

"But you don't know what's happened; there have been so many changes—"

"I don't want to know! Can't you understand? I've cut them out of my life; I don't want to know anything about them! I got over them! It took years, but I got over feeling sick from missing them, mostly because I had you to love me and help me make a new family. Katherine, you're all I want—you and the children—"

"And Elissa."

"My God, can't you let go? You *have* changed. Not just your hair and the way you walk and hold yourself—you've gotten hard. You used to be soft and loving and grateful, but that's all gone."

"Is it?"

"You act like you don't want anyone to care for you; you don't need anyone..."

I need Ross.

"Hank gave me your message; he told me you were waiting for me. What did that mean?"

"I had to talk to you."

"To finish our marriage. Right? That was how Ross put it."

"To finish with the past. I wasn't really sure about our marriage." Katherine hesitated. "Craig," she said softly. "When you left us, why didn't you go to Elissa?"

He shook his head.

"Because you love her. That's right, isn't it? You couldn't go to her because you couldn't tell her what you'd done." He sat still, and Katherine sighed. "Earlier tonight you said you didn't have to talk about your family, you didn't even think about them as long as you had me. That wasn't true. You never stopped thinking about them, you had to talk about them, and so you went to Elissa. And after a while, you fell in love with her. Why can't you face that?"

"I love you," he said. "I came back because you told Hank you were waiting for me. *I'm asking for help.* I keep running away from things— I just did it again, didn't I, trying to deny Elissa? You were leaning toward me—I saw it in your face—until I... ran away again. Katherine, I want to repair some of the damage I've done, but I can't do it alone. Don't make me do it alone. Stay with me; help me."

"I can't. I'm sorry, Craig." Katherine felt her tears again. He wasn't evil or cruel or even bad; he was a good man too easily overwhelmed by events. He was a man she no longer loved. "We'll do everything we can to help you. Whatever you need, we'll give you—"

"You're speaking for the family?"

"Yes."

"You mean you're choosing Ross."

"I mean I can't go with you; I can't live with you."

Craig pushed back his chair and stood up. "Just a minute." Katherine watched him close the door of the bathroom behind him. Her muscles ached, her head ached, and she walked through the living room to the front door, opening it to feel the cool, damp air on her face. The sky had grown light; she looked at her watch. Six o'clock. We talked more in the last six hours, she thought, than in all the years of our marriage.

Craig came out of the bathroom and stood beside her. "And the children?" he asked.

"They love you. Wherever you are, they'll come to you, as often as possible, and spend time with you—"

"Visits."

After a moment, she said, "A lot of children do that, these days."

"But they'd be visiting. I wanted to live with them again."

She felt a tug of impatience. "You'll see a lot more of them than you have in the past year and a half."

"Right," he said. "You're right. I deserved that." He went to the door of the bedroom. "I'll just take a quick look goodbye. I won't wake them— I'm not ready to talk to them—I have to figure out what to say. But when I've decided where I'll be, and when I'm settled, you'll let them come?"

"As often as possible."

He nodded. "Yes, you said that." He stood in the doorway, as he had hours before. "They curl up in their sleep. I remember that. But they're growing so fast. Jenny is going to be as beautiful as her mother. And Todd . . . Todd looks like me, doesn't he?"

Distantly, a foghorn sounded. "Dad!" Todd shouted. "Dad!" Katherine saw Craig bend down and take in his arms the pajama'd form that flung itself at him.

"*Daddy?*" Jennifer asked. Her voice was clouded with sleep and doubt. Instead of dashing to him as Todd had done, she appeared in the doorway, frowning, reaching out to touch Craig's arm, testing its solidity.

"Hello, dear Jenny," Craig said softly.

Wordlessly, she put up both arms. Craig knelt and held his children, his eyes meeting Katherine's over their tousled heads, accusing her. They love me, his eyes said. And you want to keep us apart.

"Where's your suitcase?" asked Todd as they sat on the couch. "Where are you going to put everything? We'll have to move, now, won't we, Mom? Are we going back to Canada?"

Jennifer looked at her mother and then at her father. "You're not staying," she said flatly.

"He is too!" Todd cried. "You are, aren't you, Dad?"

"No," Craig said. "I'd like to but I can't. Your mother—"

Katherine caught her breath. Don't run away from it, she begged silently. Don't blame it all on me. Face it, Craig. *Please.*

"Why aren't you?" Todd demanded.

"Are you going to get a divorce?" Jennifer asked.

"We haven't talked about it." Craig's skin was tight over his face, like a mask; his mouth worked. And then a long sigh broke from him. "But, you see, I left all of you—which was a terrible thing to do—and then I stayed away too long. And your mother and I changed. People do change, you know," he said, looking directly at Katherine. "We really aren't the same people we were. It's nobody's fault, but it happened. So that's what we're going to do. Get a divorce."

"Shit," muttered Todd, and no one scolded him.

After a moment, Jennifer asked, "Why did you go away?"

"Because I got myself into a mess and didn't know how to get out. I was scared. Too scared even to ask your mother to help me. It wasn't very smart. In fact, it was stupid. If you're lucky enough to have people love you, you ought to be smart enough to let them help you when you need it."

Katherine sat on the arm of the couch and touched Craig's cheek. "Thank you," she said softly. "I wish—"

He looked up quickly, but she stopped. It was too late for them. She clasped her hands in her lap.

Todd scowled, furiously blinking back his tears. "What's going to happen to all of us?"

"I'm going back to Canada," Craig answered. "And as soon as I find a place to live, with an extra bedroom, you'll come for a visit. Lots of visits. All you have to do is tell me when you want to come, and I'll be ready."

"Like Carrie and Jon," said Jennifer. "They see Ross a lot."

"Ross has children," Craig murmured. "Funny; in my mind he's still twenty years old, a college kid. Do you see them often?" he asked Jennifer.

"Sort of."

He gave a small smile. "It's all right if you like Ross, Jenny. He and I grew up together, you know. I always thought he was...I loved Ross and my sister better than any other people in the world. That was a long time ago."

Abruptly, Katherine turned away. Nothing is simple, she thought.

"We love him, too," Jennifer said. "Not the same as you. Different."

Craig nodded. "I'll bet he loves you, too. Hold on." He took his arms from their shoulders and stood up, wiping his eyes with his handkerchief.

No one moved. Then he turned briskly. "If I'm going to find a place to live, I'd better start. I have a lot to do. I'll call you very soon—"

"When?" Todd demanded.

"In a day or two, as soon as I've decided what I'm going to do."

"Tonight," Todd insisted.

Smiling, Craig leaned over to kiss them both. "I won't disappear again. But I'll call you tonight, if you want. And tomorrow. And as often as you like. I'll even write to you if you promise to write back."

Jennifer and Todd looked at each other. "We're not much good at writing letters," said Todd.

"Then you need practice," Craig declared. "Now, would you do something for me?" They nodded watchfully. "Go on into your bedroom. I want to say goodbye to your mother."

Todd sprang up and threw his arms around him. "You'll call *tonight*."

"I promise," Craig replied, holding him tight. "I love you, Todd." He let him go and held Jennifer. "Goodbye, my lovely Jenny. I'll see you soon."

When they were gone, he said, "They're so wonderful. Like their mother." He cleared his throat and tried to smile as he and Katherine walked to the door. "A man couldn't ask for a better family. And I threw it away. Dear God, Katherine" —he put his arms around her— "isn't there any way—?"

"No." She raised her hand to brush the hair back from his forehead, as she had done countless times in their years together. "*You* were wonderful, with them. Thank you."

He grimaced. "What difference does it make? It's too late."

"Not for the life you make from now on. And I'll help you, any way I can." She smiled. "You can tell me anything now. I'll be here, if you need to talk—"

"But that's all," he said.

"That's all. But I care about you. You'll always have that."

He tightened his hold, pulling her close again, and Katherine put her arms around him, her cheek against his. They stood that way, without speaking, as the air grew lighter and the fog pushed in from the ocean, and then they moved apart, and in another moment he was gone.

CHAPTER 23

THE night was so quiet Ross heard his footsteps echo through the house and out to the hushed coolness of the deck. He had tried to sleep and given up; some nights were worse than others, and this night, for some reason, seemed the worst of all: filled with longings and memories.

In the living room he poured himself a drink, then wandered through the rooms, turning lights on and off, seeing Katherine wherever he looked.

In his bedroom, an enlarged, framed photograph stood on the dresser: Katherine, on the boat, her hair lifted by the wind, her eyes laughing into his. Beside it was another, snapped surreptitiously by Carrie on the terrace in Menton: Ross and Katherine in conversation, absorbed in each other, smiling, in love. He ran his finger along the glass over their two faces. *Katherine.*

On the living room desk was a lucite paperweight Katherine had made in the shape of a curved sail; engraved on it was a sketch of Ross's boat, with a seagull wheeling above. Holding the polished curve on his hand, Ross sat on the couch, staring at the wall. *To take up such a large space in my life, in so short a time...*

The telephone was beside him. His hand touched it, then drew back. Ridiculous; it was two thirty in the morning; she'd be sound asleep. Besides, he had promised he would not call. He'd gone too far as it was, at the Halloween ball; because he was so damned impatient.

On the table was a book he had bought the day before; he lay back on the couch and opened it. And then suddenly a misty early morning light was coming through the glass doors and Ross awoke, the book still in his hands, and thought, as if he had not slept at all, *Katherine.*

It was six o'clock. The bridges were shrouded in fog, their towers jutting above it like miniature steeples floating above the clouds. Ross went through his morning routine, listening to a newscast as he dressed, reading the newspaper while drinking his coffee. And then he left the house.

He was backing his car out of the driveway when a taxi approached. He stopped to let it go by, drumming his fingers on the steering wheel as it slowed to a crawl, but in the next moment he knew. *Katherine.* And then she was there, opening the door and jumping out before the taxi came to a full stop.

After all the hours of imagining her before him, he could not move. Then he saw her smile. Through the pounding of his heart he took a deep breath and threw open his car door to take long strides across the grass, his eyes on hers.

"Lady?" The taxi driver's voice was rising. "Lady, did you hear me? You owe me—"

"I heard you," said Ross, and pulled out his wallet.

"No," Katherine said. "Wait. I have it, I just—for a minute, I didn't hear him."

Ross held out some bills. "Keep it."

The driver's eyes brightened. "No kidding. You want a receipt?"

"No. This is a special occasion."

"No kidding. That's what the lady said."

"Did she," Ross murmured. He put his arm around Katherine to lead her to the house. "You look like you didn't get enough sleep."

"I didn't get any."

He stopped, his hands on her shoulders, searching her face. "He called? Or came to you?"

"He came about midnight. We talked all night."

"And he left?"

"Yes."

Ross felt his pounding heart slow; he took a long breath, almost weightless with relief and love. With their arms around each other, they walked through the house to the deck. Looking at her pallor, he asked, "Have you had breakfast?"

She shook her head. "Jennifer and Todd had an early rehearsal at school, and I fixed them something, but I wasn't hungry. And I was in a hurry to get here, before you left."

"I would have waited if you'd let me know you were coming."

"I didn't want to let you know. I wanted to surprise you."

He laughed softly. "And so you did. Wait here; I'll get you some food."

"Just coffee would be fine." When he was gone, Katherine lay back on the chaise. "Don't do that," she said aloud. "You'll fall asleep." She forced herself upright, half-closing her eyes against the glare of the sun, floating on the golden light and the early-morning fragrance of roses and carnations. She took off her jacket, the heat flowing through her, making her bones feel liquid. Her head began to droop and then she heard footsteps and opened her eyes to see Ross putting a tray on the table in front of her.

"Orange juice and coffee. I didn't want to take the time for something dramatic, like waffles. Are you all right?"

"I came to propose to you," she said.

"Yes."

"You knew that?"

"I mean, my answer is yes."

She laughed and rested her cheek against his tweed jacket. "I was hoping it would be."

Ross kissed the top of her head. "Can you tell me what happened?"

"So much happened. It seemed like a lifetime, in one night." Waves of sleepiness lapped at Katherine and she swayed against Ross. "I didn't really understand how much I'd changed until I talked to Craig—heard him talk—about himself, and us."

"We've all changed," said Ross. "But you more than anyone. I tried to tell you that."

"I know. But I couldn't put it all together—what I had been and what I'd become and why I hadn't been able to do it before. Then Craig came and every time I looked at him it was as if I were looking at what I used to be. Remember," she went on sleepily, "once I told you I missed being able to predict tomorrow? That was only because I was afraid."

"And you're not afraid now?"

"No. Not since some time last night, when I saw how far I'd come by myself. That was when I knew I wanted you." Over the edge of her coffee cup, she smiled at Ross. "I knew I could be a whole person by myself, but I knew my life would be richer with you in it. I want you to let me face things on my own, the way you did when you said we should stay away from each other, but I want you to care about me, too, and protect me—and I want to help *you* when you need it . . . the two of us, sharing the good times and helping each other through the bad ones . . . Ross, I'm so sleepy . . . am I making sense?"

"You're promising," he said gravely, "to be less fierce about your independence as long as I help you without diminishing it—and let you do the same for me. As long as we keep a balance between us."

"Not easy," she murmured.

"We'll probably manage it about half the time, and work on the rest. Is that good enough?"

"It's wonderful." Katherine laughed, her love for him welling up through her sleepiness, making everything seem possible. She looked at the fog, burning away in the hot sun, and the skyscrapers across the bay, shimmering like an enchanted city filled with happy endings. "If you're lucky enough to have people love you," she said softly, "you ought to be smart enough to let them help you when you need it. Craig said that, when he was explaining to Jennifer and Todd why he'd been wrong."

"Then he's learned more than I thought he could. Will he go to Elissa?"

"I don't know. I hope so."

"And Jennifer and Todd?"

"They told him they love you. Not the way they love him, but... Oh, *damn*, I wish there was a way to build happiness without sadness somewhere underneath."

Ross took her in his arms and they held each other. "Katherine, I love you," he said, moving his lips slowly against hers. He kissed her eyes as she fought to keep them open. "My sleepy darling, I promise to share with you everything I am and everything I dream of, if you'll do the same for me."

Katherine's eyelids flew open. "I forgot to tell you. Xavier's called. I have an appointment tomorrow."

"Another beginning." He smiled. "We'll have a celebration. Trumpets and fireworks and champagne. And eventually, when the laws of California are satisfied, a wedding. With four offspring in the cheering section."

Katherine put her arms around him and opened her mouth beneath his. Their bodies met, remembering, and they stood together and walked with their arms around each other into the house, to the shadowed coolness of Ross's bedroom. But the instant the mattress yielded beneath their weight, Katherine drooped.

"Ross, do you mind—?" she asked. "I'm so sorry, but would you mind very much if I just went to sleep?"

Holding her, he laughed with pure joy. "Dear one," he said, "we have a lifetime ahead of us." He took off her shoes and laid her on the bed, her head on his pillow.

"But wake me up," she said drowsily. "I promised Jennifer and Todd I'd be there at three..."

"I'll go. I want to stop at the office; I'll pick them up and bring them here."

"And we have to call Victoria and Tobias." Her voice was barely a murmur. "They'll be hurt if we don't tell them right away..."

"I'll invite us there for dinner tonight. Would you like that? The four of us, and Carrie and Jon, and Victoria and Tobias. A family dinner."

Katherine's lips curved in a smile. "A family dinner. I love you, Ross."

He put a light blanket over her and drew the drapes, then stood for a moment beside the bed. Katherine held up her arms. Bending down, Ross kissed her closed eyes. "Sleep well, my love, You've come home."

About the Authors

JUDITH BARNARD and MICHAEL FAIN—the two halves of "Judith Michael"—are husband-and-wife partners whose first novel was the best-selling *Deceptions*. Judith Barnard is also the author of the novel *The Past and Present of Solomon Sorge* and has been a journalist and literary critic. Michael Fain, a former aerospace scientist and science writer, is also a professional photographer whose work has illustrated the couple's magazine and newspaper articles. They are currently at work on a new novel, to be set in Europe and America.

CHURC

BARBARA LEAMING

Churchill Defiant

Fighting On
1945–1955

Harper
Press

Harper*Press*
An imprint of HarperCollins*Publishers*
77–85 Fulham Palace Road
Hammersmith, London W6 8JB

www.harpercollins.co.uk

Visit our authors' blog: www.fifthestate.co.uk
Love this book? www.bookarmy.com

First published in Great Britain by Harper*Press* in 2010
Copyright © Barbara Leaming 2010
1

Barbara Leaming asserts the moral right to
be identified as the author of this work

A catalogue record for this book
is available from the British Library

ISBN 978-0-00-725790-4

Set in Minion by Palimpsest Book Production Limited,
Falkirk, Stirlingshire

Printed and bound in Great Britain by
Clays Ltd, St Ives plc

Mixed Sources
Product group from well-managed
forests and other controlled sources
www.fsc.org Cert no. SW-COC-001806
© 1996 Forest Stewardship Council
FSC

FSC is a non-profit international organisation established to promote the
responsible management of the world's forests. Products carrying the FSC
label are independently certified to assure consumers that they come
from forests that are managed to meet the social, economic and
ecological needs of present or future generations.

Find out more about HarperCollins and the environment at
www.harpercollins.co.uk/green

CONTENTS

I

You Will, but I Shall Not

Berlin, July 1945

A flashlight revealed the stairs to the concrete underground air-raid shelter. Pools of stagnant water made the steps slippery. For an old man, uneasy on his feet, the descent was treacherous. Late in the afternoon on 16 July 1945, Britain's seventy-year-old wartime Prime Minister, Winston Churchill, picked his way with a gold-headed walking stick to the dark, dank bunker where Adolf Hitler had put a bullet into his right temple two and a half months before.

Word had spread quickly that Churchill was in Berlin. By the time his convoy reached the Reich Chancellery, the small British party had swelled to a jostling mob as war correspondents and numerous Russian officers and officials pressed forward to join Churchill's entourage. Anxious to witness the final scene of one of history's greatest dramas, they followed the Prime Minister, who wore a lightweight military uniform and visored cap, into the sacked remains of the Chancellery and, later, out to the garden where the entrance to the bunker was located.

In one of his most famous wartime broadcasts, Churchill had said, 'We have but one aim and one single irrevocable purpose. We are resolved to destroy Hitler and every vestige of the Nazi regime. From this nothing will turn us. Nothing.' Now, the reporters hoped for a curtain speech from this master of the spoken word as he inspected the tangible evidence of his triumph. He had been fighting his way here in one way or another for more than a decade, and a statement from him would provide a thrilling end to the story.

Churchill had been a lonely voice in the wilderness during most of the 1930s, when his warnings about Hitler had gone unheeded. In 1940, Britain was already at war when he was called to serve as Prime Minister. Against seemingly impossible odds, at a time when France had fallen and Hitler's armies had overrun the Continent, Churchill led Britain as it fought alone. While Nazi bombs rained on London and Hitler boasted that he had crushed the panic-stricken British in their holes, Churchill's flights of oratory rallied his countrymen and offered hope that their plight might yet be reversed. After the Russians and then the Americans joined the fight on Britain's side, Churchill battled the 'bloodthirsty guttersnipe' – as he referred to Hitler – for an additional four years.

By the end of the war in Europe, Churchill had accomplished what many people had once believed he could never do. At home in Britain, even long-time detractors agreed that he had saved the country. His personal story was all the more remarkable because he had spent so much of his adult life in political disrepute. The road to the premiership had been long, 'and every foot of it contested'. Frustration, exclusion, and isolation had often been his lot before he became Prime Minister when he was sixty-five, an age that qualified him to draw an old-age pension.

The man who visited Hitler's bunker had recast himself in just five years as one of history's titans. Had Churchill died before 1940, he might have been remembered as a prodigiously gifted failure. On this day, he was at the apex of his glory. Yet thus far, he had appeared oddly detached and distracted. His bulbous, bloodshot, light blue eyes surveyed the devastation at the Chancellery, and he quietly asked a few questions of the Russian soldier who served as his guide, but he made no public comment. Finally, Churchill left reporters outside the bunker entrance as he followed the Russian soldier into the blackness.

He slowly made his way down the first flight of stone steps towards the chamber where Hitler's body had been discovered, slumped over a sofa beside the lifeless form of his bride, Eva Braun, her lips puckered and blue from poison. Churchill hesitated when the Russian told him that two additional water-soaked flights remained. As if it were no longer worth the effort, he abandoned the tour without having seen for himself the site of his mortal enemy's suicide. Churchill sent the others in his party, which included his youngest daughter, Mary, to view it without him. Then he turned and slowly began to make his way back up.

He climbed with difficulty. Five years of war had left Churchill in ravaged physical condition. In 1941, he had suffered a heart attack, the first of several episodes of heart trouble. He had repeatedly been stricken with pneumonia; on one occasion, in 1943, he had lain at the brink of death, at General Eisenhower's headquarters in Carthage. There had been moments during the war when Churchill was so exhausted that he could barely speak, walk, stand, or concentrate. In 1944, Clementine Churchill had told a friend resignedly, 'I never think of after the war. You see, I think Winston will die when it's over.' She knew better than anyone that her husband had put all he had into this war, and she was convinced it would take everything. She had watched as, whatever the state of Churchill's health, the phones kept ringing and the red boxes laden with official papers were rushed in. When illness sapped his energies and made it difficult to work, he pressed harder. Defying predictions that he would soon have to hand over to a younger, stronger man, he had fought on with the whole strength of his gargantuan will. Lady Violet Bonham Carter, a friend of four decades, feared what the 'last pull up the hill' must have cost him. As victory drew near, Churchill was so physically weak that soldiers had to carry him upstairs in a chair after Cabinet meetings.

Churchill emerged from Hitler's bunker under his own power, but when at last he reached the top of the stairs and passed through the door of a concrete blockhouse into the daylight, his hulking frame appeared so shaky and depleted that a Russian soldier guarding the entrance reached out a hand to steady him. The Chancellery garden was a chaos of shattered glass, pieces of timber, tangled metal, and abandoned fire hoses. Craters from Russian shells pocked the ground. In one of those craters, Hitler and his wife had supposedly been buried after Nazi officers burned their corpses. The rusted cans for the gasoline still lay nearby. Russians pointed out the spot where the bodies had been incinerated. Churchill paused briefly before turning away in disgust.

He moved towards a battered chair that had been propped against a bullet-riddled wall. One of the Red Army men claimed that it had belonged to the Führer. The hinges of its back were broken and the rear legs had buckled. Churchill tested it first with one hand before sitting. Gingerly perched on the front edge of the seat, he mopped his forehead with a handkerchief in the withering heat as he chewed on a cigar. When at length his daughter and the others came out of the bunker, Churchill was visibly eager to leave.

In front of the Chancellery, he was met by a cheering crowd of sightseeing British sailors and Royal Marines. The street was a sea of devastation, every roof bombed out. The glassless windows of gutted buildings stared blindly. Despite the applause that greeted him, Churchill's mind was in turmoil; his heart ached with anxiety. This uncomfortable, even painful feeling of disconnection from the general rejoicing was not a new experience. For months, he had lived with the thought that in spite of what others might believe, the struggle was far from over. As the war came to an end, he saw that Soviet Russia, still ostensibly Britain's ally, was fast becoming as dangerous poten- tially as Hitler's Germany had been and that a third world war was already in the making. Worse, he knew that the Americans did not understand, indeed did not wish to be told, what was happening. As in a nightmare, the man who had warned in vain of the Nazi threat was again trying desperately to call attention to an emerging enemy.

4

In no mood to speak of victory, he acknowledged the cheers by mechanically raising his right arm and forming the familiar V-sign. Then he climbed into a waiting car for the return trip to Potsdam, outside Berlin, where he was due to face his Soviet and American counterparts. The talks, for which Churchill had been militating since May, were to have begun that afternoon, but the arrival of the Soviet leader, Joseph Stalin, had been inexplicably delayed. Potsdam was being billed as a victory conference, but Churchill privately regarded it as a chance to stage a 'showdown' with Stalin about Soviet territorial ambitions.

The Big Three – Churchill, Stalin, and President Franklin Roosevelt – had last met at Yalta, in the Crimea, in February. But by the time he had assured the House of Commons that Stalin meant to keep his promise given at Yalta of free elections in the countries the Soviets had liberated from Germany, Churchill had already begun to be troubled by doubts. He worried that by trusting Stalin he might have made the same mistake that his predecessor, Neville Chamberlain, had committed with Hitler.

In March, Berlin became the focal point of Churchill's concerns when the Supreme Commander of the Allied Forces in Europe, Dwight Eisenhower, informed him that rather than try to take the Reich capital with American and British forces, he intended to let the Russians get there first. Churchill moved at once to persuade Eisenhower that he was about to make a calamitous error with far-reaching consequences. In separate messages to Eisenhower and Roosevelt, Churchill argued that, as the Soviet armies were about to enter Vienna and overrun Austria, should they also be permitted to take Berlin it would strengthen their conviction, already alarmingly in evidence, that they were chiefly responsible for Hitler's defeat and that the spoils were rightly theirs.

Churchill had no doubt that Stalin, whom Eisenhower had also informed of his intentions, well understood the symbolic and political significance of the Reich capital falling into Soviet hands. So when

Stalin fulsomely complimented Eisenhower and assured him that the Soviet Union would send only second-rate forces to Berlin – which, he underscored, had 'lost its former strategic importance' – Churchill's worst suspicions were confirmed. Churchill implored Eisenhower to pay particular attention to what was obviously a lie on Stalin's part. But Eisenhower flatly refused. Eisenhower had Roosevelt's backing when he declined even to attempt to race the Russians to Berlin. The Americans were not a little annoyed at Churchill's insinuations about their Soviet ally's postwar designs. Roosevelt had long insisted that Stalin was a man of good will and good faith who wanted nothing but security for his country, and that if the US gave him whatever he asked for, he could be counted on to work for a world of democracy and peace after the war and to refrain from annexing any territory. Meanwhile, on the very day – 1 April 1945 – that Stalin had written to congratulate Eisenhower on his sound thinking, he ordered two of his top military chiefs to capture Berlin post-haste.

Driving through the ruins of the former Reich capital, Churchill sat in silence. His car passed endless rows of saluting Russian soldiers, directional signs printed in Cyrillic characters, and red-bordered posters bearing the sayings of Stalin translated into German above his signature etched in vivid red. It was as if Stalin had branded Berlin, fashioned it into his personal war trophy. The Russians all seemed 'high as kites', convinced, as Churchill had predicted they would be, that they were principally responsible for having won the war. The shattered capital, where street after street had been reduced to rubble and where the stench of putrefying corpses and broken sewer lines fouled the air, was an image of the collapse of the Nazi empire. Churchill grimly perceived something more. To his eye, the ubiquitous, overpowering Red Army presence augured the rise of Soviet power in postwar Europe.

Hardly had Berlin surrendered to the Russians, on 2 May 1945, when Churchill had hatched a plan. Experience had taught him that Stalin was not a man to be swayed by arguments based on abstract principles. 'Force and facts' were his only realities. Brutal and unscrupulous, Stalin would do whatever he perceived to be in his own interest. The Americans had penetrated 120 miles deeper into Germany than originally planned. Churchill believed that gave him the leverage he needed to settle things peacefully with Stalin. The trick was to postpone pulling American troops back to the previously agreed-upon lines until Churchill was satisfied about both the temporary character of the Soviet occupation of Germany, and conditions in the countries liberated by the Red Army. Germany as a whole had yet to surrender when Churchill urgently contacted President Harry Truman, who had succeeded to office upon Roosevelt's death in April. He urged the former vice president that they invite Stalin to a heads of government meeting to take place as soon as possible and that in the interim they maintain their troops in existing positions in order to show the Soviets 'how much we have to offer or withhold'. From this point, everything depended on Truman. Roosevelt and Eisenhower had failed to listen to Churchill about Berlin. Could he hope for a better response from Truman, whom he had not yet met?

Churchill's telegram was sent on 6 May. The following day, German generals signed the act of unconditional surrender of all German land, sea, and air forces in Europe. On 8 May, Victory in Europe Day, Churchill announced in a radio broadcast that the German war was at an end; only Japan remained unsubdued. London exploded in a paroxysm of celebration. From first to last, the Prime Minister was at the centre of the festivities. When he cried out to a vast crowd assembled beneath his balcony, 'This is your victory,' the people roared back, 'No, it's yours!' A tender man easily moved to tears whether of joy or sorrow, Churchill made no secret of his pleasure in lapping up the affection and admiration, yet he remained oppressed by forebodings as he awaited Truman's answer. He ended the long, emotionally charged day by sharing his concerns with a friend, the newspaper proprietor Lord Camrose, who had come to dine at 10 Downing Street.

While the noisy celebrations continued in the streets, Churchill spoke sombrely and confidentially of what would happen if Truman turned him down and the troops were withdrawn. Stalin would control seven European capitals in addition to Berlin: Prague, Budapest, Warsaw, Belgrade, Bucharest, Sofia, and Vienna. As far as Churchill was concerned, that could not be permitted.

When Truman replied the next day that he preferred to wait for Stalin to propose a meeting, Churchill refused to take no for an answer. He wanted a leaders' meeting as soon as possible and suggested that he and Truman confer first in London in order to present a united front. The new president, who seemed to have inherited his predecessor's unrealistic view of Stalin, demurred on the grounds that he wished to avoid any impression of 'ganging up'. Churchill warned bluntly that the Soviets had drawn down an 'iron curtain' upon their front and that the rest of humanity had no idea of what was going on behind it. He argued that surely it was vital to come to an understanding with the Soviet Union or at least see how things stood before American troops retired to the agreed zones of occupation.

Truman sent an emissary to London to convey what he did not wish to put in writing: Truman wanted to see Stalin first – without Churchill. The British Prime Minister could join them later. When Churchill waxed indignant, the emissary, Joseph Davies, went so far as to blame him for having provoked Stalin with his abiding hostility towards the Soviet Union. Truman's representative maintained that in fact it was Churchill's attitude that 'placed not only the future, but possibly the immediate peace in real danger'.

Furious at being told that he, not Stalin, was threatening the peace, Churchill reminded Truman that a shared love of freedom ought naturally to align their two nations against the Soviet Communists, who followed a different philosophy. With Churchill threatening to break publicly with Washington if Truman dared to see Stalin alone, the President appeared to back down. He agreed to three-power talks, but at the last minute he declined Churchill's pleas to postpone the retreat of the American army at least until after the conference.

When Churchill returned to his rose-pink, lakeside villa in Potsdam following the visit to Hitler's bunker, he learned that Stalin had arrived in Germany. The leaders were to meet the following day at 5 p.m. in the former palace of the German crown prince. Due to Truman's decision to withdraw his troops, however, Churchill was to face Stalin without the bargaining counter he had been hoping for. As he prepared to go into the talks, he was further wrong-footed by the fact that he had no idea of how much time he had to get what he wanted from Stalin. Prior to coming to Potsdam, Churchill – who had promised the British people a general election as soon as Hitler was defeated – had fought the first general election campaign in a decade. Polling day had been 5 July, but three weeks had been allotted to permit the service vote to come in before the total vote was counted. On 25 July, while the Potsdam Conference was still in progress, Churchill was due to fly back to Britain (briefly, he hoped) to learn his political fate.

The rapturous reception he had received in the course of his thousand-mile electoral tour strongly suggested to him that he would still be prime minister when the second round of talks began. Everywhere Churchill had travelled that spring, multitudes had come out to see and thank him for what he had done in the war. Standing nine and ten deep, enthusiasts had waved flags, sung patriotic songs, and cried out, 'Good old Winnie!' Repeatedly they had closed in on the hero's open car and the progress of the motorcade had been slowed to a walking pace. Churchill had commented at the time that no one who had witnessed his reception could have any doubt about the outcome of the poll.

But what if there was an upset? What if poor Conservative showings in recent by-elections foretold a general swing to the left in British politics, as certain commentators were suggesting? Churchill had encountered some heckling, particularly in the last days of the campaign. Had these been isolated incidents, or did they reflect broad sentiment for change as Britons considered what they wanted their lives to be like after the war? Churchill had brought his Labour opponent, Clement Attlee, to Potsdam to make it clear that all of Britain was being represented at the conference table, as well as to ensure that there would be no break in Attlee's knowledge of affairs. But by his very presence, Attlee was also a reminder that when Churchill went home for the election results, they might prevent him from completing what he had begun with Stalin.

Attlee, who had been deputy prime minister in Churchill's wartime coalition government, attended a small luncheon at the Prime Minister's villa on the afternoon of 17 July. Also present was US Secretary of War Henry Stimson. Churchill lingered at the table bantering with his guests until half an hour before he was scheduled to see Stalin and Truman. With Attlee, he joked about the British general election as if there had not been a harsh word between them during the often exceptionally bitter campaign; and with Stimson, he exchanged light-hearted personal reminiscences about their younger days. In the leisurely course of the meal, Stimson gave no sign that he had anything urgent to convey to his host or that he desired to speak to him privately. Only when Churchill was showing Stimson out did the latter inform him that the world's first atomic bomb had been successfully tested the day before in New Mexico. Though Britain had been a partner in the secret project to develop the new weapon, deadlier than any yet in existence, Churchill had not known in advance the date of the test. If the bomb worked, it promised to end the Pacific war quickly and to spare a great many Allied soldiers' lives. In his present predicament, Churchill also sensed that it might be capable of something more. Nothing could be certain for there were no details as yet, but here potentially was the card he needed to persuade Stalin to come to terms in Europe.

Until Churchill had additional information, he was intent that this first bit of news from New Mexico be withheld from Stalin.

Truman had already thrown away one bargaining counter, and Churchill wanted to be sure that it did not happen again. Stimson's insistence that the Soviets really ought to be notified of the test left Churchill to go off to his meeting both excited about the new development and worried that the Americans might be about to squander another opportunity. Churchill, who had met with Truman the previous day, knew that the President had been lunching with Stalin that afternoon. Churchill had no idea whether Truman, who had had the information since the previous evening, might already have told Stalin about the bomb or even agreed to share its secrets with his Soviet ally, as Roosevelt had once been inclined to do. The last-minute timing of Stimson's disclosure made it impossible for Churchill to talk to the President beforehand.

At the first plenary session at the Cecilienhof Palace – in whose courtyard the Russians had planted masses of geraniums in the form of a 24-foot-wide red star – Churchill played for time. For weeks, he had been pressing Truman to agree to the earliest possible meeting; now, he meant to go as slowly as possible. Previously, he had been insistent that the most contentious issues be addressed without delay; now, he told his fellow leaders, 'We will feel our way up to them.' Truman was in a difficult, almost impossible position at Potsdam. In the days before the conference, he had been nervous about facing giants like Churchill and Stalin, and with good reason. Though a dying man, Roosevelt had done nothing to prepare his successor for the presidency. Roosevelt never spoke to Truman confidentially of the war, of foreign affairs, or of what he had in mind for the postwar world. When Truman suddenly landed in the Oval Office after only three months as vice president, he had to struggle to catch up. Devoid of foreign policy experience, he pored over memoranda, briefs, and correspondence on international affairs. He conferred with presidential advisers, who, to his perplexity, offered conflicting advice. On the voyage to Europe, he absorbed as much information as he could from various coaches. At his first meeting with Stalin and Churchill together, he read aloud from prepared statements and thereafter was careful to stick to positions that had been well worked out in advance.

Churchill's newly unhurried pace irked Truman, who protested, 'I don't just want to discuss. I want to decide.'

Churchill came back impishly, 'You want something in the bag each day.'

Looking ahead to subsequent plenary sessions, Truman went on, 'I should like to meet at four o'clock instead of five.'

'I will obey your orders,' Churchill replied.

Clearly amused, Stalin interjected, 'If you are in such an obedient mood today, Mr Prime Minister, I should like to know whether you will share with us the German fleet.'

When the meeting concluded, Stalin invited the others to the banquet room, the length of which was filled by a table loaded with caviar, cold meat, turkeys, partridges, and salads, as well as vodkas and wines 'of all hues'. Truman stayed less than ten minutes. Churchill, though he had previously complained of indigestion, happily ate and drank with Stalin. Pointing out that they had much to talk about privately, Stalin asked Churchill to have dinner with him the following evening. It promised to be a late night. In contrast to Truman, who preferred to go to bed early, Churchill and Stalin were both night owls. On the present occasion, Stalin remarked to Churchill that he had grown so accustomed to working late during the war that even though the necessity had passed, he could never get to sleep before 4 a.m.

By the time Churchill dined with Stalin on Wednesday, 18 July, he had had a chance to talk to Truman, who assured him that he had not informed the Soviet leader about the bomb. Churchill had concluded overnight that, once they were certain of the test results, it would actually be a very good idea were Stalin to be made aware that the Western allies had a singular new weapon. What continued to worry him, however, was the possibility that Truman would agree to share technical information with Moscow. Truman said he would not, but Churchill remained uneasy. Western possession of the bomb would be of little use in the negotiations if Stalin could count on being able to build one as well.

When Churchill arrived at half past eight, Stalin's two-storey stone villa was surrounded by machine-gun-toting thugs. A phalanx of seven NKVD – secret police – regiments and nine hundred bodyguards had accompanied the dictator to Potsdam. Stalin had lived a life of violence, fighting off rivals and would-be usurpers with murder and blood-shed, and he was perpetually fearful of being treated in kind. In the present setting, the savage vengeance the Red Army had wreaked on the Germans provided an additional motive for an assassination attempt. Still, once through the numerous layers of security, Churchill was welcomed with friendly informality. Stalin had no other guests. Only the leaders' interpreters, Birse and Pavlov, were scheduled to join them at dinner.

Though the surviving members of the original Big Three had become antagonists, they were bonded by a sense of themselves as men apart, the last of a superior breed that had included Roosevelt. As Churchill later said, together they had had the world at their feet and commanded many millions of men on land and sea. Churchill's personal history with Stalin had begun with their written exchanges in 1941 after Germany's surprise attack on Russia. When they first met, in Moscow in 1942, Stalin's insults had nearly caused Churchill to break off their talks and fly home at once. The British Ambassador, Archibald Clark Kerr, had worked hard to assuage Churchill's fury. Kerr urged him to reflect on the relative unimportance of his own wounded feelings weighed against the many young lives that would be sacrificed if he did not swallow his pride and return to the talks. Churchill resolved that in the interest of advancing their shared objective of defeating Hitler he would do what it took to build a relationship with Stalin, even somehow find a way to 'like' him. In subsequent meetings – at Tehran, again in Moscow, and at Yalta – Churchill and Stalin had devel-oped a deep fascination with and respect for each other.

Though Churchill had no idea that Stalin's late arrival at Potsdam had been due to a minor heart attack, he thought his host tonight looked ill and 'physically rather oppressed'. Stalin's once black hair was a grizzled mop, as were his shaggy moustache and eyebrows. His narrow, evasive eyes were yellow, his teeth stained and broken. Short and stocky, he had a withered left arm that he held woodenly in his right hand, palms up. War had aged the sixty-seven-year-old Generalissimo prematurely. He had worked too hard, slept too little, and not had a holiday in years. Despite his physical condition, he had made no more effort to moderate his appetites than Churchill had. In the course of the dinner, which extended to the next morning, there was a prodigious amount of smoking, eating, and drinking by both men.

When Churchill and Stalin last saw Roosevelt, at Yalta, the President had been a cadaverous figure with waxen cheeks and trembling hands. At times he had been lucid, but at other moments he sat with his mouth open, staring ahead, unable to follow the discussion. Roosevelt had clung to office in the belief that he was indispensable. Five months later, the conversation between Stalin and Churchill naturally turned to the death of great men and the problems of succession. A discussion of how Roosevelt's successor was doing under the circumstances prompted Churchill to ask if Stalin had given any thought to what would happen at the Kremlin after he died.

Churchill had designated his own political heir. In 1942 he had written to King George that in the event of his death he wanted Anthony Eden to carry on as prime minister because he possessed the 'resolution, experience and capacity' the times demanded. Tall, slim, graceful, debonair, the forty-eight-year-old Foreign Secretary accompanied Churchill to Potsdam. Eden had a furrowed but handsome face with penetrating pale blue eyes and a carefully trimmed grey moustache, and he spoke in a mellifluous baritone. Stalin too had brought an heir apparent to the Potsdam Conference: Eden's opposite number, the fifty-five-year-old Soviet Foreign Minister Vyacheslav Molotov. Recently,

Stalin had anointed Molotov with the words, 'Let Vyacheslav go to work now. He is younger.' Small and chunky, Molotov spoke with a slight stammer and had an impassive, 'lard-white' face. When he was upset, though his countenance remained stony, a telltale lump in his forehead swelled and throbbed alarmingly.

Stalin insisted to Churchill that he had arranged everything. He claimed to have groomed good men and thereby to have guaranteed the continuity of Soviet policy for thirty years. He made it all sound so sensible, but then Stalin was adept at portraying himself to foreigners as utterly reasonable and rational. In fact, in the words of the American diplomat George Kennan, he was 'a man of absolutely diseased suspiciousness'. Stalin had a history of exterminating not only his opponents but also those whose character suggested that they might oppose him later. He sniffed plots and cabals everywhere, and never more so than after the war. In 1945, the leader widely venerated as his nation's saviour was at the pinnacle of his power. At the same time, his own physical decay left him feeling vulnerable to the machinations of the ambitious younger men who formed his circle. As the fawning Molotov and other contenders for the postwar Soviet leadership well knew, Stalin was capable of ordering their arrest or execution at any time, 'no questions asked'. (As a precaution, Molotov slept with a loaded revolver under his pillow and never permitted his sheets or blankets to be tucked in lest he have to leap out of bed and defend himself in the middle of the night.) Stalin spoke matter-of-factly of retiring on a pension in two or three years, but he was no more inclined to leave office willingly any time soon than Churchill was.

This evening, when Churchill voiced anxiety about the British election, Stalin expressed confidence that the Conservative leader had nothing to worry about. The concept of free elections meant nothing to Stalin. Churchill was in power; surely he had arranged to stay there. The only real mystery as far as the dictator was concerned was why Churchill would go to the trouble of flying home for the result. Characteristically, Stalin suspected a ploy on Churchill's part.

Stalin was right to sense that Churchill was up to something, though at this point the latter's calculations had nothing to do with the British election. Churchill asked whether there would be free elections in the territories under Soviet control, and he raised concerns that the Red Army was preparing to surge westward across Europe. When Stalin sought to reassure him on every count, Churchill took care not to provoke an angry confrontation by too directly challenging anything the Generalissimo said. Churchill was biding his time until he knew what kind of hand he had to play with Stalin.

Exactly a week remained before Churchill was due to fly to London. Every day that passed without news from New Mexico with precise details of the bomb test was an agony to him. There were plenary sessions on Thursday and Friday, but still no additional information came in. At half past four on Saturday, Churchill was about to leave for the Cecilienhof when Stimson arrived with the full report. This was the document the Prime Minister had been waiting for since Tuesday; everything depended on its contents. But no sooner had he begun to read than an aide reminded him that if he did not go now, he would be late for his 5 p.m. meeting. Following the day's talks, Stalin was due to host a party for all of the conference's participants, and Churchill naturally was expected to attend.

As the report was of the highest secrecy, Stimson had shown the single copy personally to each individual on his list, beginning with Truman. There was no question of his leaving the document for Churchill to study later, so it was agreed that he would return to the Prime Minister's villa in the morning. Churchill reluctantly handed the report back to Stimson. Impatient to resume reading, he found the evening that followed interminable.

It was not until 11 a.m. on Sunday that Stimson reappeared and Churchill at last had a chance to study the report in full. The details of the atomic bomb gripped him: the lightning effect equal to that of seven suns at midday; the vast ball of flame which mushroomed to a height of more than ten thousand feet; the cloud which shot upward with immense power, reaching the substratosphere in about five minutes; the complete devastation that had been wrought within a one-mile radius. Immediately, Churchill saw that this was the card he had been hoping for. The bomb completely altered the balance of power with the Soviets. Stalin's vast armies were negligible compared to it. Truman no longer had to worry about Stalin's willingness to fight the Japanese, and Churchill hoped that that would translate into real support for some tough bargaining to get a viable settlement in Europe. He rushed over to see Truman, both to discuss a speedy end to the war in the Pacific and to confirm that the Americans were not intending to share the bomb's secrets.

Churchill spoke excitedly of the bomb to his physician, Lord Moran, the following morning. He swore the doctor to secrecy and assured him that it had come just in time to save the world. Again, at lunch, he laid out the new situation to Field Marshal Sir Alan Brooke, General Hastings 'Pug' Ismay, Eden, and other key members of the British delegation. Referring to the sudden shift in the diplomatic equilibrium, Churchill thrust out his chin and scowled. He spoke of threatening to blot out Russian cities if the Communists refused to behave decently in Europe. But for all his talk of bullying Stalin with the bomb, Churchill's aim was not to start another war. As he had told Eden early on, he believed that the right bargaining counter might make it possible to secure a 'peaceful agreement'. He calculated that Stalin did not want war any more than he did, only the fruits of war, which the Soviets felt they had earned by their signal contribution to the defeat of Hitler. If Stalin could not be persuaded to settle, it might be best, as Churchill had previously told Truman, at least to know where they stood with him – and to know it sooner rather than later.

Churchill's optimism about what he would be able to achieve with both his fellow leaders provoked intensely sceptical reactions from

British colleagues. There was sentiment in the British camp that Truman (who controlled the bomb, after all) would never provide the backing Churchill needed, that Stalin would simply shrug off any real or implied threat, and that the details in the report from New Mexico might yet prove to have been exaggerated. Still, Churchill had found reason to hope, and to him that was all that mattered. On Monday night he called Lord Beaverbrook, who had had a hand in shaping the Conservatives' electoral strategy, for the most up-to-date predictions. Churchill had come to Potsdam empty-handed; now that he had what he believed was the basis of a real negotiation, nothing must be allowed to interfere. Beaverbrook told his friend that the Conservatives were expected to win, though perhaps by a smaller majority than first predicted.

Having proposed at the outset that the leaders take their time moving towards the most difficult questions, Churchill was ready to step up the pace and intensity of the talks. But the moment was still not right for what he saw as the climactic confrontation about Soviet intentions in postwar Europe. That, he believed, must wait until the British election results were known and the people had affirmed their confidence in him. Fresh from having submitted himself to their judgement, he would be in an optimal position to demand free elections in the territories liberated by the Russians.

He managed to put off the sharpest exchanges of the conference until Tuesday, 24 July, the eve of his departure. Speaking of reports from Romania and Bulgaria, he charged that an 'iron curtain' had descended in those countries. Until this point in the talks Stalin had been inclined to speak in a low, controlled tone of voice, but Churchill had succeeded in arousing his ire, and he shot back, 'Fairy tales!' A fierce dispute about the veracity of Churchill's claims followed. There was a good deal of pique and perspiration on the Soviet side of the large round table, which was covered with a dark red felt cloth and arrayed with offerings of pungent Russian cigarettes. Both Molotov and Eden grew indignant on behalf of their respective masters. Eventually Stalin declared that his and Churchill's views were so far apart that the discussion ought to be broken off – for now.

After everyone rose, Churchill watched anxiously as Truman walked over to Stalin. Churchill and Truman had previously agreed that at the close of that day's session the President would tell Stalin about the bomb and the plan to use it on the Japanese. (In fact, Stalin's spies had already notified him of the successful test blast, but neither Churchill nor Truman knew that.) There was high tension as Churchill looked on from a distance of about five yards. He longed to see Stalin's reaction, but he was also watching Truman. What would the President do if pressed for technical information? Would he agree to a meeting of American and Soviet experts? Truman had said in advance that he would not, but Churchill was aware that there had been no firm promise and that Truman did not yet perceive the Soviet threat as he did. Both participants in the silent scene were acting: in an effort to seem as casual as possible, Truman had left his own interpreter behind and depended on Stalin's man to trans-late his remarks, while Stalin made a point of appearing by turns genial and nonchalant.

Later, as the leaders waited for their cars, Churchill found himself beside Truman. He inquired how the conversation had gone. Truman reported that Stalin had not so much as asked a question. Stalin had said only that he was glad to hear the news and that he hoped they would make good use of the new weapon against Japan.

In any event, the information had been conveyed, and every element was finally in place for the dramatic confrontation Churchill expected would occur after a forty-eight-hour intermission. He was in buoyant spirits when he dined with Lord Mountbatten, the Supreme Commander in South-East Asia. Churchill again had much to say about the bomb and his plans for the future, though Mountbatten wondered whether the Prime Minister might not be assuming too much about the election outcome. That Churchill may have had deep doubts of his own is suggested by a disturbing dream he had that night. Six nights after he and Stalin had talked of death and succession, he dreamed that he too had died. He could see his corpse laid out beneath a sheet in an empty room. The face and body were draped, but the feet that stuck out were recognizably his own. On Wednesday morning, as he prepared to attend a final brief meeting with Stalin and Truman, he feared the dream meant that he was finished.

To all outward appearances his confidence had been restored by the time of the ninth plenary session. At a quarter past twelve, when Truman adjourned the meeting until 5 p.m. on Friday, Churchill added crisply that he hoped to be back. His mood on the flight home with his daughter was one of certainty that he would soon return to complete what he had begun. In London, Churchill went to Buckingham Palace to report to the King on the talks thus far and on the changes in the international situation that the bomb had wrought. Before Churchill retired for the evening at the Annexe facing St James's Park, he was pleased by the political gossip that even Labour headquarters was predicting a Conservative majority. Fittingly, he intended to monitor the figures from the Map Room, where once he had tracked the unfolding of the Allied victory over Hitler. Family members and close friends had been invited to sit with him as numbers streamed in throughout the day on 26 July.

Churchill went to bed on Wednesday night convinced that those numbers would favour the Conservatives. Sometime before daybreak, he awakened suddenly with a stabbing pain that told him the election was lost and the power to shape the future would be denied him. In anguish, he rolled over and slept until nine. About an hour later, Churchill was in his bath when he learned from an aide that his premonition of disaster was being amply confirmed by the early poll figures.

After he had dressed in a blue one-piece zip-up siren suit, he went to his Map Room. Over the next few hours, Churchill, surrounded by charts of constituencies and of the most recent state of the election, reacted to the news of each Labour gain by silently, stoically nodding his head. He complained only of the heat and the want of air. The Conservatives were out. Churchill had been returned in his constituency, Woodford. But overall there had been a Labour landslide, and Britain was to have a new prime minister.

Mrs Churchill, tall, silvery-haired, with proud posture and a profile said to resemble a ship's prow, suggested to her husband that the outcome of the election might prove to be 'a blessing in disguise'.

He replied, 'At the moment it seems quite effectively disguised.'

It was inconceivable that he had been cut off altogether from Potsdam. Initially, he insisted he would wait to take his dismissal from the House of Commons, as he was entitled to do. Then in his pride he declared that nothing would induce him to go back to Potsdam, though he was not yet ready to resign immediately either.

He spoke vaguely of stepping aside on Monday, though that would mean asking Stalin and Truman to wait in Germany until he made up his mind. Finally, Churchill accepted that under the circumstances he really had no choice but to resign at once – and let the talks go on without him. All of his great plans, everything he had so carefully set up, must remain unrealized.

Some twenty-four hours after he had raced to Buckingham Palace to speak to the King of his hopes, Churchill returned to tender his resignation. The King offered him the Order of the Garter but Churchill declined the high honour in the belief it would be wrong to accept it after what he saw as a public rebuff of his leadership. He drafted a statement to be read aloud to the nation on the BBC at 9 p.m. He stated that as a consequence of 'the decision of the British people', he had laid down the charge which had been placed upon him in darker times.

Thursday was devoted to immediate concerns. The next morning, he awakened to the realization of what the people's decision meant for him personally. In years past, Churchill had been known to declare that in war one can only be killed once, but in politics many times.

Politicians, he once wrote, expect to fall and hope to rise again. In the face of staggering rejection, numerous setbacks and many apparent dead ends, obstinacy had kept Churchill pounding on when fainter spirits might have given up. 'No' was an answer he had repeatedly refused to accept. 'Unsquashable resilience' had long been among his defining characteristics. He had justly been said to have more lives than a cat and to have survived as many arrows as legend planted in the flesh of Saint Sebastian.

This time, everything seemed different to him, and it was his age that made it so. By most estimates the magnitude of the Labour victory, a majority of 146 seats in the House of Commons, suggested that the Conservatives could not hope to return to power for at least a decade. Some people went so far as to say that Labour was in for a generation. For Churchill, as for his party, there was no avoiding the likelihood that by the time he had another chance at the premiership – if he ever did – he would be at least eighty.

Throughout the day, as he said goodbye to some of the people who had worked most closely with him during the war, he seemed absorbed by the idea that a comeback was impossible. The previous night he had briefly thought the new Labour Government might be turned out soon enough, but the final numbers left no such hope. After a farewell meeting with his Cabinet, he lingered privately to talk to Eden. Churchill expressed confidence that the Conservative heir apparent would surely sit in the Cabinet Room again.

'You will,' Churchill said with more than a dash of bitterness, 'but I shall not.'

Churchill once observed that a man's only real necessities in life are food and a philosophic temperament. All day Saturday at Chequers, which he had yet to vacate, he appeared remarkably cheerful and controlled, but after dinner and a film screening, his mood darkened noticeably. Attlee had returned to Potsdam a day later than scheduled and the talks resumed that very night at ten.

The new Big Three worked at the conference table in the Cecilienhof until after midnight.

Cut off from all that forever, it seemed, Churchill sat into the night listening to Gilbert and Sullivan and other recordings on his gramophone.

II

Face Facts and Retire

London, 1945

During the war, Churchill had always slept with the key to the Cabinet boxes. He kept it on his watch chain. Suddenly, the key was gone. There were no more boxes, no constantly ringing phones, no telegrams requiring his immediate attention. From the first, he found it impossible to adjust to a new tempo of life. It was as if his heart was still pounding at the maximum rate, though his body had been forced to a standstill. Previously, Clementine Churchill had doubted that he could survive the intense demands on his time and energy. The question now was whether he could live without them.

Churchill returned to London on Monday, 30 July. While Clementine supervised the removal of their possessions from 10 Downing Street, the couple took up temporary residence in a sixth-floor penthouse at Claridge's hotel in Mayfair. Long prone to bouts of depression, Churchill worried about sleeping near a balcony at a time when he was haunted by what he described as 'desperate thoughts'.

A sense of incompleteness gnawed at him. He could hardly believe that other hands had taken over with Stalin when it was he, Churchill, who had established a relationship with the Soviet leader, understood him, and saw what needed to be done. Not for the first time in his life, Churchill despaired that his peculiar powers and gifts were being wasted.

The shift in his political fortunes had left him feeling hurt, humiliated, and confused. Because he had cast the election as a referendum on his conduct of the war, he was tortured by the idea that the outcome had called his record into question. Though he was no stranger to rejection, he had never developed the thick skin that is so useful to a politician. No analysis of the Labour vote prevented him from interpreting the numbers as a personal disgrace. No references to an overall leftward swing in British politics, to the public's desire for a better material life after the war, or to festering public resentment of previous Conservative leaders' failure to prepare adequately for the struggle against Hitler were capable of lessening the blow to Churchill's ego.

For all that, he was able to make light of his defeat, as when he sang an old music hall song to the doorman at Claridge's:

> I've been to the North Pole
> I've been to the South Pole
> The East Pole, the West Pole
> And every kind of pole
> The barber's pole
> The greasy pole
> And now I'm fairly up the pole
> Since I got the sack
> From the Hotel Metropole.

Sometimes, others sang to him. On 1 August, six days after the Conservative rout, the new Labour-dominated Parliament assembled to elect the Speaker of the House of Commons. The chamber was packed and tensions ran high as, flushed with victory, the 'new boys' on the Labour benches taunted and jeered at the Conservatives sitting across from them. At a quarter to one, when everyone else was in place, Churchill made his much-anticipated entrance. With chin up, he sauntered to his seat on the Opposition front bench.

Conservatives greeted him with raucous cheers. One Tory began to sing 'For He's a Jolly Good Fellow' and others heartily joined in.

Labour countered with their party anthem, 'The Red Flag'. In boisterous spirits, a Labour member dashed to the front to pretend to conduct what a witness likened to 'the chorus of birds and animals sometimes to be heard in a Disney film'. Some of the newcomers did not really know the words and struggled to improvise. Meanwhile, whenever the Labour majority threatened to drown the Conservatives out, the latter raised their voices.

At Chequers the previous weekend, Churchill had made it clear that he hoped to go on leading the Opposition and the party as long as Conservatives wished him to and as long as his strength held. The cheers from the Tory benches suggested that he had his party's unanimous support. The British people might have rejected him, but the warm emotional reception accorded him by fellow Conservatives left him in no doubt that they at least wanted him as their leader.

Sadly, as he had done at the time of his electoral tour, he misconstrued the meaning of those cheers. Now, as then, the fact that people were grateful to their wartime prime minister did not necessarily mean that they wanted him to remain in power during what promised to be very different circumstances.

Hardly had Churchill left Westminster after his debut as Opposition leader when a trio of Conservative heavyweights met to find a way to manoeuvre him out of the job. The driving force in the effort was Robert Cecil, Viscount Cranborne, leader of the Opposition peers. The fifty-one-year-old heir to the 4th Marquess of Salisbury was a grandson of the prime minister Lord Salisbury and a cousin of Churchill's wife. His politically prominent family had been advising monarchs since the sixteenth century and one ancestor had been instrumental in the accession to the English throne of James VI of Scotland. In the Conservative Party as well, the Cecils (pronounced to rhyme with 'whistles') were noted as

kingmakers and power-brokers. They had had a long and complicated relationship with the Churchill family. 'Your family has always
hated my family,' Winston was known to grumble, at which
Cranborne would 'laugh uproariously' in response. In 1886, the
prime minister Lord Salisbury had been responsible (at least as
Winston saw it) for the political ruin of Winston's father, Lord
Randolph Churchill, the second surviving son of the 7th Duke of
Marlborough. In the 1930s, Cranborne himself had done much to
obstruct Winston's career despite the fact that both men opposed
the policy of appeasement. Nevertheless, Winston had long found
it impossible to decide whether he admired the Cecils or resented
them on his late father's behalf. Salisbury had been kind to Winston
when he was in his mid-twenties, and Winston later dedicated a
book to him. Winston had enjoyed friendships with Cranborne's
uncle, Hugh Cecil, who served as best man at Winston's wedding,
as well as with, however improbably, Cranborne himself. He adored
Cranborne's wife, Betty, whose acerbic conversation he prized, and
through the years he and Cranborne had managed rigorously to
keep their political differences in one compartment and their private
friendship in another.

Known familiarly by his boyhood nickname, Bobbety, Cranborne
was tall and gaunt, with a long nose and protruding teeth. A speech
impediment caused his r's to sound like w's and he spoke at the
breakneck speed characteristic of his family, who were famous for
their ability to utter more words in a minute than most people can
in five. He was an ugly man, slightly bent and often shabbily dressed,
whose great personal charm caused many women to find him immensely attractive. He was an invalid and a hypochondriac, whose
frail frame housed a will of iron. And he was a political powerhouse,
who, like other Cecils before him, preferred to operate behind the
scenes, often so subtly that it was difficult to perceive his hand in events.
Invisibility appealed to him because he prided himself on basing his
actions not on the dictates of personal ambition, but on duty and

principle. Since he ostensibly wanted nothing for himself, he had a reputation in party circles for 'objectivity' that gave his pronouncements particular weight. Past disagreements notwithstanding, Cranborne warmly acknowledged the greatness of what Churchill had done in the war. He marvelled, as he later said, that in 1940 Churchill 'did not talk of facing the realities: he created the realities'. Now that victory had been secured, however, Cranborne maintained that Churchill ought to 'face facts and retire' without delay. Had not Churchill himself taken a similar view of Cranborne's grandfather in the twilight of his career?

During the war, the Tory party had been allowed to disintegrate on almost every conceivable level. Churchill was not a party man and never had been, and from the time he became the party's leader in 1940 he had shown no interest in overseeing its affairs. As a consequence, by 1945 there was no management, no organization, and no programme. Lacking specific policies, Tories had fought the general election on the aura of the Churchill name and record. In the wake of overwhelming defeat, there was broad agreement that Conservatism needed to be drastically rethought. In Cranborne's view, the effort needed to begin immediately under younger leadership. Anthony Eden had long been his 'horse' in the political race. From the outset, Cranborne's career in politics had been closely tied to Eden's. Cranborne started out as Eden's parliamentary private secretary, and Eden and he grabbed headlines together in 1938 when they resigned as Foreign Secretary and Under Secretary of State for Foreign Affairs respectively in protest at the Chamberlain Government's appeasement of Mussolini.

The description of Cranborne as Eden's under secretary belied a more intricate relationship. Cranborne was Eden's most powerful political supporter. Cranborne did not himself aspire to the premiership; influence was what he was after, and he viewed an Eden Government as the best way to secure it. As a politician, Eden benefited from the prestige of a connection to the house of Cecil, as well as from Cranborne's superior intellect and cunning. Cranborne was also the nervier by far. He often quietly but insistently pressed Eden to act as Eden almost certainly would never have dared on his own. Eden, whose theatrical good looks and sartorial elegance contrasted sharply with Cranborne's less photogenic appearance, attended the meeting on 1 August 1945 to discuss Churchill's future.

Also present was Britain's Ambassador to the US, Lord Halifax, who had returned from Washington on leave the previous day. When Chamberlain resigned in 1940, Halifax had been his choice to replace him as prime minister, as well as that of King George VI and much of the Conservative Party, but Halifax had declined in favour of Churchill. (Halifax calculated that the public clamour for Churchill was so great that any other appointment would inevitably be over-shadowed by his looming presence in the Government. Halifax took consolation in the judgement that Churchill's character flaws made it likely that his tenure would be brief.) When Churchill became prime minister, he returned the favour by shipping Halifax off to Washington lest he re-emerge as a political rival.

For Churchill, who could be as passionate about fighting off real and potential rivals for power as he was about fighting the war, there had been an additional advantage to replacing Halifax as Foreign Secretary with Anthony Eden. As the Conservative Chief Whip James Stuart later observed, Churchill 'knew he could bully Anthony . . . but not Halifax'. By exiling him to the US, Churchill lowered the curtain on Halifax's political career. Five years later, Halifax was one of those who believed the time had come for Churchill to bow out, and by his reckoning, Churchill was fortunately not one of those individuals whose sole interest in life is his work. There were many activities that afforded him much pleasure, but that he had had little time to pursue during his premiership. Among other things he was an author and painter, and Halifax believed he might actually welcome a chance to be free of the burdens of leadership and retire of his own accord.

Eden thought he knew Churchill's mood better. Cranborne, as

29

well, was far from optimistic that Churchill would willingly step down, and his strategy was to ease him out of power. Churchill had been asked to go to New Zealand to be honoured for his war service, and Cranborne was determined that he accept that invitation, as well as many similar ones that were sure to follow from around the world. While Churchill was abroad, Eden would run the party in his stead. Halifax was set to see Churchill at 5 p.m. that day, and Eden was to dine with him after that. Cranborne urged both visitors to press Churchill to go to New Zealand, and generally to entice him with the joys of retirement. Halifax readily agreed, but Eden hesitated.

This was partly a matter of propriety on Eden's part, partly a matter of self-preservation. He flinched at the unseemliness of trying to push Churchill aside in open pursuit of his own interests. He did not wish to appear vulgarly ambitious. Was that not among the very qualities in Churchill that had long repelled him and many others? At the same time, Eden longed to lead the Opposition and he did not want to do or say anything to provoke Churchill to turn against him at this late date and to name another successor. During the war, Churchill had been known to taunt him with the names of other 'possibles' – Oliver Lyttelton, John Anderson, Harold Macmillan. By Eden's lights, the wait to succeed Churchill had been long and excruciating, and he did not want to jeopardize his position before the handover actually took place. But Cranborne was insistent, and as had often been the case between the two friends, Eden reluctantly gave in to the stronger will.

As it happened, 1 August was also the closing day of the Potsdam Conference. The plenary sessions were set to wind up that night, and Halifax was scheduled to be present at the King's meeting with Truman in England the following day. The talks had failed to produce anything like the settlement Churchill had been chasing. When the newly configured British delegation returned to Potsdam, Stalin had viewed Attlee warily and had insisted on grilling him and Ernest Bevin, the new Foreign Secretary, about Churchill's fate. Long preoccupied with averting his own removal from office, Stalin was palpably shaken by the news from London. If Churchill was dispensable, presumably the same was true of Stalin. He did not like the change. He would not have it. For two days he failed to show up at the conference table. Ostensibly he was ailing but Truman suspected the real reason was that he was upset about Churchill. When Stalin did reappear, he seemed to have lost interest in the proceedings.

Under the circumstances, Potsdam and all it signified to Churchill cast a shadow over Halifax's visit to Claridge's. Rather than listen to his guest's paean to memoir-writing and other activities to be looked forward to in retired life, Churchill preferred to mourn the loss of power and efficacy. In conversation, he dwelled on the fact that only a week had passed since he had been at Potsdam. He found that impossible to believe. How could everything have changed so quickly?

By the time he saw Eden, he had begun to dwell on the mistakes that might have led to his defeat. It was widely believed that by attacking Labour too violently Churchill had diminished his hard-won status as a national hero who stood above the political fray. On the present occasion, he lamented that if only Eden had not been ill with a duodenal ulcer during the campaign he would have had the advantage of his heir's advice and avoided that perhaps fatal error. In making such a claim, Churchill was flattering Eden in the conviction – which had helped to sustain the number two man during the war – that he served as a 'restraining hand' on Churchill's often monstrously poor judgement. (As Pug Ismay once put it, 'Some men need drink. Others need drugs. Anthony needs flattery.') Over the course of the evening, Churchill clutched Eden to his bosom, insisted the younger man was his 'alter ego', and otherwise strove to convey how much he valued and depended on him. But the love fest was short-lived. When Eden dared to suggest that the party vice-chairmanship be awarded to a close friend of his own, a man associated in people's minds with Eden's interests, Churchill exploded. The charm, the flattery, the unctuous affection – all dissolved in an instant. Furious at being pushed, Churchill made it clear that he had his own candidate for the post.

After Eden left at midnight, Churchill swallowed a sleeping pill and went to bed. Since Saturday when the Potsdam talks had resumed without him, he had found that even after taking a 'red' he was unable to sleep through until morning. For the fifth night in a row, he shot awake at 4 a.m., his thoughts racing uncontrollably, and he required a second barbiturate pill to sleep.

In the days that followed, Churchill in his misery was of various minds about how to proceed. He tested some of the suggestions others had made, but none appeared to satisfy him. He spoke of his war memoirs, but despaired of the taxes he would be required to pay on the earnings. He said he might go abroad indefinitely, but complained that he had no appetite for travel. He talked of honours and invitations, but added that he was in no mood to accept them. By turns he vowed to fight to retain control of the Conservative Party and admitted that he did not know how much longer he wished to lead. He groused that it would have been better had he died during the war but also insisted that he was not ready to die.

On 6 August, the first atomic bomb fell on Hiroshima. A second bomb targeted Nagasaki three days later. The new weapon, which reduced innumerable victims to tiny black bundles of smoking char, proved to be everything described in the report Churchill had seen at Potsdam, and more. The news jolted him out of his lassitude and self-pity, for it vividly suggested what a world war fought with atomic weapons might be like. The prospect made it more urgent than ever to get a proper postwar settlement in Europe, but political defeat had left Churchill helpless to do anything except try to warn the world in time.

Japan surrendered unconditionally on 14 August. That evening, Churchill dined with Eden and other Conservative colleagues in a private room at Claridge's. After the meal, he and his guests listened to Attlee's midnight broadcast to announce the end of the war. Inviting people to relax and enjoy themselves in the knowledge of a job well done, Churchill's successor decreed two days of victory holidays.

V-J Day, 15 August, coincided with the state opening of Parliament. An estimated one million celebrants lined the route from Buckingham Palace as the King and Queen rode to Westminster in an open red-and-gold coach drawn by the Windsor greys. Elsewhere, in a scene reminiscent of his thousand-mile electoral tour, Churchill, travelling in an open car, was mobbed by well-wishers. Shouting 'Churchill forever' and 'We want Churchill', they greeted him as the saviour of his country, the leader who had snatched Britain from the jaws of defeat, the man who more than any other had made this day possible. Three weeks after he had been hurled from power, the ovations comforted and reassured him. When he went to the Palace afterwards to congratulate George VI on his address in the House of Lords, it was evident that Churchill was 'gleefully anticipating' the speech he planned to deliver in the Commons the next day. That evening, London, which had spent so many nights in darkness, became a city of light. Great buildings were floodlit, bonfires blazed, and fireworks streaked the sky. All across the city there was singing and dancing in the streets.

The celebrations were still going strong on 16 August when Churchill spoke in Parliament of the danger of a new war more terrible than any in the past. He gave thanks that the atomic bomb had brought peace to the world, but he cautioned that it would be up to men to keep the peace. He called the bomb 'a new factor in human affairs' and emphasized that with the advent of such a weapon it was not just the survival of civilization that was imperilled, but of humanity itself.

Hours after Attlee proclaimed that the last of Britain's enemies had been laid low, Churchill pointed out that significant differences had already arisen with their Soviet ally about the state of

33

affairs in Eastern and Central Europe. He noted the emergence of police governments and he observed that it was 'not impossible that tragedy on a prodigious scale is imposing itself behind the iron curtain which at present divides Europe in twain'.

A fortnight after the conclusion of the Potsdam Conference, he lamented that instead of resolving the most serious questions, the three leaders had handed them off to a committee of foreign ministers, which was to meet in September and was gifted with less far-reaching powers. As he had at Potsdam, he perceived a unique opportunity in the fact that thus far only the US had the bomb. He warned that the time to get a settlement was during the three or four years that remained before any other power was likely to catch up. There was not an hour to be wasted, he cautioned, and not a day to be lost.

Despite the gravity of what Churchill had to say, he enjoyed parrying interruptions by some of the new Labour members. With a puckish grin he played up the irony of being the man to press for free elections elsewhere in the world when he had just been overwhelmingly defeated at home. Thumbs in lapels, he avowed his faith in democracy, whatever mistakes the people might be inclined to make. Speaking of the ideal of 'government of the people, by the people, for the people' that he hoped to see implemented everywhere in Europe, he delighted listeners of all political persuasions with the self-mocking aside, 'I practise what I preach!'

One young Labour member wrote in his diary afterwards that Churchill's speech had been 'a real masterpiece'; the *New York Times* called it 'one of the greatest speeches of his parliamentary career'. Still, on a day of merrymaking in the streets, his words of warning were fatally out of sync with the national mood. Part of the power of Churchill's iconic wartime speeches was the extent to which they captured the nation's mood and gave magnificent voice to the hopes and ideals of the people. By contrast, the 16 August address was a throwback to his speeches in the 1930s, which had taken the form of warnings that no one wanted to hear, particularly so soon after the carnage of the First World War. In 1945, eager to start a new life under Labour, the war-weary British did not want to be informed that their trials had only just begun.

Clementine Churchill exulted that her husband's 'brilliant moving gallant' speech had been on a par with his best work, but she too was ready for a new life after the war. The Churchills had left Claridge's for their eldest daughter Diana's flat in Westminster Gardens, where they were to stay while Clementine worked on reopening their country house, Chartwell, in addition to readying a new house in London. The couple had settled on a brick house in a cul-de-sac at Hyde Park Gate, off Kensington Road, but the sort of life they intended to have there remained a point of contention.

While Clementine, aged sixty, saw Hyde Park Gate as a retirement haven, Winston emphasized its proximity to the House of Commons. He assured fellow Conservatives that he would be able to get to the House in less than fifteen minutes. By the use of certain shortcuts, the driver could probably do it in seven.

In the course of Churchill's long and tempestuous career, the one person whose backing he had always been able to count on absolutely was his wife. Through thirty-six years of marriage, Clementine had never lost faith in what together they called his 'star', and never wavered in the mystical conviction that Winston was destined to accomplish great things. Repeatedly, in the face of political disappointment, she had soothed his bitterness and encouraged him to carry on. Consistently, she had put him above their children's needs and her own. She once told him that if to help him or make him great or happy she had to sacrifice her life, she would not hesitate.

Clementine also saw his flaws and did not fear to point them out to him. She was nothing if not critical. Nonetheless, whatever he wanted for himself this imposing and formidable woman had learned in some sense to want as well. His trials had been her trials, and his enemies had been her enemies. At least, that had always been the case – until now.

The present situation was lonelier and more personally painful than anything the Churchills had experienced to date because, suddenly, husband and wife were in open and irreconcilable conflict about how to spend the rest of their lives. During the Second World War, Clementine had worried about Winston's health to the point that her own was affected. Still, as long as the Nazi menace remained she had found a way to accept that her husband must put himself at risk and that she might lose him in the process. After the war, she saw things differently. Winston was old and ill. She loved him and she wanted them to be able to enjoy the few years they still had together. As far as she was concerned, his wartime leadership had vindicated the decades when they had sometimes been almost alone in the world in believing in him.

Though Winston persisted in dwelling on unfinished business, Clementine was confident that he had fulfilled his destiny at long last and that he – no, they – had earned a quiet, happy retirement.

While he certainly did not always do as his wife suggested, he prized her judgement and political acumen. He was always eager to know what she thought, and he would grow annoyed if she refused to tell him. In early 1945, Clementine had counselled her husband to retire as soon as the war was won and to refrain from seeking re-election. She wanted him to leave office, but that did not mean she wished to see him defeated in Britain's first postwar general election. On the contrary, when he insisted he was not ready to be 'put on a pedestal', Clementine supported his candidature unreservedly.

Still, her comment that the election loss might prove to be a blessing in disguise went to the heart of a new kind of sadness in their marriage. Much as Clementine ached for him in defeat, she earnestly believed that they would both be better off in private life. Much as it pained her to see him again feel rejected and unappreciated, there could be no denying that in some sense she had got what she wanted. From this point on, the burdens of the premiership would fall to others.

After Parliament went into recess on 24 August, Churchill had nothing to absorb and distract him. It was almost worse that he had known the fleeting joy of preparing and delivering his big speech. The letdown was stunning in its ferocity. As he once wrote, he found it very painful to be impotent and inactive. In the emptiness of his days he brooded about the election, but even in private he could barely bring himself to criticize those who had cast him out. (Clementine, interestingly, was less forgiving of the British public.) In his view the people's right to choose their leaders was the very thing he had fought the war to protect, and he struggled to suppress his bitterness at what he could not help but perceive as their ingratitude.

He was mightily unhappy, and his wife observed that that made him very difficult at home. Clementine regretted that rather than cling to each other in their sorrow, they seemed always to be having scenes. He fought with her, with her first cousin Maryott Whyte, with their son, Randolph (always an eager sparring partner), and with others. He complained about the food he was served; he protested at the lack of meat now that he had to endure the same physical shortages as other men; he imagined that the 'gruff bearish' cousin, an impoverished gentlewoman who assisted Clementine in household matters, was intent on thwarting him at every turn. He wanted to have cows and chickens at Chartwell. 'Cousin Moppet' maintained it would never work. Feathers flew. Clementine said she was sure it was her own fault, but suddenly she was finding life with Winston more than she could bear.

The people had spoken, and by any realistic assessment Churchill was never going to be prime minister again. Eventually, even he accepted that no one could go on being this miserable and that he had to come to peace with what had happened to him; but how?

III

Sans Soucis et Sans Regrets

Lake Como, September 1945

During the five-and-a-half-hour flight to Milan in a Dakota aircraft provided for his personal use by the Supreme Allied Commander for the Mediterranean, Field Marshal Alexander, Churchill pored over five years' worth of his wartime minutes. This was the torrent of dictated notes, consisting of comments, questions, and requests to individual ministers, to the Chiefs of Staff, and to others, by which he had brought his powerful personal impact to bear on every aspect of the conduct of the war.

Churchill had used his minutes the way an octopus uses its tentacles – to reach everywhere, to be in many places at once. Throughout his life, he had been constitutionally incapable of sitting back and letting others do what he usually believed he could better accomplish himself. Where problems existed, he was driven to grapple with them directly, so much so that at times even his admirers had been known to question his sense of proportion. He craved responsibility, which he once tellingly described to his mother as 'an exhilarating drink'. His minutes allowed him to be involved in anything that concerned the fight against Hitler, to shine a searchlight into the most obscure corners of the war effort, and not only to learn about, but also to manage details which other, less controlling personalities might have been inclined to leave to the judgement of subordinates. Now, all that power had fallen away from him.

Still, he had not brought printed copies of his minutes just to brood over what had been lost. Faced with the likelihood that his political career was at an end, Churchill insisted he could not simply be idle for the rest of his life. More and more, it seemed as if he was weighing the possibility of a memoir along the lines of *The World Crisis*, his highly personal multi-volume chronicle of the First World War. Fellow Conservatives – most, apparently, with the ulterior motive of edging him aside as party leader – had suggested that he undertake to tell the story of the Second World War as only he could. At a time when Churchill was deeply upset that the election had called his record into question, a memoir held the distinct attraction of allowing him to defend his actions, both during the war and in the immediate aftermath, in the courtroom of history.

Could such an undertaking fill the vacuum in his life that had been created when he lost the premiership? Would a memoir be enough to absorb the energies of a man of Churchill's temperament? In part, that was what he was on his way to Italy to find out.

As Parliament was in recess until 9 October, Alexander had offered him the exclusive use of the Villa La Rosa, the commandeered property above Lake Como which had served as the Field Marshal's headquarters in the war's final days. In anticipation of his stay there, Churchill had had bound copies of his minutes and telegrams specially prepared; these would form the spine of any autobiographical work. The Churchills' middle daughter, red-headed Sarah, was with her father on the flight on 1 September, along with his physician, his secretary, his valet, and a detective. He had wanted Clementine to come as well but she refused, explaining that she would be able to accomplish more in his absence. She too was exhausted and dejected, and felt that she would be unable to enjoy a holiday in the sun.

On the plane Churchill barely said a word to the others, but in the car afterwards it became apparent that in the course of reading he had already seized on the narrative possibilities of one part of the Second World War saga. He spoke excitedly of the Dunkirk evacuation, testing the story, feeling for the drama. At the Villa La Rosa, after he learned that one of the aides-de-camp assigned to him for the occasion had been at Dunkirk, animated talk of the episode continued over dinner. Seated at a huge green glass table in the ornately-mirrored and marbled pale green oval dining room, Churchill interrogated the nervous twenty-four-year-old. How long had he waited on the beaches? What kind of vessel had rescued him? Churchill, in his enthusiasm, wanted to hear every detail.

Previously, he had been in such low spirits that Sarah had feared time would pass slowly and dully. Already, that was far from the case. But any hope that a change of scenery was all that it would take to cure her father was soon dashed. After dinner, Churchill put on a dark hat and coat over his white suit and padded out onto the balcony in bedroom slippers to sit. As he puffed on a cigar, his interest in a memoir seemed to evaporate with the swirls of smoke. He insisted to his doctor that he was in no mood to write, especially not when the Government was poised to take so much of his earnings. Suddenly, he was back to rehashing the election, brooding aloud about what had gone wrong and what might have been.

Early the next morning, the sun was warm and bright and a soft breeze rippled the lake as a tiny caravan assembled in front of the Villa La Rosa, which gave long views of villages and mountains on the opposite shore. An aide-de-camp loaded one of the cars with Churchill's painting apparatus. An elaborate lunch was packed in an accompanying station wagon. Through the years, Churchill had often sought relief, repose, and renewal through painting. He first picked up a paintbrush in 1915 after the loss of his position as First Lord of the Admiralty at the time of the calamitous Dardanelles campaign affected him so strongly that Clementine worried he would 'die of grief'.

Then, as now, he had been cut off in the midst of a great and urgent undertaking. Then, as now, it galled him to be deprived of control while the fate of the enterprise was still in suspense. Then, as now, he felt as if he 'knew everything and could do nothing'. Then, as now, at a moment when every fibre of his being was 'inflamed to action', he was forced to remain 'a spectator of the tragedy, placed cruelly in a front seat'.

In a period when dark broodings about his predicament had allowed him no rest, painting had come to his rescue. Thirty years later, his daughter and others in the group, not to mention Churchill himself, were hoping it might do so again. The vehicles were packed and ready to go by 10 a.m., but Churchill did not enter the open yellow car until almost noon.

They drove along the lakefront while Churchill scouted for what he liked to call a 'paintaceous' scene. Before long, he announced that he was hungry, so the procession halted and a table was set up. About twenty Italian peasants formed a circle around the English travellers and watched them eat and drink. At length, the Churchill party drove over the mountains to Lake Lugano. It was late afternoon before he found a view that pleased him. His easel, canvas, paints, and brushes were laid out, along with the tiny table he liked to have nearby for whisky and cigars. The paints were arrayed on a tray fitted to stand slightly above his knees. The brushes went in a ten-inch-high container. Finally, wearing a white smock and a straw sombrero, Churchill settled into his cane painting chair and began to work.

When his sister-in-law Gwendeline Churchill, known as Goonie, introduced the middle-aged Churchill to painting in 1915, he found that he needed only to concentrate on the challenge of transferring a scene to his canvas in order to put politics and world problems out of his thoughts. For a man who worked and worried as much as he did, the discovery was a revelation. His private secretary later said that it was as if a new planet had swum into his ken.

Then and on many subsequent occasions, though not during the Second World War when the magnitude of his burdens allowed no interruption, the balm of painting healed Churchill both mentally and physically. He painted in rapt silence. As he focused on a composition, all of his cares and frustrations appeared to vanish. He revelled in the physical and tactile aspects of the process, from the 'voluptuous kick' of squeezing the fragrant colours out of their tubes, to the capacity for building the pigment 'layer after layer', to the wondrous ability to scrape away one's mistakes with a palette knife at the end of the day. When he inspected a finished painting, he was known not just to look but also to touch the surface of the canvas, caressing the whorls of dry paint with his fingertips.

Churchill theorized that when he painted, the use of those parts of the mind which direct the eye and hand allowed the exhausted part of his brain to rest and revive. A change of scenery alone would not have sufficed, for he would still be condemned to think the same thoughts as before. Nor would activities like reading or writing, for they were too similar to the sort of work that had worn him out in the first place. Nor would it help simply to lie down and do nothing, for the mind would keep churning. Painting offered a complete change of interest. It was not that his thoughts stopped; he was thinking, to be sure, but about matters other than those that had been preoccupying him.

At Lake Lugano in 1945, painting again seemed to work its magic. Eyeglasses partway down his nose, Churchill paused at intervals to push back his straw hat and wipe his forehead, but otherwise he laboured continuously, utterly engrossed. Another group of Italians, mostly children no more than twelve or thirteen years old, sat on the ground and observed. By the time he put down his brush at last and the spell was broken, five hours had passed and it was early evening. Later, Sarah was pleased to hear her father exclaim, 'I've had a happy day.' As she reported to Clementine, she had not heard him say that 'for I don't know how long!'

Churchill continued to paint in the days that followed. The only drawback was that at his age too much sitting threatened to stir up the hot lava of his indigestion. In the evenings, he would prop up his canvases in the dining room and appraise them during dinner. He transformed his huge bathroom, which had mirrors on every wall, into a studio with makeshift easels, and he would stare at works in progress while he soaked in a marble tub. He rejoiced that in Italy he felt, as he had not in many years, as if he were entirely out of the world. At home he was an obsessive reader of newspapers, which he marked up with slashes of red ink before dropping them on the floor for someone else to collect. Here he saw no newspapers for days at a time. When they were delivered, he claimed to be so busy with his painting that he hardly had time to read them.

In this spirit Churchill was soon insisting he was glad to have been relieved of responsibility for how things turned out after the war. He claimed as much in separate conversations with Moran and with another physician, who came to the villa to fit him with a truss. He wrote to Clementine of his own steadily growing sense of relief that others would have to deal with the problems of postwar Europe. And he told Sarah one evening, 'Every day I stay here without news, without worry I realize more and more that it may very well be what your mother said, a blessing in disguise. The war is over, it is won and they have lifted the hideous aftermath from my shoulders. I am what I never thought I would be until I reached my grave "sans soucis et sans regrets".' In a good deal of this, Churchill was probably trying to convince himself as much as anyone else of his change of heart. Certainly he had gone through this very process at the time of the Dardanelles disaster, pretending to be content with the loss of high office when in fact he was waiting and hoping for an opportunity to regain power and influence.

Unlike his air of calm acceptance, the healing effects of his artist's holiday were no pose. Churchill had long been blessed with remarkable powers of recuperation. At Lake Como, his absorption in something other than personal and professional issues allowed those powers to kick in. At the end of eighteen days he seemed so much better physically and mentally that he decided to extend his trip, sending his doctor back to England along with Sarah and nine finished canvases. Accompanied by his remaining entourage, he drove along the Italian and French Riviera in search of new scenes to paint.

On his first day out he motored for four hours through ravishing countryside to Genoa. He arrived after nightfall to find the British officer who was in charge of the area ensconced at the Villa Pirelli, an 'incongruous' mix of marble palace and Swiss chalet perched on a rocky bluff above the sea. Churchill's host marvelled at how healthy and vigorous he looked after so many years of war. But admiration turned to alarm when Churchill proved rather too active for his host's comfort. In the morning, Churchill insisted he wished to swim despite the fact that the clear, pale green water below was said to be somewhat rough and the bathing place rocky. Refusing to be talked out of his plan, he climbed down nearly a hundred steps, followed by his valet carrying a massive towel. Soon, Churchill had doffed his silk dressing gown and bedroom slippers and was splashing about, porpoise-like, enjoying himself immensely. At the end of the session, an awkward logistical problem required the poor beleaguered host to push Churchill's boyishly pink-and-white, five-foot-six, 210-pound figure up from the water, while an aide-de-camp tugged from the shore.

After two days in Genoa, Churchill and company proceeded to the half-empty Hôtel de Paris in Monte Carlo, where he dined lavishly on a veranda overlooking the casino and confronted a stack of newspapers from London. He had seen some press at Lake Como, but in that setting the information had struck him as oddly remote. Now, revived in body, mind, and spirit, he took in the first British reports of discord and deadlock at the Council of Foreign Ministers which had been meeting in London in his absence. Molotov had thrown every obstacle he could think of in the path to progress (even so, as was later discovered, Stalin had berated him in secret messages for being too soft and conciliatory). For many observers in Britain and elsewhere, the talks' failure amounted to a first disconcerting glimpse of the sharp divisions that had already emerged between the Western democracies and their wartime ally the Soviet Union. The fiasco came as no surprise to Churchill. He had predicted as much in the House of Commons on 16 August, when he publicly lamented the handing off of the most serious questions at Potsdam, questions the heads of state themselves ought to have settled. Once again, his warnings about events in Europe were starting to come true.

When he moved on to Cap d'Antibes, where he stayed at a fully staffed villa on loan from General Eisenhower, he wrote to Clementine in a voice markedly different at times from that of his letters from Italy. Previously, he had claimed to be interested solely in painting and to have little appetite for news of the outside world. Now, he spoke of how certain he had been that the foreign ministers' talks would fail, of his understanding that the Soviets had no need of an agreement as they actually welcomed the chance to consolidate themselves in nations already in their grasp, of his concern that so little was known about what was happening to the Poles, the Czechs, and others trapped behind the iron curtain, of his sense that the future in Europe was full of 'darkness and menace', and of his feeling that there would be no lack of subjects to discuss when Parliament reconvened. Clearly, this was the letter of a man ready to re-engage.

Churchill had gone to Italy in the hope of coming to peace with the people's decision. He had tried very hard to concur with his wife that the loss of the premiership was indeed a blessing in disguise. At last, he found he could do neither. The threat of another war was too great. His confidence that he was the man to prevent it was too strong. For better or worse, it simply was not in his character to remain detached for long.

When Churchill returned to Britain on 5 October 1945, his family understood that he had made an important decision while he was abroad. Once again, in defeat he would be defiant. Whatever the obstacles, he intended to fight on. He refused to retire.

IV

Old Man in a Hurry

London, October 1945

It was one thing to decide to fight on, quite another to stage a political comeback in his seventies.

During his first week in London, Churchill was a whirling dervish of activity, leaving no doubt in anyone's mind that he meant, and retained the capacity, to lead. He set policy with his Shadow Cabinet. He cut a lively figure on the Opposition front bench. He offered the first Opposition motion and he directed all Conservatives to be present the following week when he assailed a bill to prolong government controls on labour, rations, prices, and transport for five additional years. Parliamentary commentators noted his bronzed, robust appearance, and King George remarked privately that Churchill had returned from Italy and France 'a new man'. As if he had energy to spare, Churchill capped off a busy week by attending a Friday evening performance of Oscar Wilde's *Lady Windermere's Fan.*

By the next morning, however, his efforts began to unravel. While her husband was at Lake Como, Clementine Churchill had worried that in his passion to transfer a scene to the canvas he might labour on oblivious to the chill of the evening air. Given his medical record, there was always anxiety that were he to catch cold it could escalate into pneumonia. As feared, he returned from the South of France with a cold. Despite promises to be careful, he largely ignored it.

By Saturday, he had lost his voice. By Sunday, a statement went out that he was confined to his house on doctor's orders due to an inflamed throat.

Churchill had rallied the troops, but in the end he would not be there to lead them. Instead, to his frustration, he spent the week in his sickbed unable to speak. At a moment when he had been eager to fashion an image of vitality, press reports brought up his prolonged bouts of pneumonia during the Second World War, his impending seventy-first birthday, and the undeniable fact that for a man of his years a tiny cold could prove to be a very big deal. In view of his comeback plans it was all a bit of a disaster, but as a friend once said, Churchill 'produced his greatest efforts in disaster'. Adversity tended to stimulate him.

While he was abroad, a stack of invitations to speak had accumulated at Hyde Park Gate. One request in particular fired Churchill's imagination by appealing to his sense of drama. F. L. McLuer, the president of Westminster College in Fulton, Missouri, asked him to lecture on international affairs. The proposal dovetailed with Clementine Churchill's wish that they spend part of the winter in Florida for his health. Still, McLuer's letter is likely to have been of little interest had it not been for an addendum scribbled across the page: 'This is a wonderful school in my home state. Hope you can do it. I'll introduce you. Best regards, Harry Truman'. Even Truman's seconding of the invitation would have made little impact on Churchill without the offer, however casual and offhand, to introduce him.

Churchill instinctively grabbed on to those three words as if they were a lifeline, and he refused to let go until he had used them to hoist himself back up onto the world stage. Truman's presence on the same platform would call world attention to his message about the looming Soviet threat in a way he could never hope to achieve by himself. In his present circumstances, it would mean everything to Churchill, a defeated politician after all, to be able to borrow and bask in the American leader's power.

As Churchill crafted his reply, he went significantly beyond an attempt to formalize Truman's commitment. He tried to draw the President further into the picture, to suggest that Truman had intended a good deal more by his words than he probably had. (In fact, Truman as yet had no real investment in the visit. An intermediary, a Westminster alumnus, had solicited his involvement in the invitation. Truman had merely added his hasty endorsement and passed the letter on as a favour to a friend.) Though it was McLuer who had written to him, Churchill cut the college administrator out of the loop by addressing his letter, dated 8 November 1945, directly to Truman. He wrote as if he had in hand an official presidential invitation to speak under Truman's 'aegis'. Careful to refer to his understanding that Truman planned to introduce him, Churchill insisted it would be his 'duty' to come to the US and do as the President requested. He pledged to Truman that the Fulton speech would be his only public address in America 'out of respect for you and your wishes'.

Churchill was unquestionably distorting the tenor of Truman's message, and his decision to point out that he had praised Truman in the House of Commons the previous day was also risky. At Potsdam, Truman had complained in his diary of what he perceived as Churchill's efforts to soft-soap him. Nevertheless, having cleared the speaking engagement with his successor, Churchill sent off his answer via Attlee's secretary, to be hand-delivered when the American and British leaders met presently to discuss atomic policy and related matters in Washington.

While Churchill waited for Truman to respond, he went to Paris and Brussels for a week to speak and be feted. His painting holiday had helped him regain perspective and confidence after the election and he was happy once again to receive honours. Now, with an eye towards a comeback, it suited him to shift public attention back to his war triumphs.

In Brussels, adoring crowds waited for hours to catch a glimpse of him. They fought their way past police and tossed flowers at his car. A girl managed to hurl herself onto the running board and kiss him, and an old woman was heard to declare that now that she had seen Churchill she was ready to die. He was made an honorary citizen and proclaimed 'the saviour of civilization'. Hailed for his war leadership, Churchill missed no opportunity to showcase his achievements in the run-up to war as well. When he told a joint session of the Belgian Senate and Chamber on 16 November that had the Allies moved to stop Hitler early on, the Second World War ('the unnecessary war') would probably never have had to be fought in the first place, he was reminding people that he had been right in the 1930s and letting them know that he was right now.

In contrast to his rapturous reception abroad, there were no cheers for Churchill when he returned to London on 20 November. Immediately, he faced a new challenge to his leadership. This time the malcontents were younger parliamentarians who mocked their tired elders in the Conservative Party as 'Rip Van Winkles', content to sleep through the socialization of Britain. To the young Tories' outrage, Churchill had been absent from Parliament on 19 November, resting at Chartwell after his trip, when Labour unveiled further nationalization plans. The party's number two man, Anthony Eden, had been missing as well.

At a meeting of the backbenchers, Churchill slouched in a red leather armchair for an hour and a half, but he might as well have been enduring a slow stretch on the rack as his juniors by many years criticized his leadership. At the time of the general election, Churchill's belligerence had landed him in trouble; now the complaint was that he was not belligerent enough. The man of blood had gone anaemic. The young people wanted him to set off a debate in the House of Commons on the broad matter of nationalization by introducing a motion of Government censure.

No one can have wanted to turn out the Government more than Churchill. No one can have had greater reason to be impatient. He was truly, as his father had said of Gladstone, an 'old man in a hurry'. Still, he protested, the timing was all wrong. The Attlee Government had only been in power for a few months and it was too soon to argue that they had failed. Like it or not – and Churchill did not like it – the Opposition had little choice but to wait upon events. The Conservatives needed to let some time pass and give things a chance to go wrong. Far from benefiting Conservatives, Churchill argued, a premature confrontation would spotlight Tory weakness, allowing Labour to emerge even stronger than before.

Churchill suggested that when his critics had had more experience they would see that he had been right, but they were unyielding. At last he reluctantly consented to go on the warpath against Attlee; it was either that or allow the charge to stand that somehow he had lost the will to fight.

On the evening of 27 November, three days before his seventy-first birthday, Churchill placed a motion of censure before the House, which claimed that the Government had focused on long-range nationalization plans at the expense of the people's immediate postwar needs. Churchill filed the motion without comment in expectation of a full-dress debate the following week.

Robert 'Rab' Butler, Churchill's wartime Minister of Education, established the tone at the next day's Conservative Central Council meeting in London. The pale, balding, pouchy-eyed Butler introduced Churchill as the 'Master Fighter'. Churchill's mockery of Socialist ministers elicited peals of delight, and when he slowly, mischievously flapped his arms to help listeners visualize 'the gloomy vultures of nationalization' hovering over Attlee's Britain, the hall echoed with appreciative laughter. Delegates from throughout Britain insisted they had never known Churchill to be in better form.

He met a less enthusiastic reception in the House of Commons. Labour shot down Churchill's motion – by this time, despite its genesis, it was very much identified in the public mind as his motion – by a vote of 381 to 197. But then, he had expected it to fail. What he could not have expected was the wit and ferocity of Attlee's counterattack. Churchill was known to view his successor as 'a sheep in sheep's clothing', but there was nothing sheepish about Attlee's devastating performance on 6 December.

Clementine Churchill watched from the gallery, and more than a hundred politicians had to stand or squat on the floor for want of seats, as the small, spare, fidgety Attlee, who had a reputation as a lacklustre speaker, gave what was widely received as the best speech of his parliamentary career to date. Attlee made Churchill seem ridiculous for asking why a Government that had been elected to carry out a socialist programme did not carry out a Conservative programme. He avowed that Britain disliked 'one-man shows' and he characterized the motion of censure as nothing more than 'a party move by a politician in difficulties'.

Every time Attlee scored a hit – and there were many – the Labour benches roared. His plush pink target looked on in silence. Churchill made a point of rising above the abuse. Still, that Attlee had outdebated him was a blow to his prestige. Soon, it looked as if it might even have been a knockout, and the talk in political London was that Churchill might be preparing to step aside.

In fact, that was the last thing he meant to do. While Churchill had been managing the unrest in his party, Truman had officially confirmed his offer to introduce the Fulton speech. Since then, Churchill had been back and forth with Washington to press for a firm date, to ask that the event be announced simultaneously from the White House and in London, to urge Truman to make public his endorsement of the invitation, and to express a wish for talks between the President and himself. Ironically, when Truman granted all of these requests, the news of Churchill's impending trip, to speak in Missouri and to enjoy a rest in Florida with Mrs Churchill, sparked new rumours of resignation.

Speculation was rife that Churchill's willingness to leave Britain at a time of deep division in the Conservative Party meant that he intended to give up the leadership upon his return. There were reports in the world press that he was travelling to Florida on doctor's orders and that the state of his health might soon force him to retire. Meanwhile, mindful of the havoc that had ensued when both he and Eden were missing from Parliament on 19 November, Churchill reassured a large gathering of Opposition members that Eden was set to lead in his absence. Instead of allaying fears, however, his comments provoked upset in certain Conservative quarters.

Eden enjoyed broad support in the party, but if indeed Churchill was preparing to hand over, not everyone was pleased with the prospect of power passing to Eden. His critics dismissed him as a lightweight who possessed more style than substance and who had risen only because so many of the best young men of his generation had perished in the First World War. In a public challenge to received wisdom about the succession, the *Evening Standard*, which was owned by Lord Beaverbrook, questioned whether Eden was quite up to the task. There followed a round of press comment, both at home and abroad, about Rab Butler and other possible successors should Churchill retire.

As 1946 began, representatives of fifty-one countries gathered in London for the first United Nations General Assembly. On 9 January, final preparations were under way at St James's Palace for that night's state banquet on the eve of the historic session when the Churchills sailed for America. Their giant liner, the *Queen Elizabeth*, which had delivered Eleanor Roosevelt and other members of the US delegation four days previously, was part of the effort to repatriate nearly two million American and Canadian troops that had begun after the surrender of Germany. On the present westward crossing, more than twelve thousand Canadians were finally on their way home. The day before they reached New York, Churchill addressed the troops over the ship's loudspeaker system. In the course of speaking to them of their future, the old warrior offered some hints about how he saw his own.

As the young men prepared to begin new lives after the war,

Churchill promised them that the future was in their hands and that their lives would be what they chose to make them. The trick, he told them, was to have a purpose and to stick to it. He recalled that the previous day he had been standing on the bridge 'watching the mountainous waves, and this ship – which is no pup – cutting through them and mocking their anger'. He asked himself why it was that the ship beat the waves, when the waves were so many and the ship was one. The reason, he went on, was that the ship has a purpose while the waves have none. 'They just flop around, innumerable, tireless, but ineffective. The ship with the purpose takes us where we want to go. Let us therefore have a purpose, both in our national and imperial policy, and in our private lives.'

Some people at the time interpreted those remarks as Churchill's 'farewell to politics'. In retrospect, they appear to have been anything but that. Far from being inclined to shut down his political life, Churchill, though he too was no pup, was about to restart it.

V

The Wet Hen

St James's Palace, 1946

A cold rain pelted London on the night of Britain's first state banquet since 1939. Inside St James's Palace, crackling wood fires perfumed the air. Servants wore prewar red-and-gold and blue-and-gold liveries, and royal treasures that had been stored away for the duration of the war were once again on display. Candles twinkling in gold candelabra illuminated a banquet table set for eighty-six with heavy gold plate. As each of the fifty-one chief UN delegates and other guests entered, they were taken to a cavernous, tapestry-lined room where they were presented to the King. The fifty-year-old George VI wore the uniform of an Admiral of the Fleet. The Colombian delegate responsible for overseeing the preparations for the first General Assembly sat at his right, and the Belgian who was expected to be elected its president the following day sat at the King's left. Among the topics dominating the delegates' conversation was who would be appointed to the post of Secretary General.

Hours after Churchill sailed, Anthony Eden arrived at the UN dinner for what would be his first public appearance as deputy leader of the Opposition. For at least a week he had been fuming at the prospect of being left in charge, as he complained to Cranborne, 'rather like a governess on approval'. Unlike Churchill, he lacked the stomach to prove himself again. Eden believed that as Foreign

Secretary, as well as Leader of the House of Commons, he had demonstrated his abilities and should not have to endure another round of tests. Had not a decade passed since Stanley Baldwin made him Britain's youngest Foreign Secretary since the mid-nineteenth century? Had not Churchill singled out his experience and capacity when he anointed him heir apparent?

There had been a time before the war when Eden struck many of the anti-appeasers as a more viable candidate for prime minister than the pugnacious, provocative, unabashedly and carnivorously ambitious Churchill. There had been a time when Cranborne, Eden, and others in their circle had barred Churchill from their meetings because they thought him unstable, untrustworthy, and unsound, and because they feared he would dominate their discussions and corrupt their cause by involving them with the adventurers who formed his claque. There had been a time when Eden's determination to bring Conservatives together and to formulate a unified Tory position on the Fascist threat had seemed much more sensible and appealing than Churchill's willingness, even eagerness, to split the party asunder.

Cranborne believed that when he became prime minister Churchill never really forgave the Edenites for shutting him out. Close observers would long suspect that however highly and affectionately Churchill spoke of Eden, he truly 'despised' his second-in-command. One could never be sure: when Churchill ostentatiously referred to Eden as 'my Anthony', was that a note of contempt in his voice? Nevertheless, from early on the matter of the succession in general and of Eden's claims in particular had been prominently in play. At the outset of his premiership, Churchill had spoken of his intention to resign at the end of the war to make room for younger men. In 1940 he told Eden that he regarded himself as an old man and was not about to repeat Lloyd George's error of attempting to carry on after the war. On various occasions and in various ways he made it clear that he wanted Eden to succeed him.

As the war dragged on, it seemed as if Eden would not have to wait for the peace after all. When there was broad dissatisfaction with aspects of Churchill's leadership and the progress of the war, when the old man was gravely ill, and when there were fears he might soon die, Eden had had reason to believe the handover would occur at any moment. Both verbally and in his letter to the King, Churchill spelled out his wish that should anything happen to him Eden would take his place.

Despite Churchill's assurances to Eden that it would not be long before the younger man took control, somehow that golden day always failed to arrive. There were persistent grumblings in certain quarters that the Prime Minister was 'losing his grip' (Sir Alexander Cadogan, 1942) and 'failing fast' (Field Marshal Sir Alan Brooke, 1944), that he had grown too old, sick and incompetent, and that he really ought to 'disappear out of public life' (Brooke) before he damaged both his reputation and the country; but still Churchill managed to endure. As a friend of Eden's later said, 'Waiting to step into a dead man's shoes is always a tiring business, but when the "dead" man persists in remaining alive it is worse than ever.' Ironically, in 1944 it was Churchill who took on Eden's duties in addition to his own when the ill, exhausted heir apparent, twenty-two years his junior, needed to go off for a rest.

When Churchill battled to retain the premiership in Britain's first postwar election, Eden was perhaps only being human when he discovered that he could not stifle 'an unworthy hope that we may lose'. And when he did get what he had guiltily wished for, he confided to his diary that while history would dub the British people ungrateful for having dismissed Churchill, perhaps they had, in reality, only been wise. Believing that the Tories would be out for ten years, Eden spoke to friends of his fervent desire to lead the Opposition and mould the party for the future, but he also voiced concern that Churchill would insist on holding on to the job – 'and get everything wrong'. By the time six months had passed, Eden's fears – at least, those about Churchill's intentions – seemed to have been realized.

As far as Eden could tell, at the start of 1946, Churchill had not even contemplated the possibility of retirement. Eden whined to Cranborne that Churchill meant to go on 'forever'. He was sure that the Conservative Chief Whip James Stuart and the party chairman Ralph Assheton were encouraging Churchill to hold on to the leadership for as long as possible in the interest of putting off the 'evil day' when Eden took over. And even if Churchill were miraculously to step down, Eden was no longer confident that the party leadership, not to mention the premiership, would ever be his. He worried about being displaced by the likes of the forty-two-year-old Rab Butler or the fifty-one-year-old Harold Macmillan, though neither man was generally regarded as ready to lead. He also worried about the impatient young Tories who, when they mocked the party's Rip Van Winkles, meant the second-in-command and other venerable Conservatives no less than they did Churchill. To make matters worse, Eden's tumultuous personal life threatened to bar him from the premiership for good. His marriage was in tatters; Beatrice Eden wanted to marry her American lover. A divorce could sink Eden's political dreams. Had he worked and waited all this time, for nothing?

Eden's complaint was not that he could have been a contender. It was that he had been one for too long. At a moment when he felt 'fed up with everything', the prospect of a new job suggested a way out of the succession trap. Even as Churchill had been using Eden to allay concerns about his own impending absence in America, Eden had been hoping he might soon be in a position to bolt. Nothing had been settled and other names were still prominently in play, but on 2 January 1946, Ernest Bevin confirmed to Eden that he was a candidate to become the United Nations' first Secretary General. Following their talk, Eden let it be known at the Palace that he was 'anxious' to be considered.

Characteristically, he was not without ambivalence. Eden had a lifelong tendency to vacillate that had prompted Lady Redesdale, the mother of the Mitford sisters, to dub him 'the wet hen'. In the present instance, he seemed to be scurrying in all directions at once. Eager as he was to escape to the UN, he hesitated to abandon his prime ministerial ambitions after all that he had done and endured to realize them. By turns he insisted that he longed to extricate himself from the rough and tumble of British politics and vowed to return to lead his party when Churchill was gone at last. Eden's former boss, Stanley Baldwin, warned that if he joined the UN, Butler was likely to claim the Tory leadership; once Eden made the move, there would almost certainly be no coming back.

Cranborne huffed to Conservative colleagues that if Eden took the UN job he was 'through with him'. Typically, however, Cranborne assumed a very different posture in conversation and correspondence with Eden himself. Rather than threaten Eden, he flattered him. In his most narcotic tones, Cranborne encouraged Eden in the belief that he was indispensable to the party's prospects. He maintained that only the designated heir could keep Conservatives together and that only he could lead them to victory in a new general election. For Cranborne, the UN episode was a flashback to the offstage tempest three years previously when Eden, already maddened by Churchill's staying power, had considered becoming Viceroy of India. At the time, Eden had assumed that his position as Conservative heir apparent would be waiting whenever he saw fit to return. Now, as then, Cranborne, acting in his accustomed role of providing 'the backbone to Eden's willow', worked hard to disillusion him. In the process, Cranborne may merely have substituted one illusion for another. He reassured Eden that Churchill's day was finally over, that Churchill now belonged to the past, and that even he was bound to find this out. Cranborne made the case Churchill had often made himself: that Eden needed only to be patient and wait a little longer as number two.

Eden was a figure of stark contradictions. As a diplomat he was a nimble negotiator gifted with an ability to mitigate tensions and always to seem cool and composed. As a man he was also vain, touchy, and hysterical. Alcohol brought out the worst in him. When Eden arrived at St James's Palace on 9 January, the King's private secretary, Sir Alan Lascelles, guessed that he had been drinking. Immediately, Eden ripped into two of the King's equerries as they showed him to his place at the banquet table in the William IV Room. Loudly complaining that he had been seated next to the head delegate from Nicaragua, the would-be leader of the new world peacekeeping organization made no secret of his conviction that he rated a more important dinner partner. He also seemed unhappy that he had been placed in the vicinity of Attlee.

Dinner began; the Krug 1928 champagne and other wines from the cellars at Buckingham Palace flowed; and George VI, a slight man with prominent teeth who suffered from a nervous stammer that tended to affect him when he addressed the public, spoke of the momentous tasks facing the delegates and of the need to put petty, selfish concerns aside in the interest of making the UN a success.

After dinner, the company moved to the Queen Anne Room, where the King planned to talk individually with certain guests. He was especially keen to speak to the dark-eyed, sallow-faced Russian, Andrei Gromyko (said to call to mind 'a badger forced into the daylight'), to urge that the wartime contact between London and Moscow not be lost. George VI's press secretary, Lewis Ritchie, brought over each of the chosen delegates, and photographs were taken at the King's request. The bright flashes provoked a new hissy fit from Eden. Using filthy, abusive language, he protested to Ritchie that the camera lights were bothering him.

Butler, one of a small number of Opposition members present, sprang forward to apologize on Eden's behalf, pointing out, in case anyone had failed to notice, that the man he hoped to replace as heir apparent had had too much to drink.

The next day, Lascelles drafted a stinging letter of rebuke to Eden.

Realizing that he had 'made an ass' of himself, Eden, before he heard from the Palace, wrote an abject letter of apology. Not only had he sabotaged his candidacy for the UN job, but he had also provided ammunition to those who questioned his capacity to lead the Conservative Party.

As it happened, Churchill was asked for his thoughts on both the secretary generalship and the Tory leadership when the *Queen Elizabeth* docked in New York on the evening of 14 January. Flags whipped in the frosty Hudson River winds and a US Army band struck up 'Hail, Hail, The Gang's All Here' as he descended the gangplank. Observed by the Canadian troops, whose heads stuck out of many of the ship's portholes, Churchill made one of his dainty half-bows to a large crowd of press and American, British, and Canadian officials.

Afterwards, in a heated waiting room on the pier's upper level, he thanked reporters for coming out on such a cold night and gamely took their questions. Clementine Churchill, swathed in black furs, helped with any words he failed to hear. In the course of bantering with reporters, Churchill addressed topics that had been the subject of speculation and gossip in London for weeks. His remarks were of particular concern to certain personally interested parties at home.

Did Churchill plan to retire from active politics? 'I know of no truth in such reports,' he fired back. Was he going to hand over the Tory leadership? 'I have no intention whatever of ceasing to lead the Conservative Party until I am satisfied that they can see their way clear ahead and make a better arrangement, which I earnestly trust they may be able to do.' Was Churchill prepared to serve as the first UN Secretary General? This question appeared to puzzle him. Churchill knew that Eden wanted the job, and before he left the country he had 'strongly' advised him to accept were it to be offered. (Eden, for his part, assumed Churchill wished to see him settled elsewhere so he would feel easier in his mind about staying on. Churchill similarly had counselled Eden to take the viceroyship in 1943 on the explanation that he hoped 'to go on some years yet'.) At the time of the press conference in New York, Churchill had no idea that Eden had already torpedoed whatever chance he might have had to go to the UN. It was only now he discovered that one day previously in London some of the South American delegates had put forth the name 'Winston Churchill' as the latest candidate for the post. After a second's reflection, he swatted the question aside: 'I never addressed my mind to such a subject.'

The following day in London, Eden chaired a meeting of the Shadow Cabinet. Cranborne hovered about Eden to be sure he made better use of Churchill's absence. In the wake of Eden's suicidal performance at the state banquet, Cranborne was pleased to see him act calmly and effectively to consolidate his position in the party. Where Eden had bristled at suggestions that he had yet to prove himself fully, Cranborne saw the deputy leadership as a huge opportunity for their side. Whatever assurances Cranborne had previously offered to Eden in the interest of dissuading him from accepting the post of UN Secretary General, Cranborne did not really believe that Churchill would readily hand over any time soon. He did, however, hope that if the deputy leader performed well, Eden would be in a strong enough position to push Churchill out when the old man came home.

VI

Winnie, Winnie, Go Away

Miami Beach, Florida, 1946

Seated beside a bed of red poinsettias near the pink brick seaside house his wife had arranged to borrow from a friend, Churchill contentedly scanned the coconut palms overhead in search of a 'paintaceous' angle. His tropical-weight tan suit fit snugly across his stomach. The deep creases radiating from the centre button, which looked as if it was about to burst, testified that he had grown thicker since he acquired the suit in North Africa during the war. In the white patio chair beside him, Clementine Churchill wore one of her customary headscarves, big round white-rimmed sunglasses and wrist-length white gloves. After the bone-chilling cold they had had to endure in New York harbour and the rain-splashed train windows en route through Virginia and the Carolinas, she proclaimed the intense heat and sunshine on the day they arrived in Miami Beach 'delicious'. Churchill had lately suffered his share of colds and sore throats, and in keeping with his wife's wishes he intended to rest and to enjoy the good weather in Florida. Still, from the outset the couple had contrasting perspectives on their stay. She saw their holiday as an end in itself, he as a chance to get in shape for the main event in Missouri.

The next morning, the Churchills were unhappily surprised. The sky had darkened and the temperature had plummeted. There followed a day and a half of shivering cold and rustling palm fronds until the afternoon emergence of the sun prompted Churchill to rush off with his painting paraphernalia. He worked for hours in the shade on a picture of palms reflected in water. Despite the knitted afghan which Clementine draped around his shoulders when she brought him his tea, he caught another cold and was soon running a slight temperature. The episode was exactly the sort of thing they had come to Florida to avoid. At a time when he was supposed to be gearing up for Fulton, the usual concerns about pneumonia plunged him into a fit of agitation. For all of his philosophy, he always found it maddening when illness threatened to get in the way of his great plans. Friends affectionately called Churchill the world's worst patient. This time, he alternated between insisting he wanted no medicine and taking several conflicting remedies all at once.

His fever broke after thirty-six hours. The perfect weather resumed and Churchill was able to paint again and to swim in the ocean. Welcome news arrived in the form of a message from Truman that he would soon be on holiday in Florida and would be happy to dine with Churchill on the presidential yacht. The prospect freed Churchill from the need to brave any more bad weather were he to have to fly north to confer with Truman. In the meantime, Truman sent a converted army bomber to transport the Churchills to Cuba for a week of painting and basking in the sun. The President and the former Prime Minister were set to meet after that, but when Churchill returned from Havana he discovered that Truman had had to cancel his holiday because of the steel strike. Churchill insisted he would fly to him the next day.

The exceptionally rough five-hour trip proved to be an ordeal. Churchill was finishing lunch when the B-17 bomber passed into a sleet storm above Virginia. Suddenly, plates and glasses pitched in all directions and Churchill was thrown against the ceiling. Not long afterwards, the aircraft landed safely amid a swirl of ice pellets. Churchill rose amid the shattered glass that covered the cabin and relit his cigar by way of composing himself. He descended the steps at National Airport beaming and waving his hat to Lord Halifax and other official greeters as if he had just enjoyed the most tranquil of flights. After he had bathed and dined at the British Embassy, he was off to the White House to meet Truman for the first time since Potsdam.

When Churchill last saw him, Truman had recently inherited Roosevelt's unrealistic perception of Stalin, as well as his predecessor's tactic of dissociating himself from Churchill in an effort to win the Soviet leader's confidence. Accordingly, Truman had had little use for Churchill's perspective or advice. By early 1946, however, Moscow had given the President reason to reconsider. A series of speeches in January and February by Molotov and other of Stalin's lieutenants warning of the peril of an attack from the West had culminated, the previous day, in a bellicose address by Stalin himself. A translation appeared in American newspapers on 9 February, the day Churchill flew into Washington. Stalin's enunciation of a tough new anti-West policy was a throwback to prewar Soviet attitudes. Immediately, as Halifax pointed out, the speech had the effect of 'an electric shock' on the nerves of a good many people in Washington. Could this possibly be the wartime ally with whom they had been looking forward to close future cooperation?

In part, Stalin's confrontational tone had its origins in a two-month holiday he had taken starting in early October 1945. While the ailing, exhausted Stalin rested near Sochi at the Black Sea, he had left Molotov in charge of daily affairs at the Kremlin. The arrangement set off a chain reaction of rumour and gossip in the international press. By turns, Stalin was reported to be contemplating retirement, about to hand over to Molotov, and nearly or already dead. There were news profiles of Molotov and some of the other possible contenders should a fully-fledged succession struggle erupt on Stalin's demise. Though he was supposed to be resting, Stalin obsessively pored over a dossier collected under the title 'Rumors in Foreign Press on the State of

Health of Comrade Stalin'. References to the second-in-command's ever-expanding prestige both at home and abroad fired Stalin's suspicions. Was Molotov behind the reports? Why had he not censored such material? Was the anointed heir using Stalin's absence to consolidate his position?

The rumours about Stalin's health had also distressed Churchill, who continued to hope that he might one day face him across the conference table and pick up where they had left off at Potsdam. Churchill therefore had been greatly relieved when the US Ambassador in Moscow, Averell Harriman, announced that he had visited Stalin's seaside retreat and found the Soviet leader in good health. In the House of Commons on 7 November 1945, Churchill had expressed gratitude that Stalin was well, offered some kind words about his leadership, and voiced a wish that the bond that had developed between their two peoples during the war be allowed to continue in peacetime. On the face of it, Churchill's remarks were innocuous. Nonetheless, when Molotov directed that they be published in *Pravda*, Stalin breathed fire and fury. Such praise would have been welcome during the war, but now Stalin insisted that it was simply a cover for Churchill's hostile intentions and that Molotov should have recognized it as such.

Soon, it was reported in the British press that, according to high-level sources in Moscow, Stalin's power was not as great as many outsiders believed and government affairs were perfectly capable of being carried on without him. Incensed, Stalin lashed out at his designated heir, who, even if he were not the actual source of such statements, should have undertaken to suppress them. Stalin set his other satellites, Georgi Malenkov, Lavrenti Beria, and Anastas Mikoyan, against Molotov. They vied to denounce him for, among other outrages, consenting to an interview with the journalist Randolph Churchill. ('The appointment with Churchill's son was cancelled because we spoke against it.') At length Molotov managed to stay afloat by tearfully admitting his mistakes to his rivals and penning a cringing letter to Stalin. Molotov kept his job, but from then on Stalin refrained from speaking of him as his successor.

Thus Stalin had put Molotov and the others on notice that he was always watching and that they ought not to grow too lax or too ambitious. Now, he had to dispel the rumours and to leave the world in no doubt that he, Stalin, was still number one and that he meant to keep things that way. By insisting to the Soviet people that their wartime allies in the West had already become their postwar adversaries, Stalin set himself up as the warrior whose duty it would be to drive back the enemy and save the Communist motherland – again. Under the circumstances, he simply could not contemplate retirement.

In this speech, Stalin bore no resemblance to the man Roosevelt had mistaken him for. Truman was beginning to recognize the need for a new approach to Soviet relations, one based on facts rather than on wishful thinking. Analysis of Stalin's presentation having yet to arrive from the US Embassy in Moscow, Churchill's take on what was going on at the Kremlin was suddenly of particular interest. And the visitor had something even more important to offer. At a time when Truman had yet to emerge from Roosevelt's shadow, it might be difficult politically to depart from his predecessor's Soviet policy. The Fulton speech, delivered by a private citizen who also happened to be a master of the spoken word, as well as a figure of exceptional appeal to Americans, would allow Truman, at no political cost to himself, to see if the public was ready to accept a change.

After he met with Truman, Churchill spent the night at the British Embassy. He had planned to return to Florida the next day, but snowbound airfields caused him to stay an additional night. Besides, the difficult trip north had left him feeling bilious and unsteady on his feet. His condition persisted in the days that followed. Back in Miami Beach, he remained in bed when he received James Byrnes, the US Secretary of State, for two hours of talks. Following Churchill's White House visit, an announcement had gone out that he and Truman would fly to Missouri together on 4 March. In view of his health, it was later quietly agreed that they would travel by train instead. Less than forty-eight hours before he and Clementine Churchill left for Washington on the first leg of his trip, he was coughing and complained on the phone to a friend that he was unwell.

Again, the timing of Churchill's appearance in the capital was fortunate. Again, actions taken by Stalin the day before Churchill arrived gave point to the visitor's argument. On 2 March, the Churchills were en route from Florida when Stalin failed to heed the deadline by which it had long been agreed that all Red Army troops would be withdrawn from Iran. It was the first flagrant violation of a treaty obligation since Hitler, and commentators in the US and Britain were soon anxiously comparing it to the Führer's march into the demilitarized Rhineland in violation of the Treaty of Versailles a decade before. The Rhineland episode had been only the first of many such unilateral violations. Would Iran prove to be the same?

In the fortnight since Churchill's visit, the State Department had received an eye-opening message from the US Embassy in Moscow. US chargé d'affaires George Kennan had long been frustrated by his government's naive view of Stalin. He used the present opportunity to put his considerable literary skills to work limning the postwar Soviet mind-set. Widely distributed and much read within the administration, the 8,000-word cable known as the Long Telegram did much to alter attitudes left over from the Roosevelt era. It fell to Churchill, however, to test the waters publicly. When Truman reviewed the final draft of the Fulton speech as they travelled on the ten-car presidential special to Missouri on the 5th, he called it admirable, said it would do nothing but good, and predicted it would cause a stir. Nevertheless, Churchill understood from the outset that he could count on White House support only if his presentation was well received. If he sparked off a controversy, he was on his own.

Resplendent in red robes that prompted some spectators to remark that he resembled a well-fed cardinal, Churchill made his case about time, the bomb, and the Soviet menace to an audience of 2,600 in the college gymnasium. Billed as the opinions of a private individual with no official mission or status of any kind, his comments were broadcast on radio across the US and reported around the world. As he talked on, he alternated between holding the chubby fingers of his left hand splayed across his round torso and using that hand to drive home a point.

He spoke again (though most listeners would be hearing that arresting phrase for the first time) of an 'iron curtain' that had descended across the continent from Stettin in the Baltic to Trieste in the Adriatic. As he had done with Stalin at Potsdam, he ticked off the names of the Eastern and Central European capitals now under Soviet control. 'This is certainly not the liberated Europe we fought to build up. Nor is it one which contains the essentials of permanent peace.' He rejected the idea that another world war was either imminent or inevitable, and he argued that Soviet Russia did not at present desire war, but rather 'the fruits of war and the indefinite expansion of their power and doctrines'.

Churchill observed that in his experience, there was nothing the Soviets respected so much as strength and nothing for which they had less respect than weakness, particularly military weakness. He called on Britain and the US to emphasize their 'special relation-ship', in the interest of being able to negotiate from a position of strength. The danger posed by Soviet expansionism would not be removed by closing one's eyes to it; it would not be removed by waiting to see what happened or by a policy of appeasement. What was needed was a settlement. The longer a settlement was put off, the more difficult it would be to achieve and the greater the danger would become.

Returning to the theme of fleeting time which he had sounded in his address in the House of Commons on 16 August 1945, he emphasized the necessity of acting in the breathing space provided by one side's exclusive possession of the atomic bomb. 'Beware, I say;

time is plenty short. Do not let us take the course of allowing events to drift along until it is too late.'

The Fulton speech set off an avalanche of criticism and controversy in the US. In the wake of Stalin's remarks the previous month and of the Red Army's failure to leave Iran, there was perhaps little room to quarrel with Churchill's blunt review of the unpleasant facts. His recommendations were another matter. Members of Congress lined up to administer a vigorous spanking to Churchill for – as they had heard him, anyway – proposing an Anglo-American military alliance, calling on Washington to underwrite British imperialism, and nudging the US in the direction of a new war. At the time, Halifax privately compared Churchill's situation in the US to that of a dentist who has proposed to extract a tooth. His many detractors were not so much claiming that the tooth was fine (given the recent news, how could they?), only that the dentist was 'notorious for his love of drastic remedies' and that surely modern medicine offered 'more painless methods of cure'.

When he spoke in Missouri, Churchill had been careful to call attention to Truman's presence on the same platform and to point out that the President had travelled a thousand miles 'to dignify and magnify' the occasion. Truman had applauded Churchill's address for all to see and he had praised it to him afterwards in private conversation. In view of the uproar, however, he was quick to distance himself publicly. Three days after Fulton, he claimed not to have read the speech beforehand, and he declined to comment now that he had heard it. He wrote to his mother that while he believed the speech would do some good he was not ready to endorse it yet. Other figures associated with the administration also ostentatiously backed off. Secretary of State Byrnes denied advance knowledge of the content of the speech, though he, like Truman, had been shown a copy by Churchill himself. Under Secretary of State Dean Acheson abruptly cancelled a joint appearance with Churchill in New York.

In the belief that his views had been misrepresented in Congress and in a broad swathe of the American press, Churchill spent the next two weeks trying to undo some of the damage. He made widely reported speeches and public appearances, but he also did some of his most important and effective work behind the scenes in Washington and New York. In one-on-one sessions with journalists, government officials, military leaders, and other opinion-makers, he patiently and methodically pointed out that he had called for a fraternal association, not a military alliance or a treaty. He maintained that, contrary to popular fears, he did not expect the US to back British foreign policy in every respect, or vice versa. He clarified that he had asked for a build-up of strength in pursuit of negotiations and that his purpose, as laid out in the text of the speech, was to prevent another war, not to start one. Throughout, Churchill toned down his language considerably; it was not his natural idiom perhaps, but it was what he felt people wanted to hear.

Halifax judged that by the time Churchill finished meeting with everyone on his long list he had made himself 'a far more popular figure' than he would have been had he returned to England immediately after Fulton. And he had done much to put across his argument that Soviet expansionism was a topic the US was going to find it impossible to evade. All in all, Churchill had provided, in Halifax's view, 'the sharpest jolt to American thinking since the end of the war'.

He also produced a jolt in Moscow, though the Soviets waited several days to speak out. Churchill was in Washington preparing to go on to New York when the news broke that *Pravda* had run a front-page editorial headlined 'Churchill rattles the saber'. The piece denounced him for calling for an Anglo-American military alliance directed against the Soviet Union. A similar assault ran in the newspaper *Izvestiya* the following day. The day after that, Moscow radio broadcast a blistering attack by Stalin himself.

Speaking to an interviewer, Stalin called Churchill a 'warmonger', compared him to Hitler, and accused him of seeking to assemble a military expedition against Eastern Europe. He seized on Churchill's address as an opportunity to put a face on the danger from the West which he had evoked in his speech of 9 February to the Soviet people. George Kennan characterized Stalin's comments as 'the most violent Soviet reaction I can recall to any foreign statement'. In a curious way, Churchill had actually done Stalin a favour. The potential aggressor that Stalin had set himself up to defeat need no longer be an abstraction; Churchill was the threat personified. As Molotov later said, the Fulton speech made it impossible for Stalin to retire.

Stalin in turn gave Churchill a boost when he attacked him. Bypassing the elected leaders of Britain and the US, Stalin portrayed the emerging East–West conflict as a personal contest between Churchill and himself. At a moment when the news of Soviet troop movements in Iran and of US protests to Moscow over its actions not only there but also in Manchuria and Bulgaria were heightening public fears about Soviet intentions, Stalin drew Churchill into a debate that conferred upon him the unique status of the voice of the West. When Stalin pounced on what were after all the remarks of a private citizen, he ratcheted up the drama as Churchill could never have done alone.

On 14 March, after a stack of evening newspapers with articles about the Stalin interview had been delivered to Churchill's twenty-eighth-floor suite at the Waldorf Towers, he sent word to reporters in the lobby that he would make no statement – yet. He was, however, set to speak at a banquet in his honour the following night in the hotel's grand ballroom, and he let it be known that he believed his comments would be of world interest.

Friday, 15 March, proved to be foggy, rainy, and windy. In spite of the downpour, Churchill insisted on sitting on top of the back seat of an open touring car at the head of a twelve-vehicle motorcade which advanced at a walking pace. On both sides, a row of raincoated policemen flanked the car, provided by the city of New York, which flew an American flag above one headlight and a British flag above the other. The rain flattened Churchill's few remaining wisps of ginger-grey hair and streamed down his snub nose and jutting lower lip. Confetti clung to his blue overcoat as he held up a soggy black homburg to New York.

That evening, double rows of as many as a thousand demonstrators, dubbed 'Stalin's faithful' by the local press, formed outside Churchill's hotel two hours before the banquet. Protestors carried picket signs, chanted, 'GI Joe is home to stay, Winnie, Winnie, go away,' and distributed reprints of a Communist *Daily Worker* cover showing a military cemetery with the headline, 'Churchill wants your son'. Mounted police maintained order, especially near the revolving doors where invited guests, including the Mayor, the Governor, and numerous ambassadors and other diplomats, were to enter. (The Soviet Ambassador, notably, had sent last-minute regrets.) Inside, police detectives dressed in evening attire guarded the grand ballroom where four orchid- and carnation-laden daises had been set up in tiers on stage. A tangle of microphones marked the spot where it was widely expected that Churchill would reply to Stalin.

As the hour of Churchill's talk drew near, Manhattan bars and restaurants filled with people eager to hear him. One midtown restaurant promptly lost much of its business when its radio failed to work at half past ten. The proprietor of another East Side spot marvelled that he could not recall a broadcast listened to by so many people or with such avidity since late 1941. Churchill came on the air twelve minutes later than scheduled, and the ovation he received at the Waldorf kept him from starting for an additional minute. At last, the familiar dogged, defiant voice on the radio answered Stalin's challenge to the Fulton speech by saying, 'I do not wish to withdraw or modify a single word.'

Churchill was back at the centre of great events, where he loved to be, but the exertions required to get there had cost him dearly. On the night of the broadcast he was in splendid form, but in the days that followed he experienced dizzy spells. Once or twice, as he rose from a sitting position he began to fall forward and had to steady himself by grabbing his chair. He later said that acting as a private individual rather than a prime minister had been like 'fighting a battle in a shirt after being accustomed to a tank'.

VII

Imperious Caesar

Southampton, England, 1946

A fur coat draped over his bowed shoulders, Churchill waited in the disembarkation shed at Southampton for his car to be brought round. During his nine weeks abroad, the political landscape at home had altered subtly but significantly. It was a measure of how much had changed that, two days before, when Stalin announced plans to withdraw from Iran he had felt the need to tell the world that his decision had not been prompted by anything Churchill had said in America.

On the other hand, much in political London remained the same. The Edenites were hoping to oust Churchill; Macmillan and Butler, perceiving elements of dissatisfaction with the interim Tory leadership, were jockeying to undermine Eden; and Eden himself was intent that that night, 26 March 1946, was the night when he would finally (in Cranborne's words) 'grasp the nettle' and make a forceful case to Churchill about why it would be best if he retired.

At a moment when Churchill had begun again to feel his power, he was coming home greatly alarmed by how physically weak he felt. The dizzy spells had persisted, and there was concern that they could be the precursors of a stroke. At the Southampton quayside, he deflected questions about when he would next appear in the House of Commons by saying that he did not yet know the state of business in the House.

75

He would have more information as soon as he had dined with his deputy.

A soupy fog in the English Channel had caused Churchill's ship to dock two hours late, so Eden was already waiting for him at Hyde Park Gate. On various prior occasions Eden had struggled to suggest that Churchill stand down in his favour. At the last minute, something had always caused him to hesitate. This time, he was confident things would be different – not because of any change in himself, but because Churchill's circumstances had changed. Initially Eden had taken a cynical view of the Fulton speech. He had remarked in private that he feared Churchill might actually be willing to set off another war in the hope of regaining the premiership. In the three weeks since Fulton, however, Eden had begun to sense that all the attention Churchill had been getting of late could prove useful to those who wished to force him out as Tory leader. In the past, Churchill had resisted any suggestion that he abandon power. But given his egotism and love of the limelight, might he not now be inclined to concentrate on his headline-making Soviet crusade and leave the conduct of party affairs to Eden?

Despite the long wait, Eden was in a hopeful mood when Churchill arrived at nine, but his plans quickly went awry. Before Eden could bring up the subject of Churchill's retirement, Churchill caught him by surprise. He, too, had a proposal to make this evening. Concerned about his waning strength, Churchill had devised a plan to allow him to hold on to the Conservative leadership without overtaxing himself. Just when Eden was about to ask the old man to step aside, Churchill asked Eden to help make it possible for him to keep his job. Churchill wanted Eden to take over for him officially in the House of Commons, as well as to assume the day-to-day work of running the party, while Churchill retained the overall party leadership. As he was aware that Eden was financially pressed, he had already asked James Stuart, the Chief Whip, to see if a way might not be found to pay Churchill's salary as Opposition leader to Eden instead. He went on to assure Eden that the arrangement was temporary, that he intended to keep the leadership for just a year or two, and that his successor would benefit from having an opportunity to establish himself.

Few things could have been more insulting to Eden than the suggestion that he still had anything to prove, and few could have been more exasperating than the implication, heard so many times before, that he need wait only a bit longer before the prize was his. Again, the details of the handover were hazy. Again, Churchill set no firm date for his departure.

There was resentment on Churchill's side as well. An old man does not like to feel that he is being watched by 'hungry eyes'. When at some point in the discussion Eden managed to suggest that Churchill give up the leadership altogether, Churchill refused. And Eden, though he did not reject Churchill's offer in so many words, did not accept it either. The encounter on which Eden had pinned his hopes ended in bitter stalemate.

Having informed the press that he had no idea when he would next visit the House of Commons, Churchill disregarded his state of exhaustion and made a strategic surprise appearance on the Opposition front bench the next day. Entering to his usual ovation, he let it be known that he intended to make his first speech in April during the budget debate. Eden, whose deputy leadership was widely deemed to have been a success, shrank to a subordinate position beside Churchill.

Moran arranged for his patient to be examined by the neurologist Sir Russell Brain, who concluded that the dizzy spells were nothing to worry about, that Churchill had merely overstrained himself in America, and that the episodes would soon pass. Thus reassured, Churchill seemed to forget his worst health worries and began to recover. He did not, however, forget Eden's bid to unseat him. When, over the vehement objections of his wife, Churchill took on the party leadership in 1940 in addition to his duties as wartime prime minister, it had been in part to keep the job from going to a younger rival who might later pose a threat to his premiership. In a similar vein, when he anointed Eden during the war he had been blocking the emergence of a more potent rival, someone less reluctant to seize the crown. In that sense, Eden's designation as heir apparent had been far from a sign of approbation.

Eden was still stoutly insisting to supporters that he would never accept Churchill's offer of the Opposition leadership in the House without the party leadership overall when Churchill tripped him up by abruptly withdrawing it. Suddenly it was no longer in Eden's power to accept or refuse. Churchill indicated that as he was already feeling better, a formal arrangement was no longer necessary. Eden would still be called on 'in an ever-increasing measure' to fill in for him in the House, but without any official status or salary. Churchill now expected Eden to do it all for nothing. The object of this division of powers was no longer to conserve an ailing man's strength; it was to spare Churchill what he saw as the drudgery of routine party business. In essence, Churchill wanted to do the work he chose, when he chose to do it. He wanted to speak and act when the spirit moved him – and to dump the rest of the job on Eden.

This time there was no display of temper on Churchill's side. On the contrary, in his note to lay out the new terms, he addressed Eden with ironic courtesy, assuring him, even as he joyously twisted the screws, that he looked forward to working together 'in all the old confidence and intimacy which has marked our march through the years of storm'.

Still, Churchill made it clear that this was an offer Eden could not refuse – if, that is, he hoped to retain his claim to the succession. As if Churchill were innocent of Eden's nightmare of being overtaken by other claimants, he went on enthusiastically to propose Macmillan ('certainly one of our brightest rising lights') as a candidate to become the next party chairman. There was probably only one other name

Churchill might have mentioned that would have been as likely to cause Eden to gag. Reminded that he was dispensable, Eden backed away from his demands. Eden timidly assured Churchill that he could count on him 'to play my part'.

Cranborne was horrified. He had spent the past few weeks in Portugal for his always precarious health, but he had been avidly monitoring all the moves and counter-moves from afar. He worried that under Churchill's leadership the postwar Conservative Party was fast becoming a kind of dictatorship. Cranborne fully shared Churchill's anxiety about the Soviet threat in Europe. Nevertheless, he was appalled that Churchill had delivered the Fulton speech without bothering to consult his Conservative colleagues beforehand. In the process, Churchill had committed what Cranborne saw as a political blunder which could have been avoided had Churchill taken the trouble to listen to other views. To date, Cranborne had been pleased to see the Labour Foreign Secretary consistently stand firm against the Soviets. On this matter at least, the Conservatives had been in the position of being able to sit back and support Bevin when necessary. Bevin had had to endure a good deal of sniping from the left wing of his own party, which remained infatuated with Moscow, but the broad unity of the country had been maintained. To Cranborne's eye, Churchill had unwisely destroyed that 'happy unity': thanks to Churchill, opposition to the Soviet Union had become the policy of the party of the right, and not of Bevin, whose position with his own supporters had thereby been made vastly more difficult.

Apart from all this, Cranborne believed there was a larger issue at stake. In important respects, Churchill was a lone wolf who disdained the pack. Cranborne regarded the Fulton speech as typical of Churchill's lifelong tendency to act without concern for his colleagues' opinions or his party's best interests. As far as Cranborne was concerned, this was the sort of high-handed, self-serving behaviour he and Churchill's legion of other critics had long fervently complained of. Churchill for his part shrugged off such criticism. In the present instance, he saw it as a matter of perspective: why concern himself with relative trifles like party interests or colleagues' wounded feelings when he was trying to head off another world war?

Thus the battle lines were drawn. Cranborne viewed Churchill as 'imperious Caesar' who simply had to be stopped. If Eden lacked the will to force the issue of Churchill's retirement, it seemed to Cranborne that others were going to have to do it for him. Within days of his return to London, Cranborne was discreetly proposing that party leaders 'take their courage in both hands' and make a joint approach to Churchill. He acknowledged that Churchill would probably never forgive them and that they might very naturally hesitate to participate. But, Cranborne stressed, he saw no alternative. When Eden discouraged him, Cranborne wrote in disgust to his father, Lord Salisbury, that he had been ready to lead a cabal against Churchill but that there was no reason to go forward as long as Eden refused to act.

Some of Churchill's long-time friends were also quietly advising him to retire, but their motives were very different from those of the Edenites. There was feeling among some of Churchill's contemporaries, such as the seventy-six-year-old South African Prime Minister Jan Smuts and the seventy-one-year-old Canadian Prime Minister Mackenzie King, that by allowing himself to be caught up in party strife he was tarnishing his reputation. An incident in the House of Commons on 24 May was a case in point. Churchill had caused a furore when, during a particularly fierce dispute, he stuck out his tongue at Bevin.

In contrast to those who wished to give Churchill the hook for personal or party ends, Smuts and King, who were in London for a meeting of Dominion leaders, were concerned solely with what was best for him. Churchill was especially fond of the South African leader, of whom he once said, 'Smuts and I are like two old love-birds moulting together on a perch but still able to peck.' On the present occasion, Smuts advised Churchill to retire immediately.

In a similar vein, Mackenzie King, who was then beginning his twentieth year in office, recommended that Churchill remove himself from the hurly-burly of domestic politics in favour of taking a larger view in keeping with his titanic stature. Both he and Churchill were now the very age Lord Fisher, the former First Sea Lord, had been in 1911, when, Churchill recalled in *The World Crisis*, 'I was apprehensive of his age. I could not feel complete confidence in the poise of the mind at 71.' As Churchill well knew, King had begun to worry about his own fading powers. As a consequence of the uproar over Churchill having stuck out his tongue at Bevin, claims had been heard from the Labour benches that Churchill had entered his 'second childhood'. Might the time have come to bow out for dignity's sake? Churchill was firm that it had not.

He made his intentions clear at a dinner party on 7 June in honour of Mackenzie King's long service, hosted by Clement Attlee in the panelled dining room at Number Ten. Field Marshal Smuts was present as well. When the conversation among the old men turned to Roosevelt's state of mental and physical deterioration at Yalta, Churchill suggested that he could close his eyes and see the ruined President as he was then. Someone chimed in to speak of Gladstone, who had been returned to power at a great age. In response, Churchill expressed confidence that he had time yet. But did he really mean to suggest that he believed he could be prime minister again? When King urged him to devote himself to authorship rather than politics, Churchill shot back that he had no intention of abandoning the fight and planned to lead his party to victory at the next election. In a separate conversation, he told Betty Cranborne (who later repeated it to her husband) that nothing would induce him to retire.

He dropped his bombshell to Eden when the latter returned

from a three-week trip abroad. Mindful of the work that faced him in preparing his memoirs, Churchill suggested that he might be willing to renew the offer of officially dividing the Tory leadership and of transferring his salary to Eden. This new offer would differ from the previous one in a crucial respect. In March, Churchill had assured Eden that he meant to keep the leadership for a limited time. Three months later, he told him what he had already told Mackenzie King and others about his determination to recapture the premiership.

It took Eden a while to absorb the astonishing news. Churchill, after all, had gone from pledging to retire at the end of the war, to promising to stay on as party leader for no more than two years, to this. After the Conservative rout, Eden's sole consolation had been that when next the tide of Toryism came in, Churchill could not possibly still be in position. Now, Churchill was confidently suggesting it was possible.

In the tortured weeks that followed, Eden by turns doubted that Churchill could be right about his prospects, wondered whether in light of Churchill's comments he had better give up politics in favour of a career in finance, told himself and others that Churchill was likely to take a more realistic view by the end of the summer, and strongly considered trying to find a way to accept Churchill's offer – if, that is, he ever actually made it.

Cranborne suggested to Eden that, under the circumstances, it might be best at this point simply to stand down as second-in-command and take his own independent line in Parliament. He was urging Eden, in effect, to abandon the security of his role as designated heir and to fight for the crown alongside any other contenders. The proposal reflected the considerable freedom of action Cranborne's position as heir to the Marquess of Salisbury conferred. He cared a good deal less about office and security than Eden, but then he had the luxury to be inflexible and to put practical considerations aside. In 1938, when Eden and Cranborne resigned as Foreign Secretary and Under Secretary respectively, some observers who knew both men believed that Eden had bailed out only because he had been pushed (or was it shamed?) by Cranborne. Eden's resignation speech in the House of Commons had been, to some tastes, disappointingly soft and vague in contrast to his friend's forthright remarks. Cranborne had bluntly accused the Prime Minister of surrendering to Italian blackmail. (Chamberlain said of Cranborne: 'Beware of rampant idealists. All Cecils are that.') Hoping to protect his claim to succeed Chamberlain, Eden had been careful not to burn his boats irretrievably with the party. In any case, Eden would long be distressed by the perception that he had been – indeed, still was – in thrall to Cranborne's more powerful personality.

What made this all so painful was that there was much truth to the picture. To Eden's simmering frustration, with Cranborne, as with Churchill, he was and perhaps always would be number two. On the kingmaker's side there was friendship and loyalty, to be sure, but there was also a tendency that did not go unnoticed in their inbred aristocratic world to treat Eden 'rather as if he were the head butler at Hatfield House' (the Cecil family seat).

Eden, meanwhile, continued to vacillate, and Churchill went off to Switzerland without having made another concrete offer to share power. Churchill drew more world headlines when he spoke at the University of Zurich on 19 September. His remarks were the second instalment of his prescription for confronting the Soviet danger. Having already called for an Anglo-American partnership to counter the massive Soviet presence in the occupied territories of Europe, he now proposed an end to retribution against vanquished Germany. He declared that Germany must be rebuilt and he argued that France must lead the effort. Churchill urged listeners to turn their backs on the horrors of the recent past and to look to the future – in other words, to welcome the Germans into the community of nations. So soon after the war, his recommendations were strong medicine, but, as he admitted privately, he saw a rebuilt Germany as a necessary defence against the Soviet Union. It was Churchill's hope that the creation of a strong Europe led by a revitalized France and Germany would do much to avert a war with the Soviet Union, and to produce a lasting settlement at the conference table.

In reaction to Churchill's call for the rebuilding of Germany and the formation of a 'United States of Europe', Moscow radio accused him of seeking to unite the continent in preparation for war. When Churchill went on to ask publicly why the Soviets were maintaining so many troops on a war footing in the occupied territories of Europe, Stalin called him the worst threat to peace in Europe.

Churchill was already under heavy fire from Moscow when he turned up in Paris to discuss the situation in Europe with US Secretary of State Byrnes, who was there for the peace conference. Frustrated by his inability to extract the information from his own Government, Churchill was eager to be brought up to date on current thinking in Washington. He also wanted to maintain his personal contacts with the Americans. Bevin, for his part, could not see why. Was Churchill's party not out of power? What business did he have in Paris? To the acute irritation both of the Labour Government and of certain of his Conservative colleagues, Churchill seemed to be running some sort of high-flying, out-of-control, one-man foreign policy shop. Official negotiations with Molotov continued to drag, and the British Foreign Secretary was furious at the prospect of Churchill, who had not been invited to participate, doing or saying anything in the course of his short stay to complicate matters.

In anticipation of Churchill's arrival in Paris, there had been much agitated discussion within the British delegation about how best to cope. Bevin worried that allowing Churchill to stay at the embassy would seem to confer Government approval on his private talks with Byrnes and other officials, when in fact Britain had no control over anything he said. Duff Cooper, the British Ambassador, successfully argued for accommodating him there, the better to manage him. Afterwards, the Ambassador wrote of his fellow

Conservative's whirlwind visit with a mixture of amusement and annoyance (clearly more of the former than the latter), 'Having possibly endangered international relations and having certainly caused immense inconvenience to a large number of people, he seemed thoroughly to enjoy himself, was with difficulty induced to go to bed soon after midnight and left at 10 a.m. the next morning in high spirits.'

A year after Churchill returned from his Italian holiday, he had reason to be high-spirited. Though out of office, he had handily regained influence. Though Britain had a new Government, he regularly managed to upstage it. Whether or not one sympathized with his arguments in Fulton and Zurich, there could be no denying that he had framed the international debate on such matters as Soviet expansionism and European reconstruction and unification. At the first annual Conservative Party conference since the war, held in Blackpool in October 1946, Churchill avowed that while it would be easy 'to retire gracefully', the situation in Europe was so serious and what might be to come so grave that it was his 'duty' to carry on. As he approached his seventy-second birthday, he spoke with assurance of turning out the socialists and he remained confident of his ability to secure the peace if only he could get back to the table with Stalin.

Still, there was growing dissatisfaction in Conservative quarters with a leader who was absent much of the time, travelling, speaking, writing, and collecting awards. A fresh round of defeats in the December by-elections intensified Conservatives' hunger for a leader willing to devote his energies to remaking the party. It was a measure of how much the tide had begun to turn against Churchill that the Conservative Chief Whip, James Stuart, went to Cranborne to discuss the need for a change of leadership. Though at the end of 1946 Stuart remained distinctly unimpressed by Eden, he had sadly concluded that Churchill's spotty attendance in the House of Commons was making the conduct of business almost impossible.

In conversation with Cranborne, Stuart proposed to speak to Churchill. He wanted him to revive his plan to hand over the Opposition leadership in the Commons to Eden while retaining the broader leadership of the party. At least that way, someone other than Churchill would have real authority to lead in the House. Stuart judged that Churchill might be more amenable to sharing power now that he was so effectively influencing international opinion. Cranborne was a good deal less optimistic about what amounted to a first approach to Churchill by his colleagues, on Eden's behalf. Nevertheless, he gave the mission his blessing. It was a mission that few would have taken on willingly, but Stuart, a raffish Scot, had a reputation for fearlessness. The very fact that someone unaffiliated with the Eden faction was prepared to make the proposal might signal to Churchill that it was indeed time to think about going.

To Stuart's relief, Churchill responded calmly to the suggestion that he had already done so much for his country that he could retire and enjoy the rest of his life without regrets. Still, when Stuart proposed that for the good of the party Churchill consider reviving his plan to share the leadership with Eden, Churchill would not hear of it. Churchill explained that great events were pending, though not immediately, and that he wanted to be in a position to handle them himself. His answer went to the heart of what power meant to Churchill. Through the years, he had often suggested that office and title meant nothing to him; what appealed to him was the opportunity to direct events and to shape the future. And so, he made it clear to Stuart, it was now.

On a lighter note, Churchill addressed his colleagues' concerns about whether he was still up to the burdens of the Opposition leadership by informing Stuart that he meant to install a bed in his room at the House of Commons. He assured the vastly amused Chief Whip that this would allow him to take naps there and no one need worry that he would be too tired to attend. Churchill insisted that Eden could wait a little longer to enter his inheritance and that Eden knew he was devoted to him. At the end of the hour, Stuart, veering between laughter and tears of frustration, had got absolutely nowhere. The most he could say was that at least the old lion had not bitten off his head.

For Cranborne, the news that Stuart had failed was unwelcome but not unexpected. By the end of 1946, he had explored what seemed like every option: he had prodded Eden to approach Churchill on his own; he had volunteered to organize a cabal; he had suggested to Eden that he abandon his role as designated heir and fight for power in the House; he had given the nod to the Chief Whip to act on Eden's behalf. Nothing had worked.

Cranborne lamented that Eden was 'rapidly losing ground'. He reckoned that the only way Eden could re-establish himself was 'by some resolute step, such as he took when he resigned in 1938. That got him the reputation of a strong man, but he cannot live on this one incident in his career forever.' It was a disturbing assessment of the man Cranborne still hoped to make the next prime minister of Great Britain. Cranborne insisted that if Eden wanted to be perceived as a leader he had better begin to act like one; until Eden made his move, there was nothing anyone else could do for him. In the interval, Churchill clearly meant to hold on to the party leadership 'at all costs'. For one thing, Cranborne reflected, Churchill liked power. For another, Churchill was convinced that 'like Lord Chatham he can save England & no one else can'. Cranborne did not intend the comparison to the aged, ailing eighteenth-century statesman who pushed himself to the limits of his physical endurance, collapsed on the floor of Parliament, and died soon afterwards to be flattering. Nevertheless, Cranborne recognized that part of what made Churchill an especially formidable opponent in any attempt to challenge his leadership was that he really did think he was the one man to save his country.

Still, at that point there was no rational reason to believe that Churchill could ever be prime minister again. Labour remained overwhelmingly popular, and the wisdom continued to be that the Conservatives could not hope to recapture Number Ten for at least two five-year election cycles. For all that Churchill had accomplished since he left office, the arithmetic continued to be against him.

VIII

Plots and Plotters

Hyde Park Gate, 1947

The downstairs rooms of the house in Hyde Park Gate were dark and unbearably cold. It was Sunday, 16 February 1947, and ordinarily the Churchills would have been at Chartwell, but they had decided to stay in London on account of the heavy snow and freezing temperatures. Since the last week of January, Britain had been suffering the most brutal weather conditions anyone could recall. Government mismanagement of the recently nationalized mines had left the country without a sufficient supply of coal. The power system was at breaking point and heavy restrictions were in effect. Clementine Churchill had secured a doctor's certificate to allow her husband's bedroom to be minimally heated. Even so, as the use of electricity was prohibited from 9 a.m. until noon and again from 2 p.m. until 4 p.m. on pain of a heavy fine or imprisonment, she had also arranged to have Winston's bed moved near the window so he could work by natural light.

Churchill liked his comforts, and one might have expected to find him in a petulant mood. On the contrary, the former prime minister, propped up against a mountain of pillows, his elbows resting on sponge pads on either side of his bed table, was sunshine itself. It is unattractive to gloat over other people's misfortunes, especially when one is poised to profit from them; but under the circumstances, who could blame him? After the Labour landslide he had argued that, like it or not, the Opposition would have to wait upon events. Those events had come in force. The Government was blaming its troubles on an act of God. For Churchill, the arctic weather was a godsend. Suddenly, it seemed as if Labour might indeed be vulnerable at the next general election.

The revelation of official ineptitude in miscalculating both the amount of coal needed to sustain Britain that winter and the productive capabilities of the mines shattered public confidence in the socialists. Popular disappointment was so enormous because the expectations of a better material life after the war had been unrealistically high. The continuous snowfall paralysed the already feeble economy, and, rightly or not, many Britons blamed Number Ten for the stalled train lines, business closings, mass unemployment, food and water shortages, long sluggish queues, and overall discomfort and deprivation. They also blamed the Government for their nation's abruptly diminished place in the world when, in the midst of the crisis, Britain made it clear that it could no longer afford to keep up its military commitments in Greece and Turkey.

In March the snow and ice gave way to pounding rains and catastrophic floods. Again the economic consequences were devastating, and again the Government struggled to cope. Churchill asked the House of Commons for a vote of censure. The Conservatives were still vastly outnumbered and, as he knew it must, the vote on 12 March went against him, but this time anti-Government sentiment was more pervasive than before. He had the support of Liberals and some independent MPs, and there was fierce disagreement among the Labour members about how best to respond to the crisis. The day after the vote in Parliament, both Macmillan and Butler confidently suggested to a large and enthusiastic Conservative meeting in London that a new general election could be in the offing sooner than anyone had thought. If the economy continued to deteriorate and the socialists persisted in fighting among themselves, the Government might be brought down even before 1950.

Conceivably, the coal crisis had gained Churchill five years or more – no small gift to an old man. But the events that had caused him to smell Attlee's blood also made it seem more urgent than ever to his Tory adversaries to dislodge him lest he still be in place when a new election was called. It had been one thing for him to cling to his job when the party had no realistic chance of being returned to power. But everything had changed, and beginning in late February, there was a flurry of small private meetings of Conservatives, most but not all of them Edenites, anxious to see Churchill go.

When Churchill absented himself in June for five weeks after a long-postponed hernia operation that had been troubled by complications, his opponents thought they might have caught a whiff of his blood as well. After all, the announcement had lately been made of Churchill's deal to be paid more than a million dollars for the US book and serial rights to his war memoirs, the first volume of which was scheduled for publication in 1948. Researchers and other staff had been hired, permission to draw on his official wartime papers had with much difficulty been obtained, and work on the text was under way. Given the deadline and Churchill's always precarious finances, not to mention his health, might he not be amenable to a plea that it really would be best for everyone if he stepped aside sooner rather than later?

Eight senior Conservatives gathered in the upstairs drawing room of the Tory MP Harry Crookshank to select an emissary to make the case to Churchill. Crookshank, who had been castrated by a burst shell during the First World War, lived with his mother in Knightsbridge. Eden, notably, skipped the meeting on the grounds that his direct participation in a plot to install him would be awkward. But, though he had previously vowed to do no more until Eden acted, Bobbety Cranborne – who had become the 5th Marquess of Salisbury on the death of his father in April – was again a key player in the machinations.

Why did Salisbury (as Cranborne was now known) stick with Eden when he perceived his flaws so clearly? Quite simply, in Salisbury's view there was no other viable candidate. He was opposed to Butler because of his history as an appeaser in the 1930s. Nor was he prepared to back Macmillan, whom he disliked and distrusted. Salisbury's wife, whose opinions meant much to him, was also no fan of Macmillan's. The reasons for Lady Salisbury's antipathy were strange and complicated. Early in her marriage, she had lost interest in Bobbety and began to have affairs with other men. Her husband's rise to political prominence rekindled her interest, and she became fiercely possessive of him. She even resented his lifelong affection for his sister, Mary, Duchess of Devonshire, with whom Macmillan, who was married to the Duke's sister, enjoyed a close, confiding friendship as well. Macmillan's association with 'Moucher' Devonshire doomed him in Betty Salisbury's unforgiving eyes.

Though Salisbury would never have admitted as much, there was another compelling reason to keep coming back to Eden. Salisbury could never have pushed around Butler or Macmillan the way he did Eden. They would not have tolerated it. The very weakness that Salisbury deplored in Eden in some respects made him a most attractive candidate in others. If it was influence Salisbury hankered for, Eden was assuredly his man.

There was unanimous agreement among Crookshank's guests that Churchill must go, but most were unwilling to face him. It was not just his epic temper that daunted them. If Churchill survived the putsch, the mission might be a career-destroyer for any ambitious Tory who consented to undertake it. Finally, James Stuart agreed to try – again.

Interestingly, Butler, who attended the Crookshank luncheon, also threw in his lot with a group of Labour members who, in the hope of saving their own hides should Attlee fall, aimed to bring down the Government themselves in favour of a coalition headed by Ernest Bevin. Because of the hard line he had taken on the Soviets, Attlee's

Foreign Secretary was perhaps the one Labour figure capable of commanding substantial Tory support. What was in it for Butler? As matters stood within the Conservative Party, his way to the top was blocked by a number of factors. One objection was that his résumé was too thin. Another, which threatened to be insurmountable, was that he had been too closely associated with the policy of appeasement when he served in the Chamberlain Government. Then, quite simply, there was the perception that the succession had long been fixed. Were Churchill to go, Eden was ready, as well as widely expected, to take his place. Should Butler be part of a coalition that bypassed Churchill, neither Churchill nor his designated heir would any longer stand in Butler's way.

In July, Churchill returned from his convalescence to be greeted by applause from all parties – and by a whirligig of plots and plotters. He was sitting in his room at the House of Commons when Stuart came in. Stuart began by saying that he had a difficult task to perform and that he hoped Churchill would bear with him without being annoyed. When last they spoke of retirement, Churchill had reacted calmly, and Stuart hoped that might be the case again. He repeated what he had said previously about no other man having done more for his country than Churchill. Then he went on to report the view of their colleagues that the time had come for a change of leadership.

'Oh, you've joined those who want to get rid of me, have you?' Churchill exploded.

'I haven't in the least,' Stuart protested, 'but I suppose there is something to be said for the fact that change will have to take place sometime and you're not quite as young as you were.'

Churchill responded by angrily banging the floor with his walking stick. With that emphatic gesture, he put an end to the cabal to unseat him in favour of Eden. The plotters acknowledged that Churchill was too beloved a figure, both within the Tory rank and file and the country at large, for there to be any public perception that party leaders had forced him out. If he went, it had at least to appear to be of his own accord. And he was unlikely to go anywhere at a moment when the premiership seemed achingly and unexpectedly within grasp.

Churchill was not supposed to have learned of the negotiations between Butler and other Tories, on the one side, and Attlee's Chancellor of the Exchequer Hugh Dalton, on the other, but there had been much open talk of them, including some indiscreet remarks by Butler's wife. Sydney Butler could not resist broadcasting the news to at least one lunch partner that Churchill was about to have a 'rude awakening' when a coalition government was formed with someone other than himself at the top. In the end, however, it was Sydney's husband who was in for a jolt when Churchill appeared unannounced on 31 July at a meeting of the 1922 Committee, the official Conservative organization for backbenchers. Without referring to Butler or the others by name, he put the plotters on notice that he knew of their machinations. Speaking as if it were a foregone conclusion that were there to be a coalition he would be at the head of it, Churchill warned against any such arrangement with Labour on the grounds that it would deprive the country of an effective alternative government. He made many of his listeners' mouths water at the prospect of their party's imminent return to full power if only they proceeded judiciously – under his leadership, of course. Why agree to share power, Churchill suggested, when Conservatives could have it all? Why indeed, many backbenchers concurred.

Having outmanoeuvred the conspirators in his own party, Churchill went on to leave no doubt in the minds of Britons that he and no other man would lead the Conservatives to victory. At a time when the Government was announcing stringent emergency measures that included longer working hours and extensive further rationing, Churchill publicly declared his intention to fight the next election on the matter of the economic crisis.

Eden, who had just turned fifty, alternated between threatening (again) to forsake politics altogether and making it plain to friends that even now he thought 'of nothing except becoming leader of the Conservative Party'. The ageing 'boy wonder' seemed to be of two minds about his personal life as well. One minute he was pining for Beatrice Eden to return now that her American lover had gone back to his wife, and the next he was chasing young women, including Kathleen 'Kick' Kennedy, the twenty-six-year-old daughter of the former US Ambassador to Britain, and Churchill's twenty-six-year-old niece Clarissa Churchill. In private, Eden made no bones about the fact that he loathed Churchill, yet he cheerfully played his part at the Tories' annual conference, held in Brighton that October, where Churchill was set to challenge the Government to call a new election.

Churchill liked to use a basket of bread on his arm to lure and coax his pet birds at Chartwell – geese, black swans, sheldrakes, white swans, and ducks – and, finally, to set them all fighting. He enjoyed watching his would-be successors in the Conservative Party battle over crumbs as well. Eden and Butler vied for the party's attention in speeches, to some three thousand delegates from every corner of the nation, about Conservative ideas and how they might be applied in a new Government. But it was Macmillan, the new party president, whose remarks seemed to claim the greatest share of the spotlight at Brighton.

The adroit, confident performer who introduced Churchill on the third and final day bore little resemblance to the shy, often ineffectual, even buffoonish figure Macmillan had cut before the war, when he had had a reputation as 'the most boring speaker in the House of Commons'. By Macmillan's own reckoning, he had all but reached a dead end in his career when, in 1942, Churchill assigned him to North Africa as the British Government's Representative to the Allies in the Mediterranean. At first he feared he had been sent to languish in 'political Siberia', but it rapidly became apparent that the position would be the making of him. He gained stature and confidence on the job and earned the respect and affection of colleagues like Dwight Eisenhower. By 1944, Lady Diana Cooper, who had gone to Algiers with her husband, Duff Cooper, was predicting something that would have been unthinkable just two years before. She prophesied that Macmillan was going to be prime minister someday.

Macmillan, who had thinning grey hair which he brushed straight back from a high forehead, drooping eyelids, and a bushy moustache arranged to conceal irregular teeth, came home in 1945 with great hopes. But it soon seemed as if the late-starting momentum of his career might have been fatally interrupted. He lost his seat in Parliament in the general election that swept the Conservatives from power. The setback prompted Macmillan to brood about how little he had accomplished in life to date. Eden at least had been Foreign Secretary; but despite being past fifty, Macmillan believed that he himself had only just begun. As it happened, a safe Tory seat fell vacant shortly thereafter. Macmillan fought a by-election and was back in Parliament soon enough, but the effect upon him of the general election was very severe. Having briefly been convinced that his political life was over, Macmillan felt as never before the need to propel himself forward while he had the chance. He emerged as a shrewd operator, always manoeuvring, always watching. Some people thought him devious and unscrupulous, but as far as Macmillan was concerned he was only making up for lost time.

Though Harry Crookshank was his close friend and James Stuart his brother-in-law, Macmillan refused an invitation to the witches' Sabbath to plot Churchill's ouster. But was it, as he professed, solely (or even largely) devotion to Churchill that motivated him?

When Macmillan first began to attract praise for his achievements in North Africa, Eden had pricked up his ears – and they stayed up for years to come. The Foreign Secretary became wildly jealous of the Minister Resident, a situation that was not helped by Churchill's habit, then and later, of taunting his heir with references to Macmillan's rising fortunes. As a consequence, were the prize to fall into Eden's hands at this point, he was unlikely to do any favours for Macmillan. From the perspective of Macmillan's ambitions, it therefore seemed better that Churchill be allowed to carry on, giving Macmillan a chance to overtake Eden, precisely as Churchill himself had once done.

At a moment of much discontent among senior Tories about the leader's refusal to hand over before the next general election, Macmillan cast himself as the most outspoken supporter of Churchill's ambitions to return to Number Ten. The other 'possibles' and their associates had no alternative but to cheer along with the Conservative rank and file when Macmillan pointedly, some claimed unctuously, introduced the closing speaker at the Brighton conference: 'We need a Prime Minister – Mr Churchill.'

IX

Before It Is Too Late

Westminster Abbey, November 1947

Churchill tended to operate on his own timetable, and it often fell to Clementine (or to one of his daughters when they were 'in attendance') to make sure that he was reasonably punctual. On the morning of 20 November 1947, not even Clementine's best efforts prevented the couple from arriving at Westminster Abbey after the approximately 2,500 other guests at Princess Elizabeth's wedding were already seated. The organist had begun to play, the scarlet-and-white-clad choirboys had filed in, and Prince Philip and his best man, both in naval uniform, were in position at the altar steps.

Guests on either side of the nave stood up for Churchill as he was escorted to his place beside Jan Smuts and Mackenzie King in Clement Attlee's pew. Mrs Churchill was seated separately, with Mrs Attlee. In the seconds before a roll of drums and a fanfare of trumpets announced the appearance of the bride in the west door of the abbey, the three old men chatted affectionately. Field Marshal Smuts, wearing an overcoat and high boots, sitting between Churchill and King, said in a parched voice, 'We shall not see the likes of this again. We shall soon be passing away.'

This of course was far from how Churchill preferred to view his own immediate future. At a moment when both Smuts and King recognized philosophically that the time was fast approaching when they must allow younger men to have a chance, Churchill burned to lead Britain again. He reckoned that Labour was likely to put off a new general election as long as possible, which meant that he might have to wait until the summer of 1950 before he had a chance to reclaim power.

Churchill's sense of frustration was particularly acute in advance of the fifth session of the Council of Foreign Ministers, scheduled to open in London on 25 November. Germany was the main topic on the agenda, and Churchill was hardly alone in his concern that a failure to reach an agreement there could set off another war. Failure, at any rate, seemed assured. In the belief that prolonged chaos would spur the Germans to go Communist, the Soviets did not see it as in their interest to rebuild Germany physically and economically as the US, Britain, and France proposed to do.

By this point, the Kremlin had reacted to extensive new US initiatives to limit the spread of Soviet power in Europe – the Truman Doctrine and, in particular, the Marshall Plan to rebuild Europe, for both of which Churchill could lay claim to having been an inspiration – by dropping any remaining pretence that the wartime alliance remained intact. The previous month, Moscow had decreed that the postwar world was divided into two camps, one led by the Soviets and the other by the Americans. Smuts and Mackenzie King were among the Dominion leaders who, during their visit for the royal wedding, received secret briefings at Number Ten which conveyed the Attlee Government's intense pessimism about the situation in Europe. Bevin, set to face Molotov at the foreign ministers' talks, told the Dominion leaders that, in the event the Soviets moved to block the Western powers' access to Berlin, fighting could break out as early as the following month. Nerves were on edge as a confrontation over Berlin threatened to spark off a third world war.

As far as Churchill was concerned, Germany was among the critical issues that should have been resolved by the leaders at Potsdam and ought never to have been passed on to foreign ministers. In his analysis,

Soviet Russia, like Hitler's Germany at the time of the Rhineland episode in 1936, was not ready to fight another war. He believed that this was the moment to call Stalin's bluff and use America's exclusive possession of the bomb to force the Soviets to release their grip on their satellite states in Europe and retire to their own country. Based on his assessment that the Soviets feared the bomb too much to face a war, he predicted that they could still be made to retreat without bloodshed.

It pained Churchill to be out of office while others undertook crucial negotiations he was convinced he could handle much more effectively himself. He believed that, faced with anyone else at the conference table, the Soviets might yet be inclined to seek further appeasement in Germany or elsewhere. 'If I were there,' Churchill told Violet Bonham Carter, 'they would know very well what to expect from me.'

On the day the foreign ministers' talks began, Churchill did most of the talking at a small farewell lunch party for Smuts and King at the home of Churchill's former Chancellor of the Exchequer John Anderson and his wife, Ava. Also present were Clementine Churchill and Harold Macmillan. Churchill argued that if their side failed to make it clear that the Soviet presence in Europe was unacceptable, another world war was a certainty, either directly or in a few years' time: 'I am telling you now that I see the coming war as plainly as I did the last one.' As Churchill held forth at the Andersons' table, his fervour and frustration were such that King, seated to his left, could see the greater part of the whites of his bulging eyes, which looked as if they were about to pop out of his head. 'The gleam in his eyes was like fire,' the Canadian Prime Minister wrote in his diary afterwards. 'There was something in his whole appearance and delivery which gave me the impression of a sort of volcano at work in his brain.'

The foreign ministers were still closeted at Lancaster House, when, on 10 December, Churchill flew to Paris en route to Marrakesh. There he meant to 'bulldoze' a finished manuscript, or something very close to that, of volume one of his war memoirs, which portrayed his role in the 1930s as a truth-teller and a prophet and ended with him becoming wartime prime minister. When, previously, Churchill's colleagues had urged him to devote himself to his memoirs, it had been their way of trying to persuade him to fade from the scene. Churchill had come to view the project very differently. Far from being an activity to occupy his time in retirement, the preparation of his Second World War history became an integral part of his campaign to catapult himself back into office.

As a politician, Churchill was gifted with the ability to reach people powerfully and directly in his capacities as an orator and an author. There could be no denying that the Fulton speech had done much to transform public opinion, both in the US and Britain. Now that people perceived the developing danger, Churchill used his war chronicles to help make the case that he was the leader to confront it.

After the party's defeat in 1945, senior Conservatives had been eager for Churchill to travel abroad and leave the management of party affairs to Eden. Much had altered since then, and Churchill's regular and prolonged absences had become a source of aggravation to some of the very people who had once hoped to see him go off for as long and as often as he liked. Bitter complaints were heard that Churchill was not in the least interested in politics, that he was preoccupied with his memoirs, and that he insisted on retaining the party leadership largely because he hoped to wipe out the disgrace of the general election. There was also annoyance at the prospect of his earning so much money from his books when he ought to have been looking after Conservative affairs in the House. There was upset that when he did make the occasional grand parliamentary appearance, he seemed to take an interest in no one's speeches or opinions but his own. And there was indignation that he failed to mingle with his party in the Smoking Room, only with the 'admirers and hangers-on' who formed his claque.

These charges pumped new life into decades-old questions about Churchill's party loyalty; he had had a long and difficult association with the party he blamed for having forsaken his father. As a young man, Churchill had quit the Tories supposedly on a matter of principle, but some people insisted it had been to further his own personal interests. After he returned to the Tory party, he never entirely shook off the stigma of having crossed the aisle to the Liberal side. Now, fellow Conservatives asked again whether he was out to help his party or himself. The crusty veteran Tory MP Cuthbert Headlam complained that Churchill had 'always been too much interested in himself to run a party'.

Churchill's unabashed egocentricity did make him a less than satisfactory party leader, but, as even certain of his critics acknowledged, it gave him the strength and pertinacity that had allowed him to carry on in the face of apparently insurmountable obstacles. The conviction that he had been put on earth to do great things had sustained him during his wilderness years (when he had been violently at odds with his party on the matter of the German threat) and during his wartime premiership. It sustained him now.

By the time Churchill returned from his working holiday, the foreign ministers' talks had failed, precisely as he had predicted they would. When he rose to speak in the House of Commons on 23 January 1948, he asked the question that was on many people's minds: 'Will there be war?' He reminded listeners of what he had said at Fulton, that he did not believe the Soviet Government wanted war, but the fruits of war.

It would be idle to try to reason or argue with the Communists, he maintained. It was, however, possible to deal with them on a realistic basis. The best chance of avoiding a war was to bring matters to a head and to come to a settlement with the Soviet Government 'before it is too late'. He recalled his speech on 16 August 1945, during the V-J Day celebrations, when he observed that America's exclusive possession of the bomb would provide a three- or four-year breathing

102

space. He noted with alarm that more than two of those years had already passed.

He did not think that any serious discussion which it might be necessary to have with Moscow would be more likely to reach a favourable conclusion if their side waited for the Soviets to get the bomb as well. 'You may be absolutely sure that the present situation cannot last.'

The appearance that spring of the advance excerpts from volume one of Churchill's memoirs hammered home his case that steps must be taken at once to avert a new war. The *Daily Telegraph* published a total of forty-two extracts from Churchill's depiction of the run-up to the Second World War, the *New York Times* published thirty, and *Life* magazine serialized the book over the course of six weeks. The narrative spanned events between 1919 and 1940, but from first to last the story was framed in terms of what Britain's early mistakes with Hitler had to teach the world about present problems.

The timing of its publication caused the serial to resonate inescapably in terms of the Berlin crisis. Churchill noted in his introduction that after all the exertions and sacrifices that had been made in the last war, neither peace nor security had been attained, and mankind was at present in the grip of even worse perils than those it had just surmounted. He expressed the hope that 'pondering upon the past may give guidance in days to come'. The *Daily Telegraph* billed the work as an unchallengeable case against any repetition of the appeasement that had led to the Second World War. The *New York Times* cast it as a solemn warning that 'unless we are able to learn from the past and avoid its mistakes, we stand in danger of seeing history repeat itself'.

On the political front, the serial sparked outrage among Conservatives, who worried that it would jeopardize party prospects in the 1950 general election. When they had first advised their leader to produce a history of the last war, they had assumed the story would be limited to the war itself and, especially, to his premiership. Instead,

Churchill's first volume chronicled his failed efforts to warn of the looming Nazi danger. He aimed his harshest criticism at the Tory party and its leaders, who had not only ignored but disparaged him. In Churchill's telling, he was the hero of the tale and fellow Conservatives emerged as its villains. Following the 1945 general election, public displeasure with the shortsightedness of the prewar regimes of Stanley Baldwin and Neville Chamberlain had been one of the factors generally assumed to have contributed to the Conservative defeat. Three years later, at a moment when Conservatives had reason to believe they could return to power sooner than previously expected, Churchill had focused renewed attention on the party's mistakes in the 1930s. Tory upset with this approach was by no means confined to those, such as Lord Halifax, who had themselves embraced the policy of appeasement. There was also much distress among the party's young bloods. They feared that their leader had wantonly and selfishly put their chances in a new general election at risk.

The extracts revived the charges of self-centredness and of a fatal lack of judgement that had clung to Churchill for decades. Had not the party's belief that Churchill's prestige and popularity would be enough to assure victory been one of the factors behind the cataclysm of 1945? And now, by enhancing his personal stature at the expense of his party's, had the Conservative leader not ensured that Tories would again have to depend on the glamour of his name and reputation to carry them back to power?

The week Churchill's book, *The Gathering Storm*, was published in the US, tensions over Germany, which had been escalating since the foreign ministers' talks, came to a head. On 24 June, in response to an American, British, and French decision to merge their occupation zones and to introduce a new currency that would render an independent Germany economically viable, Stalin cut off road and rail access to Berlin. The long-feared blockade had become a reality.

Churchill had often been accused of the rhetorical trick of exaggerating dangers, of always seeming somehow to claim that it was 'the hour of fate and the crack of doom'. The Berlin blockade gave point to his argument about the parallels between the run-up to the Second World War and the present. Speaking at a mass rally after the blockade went into effect, Churchill noted that the issues at stake were as grave as those in play at Munich ten years previously. He argued that only firmness, of a sort that had not been demonstrated early on with Hitler, would be capable of preventing another world war.

That same day, Harry Truman launched the Berlin airlift. American and British fliers undertook to provision West Berlin, thereby asserting the Western powers' right to be there. As usual, it frustrated Churchill to be out of office when great events were unfolding. While he was delighted that Truman had taken action and while he quickly moved to praise the President's response, Churchill was certain that had he been in power he would have done things differently. He thought it would have been better to respond to the blockade with counter-measures against Soviet shipping and imports that might be useful for war purposes, giving the Western powers 'something practical to bargain with'. Nevertheless, he was emphatic in his support for the show of resolve represented by the airlift.

How would Stalin react to the airlift? Would he dare shoot down an American or British aircraft, and what would Washington's response be if he did? These questions remained in suspense when Churchill went off to Aix-en-Provence to 'bulldoze' volume two of his memoirs – which was to cover Britain's 'finest hour' in 1940 – for publication early the following year. There was, in Salisbury's words, 'much heartburning' among Conservatives when their leader accepted an invitation to stay at La Capponcina, Lord Beaverbrook's villa at Cap d'Ail near Monte Carlo. The Canadian-born press lord, who had served as Minister of Aircraft Production in Churchill's wartime Government, had bitterly withdrawn from politics after the general election and now spent much of the year abroad. Beaverbrook remained a controversial figure in a party that still blamed him for, among many other sins, its disastrous electoral strategy in 1945.

It had been 'the Beaver', as he was known, who had encouraged Tories to see Churchill as their sole asset. And it had been he who had encouraged Churchill (as if he had needed any encouraging) to target the socialists with invective. Three years later, Churchill's sojourn at La Capponcina caused his party to fear that he was again in league with Beaverbrook.

Salisbury, who, with Eden, had long disdained Beaverbrook as an adventurer, denounced Churchill's stay with him as a 'criminal error'. To add insult to injury, when Churchill returned from his five-week working holiday for the yearly Conservative conference, he emerged from Beaverbrook's private plane.

Churchill had come home in time for the British publication of his book. It was said that when *The Gathering Storm* appeared in London shops every copy was snatched up by evening. The following day, the train from London to Llandudno was filled with delegates to the party conference carrying the book. When Churchill wound up the proceedings on 9 October, he used the occasion to explicitly tie the subject matter of his memoir to the combustible crisis in Berlin in 1948. He reminded his audience that it had not only been in the 1930s that his warnings had been ignored. He recalled that in 1945 he had similarly pointed out the error of allowing the Russians to take Berlin, and that he had opposed pulling back American and British troops in Germany until a postwar settlement was secured. Churchill expressed wonderment that it had taken the British and American people so long to perceive the Soviet threat after having made the same mistake before with Hitler. So, when he offered advice on how best to handle present problems, he asked his audience to consider an undeniable fact: 'I have not always been wrong.'

The speech did not play quite as Churchill had expected. Bursts of applause interrupted his presentation, but there was an undercurrent of disappointment among those Conservatives who wished that Churchill would spend less time focusing on a coming war and more on the 1950 election. Many members had been eager to hear a statement of Tory beliefs that might serve as a manifesto. They wanted him to comment on domestic policy. They expected him to offer specifics about what Conservatives would do to improve people's lives in an era of hard times. Instead, Churchill spoke entirely of the crisis with the Soviet Union, which, as Salisbury complained, was not at present an issue between the Conservatives and the Government. Afterwards, Viscount Kemsley, the newspaper proprietor, gave voice to the discontent with Churchill's leadership when he publicly called on him to share his responsibilities with younger colleagues. Kemsley was widely understood to mean Eden.

The Conservatives were not alone in criticizing their leader's speech or in viewing it in terms of party prospects. On the basis of his remarks in Llandudno, Moscow radio declared it obvious that Churchill hoped 'to return to power on the crest of a new war'. Three years after Stalin had incorrectly called the 1945 British general election, he predicted that Churchill would again be rejected by his people, for whom the horrors of the Second World War were still fresh.

Eisenhower entered the fray the following month with the appearance of his war memoir, *Crusade in Europe*. He had begun the book the previous February at a time when the brewing Berlin crisis made it likely that certain of his wartime decisions would be re-evaluated in the light of postwar realities. Dictating at a pace of some five thousand words a day, he produced a manuscript in forty-six days. The book cited a range of wartime strategic disagreements with Churchill and the British. On the sensitive subject of Berlin, Eisenhower vigorously defended his refusal to listen to Churchill about the need to take the Reich capital before their Communist allies did. Eisenhower maintained that military plans should be 'devised with the single aim of speeding victory' and that the sort of political considerations expressed by Churchill ought to have had no place in his own calculations.

In fact, Eisenhower argued, it was Churchill who had made a terrible mistake with far-reaching repercussions when he refused to listen to Eisenhower about the cross-Channel invasion. According to Eisenhower, Churchill's pessimism about Operation Overlord had resulted in the fatal error at Yalta of setting the occupation line in Germany too far to the west. At Llandudno, Churchill had hit hard at the American miscalculations which, in his view, had contributed to the current crisis. In Eisenhower's telling, it was really Churchill's fault that the Western allies had missed the critical opportunity to occupy more of Germany.

Speaking in the House of Commons on 10 December, Churchill said that he preferred not to respond to Eisenhower until he published the relevant volumes of his own war memoirs: 'I did not always agree with General Eisenhower on strategic decisions, and I shall take an opportunity of expressing my views if my life – and the life of the Government – are suitably prolonged.' The chamber erupted in laughter at the half-bantering suggestion that Churchill might have to put off completing his memoirs if the Conservatives regained power in 1950.

He certainly hoped to have to put it off. After Christmas, as Churchill left for a short holiday in France, he sent a New Year's message to party members expressing the wish that 1949 would prove to be their 'year of destiny'. But a Labour triumph in the bellwether South Hammersmith by-election in February 1949 prompted renewed calls, from Kemsley and others, for Churchill to shed at least some of his power in anticipation of handing over the leadership altogether. The by-election had been deemed so important that, at the behest of campaign managers, Churchill had toured the London borough in an open car on the eve of the poll. As in 1945, the crowds who came out to welcome their beloved wartime leader did not necessarily cast their votes for his party. Despite the austerity that continued to grip Britain, Labour romped to victory in South Hammersmith. The Conservatives had been highly optimistic about their chances of winning back the seat, and the defeat occasioned what was said to be the worst crisis of faith in Churchill since he left office three years previously. There was much feeling in the party that as the general election drew near, Churchill's aloof, absentee, haphazard leadership was no longer tolerable.

On the evening of Thursday, 3 March, the 1922 Committee conducted an inquest into the by-election loss that key party members were blaming outright on Churchill. Unperturbed, Churchill made a show of savouring a cigar for over an hour as his critics aired their complaints. When at last he rose to reply, he was all optimism and good cheer.

Were his colleagues downhearted? He coolly insisted that the outcome in South Hammersmith in no way contradicted what he saw as a national trend towards the Conservative Party. Were they pessimistic? He asserted that there was no reason to feel so and that Labour was sure to suffer heavy defeats later on. Did they think he was too often absent from the House? He expressed confidence that in his stead Mr Eden gave 'great satisfaction'. (Like his father before him, Churchill found it impossible to enunciate the sibilant 's'.) Did they wish him to spell out domestic policy details for use in elec-tioneering? He pledged to do so before long. Did they want him to concentrate on the general election? He promised to clear his own 'personal decks' and to throw his energies into home politics as soon as he returned from a crucial visit to the US.

Churchill warned the backbenchers not to be 'cowed because of a bump here and there'. He was so incongruously perky and positive in the face of defeat that Cuthbert Headlam, who attended the crowded session, remarked that the members were fortunate he had not given the V-sign.

At the time, Clementine Churchill seemed a good deal more concerned about her husband's troubled relations with his party than he was. It was not that she had any particular attachment to the Tory party. Clementine was a Liberal, read the Liberal press, and tended to have a low opinion of the Conservatives. On the grounds that they did not deserve Winston's help after the war, she had lamented the prospect of his using his 'great prestige' to return them to power in 1945. And she certainly did not hope to see him become prime minister again in 1950. As much as any of his Tory critics, she would have liked him to give up the party leadership before the next general election. As much as any of the men who had plotted to oust him, she was eager that the succession finally occur. But she wanted him to be able to hand over on his terms, not because he had been pushed out or because the party had grown disenchanted with him. She wanted the decision to be his alone.

So long as her husband remained in public life Clementine was ready to put her own interests aside. Though she suffered inter- mittently from low spirits and poor health, and though she had often felt, in her daughter Mary's words, as if she would 'gladly exchange the splendours and miseries of a meteor's train for the quieter more banal happiness of being married to an ordinary man', she did what it took to help him prevail. Visiting his constituency and attending to his constituency correspondence were the least of it. In important ways, Clementine kept her ear to the ground as he simply did not.

To counter the oft-heard charge that her husband held himself apart from all but a few members of his party, she presided over numerous small, elaborately choreographed luncheons in the dining room overlooking the walled rear garden at Hyde Park Gate, where backbenchers whose names Churchill might otherwise be unlikely to remember could be made to feel that they were on intimate terms with the leader and his wife. 'Clemmie' Churchill warmly greeted them at the front door and during the course of the meal 'Winston darling', as she referred to him, talked confidingly of politics new and old. He even sang a song or two. 'Very successful,' the MP Henry 'Chips' Channon noted in his diary after one such luncheon, 'but I still wonder why I was asked?'

Two days after her husband faced down the 1922 Committee, Clementine wrote the first of a pair of letters to warn him of an impending problem. She often put such ideas on paper even when she and Winston were living under the same roof. He believed he had already done more than enough to pacify his critics in the party. Clementine disagreed. When the backbenchers broached the matter of his absences from Parliament, he had assured them that his trip to the US promised to be of great benefit to the party. He naturally preferred not to speak of his plan to enjoy a holiday afterwards in Jamaica, where Beaverbrook had invited the Churchills to stay at Cromarty House, his residence near Montego Bay. Clementine had long disapproved of her husband's friendship with Beaverbrook, whom she thought dissolute and disreputable, but in the present instance her concern was not so much personal as political. She warned that Winston's acceptance of his hospitality would come off as cynical and that it would further alienate Conservatives at a moment of considerable doubt and discouragement among them. 'I do not mind if you resign the Leadership when things are good,' she said, 'but I cannot bear you to be accepted murmuringly and uneasily.' In the interest of averting what threatened to be construed as an insult to the party, she persuaded him to send his regrets to Beaverbrook.

Churchill sailed to America in mid-March in the belief that he and Truman were to speak on consecutive days at the Massachusetts Institute of Technology. He hoped to repeat the impact of their joint appearance in Fulton, but before his ship reached New York the White House announced that the President would not be able to speak at MIT after all. British Foreign Secretary Bevin was due in Washington to sign the North Atlantic Treaty and, though it was not stated publicly, there was concern that Truman's sharing a podium with the Tory leader might cause distress at Number Ten.

Following this disappointment, Churchill had some very good news when he returned to England the following month. On 8 April, as the *Queen Mary* docked eighteen hours late due to heavy gales, he received word of a surprise Tory success in London's municipal elections. The mood in the party was one of jubilation. Lord Woolton, the national chairman, crowed that the municipal elections offered a more accurate picture of broad public opinion than any parliamentary by-election. Suddenly, Churchill's calm, confident assertion that there was a national trend towards the Conservatives did not seem so far-fetched after all, and the way seemed clear for him to lead the Tories to victory. At any rate, he was the leader they had, and they were unlikely to find another in time for the general election.

In Conservative circles, the election upset temporarily silenced a good deal of the most conspicuous 'anti-Winstonism'. The news that Eden, overstrained by his several responsibilities, had fainted not once but twice in the course of an address to the United Nations Assembly made it difficult to argue, at least for now, that the party would perform better under the younger, supposedly more vigorous man. Overseas as well, events seemed to arrange themselves in Churchill's favour. On 9 May, the Soviets lifted the Berlin blockade. In the face of strength, Stalin had backed down from his bluff. The Soviet leader was left in what was widely viewed as a dramatically weakened position – exactly where Churchill wanted him when they met again at the conference table, which, he hoped, might be very soon.

Despite his vow to refocus on home politics, Churchill returned to the international stage in August. In Strasbourg, he participated in the first sessions of the Consultative Assembly of the Council of Europe. After he had spoken on the need to organize Western Europe against the threat of tyranny, he flew to Monte Carlo, where he planned to write, paint, and relax for a few days before he returned to the assembly to press for the inclusion of the Germans in the new European community. Churchill's exultant mood in Strasbourg – 'like a schoolboy', Macmillan described him – persisted at Cap d' Ail. Beaverbrook, his host, had recently turned seventy and had proclaimed that he intended to give up neither his passions nor his prejudices nor his work. On the hot, windy afternoon of 23 August, Churchill performed somersaults in the sea for the entertainment of the actress

Merle Oberon. After four years, everything pointed to the political comeback that had once seemed impossible. The cup was almost at his lips.

That night in his bedroom at La Capponcina, Churchill, aged seventy-four, had a stroke.

X

The Dagger Is Pointed

La Capponcina, Cap d'Ail, France, August 1949

23 August 1949 was to have been Churchill's last night in Cap d'Ail. The first sign that anything might be wrong came at about 2 a.m. He and Beaverbrook's friend, Brigadier Michael Wardell, were sitting up late playing gin rummy after dinner. Suddenly, Churchill heaved himself up from his chair. As he did, he reached out to steady himself on the edge of the table. He bent his heavy right leg a few times, as if it had fallen asleep. Complaining of cramps in his arm and leg, he clenched and unclenched his right fist. He sat again and finished the card game, though the cramps persisted.

'The dagger is pointed at me,' he said before he retired for the night. 'I pray it may not strike.' Uncharacteristically, he asked an aide to remain with him in his room while he bathed.

On the afternoon of 24 August, Churchill was scheduled to return to Strasbourg, where he planned to dine with Macmillan and some others whom he had left to pursue the German issue. But when he awakened at about 7 a.m., he found that his arm and leg were still troubling him. He tried to write his name, but could not form the letters with facility. Beaverbrook summoned a local doctor. Finding that Churchill had suffered a stroke, the physician asked Moran to come without delay.

In Marrakesh the year before, when Churchill developed a fever and a hacking cough, the sudden arrival from England of his wife and his personal physician had set off what amounted almost to a death-watch in the international press. The daily reports on Churchill's condition had caused much alarm to his friends and supporters at home. The news coverage, not to mention the swarm of reporters and photographers who descended on his hotel, had also greatly upset Churchill. Above all, he had worried about the repercussions to his political career of all that newspaper ink devoted to his ill health.

This time, Moran arrived at the airport in Nice lugging a set of golf clubs, and Clementine Churchill, though anxious about her husband and eager to join him, stayed away lest the sight of her trigger alarms. Moran's conclusion was the same as the local doctor's. It had been a stroke, a slight one fortunately, but a stroke nonetheless. Churchill's first reaction was to ask if he was likely to have another, a fear that would haunt him from then on. He spoke of the general election and of the possibility that he might soon be called on to lead the country. He managed a grin and suggested that he felt as if he were balanced between the premiership on one hand and death on the other. He insisted, as in the past, that he was not worried and that fate must take its course. He struck the doctor as calm, but also perhaps a bit fearful.

Moran reassured him that the episode had been limited to a small clot in a small artery. The artery had not burst and there had been no haemorrhage in the brain. Neither his speech nor his memory appeared to have been affected, and there seemed to be no paralysis. Churchill did, however, complain of a veil that seemed somehow to separate him from things. He reported an uncomfortable sensation of tightness over both shoulders. He was also concerned that his physical appearance would alert people to the fact that he had suffered a stroke, and that his bid to regain the premiership would thereby be doomed. It was not just the electorate he had to worry about; it was his party as well. According to Churchill's doctor, for now the best – and the only – thing he could do was rest.

On 25 August, Moran released a statement that the Conservative leader had contracted a chill while bathing on the Riviera. At the Council of Europe, rumours predictably flew that Churchill was gravely ill. Some said he had developed pneumonia, others that he had had a stroke. On the morning of the announcement, Churchill's son-in-law Duncan Sandys, Diana's husband, informed Macmillan that he had spoken to Churchill on the telephone and that he had indeed caught a chill. According to Sandys, he was in fine form, but was unlikely to be permitted to return to the assembly for some days at least, if at all. The report, though comforting, did not altogether dispel the rumours.

For the first three days after his stroke, Churchill remained in seclusion at La Capponcina, where he practised signing his name obsessively. Again and again, he showed his efforts to a secretary and asked whether the signature seemed normal.

In the days that followed, he tested himself in other ways. He had to find out if he could show himself in public. He had to know if his secret could be kept. One lunchtime outing, at the Hôtel de Paris in Monte Carlo, went well. As Churchill entered, the other diners rose respectfully, and no one seemed to notice that he had some trouble walking to his chair. Dinner the next evening was less successful. He was in a touchy mood, and when a woman at a neighbouring table asked him to autograph her menu he could not hide his anger.

At times, Churchill seemed to think that he would be able to put the stroke behind him. 'The dagger struck, but this time it was not plunged in to the hilt,' he told Wardell. 'At least, I think not.' At other times, he behaved as if he knew that he had had his 'notice to quit the world'. To an aide, he spoke sadly of his four 'wasted' years out of office, fighting his way back to power when there had been so much else that needed to be accomplished before it was too late. Would he be able to accomplish any of it now? For the moment, he was not even sure of his ability to walk properly when he got off a plane in England.

Churchill was eager to get home, but he worried that the inevitable press contingent at the airport would spot that something was amiss. He was so nervous about faltering in public that when he flew back on 1 September, he furiously gestured to the photographers waiting at RAF Biggin Hill to leave him alone.

For the entire month, he continued to assess his ability to carry on. The question for Churchill was never whether he should continue in politics, but whether he could. The answer depended in part on his ability to conceal what had happened at La Capponcina. Significantly, both key witnesses were prepared to keep his secret. Unlike Smuts and King, who had previously advised Churchill to retire for his own sake, Beaverbrook and Moran were convinced that retirement would almost certainly be the death of him.

Nine days after Churchill returned to England, he made a first sustained public appearance that involved a good deal of walking. Lest he stumble, Clementine Churchill hovered protectively at his side when he attended the Lime Tree Stakes to cheer on his grey three-year-old, Colonist II. The Churchills arrived three-quarters of an hour early to allow the former prime minister to show himself on the clubhouse balcony to an enthusiastic crowd below. After his horse outran four rivals, Churchill set off to visit the paddock. On his way there, he was pleased to hear one racing fan call out, 'I hope you can win the election just as easily!' Days like this bolstered his confidence immeasurably.

He also had dark, despairing days. A meeting in London with Sir Stafford Cripps, the Chancellor of the Exchequer, was one of the worst. It had fallen to Cripps to inform Churchill of the impending devaluation of the pound. The Government's decision, and the spike in prices it threatened to produce, suggested that Labour would soon have little choice but to submit their case to the nation. Churchill for his part could count nine separate occasions on which Cripps had said he would never devalue. As recently as July, the Chancellor had claimed that he would prefer to die first. Churchill's encounter with him therefore should have been a pure triumph for the Conservative leader. Instead, when the two men faced one another on 18 September, it was Cripps who managed to seem cool and in control and Churchill who was palpably nervous. Afterwards, Churchill blamed his inadequate performance on his health. How could he fight an election, no less resume office and take on Stalin, if he felt like this?

At a moment when Churchill was weighing the possibility of handing over the party leadership after the general election, major news arrived from Washington. On 23 September, Truman announced that an atomic explosion had occurred in the Soviet Union sometime within the past few weeks. The news that Moscow had acquired the secret of the bomb galvanized Churchill. He had warned of precisely this development when, in 1945, he addressed the House of Commons on the need to reach a postwar settlement while America alone had the bomb. Now, the Soviets had tested a bomb; soon they would be able to build their own arsenal, and the breathing space would be at an end. After he learned of the Soviet breakthrough, the possibility that Churchill, weakened by a stroke, would throw in his cards anytime soon was no longer seriously in play.

Ten days after the encounter with Cripps that had filled him with self-doubt, Churchill was by all accounts at the height of his powers when he held the House 'entranced' for more than an hour. Officially he was there to attack the Government on the matter of devaluation and to argue that Labour had brought the country to the brink of bankruptcy. But, as most listeners understood, his real purpose was to militate for an early election, a chance to get his hands back on the levers of power sooner rather than later.

And for all his talk of the financial crisis, his abiding preoccupation was clear: 'Over all there looms and broods the atomic bomb.'

Churchill's assault on the Government was greeted with catcalls from the Labour benches. Speaking in a high-pitched voice with a Welsh lilt, the podgy, red-nosed Minister of Health Aneurin Bevan, who had harassed Churchill brutally during the war, called on him to retire at once before he damaged his reputation further. Bevan predicted that should the Conservatives get back in they would promptly fling their leader aside 'like a soiled glove'. Nevertheless, there appeared to be broad consensus in the House that, with Churchill's speech, a watershed had been reached and an election would probably take place in October or November.

The Tories gathered in London at their annual conference in the expectation that Attlee was likely at any moment to advise the King to dissolve Parliament. Instead, the Prime Minister surprised them by declaring that there would be no election until the following year.

On 30 November, Churchill turned seventy-five. In contrast to his gust of anger at the airport two months previously, he gamely posed for photographers at his front door in Hyde Park Gate.

'I hope, sir, I will shoot your picture on your hundredth birthday,' said one member of the press.

'I don't see why not, young man,' Churchill replied. 'You look reasonably fit and healthy.'

Did Churchill at his great age have any fear of death? 'I am prepared to meet my Maker,' he answered. 'Whether my Maker is prepared for the great ordeal of meeting me is quite another matter.'

Publicly, Churchill still claimed to have no immediate plan to retire. In private, he told a different story. He informed his friend Brendan Bracken, who passed the information on to Beaverbrook, that in the event the Conservatives lost the 1950 general election he would indeed step aside as party leader.

On New Year's Eve, the Churchills travelled to Madeira, Portugal, where Winston intended to work on his Second World War memoirs until about mid-January. On the 10th, word reached him that Attlee had given in at last. Polling day was set for 23 February 1950. This was the chance that, given the mathematical realities of Churchill's age and the size of the Labour victory in 1945, it had once seemed inconceivable he would ever have again. 'I heard there was going to be a general election,' said Churchill, in a mellow mood, on his early return to London, 'so I thought I had better come back in case I was wanted.'

The election campaign would begin officially on 3 February, when the King dissolved Parliament. In preparation, Churchill plunged into a crowded schedule of 'toil and moil', as he reported to Clementine, who had remained behind in Portugal. Was it all not too much for a man who had suffered a stroke five months previously? He struggled to reassure her that his 'immense programme' was not more than he was capable of. He was acutely aware of the risks, but as he told Violet Bonham Carter, who visited him at Chartwell on 16 January, 'When great events are moving, one must play a part in them.' He would probably never have another such opportunity again and he was determined to seize it with all his strength.

On one occasion, he and Rab Butler, whose expertise was in domestic affairs, worked all evening preparing the party manifesto. Finally, Churchill looked up and said, 'It must be nearly eleven, we must think of moving.' In fact, it was 4 a.m. Another day, Churchill and his team worked for nine consecutive hours at the massive oak dining table at Hyde Park Gate.

On the morning of 24 January, Churchill was working at Chartwell when suddenly everything went misty. He could still read, but with difficulty. Frightened that this could be the prelude to another stroke, he summoned his doctor. Moran diagnosed an arterial spasm, a disturbance of the cerebral circulation brought on, almost certainly, by overwork. He suggested that Churchill could expect to have other arterial spasms if he persisted in exhausting himself.

The official launch of the campaign was still eleven days away. The travel, the speeches, the cut-and-thrust of a hotly contested election had not even begun. Yet already his body was emitting unambiguous danger signals. Churchill's instinctive response was one of defiance. As he once said, 'I am not a submissive man.' He did not easily give in to other people, to circumstances – or even to his own body. No sooner had he finished conferring with his doctor than he plunged back into the maelstrom of activity. Later, he ignored Moran's suggestion that, as much as possible, he substitute radio broadcasts for public appearances.

Churchill claimed to be invigorated by the crowds – admirers and hecklers alike. But the fact was that, as the electioneering began, he did appear to be markedly off his game. The problem at this point was not so much physical as it was psychological. More than ever, the possibility that he might have another, perhaps more serious stroke shadowed his every move.

Overall, the Conservative campaign opened weakly. National polls that suggested an upswing in support for Labour candidates were causing many frowns at Tory headquarters. A mood of defeatism afflicted the Conservative rank and file. In his remarks to voters throughout the nation, the Conservative candidate for Woodford dutifully concentrated on bread-and-butter issues. These were the matters Churchill had been assured repeatedly that people cared about most, yet his oratory never really caught fire.

Across the Atlantic, Truman had announced that the US was developing a hydrogen bomb more powerful than the weapon that had destroyed Hiroshima and Nagasaki. The President's message was meant to reassure Americans and their allies that their side still enjoyed superior strength. Britons, however, found the news, which came on top of some much-publicized Soviet chest-thumping about their new weaponry, anything but calming. For a broad swathe of voters, the prospect of another world war even more destructive than the last overrode all other issues. The outcome of the 1945 general election had fatally interrupted Churchill's plan for a diplomatic showdown with Stalin. Five years later, he sensed that the electorate, horrified by the arms race, might be ready to send him back to the mat.

Churchill was hardly alone in perceiving that a shift in public opinion about national priorities had begun. He was, however, the first politician to tap into it. He sculpted a speech, to be delivered in Edinburgh, calling for a new Big Three conference, and the Tory hierarchy found themselves counting on his words to re-energize the party's campaign. The day before Churchill's address, Anthony Eden, speaking in London, signalled the world to pay particular attention to what Churchill was about to say. Privately, Eden had long maintained that Churchill was far from indispensable and that he, Eden, was ready and amply equipped to replace him. He regarded Churchill as delusional for believing that he alone could head off a war with the Soviet Union. He believed that Churchill suffered from what amounted almost to an infatuation with Stalin. He was convinced that Churchill had actually done a poor job at Potsdam. And, he also thought foreign ministers' talks preferable by far to the top-level contacts Churchill favoured. At the moment, however, Churchill's call for a rematch with Stalin did appear to be the Conservative Party's best chance to return to power. Eden therefore played his part by lauding Churchill as the only world leader capable of ending the Cold War and by suggesting that a Conservative victory would lead to a bold new initiative to avert an atomic war.

On 14 February, Churchill began by delivering some of his usual blood-and-thunder anti-socialism to an overflowing crowd at Edinburgh's Usher Hall. Thousands who could not gain admittance stood outside in the rain listening to his remarks on loudspeakers. During the speech, Churchill's attack mode dissolved and his voice became grave. He conceded that he was privy neither to the Government's secret information nor to US intentions.

'Still,' he went on, 'I cannot help coming back to this idea of another talk with Soviet Russia on the highest level. It is not easy to see how things could be worsened by a parley at the summit, if such a thing were possible.'

The effect of his words on the general election campaign was electrifying. To the Government's chagrin, his call for direct talks with Stalin – a 'summit' conference, as top-level discussions came to be called – proved immensely popular, but by no means with everybody. Foreign Secretary Bevin dismissed his proposal as an electioneering stunt. Sir Stafford Cripps scoffed at the idea that Churchill–Stalin talks would bring salvation to the world, and another prominent Labour politician assailed Churchill's brand of 'soap-box diplomacy'.

And that was just what was being said openly. Whispers emanated from the Labour camp that Churchill would have the nation at war within eighteen months of his return to Number Ten, that he was motivated not by any true love of country but rather by a lust for power and a craving for retribution, and that he was simply too old and ill to form a new Government.

Finally, some forty-eight hours after Churchill's Edinburgh speech, rumours swirled that he was dead.

On 16 February, Churchill commented humorously from Chartwell, 'I am informed from many quarters that a rumour has been put about that I died this morning. This is quite untrue.'

In a radio address the next day – his last of the campaign – he sought to turn the issue of his seventy-five years to his advantage. 'Of course, as I am reminded, I am an old man,' Churchill said. 'All the day dreams of my youth have been accomplished. I have no personal advantage to gain by undertaking once more the hard and grim duty of leading Britain and her Empire through and out of a new and formidable crisis. But while God gives me the strength and the people show me their good will, it is my duty to try and I will.'

On polling day, Churchill visited his constituency before returning to Hyde Park Gate to await the results in the company of Salisbury and other prominent Conservatives. In the last lap of the campaign, Salisbury, though he had previously opposed further talks with Stalin on the grounds that they would be akin to the negotiations with Hitler before the war, had spoken out to support Churchill's 'summit' proposal. If the Conservatives managed to regain power, there was acknowledgement in the upper reaches of the party that it would be largely thanks to Churchill.

There was also a sense, both on Churchill's side and on that of the men who had previously worked to oust him, that the 1950 general election was his last chance. Even Churchill seemed to accept that he could hardly afford to wait another five years to begin a new Government. By the time another full election cycle passed he would be eighty, so it was now or never. If the Conservatives were unsuccessful tonight, he would have little choice but to finally hand over.

As the evening began, it appeared that Churchill was already finished. Early reports showed strong figures for Labour. Then matters began to improve as Conservatives scored heavy gains. The vigil stretched into morning, when it seemed as if Labour might have lost its majority. But by noon on the 24th, it was clear that the socialists had managed to hold on to power after all. This time, however, their majority over all parties combined was only six – hardly enough to maintain anything like a stable Government.

Among Conservatives, there was frustration at having come so close to winning, but there was also elation that another Labour landslide had been averted. Five years previously, the wisdom had been that the socialists would be invincible for at least a decade. That apocalyptic assessment had been disproved. Lord Woolton, who had done much to reorganize and revitalize the party in the wake of 1945, called the 1950 general election 'a moral victory for the Conservatives if there ever was one'.

Because of the precarious Labour majority, the contest was immediately and universally regarded as, in Macmillan's words, 'the prelude to another round'. Less certain from the Tory point of view was when that next round ought optimally to take place.

Churchill believed that another general election in the next few months was inevitable. In light of that estimate, he was quick to reconsider his previous intention to shut up shop in the event of a Labour victory. Five years was one thing, a few months another. To the embarrassment of Conservative colleagues, it soon became apparent that, whatever he may have suggested beforehand, he had every intention of continuing as party leader.

Cheered on by Macmillan, who urged him to press for a Government defeat on an issue of major policy within three weeks of the opening of the new Parliament, Churchill aimed to force an election as soon as possible. He calculated that it could take as many as three, but probably no more than six months. In the first month alone, he would lead four determined efforts to overthrow the Government.

In Conservative quarters, Eden questioned the wisdom of Churchill's determination to go against Labour so hard and so fast. Part of this, no doubt, was Eden's sincere distaste for pugilistic politics. He had long striven to distance himself from Churchill the 'political warrior'. In the present instance, however, Eden targeted not just Churchill's tactics but also his motives. A few weeks after he had hailed Churchill as the only world leader capable of ending the Cold War, the leader in waiting could not comfortably argue that Churchill ought to hand over at once when a new election and conceivably a meeting with Stalin were only months away. Eden made the case that Churchill, mindful of his age and declining powers, was aware that unless he could get the Government out quickly, time would prevent him from ever becoming prime minister again.

There was truth to the charge that Churchill was prepared to allow his personal timetable to dictate political decisions. When Churchill spoke of the need to act before it was too late, it was sometimes hard to know whether he was referring to the world situation or his own. For an 'old man in a hurry', the two can seem perilously interchangeable.

Yet, in arguing for a more cautious approach, Eden was not exactly disinterested either. Just now, it served him to proceed slowly as much as it served Churchill to move quickly. The longer the Labour Party managed to hang on to power, the less chance there was that Churchill would still be in place to carry the flag at the next election.

XI

Another Glass of Your Excellent Champagne

Venice, 1951

On 23 August 1951, a train carrying Winston and Clementine Churchill, along with their fifty-five suitcases and trunks, was approaching Venice, where guests had already begun to arrive for the masked ball at the Palazzo Labia that promised to be the most extravagant party in all of Europe since before the Second World War. Lady Diana Cooper was going as Cleopatra; Deborah, Duchess of Devonshire, as Georgiana, the wife of the fifth Duke; and the American socialite Barbara Hutton as Mozart. The evening's flamboyant Mexican host, Charles de Beistegui, intended to preside over 'the party of the century' in the garb of a Venetian procurer, with flowing red robes, a curly wig, and platform soles that increased his height by sixteen inches.

Many of the guests stayed at the Excelsior Palace Hotel on the Lido, which was also swarming with visitors who had neither received one of the 1,500 invitations nor purchased one on the black market but hoped that one might yet be had. The aspirants need not have bothered to come all the way to Venice. For weeks, bona fide invitees had been begging to be allowed to bring guests of their own. Beistegui replied indignantly that if he let in everyone who wished

127

to be admitted, his eighty-nine-room palazzo, which housed Tiepolo's frescoes of Antony and Cleopatra, would sink into the Grand Canal.

There was to be an official welcoming ceremony for the Churchills at the train station, after which they were due to proceed by motor launch to the Excelsior. Shortly before they arrived, Clementine Churchill left the compartment to prepare. In her absence, Churchill, who hoped to do a bit of painting in the city of the doges, leaned out the carriage window for a better view.

He had been discussing art materials with his bodyguard when suddenly the latter rushed forward, grabbed his right shoulder, and pulled him back in. A fraction of a second more and Churchill's head would have hit a concrete post that held up some electrical wires only a few inches from the side of the train. When Churchill grasped what had just happened, he said with a smile, 'Anthony Eden nearly got a new job then, didn't he?'

Eighteen months after the general election, British political life remained deeply unsettled. In spite of Churchill's confident prediction in February 1950 that a new election was imminent, his efforts to bring down the Government had so far come to naught. Labour retained its gossamer hold on power. Churchill compared the prolonged physical and mental strain of waiting for an election that might be called at any time to 'walking under a tree with a jaguar waiting to pounce'. George VI, meanwhile, had begun to question how much longer Churchill could possibly go on in politics. Though he had been opposed to Churchill in 1940, he had become devoted to him during the course of the war and had been stunned and dismayed when the people turned him out in 1945. Nevertheless, several times in recent months, King George had conveyed his anxieties about Churchill to Eden. On one such occasion, to the fascination of onlookers at a reception at Buckingham Palace in February 1951, the King conferred for a good twenty minutes with the Conservative heir apparent. The scene prompted suspicions that a new alliance might be in the making, one that could mean trouble for Churchill.

Seeking to counter sentiment that he was already too old to form a Government, Churchill led the Opposition in turbulent all-night sessions in the House of Commons in June, including one that lasted nearly twenty-two hours. To his party's delight, he voted in every division, gave marvellous speeches, and spiced his remarks with jokes and raillery. Afterwards, rather than go home, he would make a show of devouring a huge breakfast that began with eggs, bacon, sausages, and coffee, followed by a large whisky and a cigar.

That, at least, was the robust image Churchill hoped to project. The *Daily Telegraph*'s Malcolm Muggeridge managed to extract from Eden the information that Churchill's health was not as good as the public seemed to believe. Eden was right, of course. Few people outside Churchill's intimate circle knew about his wartime heart attack. And few knew that he had since had a stroke, let alone that he lived in perpetual anxiety that another stroke might yet keep him from returning to power.

As it happened, Churchill was arriving in Venice two years to the day since he performed somersaults in the sea hours before the first stroke. On 21 August, prior to leaving the rainy French Alps en route to Italy, he had written to ask Sir Russell Brain whether he might safely swim at the Lido. Churchill promised not to go in unless the water was well over seventy degrees, and he made it clear that he had no intention of plunging in, but rather of acclimatizing his body slowly over a period of two minutes or more. Would Brain please consult with Moran and telegraph his opinion to the Excelsior?

An army of press photographers had descended on Venice, both for the masked ball and for the Venice International Film Festival. There were many actors to take pictures of, including Vivien Leigh, Orson Welles, and Errol Flynn. But no sooner did Churchill appear in town than a picture of him on the Lido became the most ardently sought-after image. Every day, boxes filled with ornate period costumes for the masquerade were unloaded from motor launches at the Excelsior and other hotels. But the one costume every cameraman wanted a shot of was Churchill's 'flaming-red' bathing trunks. A picture of the Conservative leader shirtless, with a towel draped round his opulent waist, would also do. On his strict orders, two English bodyguards and half a dozen Italian helpers kept the press away from his canvas cabana and from the strip of beach where he and Clementine swam together every day, as they had done when they came to Venice on their honeymoon in 1908.

Churchill made a point of skipping the masked ball that everyone else seemed so frantic to attend. Despite this, he was much on view during his fortnight in Venice: painting a landscape on Torcello, seated beside his wife at a Dior fashion show, dictating portions of the fifth and penultimate volume of his Second World War memoirs to a secretary as they flew along in a motor launch.

Duff Cooper, who had retired as Ambassador to France and now worked for the British Film Producers' Association, saw a good deal of Churchill privately that August. Cooper had last encountered Churchill in May, when they had lunch together in London, and he was struck by his deterioration since then. 'I found him much older and very deaf,' Cooper noted in his diary. 'He depends on champagne and is morose and gloomy until he has had a good deal.'

It often fell to Clementine Churchill, who was herself in delicate health after gynaecological surgery that had kept her in hospital for three weeks in May, to 'run interference' for her husband, warning friends like the Coopers that he was in ill humour. When the Churchills dined with Duff and Diana at the Gritti Palace in Venice, Winston was silent and detached at first. Not even Diana, whom he adored and who adored him, was capable of bringing him out of his gloom. In years past, he would have been happy just to sit beside her and talk; he would innocently beg her to give him her 'paw' or a little kiss. But there was none of that tonight. Instead of smiling with pleasure as he tended to do in Diana's company, he did little but scowl. The Coopers' son, John Julius, watched his mother grow desperate as she tried everything, but to no avail. Each painful attempt at conversation was met with a grunt. Churchill's black mood swept over the table, reducing everyone to an awkward silence, until finally he addressed his hostess.

'I shall be much better when I have had another glass of your excellent champagne.'

Churchill drank. And in the course of about five minutes he was indeed transformed. Suddenly he was himself again, laughing, joking, and telling stories. He sang some music hall songs from his repertoire, and half in earnest, half in jest, he told Duff that he feared Clemmie would reproach him on the way back to the Excelsior for 'lacking in dignity'. The evening ended most happily. Still, there could be no avoiding the conclusion that in important ways Churchill simply was not the man he had been in 1945, 1950, or even the first half of 1951.

Soon after the Churchills returned to England on 12 September, Attlee announced that he had asked the King to dissolve Parliament and that a new election was to take place on 25 October. Immediately, Churchill summoned Eden and other members of the Tory hierarchy to launch the campaign. Polls suggested that the Conservatives were likely to secure a working majority of thirty to forty seats (Beaverbrook went so far as to put the number at fifty), so there was huge optimism among them. Understandably, there was also considerable anxiety about Churchill's fitness. As he had done many times in the past, he sought to assuage his colleagues' worries by indicating that he planned to stay in power for a limited time. He put out the word in the party that in the likely event of a Conservative victory he intended to lay down the burden within a year to eighteen months.

Nevertheless, the awkward questions kept coming. Citing Churchill's demeanour when they met in Paris on 11 September, NATO Supreme Commander Dwight Eisenhower asked Macmillan point-blank whether the Tory leader was 'physically able' to take up the work of government. Eisenhower suggested that it might be best for Churchill to announce that after setting up things properly in the new Government he would transfer the reins 'to younger hands'.

Closer to home, both Churchill's wife and doctor had grave concerns of their own. Moran confided to his diary that Churchill had lost ground in recent months and was probably no longer equal to the tasks that faced him as Britain's leader. Clementine Churchill worried that were her husband to become prime minister in his late seventies, it might no longer be possible to operate 'at his best'. Loving him as she did, she could not bear to see that happen.

Churchill's first campaign appearance, in Liverpool on 2 October, left him feeling depleted and quite glad that he had nothing on his schedule the next day. When Moran visited him afterwards at Hyde Park Gate, Churchill confessed that he was no longer as sure as he had once been of his ability to see things through. By degrees, his self-confidence began to be undermined in other critical areas as well: notably the assumption, in play since 1945, that he was his party's greatest asset.

Nineteen months previously, Churchill had nearly managed to beat the socialists by appealing to voters' desire for peace. This time around, Labour hijacked the issue and used it against him. Preferring to side-step domestic and economic matters at a moment of broad public dissatisfaction with Government policy, the socialists focused on the claim that Churchill's return to power would plunge Britain into another war. The whispering campaign of 1950 burst into the open with slogans like 'A third Labour Government or a third world war' and 'Vote Tory and reach for a rifle, Vote Labour and reach old age'. The *Daily Mirror*, which supported Labour, asked readers, 'Whose finger do you want on the trigger, Attlee's or Churchill's?' And Labour Defence Minister Emanuel Shinwell sniped that it would not be long before Britain's wartime leader would seek again to show off his talents.

By harping on the warmonger theme, Labour managed to

dominate and drive the election campaign as Churchill had done in 1950. They put him on the defensive, and there he miserably remained until polling day.

At first, Churchill struggled to answer the charges dispassionately. Since Fulton, many at home and abroad had concentrated on his call for strength and ignored his equally important plea for negotiations. In a radio broadcast on 8 October, he sought to correct that mistake. 'I do not hold that we should rearm in order to fight,' he explained. 'I hold that we should rearm in order to parley. I hope and believe that there may be a parley.' He reminded listeners of his proposal, at Edinburgh in 1950, of a top-level meeting with Soviet Russia. He recalled that the socialists had dismissed the idea as an electioneering stunt, and he suggested that had such a meeting taken place, the Korean War might have been avoided.

On 17 October, at the close of three days of electioneering in the north of England and Scotland, Churchill renewed his appeal for a meeting with Stalin. Labour shot back that far from intending to press for a peace settlement, Churchill really planned to use a summit meeting to provoke another war. The *Daily Mirror* ran a story claiming that Churchill had plans to issue an ultimatum to Stalin.

By this time, Churchill's blood had begun to boil. When Stalin called him a warmonger, Churchill had managed to laugh it off. He found that he could not be so blithe when his own countrymen repeated the accusation. As he never tired of arguing, had they listened to him in the 1930s, the Second World War might never have had to be fought in the first place. Then, as now, he had been a proponent of strategic thinking as a means of preventing war. Nonetheless, the warmongering campaign seemed to have taken hold with voters.

On 20 October, when a pollster visited Hyde Park Gate to review the Conservatives' chances of success, he found Churchill drinking a whisky and soda in bed at half past ten in the morning. This being Churchill, there was certainly nothing unusual about that. (He had long claimed that he drank in the morning strictly to 'moisten' his throat.)

What was out of the ordinary was the urgent question he put to his visitor, after the latter cautiously suggested that an overall Tory majority of about forty seemed probable.

'Do you think I am a handicap to the Conservative Party?' Churchill asked in a low, sober tone of voice.

The pollster was silent at first, but Churchill reassured him that he need not be afraid to give an opinion.

'Well,' said the pollster, 'I do not think that you are the asset to them that you once were.'

Forty-eight hours before polling day, Churchill gave vent to his anguish over the 'cruel and ungrateful accusation' that, he was convinced, had caused his stock to plummet. Speaking to an audience of six thousand in Plymouth, Churchill made it clear that he was so frustrated and upset because he believed himself to be the very opposite of a warmonger. At Fulton and on subsequent occasions, Churchill had claimed that at his age all of his personal hopes and dreams had long been fulfilled. Today, however, he confessed that he had one great ambition still. The man who had led Britain to triumph in the previous world war pleaded for the opportunity to try to avert another.

'It is the last prize I seek to win.'

Churchill was furious when the *Daily Mirror* responded by repeating the 'Whose finger on the trigger?' theme on its front page on polling day. There was speculation at the time that the newspaper cover alone cost the Tory party a great many votes. In any case, when the first figures came in that evening, it was apparent that the generous lead the Conservatives had enjoyed in the polls had evaporated. The close race continued through the night. Not until the following day, Friday, did a Tory victory in the constituency of Basingstoke give the party a thin majority.

When Churchill learned the news, at Conservative headquarters in London, tears coursed down his face. By an act of will, he had accomplished what the world had once (quite reasonably) believed he could never do. Within weeks of his seventy-seventh birthday, he was to become prime minister again, the oldest man to lead Britain since Gladstone. To reach this point, he had defied time, ill health, the opposition of colleagues, family and friends, the mockery of opponents, and, at last, his own festering doubts.

In the years before his first premiership, the middle-aged Churchill had had occasion to reflect on the amount of energy some uniquely gifted people are required to waste before they even have a chance to accomplish what they want to do in life. He wrote, 'One may say that sixty, perhaps seventy per cent of all they have to give is expended on fights which have no other object but to get to their battlefield.' When Churchill made that observation, in an essay on the British politician Joseph Chamberlain included in *Great Contemporaries* (1937), he had himself been caught up in precisely the sort of long, draining preliminary struggle to which he referred. The observation nicely described what, in the end, was to emerge as the arc of Churchill's own political career. By the time he had realized his supreme ambition of becoming prime minister, in 1940, he had spent decades fighting to reach his particular battlefield. Again, after being hurled from power in 1945, Churchill dedicated an additional six years to fighting his way back.

On 26 October 1951, the battlefield was in sight, but did he have enough strength left for the battle?

XII

White with the Bones of Englishmen

London, October 1951

Hours after Churchill learned that the Conservatives were back in, he crossed the red carpet at the entrance to Buckingham Palace on his way to see the King. Only a few months previously, George VI had sensed that the Churchill era in British politics might be coming to an end. This evening, the King, who was recovering from surgery for lung cancer, asked Churchill to form a new Government.

Later that night, over dinner at Hyde Park Gate, Churchill made the first appointment of his peacetime administration, inviting Eden to resume his old job as Foreign Secretary. Eden also insisted (though Salisbury thought him 'rather an ass' for doing so) on being Leader of the House of Commons. It was no secret that serving in both capacities had proven a nearly impossible strain during the war. Still, at a moment when Churchill professed to be ready to hand over in a matter of months, Eden's overriding concern was to safeguard his claim to the succession by grabbing as much power as he could. He also asked Churchill to make a public gesture that would leave no doubt in people's minds that Eden was next in line. In addition to the titles of Foreign Secretary and Leader of the Commons, Eden wanted to be appointed deputy prime minister.

Churchill, a devout royalist, knew that the title had no constitutional validity and might be viewed as an infringement on the royal prerogative. When Attlee held that appellation in the wartime coalition government, it had referred strictly to his focus on domestic matters, freeing Churchill to concentrate on the war effort. There had been no implication that Attlee would become prime minister should anything happen to Churchill. By contrast, in 1951, Eden construed the title wholly in terms of the succession.

Eden could be a prickly and peevish character, yet in his relations with Churchill he had rarely, if ever, been as personally demanding. (He was notorious, in the words of one observer, for 'bullying people who could be bullied and collapsing before those who couldn't'.) It had long been a source of frustration to Salisbury that Eden, for all his plots and plans, had so often failed to convey exactly what he wanted to Churchill. Time and again, as soon as he actually had to face Churchill, Eden's courage had deserted him. Time and again, Eden had proven willing to go only so far, apparently fearful of putting everything 'into one throw' and it not coming off.

What emboldened Eden now? What accounted for the new firmness, the new insistence on having exactly the jobs and titles he wanted? Churchill was visibly exhausted after an election campaign that had required him to speak nearly every day for five weeks and that had played havoc with his hearing, which was even worse than before. One witness compared his bedraggled appearance in the first few days of the new Government to that of 'a sea captain who had just come out of a very heavy storm and was glad to be in harbour again'. Another observer went so far as to wonder in all seriousness whether Churchill might die during the new Parliament. Confronted with this diminished figure, Eden became assertive and aggressive. Confronted with this new Eden, Churchill gave him everything he asked for.

Wearing a 'quilted flowered' bed-jacket, Churchill spent the better part of Saturday morning at home in bed. A sheet of writing paper with a list of names and offices printed in oversized type lay on the coverlet. A cat sprawled across Churchill's feet in lieu of a hot water bottle as he interviewed some of the men who were to be Cabinet ministers. As if he meant to exert himself as little as possible, he accompanied his remarks with small, sharp hand gestures that began emphatically at the wrist, not the arm.

The key appointment after Eden was considered to be that of the Chancellor of the Exchequer. The financial situation was far worse than Churchill and his party had previously thought; the country was on the verge of insolvency. Attlee, now Opposition leader (though his wife had hoped he would retire), was rumoured to be relieved to have handed over the mess to the Conservatives; the expectation was that they would botch the job and that Britons would soon turn back to Labour. Churchill surprised a good many people by passing over the obvious candidate for Chancellor, Oliver Lyttelton, in favour of Rab Butler. Butler himself was astonished to be offered the post, Lyttelton being his superior both in age and knowledge of finance, as well as a favourite of a number of the Tory leaders. Butler, however, had a well-established profile as a key Conservative policy-maker and as a spokesman for the party's impatient young bloods. Since 1945, he had also received a good deal of popular attention as Eden's main rival to succeed Churchill.

A preliminary list of Churchill's appointments was sent to Buckingham Palace. Immediately, both George VI and his private secretary objected to one of the notations beside Eden's name. The King was free to choose whoever he wished to succeed as prime minister. He could consult anyone he liked about the matter – or no one at all. He and Lascelles perceived the title of deputy prime minister, with all that it seemed to suggest in Eden's case, as an invasion of the royal prerogative. Lascelles went at once to Hyde Park Gate to convey the King's insistence that Eden be denied the appointment.

At lunchtime, high words were exchanged in a telephone conversation between Eden on one end and Lascelles and Secretary to the Cabinet Norman Brook on the other. Brook seconded Lascelles's view that Eden's appointment infringed on the royal prerogative. Eden, speaking from his house in Mayfair (which had once been home to Beau Brummell), angrily countered that he had been promised the title and that he saw no reason why he should not have it. Despite the vehemence of Eden's protests, Lascelles, who had had his troubles with Eden in the past, remained firm.

The deadlock persisted until Churchill intervened. As on the previous evening, the Prime Minister was courtesy itself to his heir apparent. He got on the phone to reassure Eden that he would have his title after all. Churchill kept his word, for that afternoon George VI approved the original list at a Privy Council meeting, and the news of Eden's appointment was duly announced.

Churchill, in the meantime, transferred his base of operations – to his bed at Chartwell. Harold Macmillan, who initially feared that he had been passed over altogether, found himself summoned to Kent on Sunday morning. Lady Dorothy, Macmillan's wife, drove him there. She strolled in the garden with Clementine Churchill (who tended to be cool to Harold, whom she did not trust) while he went in to his meeting.

Not long after he had gone upstairs to see Churchill, Macmillan, whose walk was a slow, stiff shuffle, emerged in a fit of temper. 'If he wants to kill me politically, let him do it, but not this way!'

Macmillan had originally hoped to be appointed Minister of Defence, a position that Churchill had wasted no time claiming for himself. Instead, after all that Macmillan had done to support Churchill when few others had been willing to back him, Churchill – 'in a most pleasant and rather tearful mood' – had repaid the favour by inviting Macmillan to become Minister of Housing. Though Macmillan, by his own account, knew nothing about the housing problem, Churchill asked him to take responsibility for fulfilling the Conservative Party's campaign pledge to build 300,000 houses a year. Few people, including Macmillan himself, believed that target capable of fulfilment. Assured that the job was a gamble and would 'either make or mar' his political career, Macmillan asked to have a bit of time before he gave his answer.

In the garden at Chartwell, Macmillan discussed the offer with his wife. It was well known in the world of Westminster that Lady Dorothy, stout and frumpy with a nest of brittle grey hair, had long been unfaithful to her husband. Her lover, Robert Boothby, was one of the adventurers in Churchill's orbit whom the Eden faction had been desperate to bar from their anti-appeasement meetings in the 1930s. The affair, which neither she nor he took any particular trouble to conceal, was still going on. Through the years, Macmillan had poured out his anguish to his sister-in-law, Moucher Devonshire (now the Dowager Duchess), to whom he confided his belief that the Macmillans' daughter Sarah had actually been fathered by Boothby. Still, for all the hurt Dorothy had caused her husband, she was a fervent supporter of his career. She adored politics, advised him sagely, and laboured tirelessly and effectively on his behalf. She was a far better campaigner than Macmillan, who tended to be stiff and overly intellectual with voters.

For better or worse, Macmillan was also inclined to be extremely cautious. Dorothy, it need hardly be said, was more of a risk-taker. During the war she had immediately perceived what Churchill's offer to send Macmillan to North Africa could do for her spouse's stalled career. Now once again, she grasped that, though certain of his colleagues might be inclined to perceive the position of Minister of Housing as a backwater, it could in fact prove to be a tremendous opportunity. At a time when England suffered from an acute housing shortage, Macmillan's efforts, if successful, could make him highly popular with the electorate. Additionally, the job would afford him the crucial domestic experience that, in contrast to Butler, both he and Eden lacked.

On 30 October, a remarkable scene unfolded in the columned Cabinet Room at Number Ten, which Churchill had once lamented he would never sit in again. Enthroned with his back to the fireplace, he met with his new Cabinet for the first time. Despite his image over the past four days of a man in decline, Churchill had moved swiftly and shrewdly to set the various aspirants against one another. The cosy picture of the teary-eyed old fellow in a bed-jacket camouflaged the characteristic ruthlessness with which he had acted to protect himself against those who hoped to replace him.

Churchill had allowed, even encouraged Eden to poison his relations with Buckingham Palace by insisting on a title that gave offence to the King. He had further checked the heir apparent by placing the latter's most feared rival in a position of power that most observers had expected to go to another man. And he had checked Butler by placing the driven, determined Macmillan in a job that would require him to fight to the knife for a disproportionate share of government funding when it was Butler's mission to re-establish financial stability.

Churchill had named Salisbury, who had been hoping to oust him since day one of the postwar Parliament in 1945, to the position of Lord Privy Seal, but by the gambit of these other appointments he had left his old antagonist little room to manoeuvre. (The Conservative victory also meant that Salisbury again became Leader of the House of Lords.)

At the beginning of Churchill's wartime premiership, there had been many comments about his renewed vitality and sharply improved physical appearance. Now, once more, power seemed to re-energize him. In sharp contrast to his air of exhaustion in recent days, he was 'in great form' today, merrily quoting Machiavelli, urging his colleagues to leave things to him, and declaring his intention to travel to the US and Canada as soon as Parliament was 'up'.

The Americans had been anticipating Churchill's arrival for some time. Long before the Conservative Party returned to power, the Truman administration had determined that in the event of a Tory victory Churchill was 'almost certain' to try to arrange the meeting with the Soviets he had spoken of so often. There had been much internal debate on the American side about how the US ought to respond. The various reasons for and against a parley at the summit had been weighed extensively, and by the time Churchill was back at Number Ten, Washington had taken a firm decision. Churchill had regained office just as the Americans were about to enter a presidential election year. Whether or not Truman decided to seek another term, it would be politically impossible to agree to talks that could subject the President and his party to a serious attack by the McCarthyites. But there was also international opinion to consider. The administration foresaw that should Churchill suddenly make a speech suggesting that he and Truman go to see Stalin, it would be difficult in view of Churchill's personal prestige for Truman to decline. Washington therefore was keen to make Churchill aware of its opposition without delay. It fell to the US Ambassador in London, Walter Gifford, to warn Churchill against any 'hasty public' move towards a top-level meeting before the new Prime Minister had had an opportunity to review the pros and, more importantly, the cons with his American allies.

Under the circumstances, the best Churchill could hope for was that the American stance might alter after the presidential election in November 1952. He was going to have to wait a year or more before there was even a chance of returning to the table with Stalin, hardly an appealing prospect to a man about to turn seventy-seven. Meanwhile, in the hope of convincing Truman of the desirability of talks with Stalin at some later date, and of re-establishing the kind of intimate bond he had enjoyed with Roosevelt during the war, Churchill was eager to get to the US prior to the onset of election fever.

Before he invited himself to Washington, he was careful to do some-thing else first. Churchill dashed off a telegram to Stalin. By reaching out to Stalin before he contacted Truman, Churchill ensured that should the Americans object it would already be too late.

'Now that I am again in charge of His Majesty's Government,' Churchill wrote to his Soviet counterpart on 5 November 1951, 'let me reply to your farewell telegram from Potsdam of August 1945. "Greetings. Winston Churchill."' But would it really be possible, as Churchill seemed to believe, to ignore the years in between and pick up where they had left off? At Potsdam, Churchill had acted on the premise that Stalin, though far from the man Roosevelt had imagined him to be, was capable of discerning what was in his own interest and that he would negotiate based on that understanding. Was Stalin any longer able to make such judgements in 1951? He was sicker and if possible more paranoid and frenzied than when he and Churchill last met. He suffered from hypertension, arteriosclerosis, and a host of other afflictions. He had had several minor strokes, his memory often faltered, and he was liable to lose his balance or pass out at any time. When he took a solitary walk in the country, the paths were specially equipped with telephones in green metal containers so he could call for assistance if he fell ill. Stalin lamented that 'cursed old age' had caught up with him and he claimed to accept that he was 'finished'. Yet he gave no sign of being ready to hand over. Stalin seemed as fearful of the loss of power as of death itself.

Unlike Churchill, who clutched his heir apparent with hoops of steel lest a more potent rival for the Conservative leadership materialize, Stalin was constantly anointing some new chosen one. Unlike Eden, who seemed always to be jockeying to retain the number two spot, Stalin's minions preferred to avoid it. In their case, Stalin's 'persecution mania' being what it was, the designation of heir apparent was as likely to lead to a death sentence as to the succession. Molotov, who had been Eden's opposite number in 1945, had managed to survive, but he had been ousted as Foreign Minister and he had acquiesced when his adored wife was imprisoned on phony charges of treason. Molotov later speculated that he would probably have been killed had Stalin lived a little longer.

Before a week had passed, Churchill reported to his Cabinet that he had heard back from both Truman and Stalin. Truman invited him to confer in Washington beginning on 3 January 1952. The old

Bolshevik's reply was less encouraging. 'Thank you for greetings' was all that it said. Churchill laughed that at least he and Stalin, who had had some pretty harsh things to say about him since Fulton, were again on speaking terms.

In the opening weeks of the premiership, Eden too was looking ahead a year to eighteen months, but he was still acting on the assumption (of which Churchill made no effort to disabuse him) that the handover would have taken place by then. Churchill had reneged on previous pledges to retire, but this time a good many people besides Eden wanted to believe that, having wiped out the disgrace of his 1945 defeat, Churchill sincerely intended to let go.

Eden cut a glamorous and popular figure as head of the British delegation at the tumultuous Sixth Session of the General Assembly of the United Nations in Paris that November. When he first entered the Assembly, foreign ministers and diplomats from many nations rushed up from all sides to pat him on the shoulder and welcome him back to the fray. He quickly earned lavish praise in the international press for his efforts to improve the tone of the proceedings after bitter charges flew between his Soviet and American counterparts, Andrei Vyshinsky and Dean Acheson. When Britain's suave new Foreign Secretary calmly but firmly recommended a truce to all the shouting, he seemed the very soul of moderation and good sense.

That, at least, was his public persona. In private, Eden was anything but calm. On the eve of the speech that was to mark his return to the international stage, he collapsed in his bedroom with stomach spasms. Initially, he feared the episode might be a recurrence of the duodenal ulcer that had sidelined him during the war and had required Churchill to take over for him.

Eden's aides summoned a doctor in the middle of the night. While the physician treated him with injections, Churchill and Acheson were notified of his ordeal, the latter in strict confidence. From then on, Churchill was far from the only one in the new Government whose health was not as good as the public was led to believe.

In the end, on 12 November, Eden managed to give his speech. It was warmly received, and most observers had no inkling that he had nearly had to cancel his appearance. Still, for those few who knew about it, the previous night's episode underscored just how unwell the fifty-four-year-old Eden really was as he launched into the punishing sixteen- and seventeen-hour days his new job entailed. When Eden had demanded the leadership in the House of Commons on top of the post of Foreign Secretary, Salisbury had worried that in addition to not being able to devote enough time to both jobs Eden was likely to kill himself in the bargain. Early on, in a concession to his health Eden had agreed to transfer the leadership in the Commons to Harry Crookshank. Whether that would be enough to save him was an open question.

More and more, any amount of stress or anxiety seemed capable of triggering another bout of paralysing pain. Eden now travelled with a black tin box that contained a smorgasbord of painkillers provided by his doctor. When he required a dose of morphine, a detective in his employ was summoned to give him a shot. By the time he landed in Rome in the last week of November for the Eighth Session of the North Atlantic Treaty Organization Council, he was in such agony that at night his loud groans could be heard through the wall in the adjoining bedroom where his private secretary, Evelyn Shuckburgh, was trying to sleep.

In Rome, there was much to make Eden nervous, not least his break-fast with Eisenhower on 27 November, four days after Churchill had begun to fulfil his 1948 promise to rebut Eisenhower's *Crusade in Europe* by publishing the relevant volumes of his own war memoirs. In volume five, *Closing the Ring*, which had been serialized in twenty-four pre-publication instalments (advance copies of which Eisenhower had seen), Churchill accused Eisenhower of inaccuracy when he portrayed him as having lacked confidence in the cross-Channel invasion. The debate was about much more than whether or not Churchill had believed that Overlord could succeed. His scepticism then was the linchpin of

Eisenhower's argument that it had been Churchill's fault that the lines of occupation in Germany had been set too far to the west. But the battle for history's verdict on who had been principally responsible for some of the worst problems of postwar Europe was far from finished. Volume six of Churchill's memoirs promised to chronicle his differences with Eisenhower and Truman over Berlin and the pre-Potsdam troop withdrawal respectively, and to make the case that he had seen the Soviet danger in time but that they had refused to listen.

Eisenhower's reaction to *Closing the Ring* was fury. In his current role as NATO's military chief, he was responsible for organizing the defence of Western Europe against the Soviets. The task promised to be a stepping-stone to the US presidency should he be called on, as was widely expected, to be the Republican candidate in 1952. Yet here was Churchill not only accusing him of misrepresentation in his book, but also threatening to embarrass and undermine him in other ways.

By the time Churchill returned to office, how best to defend Western Europe had become a deeply contentious issue. Eisenhower and the Americans were backing a plan that had originated the year before with the French and aimed to deal with fears about a rearmed Germany. The plan, which had come to be known as the European Defence Community (EDC), called for a European army, which would include West Germany, France, Italy, and the Benelux countries. The Germans would not have an independent national army, but rather would be part of an integrated European force. Churchill opposed this plan. It was not that he was against the idea of rearming Germany (he advocated it), nor that he opposed a European army per se (he had called for one in his Strasbourg talk in 1950). He was against the kind of integrated force Eisenhower favoured; Churchill preferred a coalition force. In other words, once again the two men were at odds strategically.

Eisenhower was big and broad-shouldered, with a lopsided grin and warm blue eyes. When he was riled, which seemed to be more often than most men, his face flushed and his eyes went icy. He gnawed the earpiece of his spectacles; he bit his lips with nervous rage. Over breakfast with Eden, he complained about Churchill's threat to air his objections to the current European army proposal in the House of Commons. As Churchill had been an originator of the idea of European unity and indeed of a European army, his active opposition promised to be a major embarrassment, possibly even a deal-breaker.

When Eisenhower made it clear to Eden that he wanted him to get his boss in line, the Foreign Secretary leaped at the opportunity. After all, in eighteen months, by which time Eden expected Churchill to have left the stage, Eisenhower might well be Prime Minister Eden's American counterpart. Eden suggested that, unlike his boss, he very much liked the current European army plan and that he would do what he could to sway Churchill. He presented himself as the member of the British team on whom the Americans could count not only to listen to reason, but also to intervene on their behalf. As in the 1930s, Eden posed as the sane, sensible alternative to the wayward and erratic Churchill. As in the 1940s, he saw himself and encouraged others to see him as Churchill's restraining hand.

When Eden returned to London, Eisenhower wrote to remind him of the need to get Churchill into a more cooperative mood. Eden's mission proved to be a good deal less difficult than either he or Eisenhower had expected. The Prime Minister quickly agreed not to attack the EDC proposal in his defence speech in the House of Commons on 6 December. Though he liked the European army plan no better than before, he promised that, as long as Britain was not asked to contribute troops, he would make a public statement of his support when he went to Paris later in the month.

It was certainly not like Churchill to yield without a battle royal. The iron refusal to give in that had served him (not to mention the cause of freedom) so well in 1940 had proven utterly exasperating to his American allies when he directed it against them. In his wartime encounters with Eisenhower, Churchill had harangued, pleaded, wept, threatened to resign, and done anything else he thought might help carry his point. On the present occasion, if there was none of the usual Churchillian intransigence, it was not due to any mellowing on his part. Churchill regarded the public statement as a minuscule concession in the interest of keeping the Americans happy prior to his visit, and he was determined to do whatever it took to make sure his trip was a success. Principal among these measures was reassuring both the Germans and the French that they had nothing to fear from his talks with Truman. Before Churchill went to Paris, he conferred with the Chancellor of the German Federal Republic, Konrad Adenauer, who was in London at the beginning of December. Churchill hoped to allay German concerns that he and the Americans might be ready to negotiate a deal at Germany's expense.

Before he left for Paris, Churchill made a dramatic surprise move to heal the political wounds in Britain that threatened to weaken his position abroad. The slender Tory majority of seventeen reflected a nation sharply divided after a bruising election campaign. When Churchill gave his speech on defence on 6 December it was widely expected that he would begin by cataloguing the weaknesses he had discovered upon taking office. Instead, he made a point not only of complimenting Labour, but also of tearfully praising the very politician, Emanuel Shinwell, who had most savagely and personally criticized him during the general election campaign and whom he had singled out for criticism in his Plymouth speech. As a rule, Churchill believed it was wise to be magnanimous in victory. In the present instance, reaching out to the socialist Opposition at the penultimate meeting of Parliament before the winter recess had the distinct advantage that, as a consequence, he would be able to address the Americans as a national leader.

On 16 December, Churchill took the night boat train to Paris, where he hoped to ease fears that French interests would not be taken into account in his Washington talks and that France would be excluded when he and the Americans met Stalin at the summit.

The French also needed to be reassured that Britain did not oppose the present European army plan.

A cold mist enveloped the Gare du Nord the next morning when Churchill, Eden, and their staffs were met by a large official greeting party. Churchill took his time reviewing the guard of honour of the Garde Républicaine, laboriously inspecting each man's decorations. From the outset, as Eden's private secretary perceived, this was not an easy trip for the heir apparent. The previous month in Paris, Eden had had the stage entirely to himself. Now that he was here with Churchill, he inevitably reverted to playing 'second string'.

Eden need not have been jealous of all the attention Churchill received on his first trip abroad as peacetime prime minister. Some of it reflected people's fascination with the seventy-seven-year-old leader's physical and mental condition and with how it affected the power dynamic in London. From this point on, everywhere Churchill went, people would be watching, judging, evaluating. There could be no avoiding the questions. How did he look? How did he sound? Was he as sharp as he had been previously? Was he forgetful? Did he make mistakes? Had the mastermind begun to lose his mind? Did he seem overly emotional? Did he fail at times to understand what others said, or was it just that he had been unable to hear? How often did he have to leave the room to urinate?

The French ministers who faced Churchill that day whispered among themselves that he had aged 'very considerably' during the first eight weeks of his premiership, and predicted that he could not last in office for long. Still, when Churchill duelled with one of his hosts over the latter's assertion that he had been inconsistent in his views on European federation, the others took note that Churchill was still capable of defending himself 'vigorously'. Would it have been any consolation to Eden to know that the French ministers' scrutinizing eyes had been on the number two man as well? Afterwards, at least one minister expressed doubt that, when the time came, Eden would be Churchill's successor.

Having stayed up into the small hours drinking whisky at the British Embassy as he burnished the draft communiqué on his Paris visit, Churchill spent much of the next morning, as was his custom, at work in bed. Eden's follow-up meeting with the French had to be cut off early, as he and Churchill were expected at Supreme Headquarters, where Churchill was to lunch with Eisenhower. Churchill was not happy to have to take time out of his tightly-scheduled two-day visit to drive to Versailles. When Eisenhower had written to propose a meeting which would enable Churchill to see Supreme Headquarters and meet key NATO staff, the Prime Minister had asked him to lunch at the British Embassy instead, as that would be more convenient. Eisenhower fired back a 'deliberately grumpy' message to the effect that while he would always go and see his old friend he was disappointed that Churchill did not have the time to visit Supreme Headquarters. A mini-test of wills between them ended with Churchill agreeing to come to Eisenhower on 18 December.

Bundled into a heavy woollen overcoat and a felt fedora, Churchill pulled up at Supreme Headquarters twenty minutes late on account of a blinding fog. It was to be his first meeting with Eisenhower since the publication of *Closing the Ring* and Eisenhower was spoiling for a fight. The previous week, after receiving word that Churchill had agreed to come to him, Eisenhower had told seven dinner guests, including the US Ambassador in France, David Bruce, and the journalist C. L. Sulzberger, that he planned to 'to give Churchill hell' about his position on the European army. To judge by his remarks to his guests, that was by no means all that was distressing him. Again, his outrage centred on the question of who ought to have listened to whom in 1945. Sulzberger recorded in his diary afterwards: 'Eisenhower blames Churchill entirely for the political division of Germany which gave Russia such a large share. He said Churchill never had any faith in "Overlord" – the invasion of Normandy . . . As a result of Churchill's sceptical attitude, unsound political decisions were taken . . . The line was chosen largely because of Churchill's pessimism.'

Eisenhower had vowed 'to put the bite on Churchill' when he came to Supreme Headquarters. Hardly was Churchill in the door when the fighting began, but it was the Prime Minister who struck first. Reminding Eisenhower that he had advocated a European army as early as 1950, he went on to explain that it was merely the present inefficient and ineffective plan that he objected to. 'I want a fagot of staves bound by a ring of steel,' Churchill lectured Eisenhower, 'and not a soft putty affair such as is now contemplated.' Eisenhower, in turn, 'pounded' Churchill, making it clear that he did not think that the Prime Minister disagreed with the proposal so much as that he just did not understand it. In his diary, Eisenhower judged that Churchill was no longer capable of absorbing new ideas. And there was another problem: 'I am back in Europe in a status that is not too greatly different, in his mind, from that which I held with respect to him in World War II,' Eisenhower wrote. 'To my mind, he simply will not think in terms of today, but rather only those of the war years.' At a moment when Eisenhower had his eye on the presidency, being asked to revert to his former relationship with Churchill – who as far as he was concerned ought to have retired anyway – was not a pleasing situation.

Churchill returned to London in anticipation of sailing to America in a little over a week. As his departure drew near, he learned that an announcement of American economic aid to Britain would be made around the time his ship docked in New York. In his recent dealings with the Germans, the French, and the Americans, Churchill had shown that, in certain circumstances at least, he was willing to stoop to conquer. But the idea of arriving in the US in the guise of a 'penniless beggar' made him flush with anger. The humiliation, both to his country and to himself, would be too much for this exceedingly proud man to bear.

Churchill believed that during the war he had gone to Washington as an equal, and he desperately wanted that to be the case again. Britain's economic weakness was only part of the problem. He deplored the liquidation of its empire begun under Attlee. He bemoaned the loss of influence and the will to rule. His January 1952 trip was very much about recapturing lost dignity by restoring Britain to a prime role in world affairs. In Churchill's view, Britain, 'broken and impoverished' though it might be, still had something precious to offer. He hoped to align what he saw as British wisdom and experience with American military might in a concerted effort to win the peace in Europe.

On 29 December, hours before he was due to leave on the first leg of his trip, Churchill contacted the American Ambassador to say that he desired to speak to him immediately. When Gifford arrived, Churchill interrupted a rare Saturday Cabinet meeting to see him. Weeks after the Ambassador had warned against any public call for talks with the Soviets, Churchill had a warning for him. He made it clear that he did not want Britain's financial plight to be thrown in his face as he came off the ship in New York. He demanded that Washington alter the timing of its announcement. Nothing had been settled when the Ambassador left, and Churchill returned to the Cabinet Room in foul spirits. By the time he wound up a second late afternoon meeting in anticipation of temporarily entrusting Cabinet affairs to the leadership of Harry Crookshank, he had heard from the American Embassy. The offending statement would be postponed until after he came back from the US.

At the end of a long, emotionally draining day, Churchill was driven to Waterloo Station, where reporters peppered him with questions as he boarded a special coach bound for Southampton. It was nearly one in the morning when he, Eden (who had left the Foreign Office in Salisbury's care), and the rest of their party of thirty-six boarded the *Queen Mary*. The vessel had docked three days late after the roughest crossing of her captain's nearly forty-year career, but the skipper expected they would probably be able to sail by noon. If all went well, Churchill would arrive in New York on Friday in time for his first scheduled meeting with Truman that afternoon in Washington.

On Sunday morning, Churchill was in bed when the Captain came in with a sheepish look on his face. Clearly expecting Churchill to blow up when he heard the news, he informed him that the sixteen-ton port anchor had jammed. The ship could not sail until the anchor was freed. It would likely be another twenty-four hours before they finally headed out to sea. A telegram went off to Truman and the frantic juggling of arrangements began. For the rest of the day, as Cunard Line employees used acetylene torches to blast the anchor loose, Churchill did not budge from his rooms, which had been specially equipped with numerous extra-large ashtrays and a generous stock of brandy.

That evening, Lord Mountbatten, the Fourth Sea Lord, came to dine. In the course of the meal, the Prime Minister and his outspoken guest clashed over the wisdom of linking Britain's fortunes with that of the Americans. Churchill was not in the mood to hear Mountbatten's anti-American views as he waited to embark on a trip designed to strengthen the Anglo-American bond. In annoyance, he cautioned Mountbatten to avoid expressing any political opinions in future. 'Your one value as a sailor is that you are completely non-political. Take care you remain so!'

The *Queen Mary* finally sailed at noon on 31 December. At ten minutes before midnight, the Prime Minister's entourage joined him for a toast. While his guests listened to Big Ben strike a dozen times on the radio and to the BBC announcer wish listeners a happy new year, the seated Churchill looked as if he were absorbed in thoughts of his own. At last, champagne glass in hand, he hoisted himself up out of his chair. As Churchill swayed with the ship, he gave the impression of being about to give a speech. Instead, he said only, 'God save the King,' whereupon everyone drank his health.

Before long, the crowd had dwindled to a few intimates. Churchill again seemed preoccupied, and no one spoke until finally he broke the silence. He talked of his trepidation about addressing a joint session of Congress. He worried that the speech, which he had very much wanted to give but had yet to write, might not come off. Later, he returned to the subject when his doctor remained behind to take his pulse, which proved to be rapid and irregular. As Churchill began to undress for bed, he lamented that his mind was no longer as good as it used to be and that these days the prospect of delivering an address – any address – made him uneasy.

Anxiety about his speech to Congress would burden Churchill during much of the trip. In early life, Churchill had slaved to make himself master of the spoken word. Now that he was in his late seventies, however, words no longer came as freely and fluently as they had in the past. Simply to marshal them was an enormous effort. The Washington speech was especially worrisome because of scheduling problems that had required it to be put off until 17 January, extending his time on the road to more than three weeks. As it was, Churchill faced several days of difficult talks in Washington before going on to New York and Ottawa; only then would he return for his nationally broadcast congressional appearance and a crucial last session with the President.

On Saturday, 5 January 1952, the *Queen Mary* arrived in New York in a soaking rain. Churchill flew directly to Washington, where Truman hosted a dinner party in his honour on the presidential yacht. In recent weeks, as Truman prepared to see Churchill, the White House had received various reports on his condition, including one from Ambassador Gifford that stated that he was 'definitely aging and . . . no longer able to retain his full clarity and energy for extended periods'. In spite of anything those accounts might have led Truman to expect, and in spite of his being in much physical discomfort due to a boil on his leg and a chill contracted at sea, Churchill was pitch-perfect that evening.

When the table had been cleared after dinner, Churchill, Eden, and their group and Truman, Acheson, and theirs returned to the dining saloon for conversation. The President opened the discussion by inviting Churchill to give his American hosts 'the benefit of his reflections on the state of the world', with particular reference to the attitude of the Soviet Union.

The theme of Churchill's remarks was fear as the 'central factor' in Soviet policy. He suggested that at present the Soviets feared the West's friendship more than they did its enmity. Still, he hoped that an increase in Western strength would encourage Moscow to seek the free world's friendship instead. Churchill lauded Truman's decision to go into Korea, which had led to rearmament in the US and other 'freedom-loving countries'. By lessening the chances of a Soviet attack, Churchill maintained, rearmament increased the chances of peace. And that was wholly thanks to Truman. In Churchill's telling, the President's actions had been the 'turning point' in East–West relations.

Churchill sensed that the President liked to be flattered and deferred to. In his comments, the guest of honour had taken care to do both. He knew that Truman valued brevity, so he limited his talk to five or six minutes. It was no secret that Truman approached Churchill's visit warily. Where Churchill had pushed for informal talks ('so that we can work together easily and intimately'), Truman had demanded an agenda. Truman also had insisted on having his advisers present whenever he met with Churchill. For all the accounts of the aged Prime Minister's decay, Truman still seemed worried about being out-talked and outflanked.

Truman was not alone in his concern about what Churchill might yet be capable of. The British Ambassador to the US, Sir Oliver Franks, had recently reported to London on the 'nervousness' among US officials, particularly at the Pentagon, and in parts of the American press that Churchill would dominate the Washington talks 'by sheer weight of personality'. In his after-dinner remarks, therefore, Churchill did no more than set up the argument he had travelled to America to make. The actual pitch for a meeting with Stalin would come later.

Churchill viewed his first night back in Washington as an unqualified success. At the end of the Potomac cruise, he assured the President that he had never felt relations between their countries to be closer. When Churchill returned to the British Embassy after midnight, he rejoiced that he and Truman had been able to talk as equals.

In the formal meetings that followed, Churchill was a good deal less happy with his reception. At times, Truman simply cut Churchill off when he spoke emotionally of the Anglo-American bond. 'Thank you, Mr Prime Minister,' Truman would say in a loud, cheerful, patronizing voice that suggested he wanted to keep things moving. 'We might pass that on to be worked out by our advisers.'

Beforehand, the Americans had determined that any effort to recreate the intimacy of Churchill's old relationship with Roosevelt ought to be discouraged: Churchill must be made to understand that, in 1952, he would be operating under 'different circumstances' from those he had experienced in Washington during the war. That attitude did not sit well with Churchill, who bristled at their image of Britain as a junior partner. One of the principal subjects under discussion in the plenary sessions, whether or not to appoint an American admiral as Supreme Allied Commander of the Atlantic, soon became a focal point for Churchill's resentment. Attlee had been prime minister when an agreement was struck to give the sea command to an American. At the time, Churchill had regarded the arrangement as an insult to Britain and he had been on his feet in the Commons to demand that a British admiral have the job. As the Americans were in command on land, he believed it only fair for the British to lay claim to the seas. Churchill's passion on this subject had not subsided since he became prime minister. If anything, he seemed even more fervent. While he was in Washington, he made it the testing point between the Americans and himself.

Key members of his delegation thought this unwise. At the British Embassy on 7 January, they urged him not to concentrate on such a purely symbolic issue. To Churchill's horror, Secretary of State for Commonwealth Relations Lord Ismay, First Sea Lord Admiral Sir Rhoderick McGrigor, Chief of the Imperial Staff Field Marshal Sir William Slim, and Ambassador Franks all seemed to regard the appointment as not worth fighting for. The time for the British Government to press the case had been when matters were still in Attlee's hands; perhaps then the Americans might have been swayed. As far as Churchill's advisers were concerned, at this late date the only thing to do was acquiesce.

Churchill adamantly disagreed. In spite of what anyone said, he was determined to press Truman to release him from the obligation of the previous Government. After Churchill left the room, grumblings were heard that he had lost the ability to see things in perspective. (Churchill's detractors had long claimed that he never had that ability in the first place.)

That day and the next, in the presence of the very advisers who had counselled him to back off, Churchill locked antlers with the Americans. He argued that Britain had earned equality 'with British blood' and he insisted that equality was all he was asking for. It was evident to the Americans that he viewed the whole subject of the Atlantic command with a great deal of emotion – rather too much, as far as they were concerned. The Americans perceived something else as well: Churchill's own military staff did not agree with his position.

Churchill's diehard refusal to fall into step on the naval issue created an awkward situation for the British and American teams alike. On one side, his countrymen – most of them, anyway – had no wish to undermine and embarrass him in front of Truman; they just thought he was wrong. On the other side, the Americans acknowledged that Churchill's personal stature required them to secure the new Government's pro forma approval even though they had already made a deal with Attlee.

The first round of meetings ended on 8 January. At the British Embassy that evening, Churchill was so weary that he lay in bed rather than come down to dinner. To be sure, he had managed to hold his ground in the debate about the Atlantic command. He calculated that the Americans would not dare go forward without him. Yet even as Churchill fought to uphold British dignity, he had been at risk of jeopardizing his own.

There had been moments during the talks when Churchill's eyes clouded over alarmingly, moments when he seemed uncertain and confused, and moments when his own team judged that 'poor old Winston' was not the most effective advocate for his country's interests. At the fourth plenary session, Churchill had even appeared briefly to forget where he was and to be under the peculiar impression that he was speaking to the British Cabinet. Afterwards, Eden's private secretary noted in his diary that the Americans had 'bravely and loyally' extricated the British delegation from this predicament.

Tonight, when Moran came in to see him, Churchill complained that he had been kicked about so much since he left London that he could hardly any longer tell night from day. At his age, Churchill explained, the problem was not attending meetings as much as thinking out what he wanted to say.

While Churchill conferred with his doctor, Eden was downstairs airing some complaints of his own. Due to return to Europe directly from Canada, the number two man was distressed about the wording of the press communiqué to be issued before they left Washington. Like his boss, Eden harped on the theme of equality, but with a somewhat different emphasis. He noted that every paragraph began, 'The Prime Minister . . .' or 'The Foreign Secretary was instructed . . .' 'No one instructs me,' Eden railed. 'The Prime Minister and I are colleagues.'

Churchill spent 9–16 January in New York and Canada. Back in Washington on the 17th, he was still at work on his speech when Deputy Under Secretary of State Sir Roger Makins came in to announce that a car was ready to take him to the Capitol, where he was to go on in about forty minutes. Churchill, who had yet to rouse himself from bed, was absorbed in puzzling over a passage about British participation in the Korean War.

'If the Chinese cross the Yalu River, our reply will be – what?' he asked.

'Prompt, resolute, and effective,' Makins shot back.

'Excellent,' said Churchill. He inserted that phrase in the body of his speech. Then he dressed hurriedly and, assisted by a motorcycle escort, managed to get to the House of Representatives two minutes early.

In the course of a thirty-seven-minute address that was carried by all the radio and television networks, Churchill evoked a changed world in which former allies had become foes, former foes had become allies, conquered countries had been liberated, and liberated countries had been enslaved by Communism. Speaking in a firm, strong voice and rarely hesitating over his phrases, Churchill revisited the theme he had developed privately that first night on the presidential yacht. He argued that the consequences of Truman's actions in Korea extended far beyond that region. The 'vast process of American rearmament' had already altered the international balance of power and might well, 'if we all persevere steadfastly and loyally together, avert the danger of a third world war'.

A satisfied smile erupted on Churchill's face as he walked slowly but energetically through the standing, cheering crowd. When he reached his car, he sank back into the seat, visibly relieved.

He could not relax for long. The following afternoon, Friday, 18 January, he and Truman were scheduled to discuss Soviet relations. Now that he had further set up his argument in Congress, Churchill was finally about to make his case for a return to the table with Stalin. It would be but a short distance from crediting Truman with having shifted the balance of power to urging him to capitalize on that achievement by securing the postwar settlement.

On Friday morning, Churchill, Admiral McGrigor, and other military staff visited the Pentagon, where, at Churchill's request, Defense Secretary Robert Lovett briefed them on American war plans. Afterwards, Churchill went back to the embassy for a nap. The rest of the British contingent remained at the Pentagon, where, in conjunction with American officials, they drafted a joint communiqué that ratified previous decisions about the Atlantic command, including the agreement to name an American to the top post.

Shortly before three that afternoon, Churchill was shown into the President's anteroom at the White House. He was joined there by Admiral McGrigor and the other military men, who surprised him with a copy of the joint communiqué. Minutes before his climactic session with Truman, Churchill was confronted with the fact that the very advisers whom he had previously defied had now chosen to stand up to him. In full view of the Americans, his military staff had dared to take a position contrary to the one he espoused.

Because of his staff's participation, the document was no longer just about Britain's decline – it was about Churchill's. The weakness of his leadership was on display for all to see. When he finished reading, his mute comment was to rip up the text and throw the bits into the air like confetti.

'Hurricane warnings along the Potomac,' said Admiral McGrigor as the noticeably 'shaken' British delegation entered the Cabinet Room, where the Americans, with the exception of Truman, had already assembled. In the moments before Truman appeared, Churchill lingered in the anteroom to improvise a draft of his own.

When both leaders had taken their seats, the President opened the proceedings. He began by saying that it was regrettable that all good things must come to an end and that that included Churchill's visit. He insisted he would be sorry to see the Prime Minister leave, and went on to suggest that Churchill use the present occasion to speak about whatever else was on his mind. For many weeks, the White

House had been bracing for Churchill to make his case for a meeting with Stalin. Now, the President had given Churchill his cue. Truman had offered him the perfect opportunity to lay out his thoughts on East–West relations (the day's official topic, after all). That Truman was well armed with previously prepared arguments against a summit meeting, and that he was ready and eager to shoot down Churchill's proposals, would have come as no surprise to the Prime Minister. Churchill had not, however, expected to be ambushed by the members of his own team.

Hot with indignation, he began by addressing the lack of agreement on the naval issue. If Britain and the US could not come to terms, he warned, he would have to take up the matter with NATO, and the rift between the two nations would be made public. That was something neither side wanted. He delivered a 'majestic' address on Britain's proud history as a ruler of the seas. He asked the Americans, in the plenitude of their power, to allow his country to continue to play its traditional role 'upon that western sea whose floor is white with the bones of Englishmen'. Dean Acheson later went so far as to call the performance 'one of Mr Churchill's greatest speeches'. It was good enough, at any rate, to impel Sir Oliver Franks to pass a note to warn his friend Acheson to be 'very, very careful' – that is, not to allow himself to be dazzled.

Churchill made it clear that he could not accept the joint communiqué that had been prepared in his absence. In its place he had written out 'a little statement' of his own, which he proceeded to read aloud. It was a measure of Churchill's excruciating isolation in the room that it fell to Franks, who opposed him on this, to hand the Prime Minister's draft to Truman. After some discussion, Truman asked Acheson and Secretary of Defense Lovett to study the new document. Churchill's powerful presentation had sent the meeting completely off the rails. Suddenly, everyone was waiting to hear from Acheson and Lovett.

In this unsettled atmosphere, Churchill finally got around to raising the possibility of a conference with the Soviet Union. That topic was supposed to have been the centrepiece not just of the fifth plenary session but also of his entire trip. Now, it came across almost as an afterthought, a side issue. On various occasions in the past, Churchill had spoken beautifully and affectingly of his desire to return to the summit. Today, however, he had used himself up on the naval question. He had squandered his dwindling energies and capacities on a lost cause.

Truman easily brushed aside Churchill's halting comments. The fact that Moscow had recently referred to a top US general in Korea as a cannibal suggested to Truman that the Soviets were not in a conciliatory mood and that a top-level meeting would not be helpful.

Churchill had been looking forward to this conversation for months, yet instead of responding to Truman's argument he abruptly changed the subject and asked how Acheson and Lovett were doing. At length, Acheson proposed that he might be able to suggest a compromise. He, Lovett, McGrigor, Franks, Air Marshal Sir William Elliot, and some of the others went off together to the President's office to draft a new document.

While Churchill waited in the Cabinet Room for a good thirty minutes, it was as if all the juice had seeped out of him. Now that the tired titan no longer posed a threat, Truman magnanimously gave him several openings to at least complete his summit pitch, but Churchill passed up every one. Eventually, Churchill sent his private secretary, Jock Colville, to see how much longer Acheson and the others planned to take. This prompted Truman to protest that he was enjoying their talk and was in no hurry. Churchill, however, was eager for the painful and increasingly pointless encounter to end. He had failed to make his case about the Soviets. When the drafting group returned and Acheson read the revised communiqué aloud, it was evident that Churchill had been unsuccessful in this area as well.

The new document still provided for the appointment of an American admiral as supreme commander.

Churchill's antagonists on both sides of the table waited an 'interminable minute' for his response.

Unwilling to prolong this he said finally, 'I accept.'

XIII

Naked Among Mine Enemies

New York, January 1952

On the morning of Saturday, 19 January 1952, Churchill spent much of the train trip to New York gazing out the window. Ordinarily, he preferred to work, play cards, or devour a stack of newspapers, but today he was not in the mood. He made passing comments to his doctor and others in his travelling party of fourteen. Yet he seemed too weary and distracted to focus on any one topic for long. At length, he disappeared to his compartment where he slept deeply for an hour. Even that did not seem to help, and as the train drew into the station Churchill complained that he was still very tired. Before he sailed he intended to spend forty-eight hours at the home of his friend Bernard Baruch, where he hoped to recover. The eighty-one-year-old American financier – who liked to say that as far as he was concerned 'old age' was always fifteen years older than he was – arranged to have Churchill collected from Pennsylvania Station so that he could avoid a barrage of reporters' questions.

Far from reviving in New York, Churchill fell ill as the muggy weather turned icy overnight. 'Such is life nowadays,' he reflected, when a head cold required him to disappoint a great many people by failing to appear in a ticker-tape parade and a ceremony in his honour at City Hall. Not feeling well enough to rise from his bed, a blue-pyjama-clad Churchill received the Archbishop of New York and the Mayor at the Baruch residence. He leaned forward slightly from a stack of pillows as Mayor Impellitteri placed the city's Medal of Honor round his neck. Late that same day, Tuesday the 22nd, Churchill emerged onto Fifth Avenue and Sixty-sixth Street wearing a grey storm coat with a fur collar, en route to the *Queen Mary*, which was due to sail at midnight.

During much of the voyage, Churchill lay in his suite on the main deck, where late one morning he dreamed that he was so sick that he could neither see nor walk straight. Awakening with a jolt, he hurried out of bed to test his ability to walk, which proved to be unimpaired.

Two days later, on Monday, 28 January, Clementine Churchill was waiting at Southampton when the *Queen Mary* docked. He looked forward to dining alone with her. But when the couple reached Waterloo Station they were met by Eden, Butler, Crookshank, and others whose business could not be delayed. The ministers accompanied Churchill home to lay out the crisis that faced him the next day when Parliament met again after a recess of more than seven weeks.

The congressional address that had caused Churchill such anxiety beforehand had set off a political earthquake at home. Of all things, it was the four words that Sir Roger Makins had casually suggested be added to the text that had produced the most severe tremors. When Makins proposed the phrase 'prompt, resolute and effective', he had merely been trying to rush Churchill out of bed and get him to Congress on time. Churchill had liked the sound of the phrase, to which he had attached no further significance than that Britain and the US would respond firmly to any breach of a truce in Korea. The Labour Opposition, however, had since read a great deal more into it. They interpreted it to mean that Churchill had secretly agreed to an American plan to extend the Korean War to Communist China, to bomb Chinese cities, and even possibly to employ an atomic bomb. They used it to revive the charges of warmongering that had stung Churchill in the general election. In recent days, concern about Churchill's choice of words had taken root in a broad section of the press, and he was coming home to demands from various quarters, not just the left, that he immediately clarify what he had agreed to in his talks with Truman.

Churchill hoped to forestall a full-dress account for at least several days. He had recovered from his head cold but had yet to regain his strength after the trip and was not ready to take on anything like this just yet. The next morning, he told the Cabinet of his intention to reply to the four Prime Minister's Questions that he had for that day's session. Then, he would invite the House to await a complete statement to be made at the start of the foreign affairs debate the following week.

Eden said he might 'get away' with it, but went on to remind Churchill that there was a campaign against him and that the House of Commons was 'very anxious' to know exactly what guarantees he had given to Truman. Even after the Cabinet meeting had been interrupted by a message from the Labour whip asking for a statement that day, Churchill was still inclined to stall.

'Let's see what fuss they make today,' Churchill said. 'If there's great trouble, I will promise to make it tomorrow.'

'Then you will have it forced out of you,' warned the persnickety Conservative Chief Whip, Patrick Buchan-Hepburn. 'Is that good?' Churchill did not seem to think it would be a problem.

At half past two that afternoon, Parliament met for the first time since before Christmas. Back in December, Churchill had offered the socialists a peace pipe. Today, he pretended not to notice they were all wearing war paint. Asked for a full accounting of his Washington visit, he replied that he had thought it would be 'more convenient' for the House if he dealt with the matter in opening the debate on foreign affairs which was set to begin the following Tuesday.

'As, however, I learn it is the wish of the Opposition that some statement should be made,' Churchill continued, 'I should be prepared to make a preliminary statement tomorrow.'

Attlee reminded him in the tone of a stern and disapproving school-master that there was considerable anxiety about certain matters that had occurred overseas. Churchill retorted, 'It is on those points on which there is considerable anxiety that I may, in comparatively few sentences, endeavour to enlighten the House and, I trust, relieve the anxieties which prevail.'

Back in Parliament the next day, Churchill deadpanned that he had used the phrase 'prompt, resolute and effective' because he preferred those words to 'tardy, timid and fatuous'. In fact, he insisted, he had carefully chosen his language to make it plain to the Communists that Britain and the US would 'work together in true comradeship' in the event of a renewal of hostilities in Korea. He stressed that that was all he had meant and that there was no sense in which he had been signalling a shift in Far East policy. Churchill's explanation, not to mention his sometimes insouciant manner, drew a good deal of Opposition scorn.

So did his decision to send Eden to open the foreign affairs debate on 5 February, though Labour had had every reason to expect Churchill to speak first. Eden, when he faced the House, did not seem especially pleased with his assignment either. He was visibly 'irritated' when Churchill persisted in conversing with Buchan-Hepburn while Eden struggled to defend him. Labour's surprise response to Eden's efforts was to harpoon Churchill with a personal censure motion. The artfully worded motion endorsed the Government's Far East policy as stated by Eden, but regretted Churchill's 'failure to give adequate expression to this policy in the course of his recent visit to the United States'.

The claim infuriated Churchill, who set to work preparing a real fighting speech in response to what he viewed as a 'shameful' personal attack. As far as he was concerned, it was both absurd and unjust. He had gone to America in quest of peace, yet he stood accused of having set his country on a path to war. He had defied the Americans in the name of equality, yet the Opposition assailed him for having allowed Britain to drift into subservience.

167

On the morning of Wednesday, 6 February, Churchill rose early in anticipation of addressing the House that afternoon. He was at work in bed with all his papers around him and a candle for his cigar when Edward Ford, the King's assistant private secretary, was unexpectedly shown in.

'I've got bad news,' the visitor said. 'The King died this morning.'

'Bad news?' said Churchill. 'The worst!' As he cast aside the pages he had been absorbed in only a moment before, he remarked, 'How unimportant these matters seem.'

After Ford left, Jock Colville entered the bedroom, where the Prime Minister sat looking straight ahead. Tears streamed down Churchill's face as he reminisced about his wartime comradeship with George VI. Colville, who also had served as Princess Elizabeth's private secretary, tried to reassure him by saying how well he would get on with the new Queen, but Churchill was inconsolable.

'I hardly know her,' Churchill despaired, 'and she is only a child.'

At half past eleven, he opened a special Cabinet meeting by announcing that the King had died in his sleep at Sandringham the previous night. Then he turned to the enormous volume of business that suddenly confronted the Government. One week previously, Churchill had accompanied the King and Queen, as well as Prince Philip's uncle and aunt Lord and Lady Mountbatten, to London Airport to see Princess Elizabeth and her husband off on the Commonwealth tour she was making in place of her ailing father. She was still in Kenya, its first stop, at the time of his death and would have to come home at once, but the thought of her in an aeroplane filled Churchill with dread. Initially, it seemed it might be best if the Cabinet recommended that she return by sea. But the trip would take fourteen days, and even as he contemplated the idea, he doubted that they would be able to prevent her from boarding a plane immediately. By the time the Cabinet met again in a few hours, Churchill was able to report that the royal party was already en route and expected the next day.

That night, the House of Commons was filled to overflowing as Churchill slowly rose from his seat and, in a low, soulful voice, took the oath of allegiance to the new sovereign. Then he signed the roll and left the chamber.

Among themselves, a number of Opposition members admitted to being 'terribly disappointed' that the death of King George had postponed the fierce high-stakes debate that otherwise would have played out that day in the House. Churchill's wartime scourge Aneurin Bevan, whose gifts of oratory were thought by some to be on a par with the Prime Minister's, had been pumped up to lead the attack. There was upset in the Bevan camp that at the last minute Churchill had been rescued by events, and there was concern that Labour would have a hard time recapturing the momentum against the Prime Minister. 'No doubt we shall revive the issue,' Richard Crossman, a Bevanite, confided to his diary on 6 February, 'but, in the flood of sentimentality which Royal deaths and innocent young couples coming to the Throne create, we shall have to bide our time.'

Crossman acknowledged that the parliamentarians' 'hard-boiled' reaction – his own included – to the King's demise was out of sync with what most Britons appeared to be feeling at the time. 'Directly you got outside, you certainly realized that the newspapers were not sentimentalizing when they described the nation's feeling of personal loss.'

On the morning of 7 February, it fell to Eden to preside over the Cabinet. Churchill had not awakened in time – 'being much tired with the emotion of yesterday'. Hardly had Churchill cast aside his fighting speech when he had to pivot to the preparation of the first of two eulogies of George VI. Originally scheduled for Wednesday night, his nationwide address had been moved to Thursday at 9 p.m., to take place after the royal party had safely returned.

In the car to London Airport, Churchill wept as he dictated portions of that night's radio broadcast to a secretary. At the airport, where he stood on the tarmac with Eden, Salisbury, Attlee, Lord and Lady

Mountbatten, and other dignitaries, the seventy-seven-year-old Prime Minister gave a low bow as the black-clad twenty-five-year-old Queen emerged from the aircraft. Churchill was the first to welcome her, but he was too emotional to speak.

Churchill resumed dictating his eulogy as he was driven back to London. By the time he reached Number Ten, the text of the address was finished, but the effort of composition had exhausted him. While he rested, staff members were told he was still at work.

When Churchill went on the air that evening, he managed to accomplish something he had often done to great effect during the war: he connected with his audience on a visceral level. He gave voice to the feelings of the millions of Britons who had watched with anxiety – in newspaper photographs and more recently in television images on the day of Elizabeth's departure for Kenya – as George VI publicly neared the close of his life. The King, Churchill said, had walked bravely with death as if death had been a companion. 'In the end, death came as a friend; and, after a happy day of sunshine and sport, and after "good night" to those who loved him best, he fell asleep as every man or woman who strives to fear God and nothing else in the world, may hope to do.'

The emotion was deeply felt, but the calculating, political part of Churchill's brain had not stopped churning either. He moved seamlessly from evoking the past to contemplating, not to mention staking a passionate personal claim on, what was to come. For the first time the aged premier hitched his wagon to the future of the young monarch. He noted that some of the greatest periods of Britain's history had unfolded under the rule of its queens. 'I, whose youth was passed in the august, unchallenged and tranquil glories of the Victorian era may well feel a thrill in invoking once more the prayer and the anthem, "God Save the Queen".' The association was significant, it having long been Churchill's dream to secure an enduring peace such as Britain had last enjoyed in his Victorian youth.

By the time Churchill addressed the House of Commons four

days later, he had managed to insert both Elizabeth and her late father into the grand narrative of his second premiership. He spoke of the end of the war, when the surmounting of one menace had seemed only to be succeeded by the shadow of another. He recalled George VI's disappointment that victory had led neither to real peace nor security. And he expressed a wish that the accession of Elizabeth II might coincide with the beginning of a new era of true and lasting peace. Thus Churchill sought to connect the Queen to his goal of a parley at the summit.

Soon he was linking her to the question of his retirement as well. Churchill was pointedly in no rush to see Elizabeth crowned. After he had delivered his parliamentary eulogy, he discussed the date of the coronation with the Cabinet. On the argument that the economic crisis ruled out 1952, he pressed for a distant date. He maintained that were the coronation to take place the following year, it would have a 'steadying effect' on the country. The Cabinet concurred, and on 12 February he advised the Queen that the ceremony ought to be staged in the spring of 1953. After that had been settled, he set himself a new time-lock. He began saying that he intended to remain in office until the coronation.

Within a matter of days, Churchill had come a long way: from despairing about the accession of a young Queen to finding her supremely useful to his purposes. He was inclined to adopt a paternal attitude in his personal relations with her. Some observers saw his relationship with Elizabeth as a reprise of the formative role that Lord Melbourne had played with the young and malleable Queen Victoria. But there were crucial differences between Elizabeth and her great-great-grandmother at the outset of their reigns. For one thing, Elizabeth was a married woman. Though her husband's uncle, who had been like a father to him, was known to have had a hand in engineering the marriage, it was also the case that the union of Elizabeth and Philip was 'a real love-match'. 'I've seen the man I'm going to marry!' the thirteen-year-old Princess Elizabeth had told her sister, Princess Margaret, after she met their eighteen-year-old cousin in 1939.

The question of how much power Philip would exert was an important one. Churchill was also very concerned about what Mountbatten's role would be. (Macmillan was not alone in his suspicions that Mountbatten aimed to be 'the power behind the Throne'.) Churchill and Mountbatten had collided over India, and lately over Mountbatten's anti-American opinions. At a moment when Churchill was still waiting to get Uncle Sam behind his Soviet initiative, could he afford to have 'Uncle Dickie' in the mix?

In anticipation of the state funeral on 15 February, Mountbatten turned up at the Earl Marshal's meeting, where he proposed that Norwegian and Danish sailors take part in the ceremonies. When this was reported at a Cabinet session, Churchill grumbled, 'Why was he present?' 'As Fourth Sea Lord, I suppose,' said Eden, 'and also as a member of the Family.' After the funeral, Churchill's annoyance escalated to alarm when word reached him that Mountbatten had been heard to say that 'the House of Mountbatten now reigned'. Churchill learned of the episode on 18 February from Jock Colville, who had heard it from George VI's mother, Queen Mary (no friend or admirer of Churchill's, by the way), who in turn had heard it from Prince Ernst August of Hanover, who had been present at the royal house party where Mountbatten committed the indiscretion.

Immediately Churchill repeated the story to his Cabinet. Thirty-five years before, the family name Windsor had been adopted by a decree of King George V. Now, Churchill spoke of both Queen Mary's and his own vehement opposition to a name change. The ministers agreed that Windsor should be retained, and they invited the Prime Minister to communicate their views to Her Majesty. The encounter, set to take place the following evening, 19 February, was going to require a delicate touch. However Churchill cast it, he was about to have to ask her in effect to distance herself from, and almost certainly to embarrass, her husband by participating in a rebuff to his family's ambitions.

All this was taking place as the moratorium on partisan strife drew to a close. After the King's burial, Churchill had spent the weekend at Chartwell, where he resumed work on his answer to the personal censure motion that had been hanging over him for days. Back in London on 18 February, he sent a draft to Dean Acheson, who had come for the funeral. Would the US Secretary of State review Churchill's efforts to be certain he had revealed nothing to which Washington might object? To Acheson's eye, the speech did indeed contain top-secret information and he promptly wrote with his objections.

The next day, Acheson, who had just been to see the Queen about unrelated matters, was shown into the Cabinet Room. Churchill, who had yet to see her himself about the Mountbatten affair, barely welcomed him. Bent forlornly over the baize-covered table, the Prime Minister muttered not sentences but phrases. Acheson heard him say 'naked among mine enemies' and 'the sword stricken from my hand'. Determined to ignore Churchill's gloom, the visitor genially inquired how he might be of service. Churchill claimed that Acheson had vetoed the heart of his speech and asked whether he could suggest a substitute. Though Acheson had come prepared with an alternative, he protested that to revise Churchill's prose would be impertinent. Churchill waved this aside and, at length, his spirits lifted materially as he listened to Acheson's version – twice. Declaring 'I can win with that,' he seized the paper from Acheson's hand and read through it himself with pleasure.

Churchill also got what he wanted out of his audience with the Queen. Afterwards, he was able to report to the Cabinet that Elizabeth had agreed that she and her descendants would bear the name of Windsor. The battle was far from over, for the consort himself had yet to have his say, but for the moment Churchill was able to put the issue aside.

At a Cabinet meeting on Thursday, 21 February, he made it clear that he needed to focus on his appearances in the House of Commons the following week. The censure debate was set for 26 February, and two days after that he was to open the defence debate. Eden disclosed to Acheson that the Tories were allowing Churchill to fret about the charges against him, though they were confident the Labour motion would easily be defeated. Churchill knew he had the numbers as well, but it was not enough to beat his accusers; he wanted to decimate them.

Late Thursday afternoon, Churchill went upstairs to his bedroom at Number Ten for a nap. When he awoke, it was about half past six. He picked up the telephone, but when he tried to speak to the operator he could not think of the words he wanted. Other, useless words filled his thoughts. As he feared he knew what was happening to him, he remained silent.

XIV

I Live Here, Don't I?

London, 1952

After twenty-five days of running on empty since he returned from America, Churchill had suffered another arterial spasm. He let about an hour pass, and when he was able to speak again he summoned his doctor. Seated on the edge of his bed when Moran came in, Churchill recounted the telephone incident and asked what it meant. Was he going to have another stroke? And what were the chances the aphasia would recur? Moran explained that the blood flow to the speech centre had been diminished, and that as a result Churchill had been temporarily unable to find the words he wanted. By the doctor's reckoning, Churchill had two options if he wished to avoid another stroke. Either he had to retire immediately, or he needed at least to arrange matters so that he would be under less strain.

What, Moran asked, did Churchill wish him to do if he ran into Clemmie on the way out? Churchill said she was in bed with a cold and he proposed they go to her room to tell her what had happened.

Had it been up to Clementine Churchill, her husband would never have become prime minister again. He had already had one stroke, and it was her nightmare that someday he would break down during a speech, discover he was no longer capable of conducting affairs, and end up like Lord Randolph Churchill 'the principal mourner at his own protracted funeral'. Nevertheless, rather than upset him further, she listened calmly and silently to his and the doctor's account. Throughout, her demeanour was grave but composed. She judged that this was not the time to admonish, but rather to envelop her husband with care and concern.

On the assumption that not only would Churchill refuse to step aside but that the sudden loss of power could actually prove detrimental to his health, Moran acted immediately to try to give him a bit more time in office. Of course, the arterial spasm might be the harbinger of an imminent full stroke. In the event Churchill survived, he would have little choice but to hand over. If, however, a clot did not form in the next few days, major decisions would have to be taken. The episode had been a warning that unless Churchill agreed to husband his strength, there would likely be severe consequences in six months or less.

Moran, for his part, had no idea whether a prime minister's burden could be eased. He calculated that it would be best to ask someone in the Cabinet. At the same time, he was adamant that he did not want to put a weapon in the form of confidential information in the hands of any individual who might later use it against his patient. He therefore decided to confide in the one minister renowned for his objectivity and complete absence of personal ambition. On the morning of Friday, 22 February, Moran asked Jock Colville to arrange a meeting with Salisbury.

Within two hours, Moran and Colville were ushered into Salisbury's office. After the doctor revealed what had happened the night before, he asked whether Churchill's duties could be cut. Salisbury replied that a prime minister could not simply cast off his responsibilities. The solution, he suggested, might be for Churchill to continue as prime minister from the House of Lords, leaving Eden to take over for him in the Commons. This unusual arrangement would allow Churchill to realize his wish to stay in office until after the coronation, and in the meantime it would make Eden prime minister in all but name.

The others liked the idea, but the inevitable question arose: who would be the best emissary to put it to Churchill? Lord Cherwell (Churchill's friend) and Christopher Soames (the husband of Churchill's daughter Mary) were mentioned. The Prime Minister adored both men, but whether either would be able to persuade him was questionable. Finally, Moran suggested that there was only one person who would be able to convince Churchill. Three days after the Prime Minister had been in to see Queen Elizabeth about the royal family name, it was agreed that they would appeal to her to talk to him.

That afternoon at Buckingham Palace, Sir Alan Lascelles, now the Queen's private secretary, concurred that something needed to be done. Lascelles had lately noted the uneven quality of the Prime Minister's performance. There were days when he seemed fine and Lascelles asked himself why he had been worrying; there were also days when Churchill seemed incapable of grasping the point of a discussion. Even so, Lascelles refused to involve the Queen. He informed Moran and Colville that if she did speak to Churchill, he no doubt would thank her graciously for her suggestion before politely dismissing it. She was simply too young and inexperienced to have an effect. Under the circumstances, Lascelles thought Moran should be the one to approach him. The physician disagreed. He argued that Churchill would listen to him solely on medical matters. Moran was ready to warn his patient that he must not continue at his present pace, but someone else would have to broach Salisbury's plan.

At any rate, nothing could even be attempted until after the foreign affairs, defence, and finance debates. To confront Churchill beforehand would only multiply his troubles at a moment when he needed to cut back. Besides, faced with a personal censure motion, Churchill surely would not consider walking out at this point, lest it be said that he had run from a challenge. For the moment, their little group could only hope that he made it safely through the next ten days.

Deeply concerned about his boss, Colville sought to ensure that Churchill did not overtax himself. That weekend at Chartwell, where Churchill had gone to finish his reply to his accusers, Colville urged him to let someone else assume the burden of the defence speech. Churchill's antennae tended to be hypersensitive to intrigues of any kind, and the private secretary's suggestion that he delegate the speech to the Secretary of State for War, Anthony Head, fired his suspicions. As far as Churchill was aware, only his wife and doctor knew about the arterial spasm. He had no knowledge that Colville had been informed, let alone Salisbury or Lascelles. Abruptly, he turned on Colville and demanded to know whether he had been talking to Moran. Colville insisted he had not.

Instead of delegating the defence speech, Churchill postponed it until 5 March, and soon he rescheduled the finance debate to take place on the 11th. As a consequence, the critical ten days of waiting and worrying stretched to nearly three weeks.

Those of Churchill's colleagues who knew about the arterial spasm were not alone in their concern that he might not be up to the exertions that faced him. On the afternoon of the renewed censure debate, Churchill himself questioned whether he would be able to make a speech at all. Characteristically, he had lavished infinite care on the preparation of his address, but now wondered whether he would have the stamina to bring it off. The early signs were not promising. To his alarm, he was dull and listless at lunch, and he continued to feel that way after he took his place in the House. For sixty-five minutes he sat through a 'cumbrous, ill-at-ease' speech by the former Labour Foreign Secretary Herbert Morrison that not a few listeners found interminable. It enraged Churchill to hear his trip to Washington dismissed as a doubtful mission by the wrong man at the wrong time, but indignation had yet to animate him. Before he rose to reply, he noted that he was still shaky and fatigued.

Churchill warmed to the cheers that greeted him and as he began to speak he felt his strength increase. 'He is looking white and fatty,' observed the young Tory member Nigel Nicolson, 'a most unhealthy look, you would say if he were anyone else, but somehow out of this sickly mountain comes a volcanic flash.' Churchill's speech was a tour de force. He exposed his critics as hypocrites who, when they were in power, had done the very things he now stood accused of. Assailed as a warmonger, he disclosed that the Attlee Government had been secretly constructing an atomic bomb and had erected 'at the expense of many scores of millions of pounds' a facility for its regular production. Attacked for having made unprecedented commitments in Washington, he revealed that his accusers had themselves previously pledged to support US bombing across the Yalu River in the event of heavy air assaults from Chinese bases. He tartly added that he himself had yet to go so far. Pandemonium erupted in the chamber. The Labour front bench 'sat stunned and white'.

As he had been known to do, Churchill cunningly set his enemies against one another so they would have less strength left to go at him. Among his tasty revelations was that Attlee, Morrison and their group had kept both secrets not just from the Conservatives but also from Labour's own left wing. The latter faction, headed by Aneurin Bevan, was at the time vying for control of the party. Churchill's disclosures provided the Bevanites with ammunition against the more moderate Labour leadership. Privately, Churchill would not have minded if the radicals, whose ideas and leader were anathema to him, won out over Attlee. He calculated that their extreme views would alienate a good many middle-class voters who had been drawn to the Labour banner since 1945.

Conservative cheers and sarcastic Labour cries threatened to drown out Macmillan when he jauntily declared that the censure motion had backfired and urged the House to reject it with the scorn it merited. After the motion was defeated, Moran advised his patient to go home. Too worked up to leave, Churchill bustled to the Smoking Room to learn what his colleagues had thought of his performance.

A newly confident Churchill returned to the charge at the defence debate the following week. He twitted Labour about the cleavage in their ranks. The angrier they became the merrier he seemed. At one point, he managed to get so far under Emanuel Shinwell's skin that the former Defence Minister burst out, 'I wish Mr Churchill would stop interrupting in an inaudible fashion. He sits there muttering. He is smirking and grinning all over his face as if he is enjoying himself hugely.' Never was the premier's pleasure more manifest than when the Bevanites twice openly defied Attlee's voting orders.

Meanwhile, internecine warfare had also erupted in Churchill's Cabinet. In anticipation of the finance debate, Eden had targeted Butler's plan to float the pound. Macmillan, sensing that the plan posed a threat to his housing programme, formed a tag team with Eden. They took turns pummelling Butler, who tended to shrink from head-on clashes. Churchill, having initially supported the plan, stood aloof for the most part, but at length he sided with the attackers. Within the Cabinet, the Chancellor's defeat registered as a significant political victory for Eden.

The manoeuvres, however, were far from finished. When Butler lost out to Eden, he had yet to present his maiden budget in the House of Commons. After consulting with Churchill on 8 March, he produced a speech that was received triumphantly at the finance debate. As cheering MPs rose in their places to wave their order papers, the Prime Minister, near tears, offered Butler the highest form of praise. He compared him to his own father, Lord Randolph Churchill. In spite of what had gone on behind closed doors, the strength of Butler's parliamentary performance sparked a round of suggestions in the press that he had taken the lead over Eden in the race to succeed Churchill.

After the finance debate, Moran delivered his medical ultimatum in the form of a letter, a copy of which he sent to Clementine Churchill. In recent days, Churchill had spoken of being prepared to die in harness. Moran pointed out to Mrs Churchill, as if she did not know it already, that her husband was far from putting the whole case when he said that. What one dreaded much more, the physician explained, stoking Clementine's deepest fears, was an attack which would leave him permanently disabled. This was what they were striving to avoid.

Churchill was in no mood to be ordered to work less, certainly not after his latest triumphs. He brusquely dismissed the letter and when Clementine took it on herself to propose Salisbury's plan, he called the arrangement impractical and refused even to consider it. Churchill conceded to Moran that he was winding down physically and mentally. Nevertheless, he advised the doctor to stop worrying and reminded him that everybody has to die at some point.

Stalin's personal physician, Vladimir Vinogradov, did not get off so easily when his patient rejected his advice. Furious at being told to retire lest he suffer a severe stroke, Stalin destroyed his medical records and vowed to stay away from doctors in future. He later went so far as to have Vinogradov arrested and tortured for being part of a Western-inspired plot by eminent doctors to murder the nation's leaders through incorrect diagnosis and faulty treatment. As it happened, on the day Moran sent his note to Churchill, the Prime Minister was conferring with his Cabinet about a message from the ailing Stalin that had been presented to the British, American, and French ambassadors in Moscow. Reacting to Western efforts to establish a continental defence force and to rearm the Germans, Stalin proposed a four-power conference, possibly at the highest level, on the creation of a reunified neutral Germany. Churchill recognized that the offer might simply be a propaganda ploy and he saw that a neutral Germany, were it to be undermined by the Soviets, might soon go the way of Czechoslovakia. Still, another chance to face Stalin was exactly what he had been longing to arrange.

Despite this, from the moment Churchill returned to office, he had also been operating on the premise that serious settlement talks could not occur until after the US presidential elections. Although this timetable did not suit him, he remained intent on acting in tandem with the Americans, which meant he was going to have to resist Stalin's overture and wait another six months at least.

Could Churchill last? At times, he had his doubts. He had bested Labour in recent debates, but now a contingent of about fifty young socialists in the House took to heckling him regularly about his age and growing deafness. They hooted at his entrances and exits, jeered his pronouncements, and filled the chamber with derisive laughter when they caught him having to lean forward and cup his hand to his ear in order to follow the give-and-take.

It was bad enough that the Opposition openly and repeatedly questioned his competence. Before long, Conservatives were raising questions of their own and Churchill became a piñata for both sides. Young Tories in particular were unnerved by heavy Conservative losses in the county council and borough elections in spring 1952. Though Churchill had warned at the start of his peacetime Government that the economic recovery would not take place overnight, Britons were naturally impatient after seven years of postwar austerity. At a moment when jubilant Labour spokesmen were already calling for a new general election, Conservatives began to wonder whether younger, more effective party leadership might be in order. On 9 April, after being mocked and taunted by his young Labour persecutors in the House, Churchill went on to assure his young Conservative critics in the 1922 Committee that things would get better – in time. He also pledged not to cling to power if he began to fail physically or mentally.

Following a bout of bronchitis that kept him in bed for a week and excited much concern about his health, Churchill returned to

Parliament with a hearing aid in his left ear. By turns, he insisted his health was better than it had been in a long time and complained that his zest was diminished. He boasted that he could still put his enemies on their backs but lamented that his 'old brain' did not work as well as it used to. He told Eden that he looked forward to working with the next administration in Washington but suggested (for the umpteenth time) that it would not be long before he handed over. As far as the hearing aid was concerned, he found it uncomfortable and frequently tore it out in disgust.

Three months after Churchill had declined to go to the House of Lords, Salisbury, Crookshank, Stuart, and Buchan-Hepburn met to formulate a new ultimatum. Amid a blizzard of press rumours that Churchill might be about to leave office, Buchan-Hepburn called on the Prime Minister on the evening of 23 June. This time, there was no attempt to cushion Churchill's feelings. There was no pretence of approaching him out of concern for his health, no willingness to indulge his wish to remain in office until after the coronation, and no sop to his dignity such as the proposal that he transfer to the Lords had been. This was strictly about Churchill's performance and the party's ability to win elections. The Chief Whip conveyed the ministers' opinion that he ought to retire at once or at least set a firm date for his resignation. Churchill refused to do either. On this and similar occasions, he affected a frosty exterior, but, as his wife and children understood, he was desperately hurt by the efforts of fellow Conservatives to force him out.

Later that week, Churchill took revenge on Eden, though the latter had been careful to play no visible role in the machinations on his behalf. Eden's American and French counterparts, Dean Acheson and Foreign Minister Robert Schuman, were then in London. Before their meetings concluded, Churchill invited the trio to lunch. In the course of the afternoon, Churchill steered Acheson to the window of the sitting room where they had all gone to have a glass of sherry. Signalling by his tone of voice and by several conspiratorial pokes that he was about to have some fun at Eden's expense, Churchill announced that he planned to tear out a row of poplars along the garden wall because they spoiled the view. His remarks disturbed Eden, who broke off his talk with Schuman elsewhere in the room. Eden informed Churchill that he could not possibly remove the trees.

'Why not?' said Churchill. 'I live here, don't I?'

Eden solemnly reminded the Prime Minister that occupying Number Ten was not the same as owning it.

'Ah!' said Churchill, coming in for the kill. 'I see what you mean. I'm only the life tenant. You're the remainderman.'

The intriguers met again to plan their next move. Their deliberations became pointless and even a bit absurd when Eden suddenly fell ill at a meeting with Acheson on 27 June. He developed a fever and was diagnosed with jaundice. The Foreign Office announced that he was likely to be out for a month. Days after the Edenites had asked Churchill to step aside, he lustily threw himself forward in the House of Commons to take Eden's place in the debate on Korea and the Far East. On 1 July, Churchill, attired in a short coat and pale grey trousers, gave the Government's reply to a critical motion tabled by the Opposition. Churchill 'fairly pulverized his attackers', Chips Channon recorded; 'rarely has he been more devastating.' There was a sense at the time that the Prime Minister's lively riposte was aimed not just at Labour, but also at those in his own party who thought him too old to carry on.

Churchill was not always so successful, and eventually the strain of these weeks began to show. During his final address in the House of Commons prior to the summer recess, he was unable to maintain his composure when young Labour members heckled him as he struggled to survey the dire economic situation. By the time Churchill sat down, he was flushed and furious. Attlee provoked him further by commenting that while Churchill had undoubtedly accomplished great things in his day, the first nine months of his peacetime Government could only be described as squalid. When Churchill returned to his room in the House, his appearance so alarmed Colville that he sent for the doctor.

Not long afterwards, Churchill was resting at Chartwell when Eden brought some surprising news. Since January, the heir apparent (whose first marriage had ended two years before) had been secretly engaged to Churchill's niece. Clarissa Churchill, the willowy blonde daughter of the Prime Minister's late brother and sister-in-law, was twenty-three years Eden's junior. They had first met in 1936 when she was only sixteen. At the time, she had been part of the set of Salisbury's handsome teenaged son Robert, who in those days was rather in love with her himself. When Eden and Churchill's niece met again, in 1947, he became her 'latest admirer', and she was soon confiding to another admirer, Duff Cooper, that Eden never stopped trying to make love to her. Persistence paid off and Eden finally married into the Churchill family on 14 August 1952. The Churchills gave the happy couple their blessing, hosted a reception at Number Ten (which to some eyes gave the proceedings a 'dynastic' air), and presented the newlyweds with a substantial cheque. But hardly had they gone off on their honeymoon when Uncle Winston made it clear that he had no intention of treating 'my Anthony' any better than he had in the past.

Churchill contacted Truman to say that he was taking charge of Foreign Office correspondence in Eden's absence. He went on to propose that he and Truman make a joint approach to the Prime Minister of Iran in the hope of settling a dispute about Iranian oil that Eden had been working on. In one of a series of messages, Churchill said, 'I thought it might be good if we had a gallop together such as I often had with FDR.' This was no small suggestion, for if Truman signed a common telegram it would be the first occasion since 1945 that the Americans agreed to take joint action with Britain against a third party.

During Churchill's recent visit to Washington, Truman had resisted efforts to replicate the Roosevelt–Churchill relationship. Now, as he had done in advance of Potsdam, the President insisted that he wanted to avoid the impression of ganging up. Churchill replied, 'I do not myself see why two good men asking only what is right and just should not gang up against a third who is doing wrong. In fact I thought and think that is the way things ought to be done.' This time at least, Truman took his point and consented to speak in a single voice with Britain's leader. Colville noted in his diary that Eden, completing his honeymoon in Lisbon, was furious when he learned of Churchill's coup. 'It is not the substance but the method which displeases him; the stealing by Winston of his personal thunder.'

Churchill, meanwhile, was in a state of euphoria. The significance of the joint action went far beyond Iran. He saw it as a test run for a unified Anglo-American approach to Stalin after the election. Truman had already announced that he would not be a candidate for re-election, and at this point Churchill calculated that an Eisenhower presidency was probably his best hope of facing Stalin again with American power on his side. Whatever differences Churchill may have had with him in the past, Eisenhower was an internationalist. That made for a stark contrast to the isolationism of his chief rival for the Republican nomination, Senator Robert Taft of Ohio. When Eisenhower embarked on the pursuit of the presidency, he had the image of, in Sir Oliver Franks's words, 'the best man to win the peace'.

But something happened to Eisenhower on the path to power. After he beat out Taft, he made significant compromises in the name of unifying the Republican Party. He veered sharply to the right, he refused to denounce McCarthy, and his foreign policy pronouncements took on a new bellicose tone. He spoke – some thought recklessly – of US action to 'liberate' Soviet satellites. Truman accused Eisenhower and his chief foreign policy adviser, John Foster Dulles, of playing 'cheap politics' and of increasing the risk of war in a cynical effort to gain votes. The previous summer, when Eisenhower took the lead over Taft, Churchill had expressed relief to his wife. By the time Eisenhower won a landslide victory over Adlai Stevenson in November 1952, Churchill had come to view him very differently. 'For your private ear, I am greatly disturbed,' Churchill told Colville of the outcome of the presidential election. 'I think this makes war much more probable.'

In any case, Churchill had been waiting a long time for the American election to be over, and as far as he was concerned there was not a moment to be lost. It was not solely his age and health that worried him. It was also Stalin's. He expected that the international situation would become much more perilous when Stalin's sycophants began to scramble for the succession after he died.

Immediately, Churchill dictated a message to Eisenhower: 'I send you my sincere and heartfelt congratulations on your election. I look forward to a renewal of our comradeship and of our work together for the same causes of peace and freedom as in the past.' Churchill transmitted the text to the Foreign Office with instructions that it be dispatched at once, as well as made public. Eden, when he read the message, was quick to object. Eisenhower had had some vile things to say about Truman during the campaign, and Eden worried that Churchill's effusive tone might offend the outgoing president. Besides, Eden was far from pleased to see Churchill try to renew anything with Eisenhower. That sounded dangerously more like a beginning than an end. The Foreign Office advised that Franks be consulted about the wording. The recommendation made Churchill very cross and he insisted on sending the telegram precisely as he had written it.

Eden was rather cross himself afterwards when he went off to a luncheon at the Austrian Embassy. In 'a sudden burst of nerves and temper', he confided to a fellow guest that he and Churchill were on bad terms. 'I get all the knocks,' Eden complained to Chips Channon, whom he had known at Oxford. 'I don't think I can stand it much longer.'

Eden's nervous agitation persisted when, two days later, he flew to New York as head of the British delegation to the United Nations General Assembly. En route, despite being heavily drugged, he suffered an attack of severe abdominal pain. He could not sleep and had to be injected by his detective. While he was at the UN, he conducted meetings with both Dulles, who sought to allay British concerns about the foreign policy goals of the new administration, and Eisenhower. To Eden's surprise and delight, Eisenhower did not even mention Churchill. Instead, he talked entirely of working with Eden, who emerged from the meeting convinced that Eisenhower saw Churchill as already essentially out of the picture. Afterwards, an emboldened Eden spoke to his private secretary of the Cabinet appointments he intended to make as soon as he became prime minister. On the flight home he continued to speak of all that he planned to do when he took over from Churchill.

Back in Britain, Eden learned that Churchill had been speaking to Clarissa Eden of his retirement. Churchill had suggested to his niece that he wanted to give up and that he was simply looking for the right opportunity. Mrs Eden asked her husband to be gentle and allow Churchill to travel to Washington before he left office. The question of one last trip came up again presently when he and Churchill conferred. It seemed to Eden that Churchill actually 'begged' to be allowed to go. At other times, Churchill appeared almost to wink when he talked of handing over. Shortly after Eden's home-coming, he and Clarissa were included in an intimate family dinner in honour of Uncle Winston's seventy-eighth birthday. The other guests were Churchill's daughters Mary and Diana, his son Randolph, and their spouses. A great many gifts had poured in, and the Prime Minister reported that he had even received some 'rejuvenating' pills from the US. He said he dared not try them: 'Think how unfair it would be to Anthony.'

The question of when precisely Churchill planned to leave office was one Salisbury insisted must be answered without delay. Salisbury was not pleased when he learned about what was being billed as the Prime Minister's farewell trip to America. Many times in the past, Churchill had made similar vague assurances. Yet here he was, still in place, still in power. The day after Churchill's birthday, Salisbury had observed him at a reception for Commonwealth prime ministers, where he seemed sadly unable to follow the business of the conference. One participant described Churchill's lack of comprehension as 'pathetic'. Was it not his colleagues' duty to ensure that he relinquish his post? Eden was due to visit Churchill at Chequers, and Salisbury advised him to be blunt. He said that if Eden failed to extract a specific date he would convene a ministers' meeting (exclusive of the heir apparent) to discuss a new plan of attack.

In advance of the confrontation, Eden's private secretary sounded out Lascelles about current thinking at the Palace. Shuckburgh let it be known that both the President-elect and Secretary of State-designate Dulles had communicated a distinct preference for working with Eden. But when Eden's man subtly questioned the usefulness of another visit to the US by Churchill, he discovered that the Prime Minister had already been in to enlist the Queen's support.

At last, on Sunday, 7 December, Eden told Churchill that he must know something of his plans. As he had done many times before, Churchill solemnly suggested that it was his intention to hand over to Eden in the fullness of time. When exactly, Eden pressed, would that be? Both men remained silent for about a minute before Churchill remarked on there being things he could say, speeches he could make, so much more easily, were he no longer prime minister. This, too, sidestepped Eden's question, and there followed another long, tense silence. (In conversation, Churchill had a way of going dead silent at the end of a sentence, then recommencing after a few seconds. The effect could be unnerving. Ought one to speak into the silence, or ought one to wait?) Finally, it was Eden who blinked. He changed the subject once again, and the question of the succession was dropped.

When Churchill contacted Eisenhower to say that he intended to take a holiday in Jamaica and to suggest that they arrange to meet prior to the inauguration, Cabinet ministers fretted that he had revealed himself to be an 'old man in a hurry' and that his premature request might irritate the President-elect. Their concerns soon appeared to be unfounded. Eisenhower replied immediately, and he sounded almost as eager to see Churchill as the Prime Minister was to see him: 'I am delighted at the thought of a meeting with you in the first half of January.' Eisenhower, naturally, could not come to Churchill in Jamaica, but he suggested they arrange to meet in New York at the home of Bernard Baruch. 'This would not be as satisfactory as a longer and more leisurely visit over our respective easels,' said Eisenhower, who shared Churchill's love of painting, 'yet it would be, from my viewpoint, far better than no meeting at all.'

Eisenhower pressed all the right buttons. When he noted that he had managed to avoid formal meetings with representatives of a number of world governments, he was flattering Churchill's conviction that Britain had earned the right to be treated differently from other countries. And when he asserted that the future of the free world required close understanding and cooperation between the English-speaking nations, he was giving a reassuring nod to the concept of the unity of the English-speaking peoples that was so dear to Churchill's heart.

Churchill arrived in New York on 5 January 1953, full of hope that after eight years of struggle he was finally, assuredly, on his way back to the summit. To the distress of certain intensely interested parties at home, he announced that he did not plan to retire until he was 'a great deal worse and the Empire a great deal better' and that he was confident his best work was still ahead.

What Churchill did not yet know was that in spite of his warm messages, Eisenhower was determined not to allow him to recreate the close partnership with the White House that he had enjoyed during the war. In his diary, Eisenhower called the Prime Minister's hope of establishing such a relationship 'completely fatuous' and he again expressed the wish that Churchill 'would turn over leadership of the British Conservative Party to younger men'.

Eisenhower's feelings about Churchill had not been softened by the role that the Berlin controversy had played during his campaigns for both the Republican nomination and the presidency. Eisenhower had been dogged by questions – from the right wing of his party, from potential supporters and contributors, from Republican delegates, and from the voters themselves – about his 1945 decision to let the Russians reach Berlin first. In the opening salvo of his effort to secure the Republican nomination over Taft, he told an audience in Detroit that one of the questions most frequently asked of him was, 'General, why didn't you take Berlin?' Again and again, in letters, private conversations, and speeches, he had made the case that 'no political directive' had ever been given to him to take Berlin, that it had been a 'destroyed city', and that he had had no role in the unsound political decisions that had already set the lines of occupation in the Soviets' favour. The first and second points, while true in themselves, were not quite the whole story. Churchill had implored Eisenhower to take Berlin and had written to impress upon him the political and symbolic importance of capturing it, Stalin's lies to the contrary. The third point was Eisenhower's old trick of shifting the blame for postwar problems to the British Prime Minister. At times in his campaign statements, Eisenhower seemed almost to be trying to convince himself as much as anyone else that he had not simply been duped by Stalin. He could get away with making these and related claims so long as Churchill's 1945 telegrams to him were not in public circulation. That would change as soon as Churchill published volume six of his war memoirs, it being his custom to print the relevant correspondence verbatim.

Churchill had come to New York to seek the benefit of American power, without which he could not hope to negotiate effectively with Stalin. The initial signs seemed promising when he met Eisenhower in Bernard Baruch's living room, where a painted portrait of Churchill in military uniform hung above the fireplace. Eisenhower spoke with 'much vigour' of his intention to parley with Stalin after the inauguration. It seemed like everything Churchill could have wished for – but then suddenly Eisenhower struck his blow. He planned to meet with Stalin alone, cutting Churchill and the British out.

In 1945, Truman had similarly suggested that he wanted to see Stalin by himself. Eisenhower's proposal was considerably worse. Truman at least had indicated that Churchill could join them later. Eisenhower had no intention of allowing the Prime Minister to participate at any time. He had completely outmanoeuvred Churchill, who had often suggested that his reason for clinging to power was the hope that he might yet have a chance to win the postwar peace. Whether or not Eisenhower really meant to see Stalin – during the presidential campaign he had said that he did not think a meeting at this time would help solve world problems – he had effectively blocked Churchill from putting pressure on the new administration by calling for a summit conference. The Prime Minister was unlikely to demand a meeting from which he knew he would be excluded. If and when Eisenhower announced his intention to talk to Stalin, Churchill, a staunch advocate of top-level talks, could hardly argue publicly that the President ought not to go.

As if to rub salt into the wound by reminding Churchill that he was powerless without the Americans, Eisenhower politely informed him that he was 'quite welcome' to arrange to see Stalin separately, if he saw fit, at any time. Eisenhower, for his part, claimed to be contemplating an announcement in his inaugural address of his willingness to meet Stalin one-on-one in Stockholm. At this, Churchill frantically shifted gears. Suddenly, the 'old man in a hurry' was doing whatever he could to slow things down in the hope that he might yet find a way to insinuate himself into the process. He suggested that it would be wiser to keep to generalities in the inaugural speech. He reminded Eisenhower that there was no battle going on and that as a general he could wait for full reconnaissance reports. He pointed out that Eisenhower had four years of 'certain power' ahead of him, and he asked whether it might not be a mistake to seem 'in too great a hurry'.

XV

If Nothing Can Be Arranged

Jamaica, January 1953

After stopping in Washington for a farewell visit to Truman, Churchill went on to Jamaica for a two-week holiday. It was not a happy interlude. He devoted most of his time to painting, but he also corrected the last three chapters of the final volume of his war memoirs. The need to revisit the frustrations of 1945 did not help his mood in the wake of New York. In conversation with Colville and other companions, he complained bitterly about Eisenhower, calling him 'a real man of limited stature'. To the last minute, Churchill did not know whether Eisenhower would go through with his plan to immediately propose a one-on-one meeting with Stalin. In New York, he had seemed to listen when Churchill urged him to hold off, but what he would actually do on 20 January remained in suspense.

Churchill was still in Jamaica when Eisenhower was inaugurated. The inaugural address made no mention of a desire to parley with Stalin, but of course the omission did not rule out some sort of public statement in the near future. It did not bode well that Eisenhower had rejected Churchill's suggestion that rather than return directly to London after his holiday, he come to the White House for a week of leisurely talks. To make matters worse, Eisenhower had not even bothered to turn him down personally. That Eisenhower had chosen to convey the unwelcome message via Dulles further suggested that he meant to keep Churchill and the British at a distance.

Churchill returned to London on 29 January to face growing unrest in his own Government. While he was abroad, Eden had assented to a proposal by Harry Crookshank that party leaders stage a new showdown with the Prime Minister, whose fading powers made him 'an increasing liability' to the party. Even as Eden protested that he could play no direct role in an effort to force Churchill to step aside after the coronation, he agreed unequivocally that the effort needed to be undertaken. Eden had lately been subjected to a series of blistering attacks in the Beaverbrook press that he and his supporters suspected Churchill's surrogates (i.e., his son or sons-in-law) or even the Prime Minister himself of having instigated in the belief that tearing down the likely successor might prolong Churchill's tenure in office. The more Eden was criticized in print, the more Butler seemed to come in for praise. Lascelles assured Eden's private secretary that if Churchill were to die at this point, it was still certain that the Queen would send for Eden. He predicted, however, that that might change by the end of the year. According to Lascelles, were present trends to continue, at least fifty per cent of opinion in the party might favour Butler by then. Frantic that Butler might yet overtake him in the race to succeed Churchill, Eden moved to line up key support. He tempted Macmillan with the post of Foreign Secretary in an Eden Government – if, that is, Macmillan backed him over Butler.

When the retiring US Ambassador to Great Britain, Walter Gifford, lunched with Eisenhower on 12 February, he depicted Churchill as a powerless old man, whose own inner circle longed for him to hand over. The picture confirmed Eisenhower's impressions in New York, where his strategic move to block the Prime Minister's efforts to get to Stalin had left Churchill sputtering. The President's reaction to Gifford's report was clear from the entry he made in his diary afterwards: it was time for Churchill to retire.

Churchill had no intention of stepping aside, whether to please Eden or Eisenhower, but on his return to London he was still miserably in the corner Eisenhower had backed him into in New York. Soon his situation got worse.

During the night of 1–2 March, Stalin suffered the severe stroke his physician had warned of if he refused to retire. For some twelve hours, the lieutenants whom Stalin had taunted and tormented until the end put off calling a doctor for fear they would be accused of trying to grab power. When at last a decision was taken to summon help, the choices were limited. Vinogradov was being tortured in an effort to make him confess that he was a long-time agent of British intelligence. Other eminent doctors had been jailed as participants in the 'doctors' plot' to murder Stalin and other Soviet leaders. The plot had been a figment of Stalin's paranoia but the Soviet people, who had first read about 'killer doctors' in *Pravda* two months previously, did not know that. To allay public fears, Stalin's lieutenants issued a communiqué stating that his treatment would be closely supervised by the Central Committee of the Communist Party and the Soviet Government. The doctors who were brought in to save the dying Stalin had never treated him before and the pressure on them was excruciating. Though the tyrant lay helpless, his face 'contorted', the medical men trembled as they struggled ineptly to examine him.

When Stalin died on 5 March, his position did not pass to any individual. Instead, there was a joint leadership comprising Chairman of the Council of Ministers Georgi Malenkov, Minister of State for Security Lavrenti Beria, Foreign Minister Vyacheslav Molotov, First Secretary of the Communist Party Nikita Khrushchev, and Minister of Defence Nikolai Bulganin. Ostensibly, the paunchy, unkempt fifty-one-year-old Malenkov occupied the first place and Beria the second. Still, Malenkov's colleagues – especially Molotov, whom Dulles compared to Machiavelli, and whom a good many observers in the West had been betting on to come out on top – failed to accord him the degree of authority they had unhesitatingly accorded to Stalin. Already, the others were watching Malenkov 'like hawks' for any indication that he was not up to the job.

What did the change mean for the last surviving member of the original Big Three? There was reason to think that the death of Stalin might be the final nail in Churchill's political coffin. Churchill had long conceived of a parley at the summit as a personal rematch with Stalin. He had maintained, and seemed sincerely to believe, that his hard-earned visceral sense of the tyrant's cast of mind would smooth the way to agreement, and that that alone was ample justification for keeping his would-be successors waiting. Nevertheless, no sooner had Stalin been laid out beside Lenin than Churchill used his demise as an excuse to try again with Eisenhower. Malenkov became Churchill's new Moby-Dick.

On 11 March, the night after Stalin's funeral, Churchill drafted a telegram to Eisenhower. He began by saying that he was sure everyone would want to know whether Eisenhower still contemplated a meeting with the Soviets: 'I remember our talk at Bernie's when you told me that I was welcome to meet Stalin if I saw fit and that you understood this as meaning that you did not want us to go together, but now there is no more Stalin I wonder whether this makes any difference to your view about separate approaches to the new regime or whether there is a possibility of collective action.' When Churchill composed this message, he was acting on the assumption that Eisenhower had not wavered from his intention, stated emphatically in New York, to sit down with the Soviets. But when Eisenhower's reply came in the following day, Churchill rethought his whole approach. Not only did Eisenhower refuse to act jointly with the British, he also questioned the wisdom of top-level talks in general. In New York, Eisenhower had portrayed himself as eager to go to the summit; now, he seemed anxious to avoid a meeting with the Soviets on the grounds that it would merely give them another opportunity to take advantage. Suddenly, it was evident that the man who had allowed himself to be duped by Stalin in 1945 was afraid of being made a fool of again. Once Churchill grasped that Eisenhower had been bluffing in New York, he was no longer precluded from moving actively and publicly to arrange a top-level conference.

Determined to force Eisenhower to the summit, Churchill, without telling the President, set to work building momentum towards a leaders' meeting. He began by seeking to throw Eden together with his counterpart in the new Soviet Government, Molotov, who was also the one member of the new team with whom both Churchill and Eden had had extensive prior contact. In discussions with British colleagues, Churchill made no effort to conceal his view of an Eden–Molotov encounter in Vienna as only an 'interim objective' or of his hope that it would lead to a top-level meeting with Malenkov, attended by both Eisenhower and himself. Under different circumstances, Eden would likely have baulked at the Prime Minister's proposal that Eden take the lead in a new Soviet initiative. Encouraging Churchill's summit dreams and giving him a reason not to quit were the last things Eden wanted to do. Nevertheless, a chance to claim the limelight at a particularly difficult point in his career seems to have proven irresistible to Eden, who was 'very keen' from the first.

The indications from the Kremlin, meanwhile, suggested a desire to reduce East–West tensions, though to what end no one could be sure. On 15 March, Malenkov made a speech in which he maintained that there was no problem between the two sides that could not be resolved diplomatically. A Soviet offer to comply with previous requests from London that British civilian prisoners in Korea be released was soon followed by larger gestures, such as the acceptance by the Korean Communists of a long-standing UN proposal for the reciprocal release of sick and wounded prisoners and a call for the resumption of the suspended armistice talks at Panmunjon. From the time Churchill moved back to Number Ten in 1951, the Korean War had been a major obstacle to US participation in a summit meeting. Whether or not that obstacle was finally about to come down, Churchill was eager to use the Communist offer on Korea as an excuse to propose the Eden meeting to Molotov.

It quickly became apparent, however, that Eden's health ruled out a meeting anytime soon. On 4 April, the Foreign Secretary learned that he required an immediate operation on his gall bladder. The surgery would put him out of play for three to six weeks. Initially, the delay did not seem to worry Churchill. The astonishing news from Moscow that Vinogradov and other jailed doctors had been released and that the charges against them had been fabricated and their confessions obtained improperly (a euphemism for torture) suggested to Churchill that time for the moment was on his side. It struck him that in a dictatorship, an admission that the government had lied could be the beginning of the end. On the theory that the most dangerous moment for evil governments is when they begin to reform, Churchill calculated that he could sit back and let things develop until Eden recovered.

On 6 April, however, he learned that Eisenhower had been quietly planning a move of his own. The President sent word that he was contemplating a major foreign policy speech. There had been considerable upset in Washington with the impression Malenkov's speech had made in the world. Eisenhower, in particular, had been distressed that he had missed the opportunity to take the lead with a 'big' speech of his own. His forthcoming address on world peace was designed to seize the initiative from Moscow. Eisenhower also assumed it would serve as the defining statement of the West's post-Stalin Soviet policy.

Three days later, a draft of the President's speech was delivered to Churchill. When he read it, he was appalled. As he saw it, Eisenhower's speech, scheduled for 16 April, threatened to halt the flow of hopeful gestures from the East. Deeply sceptical of Soviet intentions, Eisenhower planned to argue that rhetoric was one thing, concrete acts another. The speech enumerated the specific steps Eisenhower expected the

Soviet Union's new leaders to take in Korea, Austria, Germany, and elsewhere in the world to prove their sincerity before he could even consider meeting them.

For Churchill, the most important action to take at this point was to make direct contact with Stalin's successors and to start talking informally and unconditionally. In his mind, what was needed now was an 'easement' of tensions, a period when one small agreement might lead to another, rather than a single all-encompassing agreement. Churchill hoped that in Stalin's absence the Soviet Union would allow itself to become a little less isolated and therefore more pervious to Western influences, and he worried that Eisenhower's demands might send the new leaders back into their shell just when they had been showing signs of a desire to emerge. Not for the first time, he deplored what he saw as Eisenhower's fatal lack of strategic thinking.

He reacted immediately. On the same day he read Eisenhower's draft address, he offered to let the President see a draft of something he had written. Churchill, who had previously announced that he would respond to *Crusade in Europe* in the relevant volumes of his own memoirs, sent word that the final volume was to appear later in the year. He explained that the book spanned the period from the launching of Overlord to the Potsdam Conference, a time of almost unbroken Allied successes 'but darkened by forebodings about the political future of Europe which have since been shown to have been only too well founded'. In the guise of asking whether Eisenhower wished to vet the numerous references to him in the manuscript, Churchill implicitly reminded the President of how wrong he had been about Berlin.

Two days later, Churchill followed up with a telegram beseeching Eisenhower to postpone his speech. He argued that the apparent change of mood in Moscow was so new and so indefinite and its causes so obscure that there was not much risk in allowing things to develop. 'We do not know what these men mean. We do not want to deter them from saying what they mean.' Citing the Kremlin's about-face with regard to the doctors' plot, Churchill said he did not want the world to think Eisenhower's speech had interrupted a 'natural flow of events' that might themselves lead to the undoing of Soviet Communism.

When Churchill's second message arrived in Washington, Eisenhower seemed to waver. Clearly, the controversies of 1945 continued to eat at him. Twice since Stalin's death, Eisenhower had erupted weirdly at National Security Council meetings, claiming that had Stalin been able to act freely at the close of the war, the Soviet Union would have gone on to establish more peaceful and normal relations with the rest of the world. As if he were trying to convince himself that he had not been wrong to swallow Stalin's assurances, he insisted that the Soviet leader had never enjoyed complete power and that he had had to come to terms with other members of his ruling circle. Still, in conversation with speechwriter Emmet John Hughes and other advisers on 11 April, Eisenhower was palpably nervous about making the same mistake twice by failing to listen to Churchill. He said, 'Well, maybe Churchill's right, and we can whip up some other text for the occasion.'

Hughes and certain of the others appealed to Eisenhower's ego by arguing that Churchill's motive for requesting a postponement was 'to guard and reserve for himself the initiative in any dramatic new approach to the Soviet leaders'. Determined never to have to play second fiddle to Churchill, Eisenhower finally sent word that the speech could not be put off. If Churchill wished to propose any specific changes, he ought to cable his list at once. Eisenhower stipulated that while he could not agree in advance to be guided by all of Churchill's suggestions, he would certainly consider them 'prayerfully'.

When Churchill received this message, Eden was at the London Clinic waiting to undergo a cholecystectomy. On the eve of the operation, the two men worked frenziedly to try to minimize the damage

Eisenhower was about to do. They urged the President to combine his reassertion of inflexible resolve with some balancing expression of hope that the world had entered a new era. Though Churchill had previously seen no problem in Eden being out of commission for several weeks, suddenly it seemed crucial that he be well enough to face Molotov at the earliest possible date lest the momentum towards a summit meeting be lost. Churchill lectured Eden's surgeon, Basil Hume, on the grave responsibility that had been placed in his hands and warned that nothing must be allowed to go wrong. He demanded constant updates and concerned himself with the most infinitesimal medical details. At times, it seemed almost as if the Prime Minister was about to insist on donning a surgical mask and cutting out Eden's gall bladder himself.

Churchill's efforts at micromanagement had the effect of completely unhinging Hume. On the day of the operation, Eden was already under anaesthesia when a further communication reached the operating theatre to reiterate the Prime Minister's interest and anxiety. By this time, Hume was so flustered that the surgery had to be postponed for almost an hour. At length, Eden spent over three hours on the operating table and what ought to have been a routine procedure became a fiasco. The knife 'slipped', the bilary duct was inadvertently cut, and Eden lost a bucket of blood and nearly died. He faced a second operation to repair the damage of the first.

Though Eisenhower had agreed to tone down his speech some-what, the final text persisted in demanding positive evidence of the Kremlin's desire for peace before any talks could take place. Hardly had Eisenhower delivered his speech on 16 April when Churchill undertook to spin the President's remarks. Speaking in Glasgow on the next day, he portrayed Eisenhower's address as a 'massive and magnificent' statement of the West's peace aims and downplayed, if not altogether ignored, its emphasis on tests and conditions. He stressed that Eisenhower had 'closed no door' on sincere efforts to achieve world peace. When Dulles, speaking in Washington, painted

Eisenhower's comments as a challenge to the Soviets, Churchill was quick to cast doubt on the Secretary of State's interpretation. Churchill insisted in the House of Commons on 20 April that he did not 'read' Eisenhower's speech as a challenge and that he did not expect Moscow to give 'an immediate categorical reply to the many grave and true points which his remarkable and inspiring declaration contained'. After the Prime Minister slathered on additional praise for Eisenhower, he expressed the hope that there might soon be a top-level meeting of the 'principal powers' involved in the Cold War. Eisenhower certainly had not said anything about this, though in Churchill's telling it was almost as if he had. Churchill then sent off a transcript of his remarks in the Commons to the British Embassy in Moscow to be passed on to Molotov. This was how he wanted the Kremlin to perceive Eisenhower's words. These were the positive lines along which he wanted the Soviets to be thinking.

On 21 April, he offered Eisenhower a chance to go along with the spin. He sent on a transcript of his remarks in the Commons, along with a message asking what the President thought should be the next step. Churchill was not bashful about giving his view. 'In my opinion the best would be that the three victorious Powers, who separated in Potsdam in 1945, should come together again.' He recalled that in New York the President had spoken of meeting Stalin in Stockholm, and he suggested that that might be just the place for the three leaders to meet now.

'If nothing can be arranged,' Churchill continued, 'I shall have to consider seriously a personal contact. You told me in New York you would have no objection to this.'

In New York, it had been tacitly understood that seeing Stalin separately (without the backing of American might) was precisely what Churchill did not want to do. Three months later, when it was Churchill who raised the possibility of going solo, the suggestion had the odour of a threat.

This shift in tone persisted the next day in the House of Commons, when Churchill followed up his private suggestion to Eisenhower that Britain might be about to take an independent line. The Prime Minister had lately been under considerable pressure from the Labour front bench to make good on his campaign pledge to arrange a meeting with the Soviets. In reply to Opposition members who heckled him for being overly complimentary to Eisenhower and who asked for assurance that Churchill did not plan to leave the initiative entirely in American hands, he asserted his and his country's independence: 'I do not think, looking back over a long period of peace and war, I have ever, so far as I had anything to say in matters, been willing to accept complete initiative from the United States.'

That spring, it was widely noticed that the seventy-eight-year-old Churchill seemed suddenly in better fettle. Lord Swinton, the Secretary of State for Commonwealth Relations, toasted Churchill's renewed vitality. Violet Bonham Carter thought he appeared 'extraordinarily well and buoyant – a different creature from what he was last year'. Though he was doing Eden's work in addition to his own, he seemed 'not the least overburdened'. On the contrary, the arrangement appeared to exhilarate him. Churchill savoured the irony that he seemed only to get better, while everyone around him went down: Salisbury had been sick, and Macmillan had recently spent a week in hospital with gall bladder troubles of his own. Eden would probably be away from his desk for several months, if not more.

Protesting that he could not bear a sick man, Churchill refused Eden his request to stay involved from home. Previously, Moran had been at pains to lessen the Prime Minister's load. Now, Churchill himself had gleefully added to it. Worried that, appearances to the contrary, Churchill was heading for a fall, Moran warned on 24 April that while Churchill could probably manage both jobs for a brief period, burdening himself indefinitely was surely unwise. Churchill laughed off his concerns and assured him it was not as much work as he thought.

At Windsor Castle that evening, the Prime Minister knelt at the feet of the young Queen to be made a Knight of the Garter. In the aftermath of the Labour landslide in 1945 he had rejected that high honour because 'I could not accept the Order of the Garter from my Sovereign when I had received the order of the boot from his people.' Eight years later, Churchill rejoiced that he was again at one with his countrymen. When Queen Elizabeth tapped his shoulders with a ceremonial sword and he rose as 'Sir Winston', some observers mistook his decision to accept the knighthood as a sign that he intended to retire after the coronation.

The White House certainly would not have been miserable to see him bow out. When Eisenhower's response to Churchill's latest telegram reached London on 27 April, it was far from what the Prime Minister had been hoping to hear. Now, Eisenhower was the one who spoke of not rushing. He altogether rejected the idea of a summit meeting at this time. As far as what he had said previously about Churchill being welcome to make personal contact with Stalin, he noted that the situation had 'changed considerably' in the interim. The President no longer thought it appropriate for Churchill to talk to the Soviets on his own.

Eisenhower's stance enraged Churchill. As Churchill saw it, the death of Stalin had presented the West with what was perhaps a unique opportunity to make a fresh start with the Soviets. Eisenhower seemed to be about to squander that opportunity. By Churchill's lights, the President's speech had already provoked a most unfortunate countermove from Moscow. In an apparent response to the American effort to seize the diplomatic initiative, Molotov proposed five-power talks that would also include France and the Chinese People's Republic. On 28 April, Churchill complained to the Cabinet that five big powers at the table would be too many. If there was to be a meeting, Churchill wanted it to be limited to the Soviets, the Americans, and the British, 'who could take up the discussion at the point at which it had been left at the end of the Potsdam Conference in 1945'. Just when things had been going so well, suddenly everything threatened to end in stalemate. Churchill blamed it all on Eisenhower. Exasperated, he told the Cabinet that he wished the President 'hadn't started this off by making his speech'. To his mind, once again Eisenhower was undermining his ability to deal with the Soviets. Churchill was determined not to let him succeed a second time.

After a follow-up operation on 29 April left Eden even worse than before, Churchill recast his plan to send the Foreign Secretary to see Molotov as the prelude to a top-level encounter. He now intended to wear both hats and take both meetings – first with Molotov, then with Malenkov – himself. And instead of Vienna, he was ready to volunteer to go to Moscow. On 4 May, he sent Eisenhower his draft letter to Molotov and waited for the fireworks from Washington. Churchill included no explanation or justification for his decision to charge ahead in defiance of the White House, only a line to say that he was thinking of going for three or four days in the last week of May. Eisenhower promptly advised him not to go and expressed astonishment at his willingness to meet the Soviets on their home ground, which they were likely to take as a sign of weakness. Churchill retorted that he meant to proceed in any case. This time, he did not merely ignore the President's objections; he disputed them point by point. He argued that the Western allies would gain more immediate good will by going as Moscow's guests than they would lose by seeming to court the Soviets. Taunting Eisenhower, whose refusal to face the Soviets he attributed to fear, Churchill asserted that he was 'not afraid' of risking his own reputation if he believed there was a chance of advancing the cause of peace.

Churchill went on to suggest that the only way for Eisenhower to stop him was to join him. 'Of course, I would much rather go with you to any place you might appoint and that is, I believe, the best chance of a good result.' His sole concession was to defer to Eisenhower's concern that by going to Moscow in May Churchill might jeopardize the President's budget in Congress. Churchill promised to put off his trip until late June, after the coronation. 'Perhaps by then,' he suggested, 'you may feel able to propose some combined action.'

Four days later, Churchill turned up the heat on Eisenhower. He opened a two-day foreign affairs debate in the House of Commons on 11 May by making their disagreement public in a powerful speech that recalled his greatest wartime efforts. After declaring that the US would have done well to have heeded British advice in 1945, he made a dramatic announcement: 'It is the policy of Her Majesty's Government to avoid by every means in their power doing anything or saying anything which could check any favourable reaction that may be taking place and to welcome every sign of improvement in our relations with Russia.'

The previous month, Eisenhower had undertaken to define the West's Soviet strategy. Now, the Prime Minister boldly laid out his own, very different approach in full view of the entire world. In a stunning challenge to Eisenhower, Churchill called for immediate talks at the highest level without agenda or preconditions, and he goaded the Americans by insisting that he could not see why anyone should be 'frightened' of a summit meeting. At worst, he said, the participants would have established more intimate contacts. At best, the world might have a generation of peace.

In the days that followed, the world press blazed with news of an open rift between London and Washington, and of Churchill's surprise bid for 'the diplomatic leadership of the Western world'. In a press conference on 14 May, Eisenhower rejected Churchill's proposal by reiterating that he would need to see hard evidence of Soviet intentions before he could consider top-level talks. His anger at the position Churchill had put him in was on display at a meeting of the National Security Council on 20 May. Warned by Henry Cabot Lodge, US Ambassador to the United Nations, that unless he did something quickly he would lose the initiative gained in his 'great' speech of 16 April, Eisenhower shot back that Churchill's manoeuvres to get a summit meeting made him wonder whether the Prime Minister's 'faculties and judgement were not deteriorating'.

Many Britons, by contrast, saw the 11 May speech as evidence that their leader was again at his best. Having lived through two world wars and having experienced what it means to be attacked at home, they were eager to test every possible chance for peace. Though Churchill's speech had its detractors, especially within his own party, even his critics could not deny that the broader public strongly backed him on this. Alone among Western leaders, Churchill appeared to have boldly seized the moment. As Viscount Stansgate said in the House of Lords, 'Sir Winston Churchill made a speech which suddenly put into the hearts of the people of this country that feeling of proud confidence in his leadership that we had at the time of the Battle of Britain.' Churchill's declaration of diplomatic independence dovetailed beautifully with the wave of renewed patriotic fervour associated with the coronation. The British were tired of always having to follow America's lead in world affairs. They took pleasure in the spectacle of Churchill taunting mighty Washington, and they delighted in his insistence that the US would have been wise to heed British advice at the end of the war. The speech also earned high marks throughout Europe, where popular sentiment favoured a summit meeting.

Eisenhower, meanwhile, knew what the world did not: that if he refused to participate in a summit meeting, Churchill planned to see the Soviets alone in June. Should that happen, Eisenhower would find himself cast as an obstacle to peace, rather than its champion. Desperate to regain control of the situation, Eisenhower leaped at a request by French premier René Mayer on 20 May for an early personal meeting with his American and British counterparts. Given Churchill's predilection for three-power talks on the old Churchill–Roosevelt–Stalin model, the French were nervous that they could find themselves excluded from a summit meeting where the fate of Germany was decided. By arranging to confer with Eisenhower and

Churchill beforehand, Mayer sought to ensure his country's place at the table. Eisenhower called Churchill that night at about 11 p.m. London time. He said that Mayer needed their answer by the next day, when he hoped to announce the allies' talks to the French National Assembly.

Churchill loved the idea of a meeting, but he pretended not to hear when the President suggested that it take place in Maine. Eager to be perceived as hosting the conference, Churchill suggested that the leaders assemble in Bermuda – on British territory. Though Eisenhower guessed that Churchill had heard him perfectly well, he tentatively accepted Bermuda as the venue. The President did, however, take care to stipulate and confirm in writing that the Bermuda talks were in no way a preliminary to four-power talks with the Soviets. He saw the meeting, and he made it clear that he expected Churchill to see it as well, strictly as a forum in which to discuss their common problems. Churchill solemnly agreed.

When Churchill faced the Cabinet the next day he was 'in a mood of almost schoolboy enthusiasm'. Far from having Churchill in his hand, Eisenhower had presented him with an opportunity both to portray the British as driving events and to make his case for a parley at the summit directly to the President. A number of ministers were not without ambivalence. Salisbury in particular was 'frankly scep-tical' about Churchill's claims of a change of heart at the Kremlin. Might it merely be that the Soviet Union's new rulers were seeking 'a quiet time in which to find their feet'? He was also distressed that Churchill had failed to consult the Cabinet in advance of his summit proposal. Nevertheless, when Churchill recounted his telephone conversations with Eisenhower, Salisbury chimed in approvingly, 'Eisenhower has followed the PM's lead.'

Salisbury saw Eisenhower's decision to call an allies' meeting as 'a direct result' of the 11 May speech. While he persisted in his disapproval of Churchill's failure to check in first, he could not help but be pleased that Britain, and therefore the West, had gained the initiative in foreign affairs. A 'completely negative attitude', such as Eisenhower had taken, would have left the initiative with Moscow. That, Salisbury believed, would have been very bad indeed.

News of the conference to be held in Bermuda was met with a tremendous reception in the House of Commons later that day. Attlee asked whether it might, perhaps, be a preliminary to talks with Malenkov. Hours after Churchill had assured Eisenhower that they were in full agreement about the purposes of the conference, he sang a different song in public. 'Yes, sir, it is my hope that we may take a definite step towards a meeting of far greater import,' Churchill said, to shouts of approbation from nearly every corner of the House. The cheers from the Labour benches appeared to be the loudest despite the socialists' concern that Churchill had stolen their political thunder. With his answer, Churchill transformed the Bermuda conference into precisely what Eisenhower had stipulated it must not be. From this point on, it would be up to the Americans to counter the perception of Bermuda as the prelude to a summit meeting.

Five months had passed since Eisenhower, in New York, had moved to shut Churchill out by declaring that he intended to meet Stalin alone. In the interim, Churchill had argued, cozened, cajoled, threatened, and, finally, muscled his way back into the game.

XVI

The Abdication of Diocletian

Buckingham Palace, 1953

Shortly before midnight on 5 June 1953, the Prime Minister's car pulled up at a side entrance to Buckingham Palace. Three days after the Archbishop of Canterbury had placed the heavy crown of Edward the Confessor upon the head of Elizabeth II, she was to preside over a reception for some two thousand envoys, princes and other dignitaries as many of them prepared to leave London. An estimated fifty thousand people waited in front of the Palace to see the guests, who wore all manner of uniforms, evening attire, and jewels. Churchill was swanked out in his dress uniform of Lord Warden of the Cinque Ports. He had a cocked hat, a sword, heavy gold epaulettes, and gold braid, and his chest glittered with medals and a blinding 150-diamond Garter star.

Inside, as Churchill headed to the white-and-gold state ballroom, the detective who accompanied him suggested that he might want to visit the Gents' first.

'Well,' Churchill replied, 'just as a precautionary measure you might be right.'

When Churchill emerged from the men's room, he came face to face with his long-time political foe Aneurin Bevan, on the way in. Bevan had annoyed not a few people by attending the coronation at Westminster Abbey in a business suit, and he was similarly attired this evening. Churchill, whose fondness for uniforms Bevan had been known to mock, stared at him frostily and said, 'You might have taken the trouble to dress correctly on this occasion at least.'

Bevan retreated slightly, surveyed him from top to bottom, and called out, 'Winston, your flies are undone!'

'Do not concern yourself too much about that,' Churchill replied, 'dead birds never fly from their nest.'

He walked off, doing up his trousers as he went.

Churchill was in a wonderful mood that night, and he was not about to let anyone spoil his pleasure. Nobody truly believed that he would retire now that the coronation festivities were drawing to a close. Instead, he was headed to Bermuda with overwhelming popular support – and then, if all went well, back to the summit.

In recent days, as he played a prominent part in the royal rituals (and as he fought off the waves of fatigue that had nearly prevented him from attending the coronation), he was also working methodically to keep up the post-11 May momentum. He had leaned on the Soviets to break the deadlock over the prisoner exchange in Korea that threatened to provide the White House with an excuse to reject a summit meeting. He had been in contact not only with Molotov, but also, for the first time, with the little-known Malenkov. He had sold the concept of East–West talks to the visiting Commonwealth prime ministers, so that when he reached Bermuda he could tell Eisenhower that he was speaking not just for himself but also for them.

Even if Churchill had been of a mind to hand over power, he could hardly have done so when the second-in-command whose political interests he had pledged to protect was too ill to replace him. On 5 June, Churchill had begun his day with a trip to the airport to bid farewell to an emaciated Anthony Eden as he left for the US to undergo the operation his new American doctor described as the only hope of saving his life. If Eden survived, he was likely to be out of commission for much of 1953. Under the circumstances, none of the Cabinet ministers who had plotted to force Churchill out in favour of Eden would have been pleased to see Churchill go. That did not mean there was not acute nervousness among them about, in Macmillan's words, the 'big game' he was playing. Was it all about to degenerate into a high-risk game of chicken? Churchill was confident that, face to face, he would be able to change Eisenhower's mind. But what if he was wrong?

When they met at Epsom Downs the next day, Macmillan and Salisbury discussed their concerns about what Churchill would do if Eisenhower proved to be as obstinate as he was. Macmillan, who, unlike Salisbury, knew Eisenhower well, was of the opinion that the President 'would not trust himself' to go to a high-level meeting. In contrast to Churchill, who preferred to do everything himself, Eisenhower's modus operandi was to work 'through' others. That afternoon, the sun shone brightly and by some estimates the crowd was the largest and quite possibly the noisiest in Epsom history. Queen Elizabeth had arrived in the royal train with Prince Philip, Princess Margaret, the Queen Mother, and other members of the royal family. Churchill, who as usual had been late to get started, had had to be driven post-haste on the wrong side of the road to get him to Epsom in time to watch the race from the Queen's box. As it happened, Elizabeth II had a horse of her own in the competition. The co-favourites in a field of twenty-nine were the Queen's chestnut colt Aureole and Sir Victor Sassoon's brown colt Pinza. The latter was to be ridden by the forty-nine-year-old Gordon Richards, whom many racing enthusiasts regarded as the finest jockey of all time. Now approaching retirement, Richards had won more races than any of his peers. One accomplishment had long eluded him, however: he had yet to win a Derby. That changed when Pinza won by four lengths and Richards was called from the winner's enclosure to receive the Queen's congratulations.

In the midst of the excitement, Macmillan and Salisbury talked of Churchill's recent efforts to set the seal on his own career. Salisbury worried that Churchill would go ahead and meet the Soviets even if he failed to win over Eisenhower. In his view, a summit meeting without Eisenhower would be hugely destructive to the Anglo-American alliance. Macmillan opined that that would be 'a most serious step' which could not be taken in the absence of Cabinet approval. After the Derby, Salisbury communicated his concerns in a private letter to Churchill. He suggested that the present state of public opinion in the US made a joint approach unlikely. And he argued that even if there was enormous pressure from the British left to go on alone and even if Eisenhower showed 'an understanding attitude', Churchill must resist the 'great temptation' of a bilateral meeting with Malenkov. 'I am sure that the only safe line is to move only on all fours with the Americans, prodding them no doubt at intervals but never advancing without them.'

To Churchill's frustration, the Bermuda talks, which were to have taken place in the middle of June, had to be postponed twice due to the fall of the Mayer Government. Finally, though a new regime had yet to materialize in Paris, he and Eisenhower agreed to a firm set of dates. Churchill would arrive in Bermuda on 6 July and welcome Eisenhower there the next day. Presumably by then France would have a new leader, who would be arriving as well.

On the evening of Tuesday, 23 June, a week before he was due to sail, Churchill undertook one last formal engagement, presiding over a large dinner party in honour of Alcide de Gasperi, the Italian Prime Minister. Though Churchill had seemed fatigued earlier in the day, he held forth with brio, delighting his guests with a witty after-dinner speech about the Roman conquest of Britain. Later, the ebullient host was making his way to the door of the drawing room in what appeared to be good health when he slumped suddenly into the nearest chair. A number of people assumed that he simply had had too much champagne. The art historian Kenneth Clark suspected something else. Clark, who had been asked to the Gasperi dinner because he spoke fluent Italian, instructed his wife to sit beside Churchill while he looked for Mary Soames.

Churchill, barely able to move, clutched Jane Clark's hand and said, 'I want the hand of a friend. They put too much on me. Foreign affairs . . .' After that, his voice drifted off.

Christopher Soames dashed to Churchill's side, and moved quickly to bring the evening to an end. He warned Clementine Churchill that Winston could not walk and that they would have to wait until the room was cleared before they could get him to bed. Signor de Gasperi and the others were told only that their host was over-tired. On her husband's instructions, Mary Soames did her best to keep any of the guests from talking to her father, whose speech was slurred and incoherent. At last, Churchill, leaning heavily on Jock Colville's arm, struggled to his room. The doctor who had warned him either to retire immediately or lighten his load if he hoped to avoid another stroke was nowhere to be found. Colville left a message asking Moran to come in the morning.

When Churchill awoke the next day, his mouth sagged on the left side, particularly when he tried to speak, and he remained unsteady on his feet. When Moran examined him, he said that there had been a spasm of a small artery. The episode appeared to be similar to the one in 1949 in the South of France, but it would take a few days to be certain. For the moment all they could do was wait and see how his condition developed.

Immediately, Churchill approached Moran's preliminary diag-nosis as he would a negotiation. As he had lately done with Eisenhower, and with countless other opponents through the years, Churchill seized on the words that appealed to him and ignored the rest. Moran had suggested that the incident might be a reprise of 1949; as far as Churchill was concerned, so it must be. The first stroke had been minor. He had had a relatively quick recovery and had gone on from there to recapture the premiership. At a moment when Churchill was finally about to make his case to Eisenhower, he was not prepared to entertain the possibility that this new episode could in fact be the major stroke of which he had long been warned. He was intent on recovering in time to sail on Tuesday.

Hardly had Moran left Number Ten with a promise to come back later when Churchill asked to be helped down to the Cabinet Room. In spite of everything, he meant to preside over the Cabinet. He planned to be seated in his usual chair in front of the fireplace before the others came in so they would not have a chance to see him walk. And he intended to say as little as possible, the droop in the left side of his mouth being more prominent when he spoke. The point was to show himself to his colleagues and to act as if nothing were wrong.

For the most part, he succeeded. Salisbury, who had been at the Gasperi dinner, took his customary place on the Prime Minister's left and appeared to notice nothing. Butler, who also had been present the night before, registered only that the Prime Minister seemed more taciturn than usual. Macmillan, though he thought Churchill unusually pale, was not alarmed. Only later did Macmillan suspect the significance of something Churchill said to him in the course of the Cabinet: 'Harold, you might draw the blind down a little, will you?' Crookshank alone would later insist that he suspected the Prime Minister had had a stroke, but if he really thought that he did not mention it at the time.

Moran returned that afternoon accompanied by Brain. Again, Moran stressed that it would be some days before they could be certain how serious matters were. When Churchill announced plans to answer Prime Minister's Questions in the House of Commons, the doctor warned against it. Obstinacy had got Churchill through the Cabinet earlier, but that was no guarantee things might not get worse at any time. Moran cautioned that when Churchill rose to speak, the wrong words might come out – or no words at all. Still Churchill kept insisting he would go. He acted as if to acknowledge the doctor's warnings would also be to accept that this might not be the minor incident he was determined it must be. Moran persisted; and finally, rather than seem to give in, Churchill called for a list of the questions and quickly pronounced them unimportant. He made it clear that he was cancelling his appearance not because of anything the doctor had said. He planned to remain in seclusion at Number Ten and wait for the symptoms to pass.

He did not improve; far from it. On Thursday morning, Churchill's speech was thick and his ability to walk had deteriorated. He wanted to attend another Cabinet later in the day, when he was expected to fulfil his promise to Salisbury to fully discuss Bermuda and hear the views of his colleagues. When Moran suggested that it would be best to put this off, Churchill dug in. Only after the doctor mentioned that the drooping left side of his face would attract notice did Churchill relent. Salisbury, Butler, and other ministers had tried to push him out in the past. He was reluctant to let them see his condition and feel emboldened – certainly not when he would soon be better. So he agreed to postpone until the Monday.

At this point, Moran remained unsure of just how the situation would develop. There might indeed still be a chance that Churchill's formidable powers of resilience and recuperation would permit him to sail. But if he were to carry on, it was important that he stay out of sight until he looked and felt better. Concealing his condition was almost impossible as long as he remained at Number Ten. It would all be much easier if he were to hide out at Chartwell. Churchill initially resisted the suggestion. If he were to leave London unexpectedly, would that not create suspicion? Finally he gave in, and Lady Churchill went on ahead to prepare the house for his arrival. To explain the Prime Minister's sudden departure it was announced that he was going off to prepare for his talks with Eisenhower. The plan was to return for the Monday Cabinet and sail the next day.

At about noon, Churchill emerged from Number Ten in plain sight of any members of the press or public who happened to be outside. Happily, he was able to walk unaided to his car and his condition went undetected. Colville accompanied him on the trip, and en route Churchill gave strict orders that no one was to be told that he was 'temporarily incapacitated'. He directed Colville to see to it that the Government continued to operate as though he were still in complete control. Churchill was going to Chartwell to rest and recover, but by the time they got there his condition had worsened substantially. He could not get out of the car or walk to the house without help. Had he left London just a bit later, people would have seen his incapacity and the game would have been up.

In defiance of Churchill's instructions, Colville contacted three press barons who were the Prime Minister's friends. Lords Beaverbrook, Bracken, and Camrose came at once to Chartwell, where they hatched a plan to keep the news of the stroke out of the papers. While they were there, the hope remained that if Churchill could be got onto the waiting ship he might yet have enough time at sea to recover sufficiently for the Bermuda conference. By Thursday night, it became apparent that in the absence of a miracle there could be no question of his meeting Eisenhower and little, apparently, of his remaining in office. His left side was now partly paralysed and he had lost the use of his left arm.

When Moran examined his patient on Friday morning, he determined that the thrombosis was spreading. Seventy-two hours before, Churchill had been hoping to move nations and save the world. Now, he found it difficult just to turn over in bed. No amount of willpower or positive thinking had been capable of halting the slow spread of the paralysis. Churchill had been unable to out-talk and outwit his body. The force of facts had reasserted itself: he had sustained a serious stroke and even he acknowledged that Bermuda had to be cancelled. Recovery – if he did recover – was going to take much more than a weekend in the country.

Under ordinary circumstances, there would have been no doubt that Eden's moment had come at last. The trouble was that the heir apparent was then in the US recovering from an eight-hour operation, which he had been given only a fifty-fifty chance of surviving. Eden was not scheduled to leave his Boston hospital until the following week, when he planned to travel to Newport, Rhode Island, to recuperate at the home of friends. Even if everything went smoothly, it would be at least October before he could return to work. Whether he would ever really be able to resume his burdens was an open question. Eden's American doctor had warned the British Ambassador to the US, Sir Roger Makins, that there was only a ten per cent chance of full recovery.

Eden's predicament gave Churchill room to manoeuvre. Even now, he was determined not to have to resign. Were it to be announced that Churchill had had a major stroke, he surely would have to hand over, if not to Eden then to Butler or some other successor. Instead, Churchill decided, in a favourite phrase, to 'pig it'. He would try to get away with holding on to power by keeping his true medical condition a secret. As he was likely to be out of commission for some time, there would have to be a public explanation, as well as some mechanism for running the Government in his absence. To the first end, Moran prepared a medical bulletin that attempted to explain why the Prime Minister who had fought so hard for a conference in Bermuda would suddenly bow to his doctors' order to cancel it.

Of course, Moran said nothing about a stroke. Instead, he wrote that Churchill had suffered 'a disturbance of the cerebral circulation' which had resulted in 'attacks of giddiness'. Both Moran and Brain signed the statement, which could not be released until after Eisenhower had been notified that Bermuda was off. Thereupon the physicians left Chartwell and the politicians took over.

At times, Churchill could barely make his words understood, yet the wheels in his brain were still spinning furiously. On Friday, urgent messages were delivered to the two adversaries most likely to rush in upon him when they learned he was wounded. Rather than keep them in the dark for as long as possible, he made sure they were among the very first to know. Salisbury was in London preparing to go off to lunch with a friend when he received a note which Colville had written in his own hand the previous evening.

Salisbury immediately cancelled his engagement and went to Chartwell. Butler was at the bedside of his dying mother when the summons reached him. He too left at once.

The Lord President and the Chancellor arrived to find the family in tears. When Churchill appeared for a late lunch, the effects of the stroke were manifest. In halting, often tortured conversation, he frankly laid out the details of his ordeal and raised the question of the future of his premiership. Given the company, Churchill was playing a dangerous game. If at any time either Salisbury or Butler insisted that Churchill's stroke be made known to the country he would only be saying what was right and proper. If either or both men chose to go public with the information, there was nothing Churchill could do to stop them. Once the news was out, there would be no way to hang on long enough to recover. He would have little choice but to retire. For the moment, if he hoped to keep his job the only card he had to play was his well-honed understanding of his guests' complicated and conflicting personal interests.

Churchill claimed to want to hold on only until Eden was well enough to return to England. He insisted that when Eden reappeared, probably in October, he would of course step aside. He cast his actions as an effort to serve not his own interests but Eden's. He pretended that, sick as he was, he was determined not to let Anthony down. If Churchill left office while Eden was incapacitated, someone else would get the top job, and that would not be fair to Eden – his 'rightful deputy', as he pointedly informed Butler.

But, Churchill went on, he could only protect Eden if he could conceal that he had had a major stroke and if he could devolve his duties to others. As Parliament was due to begin its summer recess at the end of July, there was reason to believe that together he and his lunch guests might bring off the ruse. Churchill asked them to take on the major burden of his duties. He invited Butler to fill in as head of government. In addition to his present responsibilities as Chancellor of the Exchequer, Butler would preside over the Cabinet

220

and, along with the Lord Privy Seal, Harry Crookshank, share responsibility for making any statements or answering Questions in the House of Commons. Churchill asked Salisbury to oversee foreign affairs. Since Salisbury was in the Lords, the Foreign Secretary's chores in the Commons would fall to Butler as well.

The moment of decision had come. On the face of it, that either Salisbury or Butler would do as Churchill asked seemed improbable. Even cast as a selfless action, the proposal was outrageous. Of course the country ought not to be deceived. Of course the Prime Minister should step aside now that he was unable to carry out his duties. Salisbury had been scheming to unseat him since 1945. Was this not the perfect moment to force Churchill into retirement? As for Butler, he too had plotted, both with fellow Conservatives and with Labour members interested in a coalition. Butler had long been frustrated by the wisdom that the Tory succession was fixed. Was he not likely to welcome a chance to seize the leadership at a moment when Eden was out of the country and out of commission? Why should he agree to keep the seat warm for his rival?

Actually, there were some very good reasons. For one thing, Butler's background as an appeaser threatened to make it impossible for him to form a Government at this point. While he had his supporters among Conservatives, he also had important detractors, like Salisbury, who had yet to forgive his position in the 1930s. If, however, Butler were to chivalrously step aside, he would build up future credit with the party. Besides, there was always the chance that Eden's health might prevent him from returning to work in the autumn. In that case, Butler, having won the gratitude of the Edenites and having proven his loyalty to the party, might be in a position to step in sooner than expected.

Butler agreed to assist Churchill, but his cooperation would mean nothing if Salisbury refused to go along. Salisbury was a stickler for rules and decorum. It seemed inconceivable that this most punctilious and respectable of men would even consider Churchill's proposal.

Still, the scheme had its attractions. Salisbury had striven for years to install Eden at Number Ten. Now the premiership threatened to fall into Butler's hands. In that case, Eden would hardly be the only one to suffer. Were the prize to go to Rab Butler, Salisbury was unlikely to enjoy the influence he sought in a new Conservative Government.

When Salisbury agreed to the cover-up, he was consenting to participate in precisely the sort of behaviour for which he had often criticized Churchill. As ever, Salisbury preferred to avoid the lime-light, so he asked not to be named Acting Foreign Secretary. He would be available to consult on foreign affairs while Minister of State Selwyn Lloyd would assume responsibility for day-to-day Foreign Office business. Churchill had no problem with this arrange-ment. The important thing was to feel that he had Salisbury safely in the meshes. He also wanted to be in a position to ask one other crucial favour.

Churchill was distraught that, as a consequence of his paralysis, the momentum which had derived from his speech of 11 May had been interrupted. It seemed to him, however, that the interruption need not necessarily be fatal. He had yet to tell Eisenhower that Bermuda had to be scratched, but when he did he wanted to be able to say that Salisbury was prepared to travel to Washington to express the British (i.e. Churchill's) point of view on the next step with the Soviets. Churchill was asking Salisbury in effect to represent a policy with which the Lord President privately disagreed. In the guise of protecting Eden's future, Churchill was using Salisbury, really, to safe-guard his own. He needed Salisbury, of all men, to help keep his summit proposal alive. He could not hope to secure the last prize without him.

Salisbury signed up to visit Washington in the event that the Americans agreed to a meeting. He did not, however, believe that the medical report, which Churchill planned to send along with his message to Eisenhower, ought to read quite as it did. It was not that he thought Moran had gone too far in his obfuscations; in Salisbury's view, the doctor had not gone far enough. Moran had spoken of a 'cerebral disturbance'. Salisbury worried that such language pointed all too clearly to a stroke. It was well known that Churchill had been functioning as both Prime Minister and Foreign Secretary in Eden's absence. Salisbury and Butler revised the medical report to say simply that Churchill had had no respite from his arduous duties for a long time and was in need of a complete rest; his physicians had therefore advised him to lighten his burdens and rest for at least a month. In the ministers' opinion this was all that the public, or Eisenhower for that matter, need be told.

By the end of lunch, Churchill had transformed both adversaries into ardent enablers. This time, rather than set the birds against one another, he had insidiously encouraged them to fly in formation. Despite their clashing purposes, everyone was supposedly doing this for Anthony. Having bought himself time to recover, Churchill picked up a beaker of brandy with his good arm and gingerly raised it to his twisted mouth.

For all of Churchill's cold tenacity, it soon looked as if his efforts might have been for naught. That evening, his condition worsened to the point that Moran told Colville he did not know if the Prime Minister would live through the weekend. Churchill continued to decline overnight. On Saturday, he could barely stand when the doctor got him out of bed. Suddenly, his good hand seemed to be affected, provoking concern that his right side was about to stiffen as well. The house was filled with gloom, but somehow Clementine maintained her spirits and concentrated on trying to make her husband and family comfortable. Randolph arrived at midday and Sarah was called home from America. Churchill appeared to have given up hope and the end seemed near.

On Sunday, he rallied. Though the left arm and leg remained frozen, Moran judged that the thrombosis was no longer on the move. Beaverbrook came to lunch and reminded Churchill of his complete recovery after his previous stroke. He was fibbing, of course, when he claimed that Churchill was hardly as bad as he had been in 1949, but his words seemed to have an effect. After lunch, Churchill refused his wheelchair and, though he required a helper on each side, he insisted on walking to his room. It was the first of many goals he was to set for himself. As he lurched forward, the toes of his lifeless left foot dragged on the carpet. When he finally reached his bed he dropped from the exertion – but he had made it.

At the Cabinet meeting on Monday, Butler disclosed that, contrary to the sanitized medical bulletin released two days previously, Churchill had suffered a serious stroke. When they heard the news, some of the very men who had intrigued to force Churchill out wept openly or fought back tears. Butler warned that the Prime Minister's condition must be kept secret. He went on to detail the arrangements that had been agreed to on Friday to carry on Government business. Salisbury spoke of Churchill's request that he be available to go to Washington. In the interim, Salisbury had heard twice from Dulles, agreeing to an 'intermediate' meeting of British, American, and French foreign ministers, which would be 'preparatory to a Bermuda meeting later'. Salisbury thought he should accept and the ministers concurred.

Cabinet Secretary Norman Brook went to see Churchill for himself the next day. On Tuesday, 30 June, Brook and Colville dined with the Prime Minister, who was in a wheelchair. After the meal, Churchill announced that he intended to stand without assistance. The others advised him not to try, but there was no stopping him. When his guests positioned themselves on either side for safety's sake, he warned them away with his stick. Then he lowered both feet to the floor, clutched the arms of his chair and slowly, painfully, purposefully hoisted himself up as sweat poured down his face. At last, having shown what he was still capable of, he sat and returned to his cigar. Brook viewed the scene as a demonstration of the refusal to accept defeat that had served Britain so well in the war: 'As he had done for the nation in 1940, so he did for his own life in 1953. He was determined to recover.'

Once Beaverbrook had spoken of complete recovery, Churchill made that his mantra. He could no longer pretend that he had had another minor stroke, but he could focus on all that he had managed to accomplish since the earlier episode. As far as Churchill was concerned, there was no reason it should be any different this time. The previous Friday, he had attempted to keep his stroke a secret from Eisenhower. (The medical bulletin had not fooled the President, who guessed immediately that there was something far more serious involved.) Now, Churchill took a different tack. He wrote to Eisenhower on 1 July, 'Four years ago in 1949, I had another similar attack and was for a good many days unable to sign my name. As I was out of Office I kept this secret and have managed to work through two General Elections and a lot of other business since. I am therefore not without hope of pursuing my theme a little longer but it will be a few weeks before any opinions can be formed. I am glad to say I am already making progress.' In the same strain he informed Macmillan, who came to dine the following day, 'I have had a stroke. Did you know it was the second? I had one in 1949, and fought two elections after that.'

During the weekend of 4–5 July, Churchill had a major breakthrough. Exactly one week before, it had seemed as if the old escapologist had finally run out of rope. Now he managed to walk a short distance unaided and he vowed to accomplish a bit more daily. These efforts left him exhausted and in a considerable amount of pain, but he refused to give up, intent on regaining the full use of his limbs and becoming again the man he had been before the stroke. It had long been Churchill's goal to return to the summit; it looked as if he meant to drag himself there if necessary.

As Churchill battled his way back to health, he was also micro-managing the preparations for the Washington talks. He dictated a long, lucid statement that set out what he hoped Salisbury would be able to accomplish on his behalf in the US. Although the European Defence Community proposal had originated in France, the idea of a rearmed Germany in any form remained highly controversial for many Frenchmen. As a consequence, the French had still not ratified the EDC. Churchill was convinced, however, that a rearmed Germany would put the West in a stronger position to negotiate with Moscow. He wanted Salisbury to go to Washington with two key goals: to press the French to ratify the EDC by October, and to get the Americans and the French to agree that as soon as ratification occurred, they would call for a top-level meeting with the Soviets before the end of the year.

On 6 July, two days before Salisbury was to fly to the US, he read the Prime Minister's statement aloud to the Cabinet. The ministers agreed that it would be Salisbury's mission to pursue the aims set out in Churchill's paper. The following night, Salisbury and his wife dined at Chartwell, where Churchill briefed him additionally for two hours. Salisbury by this time had had to agree to a good deal more than he had originally bargained for. The Opposition had baulked at an arrangement that divided responsibility for foreign affairs, with no one individual clearly in charge. Salisbury therefore had reluctantly accepted the title of Acting Foreign Secretary. He had had no choice if the cover-up was to work.

At this point, it seemed to Churchill that every sign pointed to success in Washington. Eisenhower had written to assure him that he looked upon the cancellation of Bermuda as only 'a temporary deferment of our meeting'. And now, as the Washington talks were about to begin, the President responded favourably to a reporter's question about whether in view of Churchill's health he might be willing to go to London. At a time when it looked as if Churchill's remaining days in office were limited, Eisenhower could afford to seem gracious. Churchill, however, was quick to pounce on the President's offhand comments. As though a decision had already been made in Washington, he spoke enthusiastically to his doctor of Eisenhower's impending visit and of the favourite dish of Irish stew Clemmie would have prepared for him.

Also propitious from the vantage point of Chartwell was the excellent press Salisbury, a little-known figure in America, received on his arrival. He was billed as a major opponent of the appeasers in the run-up to the Second World War, an image that promised to lend credibility when he made the controversial case for talks with Stalin's successors. There was some perplexity in the US press about Salisbury's rumoured differences with Churchill over the usefulness of a parley at the summit. As soon as the Acting Foreign Secretary emerged from the plane at National Airport, he therefore made it clear in conversations with reporters that he had come to argue for early four-power talks.

Before the foreign secretaries had even had a chance to confer, some startling news from Moscow scrambled everyone's calculations. The number two man, Lavrenti Beria, had been arrested as a traitor. His fall raised important questions about the stability of the new joint leadership. With things so unsettled, was this really the moment to talk to the Soviets? Who was to say that Malenkov might not be the next to go? Churchill would liken the Soviet succession struggle to a 'bulldog fight under a rug'. 'An outsider only hears the growling,' Churchill declared, 'and when he sees the bones fly out from beneath it is obvious who has won.' But at this point, nothing was obvious yet, and Salisbury drily observed that Beria's arrest did not make his task in Washington easier.

At the first session, on 10 July, Salisbury moved at once to turn the uncertain situation to Britain's advantage. He nimbly argued that the lack of clarity about events at the Kremlin since Stalin's death was precisely why Churchill had called for early contact with the new Soviet leaders, who were themselves such 'an unknown quantity'. As Salisbury explained, Churchill saw a meeting as an opportunity to explore their minds in an effort to understand what was really going on in Moscow. Salisbury urged Dulles and French Foreign Minister Georges Bidault at least to agree in principle to the desirability of leaders' talks 'when practicable'.

Salisbury's counterparts would not hear of it. Where Churchill sought a top-level encounter, the Americans and the French joined forces to propose a meeting at the foreign ministers' level. Where Churchill was adamant on the need to have a card to play with the Soviets in the form of a German army, Dulles and Bidault were ready to see Molotov before the EDC had been ratified. When it became evident that Salisbury was not about to budge them, he cabled London for instructions.

Churchill's blood rose when he learned where things stood. Since 1945, when Truman, Attlee, and Stalin had concluded the Potsdam Conference by handing off the most contentious questions (including Germany) to foreign ministers, Churchill had often made that tactic the target of his shafts; as far as he was concerned, history had amply vindicated him. Yet here were the US and France demanding more of the same. Churchill instructed Butler to convey his view to the Cabinet that any talks were better than none and that Salisbury should ask that the allies at least keep an open mind to the possibility that Churchill, Eisenhower, and Malenkov would meet later.

At London's direction, Salisbury pressed strongly, but to no avail. When in the end the Washington communiqué spoke only of foreign ministers' talks, Churchill commented disgustedly, 'They've bitched things up.' That, at any rate, was what he said privately at Chartwell. He adopted a very different tone in a telegram to Eisenhower on 17 July.

Churchill informed the President that he had made a great deal of progress physically, that he could now walk about, and that the doctors thought he might be well enough to appear in public in September. 'Meanwhile, I am still conducting business.' Indeed he was. Though the Washington communiqué had made no mention of leaders' talks to follow, Churchill craftily wrote as if Eisenhower had already accepted that the top men would come in later: 'Please consider at your leisure whether it might not be better for the Four-Power Meeting to begin, as Salisbury urged, with a preliminary survey by the Heads of

Governments of all our troubles in an informal spirit. I am sure that gives a much better chance than if we only come in after a vast new network of detail has been erected.'

While Churchill waited for Eisenhower's reply, he confronted the problem of how to present the Washington agreement to the House of Commons. Obviously, there would be much disappointment with the mission's failure. Churchill was inclined to truthfully inform the House that Salisbury had agreed to foreign ministers' talks only after it became clear that the US and France would not accept the British proposal. The Foreign Office objected to this approach on the grounds that it would give offence to Washington and Paris. So, when Butler dined at Chartwell on the evening of 19 July to go over his speech, the wording he and the Prime Minister agreed on made a tortuous case for the supposed continuity between Churchill's 11 May address and the Washington communiqué.

Butler's speech on 21 July was a fiasco. The Opposition bayed that in spite of anything the Chancellor said, foreign ministers' talks were far from what Churchill had proposed. Attlee spoke of the great hopes that the 11 May speech had aroused and of the way in which the Washington talks had dashed those hopes by reverting to an approach that had failed in the past. The Labour member Ian Mikardo accused Butler and Salisbury of having sold out Churchill on behalf of a broader Conservative conspiracy against the Prime Minister. According to Mikardo, as soon as Churchill fell ill 'the lesser men all round him got to work to tear down what he had been trying to build up. It was the mediocrities of the Conservative Party, the same people who had kept the Prime Minister out of office for all those years before the war, who seized the opportunity presented by his illness to betray those hopes.'

In his absence, Salisbury came in for some particularly harsh personal abuse. Labour members gleefully mocked him as 'limp' and untrustworthy, and claimed he had gone to Washington not to serve Churchill's Soviet initiative but rather to sink it. Part of this, naturally, was an effort by Labour, which had recently been weakened by party infighting of its own, to wreak similar havoc among the Tories by dividing Churchill from his party. But Labour also had reason to be suspicious of Salisbury. They knew of his opposition to the whole idea of top-level talks as articulated by Churchill. They had no inkling, however, of his and Butler's compact with Churchill or of both men's motives for faithfully doing the Prime Minister's bidding while they waited for Eden to regain his health. Contrary to Labour claims, Salisbury and Butler had made no effort to take advantage of the Prime Minister's illness. Ironically, it was Churchill who had used Eden's malady to neutralize the Lord President and the Chancellor.

At Chartwell, Churchill was impatient to hear how Butler's address had been received. Unable to reach either Colville or Soames, he finally managed to talk to Buchan-Hepburn on the phone. Hardly had he received a preliminary account of the debate, in which both sides had vied to associate themselves with his summit proposal, when he heard back from Eisenhower, who fully and finally rejected it. Eisenhower pretended to have believed that the four-power meeting agreed to in Washington was consonant with what Churchill had wanted. He assured Churchill that it was all he would have consented to in Bermuda in any event. 'I like to meet on a very informal basis with those whom I can trust as friends. That is why I was so glad at the prospect of a Bermuda meeting. But it is a very different matter to meet informally with those who may use a meeting only to embarrass and entrap.'

Salisbury came to Chartwell on 23 July to report on the Washington talks. He painted a vivid and disturbing picture. Since the 1952 presidential election campaign, the assumption in London had been that Dulles must be behind Eisenhower's more extreme foreign policy positions. Salisbury sought to correct that view. Based on what he had seen of the President in Washington, he now believed him to be the source of some of the administration's most dangerous ideas and attitudes. Eisenhower struck Salisbury as more 'violently

Russophobe' even than Dulles. The President spoke of harassing the Soviets 'by every possible means' and of applying a policy of pin-pricks designed to bring down a Communist regime that Washington (though not London) suspected was already on the verge of collapse.

Salisbury and Churchill concurred that this ill-conceived strategy might have the quite unintended effect of setting off a third world war. But they differed sharply on how to follow up on Salisbury's sense that no argument of Churchill's would be capable of persuading Eisenhower to accompany him to the summit. Eisenhower opposed a leaders' meeting on constitutional grounds – the head of state must not argue. Salisbury believed that the danger from Washington made it more important than ever for the British to allow nothing to separate them from their American allies. As far as Salisbury was concerned, Churchill must altogether abandon the idea of seeing Malenkov on his own lest he put at risk Britain's ability to exert a beneficent restraining influence on the US. Churchill vehemently disagreed. For Churchill, the American danger made it more important than ever to get to the Soviet leader himself – before the world situation had a chance to ignite.

On the day of Salisbury's visit, reports in the French and American press quoted French Foreign Minister Bidault to the effect that though Churchill remained intact intellectually he suffered from complete paralysis, and that Eden was therefore urgently flying back from the US. It was true that Eden was due in London presently, but the reasons for his decision to put in an appearance before resuming his recuperation, on a Greek island cruise, were not as reported. In the six weeks since his third operation, Eden had had messages from well-wishers assuring him that Churchill meant to keep his place until October, that Salisbury was working to protect his interests, that Butler did not intend to move against him, and that all in all, his position was secure. Some supporters, however, were of the opinion that Eden would do well to show himself in London before Parliament rose for the summer recess or in early August at the latest. In line with this advice, Eden, who remained far from well, planned to stage a 'triumphal' homecoming on 26 July.

The stories that Churchill was unable to move without assistance so annoyed the Prime Minister that he spontaneously climbed up onto a chair and, as he stood erect with nothing to hold onto, challengingly asked his doctor what he thought of that. Reports that Eden was returning to take over from him prompted Churchill to try to tamp down the worst rumours about his condition. His wife had insisted that the staff at Chartwell must have some respite, so Churchill was set to transfer his base of operations to Chequers on the afternoon of Friday, 24 July. The move provided an opportunity to be photographed in the doorway as he prepared to leave for the three-hour drive from Kent to Buckinghamshire. The carefully staged image of the Prime Minister in a summer suit and bow tie, holding his hat in his right hand and cigar in his left, was his answer to suggestions that he was on his last legs and desperately in need of being replaced. The picture, which was the first the public had seen of Churchill since the stroke, ran in all the Saturday papers, on the eve of Eden's arrival. An accompanying statement from Number Ten announced that Churchill had 'benefited greatly' from a month's rest and that at Chequers he expected to resume more of his normal work.

During this time, the Foreign Office was inundated with frantic telegrams from Eden. He expected to have radio and television coverage at the airport. He wanted photographers present when his plane touched down. These rumblings from America caused concern in both the Eden and Churchill camps that even now Eden might be expecting too much too soon. According to this view, for Eden's own good, he had to be made to understand that in spite of anything he had heard or been led to believe, Churchill was far from ready to lay down his burdens.

Evelyn Shuckburgh wrote to warn Eden that Churchill had begun to speak of plans that went well beyond October. Colville suggested that it would be best if Eden discreetly refrained from mentioning the succession when he and Churchill first met again. Norman Brook sent word that Churchill believed he had been doing Eden a favour by protecting his place and that he would not like to be asked when he could be expected to die.

Churchill was not the only one who was irritated by the timing and circumstances of Eden's return. Eden had signalled the Foreign Office that he intended to speak out about both the Washington talks and the 11 May speech when he faced the press at the airport on Sunday. At a moment when, as a consequence of the foreign affairs debate in the House of Commons, both topics had provoked a public uproar, Salisbury was not eager for Eden to weigh in and perhaps complicate matters. With a week to go before Salisbury had a chance to defend himself in the House of Lords, he urged Eden to keep his opinions to himself for the moment.

Salisbury was waiting at Heathrow Airport when the Edens flew in. As cameras clicked on all sides, Eden's wasted appearance mocked Salisbury's hopes that he would be well enough to replace Churchill in October. A thick coating of Newport tan could not conceal that Eden was a good twenty pounds below his normal weight. Churchill had done more than merely upstage Eden. In the duel of the newspaper photographs, the Prime Minister, who looked the healthier by far, was the clear winner.

When Eden came to Chequers with his wife for lunch the following day, the 'two invalids' (as Colville dubbed them) eyed each other anxiously. Eden was predisposed to discover that Churchill could not last long in office, and Churchill in turn was eager for any sign that Eden was not ready to replace him. Eden's first sight of his host, sporting an enormous Stetson hat and making his way across the lawn unaided, was not encouraging. Throughout the meal, Churchill, who still spoke thickly at times and whose mouth remained slightly crooked, taunted Eden. 'What!' Churchill exclaimed when Eden refused a nip. 'Can't you drink? I can.' At another point,

Churchill assured his niece sympathetically, 'Anthony must get his strength back.'

Churchill had vowed beforehand that should Eden bring up the succession, he would say only that the more he was hustled the longer he would be. Churchill need not have worried – yet. On this first visit, Eden spoke largely of foreign affairs, of Beria's downfall and related subjects. But Eden and his wife, along with Lord and Lady Salisbury and others, were also invited to spend the following long weekend. In spite of further warnings from Butler, Buchan-Hepburn, and Bracken, Eden let it be known to his supporters that he planned to use the occasion to beard Churchill about the handover of power.

On the night of Tuesday, 28 July, Salisbury and Shuckburgh discussed the coming collision as they worked late at Salisbury's London home. For days, Salisbury had been preparing the speech he planned to give in the House of Lords on Wednesday. This was the final run-through. Salisbury was known for his quality of reserve, his distaste for all emotional display. He could not, however, fully mask his agitation over the savage personal attack Labour had mounted against him. Unhappy about finding himself at the centre of public attention, pessimistic about the chances of Eden's recovering in time, and convinced that his own recent exertions might have been for naught, Salisbury was in no mood to pretend yet again that Eden was up to confronting Churchill.

'I have been through all this a hundred times,' Salisbury told Shuckburgh. 'The fact is that the PM is much tougher than Anthony. He very soon brings Anthony to the point beyond which he knows he will not go and then he has won the day.' It was a measure of Salisbury's exasperation that when Shuckburgh said he feared Eden would never get the premiership after all, Salisbury retorted that perhaps Eden's real role in life was to be a great Foreign Secretary – this after Salisbury had been scrambling for a month to finally install him at Number Ten.

Salisbury's performance the next day was pitch-perfect. Of the attack on him in the Commons he fairly dripped with scorn. 'I noted with some interest that I was described as a kind of Jekyll and Hyde, a kind of schizophrenic, at the same time feeble, weak, limp – "limp" I think was the word – and deep, dark and dangerous. Personally I do not want to go into that. I am quite content to leave my character in the hands of your Lordships.' Salisbury did however propose to answer head-on Labour charges that he had sold out Churchill. Mindful of the difficulties the Foreign Office had caused Butler when he was prohibited from attributing the failure of the British initiative to France and the US, Salisbury had previously secured Cabinet permission to place the blame squarely where it belonged.

In the course of his self-defence, Salisbury noted accurately that he had made the case in Washington for top-level talks with the Soviets. But, he went on, the French and the Americans had stood in the way. In short, the initiative had stalled not because of anything he had done but because of the obstructionist tactics of Britain's allies. After the speech, Salisbury was lauded in various quarters for the quintessentially Cecilian forthrightness of his remarks. Such praise had an edge of unintended irony given the circumstances that had led him to agree to travel to Washington in the first place.

As the fateful house party at Chequers drew near, Churchill had a conversation with the American Ambassador, Winthrop Aldrich, that seemed to provide the opening he had been hoping for. Over lunch on Friday, 31 July, Aldrich appeared to confirm Eisenhower's suggestion that in view of Churchill's health Eisenhower was prepared to come to him in London. Suddenly, Churchill saw a way around Eisenhower's unwillingness to risk attending a parley at the summit. While the President was in London, Churchill would seek his authorization to see Malenkov on his own.

By the time the Edens returned to Chequers on Saturday, their host was racing to orchestrate Eisenhower's invitation. The Salisburys were not due until teatime on Sunday. Eden, oblivious to what the Prime Minister was about to attempt, had decided to postpone his climactic face-off with Churchill until the reinforcements arrived. The atmosphere at Chequers was fraught. At Sunday lunch, Churchill and Eden clashed over the wisdom of meeting the Soviets. Clementine Churchill sided with Eden, though obviously for personal rather than policy reasons. She did not want Winston to risk a trip that his doctors feared could cost him his life. Churchill and Eden also differed in their views of Eisenhower, of whom Churchill declared, 'He is a nice man, but a fool.'

That evening, Churchill slipped off to the Royal Lodge at Windsor, a half-hour's drive, for his first audience with the Queen since his stroke. In their host's absence, Eden had a confidential talk with Salisbury, who had finally arrived at Chequers. Previously, Salisbury had doubted that anything would come of Eden's promised confrontation with Churchill. Now, he discovered that Eden no longer planned to broach the subject of the handover. He wanted Salisbury to do it for him. Salisbury agreed but suggested that they had better sleep on it.

Presently, the question of whether or not to press Eden's claim vanished from consideration, when an ebullient Churchill returned from Windsor. He had managed to secure the Queen's permission to ask Eisenhower for the last week in September or the first week in October. The Queen promised to return from Balmoral to welcome Eisenhower at Buckingham Palace during his stay. When Salisbury learned of Churchill's scheme to seek the President's blessing to meet Malenkov, he was horrified. Bilateral talks with the Soviets were precisely what Salisbury had warned Churchill against on his return from Washington. To add insult to injury, Churchill had enlisted the Queen's support without so much as a word to Salisbury or other colleagues beforehand. Salisbury objected immediately, but it was too late. Churchill presented the matter of the state visit as a *fait accompli*. An invitation flew off to Washington the next day and Churchill gaily bid farewell to his houseguests without their having had a chance to quiz him about his retirement plans.

All of Churchill's fighting instincts were in play, and when Violet Bonham Carter visited two days later, Clementine Churchill, who arranged to see her first, implored her not to encourage him to carry on. Clementine explained that though her husband's mind was clear, he tired easily, and she was certain he ought to give up power in the autumn rather than wait and peter out. When she saw him, Violet realized that in spite of anything she or anyone else might recommend he did not intend to go gently into that good night. After the visit, she wrote in her diary of the man she had known and adored since she was nineteen and he thirty-two, and whom she had once hoped to marry: 'I drove back feeling an unutterable sense of tragedy – at watching this last – great – ultimately losing fight against mortality. The light still burning – flashing – in its battered framework – the indomitable desire to live & act still militant & intact. Mind & will at bay with matter. At best a delaying action – but every instinct armed to fight it out until the end.'

Churchill was not altogether unrealistic about whether his body would permit him to continue in office. He told Violet Bonham Carter, as he had previously informed the Queen, that before he took a final decision he must see if he could clear two hurdles. As far as he was concerned, he had to be able both to deliver the leader's speech at the Conservative Party conference and not only to face, but also to dominate the House of Commons. He really did not know if he could manage to bring off either. When Eden left England on 8 August to resume his own recuperation in peace and tranquillity, Churchill plunged headlong into a series of what he viewed as preliminary tests. On the day of Eden's departure, Churchill presided over his first official meeting since he faced the Cabinet on the morning after the Gasperi dinner. At Chequers, he conferred for an hour with Salisbury, Butler, and William Strang of the Foreign Office.

Churchill brought the meeting off to perfection, and was in a 'sparkling mood' at the small luncheon that followed, where they were joined by some others. In the course of the meal, the conversation turned to Churchill's prose style, and Butler asked whether Macaulay had been one of his literary influences. Churchill said he had, as well as Gibbon – whereupon he launched into a recitation from memory of the opening lines of Chapter Fourteen of *The Decline and Fall of the Roman Empire*, about the eighteen years of discord and confusion that afflicted the empire after the abdication of Diocletian: 'The balance of power established by Diocletian subsisted no longer than while it was sustained by the firm and dextrous hand of the founder. It required such a fortunate mixture of different tempers and abilities as could scarcely be found, or even expected, a second time.'

As the moment approached when Churchill would be expected to hand over, this was his puckish way of reminding his two chief co-conspirators that it might not be in the country's best interests to lose him. No one savoured the performance more than Salisbury. Nonetheless, Salisbury persisted in the belief that he had never known a more dangerous situation. He insisted afterwards to Macmillan (who had not attended the luncheon) that while Churchill was 'more charming and delightful than ever', he simply had to resign as soon as Eden was ready.

Two days later, Churchill's sky darkened. Eisenhower would not be coming to London after all. He said he was afraid that Aldrich had misinterpreted a little wishful thinking on his part, growing out of disappointment at not being able to see Churchill in Bermuda; or perhaps Churchill had misunderstood Aldrich. As it was, 'a number of inescapable commitments during the foreseeable future' made it impossible for Eisenhower to leave the country. Clementine Churchill did not believe a word of it. She was sure that in fact Eisenhower did not wish to see her husband and that he had been delighted when Bermuda had had to be cancelled. She guessed that at the moment, Eisenhower was merely waiting to see which way the cat jumped and whether the Prime Minister would retire. Churchill briefly considered proposing that he come to Washington in late September. But he soon abandoned the idea, at least until he had convinced himself that he had the stamina to press on.

Against his doctor's advice, Churchill presided over his first Cabinet in London on 18 August. Though he had been uneasy about it, the session seemed to go well, and he dined with friends late that night. But when he arrived at Chartwell the next day, he looked alarmingly 'dazed and grey'. His family was dismayed by what the meeting had cost him, and he wondered aloud about his ability to tackle the party conference when a single Cabinet had been capable of depleting him so severely. The incident set off a new wave of uncertainty. In the days that followed, Churchill spoke by turns of handing over in October and of postponing his departure until May 1954, when the Queen returned from her round-the-world Commonwealth tour. He alternated between believing that he was too weak to fight on, and telling himself that it was his duty to keep his Soviet initiative alive when the Americans were so opposed to it and when Eden, if prime minister, was certain to side with Eisenhower. Churchill's family had difficulty believing he would yet be able to recover sufficiently to return to public life. He accused them of selfishness in urging him to resign when he retained the capacity to help the country.

Still, he did not wish to proceed recklessly. He did not want to attempt either the party conference or Parliament if he believed he was not up to the task. Certainly, Brain, the neurologist, was pessimistic. A great many things could go disastrously wrong at Margate, where the party conference was to be held. The stroke had diminished Churchill's control over his emotions, so he might embarrass himself on the platform. It had robbed him of strength, so he might grow exhausted and have to make an ungraceful exit. It had affected his memory, so he might forget what he had come to say. Brain also doubted that Churchill would be in any condition to return to the House of Commons. Churchill decided to wait and see how he felt in September.

When Queen Elizabeth invited Churchill to accompany her to the races at Doncaster on 12 September and to spend several days afterwards at Balmoral, he accepted despite his wife's vehement objections. Clementine Churchill worried that Doncaster, which would require him to stand and walk in front of affectionate but curious crowds, would be too much for him. Nor was she pleased to see him subject himself to the strain of an overnight trip in the royal train to Scotland. As the outing approached, Clementine's anxieties mounted. During this time, she herself suffered a bad fall and cracked her ribs. On 2 September, she was in London to see her doctor when she telephoned Winston at Chequers to urge him again to send his regrets to the Queen. Winston dug in and the couple quarrelled bitterly. Before the evening ended, however, he called her back full of apologies and tender words.

The morning after, Clementine composed a note in the same loving spirit. She warned him not to risk a setback before Margate and Parliament. He, however, would not be deterred. In the end, Clementine joined him at the races – which by chance took place on their forty-fifth wedding anniversary – and at Balmoral. He did exceedingly well at Doncaster; and in Scotland, rather than permit himself to be treated as an invalid, he insisted on trudging at the Queen's side through the heather for some three-quarters of a mile. He seemed a good deal more confident when he returned from Scotland, yet there could be no denying that, much as Clemmie had feared, the expedition had overtaxed him.

On 17 September, Churchill went off for two weeks to La Capponcina, during which time he would take a decision about the party conference. From the moment he arrived it was evident that his energy and stamina were, as he told his daughter Mary, who accompanied him, on an ebb tide. He had hoped to paint but found that he was unable to marshal the strength even to go outdoors and sit at his easel. He was often depressed, and though he persisted in working on a speech for Margate he questioned how long he could stand on his 'pins' to deliver it. 'I still ponder on the future,' he wrote to Clemmie, 'and don't want to decide unless I am convinced.' Finally, he did manage a bit of painting. Working on a picture was a great relief, he reported, 'and a little perch for a tired bird'. Churchill's agonizing indecision persisted for the better part of his stay, but by the time he flew home on 30 September he had made up his mind to try both hurdles. He promised himself that if his body failed him during either ordeal, he would step aside.

Margate loomed in ten days. First, however, he had to handle Eden, who flew in from Athens shortly after the Prime Minister returned from the South of France. During his sojourn in Greece, Eden had had ample warning, from Salisbury and Macmillan among others, of what faced him. Nevertheless, at the airport he pointedly avoided telling reporters that he was headed back to the Foreign Office. As if to leave open the possibility that the prize might yet be his, Eden would say only that he was 'fit and ready to work'. A session with Churchill the morning after his return swiftly shattered any lingering illusions he might have harboured. When Churchill and Eden talked on 1 October, the Prime Minister left no doubt that he wanted to stay put. He aimed to try himself out and he promised Eden that if he found he could not do his duty he would resign.

Churchill asked Eden to return to his old post as Foreign Secretary. Eden worried that if he declined, it would look as if he were not fit and that that might be a cue for Butler or one of the other possibles to swoop in and take his place at the head of the list. Still, the meeting concluded without his having answered Churchill one way or the other.

That evening, Eden, Salisbury, and Butler were the Prime Minister's dinner guests. In front of the two men who had done the most to keep the premiership open for him, Eden caved in to Churchill yet again. He announced that he would do as Churchill requested and resume his duties as Foreign Secretary. In short, whatever Salisbury and Butler may have thought they were accomplishing at the time, the sole outcome of the medical cover-up had been to allow the old man to cling to office long enough to engineer another comeback. In the guise of catering to their interests, Churchill had made fools of them both.

Tonight, he rubbed their noses in their deeds when he announced that now that he was back he meant to resume his pursuit of a meeting with Malenkov – with or without Eisenhower. Tempers flared at the disclosure that Churchill planned to publicly revive his 11 May proposal when he addressed the Conservative Party conference. Eden made it clear that he did not approve of the 11 May speech. When Churchill huffed that it had been very popular, Eden shot back that he did not dispute that. Popularity was not the point; he opposed Churchill's policy regardless of public opinion.

When Eden and Salisbury joined forces to question the usefulness of top-level talks, Churchill jested darkly, 'Now I begin to understand what Chamberlain felt like.' The joke outraged Salisbury, who flung back that this was just too much. At one point, Churchill and Eden debated whether the leaders' or the foreign secretaries' meetings had been the more important during the war. Churchill insisted that the Stalin–Churchill–Roosevelt meetings had made the foreign secretaries' work possible. Eden protested that it was his own discussions with American Secretary of State Cordell Hull in Moscow in 1943 that had been decisive. Nothing was resolved and the evening ended with Churchill and his guests at daggers drawn.

Eden returned to work at the Foreign Office on 5 October determined to find some way to stop Churchill from going to the summit. His instinct, as so often in their dealings, was to look for someone else to do the dirty work. Eden initially saw Eisenhower as the man for the job, and he considered pressing for an allies' meeting where Eisenhower could be counted on to torpedo top-level talks. But Eden soon grew worried that Churchill would use the announcement of a meeting with the President to build even more momentum and public support for a parley at the summit. An encounter with Dulles, which would draw less attention, might be another matter. Dulles had already suggested that he and Eden sit down to talk as soon as Eden completed his convalescence.

Churchill vetoed Eden's suggestion that Dulles be invited to London. Suddenly, the Prime Minister was touting a different idea. Why should the two top men and their foreign secretaries not meet at the same time? Three days before Margate, Churchill sent off a message to Eisenhower proposing that they meet the following week in the Azores. While the leaders conferred, Dulles and Eden, who would accompany them on the trip, could meet as well. Having renewed his 11 May proposal at the party conference, Churchill would use the opportunity to ask Eisenhower either to join him at the summit or to authorize him to see Malenkov on his own. Either way, when Churchill returned to London he would be able to make his first appearance in the House of Commons since the stroke with his return ticket to the summit finally in hand.

Mindful that Eisenhower had declined his previous invitation, Churchill meant to force the issue this time. His 7 October telegram was less a request to meet than an offer to the President to choose the venue. Churchill reminded Eisenhower that he had not troubled him with telegrams since August. He said he would be agreeable if Eisenhower insisted on including the French, though Churchill for his part would prefer to do without them. The meeting, however, had to take place the following week, before the opening of Parliament. Churchill suggested that in view of his and Eden's health it would be easier to go to the Azores than to Washington. But, he added, if Eisenhower found that impossible he and Eden would be at the British Embassy, Washington, during 15–18 October. Churchill did not say so but the implication was clear. As a matter of courtesy, the President would have to see them then.

While Churchill waited to hear back from Eisenhower, he plunged into preparations for the party conference. Two days before he confronted the first of his self-imposed hurdles, he rehearsed his big speech exactly as he planned to deliver it. On the day of the run-through, he dined at noon: a dozen oysters, a bit of steak, and half a glass of champagne. An hour later, he swallowed the pill that Moran had specially concocted to clear his head and provide a blast of energy before he spoke. An hour after that, he stood on his 'pins' and sped through the speech in a little over thirty-six minutes. Clementine Churchill sat behind him, precisely as she would at Margate. The practice session (not to mention the amphetamines) left Churchill feeling elated and confident. He planned to travel to Margate on Friday afternoon so he could spend the night there and be well rested.

On Friday morning, however, all hell broke loose. For weeks, Eisenhower had indeed been waiting to see if Churchill would retire when Eden came back. Now that it was apparent that Churchill meant to go on, the President's patience seemed depleted. Eisenhower icily refused to meet in the Azores. Nor would he agree to Washington, as he said he would be out of town during the dates mentioned. If Churchill and Eden insisted on coming anyway, the best that could be arranged was to have Dulles talk to them. If they could stay through 20 October (which Churchill had stressed they could not), Eisenhower would participate on that day, but not earlier. Though it was evident that Churchill's principal purpose was to confer king-to-king, Eisenhower suggested that it might be best to send Eden alone.

Eisenhower's answer infuriated Churchill. He decided to put Eisenhower on the spot by suggesting that he and Eden might come a week later, though that would require Churchill to miss the first week of the new parliamentary session. When Eden's Foreign Office colleagues urged him to find a way to stop Churchill from provoking Eisenhower, Eden replied gloomily, 'I haven't got a log heavy enough to hold this elephant.' Twice on Friday afternoon, Eden appeared at Number Ten with drafts of messages which reverted to Eden's original plan to invite Dulles to London. Twice, Churchill refused. Finally, the Prime Minister left for Margate, but hardly had he arrived at his hotel when he was on the phone to browbeat Eden into agreement that they try again to force Eisenhower to come to the Azores.

Eden buckled and a new message to the President was drafted. This occasioned acute anxiety at the Foreign Office about what Churchill's next step might be should the President refuse again. Nevertheless, by 7 p.m. on Friday the telegram was ready to go and was sent off to be enciphered.

At the last minute, a remark of Colville's caused Churchill to reconsider. Colville asked, 'What subjects are you going to discuss when you get there?' It occurred to Churchill that at this point anything he might say to Eisenhower face to face would necessarily elicit a negative response. Within a matter of hours, Churchill would have a platform where he could begin to apply intense public pressure on the President to be more agreeable. He therefore cancelled the first telegram in favour of a softer, more conciliatory one that offered no hint of the fireworks to come. Churchill wrote that in view of Eisenhower's schedule it did not look as if the meeting he had hoped for could be arranged. 'I am very sorry, as there are so many things I would like to talk over with you quietly and at leisure. I earnestly hope a chance may come in the not too distant future.' In the meantime, he told Eisenhower, Eden would cable separately to ask Dulles to London.

Some four thousand Conservatives gave a standing ovation and sang 'For He's a Jolly Good Fellow' when Churchill appeared on the flower-edged stage at the seaside Winter Gardens the next day. Despite the adoring reception, Churchill knew how much depended on the performance he put up. There had been rumours that he had suffered a stroke and rumours that he had been rendered unfit to lead. Aneurin Bevan had loudly demanded that Churchill 'clear out' if he was no longer capable. *The Times* had called on the Prime Minister to demonstrate that he was physically equal to the tasks ahead.

Would Churchill's many well-wishers at the conference think that he seemed different? Would they notice the faint crookedness in his mouth, the residue of stiffness in his arm? Having shown him their love, would they soon decide to show him the door? When Churchill put on his glasses and began to read from notes, none of the ministers and party officials seated behind him knew, in the words of one, 'whether he would pull through or not'.

The speech was an ordeal, but the fact that the whole world was watching made it an opportunity as well. Hours after Eisenhower had cold-shouldered him, Churchill renewed not only his 11 May proposal, but also his bid for the diplomatic leadership of the West. He announced that the reason there still had not been a parley at the summit was that Britain's 'trusted allies' had yet to agree to the idea. Churchill put those allies on notice that he meant to keep pounding until he prevailed. That meant retirement was out of the question – at least for now.

'If I stay on for the time being, bearing the burdens at my age,' Churchill continued, 'it is not because of love for power or office. I have had an ample feast of both. If I stay, it is because I have the feeling that I may, through things that happened, have an influence on what I care about above all else, the building of a sure and lasting peace.'

When Churchill concluded, the hall exploded in applause. All he had been required to do was show that he was in fighting trim. No one had expected him to come out swinging. *The Times* later called his performance a 'triumphant return to public life' and the consensus in the party was that Winston was back – again. After the young MP Edward Heath moved a vote of thanks to 'the great Prime Minister of peace', a visibly weary Churchill began to leave the platform on his way to an adjoining room, where an overflow crowd had listened to his speech on loudspeakers. He was scheduled to say a few words to them, but suddenly he realized that any further exertion was beyond his powers.

Churchill reappeared at the microphone to say, 'I hope you will excuse me. I have done quite a lot of work today. My trusted colleagues Mr Eden and Lord Salisbury will take my place.'

Yet again, Churchill had upped the ante in his long-running

struggle with Eisenhower by appealing directly to the people – not just Britons, but people everywhere – to support his initiative. Eisenhower reacted by issuing strict marching orders to Dulles on the eve of his departure for London. He assigned Dulles to put an end to Churchill's summit appeals by making it clear once and for all that the President would never agree. Dulles was to leave no doubt in Churchill's mind that coming in at the very last minute to finalize a deal that the foreign ministers had already negotiated was as far as Eisenhower would ever go.

Churchill's remarks at the party conference had angered and irritated Eisenhower, but they had also made him exceedingly nervous about what the Prime Minister might have accomplished by taking his case directly to the people. It was one thing to privately resist Churchill's arts, and quite another to refuse him with the whole world looking on. Churchill had highlighted the strategic breach between London and Washington, and Eisenhower worried that people would look badly on US opposition to the Prime Minister's proposal. So, even as he directed Dulles to decline any suggestion of leaders' talks with the Soviets, he acknowledged that the Secretary of State 'would be walking a tightrope in maintaining this position without creating the impression that the US was blocking a useful step'.

Dulles, whose breath stank and whose left eye twitched incessantly and disconcertingly, arrived in London on 15 October. That night, he dined at Number Ten, where Churchill's other guests were Salisbury and Eden. When the Prime Minister spoke of his summit proposal, Dulles moved at once to try to turn Churchill from his purpose. Churchill responded to Dulles's invocation of the constitutional argument by politely conceding that the President's position differed from his own. Then he added that, as Eisenhower felt he could not sit down with Malenkov, perhaps he, Churchill, ought to go alone. In a similarly courteous tone, Dulles observed that obviously this was a decision Churchill was wholly free to make. But, Dulles added, he was concerned that a solo mission would create the impression that Britain had assumed the role of middleman between America and the Soviet Union. He suggested that such a perception would 'seriously prejudice' America's desire to work in close partnership with Britain in areas of mutual concern.

Suddenly, the air of cordiality that had prevailed thus far in the encounter dissolved. Churchill retorted angrily that he thought the Americans could trust him not to be entrapped at Moscow. He recalled that when he met Eisenhower in New York prior to the inauguration, the President-elect had said he was free to meet the Soviets alone. Dulles in turn assured Churchill that he was certain this remained Eisenhower's view. Of course, Washington would make no effort to interfere in any decision Churchill might make. Still Dulles felt obligated to point out that as Churchill could hardly go as Washington's representative, US public opinion would inevitably cast him in the role of middleman and that that could have an undesirable effect on relations elsewhere. Dulles had just put on the table the very possibility that Salisbury, arguing from a dramatically different perspective, had warned of when he returned from Washington – that Churchill's summit strategy risked the Anglo-American alliance. When in the course of the dinner Dulles interpreted Salisbury's silence to mean that he had the Lord President's tacit support, he was right, but only up to a point. Salisbury and Dulles differed about much else, but for the moment their shared opposition to bilateral talks made them strange political bedfellows.

Eden too had remained significantly silent throughout Churchill's acrimonious exchange with the American visitor. Dulles had gone into the dinner with a comforting sense that as far as the summit debate was concerned, he and Eden were on the same side. During the drive from the airport, Eden had conveyed to Dulles that though he would of course 'loyally' support his chief, he personally doubted the wisdom of top-level talks. When in the days that followed Eden, Dulles, and Bidault sat down together, the foreign ministers, clearly operating on a very different line from Churchill, agreed to renew the Western allies' stalled offer to the Soviet Union of a second-level, four-power conference on Germany and Austria. A communiqué to announce the invitation was drafted and on 18 October Churchill hosted a farewell luncheon, where it quickly became apparent that American efforts to silence him had failed. When he reviewed the draft communiqué, Churchill immediately complained of the wording. As had been the case before, he knew he could hardly block a foreign ministers' meeting, but he did not wish the communiqué to undermine his goal of a parley at the summit. He objected strongly to the statement that the three governments agreed that a foreign ministers' meeting would be 'the most practical step toward a reduction of international tension and a solution of major European problems', and urged that the communiqué say instead that as far as their governments were concerned, a foreign ministers' meeting 'might be an invaluable step'.

Things heated up from there. Churchill went on to make his usual derogatory remarks about the usefulness of foreign ministers' talks. To the fascination of Churchill's guests, his comments provoked an outburst of annoyance from Eden. On 1 October, the two men had sparred privately and indeed rather bitterly on the subject. The difference on the present occasion was that they were openly disagreeing in front of the Americans and the French. Salisbury dived in to break up the fight, but by that time, the damage to the premiership had been done. Dulles now had no doubt that the Prime Minister was in this alone. On the matter of a summit meeting, Churchill perceptibly did not have the backing of his own key people.

Something else happened at the luncheon that raised eyebrows on the American side. After the altercation with Eden, Churchill seemed suddenly in much less good form than at the start of the meal. Aldrich, who was among the guests, gauged that Churchill was finding it hard to concentrate. At times, the Prime Minister's comments sounded suspiciously like a set speech and did not really fit into the discussion. Apart from various individuals' particular reasons for opposing a parley at the summit, episodes like these raised important questions about what could happen if Churchill succeeded in his campaign to face the Soviets across a conference table.

There was no doubt that he retained the ability to soar intellectually and strategically. But, seemingly more and more, there were also moments when he crashed, when he was simply too groggy to operate effectively. These days, one never knew which Churchill one was going to encounter at any given moment. Even if one agreed with him on the desirability of leaders' talks, the question unavoidably presented itself of whether it would be responsible to allow the old man to attend.

For the moment, it seemed as if foreign ministers' talks was the route the Western allies had chosen to go. In the days that followed, however, Churchill made it clear to the world that he had other ideas. It was as if he had not heard a word that Dulles had said in London, as if he had not been firmly warned of the consequences should he persist in badgering Eisenhower. On 20 October, during Prime Minister's Questions in the House of Commons, Churchill stressed that in spite of the foreign ministers' invitation, leaders' talks remained his goal; and again on 27 October he suggested in the Commons that he longed to have a private talk with Eisenhower, presumably to discuss the next step.

During this time, the thirty-part newspaper serialization of *Triumph and Tragedy*, the concluding volume of Churchill's war memoirs, which had begun to run on 23 October, ratcheted up the public pressure on Eisenhower by richly documenting Churchill's claims that he had seen the Soviet danger in 1945 but that the Americans had failed to listen. The passages about Eisenhower had been toned down somewhat in view of his current employment, but enough of the sting remained for the *New York Times* to have asked the President in advance of publication whether he wished to respond. Eisenhower had long and accurately maintained that he had not been ordered to take Berlin. But after Churchill published extracts of their correspondence, it could never be said that Eisenhower had not been warned of the political and psychological importance of beating the Russians to Berlin, or that he had not been cautioned that it would be a huge mistake to put his faith in Stalin. Once again, the British Prime Minister was openly battling Eisenhower on two fronts, the past and the present, for the verdict of history and for the diplomatic leadership of the West. This time, his documentation provided him with especially powerful ammunition. The fact that in October Churchill was awarded the Nobel Prize for Literature heightened the excitement surrounding his memoir.

The serialization was in progress when, on 3 November, Churchill used the occasion of the culminating hurdle, his first full-dress parliamentary speech since the stroke, to again call for a parley at the summit. Churchill alluded movingly to his own advanced age when he emphasized that at this point, it probably was no longer possible to obtain a speedy settlement: 'Time will undoubtedly be needed – more time than some of us here are likely to see.' Churchill hoped at least to have the opportunity to begin the process. But before he could even try, he had to wrest some form of assent from the White House.

Two days after his address, when Moscow responded negatively to the foreign ministers' invitation, Churchill saw a chance to appeal to Eisenhower anew. This time his proposal took the form of a private communication, but he held open the possibility that he might be forced to speak out again if he did not get what he wanted. 'The Soviet answer puts us back to where we were when Bermuda broke down through my misfortune,' he wrote to the President on 5 November. 'We are confronted with a deadlock. So why not let us try Bermuda again?' Pointedly and not a little threateningly, Churchill warned of 'serious criticism' from the public if a meeting could not be arranged.

The following day, Eisenhower capitulated. He unhappily agreed to face the Prime Minister during the first week of December, with the proviso that their talks must not be billed as the prelude to a further approach to the Soviets. As he had done six months before, Churchill offered hand-on-heart assurances that he would suggest no such thing.

Churchill had had no help from the Cabinet in this latest struggle with Eisenhower. Now that he had won, he was hardly in the mood to listen to ministers' advice about his travel plans. Churchill rejected the argument that in view of his health it would be safest to travel by sea. 'I shall go to the airport,' he told them. 'I shall board my plane. I shall go to bed and take my pill. In the morning I shall wake up either in Bermuda or in Heaven – unless you gentlemen have some other destination in mind for me.'

XVII

I Have a Right to Be Heard!

Bermuda, December 1953

Asked who exactly was standing in his way right now, the seventy-nine-year-old Churchill shot back, 'Ike'.

At dinner with his team at the Mid-Ocean Club in Bermuda on the eve of Eisenhower's arrival, Churchill had been speaking of his great plans. The goal was to get to Malenkov. To accomplish that, he had to persuade Eisenhower either to accompany him to the summit or to authorize a solo mission. It was a tall order, to be sure. Still, against all odds Churchill had managed to get this far since his stroke, and for the most part he seemed radiantly (certain of his colleagues thought unrealistically) confident that face to face he could get what he needed from the President.

When Eisenhower flew in on 4 December 1953, it was no secret that he was a reluctant participant in the conference. This was to be his first encounter with Churchill since the 11 May speech and the publication of *Triumph and Tragedy*, in both of which the Prime Minister had posed a controversial and highly effective public challenge to the President's authority. Churchill's ability to keep returning from the dead (political and otherwise) had long been maddening to his antagonists, and so it was now to Eisenhower. Yet again in the Churchill story, the funeral had been premature, the coffin empty. Eisenhower was furious that Churchill had ignored Dulles's warnings and had persisted in pressuring him to meet. In the weeks since Bermuda had been agreed to, Eisenhower had sought repeatedly to douse press expectations of what might be accomplished there. When Eisenhower emphasized that the whole idea had been Churchill's, when he predicted that no real news would emerge from their discussions, and when he stressed that he had consented merely because he wanted to be agreeable, he made the conference sound like nothing more than an old man's folly.

In fact, Eisenhower looked anything but agreeable when he emerged from his aircraft with a grin that struck observers as forced. After he greeted Churchill, he strode off to inspect an honour guard of Welsh Fusiliers. Churchill was left 'trotting behind, neglected and pathetic'. The Prime Minister refused to be offended and finally 'pirated' Eisenhower and arranged a tête-à-tête lunch in his suite.

At half past one, when he finally had Eisenhower to himself, Churchill promptly broached the possibility of a meeting with the Soviets. Since the Bermuda conference had been arranged, Moscow had reversed its earlier rejection of foreign ministers' talks. As a consequence, part of its purpose had become to draft the West's reply to the most recent Soviet note. When Churchill immediately spoke of keeping the door open to top-level discussions, Eisenhower was just as quick to cut him off. He reiterated what he had previously sent Dulles to London to convey: he would not participate in a leaders' meeting until Moscow had shown good faith at the foreign ministers' level. If Churchill thought he could continue to badger him in the press, Eisenhower had a surprise waiting.

When the American, British, and French delegations convened that evening, the President disclosed that he had received an invitation to address the United Nations. Though he emphasized that he had yet to accept, he reported that he had already drafted a speech on the peaceful use of atomic energy. His address would present the US as it really was – 'struggling for peace, not showing belligerence and truculence, but rather our will for peace'. When Churchill learned that Eisenhower was to deliver a major address on the same evening he left Bermuda, 8 December, he sensed that the President had outflanked him. Obviously, Churchill would be unable to stop him from giving the speech, the latest blow in their contest for pre-eminence. Whatever the outcome in Bermuda, Eisenhower's UN appearance would overshadow the allies' meeting and dominate the news. Should Eisenhower persist in blocking a parley at the summit, the New York speech would armour him, at least for the moment, against further charges by Churchill.

Nevertheless, following some opening remarks by French Prime Minister Joseph Laniel, Churchill methodically laid out the strategy that underpinned his desire to meet Malenkov. He spoke of a 'new look' in Soviet policy, the apparent change of heart that had occurred since Stalin's death. He proposed that the West adopt a double-barrelled policy of military strength combined with negotiations, and he suggested that it might be possible to open up the closed Communist society by contacts, meetings, trade, and other forms of 'infiltration' behind the iron curtain. Churchill argued that such infiltration was feared by everything that was bad in the Kremlin regime. Western leaders, by contrast, had nothing to fear from top-level talks.

Eisenhower sat across from Churchill at a large, round cedar-wood table that, due to a power failure, was illuminated by candles and hurricane lamps. He gave the Prime Minister all the time he needed to frame his argument. But when Churchill was finished, Eisenhower stunned the British delegation with a smackdown of a speech that witnesses characterized as 'vulgar', 'rude', and 'very violent'. In his diary afterwards, Colville expressed doubt that such coarse language had ever before been heard at an international conference. Eisenhower compared Russia to a woman of the streets and he insisted that whether her dress was new or just the old one patched she was still the same whore underneath. He said it was America's intention to force her off her current beat into the back streets.

Eisenhower's rant provoked 'pained looks all round'. Eden had hoped that the President might be the man to stop Churchill. He shared Eisenhower's antipathy to leaders' talks, as well as his belief that Moscow's somewhat more reasonable attitude lately was attributable less to Stalin's absence than to constant pressure from the West. He also shared Eisenhower's ineffable frustration at Churchill's refusal to vanish into retirement and at the persistence, bordering on effrontery, with which the old man had forced this conference to take place. Still, the tenor of Eisenhower's remarks rattled him. In an effort to wind up the proceedings on a note of dignity and decorum, Eden leaped in to ask when the next meeting would be.

'I don't know,' Eisenhower snapped, before he rose to leave. 'Mine is with a whisky and soda.'

The rancorous session set the tone for a conference that would be marred by frayed tempers on both the American and British sides. (The French amused themselves by leaking choice bits to the press.) The next day, when Churchill and Eisenhower squared off on atomic policy, it seemed to Churchill that all else shrank in significance alongside Eisenhower's declared determination to unleash atomic weapons on Chinese bases should the truce in Korea break down. China did not have the bomb but the Soviets, who did, were pledged to come to their Communist ally's defence, and Churchill saw Britain as a likely first target.

Churchill warned the President that the use of atomic weapons in Korea could trigger a third world war. Throbbing with emotion, he explained that the defences in London were inadequate against such weapons and that he could not bear to think of 'the destruction of all we hold dear, ourselves, our families and our treasures'. He went on, 'Even if some of us temporarily survive in some deep cellar under mounds of flaming and contaminated rubble there will be nothing to do but take a pill to end it all.' Eisenhower's response was to scoff at the notion that the use of atomic weapons in Asia would provoke the Soviet Union to attack the West.

Churchill despairingly produced a copy of the Quebec Agreement of 1943, signed by himself and Roosevelt. That agreement had given Britain veto power over the use of the bomb. Had it still been in effect ten years later, Churchill could simply have nixed the whole idea of strategic bombing and Eisenhower would have had little choice but to back off. As it was, the Attlee Government had abandoned the British veto, so all Churchill could do now was plead.

On this and related matters, he pleaded in vain. After his stroke, Churchill had pulled himself back from the brink of death. He had persisted in fighting and scheming when other men might have long given up. Yet, in the end, he had failed with Eisenhower in every significant respect. The President had agreed neither to meet Malenkov nor to give his blessing to Anglo-Soviet talks, and he had not backed down about using atomic weapons in Asia. The sole positive outcome of the conference was to begin preparations for another foreign ministers' meeting with the Soviets, this one to take place in Berlin in January.

Churchill bitterly attributed his failure in Bermuda to age and incapacity. He began to accept what his doctor had known for some time, that no matter how hard he pushed he would never again be the man he was before the stroke. Reflecting on his dashed hopes for the conference, Churchill tearfully told Moran, 'I have been humiliated by my own decay.'

In London, the excitement and optimism that had surrounded Churchill's departure for Bermuda had fizzled out by the time he came home empty-handed. To his family and close associates he spoke often of retirement. No one really expected him to lead the party into a new general election, which had to be held by the fall of 1956. It was tacitly understood that Churchill would not want to risk ending his career with another defeat. The hope among party leaders was that he would retire decently in advance of the next election in order to give Eden time to establish himself. Churchill went so far as to mention various dates when he thought he might like to go. Colville conveyed to Shuckburgh that the Prime Minister would be much more likely to relinquish power if Eden was 'kind' to him and that every time Eden acted too aggressively Churchill saw it as evidence that he was still not ready to be left in charge.

Eden for his part complained to colleagues that Churchill was 'gaga' and that the situation must not be allowed to go on. There was no question that Churchill was suddenly much deafer, that he repeated himself incessantly, and that he conducted Cabinet business at a glacial pace. Slumped in his seat, with his shirt front gathered in a large roll, he seemed robotic at times and appeared not to recognize people he ought to have known. In the House of Commons, he made a show of laughing off a Labour backbencher's questions about when he might be expected to stand down. Yet he could not disguise his hurt when *Punch* ran a controversial cartoon that cruelly suggested the effects of the stroke on his face. An accompanying text penned by the editor, Malcolm Muggeridge, accused Churchill of clinging to office with faltering capacities. In this increasingly ugly and harassing environment, Christopher Soames, privately acknowledging that his father-in-law had deteriorated significantly during the first few weeks of 1954, concluded that it should be Churchill's friends rather than his adversaries who convinced him to go.

There was little chance that Churchill would agree to do any such thing after a strange and disquieting message arrived from Washington on 9 February. Suggesting that he and Churchill shared a responsibility to protect civilization against the incursions of 'atheistic materialism', Eisenhower spoke of the need to seek renewed faith and strength from God and to sharpen their swords 'for the struggle that cannot possibly be escaped'. What did Eisenhower mean by that last phrase? Was he talking (as Churchill hoped he was) about a spiritual struggle with the Soviets – or did he mean inevitable war? Salisbury, when at length he saw what Eisenhower had written, was if possible even more alarmed.

Churchill had yet to make up his mind about quite how to reply when a newspaper report of a speech by the chairman of the Joint

Congressional Committee on Atomic Energy made the eyes 'start out' of his head. Addressing a group of businessmen in Chicago, Representative W. Sterling Cole offered the first extensive public account of a US hydrogen bomb test eighteen months previously that had obliterated a Pacific island and torn a vast cavity in the ocean floor. The congressman noted that the Soviet Union was also engaged in H-bomb research and was perhaps a year behind the Americans. When Churchill contacted the White House on 9 March, he had a simple, powerful new argument. He believed that the Cole revelations had shifted and narrowed the topic of the conversations he and Eisenhower needed to have with Malenkov. To Churchill's mind, the Soviet leadership must be made to understand that the hydrogen bomb, with its vast range of annihilation and even broader area of contamination, rendered the scattered population of the Soviet Union vulnerable as never before.

Churchill was waiting to hear back from Eisenhower when, on 17 March, the Soviet chargé d'affaires in London transmitted a cryptic message to the effect that Malenkov 'would be willing to consider meeting him'. Churchill took this to mean that Malenkov was interested in talking to him alone. When he reported the development to Eden, the Foreign Secretary was most discouraging. The Berlin foreign ministers' conference (25 January–19 February) had produced no results, but before it ended Eden had succeeded in the delicate task of getting all parties to agree to a five-power conference on Korea and Indo-China, to take place in Geneva in the latter part of April. The upcoming meeting was widely thought of as Eden's conference, and the last thing he wanted right now was for Churchill to go off for talks that threatened to steal some of that precious limelight. Eden told the Prime Minister that he considered the message from Moscow an insulting way to put things to Britain's leader. The most Churchill would concede was that while he would not attempt to pursue the idea of bilateral talks before Geneva, he might well return to it down the line.

Eisenhower checked in two days later. The answer, again, was negative. But while Churchill had been awaiting his response, word had broken of a new US hydrogen bomb test. At the beginning of the month, a Japanese fishing boat had been deluged with radioactive ash though the vessel was some eighty miles outside the test zone at the time of the explosion. The news that twenty-two crew members had been burned and their cargo of tuna and shark poisoned provoked mass outrage in Britain. The British were so upset because they were so vulnerable to a nuclear attack. Eisenhower inadvertently made things worse when he disclosed at a press conference that the magnitude of the hydrogen blast had far surpassed scientists' expectations. The President's remarks, delivered in an incongruously by-golly tone, created the impression that the test had spun wildly and perilously out of human control.

Much had changed since Churchill, in his message to Eisenhower, expressed astonishment that the Cole disclosures had attracted so little public comment. Britons were now in full outcry and Churchill perceived an opportunity to cast himself as their voice. As he had done in May 1953, he planned to counter Eisenhower's intransigence by appealing directly to the people about the urgency of a summit meeting. This time, the occasion would be a House of Commons debate on the H-bomb on 5 April. On that day, Churchill meant to regain the ground he had lost in Bermuda.

The Opposition continued to support Churchill's Soviet initiative, but they were not eager to let him make political hay of the H-bomb debate. For days on end the Labour press upbraided Churchill for having allowed Britain to become a powerless, voiceless satellite of the US. Labour MPs amplified the charges on television and in the House of Commons. Why had Churchill acquiesced to the H-bomb experiments? Why had he taken no action to halt them? Why, again and again, did Britain's great ally act unilaterally? Why did Churchill not talk 'straighter and harder' to the Americans? According to his attackers, the answer to each of these questions was that Churchill was too old and impotent to carry on.

'His battles are past,' the mass-circulation *Daily Mirror* editorialized. 'This is the Giant in Decay.'

The Giant was not amused. At the end of the Second World War, Clementine Churchill, along with certain of Winston's friends, had been known to wince at the national hero's willingness, even eagerness, to shape-shift into a vituperative, if ineffectual, partisan battler. Some Tories still blamed the Conservative rout of 1945 on the violence of Churchill's invective during the general election campaign, which had contrasted unfavourably with Attlee's 'more statesmanlike' demeanour. In 1954, did Labour calculatedly goad the Prime Minister to self-destruct, as some Opposition members later claimed to have done? However it happened, the angry apostle of peace arrived in the Commons on 5 April with an ill-considered speech that lurched between calling for three-power talks on the H-bomb – his principal purpose – and dropping a super-bomb or two of his own on the Opposition.

Attlee spoke first, and wrong-footed Churchill with a grave, impeccably patriotic speech that was widely hailed as the most statesmanlike of his career. In contrast to the scurrilities of recent days, Attlee served up no criticism of Churchill. This afternoon at least, he had only praise for the Prime Minister, whose grasp of history and experience of world problems he painted as unsurpassed. Emphasizing that the international situation was suddenly too dangerous for politics as usual, Attlee insisted that he offered his party's resolution 'in no party spirit' and that he sought 'no party advantage'. The Opposition called for an immediate initiative by Her Majesty's Government to put Churchill together with Eisenhower and Malenkov.

Was that not exactly what Churchill wanted? As he was the first to admit, there was almost nothing in the Opposition leader's speech with which he could find fault. When Attlee sat down, it was widely expected that the Prime Minister would follow with an even better speech, though in the same noble, nonpartisan vein. Many listeners expected that he would deliver another 'epoch-making' performance along the lines of 11 May.

Instead, hardly had Churchill begun when he launched into a slashing partisan denunciation of the Attlee regime for having abandoned Britain's veto over the use of the bomb. The loss of the veto had been eating away at him since he sat helplessly opposite Eisenhower that terrible day in Bermuda, when the President spoke of unleashing atomic weapons. Today, Churchill asked why Labour blamed him for a lack of influence, when it was they who had fatally weakened Britain's hand. As it became apparent that he was in full attack mode, the House went wild.

The Opposition pelted Churchill with cries of 'Resign!' and 'Retire!' They accused him of acting disgracefully, of dragging the debate into the gutter and of sacrificing the interests of humanity to make a cheap party point. The cacophony seemed to stagger Churchill physically. Unable to hear what some of the members were shouting at him, he looked helpless and confused.

Overcome with frustration, Churchill stretched out both hands and beseeched the House, 'I have a right to be heard!' The Opposition persisted in hooting him down.

Macmillan guessed that a few years previously, Churchill, though never the nimblest of debaters, would still have been flexible enough to readjust himself to the situation and depart from his script. Today, he dutifully, doggedly hewed to the prepared text. White-faced, he swayed slightly as he soldiered on in a tired, tremulous voice. Most Tories sat out their leader's martyrdom in grim silence. Woolton, concerned about the strain on Churchill in his present state of health, was relieved to spot Moran in the visitors' gallery. The doctor worried that the ordeal might trigger another stroke. Boothby drew a good deal of attention by flamboyantly rising from his seat below the gangway, turning his back on the Prime Minister in what many witnesses interpreted as a display of naked disdain, and marching out of the chamber. Boothby later claimed to have undergone periodontal surgery earlier in the day and to have had to leave suddenly on account of the pain.

People of all political stripes agreed that Churchill had made a fatal mistake in exposing his debility to the House and the public. He had intended to smite his enemies, but the only person he managed to damage with his cringe-inducing performance was himself. He had hoped to instil confidence, but he had undermined it instead. He had previously conceded that he could not go on after his stroke if he failed to exhibit his usual mastery of the House. Lord Layton, a leading member of the Liberal Party, predicted that the day's brutal spectacle would hasten the Prime Minister's resignation. Had Churchill fought his way back from the brink of death only to commit political suicide?

The H-bomb debate raged on for several hours more. Eden, set to wind up for the Tories, conferred with fellow Conservatives in his room at the House. In recent weeks, 'poor Anthony' (as colleagues referred to him) had grown so exasperated with Churchill that he seemed at times to be on the verge of another physical collapse. Two ministers recommended that he make no effort to rescue Churchill. Churchill had brought himself down; why not just let him stay down?

Under the circumstances, Eden preferred to be kind. That evening, he took the high road that Churchill had so disastrously spurned earlier. He argued that the Prime Minister had had every reason to be upset about the vicious attacks on him in the Labour press. Eden's remarks may have done little to help Churchill, but they immediately and immeasurably enhanced the heir apparent's standing in both the party and the House. Where Churchill had been rabid, Eden had seemed measured. Where Churchill seemed scattered and confused, Eden came off as reassuringly controlled.

The morning after Eden spoke up for Churchill in public, he moved against him behind the scenes. Having magnificently defended his chief's 5 April performance, he now offered it as evidence that Churchill must be made to go. Previously, Eden had been careful to distance himself from the machinations. It was a measure of how much the Prime Minister's stock had fallen that Eden was now actively driving the efforts to remove him. In the course of the day, he checked in with Butler, Salisbury, Macmillan, and others. That evening, he, Buchan-Hepburn, and Brook (who as recently as Bermuda had maintained that it was still best that Churchill stay on) agreed that Churchill must leave office no later than Whitsun, 6 June. Eden and his colleagues also concluded that as long as Churchill remained in power he must not under any circumstances be allowed to attend a summit meeting.

As if he were living in a parallel universe, Churchill viewed 5 April very differently from most people. Where others heard taps, Churchill heard reveille. Instead of focusing on his mortifying performance and on the personally devastating newspaper coverage, Churchill riveted his attention on an indisputable fact: in the end, the Opposition motion calling for the Prime Minister to press for a Churchill–Malenkov–Eisenhower meeting had carried unanimously. As far as Churchill was concerned, that gave him a 'warrant' to carry on. Ironically, Eden and other leading Conservatives who saw the debacle as proof that Churchill was not fit to meet the Soviets had just voted along with the rest of the House instructing him to seek a summit meeting. Churchill thanked Eden for his speech (which, he took note, had endorsed the motion) and suggested that he was more disposed on account of it to regard Eden as fit to lead. The timetable Churchill had in mind for the succession, however, did not coincide with Eden's plans. After 5 April, Churchill took a new line: how could he even consider handing over until he had accomplished what the House had demanded of him?

The day after the H-bomb debate, Eisenhower asked Churchill to join him in threatening the Chinese in Indo-China. 'I know of no man who has grasped more nettles than you,' the President wrote to him.

'If we grasp this one together I believe that we will enormously increase our chances of bringing the Chinese to believe that their interests lie in the direction of a discreet disengagement.' Should China refuse to discontinue support of the Viet Minh rebels, Eisenhower wanted Britain to be prepared to participate in military intervention. Coming on top of Eisenhower's talk at Bermuda of unleashing missiles on Chinese bases, this new proposal horrified Churchill. At the same time, he was not anxious to displease the Americans just when he was gearing up to come back to them with a new summit pitch.

Eden too was appalled, both because he also vehemently disapproved of the American proposal and because he feared its potential impact on his own immediate plans. He had been hoping that a productive Geneva Conference would set up his homecoming as Churchill's successor nicely. The last thing he wanted was for China and the Soviet Union to pull out at the last minute. Both Churchill and Eden were conspicuously antsy and conflicted when Eisenhower's request was discussed at the 7 April Cabinet. It therefore fell to Salisbury to voice the most forthright objections. Salisbury demanded to know exactly what Eisenhower meant when he spoke of 'air action' against China. Was he referring to atomic bombs?

As Churchill stealthily crafted a new campaign to sell Eisenhower on a bilateral meeting, he was careful to take the President's psychology into account. In the past, when Churchill had spoken of a solo mission to see the Soviets, he had cast the suggestion in the form of a threat, as the alternative strategy it would be his duty to pursue if the President refused to accompany him. This time around, he repackaged it as a favour. If Churchill struck out with Malenkov, the onus would be solely on Churchill. If, however, he managed to secure the token of good faith Eisenhower had demanded, the President would have the political cover he needed. He would be able to go to the summit without fear of criticism that he had allowed himself to be conned by the Soviet leadership.

There was another significant difference between Churchill's new proposal and past appeals. To date, Churchill had been seeking Eisenhower's immediate commitment to top-level talks. Here, he split his request in two. First he planned to ask Eisenhower to give him the go-ahead to see the Soviets alone. If, however, Churchill managed to secure an Austrian treaty (one of the proofs of good will Eisenhower had suggested in his April 1953 speech), only then would he seek a commitment to three-power talks.

Churchill knew that, given his own age and health, this might well be his last chance to win over the President. It was likely now or never, so he was determined to argue the point in person. On 22 April, without advising anyone, he wrote Eisenhower to suggest that he come to Washington in May. Churchill said only that he would 'very much like to have some talks'. About what specifically he did not say. 'I should keep the plan secret till the last moment. Do you like the idea?' For the past few weeks the White House had continued to militate for British support in Indo-China, so Eisenhower naturally assumed that this was what the Prime Minister wished to discuss. Churchill for his part was happy to have Eisenhower believe so. At length, Eisenhower suggested he come in June. When Churchill wrote to inform Eden of the trip, without of course spelling out what he hoped to accomplish in Washington, it became clear that there was no longer any possibility that he would hand over before Whitsun, as the heir apparent and his supporters had been hoping.

Churchill told the Cabinet about his trip on 5 June. Addressing the ministers, he was as vague and evasive about his purposes as he had been with Eisenhower. He indicated that he wished to talk to the President about atomics and Egypt. About his new summit proposal, however, he uttered not a syllable. He noted that he had originally planned to have Eden accompany him to Washington, but as the Geneva Conference was dragging on he now proposed to go alone.

Salisbury would not hear of it. In Cabinet discussions to date, Salisbury had been a fierce advocate of doing everything possible to discourage the US from 'precipitate action', whether in Indo-China or other hot spots. Salisbury's concerns had resonated strongly with Cabinet colleagues. He regarded Eisenhower as a 'prize noodle' and he worried desperately that even without British support the US might bomb China on the rationale that the international situation threatened to become much more dangerous when the Soviet Union was further along in the nuclear arms race. Salisbury maintained that, on the contrary, the danger of war would be less when there was 'a strong deterrent to all'. In the meantime, he argued, the British must make it their mission during the next two or three years to stay close to the Americans. At the Cabinet on 5 June, Salisbury pointed out that Indo-China was sure to be spoken of while Churchill was in Washington. Salisbury wanted Eden to be there to counter any arguments Dulles might make in favour of military intervention.

In the ensuing discussion around the Cabinet table, there was a subtext of concern that it really would be best if Eden (who was present) went to Washington in his long-time capacity as Churchill's restraining hand. No one said as much in front of the old man, but the feeling in the room was palpable. Churchill raised no objections, and at length it was agreed that Eden would somehow arrange to go as well.

After the Cabinet, Churchill and Eden had a private talk about the succession. Churchill said he now intended to leave office at the end of July when Parliament rose for the summer recess. Eden protested that that would not be an ideal time to form a new Government, but Churchill was, or pretended to be, oblivious to his objections. Later, Churchill told his wife how well the talk had gone. He insisted that he and his successor had reached 'a very perfect understanding'. Eden certainly did not see it that way. On his return to Geneva, he wrote to complain further. He asked Churchill to step aside as soon as he came back from Washington, preferably before the end of June. The request so offended Churchill that he withdrew his offer to go in July. Suddenly, he refused to commit to any date at all. The most he would say was that he hoped he would not have to remain in power beyond the autumn. He informed Eden that he must 'see what emerges from our talks in Washington and how they affect the various schemes I have in mind'.

On 25 June 1954, when Churchill emerged from a black Lincoln convertible at the North Portico of the White House escorted by Vice President Richard Nixon, neither the Americans nor the Cabinet in London had a firm grasp of his intentions. In the run-up to the Washington meetings, Sir Roger Makins had wittily observed that the Americans tended to be 'terrified' of Churchill's visits and that they liked to take protective actions, 'like squids or skunks', in advance. To judge by Churchill's fragile appearance, however, there seemed to be nothing very much to guard against. In contrast to the beaming, effusively smiling Eisenhower, who trotted down the marble steps to welcome him, Churchill ascended with the gingerliness of great age. His head was bent and his eyes, with their pale lashes, were down-cast lest he stumble. At moments, he resembled a marionette whose cords had been cut. As Eisenhower hovered protectively at his side, Mamie Eisenhower, standing at the top of the stairs, leaned forward, grasped Churchill's hand and helped guide him the rest of the way up.

Offered a choice of accommodations in the family quarters, Churchill asked for the Queen's Suite, where he had stayed during the Roosevelt presidency. When he was shown to his rooms, which had rose-coloured walls and a canopied four-poster bed, his hosts assumed he would need to rest before the business of the conference began. Eden and Dulles closeted themselves in the presidential study on the second floor of the White House to discuss Germany. They too assumed that it would be at least an hour before the Prime Minister was ready.

Churchill surprised everyone. Given his admittedly waning strength, it was far from ideal that, as matters stood, he might not have an opportunity to make his summit case to Eisenhower until the end of seventy-two hours of tightly scheduled meetings on Indo-China,

Europe, and a raft of other topics. Thus, as soon as he reached his rooms, he changed into a fresh shirt and fawn-coloured tropical suit and waddled off in search of the President. When the leaders found themselves alone in the Oval Office for three-quarters of an hour, Churchill briefly outlined his new summit proposal. This time, he found that he did not have to do very much. He was elated, relieved, and not a little flabbergasted when Eisenhower's answer – immediately – was yes. Eisenhower accepted that Churchill would see Malenkov first. If Churchill managed to wrest a token of good faith from the Soviets, Eisenhower would join in later.

Why the abrupt pivot? It was not really anything Churchill said or did. Rather, it was what Eisenhower expected to get from him that seems to have made the difference. While Churchill was at the White House, Eisenhower hoped – vainly, it turned out – to convince him to sign off on a unified Anglo-American position on Indo-China. Congressional support for intervention was contingent on British involvement. What harm could there be in putting his guest in a good humour by agreeing in principle to a summit meeting that was never going to happen on Churchill's watch anyway?

By the look of him, Churchill was unlikely to be in office long enough to arrange two-, let alone three-power talks. Even if he managed to hang on, Eden and the Cabinet were sure to block him before things went too far. Besides, Churchill could not take any further action until he had checked in again with the White House, could he?

Churchill emerged from the encounter in roaring spirits. The official sessions had not even begun, but as far as he was concerned he already had what he had come to Washington for. Eisenhower, by contrast, was not so pleased. Hardly had he assented to Churchill's proposal when he began to have second thoughts. When, after lunch, he and Churchill met with the others, he struggled perceptibly to slow things down. He asked Churchill to put his proposal in writing and he suggested that it would be best to reach out to the Soviets through normal diplomatic channels.

Churchill sensed what Eisenhower was trying to do. But, like a dog with a bone, he was not about to give up what he had won earlier; he would not let Eisenhower turn that yes into a no. Churchill nimbly sidestepped the President's many cavils and caveats. He offered only enough information so that later no one could claim that he had failed to spell out his intentions. He mentioned no dates other than to assure the Americans that he would do nothing until he was back in Britain.

Finally, after repeated efforts to regain control of the situation, Eisenhower sent in the reinforcements. The Prime Minister had mentioned a 'reconnaissance in force' and Dulles had privately told Eisenhower that he found the idea alarming.

'You are to be a go-between,' said Dulles with undisguised distaste when he sat down with Churchill on the third day of the visit.

'No,' Churchill replied cheerily. 'For I know on which side I stand. I will be a reconnoitring patrol.'

Dulles expressed doubt that Churchill could get an Austrian treaty. The foreign ministers had already tried that with Molotov. He warned that were Churchill to fail as well, an impression might be created in the world that the only alternative was war. He predicted that a solo mission would not play well in America and that the White House might be compelled to announce that Churchill did not speak for the US. Though – crucially, in Churchill's view – Dulles never asked him in so many words not to contact the Soviets, the Secretary of State urged that the matter be 'very carefully weighed before any positive decision was made'.

Afterwards, Dulles reported the conversation to Eden when the Foreign Secretary visited him at home in Georgetown. Relations were icy between Dulles and his British counterpart. They had collided often and acrimoniously in Geneva, where Eden had been at pains to convey that British foreign policy would be set in London, not Washington. Though Dulles was rooting for Butler to succeed Churchill, he knew Eden to be no advocate of top-level talks and therefore a useful ally.

Previously, Eden had looked to Eisenhower to block Churchill's path to the summit. Now, the Americans were looking to Eden.

The long-suffering protégé was indeed eager for a heart-to-heart with Churchill after they left Washington. But it was the succession, not the summit, he burned to discuss. Had Churchill not said that that conversation would have to wait until he had finished with Eisenhower? Eden, who had been scheduled to fly home, decided to join Churchill on his ship in the hope of extracting a firm date for the handover.

Where Eden looked upon the Washington visit as an end, Churchill, characteristically, saw it as only a beginning. In contrast to his mood after Bermuda, he left the US a happy man. Churchill knew full well that Eisenhower was far from pleased and that there might be trouble down the line, but by his lights he had the President's blessing nonetheless.

At least, he could claim that he did. Having got what he needed at the White House, Churchill panted to be in touch with the Kremlin. As far as he was concerned, he did not have time to waste on the five-day sea voyage his doctor had strongly recommended for his health. Besides, he was in no mood for another confrontation with Eden. At the last minute, Churchill thought he might duck the heir apparent and fly home instead.

XVIII

An Obstinate Pig

Aboard the *Queen Elizabeth*, July 1954

In a loud voice that carried through the small, hot, crowded grill room on the sun deck of the *Queen Elizabeth*, Churchill protested that he did not know why he had allowed himself to be persuaded to travel by sea. It was lunchtime, 1 July 1954. The Prime Minister's party had boarded in New York the night before, and Churchill grumbled that he would have been at Chartwell already had he flown.

Angrily, he complained that the restaurant had no fan, that the windows were sealed, and that the sun was beating on him through the glass. Suddenly, to the embarrassment of his companions, he fled to another table, and then another. But nothing seemed to comfort him.

Seated at the original table with Soames and Moran, Colville suggested that the real reason Churchill was so on edge was that he knew matters were about to come to a head with Eden. Indeed, that night a 'bashful' Eden sought Colville's advice about the best time to speak to Churchill.

Meanwhile, Churchill had a chance to completely rethink his attitude towards the sea voyage. Instead of regarding it as a waste of precious time, he came to view it as an opportunity. And instead of being aggravated and offended by Eden's impatience, he found a way to use it to his advantage.

Churchill faced a huge problem at home. He had not told the Cabinet beforehand about his new summit pitch, and he expected they would raise objections and cause delays. So, though he had assured the Americans that he would wait until he reached London, he decided to contact the Soviets from the boat. Cabinet ministers would no doubt be incensed when they learned what he had done, but by then it would be too late to stop him. The scheme had the further advantage of boxing in the Cabinet in the event of a favourable response from Moscow. At that point, ministers would find it difficult to block Churchill without endangering themselves politically.

On the morning of 2 July, when Eden finally worked up the courage to approach him, Churchill was unusually welcoming. He offered to retire in September – if, that is, Eden made no objection to his contacting the Soviets to float the idea of a meeting. When Eden agreed to the horse trade, Churchill closeted himself with Colville to dictate a telegram to Molotov. He proposed two-power talks that could lead to a reunion of the Big Three 'where much might be settled'. How, he wanted to know, would Moscow feel about such a plan? Churchill was proceeding on the assumption that after three years of stall tactics, the French were finally about to ratify the EDC by the end of the summer. With the German problem resolved, he could see Malenkov in late August or early September – in time (theoretically anyway) to deliver on his part of the bargain with Eden. It was a tight schedule, to be sure, but it just might work.

Tempted with a definite date, the restraining hand had been unable to restrain himself. Yet hardly had Eden made his deal with the devil when second thoughts consumed him. After Churchill, Eden, and the others in their travelling party had a high-spirited lunch in the Prime Minister's dining room, Eden tried to claw back what he had agreed to earlier without jeopardizing the September date. Eden urged Churchill to wait until he had had a chance to check in with the Cabinet, in keeping with constitutional proprieties. He offered to personally deliver Churchill's message to Molotov when the foreign ministers reconvened in Geneva.

Churchill refused to consider it. He insisted that his message was not an official proposal and that he was only asking if the Soviets would care to have a visit. If the answer was no, he need not trouble the Cabinet. If it was yes, and the Cabinet disapproved, he could easily get out of the whole thing by notifying Molotov of his colleagues' point of view.

The crossfire continued all afternoon and evening. Eden persisted in recommending delay. Churchill demanded to telegraph at once. Eden warned that if Churchill went forward it would be contrary to his strong advice. When Colville and Soames sided with Eden, Churchill angrily threatened to throw both his private secretary and his son-in-law out the porthole.

For all the bluster on Churchill's part, there was a good deal of quiet calculation. At length, he offered to show the telegram to Butler and to invite his comments – if, that is, Eden would allow him to say that he agreed with it 'in principle' (which, they both knew, he did not). By his acquiescence, Eden permitted Churchill to make him complicit in the decision to act before they reached London. Churchill had fashioned a piece of evidence that he had proceeded not just with Eden's knowledge but with his support.

Churchill ran a considerable risk, however, that Butler might decide on his own to summon the Cabinet. That was why Churchill worded his covering message as he did: 'I propose to send this personal and private telegram, with which Anthony agrees in principle, to Molotov. I hope you will like it. The matter is urgent.' The telegram went off to London at half past ten that night. Churchill hoped that Butler would get back to him immediately, while Eden hoped that he would share the document with Cabinet colleagues and that they would move in unison to stop Churchill before it was too late. Eden did not, however, press Churchill to direct Butler in so many words to show the telegram to anyone else.

Everything depended on Butler, but by the following afternoon he had yet to respond. Eden's and Churchill's behaviour in the face of his thundering silence was typical of both men's natures. Eden pouted about how badly Churchill had treated him the previous day, but otherwise waited passively. Churchill grumbled that he had allowed himself to be trapped into querying Butler, but he also took action to make things go his way. The longer the delay, the likelier it seemed that Butler had summoned the Cabinet. On the chance that Butler had yet to do anything irrevocable, Churchill fired off a deviously worded telegram at a quarter to three that afternoon: 'Presume my message to the Bear has gone on. It in no way commits the Cabinet to making an official proposal. Time is important.'

For the moment anyway, time was on Churchill's side. This was a Saturday and Butler was in Norfolk for the weekend. Churchill's first telegram had arrived in London shortly after midnight, but it had had to be sent to the country by dispatch rider and did not reach the Chancellor until nearly 5 p.m. on Saturday. That evening, Butler conferred with the Foreign Office. On their advice, he was about to urge the Prime Minister to wait until he had had a chance to talk to the Cabinet when Churchill's misleading second telegram arrived. Told that Churchill assumed he had already sent on the Molotov telegram, Butler fretted that he had somehow misunderstood everything. Without delay, he sheepishly sent Churchill some suggestions for minor edits, along with the assurance that he would transmit the message to Moscow as soon as he heard back from him.

Churchill had brought it off. Not only had he managed to circumvent the Cabinet, he had also added the Chancellor to the list of those who had had a hand in the affair. On Butler's instructions, the British Ambassador in Moscow, Sir William Hayter, went to the Kremlin on Sunday afternoon to deliver Churchill's missive.

Two days later, the *Queen Elizabeth* docked in Southampton, where Churchill and Eden boarded a special train to London. Butler was waiting at Waterloo Station at seven that evening, and he accompanied them to Number Ten. There, Churchill hardly had a chance to catch his breath when the Soviet Ambassador, Jacob Malik, arrived with a message from Molotov. Churchill had not expected to have his reply so quickly. Molotov wrote, 'Your idea about a friendly Meeting between you and Premier G. M. Malenkov as well as the considerations expressed by you regarding the aims of such a Meeting, have met with sympathetic acknowledgement in Moscow.'

Molotov's answer sent Churchill into overdrive. Suddenly, he had what he believed he needed from both the Americans and the Soviets. Ironically, the main obstacle that faced Churchill now was his own Cabinet.

The Prime Minister had already entangled Eden and Butler in his web. Immediately, he moved to draw in Salisbury and Macmillan as well before he faced the full Cabinet the next morning. In the past, both men, Salisbury in particular, had vehemently opposed any talks that did not include the Americans. It was after 10 p.m. when Churchill summoned Salisbury and Macmillan to the Cabinet Room. Ostensibly, he wanted them to consult, along with Eden and Butler, on the delicate task of informing Eisenhower that he had already contacted Molotov. But since when did Churchill need help crafting wily telegrams?

Salisbury arrived first. Macmillan, who had just been getting into bed when the phone rang, entered a bit later. Eden and Butler, both looking the worse for wear, were also at the table. The file the Prime Minister passed around, comprising the shipboard messages to Butler and Molotov, did not display either Churchill or Eden in an especially flattering light. Clearly, Churchill had flouted constitutional proprieties by acting on a major foreign policy initiative he had yet to discuss with the Cabinet. Clearly, he had been far from straightforward in his arrangements with Butler. And clearly, Eden had countenanced Churchill's actions, whether out of weakness, ambition, or both. After Salisbury examined the documents, he was visibly distressed. But it was only when Churchill spoke of the need to explain himself to Eisenhower that the full dimensions of what the Prime Minister had done began to sink in.

It was not just the Cabinet whom Churchill had put in an awkward position by presenting his correspondence with Molotov as a done deal. That in itself was bad enough. Even worse was the fact that Eisenhower had as yet no inkling that Churchill had made an overture to Moscow, though he had been the President's guest only a few days before. While Churchill believed that he had acted in the interest of peace, Salisbury judged that his behaviour at sea had made the world more rather than less dangerous. In the interest of minimizing the damage to the Anglo-American alliance, Salisbury stifled his indignation and joined forces with Churchill in an effort to finesse Eisenhower.

At length, the ministers approved a message to Eisenhower that was as guileful as those Churchill had written to Butler from the boat: 'In the light of our talks and after careful thought I thought it right to send an exploratory message to Molotov to feel the ground about the possibility of a two-power meeting. This of course committed nobody except myself.' Churchill spoke as if his actions flowed directly from the Washington talks and as if he had complied fully with Dulles's request that he consider carefully before he took a decision. He pretended that he had not said that he would wait until he returned to Britain, and he prompted Eisenhower to comment not on what he, Churchill, had done, but rather on Molotov's reply. What, he asked, did Eisenhower make of the message from Moscow?

Churchill had moved slyly and swiftly to bind the President to him, to make Eisenhower a partner rather than an opponent. Whether the stratagem would work remained to be seen. At the same time, as Macmillan perceived, Churchill had acted along similar lines with Salisbury and himself.

The ministers left Number Ten after midnight. Salisbury and Macmillan accompanied Eden to the Foreign Office to hear his side of the story. It turned out that they were not the only ones who were disappointed in Eden. Awaiting him was a stack of messages from Foreign Office colleagues who were appalled by Churchill's actions on the boat and troubled by Eden's failure to restrain him. Eden alternated between insisting that 'no power on earth' could have stopped Churchill and blaming Butler for his failure to go to the Cabinet when he had the chance.

Macmillan wondered why Eden had not simply threatened to resign, the final option when one cannot live with a prime minister's decisions. But then, had Churchill called his bluff, Eden would have left office just when it seemed as if his accession was – really, this time – about to take place.

Churchill's telegram went off to Washington at a quarter to three in the morning. At half past eleven, he was back in the Cabinet Room. Of the fifteen ministers seated around the table, only those who had attended the previous night's session at Number Ten knew about the 'bombshell' he was about to drop. The others were still 'blithely unconscious' of what awaited them. This was the first time most had seen Churchill since his journey, and the room echoed with congratulations on a job presumably well done. Those few in the know made no effort to disillusion their colleagues; they would find out soon enough. For an hour and ten minutes, Churchill meandered through various less incendiary topics before he came to the fifth and penultimate item on the agenda, the Washington talks. As he began to speak, his nervousness was perceptible. Before long, the reason for his unease became clear.

He opened by saying that while he was not ready to give a full account of his trip he 'must, however, inform the Cabinet of a project for a meeting with Russia'. As he offered ministers their first glimpse of his retooled Soviet initiative, he emphasized that Eisenhower had admitted his right to go and that Dulles had 'tacitly' accepted the possibility that he would go. Churchill went on to disclose that he had contacted Molotov from the ship and that he had already had an answer.

His audience reacted to these revelations with looks of 'blank surprise'. Crookshank, who sat to one side of the Prime Minister, radiated 'disgust'. Churchill sought to obfuscate his failure to consult the full Cabinet beforehand by highlighting the various consultations he had undertaken – with the Foreign Secretary, the Chancellor of the Exchequer, the Lord President and the Minister of Housing. None of this was enough to dissipate the gathering storm.

When Churchill finished, he asked Eden to comment. Eden spoke briefly and anxiously. He said a few words about possible European reactions and he seconded Churchill's point that it would be best to wait to hear back from Eisenhower before the Cabinet took a decision about a reply to Molotov. But what, really, could Eden say after he had allowed Churchill to go forward on the boat? As at the time of his 1938 resignation speech, there was the uncomfortable appearance of Eden having been at pains to guard his claim to the succession.

Also as in 1938, it fell to Salisbury to speak the harsh words that Eden dared not utter. Clearly, Churchill's attempt to defang Salisbury had failed. Just when a parley at the summit seemed achingly within grasp, Salisbury put Churchill on notice that he was prepared to stop him. Acting as if he had no doubt that his was the opinion that counted in the room, Salisbury stated that he had reflected overnight and that his attitude would turn largely on the 'temper' of Eisenhower's answer. If the answer were 'critical or hostile', Salisbury would advise the Cabinet to vote against going forward with the Malenkov meeting because it would damage 'the US/UK relationship'. That relationship, Salisbury made it clear, overrode everything else. 'Meanwhile, I reserve my attitude.'

Macmillan began to speak, but Churchill cut him off to counter what Salisbury had just said. 'The United States can't veto my visit,' Churchill pointed out. 'They accept that.' The Prime Minister made no reference to what Salisbury had heard Dulles tell him the previous October – that, while the Americans accepted that the decision was wholly Churchill's to make, a solo mission would jeopardize the Anglo-American alliance.

After the Cabinet agreed to wait to hear from Eisenhower, Churchill turned to the last item on the agenda, the question of whether Britain ought to manufacture its own hydrogen bomb. He laid out the strategic argument that such a weapon would assure Britain's place at the table in all subsequent East–West negotiations. But he mischievously left it to Salisbury to disclose that the defence policy committee had already decided to build an H-bomb and to carry on with active preparations. In his capacity as Lord President and minister for the bomb, Salisbury had participated in the secret deliberations in June. The revelation that there had been no Cabinet consultation on this matter as well left several ministers reeling. They were upset on account less of the decision itself than of the improper way in which it had been made. When Crookshank angrily protested that such a momentous decision had been communicated to the full Cabinet in so cavalier a fashion, it became evident that Churchill was up to his old tricks. He had set the birds against one another. Crookshank stalked out, others followed, and the meeting broke up unceremoniously.

By this pretty manoeuvre, Churchill put Salisbury on notice that if the noble lord really meant to go up against him, he had better watch his back. Macmillan spotted a disaster in the making. If two such uncompromising characters went to war, the effect on both the Government and the party could be disastrous. All this was coming at a most inconvenient time for Macmillan personally. Just when the post of Foreign Secretary in an Eden Government was conceivably about to be his, he was distraught at the prospect that the Government might fall.

Churchill, by contrast, seemed as though he had not a care in the world when he hosted a dinner party in honour of Pug Ismay that evening. He knew precisely what he had and had not said in Washington. He was sanguine that in the end Eisenhower would accept that it was not within his power to prevent Anglo-Soviet talks. He was also optimistic that Salisbury could be mollified and that the crisis would end with a whimper. After dinner, Macmillan, who was one of the guests, had a talk with Colville about (what else?) the Cabinet crisis. When Colville pointed out that Churchill intended to retire in September in any case, Macmillan warned that the Government and probably the Tory party would have broken up before that. Macmillan alternated between viewing Churchill's actions on the boat as evidence of almost demoniacal cunning on one hand and of senility on the other.

'He must go at once, on grounds of health, to avoid a disaster,' Macmillan declared.

'You are very severe,' Colville protested.

'As you know,' said Macmillan, 'I am devoted to Winston and admire him more than any man. But he is not fit. He cannot function. If there were a strong monarch, of great experience, he would be told so by the Palace.'

When Colville refused to ask Churchill to leave office before September, Macmillan proposed that he at least speak to him about the gravity of the crisis. 'I beg of you to urge him not to try to ride this one off too easily. He must take it seriously and realize how deeply he has hurt us.'

Meanwhile, Churchill's telegram had reached Washington. Far from sharing Churchill's delight in Molotov's friendly reply, Eisenhower regarded it as proof that Moscow aimed to drive a wedge between the Americans and the British. No one, not Eisenhower or Dulles, not Eden or other Cabinet ministers, had been able to stop Churchill. The one remaining hope seemed to be a higher power. Eisenhower and Dulles agreed that 'only another stroke' would be capable of preventing Churchill from going to Malenkov.

Eisenhower complained to Makins that Churchill had confronted him with a tricky political problem. Anglo-Soviet talks were sure to play poorly with the American people. In anticipation of the inevitable questions from press and public when the news broke, the President wondered whether it might not be best if he simply 'went fishing'. Eisenhower ruefully acknowledged to Makins that in the end he 'could not prevent the head of a friendly state from doing what he thought right'.

Before the day was done, Eisenhower wrote to Churchill in a tone of annoyance: 'You did not let any grass grow under your feet. When you left here, I had thought, obviously erroneously, that you were in an undecided mood about this matter, and that when you had cleared your own mind I would receive some notice if you were to put your programme into action.' Eisenhower conceded, however, that that was now 'past history'. Treating it as a foregone conclusion that Churchill would soon publicly announce his plans, Eisenhower asked only to be told the date so that he could prepare a statement of his own. He would probably say that while Churchill was in Washington the possibility of a Big Three meeting had been spoken of, that he had been unable to see how it could serve a useful purpose, and that he had indicated that if Churchill did undertake such a mission the plan would carry Eisenhower's hopes for the best but that it would not engage his responsibility.

Eisenhower's missive reached the Foreign Office after midnight. When he read it, Churchill was thrilled. He had endured enough of Eisenhower's emphatic nos in the past to recognize that this message was something else entirely. And he sensed that with a bit of fancy footwork he might be able to coax an even more useful answer out of the President. When he began a new telegram, 'I hope you are not vexed with me for not submitting to you the text of my telegram to Molotov,' he was prompting Eisenhower to say that of course his anxieties were baseless.

In this slippery vein Churchill continued, 'I felt that as it was a private and personal enquiry which I had not brought officially before the Cabinet I had better bear the burden myself and not involve you in any way. I have made it clear to Molotov that you are in no way committed. I thought that would be agreeable to you, and that we could then consider the question in the light of the answer I got.'

Did Churchill really expect Eisenhower to believe much of this? Probably not, but at least there was the veneer of a decent explanation and perhaps they could proceed from there. Now that a parley with the Soviets was in play, Churchill suddenly was all for full and frank consultation with the Americans. He promised not to seek an official decision from the Cabinet until he had heard again from Eisenhower. And he insisted that there would be no question of an announcement until their two governments had consulted together and agreed on what it would be best to say.

When Churchill faced the Cabinet on the morning of 8 July, he read aloud the full text of Eisenhower's telegram. Then he read his own draft reply and suggested that they wait to take a decision until they had had Eisenhower's further comments. He voiced confidence that he could get a 'better' answer from the President – that is, an answer that put to rest any fears about Anglo-American relations.

Churchill went on to paint himself as blameless in having contacted Molotov without Cabinet consultation. He argued that the telegram had been a personal message no different from those he had exchanged with foreign leaders in the past. He emphasized that he had long reserved the right to communicate personally with his counterparts abroad, and he denied that in the present instance he had felt any obligation to go to the Cabinet.

The truth of course was more complicated. A few days after this, he privately confessed to Colville that he had deliberately gone around the Cabinet. Offstage, Churchill disclosed his abiding belief that had he waited to consult them until after his ship returned, they would almost certainly have held him up with objections and delays. He suggested that the stakes had been so high and the possible benefits so crucial to human survival that he had been prepared to use any methods to secure a meeting with Malenkov. Throughout Churchill's career, his willingness to take ethically questionable shortcuts had incensed countless critics. If he thought he was doing something important, his attitude was let the rules be damned. He dismissed those who had a problem with this approach as nitpickers.

Salisbury had been wincing at Churchill's bad behaviour since at least the 1930s. This morning, Salisbury weighed in that Churchill's telegram to Molotov had constituted an important act of foreign policy which involved the collective responsibility of the Cabinet. Taking Churchill at his word that he believed he had the 'absolute right' to conduct such correspondence, Salisbury pointed out that it was the remedy of ministers to resign if they disagreed. He did not say that he or any other minister would resign, with all that that might mean for the viability of Churchill's postwar Government – only that it was an option.

At first, Churchill ignored the fact that the threat of resignation was now on the table. (As far as he was concerned, the Cecils had long debased the currency of that threat by using it too often.) Resuming his self-defence, Churchill argued that what he had done on the ship was less a fully fledged act of foreign policy than an enquiry. Action, he conceded, would have required Cabinet consent. enquiry, on the other hand, was quite permissible so long as he showed the telegram to Eden. Then the zinger: 'He [Eden] could have insisted that it should come to the Cabinet.'

How was Eden to respond? As Salisbury and other supporters well knew, he had insisted on no such thing. Today, Eden's feeble claim that he had had it 'in mind' that the Chancellor of the Exchequer would show the telegram to the Cabinet prompted an indignant Butler to jump in. Creating a sideshow was a tactic that had worked for Churchill in the past, but Salisbury was determined not to let him get away with it this time.

'Only two days passed before the Prime Minister returned,' he interjected, turning the heat back on Churchill. A few minutes before, Salisbury had made the pretence of taking him at his word. Now, he implied that whatever Churchill claimed about his thinking on the boat, he had really just been trying to ram his policy through before the Cabinet could object: 'What was the urgency which precluded waiting for a proper consultation?'

Confronted with the truth, Churchill replied tartly, 'I may have exaggerated the urgency of my hope for strengthening world peace.' He went on to suggest that if the Cabinet broke on the constitutional issue, most Britons would side with him. After 11 May 1953, there could be little doubt about where the people stood on the question of a summit meeting, and he threatened to appeal directly to them. Let his adversaries cry that he had skirted the rules; Churchill was sure the public would not care. Swinton, Lyttelton, and Stuart, the Secretaries of State for Commonwealth Relations, the Colonies, and Scotland respectively, scrambled to cool things down. In spite of their efforts, Churchill went further. He hinted that Salisbury was not the only one who might soon bolt.

'If I found myself at variance with colleagues,' Churchill warned, 'I could resign.' Like Salisbury, Churchill did not say he would go – only that his resignation was on the table, with all that that might mean for his colleagues' political futures.

At a time when those colleagues had been praying that Churchill would agree to retire, he suddenly recast the possibility of resignation as a threat. Yes, they all still wanted him to go, but not this way. If Churchill resigned on this issue he would torpedo the Conservatives' chances in the next general election by making them look like enemies of the peace. Churchill had been known to abandon his party before; why not now?

At this point, Churchill did not think he would have to do anything so drastic. He calculated that with a little help from Washington he could yet defuse the crisis. On the morning of Friday, 9 July, when he received Eisenhower's second reply ('Of course I am not vexed'), he moved at once to put a few more key words into the President's mouth. Churchill opened his third message of the series, 'I am very much relieved by your kind telegram which reassures me that no serious differences will arise between our two governments on account of Russian excursion or "solitary pilgrimage" by me.' He gilded the pill by promising not to agree to meet Malenkov in Moscow, and by reiterating his plan to seek a gesture of Soviet intentions in the form of an Austrian treaty. If Churchill elicited the answer from Eisenhower that he hoped for, what choice would Salisbury have but to back off?

At half past twelve that afternoon, the Cabinet reconvened, this time in Churchill's room at the House of Commons. Churchill read aloud Eisenhower's second telegram as well as his own draft reply.

Salisbury cut in, 'I am unalterably opposed to a meeting with Russia without the United States.'

Previously, Salisbury had indicated only that he would base his decision on Eisenhower's response. Now that he had seen how effectively Churchill was playing Eisenhower, he announced that he would oppose bilateral talks no matter how good the answer Churchill managed to extract. Directly addressing Churchill, Salisbury went on, 'I told you last year why I was opposed to this.' (He meant the letter he had written to him after the Derby.)

Salisbury continued, 'Other members of the Cabinet may think it is right to go forward. But, if they so decided, I should have to resign.' As Salisbury said this, Churchill turned 'dead white' one moment and 'puce' the next. After Salisbury finished speaking, there was silence. Salisbury had just moved into open and direct conflict with Churchill over the issue dearest to the Prime Minister's heart. He had in effect asked their colleagues to choose between Churchill and himself.

Churchill took a few seconds to regain his composure. 'I should greatly regret a severance,' he said at last. 'But I hope our private friendship would survive.'

After the Cabinet, an anxious Eden asked Macmillan to come to him at the Foreign Office that afternoon. As the two soon agreed, much had altered as a consequence of the explosive morning session.

The time had been when Salisbury plotted and planned to make Eden prime minister. Now Salisbury was poised to bring down the Government on the very eve of Eden's accession. The time had been when Salisbury worried that Churchill had embarked on a dangerous game of chicken. Now Salisbury had begun to play a similar game himself. The time had been when Eden complained bitterly of Macmillan (of his rapacity for high office, his toadying, and other sins) to Salisbury. Now it was Salisbury whose actions horrified him, and Macmillan in whom he confided.

As ever, Salisbury presented himself as calmly willing to sacrifice everything for his principles. But was he really? If the Government fell, he would still be Marquess of Salisbury, a figure in both the party and the nation. Men like Eden and Macmillan stood to lose much more. Under the circumstances, their priority, as they saw it, was to keep the Government intact until Eden was safely at its head. Macmillan went to Hatfield House that evening to beg Salisbury on behalf of Eden and himself to do nothing rash. Eden was due to return to Geneva the following week and the last thing he wanted was for Salisbury to provoke a political crisis in his absence. Initially, Salisbury seemed willing to hold off until Eden came home. In the course of the weekend, he changed his mind.

Salisbury decided that if he were to avoid becoming complicit in policies he did not support, he must bail out sooner rather than later. Contemplating the speech he would deliver in the House of Lords to explain his resignation, Salisbury thought he would cite the telegram to Molotov and the 11 May speech as examples of Churchill's tendency to make major decisions without properly consulting his colleagues.

On the morning of Tuesday, 13 July, Churchill received a third message from Washington. Eisenhower wrote: 'You, of course, know that never for one moment would this create any difference between two Governments which are headed by you and me . . .' He went on to say that he could not of course undertake to deliver US public opinion, but he pledged to do his best to 'minimize' the American people's unfavourable reaction to Anglo-Soviet talks. On reading this, Churchill was ready to do a victory lap round the Cabinet table. Later that morning, he read the telegram aloud to the Cabinet and distributed copies. As he had hoped, most ministers seemed relieved. The predictable exception was Salisbury, who appeared 'glum and worried'. At this point, it certainly looked as if Salisbury was not going to be able to carry the Cabinet. Churchill calmly announced that he would wait to call for a decision until the Geneva Conference wound up in about ten days. Though he planned to go forward in any case, his proposal to Molotov would be cast differently depending on the outcome at Geneva.

Following the Cabinet, Churchill roared that he did not 'give a damn' if Salisbury resigned. Now that he had his trump card in the form of Eisenhower's telegram, he was sure that no matter what Salisbury did, the rest of the Cabinet would stay put.

Eden, Macmillan, Swinton, and other colleagues did not share the Prime Minister's optimism. They expected that Salisbury's defection would be followed by Crookshank's and then others. In the days that followed, various failed efforts to persuade either Churchill or Salisbury to back down culminated in a visit by Macmillan on 16 July to Clementine Churchill at Number Ten. It was no great secret that she longed for her husband to retire. Macmillan spoke to her of Salisbury's imminent resignation and of the likely consequences. He reported the feeling in the Cabinet that much as they all loved Churchill it would be best for both the party and the country if he handed over immediately. Would she talk to him?

Though Clementine Churchill had never warmed to Macmillan, she was cordial and composed during the visit. When he left, however, she called Colville and angrily recounted all that Macmillan had said. Her indignation puzzled Colville. He asked whether she did not herself feel that Churchill ought to step down.

'Yes, I do indeed,' she replied, 'but I don't wish to be told that by Mr Harold Macmillan.'

Clementine Churchill tended to be fearless with her husband. She was known to scold him thoroughly when it suited her, and the old couple had many stormy scenes. Yet on the present occasion she preferred not to be alone with him when she conveyed his colleagues' views. Colville joined the Churchills for lunch, but the confrontation did not go well. Colville thought she would have been wise to lead off by pointing out that ministers were anxious to avert Salisbury's resignation. Instead, her comment that the Cabinet was angry with Churchill for mishandling the situation caused him to 'snap back' at her. At length, Churchill turned to his private secretary and asked him to notify Macmillan that he would be glad if he would come and tell him in his own words what he thought – 'rather than tell my wife'.

When Macmillan reappeared, Churchill was in no mood to listen. He had already heard the particulars at lunch. Instead, he delivered an angry, rambling, repetitious defence of his actions on the boat.

As far as the Cabinet crisis was concerned, Churchill boasted that he held all the cards. He warned that neither the Conservative rank and file nor the country at large would tolerate a palace revolt by disaffected ministers. He pointed out that his personal popularity transcended party lines, and he promised that if Salisbury and others resigned he would simply form a new and more powerful Government. Possibly, he would form a coalition government with the Opposition, who, whatever their differences with him in other areas, wholeheartedly supported his Soviet initiative. According to Churchill, Salisbury's preoccupation with constitutional niceties would stir the public not at all. The only issue that would resonate was whether meeting Malenkov was a good idea.

When Churchill gloated that Salisbury's resignation would be as foolish as Lord Randolph Churchill's had been, he was referring to some highly charged family history. In 1886, Winston's father, who had been spoken of as a possible successor to Lord Salisbury as prime minister, tendered his resignation as Chancellor of the Exchequer. He claimed to be driven by differences on matters of high policy, but the Cecils insisted that his resignation had had nothing to do with principle. Lady Salisbury, the Prime Minister's wife, blamed that wilfulness said to be characteristic of the Churchills throughout history. Whatever Lord Randolph's motives, he had clearly expected Lord Salisbury to refuse his resignation. Instead, the Prime Minister called his bluff. Lord Randolph's career was destroyed in an instant. A generation later, Winston was confident that this time round it was a Cecil who was about to self-destruct and a Churchill who would endure.

About an hour into his verbal jag, Churchill began to calm down. Had he simply worn himself out? The lull in the tempest allowed Macmillan to make the case that in spite of anything the Prime Minister said the resignations would do the Government and the party much injury.

When Macmillan left, Churchill pretended to Colville that nothing of importance had been spoken of. He coyly claimed to have no idea why Clemmie had made such a fuss. Nevertheless, in important respects Macmillan's visit did seem to have an impact. Only now did Churchill begin to accept that Salisbury's resignation could have grave consequences.

Churchill moved at once to try to bind Eden and Butler to him. On the night of 16 July he composed a telegram to Eden that mocked Salisbury as 'this stickler for precise etiquette' and questioned the sincerity of his vaunted principles. He accused his opponent of being one of those men who 'compound the sins they are inclined to by banning those they have no mind to'. Salisbury's behaviour the previous summer, when he had been a principal player in the medical cover-up, gave Churchill licence to speak of him in this manner. The high-and-mighty Salisbury had been perfectly willing to get in the dirt with Churchill when it suited him, but he took a very different attitude now that strict adherence to the rules best served his interests. Churchill assured Eden that when Salisbury complained of constitutional improprieties, he was arguing on very weak ground.

That Churchill was more worried than he let on is suggested by his behaviour with Butler on 19 July. Previously, Churchill had been adamant that he had felt no obligation to check in with the Cabinet before he approached Molotov. Now, he attempted to bully the Chancellor into accepting an untruthful account that suggested that Churchill had really tried to consult the Cabinet after all. Pinocchio's nose grew longer as he claimed to have expected Butler to summon the Cabinet on receipt of the first telegram. It continued to grow when he said that he had assumed Butler's suggested edits were the product of Cabinet consultation.

In Churchill's intimidating presence, Butler made no protest. Still, he was unwilling to lie for Churchill again or, worse, to be cast as the fall guy. Two days later, Butler politely but vigorously disputed him in writing. Aware of what Churchill might yet be capable of, he took care to conclude with a gentle warning, pointing out that he was also sending a copy of his rebuttal to the Secretary of the Cabinet 'so that it may be on record'. If Churchill persisted, Butler would ask that the document be circulated to the full Cabinet.

Finally, Eden turned to the Americans for help with the old man. He asked the US representative in Geneva, Under Secretary of State Walter Bedell Smith, to come to London after the conference. Explaining that he was 'gravely concerned' about Churchill's solitary pilgrimage to meet Malenkov, Eden enlisted Smith to try to talk him out of it. Churchill was fond of Smith, who had served as Eisenhower's chief of staff during the war. Nevertheless, on Thursday, 22 July, when Smith made his pitch in advance of a dinner party in his honour at Number Ten, he was entirely unsuccessful. Churchill turned aside Smith's arguments that Malenkov was not actually filling Stalin's shoes and that at the moment it was quite possible that Molotov might be the more important figure.

He sent Smith back to Washington with a message for Eisenhower: 'I am an obstinate pig.'

After dinner, Churchill drew Eden aside. He made it clear that he expected Eden's support the following morning when the critical Cabinet meeting was due to take place in Churchill's room in the House of Commons. Following their terse little talk, Eden was so flustered that he forgot about his wife and went home without her by mistake. Churchill assumed that yet again he had bent the heir apparent to his will. Friday morning, however, Churchill was about to leave for Westminster when a note from the Foreign Secretary took him by surprise. Eden had composed the message in the middle of the night in a fit of agitation. He wrote that on reflection he would not be able to do as he had been asked. As far as the meeting with Malenkov was concerned, Churchill was on his own.

Ministers gathered at eleven. Three other items came first on the agenda. When at last Churchill reached the potentially explosive fourth item, he calmly asked the Cabinet to approve his draft telegram to Molotov. The telegram, which he read aloud, suggested that before the British made a formal proposal he and Molotov should agree on a date and place for the meeting. Churchill named early September in Bern, Stockholm, or Vienna.

No sooner had he finished reading than Salisbury jumped in. His face 'white and tense', Salisbury spoke from notes. He expressed the hope that 'no message need be sent now leading up to a firm proposal for bilateral talks'. But instead of focusing on the question of Cabinet consultation, as Churchill and the others had been expecting, Salisbury took a different tack. At the time of the previous Cabinet, it had looked as if he had no chance of persuading his colleagues to join him in trying to stop Churchill. Even ministers who agreed that they ought to have been consulted about the message to Molotov were unlikely to raise a fuss now that Churchill had Eisenhower's third telegram in hand. In the past ten days, Salisbury had had a chance to completely rethink his strategy. His comments of recent months about American recklessness had touched a chord with the Cabinet. Today, he began by recalling that initially it had been the constitutional implications of Churchill's actions that had chiefly concerned him.

'On reflection,' Salisbury continued, 'I find the international repercussions even more disturbing. Some people think Russia is now the greatest threat to peace. I don't. I think the main danger is from the United States.' Not for the first time in this setting, Salisbury expressed concern that the Americans might be tempted to bring matters to a head while they still possessed overwhelming atomic superiority.

Salisbury's remarks tapped into strong Cabinet sentiment that the Americans had been playing a dangerous game in Indo-China and elsewhere. 'During this period,' he went on, 'the supreme object of policy should be to preserve the unity of the West. How can we expect the US to respect that if we approach Russia without prior consultation?' If the British acted alone, Salisbury asked, was there not a risk that they would thereby encourage the Americans to pursue independent policies and to take less account of London's views?

In short, Salisbury was no longer attacking Churchill for having flouted the rules. He was calling him to task for having risked Britain's ability to restrain the United States. It was a potent argument and suddenly he seemed to have a real chance of defeating the Prime Minister on the central issue of Churchill's postwar premiership. Churchill could no longer sneer that Salisbury was concerned with mere questions of etiquette while he was engaged in the rather more important business of saving the world. Now, Salisbury also claimed to be trying to prevent a third world war. In closing, Salisbury urged the Cabinet not to allow Churchill to go forward with two-power talks. Churchill had boxed ministers in politically by acting first and informing them later, but Salisbury thought he saw a way out. This very morning Moscow had issued a new attack on US policies.

Salisbury proposed that Molotov be informed that in light of these statements the entire situation needed to be reviewed.

Churchill was caught off guard. Suddenly, he had a real contest on his hands. At first, he tried to recover by arguing that of course there had been prior consultation with the Americans. He ticked off examples and he read aloud from Eisenhower's third telegram.

Salisbury was unimpressed. He sniffed, 'No word was said before the approach to Molotov.'

'Much was said informally, though with no time factor, in Washington,' Churchill countered. 'I mentioned a bi-lateral reconnaissance as well as an eventual three-power meeting. They knew what was in my mind.'

At this point, Churchill abruptly shifted the ground back to the issue of Cabinet consultation, where he preferred to fight. The debate over the international repercussions of his behaviour was far more dangerous to him. Salisbury allowed himself to be lured into further discussion of the constitutional issue, and before long he had lost his edge. Lest he manage to regain it, Churchill called for a vote. Salisbury fought him off and at length Eden suggested that they postpone a final decision to give them all time to digest that morning's blast from Moscow. Churchill again demanded an immediate vote, but the ministers were desperate to stall. It was decided that they would reconvene on Monday, and the session ended with Churchill and Salisbury trading bitter threats to resign if the other prevailed.

Referring to the setting of their next encounter, Churchill declared, 'If it is to be my last Cabinet, I should like it to be at Downing Street, not here [i.e. the House of Commons].' Then he looked over at his antagonist and huffily asked, 'Will that suit Lord Salisbury?'

'Certainly,' Salisbury said, 'if I am to be there.'

'What do you mean "if I am to be there"?' Churchill fumed. 'Will you resign before that?'

Salisbury flashed a wry smile. 'I only said "if".'

As the curtain dropped, there was a sense that compromise between these two was impossible. If on Monday the Cabinet blocked Churchill, he was pledged to resign and to tell the public why. If they let the Prime Minister respond as he wished to Molotov, Salisbury would go.

That weekend, Churchill presided over a 'stag-party' at Chequers attended by several Cabinet ministers. Churchill and his guests laughed, told stories, and recited poetry. But for all the gaiety, an 'air of crisis' hung over the occasion. To their colleagues' horror, both Churchill and Salisbury seemed ready to go to the extreme if they did not get their way. Neither appeared to care if he brought the Government and the Tory party down with him. Whether it was Churchill or Salisbury who resigned, Monday looked to be a day of doom.

On Saturday evening, the unexpected happened. The Soviets delivered identical notes to the British, American, French, and Chinese embassies in Moscow to propose a thirty-two-power foreign ministers' conference on European security issues. Clearly, the proposal aimed to derail French ratification of the EDC. The Soviet note was a game-changer and it profoundly unsettled Churchill. How could he possibly go ahead with efforts to arrange a top-level meeting so long as the new proposal was in play? In his great eagerness to return to the summit, had he misread the tenor and timing of Molotov's 6 July message?

The fireworks everyone had been dreading on Monday never happened. Instead, a strangely subdued Churchill informed the Cabinet that the Soviet note, which had been made public, constituted a 'new event'. Churchill opined that it was clearly calculated to block French ratification of the EDC. He said he was satisfied that he could not go forward with his proposal for bilateral talks while this suggestion of a much larger foreign ministers' meeting was being publicly canvassed. Accordingly, he had prepared a new reply to Molotov's 6 July message. He suggested saying that his own proposal would be held in abeyance while the Soviet note was under consideration.

Churchill wanted the Cabinet to understand that he was not conceding that he had done anything wrong. 'I don't regret my approach. It was consistent with what I have said in public.' But this burst of defiance quickly died out. What was the point? The battle was over, though in the end it was not Salisbury who had shot down Churchill's summit proposal, but the Soviets. Thus far in the meeting, Salisbury had remained silent. But when Churchill suggested that the Cabinet approve the substance of his message to Molotov, its precise wording to be settled later with Eden, Salisbury piped up that he would be happy to assent.

In the days that followed, Churchill wore his heavy heart on his sleeve. He seemed exceptionally old and confused; he alternated between sitting in silence and rambling on about nothing; he looked at times as if he might be about to suffer another stroke. When Parliament adjourned at the end of the week, the table talk in political London was that Churchill would have handed over power by the time they reassembled on 19 October.

But then, on the very first day of the eleven-week recess, the situation shifted dramatically again – at least, to Churchill's eye. He was at Chartwell on Saturday night when a new note from Molotov was brought in. Molotov expressed astonishment that Churchill seemed to think that the proposed thirty-two-power conference ruled out top-level talks. Again, Churchill went into overdrive, though the Foreign Office advised that Molotov was probably just trying to preclude accusations that the Kremlin had killed the British peace proposal. Churchill moved at once to resume the Cabinet debate where it had broken off. Salisbury had come at him with a powerful new argument. Though Churchill had managed to sidetrack him, Salisbury was sure to reprise his strongest points when the contest resumed. Cabinet members had already begun to leave town, so instead of calling a meeting at Downing Street, Churchill dictated a fresh set of arguments for bilateral talks and sent them around on 3 August.

In the knowledge that Salisbury's argument about the American danger was weighing heavily with ministers, Churchill hijacked it. Churchill did not disagree that the Americans might be tempted to bring tensions to a head while they still had overwhelming atomic superiority over the Soviets. He, too, saw the American danger during the next two or three years as real and pressing. But where Salisbury cited that danger as a reason to avoid two-power talks, Churchill argued that it made those talks the more essential.

Salisbury took two weeks to respond. When he did (copying his remarks to Eden, Butler, Macmillan, and Crookshank) it was evident that his patience had worn thin and that he was determined to put an end to Churchill's summit dreams once and for all. This time, Salisbury said the unsayable. For nine years, Churchill had been fuelled by the belief that if only he could return to the summit, he could head off another world war. The particular men he wished to see and the tactics he planned to employ had changed over time. What had never altered was his confidence that summit talks were the best way to achieve a lasting peace and that his unique gifts, insights, and personal stature made him the best, no, the only figure in the West to conduct them. In 1954, as in 1945, Churchill had no doubt that face to face with the Soviet leadership he would be able to accomplish what no one else could. That clear conviction had helped him spring back from electoral defeat, two strokes, and other trials. Now, a very fed-up Salisbury bluntly informed Churchill that he had been operating on the basis of 'an illusion'.

Salisbury argued that summit talks were destined to fail and that not even someone as 'pre-eminent' and 'persuasive' as Churchill would be able to achieve anything by a personal meeting with Malenkov. Salisbury was not just attacking Churchill's core ideas. He was undermining his justification for clinging to power long past the stage when most people thought he ought to have gone. He was puncturing the myth of his indispensability. If the defining policy of Churchill's postwar premiership was indeed based on an illusion, what reason did he have to remain in the job? In closing, Salisbury renewed his threat to resign if the Cabinet sided with the Prime Minister on this.

Salisbury's attack seemed hardly to touch Churchill; at least, Churchill behaved that way. On 21 August, he replied that he planned to go forward and warned Salisbury against being too rigid in his views. (Churchill was far from the first person to accuse a Cecil of lacking flexibility.) Churchill wrote: 'In peace or war action is determined by events rather than by fixed ideas. One is fortunate when one has the power to decide in accordance with the factual circumstances of the day or even of the hour. I always reserve to myself as much of this advantage as I can get. Not only does one thing affect many others, but their proportions alter in an ever-changing scene.' Why, in short, take a position before Salisbury saw where things stood in a few weeks' time?

Churchill expected to summon the Cabinet to vote on his proposal as soon as the Western allies formally rejected the idea of a thirty-two-power conference and the French ratified the EDC. He thought both matters would be out of the way by the end of the month, or early September at the latest. Two days after he wrote to Salisbury, however, a crater opened before him. Following three years of endless delays, the French would not be ratifying the EDC after all. Western diplomats were going to have to develop a substitute plan to rearm West Germany and bring the Germans into Western Europe. Churchill gruffly acknowledged that until a new plan was agreed upon (a process that could take months, perhaps even years) he could not renew his proposal.

The day after Churchill heard about the French, he wrote to Eden that the September handover was off. He had no intention of abandoning his post during the present world crisis. As he prepared to lob this grenade into the Eden camp, he also had reason to expect quite an explosion at home. No doubt his wife would be as unhappy as his political heir about his determination to battle on. So he reprised the stunt that he had recently used with the Cabinet and with Eisenhower. He sent off the letter first and told Clementine about it later.

'It has gone,' Winston reported on 25 August when he showed her a copy of what he had written to Eden. 'The responsibility is mine. But I hope you will give me your love.'

Churchill's eightieth birthday was fast approaching, and both Houses of Parliament had commissioned the artist Graham Sutherland to paint his portrait. The picture was to be their joint gift to the Prime Minister, who agreed to sit for sketches on 26 August. At Chartwell that afternoon, Sutherland lunched with the Churchills. Afterwards, the men walked down to the painting studio together. There Churchill climbed onto a wooden platform which stood before a wall densely covered with his own framed paintings. Some of the pictures on display had been completed in Italy in 1945, after Churchill was hurled from power.

Sutherland, who had never met Churchill before this day, was encountering him at another moment of decision and defiance. Churchill had written to Salisbury and Eden. He had revealed his plans to Lady Churchill. Tomorrow, he intended to notify the Cabinet in person.

As he dropped into an armchair, he inquired whether Sutherland planned to portray him as Churchill the cherubic or the defiant. But it quickly became apparent that the sitter had his own firm ideas about how he wished to appear.

Churchill's lower lip jutted out. His eyes glowered. His head tilted challengingly.

XIX

The 'R' Word

Westminster Hall, November 1954

Westminster Hall rocked with affectionate laughter when Churchill used the 'R' word.

'This is to me the most memorable public occasion of my life,' he told the 2,500 celebrants – members of all parties and both Houses of Parliament, and their wives – who had gathered on 30 November 1954 to salute him on his birthday. 'No one has received a similar mark of honour before. There has never been anything like it in British history and, indeed, I doubt whether any of the modern democracies abroad have shown such a degree of kindness and generosity to a party politician who has not yet retired . . .'

For more than a decade, people had been asking when Churchill planned to retire. Could he last to the end of the war, or would he have to hand over to a younger, stronger man? By defeating the Nazis, had he not earned the right to a quiet, happy retirement? As the new Labour Government was likely to be in for at least ten years, would it not be wise to accept that at his age he almost certainly could never be prime minister again?

Would he go after the Fulton speech? At the end of the first year to eighteen months of his new postwar Government? At the coronation? As soon as Eden recovered from surgery in the US? When the Queen returned from her Commonwealth tour?

In September 1954? By the time Parliament reassembled after the summer recess?

At his eightieth birthday?

On the eve of the tribute, Salisbury had predicted that rather than see the occasion as 'just the moment for closing a great career', Churchill was 'much more likely' to be confirmed in the opinion that he had 'never been more necessary to the country'.

Both main speakers on the day's programme, Attlee and Salisbury, in their capacities as Opposition Leader in the Commons and Leader of the Lords, paid homage to a giant whose place in history was assured. Salisbury said tenderly and movingly that it had been the privilege of the present generation to have seen and known Churchill for themselves. 'That is something, I believe, for which we shall always be envied by those who come after.'

Churchill lapped up the praise. Nevertheless, he made it clear that for all the talk of history he was not ready to be relegated to the past. 'Ladies and gentlemen, I am now nearing the end of my journey,' he said before he added, 'I hope I still have some services to render.'

Seated behind Churchill were ministers who would have been relieved to see him tender his resignation without delay. Churchill knew how they all felt. But, as ever, he preferred to seize on anything that might be construed as encouragement.

And what could seem more encouraging than the thunderous applause, the heartfelt testimonials, the flow of presents large and small from every corner of the nation? Churchill was particularly impressed by the nearly quarter of a million donations, ranging from less than a shilling to ten thousand pounds, to the Winston Churchill Eightieth Birthday Fund.

The only black moment was the public unveiling of the Sutherland portrait. Churchill, who had already seen the finished painting, felt that the artist had betrayed him by depicting too vividly the ravages that time and illness had wrought. Lest her husband spoil the day, Clementine Churchill counselled him beforehand to pretend that he was pleased. She later quietly burned the picture because he hated it so.

In the afterglow of the all-party tribute, Churchill wrote again to Eisenhower of his abiding wish that they might yet meet Malenkov together: 'It is in the hope of helping forward such a meeting that I am remaining in harness longer than I wished or planned.' As far as Churchill was concerned, events in Europe since France's failure to ratify the EDC had confirmed the wisdom of his refusal to hand over in October. Thanks to Eden's deft diplomacy that autumn, agreements to resolve the German problem had been reached more quickly than anyone had expected. The Allied occupation was to end and West Germany to become a sovereign state and full member of NATO. Churchill was optimistic that the nine powers involved would be able to ratify the agreements early in the new year. After that, the way to the summit would be open.

Churchill reported to Eisenhower that when he had had his last audience with the Queen, she had spoken of the pleasure with which she would welcome a state visit by him to London. He went on, 'This might be combined in any way convenient with a top-level meeting.'

Eisenhower moved quickly to dash Churchill's hopes. The President pointed out that ratification was likely to take a good deal longer than Churchill suggested. He noted that even if the accords went through, the Soviets, displeased by West Germany's entry into NATO, would probably 'play tough' for a while at least. In any case, Eisenhower continued to believe that the top men ought not to meet until the foreign ministers had had a chance to lay the groundwork. Under the circumstances, he did not expect even second-level talks in the near future. 'So, I am bound to say that, while I would like to be more optimistic, I cannot see that a top-level meeting is anything which I can inscribe on my schedule for any predictable date.'

This was devastating, not because Eisenhower had again refused, but because of what he said about time. If the President had his facts right, and he seemed to, it would be many months before the Big Three could be reunited. Quite simply, Churchill did not have many months left in office. Through the years, Churchill had often warned of the shortness of time. Now, the old man sensed that time – his time – had just run out.

Churchill was not alone in grasping the import of Eisenhower's 14 December telegram. When the message came in, Eden was about to go off to Paris for defence talks. Convinced that Churchill no longer had even the flimsiest excuse to cling to power, Eden asked to see him as soon as he returned. But when Eden arrived home on 19 December he took to his bed with a chill. As a consequence, he missed the next day's Cabinet when Churchill asked Woolton, Butler, and Stuart to stay behind afterwards. To their surprise, Churchill proposed that they consider having a general election in the spring. As he did not plan to lead in a new election, the ministers understood him to have suggested that he might step down early in 1955.

It was one thing for Churchill to speak of these matters to Woolton and the others, and quite another to have to face Eden's 'hungry eyes'. The younger man no doubt would press for dates and specifics, and Churchill was far from ready to talk in those terms. Work and life were interchangeable to him. He was not anxious to sign what he bitterly described as his own death warrant. For the moment, Eden's illness suggested a convenient, if temporary way out. Today was Monday. Due to leave town on the Thursday, Churchill told Eden on the phone that there would not be time to meet before Christmas. But Eden persisted and, though he had developed a fever, he went to Churchill the following evening. Clementine Churchill expressed alarm about Eden's sickly colour. Churchill sneered that it looked as if he had been living too well in Paris.

Some men seek to bribe the grim reaper, others to trick him. Churchill tried intimidation. 'What do you want to see me about?' he demanded of Eden in what the latter described in a diary entry as 'his most aggressive tone'. When Eden pushed for a definite date, Churchill pushed back. Far from speaking of an early election, he insisted he really need not go until the end of June or July. Eden protested that that would be too late. This prompted Churchill to play a favourite mind game. Macmillan, whom Churchill had recently appointed Minister of Defence as a reward for his successes at Housing, and as part of a broader Cabinet reshuffle, had just accompanied Eden to Paris. Now, Churchill asked Eden how he got along with Harold.

'Very well,' Eden replied, taking the bait. 'Why?'

'Oh,' said Churchill suggestively, 'he is very ambitious.'

In recent months, Churchill had tried as much as possible to face his attackers separately, the better to play them 'one against the other'. This evening, he grudgingly agreed to meet the next day with a group of Eden's choosing. Ostensibly, the purpose of the session would be to consider election dates.

When Eden, backed up by the usual suspects – Salisbury, Macmillan, Butler, Woolton, Stuart, and Crookshank – confronted Churchill on the afternoon of 22 December, everyone knew that the real date in question was that of the old man's retirement.

It did not take long for Churchill to explode at Eden: 'I know you are trying to get rid of me.'

Pointedly, no one contradicted him.

Churchill said he refused to be hounded from office. He reminded the ministers that it was up to him to go to the Queen and hand her his resignation, but he vowed not to do it. He conceded that if they felt strongly they could always force his hand. Were a significant number of them to resign, an election would be inevitable.

Churchill added menacingly, 'But if this happens, I shall not be in favour of it and I shall tell the country so.'

Eden and his supporters left with their tails between their legs. If Churchill carried out his threat, he would badly, perhaps fatally damage the party in both the House and the country. The leader Eden insisted was gaga had single-handedly outfoxed them again. Eden was 'in despair'. Stuart opined that the meeting had been painful but necessary; Churchill simply had had to be told that he could not persist in a course of 'such utter selfishness'. But had the Prime Minister taken their point? Stuart feared not; he had the uncomfortable feeling that Churchill meant to remain in office until he died or until Parliament ended in 1956.

Later in the day, Churchill merrily suggested another possibility. As Eden and some of the others seemed so intent on an early election, he proposed to give them what they wanted – with one important difference. Churchill phoned Woolton to say that the size of the Winston Churchill Eightieth Birthday Fund demonstrated his high electoral value and that perhaps he should be the one to lead in an early election. He asked the horrified party chairman to look into it.

As Parliament rose on 23 December and Churchill went off to Chequers, it was clear that he had had the best of his face-off with the mutineers. While Churchill was in the country and while Eden (temporarily and not a little gratefully) withdrew from the fray, Salisbury, Macmillan, Stuart, and Butler reconvened at the home of Harry Crookshank. Seven years after this particular brain trust had first assembled there to discuss this very problem, they still lacked a better idea of how to force Churchill out.

The difference in the winter of 1954–5 was that not even the most devoted Churchillians any longer questioned that there were legitimate concerns about the Prime Minister's ability to carry on. Norman Brook judged that, though Churchill could still rise to the great occasion by a sheer act of will and the use of amphetamines, he no longer had the energy to grapple with the day-to-day demands of the premiership. Jock Colville noted that with each passing month, Churchill's powers evaporated a bit more. Was Churchill still the man to face the Soviets? Absolutely not, the Edenites insisted. Colville admitted he just did not know. On icy winter nights, as Churchill and Colville played bezique and dined together, Churchill spoke of being 'tired of it all' and having 'lost interest' now that his hopes of a Big Three meeting had been deferred. A final decision seemed to be at hand; but could he bring himself to make it?

When Churchill refused to retire in 1945, his decision had flowed from everything that was essential to his character; so had his subsequent decisions to fight on. At the beginning of 1955, the decision that confronted Churchill was different, harder. This time, rather than ride the wave of his obstinacy, he had to overcome it. He had to crush his lifelong refusal to accept defeat. He had to conquer the primal survival instinct that had allowed him to spring back so many times before. This time, Churchill's battle was not really with Salisbury, Eden, Eisenhower, or any other antagonist. It was with himself.

At length, Churchill thought he might leave office at the Easter recess. First, he mentioned the date to Colville. Then, he broached it in conversation with Butler. Finally, on 1 February 1955, Eden came to Number Ten. The Foreign Secretary was preparing to go to a conference in Bangkok and he wanted to know Churchill's plans. After sending for a calendar at Eden's suggestion, Churchill mentioned Easter. But he asked Eden to keep that date a secret so that he could tell the Queen quietly and avoid a fuss. Eden was pleased by how smoothly the meeting had gone.

Whether Churchill could be trusted to follow through was another matter. On 8 February, reports from Moscow suggested that the post-Stalin succession struggle was far from finished. Malenkov had fallen. Bulganin and Khrushchev had taken his place. Whose bones would fly out next was anyone's guess. Directly, Churchill asked to see Eden and Butler to coordinate the date for the Budget and the timing of the handover. On the evening of 14 February, Eden emerged from Number Ten convinced that he finally had a solid commitment.

A two-day defence debate loomed in the House of Commons at the beginning of March. More than half a century after Churchill had first spoken in the House, he planned to use the occasion to deliver his last great address there. He lavished twenty hours on the composition of a forty-five-minute set-piece speech, a meditation on global statecraft in the age of the H-bomb. When he ordered up the necessary medical stimulants in advance of his performance, he told Moran that before he left office he intended to make it clear to the world that he was still fit to govern. He wanted people to understand that he was not retiring because he could no longer carry the burden but because he wished to give a younger man his chance.

Slapping the sides of the dispatch box as he addressed the House on 1 March 1955, Churchill observed that a quantity of plutonium less than would fill that very box would suffice to produce weapons capable of giving world domination to any great power which alone possessed it. 'What ought we to do? Which way shall we turn to save our lives and the future of the world? It does not matter so much to old people; they are soon going anyway, but I find it poignant to look at youth in all its activities and ardour and, most of all, to watch little children playing their merry games, and wonder what would lie before them if God wearied of mankind.'

His account of the policy of defence through deterrents was lucid and effective. His phrases sparkled. His voice throbbed as strongly at the close as it had at the start. At one fell swoop Churchill reasserted his gift of oratory and his mastery of the House. Even the *Daily Mirror*, which had been calling for the Prime Minister's resignation on grounds of senility, admitted that the performance had been Churchill 'at his very best'. Afterwards, Soames assured his father-in-law, who was noticeably out of breath, that if he never made another speech in his life this had been 'a very fine swan song'.

Unexpectedly, the coda was still to come. Mission accomplished, Churchill did not plan to speak on the second day of the defence debate, only to sit beside Macmillan on the Tory front bench. But he was stung to interrupt when Aneurin Bevan insinuated that he had been dithering in the business of securing a top-level conference and that he had permitted himself to be at the beck and call of the Americans.

Churchill flung back, 'It is absolutely wrong to suggest that the course which we have followed here has been at the dictation of the United States.' The day before, Churchill had spoken with his notes laid out before him. Every element of his performance had been scripted. Nothing had been left to chance. By contrast, today's intervention was entirely off the cuff. Macmillan trembled for fear of what Churchill in his fury was about to say. Was he about to undo all of yesterday's fine work? Was this to be a rerun of the debacle of 5 April 1954? Equally nervous, Soames chewed his thumb until it bled.

Churchill spoke of his efforts to arrange a meeting with the Soviets after Stalin's death, of his original plan to meet Eisenhower in Bermuda, and of the real reason he had been unable to go. 'I was struck down by a very sudden illness which paralysed me completely, physically,' he said as he ran his right hand down the right side of his body, from shoulder to knee. 'That is why I had to put it all off.'

He talked of Eisenhower's refusal to join him in making a summit proposal and of his own attempt to arrange a bilateral meeting. His references to the tumultuous events of the previous summer, after he sailed home from the US, caused stomachs to churn on the Government bench. The Cabinet crisis had petered out without the potentially damaging details having become widely known. Was Churchill about to punish his party by revealing Eden's reluctance and Salisbury's intransigence? Would he acknowledge that the Cabinet had nearly broken up?

To his colleagues' vast relief, Churchill 'slid successfully past these traps'. He laid the blame for the failure of his Soviet initiative on the Kremlin's efforts to block ratification of the EDC. Now, he suggested, it remained only to wait until the NATO agreements were ratified. Once that process was complete, 'any Government who are responsible at that time' would be free to meet the Soviets. Most of his audience was still reeling from the first public acknowledgement that he had had a stroke, but a careful listener might have caught a hint that by the time the road reopened Churchill himself would no longer be in power.

Churchill was exceedingly pleased with himself afterwards. The two-day debate had allowed him to double-dip, both to prove that he had lost none of his old razzle-dazzle and to defend his reputation in the eyes of history. When he discussed the debate with his doctor, he even seemed capable of jesting about his departure from office. He assured Moran that he had no intention of going back on his date with Eden and that he was not considering a comeback.

Then he added slyly, 'At least not yet.'

Picturesque in a red velvet brocaded jacket and matching slippers, Churchill was full of jokes about retirement when he entertained the Edens at dinner on Tuesday, 8 March. There was much ebullient table talk of the holiday he planned to take at Easter. Following the handover, he and Clementine were to go to Sicily with Bobbety and Betty Salisbury. They were all to stay at the deluxe San Domenico Hotel in Taormina, on the island's east coast. Over lunch on Wednesday, Eden expressed confidence to Macmillan that Churchill really meant it this time. On the Thursday, Clementine Churchill gave Clarissa Eden a tour of Number Ten in anticipation of the Edens' taking up residence there in less than a month.

On the Friday, Churchill tested the new Rolls-Royce he contemplated buying as a retirement gift to himself. En route to Chequers, he spontaneously stopped off at the London Zoo to visit the lion, Rota, and the leopard, Sheba, he kept there. If retired life was going to be like this, it could not be so bad; could it?

Later, he and Colville were playing bezique at Chequers when some official papers were brought in. Churchill read both the telegram from Sir Roger Makins which had been delivered earlier at the Foreign Office and Eden's covering minute. Neither document seemed to make much impression at the time. The men completed their card game and, at length, Lord Beaverbrook joined them for dinner. Only when Beaverbrook had gone did Churchill take a second, longer look at what the Ambassador and the Foreign Secretary had written. When he finished reading he informed Colville that all bets were off. He had changed his mind about April. At the faintest flicker of encouragement, Churchill's instincts had kicked in.

That flicker had been very faint indeed – if there was a flicker at all. Makins's telegram sought London's response to the American plan for spurring France to approve the European security agreements. The White House, which at this point was unaware that Churchill had consented to leave office before Easter, suggested that Eisenhower might come to Paris on 8 May, the tenth anniversary of V-E Day. His visit would provide an opportunity to ratify the agreements alongside Churchill, Adenauer, and President René Coty of France. Makins reported that Eisenhower had also suggested that while he was in Paris they could 'lay plans for a meeting with the Soviets in a sustained effort to reduce tensions and the risk of war'.

The phrase electrified Churchill. He read it as an indication that Eisenhower was finally ready to participate in top-level talks. He saw it as a last-minute reprieve. He transformed it into a lifeline to save him from having to retire. It referred neither to a Big Three meeting nor to Eisenhower's willingness to attend, but from then on, Churchill confidently spoke and acted as if it did. On the basis of it, he informed Colville that he had decided to remain in office and to meet the Soviets with Eisenhower.

When Colville pointed out that no suggestion of a heads of government meeting had been made, Churchill was brusquely dismissive. Nor would he listen to Clementine Churchill when she too sought to tamp down his enthusiasm. The Houdini of British politics went to bed that night convinced he still had some rope left after all.

In the morning, Churchill wrote to inform Eden that everything had changed. He exulted that this was 'the first time' that Eisenhower had responded positively to his appeals. He decreed that the US proposal of leaders' talks which Eisenhower would attend 'must be regarded as a new situation which will affect our personal plans and time-tables'. He acted as if the angels had sung though only he seemed to have noticed. 'The magnitude of the Washington advance towards a Top Level meeting is the dominant fact now before us.'

Churchill was aware that Eden was inclined to call a May election to take advantage of Labour disunity, but he warned that that plan would have to be dropped. There must be no suggestion that considerations of party advantage had been permitted to override the quest for world peace. The people would not stand for it.

Eden was already in high hysteria when he received Churchill's message at lunchtime on Saturday. Makins's telegram had plunged him into 'full crisis' the day before when he realized that Churchill would no doubt use Eisenhower's Paris visit as an excuse to cling to office. After all these years, Eden knew his man. But even he had not foreseen that Churchill would go so far as to read a change of heart about summit meetings into Eisenhower's proposal. Outraged at what he took to be a nasty personal dig, Eden replied that he was not aware that anything he had done in his public life 'would justify the suggestion that I was putting Party before country or self before either'.

Eden's nerves worried Salisbury, who conferred with him several times in the course of the weekend. Along with Butler, Salisbury had agreed to join Eden in resigning if Churchill tried to wiggle out of the April date. For the moment, however, Salisbury was confident that Churchill could be stopped. The present crisis was entirely different from the one during the summer. Then Churchill had actually managed to wheedle an okay out of Eisenhower, and there had been a real possibility that he might have persuaded the rest of the Cabinet to back him on bilateral talks. This time, one needed only to examine the Washington telegram to see that Eisenhower had not proposed to meet the Soviets. Conveniently, Churchill in his exuberance had already circulated copies to the full Cabinet. As far as Salisbury was concerned, the most important thing their side could do on Monday was to coolly point out that the emperor had no clothes. But was Eden up to it? Salisbury confessed to Macmillan that he feared Eden might not be able to stand the strain.

At the Monday Cabinet, Churchill and the ministers talked past one another for the better part of an hour. The ministers concentrated on the pros and cons of an Eisenhower visit in terms of the ratification issue and of Tory election plans. Bewilderingly to some of his colleagues, Churchill kept coming back to the prospect of a summit meeting. The way he told the tale, there was a good deal more to Eisenhower's trip than an effort to prod the French. Churchill had already been to Buckingham Palace for permission to invite Eisenhower to London, so talks with the Soviets might begin at once.

Finally, Salisbury doused cold water on the Prime Minister's excitement. 'I don't think Eisenhower contemplates a top-level meeting. He never has. As a constitutional monarch, he will confine himself to formal acts. Almost certainly, he thinks in terms of a foreign ministers' level meeting.' Salisbury went on to argue that in any event the Conservatives must retain the option of calling a May election, in which case a presidential visit then would not do. The ministers discussed asking Eisenhower to put off his trip until June. When Churchill spoke, he made it sound suspiciously as if he planned still to be in office then.

'Does that mean, Prime Minister,' Eden asked slowly and unemotionally, 'that the arrangements you have made with me are at an end?'

The question took Churchill aback. 'This is a new situation,' he mumbled. 'I should have to consider my public duty.' Always at such moments he spoke in terms of duty.

Eden's brittle veneer of calm began to crumble. 'Does that mean, Prime Minister,' he challenged, 'that if such meetings were to be held there is no one capable of conducting them?'

Churchill replied, 'It has always been my ambition – this is too great a national and international opportunity to yield to personal considerations.'

Eden protested, 'I have been Foreign Minister for ten years. Am I not to be trusted?'

Churchill took this as his cue to wax indignant and to cite his even lengthier public service. 'All this is very unusual,' he blustered. 'These matters are not in my long experience discussed in Cabinets.' He put Eden and the others on notice that the decision of if and when to leave office was his alone to make.

Salisbury tried to bring down the temperature, but his remarks had the opposite effect. He pointed out that not everyone present was aware of the arrangements Churchill and Eden had been speaking of. Only Churchill, Eden, Salisbury, Butler, and Macmillan had definite knowledge that Churchill had agreed to go in April. Woolton and Swinton knew some of it. Salisbury's suggestion that the full Cabinet be apprised of his retirement plans infuriated Churchill, who had just made it clear that this was a subject he did not wish to discuss.

'I cannot assent to such a discussion,' Churchill thundered. 'I know my duty and will perform it. If any member of the Cabinet dissents his way is open.'

The Cabinet Room seethed with embarrassment. Churchill thought everyone seemed so pained because Eden had dared to raise the personal issue, but that was only part of it. The Washington telegram appeared to have pushed Churchill over the line that separates optimism from self-deception. Perhaps he really did believe that Eisenhower had made a 'new offer', but no one else did.

As the meeting broke up, Churchill asked to see Salisbury privately. When they were alone, Churchill said he hoped Salisbury still planned to go to Sicily with him. Salisbury said he did. Testing the waters further, Churchill asked, 'It isn't against your principles to fly on holiday with a prime minister?' This was his arch way of stating that he did not intend to yield. Having already made one false step, Salisbury refused to be provoked. After all, at this point Salisbury really had no need to do anything but wait. Sooner or later, Churchill was bound to crash headlong into the mountainous fact that the 'new offer' was a chimera.

The crash came that very day. Aldrich delivered a message from Washington that stated flatly that Eisenhower was not willing himself to take part in a meeting with the Soviets. That certainly would have seemed to be the end of that – at least, the Edenites thought so. But it was not quite enough for Churchill. Still scrambling to find a way out of an April handover, he insisted on going back to the Americans one more time. Again, he struggled mightily to wring a more hopeful meaning out of the words in front of him. He knew his interpretation was a stretch (he admitted as much to Clementine), but given the alternative he felt he had to try. He asked whether this latest Washington message referred exclusively to Eisenhower's upcoming visit. Did it necessarily rule out talks at a somewhat later date?

Churchill had his answer soon enough. Makins telegraphed that Eisenhower was not contemplating an early top-level meeting. The President had merely thought that while he was in Europe, preliminary arrangements might be made for foreign ministers' talks to take place in October. On 16 March, Churchill read the telegram aloud to the Cabinet. When the old man spoke the word 'October', he made 'a gesture of disappointment'. Churchill seemed to accept that the struggle was at an end. He would retire in April after all.

The mood at Chequers that weekend was very sombre. 'It's the first death,' Clementine Churchill reflected, 'and for him, a death in life.' Though she was relieved that the matter of Winston's retirement was settled at last, she shared his anguish nonetheless. He had confronted the abyss in 1915 and again in 1945. The difference in his eighty-first year was that there could be no 'next time'. Once he tendered his resignation, his political life would be over.

For ten years, the war lord had longed to 'round off' his story by making the peace. In all that time, he had never lost faith in his Soviet strategy or in his unique ability to execute it. Now that the last prize had eluded his grasp, it galled him to leave the leadership of the Western alliance in the hands of men whose expertise and understanding he did not trust. Churchill raged that Eden had done more to thwart him and to prevent him from pursuing the policy he believed in than anyone else. Nor in private did he have kind words for Eisenhower. Churchill said he would have stayed on had there been a chance of a summit meeting. 'But,' he continued, 'Ike won't have it. He's afraid – and there it is.'

Sadly, the universal applause that had delighted Churchill at his eightieth birthday tribute had faded from his ears. The sense of peace he had begun to acquire in the aftermath of the defence debate also was gone. He bristled at the political gossip that Eden had finally managed to kick him out. He brooded that in an effort to ensure his departure his own party must be responsible for leaks to the press that Eden was to succeed him before Easter. He thrashed about miserably as the countdown to 5 April began: his last weekend at Chequers, the Edens' dinner party in his honour, Queen Elizabeth's highly unusual visit to Number Ten on the eve of his resignation. Butler compared Churchill to a fish that had been hooked but had yet to be gaffed. Colville saw him as having almost been landed but still fighting to break free from the net.

On Sunday, 27 March, Churchill was spending his final days at Chequers when he saw newspaper reports that Bulganin had commented favourably on the idea of a conference of the great powers. The following day, Eden said in the House of Commons that it would be best if such contacts began at the foreign ministers' level. Churchill had been complaining of precisely that approach since 1945. That night, he told Colville that he could not possibly hand over at such a moment just to gratify Eden's personal hunger for power. When Churchill threatened to call a party meeting and ask Conservatives to choose, Colville warned that that would make an unhappy last chapter to his biography.

Did Churchill really want it to be written that at the end of his career he had brought down the party of which he was the leader? Colville assumed that Churchill's threats were nothing more than a late-night fantasy, which reflected the anguish with which he contemplated the approach of retirement. No doubt the Prime Minister would think better of it in the morning. Instead, the next day, Churchill sent Butler to notify Eden that the grim international situation made it impossible for him to retire after all.

When Churchill answered questions in the Commons that afternoon, it was evident that summit dreams were again dancing in his head. He said he hoped a leaders' meeting might yet be arranged. When a Labour member asked whether he thought he could get one in time to participate himself, Churchill answered coyly that the future was 'veiled in obscurity'. Afterwards, at his weekly audience with the Queen, he disclosed that he contemplated postponing his resignation. When Churchill asked whether she would object, the young sovereign said no. Some people at the time believed that Elizabeth's father would have been less understanding and that matters would never have proceeded to this point had he still been alive.

That night of all nights, Churchill was due at the Edens' dinner party. He rang to say he had been delayed at Buckingham Palace and would be late. Clementine Churchill phoned separately to report that her neuritis had flared up and that she could not attend. Eden, who had been frantic since morning, interpreted Churchill's call as a very bad sign. Colville sent word to remind Eden that Churchill throve on confrontation. To make a scene of any kind would only fuel his determination to battle on. When Churchill arrived that evening, Eden bit his tongue and pretended that nothing was wrong. Strange to say, so did Churchill. He sweetly inquired how his niece had enjoyed her tour of Number Ten and spoke of being in Venice in June. What did the mixed signals mean? To the last minute, Churchill seemed not to know himself what he planned.

316

At half past six the next evening, Churchill summoned Eden and Butler to the Cabinet Room. The men had been rivals since the end of the war, but at this late date almost no one believed that Butler had ever had a real chance of supplanting the designated heir. Yet, when they joined Churchill on 30 March, the Prime Minister invited Butler to sit on his right. The gesture seemed to suggest that there had been a last-minute upset and that after all these years Eden had been dealt a terrible blow. But Churchill quickly corrected himself. He signalled Eden to take the place on his right, and he seated Butler on his left. Had the incident been a slip? Or a final stab of cruelty at his political heir's expense?

For a moment, the three of them sat without speaking. Finally, Churchill broke the silence.

'I am going and Anthony will succeed me,' he declared. 'We can discuss details later.'

In the morning, Churchill sent a message to the Palace. The 5th of April it would be.

During the next four days, he alternated between groaning that he was not ready to retire and acknowledging that he could not keep others waiting, between sighing that he did not wish to live very long after he relinquished power and insisting that he would still wield great influence. Churchill had written in his biography of the 1st Duke of Marlborough (1936) that it is best for a warrior 'to die in battle on the field, in command, with great causes in dispute and strong action surging round'. But, he went on, that is not always possible. It had not been the lot of Churchill's ancestor to make such a perfect exit. Nor, he finally accepted that spring of 1955, was it to be his. Still, he did not want anyone to think that he had been dictated to or defeated by Eden, by the party, or even by age and failing health. That would be intolerable. To the end, he insisted that the timing and circumstances of his departure were his alone to choose. Even at this point, there was no individual or group in a position to force him to go. He had to surrender the seals of office of his own volition, and until the hour itself no one could be certain he really would.

Yet the momentum was steadily, relentlessly building. Shortly before midnight on 4 April, Churchill emerged from Number Ten at the close of his farewell banquet, which had been attended by fifty guests including Queen Elizabeth and Prince Philip. Churchill wore black knee breeches, long black silk stockings and his blue Garter sash. The Queen followed a few steps behind, the diamonds in her tiara flashing in the photographers' floodlights. Cameras clicked as Churchill bowed low before her and took the white-gloved hand she extended in farewell. As there would be no photographs inside the Palace the next day, this image promised to be the one that would stand in history.

After the Queen's dark red Rolls-Royce drove off, Churchill went upstairs to his room. Still wearing his breeches and Garter sash, he sat in meditative silence on the edge of the bed for several minutes. That night, glasses had been raised. Pictures had been taken. And though (alarmingly, to some ears) Churchill had not spoken the 'R' word in his after-dinner speech, the significance of the evening had been well understood by all. It would certainly seem as if there was no longer a way out of what faced him the next day.

Or was there?

As if he were still searching for an excuse to stay on, still struggling to reassure himself he was indispensable, he looked up and said, 'I don't believe Anthony can do it.'

The next day at noon, Churchill presided over the Cabinet for the last time. The showdowns, the manoeuvres, the machinations ended abruptly when he announced, 'I have decided to resign.' After the full Cabinet posed for a group photograph, each minister came up to shake Churchill's hand and say a few words. Eden, Salisbury, Butler, Macmillan, and the rest were full of praise and affection for the leader they had long hoped to unseat. At a quarter past four, Churchill donned the frock coat and top hat he customarily wore at audiences with the Queen and went to the Palace to surrender the seals of office. When he returned to Number Ten, a crowd was waiting.

'Good old Winnie!' they shouted.

His eyes filled with tears as he gave the V-sign. Then he disappeared inside and the door closed after him.

ACKNOWLEDGEMENTS

My first and greatest debt is to Deborah, Dowager Duchess of Devonshire, who did so much to make it possible for me to tell this story. She laid out the terrain, provided key insights into many of the major players in the drama, and was generous in ways too numerous to list. She helped me begin to grasp just how complicated – and exciting – were the motives and relationships, the history and politics, of Churchill's world in these years.

I would like to thank the following people for their generous help and for their patience with my endless questions:

Lady Elizabeth Cavendish and Lady Anne Tree, for filling me in on the cast of characters and their tangled web of relationships.

Lady Soames, for speaking to me about her parents, Winston and Clementine Churchill, and especially for pinpointing the moment in 1945 when her father made the decision to fight on. Her discussion of the fraught issue of retirement, of her father's focus on the Soviets during his final premiership, and of his 1953 stroke were all essential.

Sir Nicholas Henderson, for providing an eyewitness account of Churchill at Potsdam, for explaining what that conference meant to Churchill, and for illuminating the characters of Eden and Butler, for both of whom he served as private secretary.

Lord Carrington, for telling me what it was like to be a member of Churchill's postwar Government and for speaking of Churchill's situation after the war and of his relationships with Eden, Salisbury, and Macmillan.

Both Sir Nicholas and Lord Carrington talked to me about the significance of Eisenhower's mistake over Berlin, and Truman's refusal to come to London to consult with Churchill before Potsdam. It was my talks with them that made me realize that Potsdam was the place to start this story.

Lord Salisbury, for talking to me about his grandfather Bobbety Salisbury, and for clarifying aspects of his relationships with Churchill, Eden, and Macmillan, as well as of the Churchill–Cecil family relationship.

Hugh Cecil, for his insights into his uncle Bobbety Salisbury's character, and for discussing him in the context of the Cecil family.

Lord Stockton, for speaking to me of his grandfather Harold Macmillan's role and of his relations with Churchill, Salisbury, and Eden.

Lord Norwich, for sharing his vivid memories of Churchill's visits with his parents, Lady Diana and Duff Cooper, and especially for his account of Churchill in Venice in 1951.

Also, two people who were no longer alive when I began this book, but whose influence was felt throughout:

The late Lady Lloyd, for countless hours of conversation in which she made the world of this book come alive for me. I first heard many of the names in this story listening to her.

And the late and wonderful Andrew, 11th Duke of Devonshire, who – almost ten years ago – put a copy of Volume One of Churchill's *The World Crisis* in my hands and said, 'Start here.'

Finally, I wish to express my gratitude to Helen Marchant, Lindsay Warwick, and Alex Harttung. And to the essential people who understood from the first what I wanted to do with this book and helped me every step of the way: my publishers and editors Jonathan Burnham, Gail Winston, Arabella Pike, Sophie Goulden, and Allegra Huston; and my agents Michael Carlisle and Bill Hamilton.

To my husband David, my thanks for simply everything.

SOURCE NOTES

I: You Will, but I Shall Not

p. 1   background on Churchill in Berlin and Potsdam: Lady Soames, Sir Nicholas Henderson, Lord Carrington, author interviews.

p. 1   British party had swelled: Sir Alexander Cadogan, *The Diaries of Sir Alexander Cadogan*, New York: Putnam's, 1972, 17 July 1945.

p. 1   'We have . . .': WSC, 22 June 1941, quoted in *New York Times*, 23 June 1941.

p. 2   'bloodthirsty guttersnipe': *Ibid.*

p. 2   'and every foot . . .': Winston S. Churchill, *Great Contemporaries,* London: Thornton, Butterworth, 1937, p. 63.

p. 2   questioned the Russian soldier: *The Times*, 17 July 1945.

p. 2   followed the Russian soldier: Lord Moran, *Diaries of Lord Moran,* Boston: Houghton Mifflin, 1966, 16 July 1945.

p. 3   'I never think . . .': Quoted in Diana Cooper, *Autobiography,* New York: Carroll & Graf, 1985, p. 668.

p. 3   'last pull up . . .': Violet Bonham Carter, *Champion Redoubtable: The Diaries and Letters of Violet Bonham Carter, 1914–1944*, ed. Mark Pottle, London: Orion, 1998, 1 August 1945.

p. 4   turning away in disgust: *The Times*, 17 July 1945.

p. 4   tested it first: *Ibid.*

p. 5   'showdown': Prime Minister Churchill to Anthony Eden, 4 May 1945, *Foreign Relations of the United States: diplomatic papers: the Conference of Berlin (the Potsdam Conference), 1945*, Washington: United States Printing Office, 1945, vol. 1.

p. 5   troubled by doubts: John Colville, *The Fringes of Power: Downing Street Diaries*, London: Weidenfeld & Nicolson, 2004, 23 February 1945.

p. 5   Eisenhower mistake on Berlin: Sir Nicholas Henderson, Lord Carrington, author interviews.

p. 5   presses Eisenhower to take Berlin: Prime Minister to General Eisenhower, 31 March 1945, quoted in Winston Churchill, *Triumph and Tragedy*, Boston: Houghton Mifflin, 1985, p. 405.

p. 6   'lost its former . . .': Quoted in Churchill, *Triumph and Tragedy*, p. 402.

p. 6   sat in silence: Moran, *Diaries*, 16 July 1945.

p. 6   saluting soldiers: *Ibid.*

p. 6   'high as kites': Sir Nicholas Henderson, author interview.

p. 7   'Force and facts': WSC to Anthony Eden, 1 April 1944, quoted in Martin Gilbert, *Winston S. Churchill*, vol. 7, *Road to Victory, 1941–1945*, Boston: Houghton Mifflin, 1986, p. 725.

p. 7   'how much we have': Prime Minister Churchill to President Truman, 6 May 1945, *FRUS: Conference of Berlin*, vol. 1.

p. 8   Truman preferred to wait: President Truman to Prime Minister Churchill, 9 May 1945, *ibid.*

p. 8   confer first in London: Prime Minister Churchill to President Truman, 11 May 1945, *ibid.*

p. 8   'ganging up': President Truman to Prime Minister Churchill, 12 May 1945, *ibid.*

p. 8   'iron curtain': Prime Minister Churchill to President Truman, 12 May 1945, *ibid.*

p. 8   surely it was vital: *Ibid.*

p. 8   did not wish to put in writing: President Truman to Prime Minister Churchill, 22 May 1945, *ibid.*

p. 8   wanted to see Stalin first: Joseph Davies to President Truman, 12 June 1945, *ibid.*

p. 8   Churchill waxed indignant: *Ibid.*

p. 8   Davies blamed Churchill: *Ibid.*

p. 8   'placed not only . . .': *Ibid.*

p. 10   Stimson luncheon: Henry Stimson Diaries, 16 July 1945, Yale University Library.

p. 11   Stimson's insistence: *Ibid.*

p. 11   'We will feel . . .': First Plenary Meeting, 17 July 1945, *FRUS: Conference of Berlin*, vol. 2.

p. 11   nervous about facing: Charles Bohlen, *Witness to History*, New York: Norton, 1973, p. 226.

p. 12   'I don't just . . .': First Plenary Meeting, 17 July 1945, *FRUS: Conference of Berlin*, vol. 2.

p. 12   'of all hues': Cadogan, *Diaries*, 18 July 1945.

p. 12   grown so accustomed: Record of Private Talk between the Prime Minister and Generalissimo Stalin after the Plenary Session on 17 July 1945, at Potsdam, PREM 3/430/7, The National Archives, Public Record Office.

p. 13   the British ambassador: Archibald Clark Kerr Diaries, 16 August 1942 (Baron Inverchapel Papers), FO 800/300, PRO.

p. 13   build a relationship with Stalin: Lady Soames, author interview.

p. 14   'physically rather oppressed': Churchill, *Triumph and Tragedy*, p. 548.

p. 14   conversation at dinner: Record of Private Talk between the Prime Minister and Generalissimo Stalin at Dinner on 18 July 1945, at Potsdam, PREM 3/430/6.

p. 14   background on Churchill–Eden relationship: Sir Nicholas Henderson, the Dowager Duchess of Devonshire, Lord

Salisbury, Lord Carrington, Lord Stockton, Lady Anne Tree, Lady Elizabeth Cavendish, author interviews.

p. 14   'resolution, experience...': Quoted in Robert Rhodes James, *Anthony Eden: A Biography*, New York: McGraw-Hill, 1987, p. 265.

p. 15   'Let Vyacheslav...': Quoted in *Molotov Remembers: Conversations with Felix Chuev*, ed. Albert Resis, Chicago: Ivan R. Dee, 1993, p. 190.

p. 15   'lard-white': Sir M. Peterson to Mr. Bevin, 22 March 1949, in *British Documents on Foreign Affairs: Reports and Papers from the Foreign Office Confidential Print*, part 4, series A, *The Soviet Union and Finland*, vol. 6, *1949*, Bethesda, MD: University Publications of America, 2002, p. 266.

p. 15   'a man of...': George Kennan interview, National Security Archive, George Washington University.

p. 15   'no questions asked': Sir M. Peterson to Mr. Bevin, 22 March 1949, in *BDFA*, part 4, series A, vol. 6, p. 275.

p. 15   Molotov's sleeping habits: James Stuart, *Within the Fringe*, London: Bodley Head, 1967, p. 130.

p. 15   Stalin spoke of retiring on a pension: *Molotov Remembers*, p. 190.

p. 16   interminable: Moran, *Diaries*, 21 July 1945.

p. 16   study the report in full: Stimson Diaries, 22 July 1945.

p. 17   rushed over to see Truman: Truman–Churchill Meeting, Sunday, 22 July 1945, 12:15 p.m., *FRUS: Conference of Berlin*, vol. 2.

p. 17   spoke excitedly of the bomb: Moran, *Diaries*, 23 July 1945.

p. 17   laid out the new situation: Field Marshal Lord Alanbrooke, *War Diaries, 1939–1945*, London: Weidenfeld & Nicolson, 2001, 23 July 1945.

p. 18   Truman would never provide: Lord Carrington, author interview.

p. 18 Stalin would shrug off: Sir Nicholas Henderson, author interview.

p. 18 might yet prove to have been exaggerated: Alanbrooke, *War Diaries*, 23 July 1945.

p. 18 sharpest exchanges: Eighth Plenary Meeting, Tuesday, 24 July 1945, 5 p.m., *FRUS: Conference of Berlin*, vol. 2.

p. 18 'Fairy tales!': *Ibid.*

p. 20 Churchill's dream: Moran, *Diaries*, 26 July 1945.

p. 20 hoped to be back: Ninth Plenary Meeting, Wednesday, 25 July 1945, 11 a.m., *FRUS: Conference of Berlin*, vol. 2.

p. 20 mood on the flight home: Lady Soames, author interview.

p. 21 complained of heat and want of air: Nicholas Henderson, *Inside the Private Office*, Chicago: Academy Chicago, 1987, p. 20.

p. 21 'a blessing in disguise': Quoted in Churchill, *Triumph and Tragedy*, p. 583.

p. 21 stepping aside on Monday: Sir Alan Lascelles, *King's Counsellor: The Diaries of Sir Alan Lascelles*, ed. Duff Hart-Davis, London: Weidenfeld & Nicolson, 2006, 26 July 1945.

p. 21 in war one: Alfred G. Gardiner, *Portraits and Portents*, New York: Harper & Row, 1926, p. 57.

p. 22 'Unsquashable resilience': Violet Bonham Carter, *Winston Churchill: An Intimate Portrait*, New York: Harcourt Brace, 1965, p. 3.

p. 22 as many arrows: Gardiner, *Portraits and Portents*, p. 57.

p. 22 at least a decade: Henderson, *Inside the Private Office*, p. 21.

p. 22 in for a generation: Harold Macmillan, *Tides of Fortune*, London: Macmillan, 1969, p. 286.

p. 22 'You will, but I . . .': Anthony Eden, diary entry, 27 July 1945, quoted in Anthony Eden, *The Reckoning*, Boston: Houghton Mifflin, 1965, p. 639.

p. 22 food and a philosophic temperament: WSC to Lady Randolph

Churchill, 2 October 1897, quoted in Randolph Churchill, *Winston S. Churchill*, vol. 1, *Companion, Part 2, 1896–1900*, London: Heinemann, 1967, p. 797.

p. 22   Attlee arrives a day late: Telegram: Foreign Office to Terminal, 27 July 1945, FO 371/50867.

p. 22   talks resume: Record of Meeting between Prime Minister and Foreign Secretary and Generalissimo Stalin at Potsdam, 28 July 1945, at 10 p.m., PREM 3/430/9.

II: Face Facts and Retire

p. 24   slept with key: Sarah Churchill, *A Thread in the Tapestry*, London: André Deutsch, 1967, p. 86.

p. 24   sleeping near a balcony: Moran, *Diaries*, 2 August 1945.

p. 25   old music hall song: Churchill, *A Thread in the Tapestry*, p. 88.

p. 25   'new boys': Cuthbert Headlam, *Parliament and Politics in the Age of Churchill and Attlee: The Headlam Diaries, 1935–1951*, ed. Stuart Ball, London: Cambridge University Press, 1999, 1 August 1945.

p. 26   raucous cheers: Chips Channon, *Chips: The Diaries of Sir Henry Channon*, ed. Robert Rhodes James, London: Orion, 1996, 1 August 1945.

p. 26   'the chorus of birds...': Arthur Booth, *British Hustings 1924–1950*, London: Muller, 1956, p. 228.

p. 26   Churchill made intention clear at Chequers: WSC to Hugh 'Linky' Cecil, 29 July 1945, quoted in Martin Gilbert, *Winston S. Churchill*, vol. 8, *Never Despair, 1945–1965*, Boston: Houghton Mifflin, 1988, p. 112.

p. 26   his party's unanimous support: Moran, *Diaries*, 2 August 1945.

p. 26   trio of Conservative heavyweights met: Anthony Eden, diary entry, 1 August 1945, and Halifax, diary entry, 1 August 1945, quoted in Gilbert, *Churchill*, vol. 8, p. 117.

p. 26   background on Cranborne: Lord Salisbury, the Dowager Duchess of Devonshire, Lady Elizabeth Cavendish, Lady Anne Tree, Hugh Cecil, Lord Carrington, Sir Nicholas Henderson, Lord Stockton, author interviews.

p. 27   'Your family has . . .': Lord Salisbury, author interview.

p. 27   immensely attractive: The Dowager Duchess of Devonshire, author interview.

p. 27   operate behind the scenes: Lady Anne Tree, author interview.

p. 28   'objectivity': Sir Nicholas Henderson, author interview.

p. 28   warmly acknowledged: Lord Salisbury, author interview.

p. 28   'face facts and retire . . .': Cranborne to Paul Emrys Evans, 19 January 1946, Paul Emrys Evans Papers, British Library.

p. 29   'knew he could bully . . .': Quoted in Andrew Roberts, *The Holy Fox*, London: Weidenfeld & Nicolson, 1991, p. 274.

p. 30   Potsdam fails to produce settlement Churchill chased: WSC, 16 August 1945, in *New York Times*, 17 August 1945.

p. 30   viewed Attlee warily: Sir Nicholas Henderson, author interview.

p. 31   palpably shaken: *Ibid.*

p. 31   seemed to have lost interest: Sir Nicholas Henderson and Robert Murphy quoted in Alan Thompson, *The Day Before Yesterday*, London: Sidgwick & Jackson, 1971, p. 30.

p. 31   Halifax's visit to Claridge's: Lord Halifax, diary entry, 1 August 1945, quoted in Gilbert, *Churchill*, vol. 8, p. 117.

p. 31   if only Eden had not been ill: Anthony Eden, diary entry, 1 August 1945, quoted in Rhodes James, *Anthony Eden*, p. 311.

p. 31   'Some men need drink . . .': Quoted in Cynthia Gladwyn, *The Diaries of Cynthia Gladwyn*, ed. Miles Jebb, London: Constable, 1995, 9 January 1957.

p. 32   swallowed a sleeping pill: Moran, *Diaries*, 2 August 1945.

p. 32   Since Saturday: *Ibid.*

p. 33　'gleefully anticipating': Lascelles, *King's Counsellor*, 15 August 1945.

p. 33　the danger of a new war: WSC, 16 August 1945, in *New York Times*, 17 August 1945.

p. 34　'a real masterpiece': Hugh Gaitskell, *The Diary, 1945–1956*, ed. Philip M. Williams, London: J. Cape, 1983, pp. 18–19.

p. 35　'brilliant moving gallant . . .': Clementine Churchill to Mary Churchill, 18 August 1945, quoted in Mary Soames, *Clementine Churchill*, Boston: Houghton Mifflin, 1973, p. 429.

p. 35　background on Churchill marriage: Lady Soames, the Dowager Duchess of Devonshire, Lady Elizabeth Cavendish, Lord Norwich, author interviews.

p. 35　soothed his bitterness: Hugh Cecil, author interview.

p. 35　put him above their children's needs: The Dowager Duchess of Devonshire, author interview.

p. 35　she would not hesitate: Clementine Churchill to WSC, 6 April 1916, in Mary Soames, ed., *Winston and Clementine*, Boston: Houghton Mifflin, 2001.

p. 36　would grow annoyed: Lady Soames, author interview.

p. 37　painful to be impotent and inactive: Martin Gilbert, *Winston S. Churchill*, vol. 3, *Challenge of War, 1914–1916*, Boston: Houghton Mifflin, 1971, p. 501.

p. 37　less forgiving: Clementine Churchill to Mary Churchill, 18 August 1945, quoted in Soames, *Clementine Churchill*, p. 429.

p. 37　Clementine regretted: *Ibid.*

III: Sans Soucis et Sans Regrets

p. 38　flight to Milan: Moran, *Diaries*, 2 September 1945.

p. 38　'an exhilarating drink': WSC to Lady Randolph Churchill, 12 February 1897, quoted in Randolph Churchill, *Winston*

S. *Churchill*, vol. 1, *Youth, 1874–1900*, Boston: Houghton Mifflin, 1966, p. 315.

p. 40   dinner at Villa La Rosa: WSC to Clementine Churchill, 5 September 1945, in Gilbert, *Churchill*, vol. 8, p. 137; Sarah Churchill, *Keep on Dancing*, New York: Coward, 1981, p. 137; Moran, *Diaries*, p. 315.

p. 40   feared time would pass slowly: Churchill, *A Thread in the Tapestry*, p. 90.

p. 40   'die of grief': Clementine Churchill quoted in Gilbert, *Churchill*, vol. 3, p. 473.

p. 41   'knew everything and . . .': Winston S. Churchill, *Painting as Pastime*, New York: Cornerstone Library, 1950, p. 16.

p. 41   first day of painting in Italy: Sarah Churchill to Clementine Churchill, 3 September 1945, quoted in Churchill, *Keep on Dancing*, p. 136; WSC to Clementine Churchill, 3 September 1945, in Soames, ed., *Winston and Clementine*; Moran, *Diaries*, 3 September 1945; Churchill, *A Thread in the Tapestry*, pp. 91–3.

p. 42   'voluptuous kick': Bonham Carter, *Winston Churchill*, p. 381.

p. 42   'layer after layer': Churchill, *Painting as Pastime*, p. 18.

p. 42   'I've had a . . .': Sarah Churchill to Clementine Churchill, 3 September 1945, quoted in Churchill, *Keep on Dancing*, p. 139.

p. 43   He rejoiced: WSC to Clementine Churchill, 5 September 1945, in Soames, ed., *Winston and Clementine*.

p. 43   no newspapers: WSC to Clementine Churchill, 5 September 1945 and 13 September 1945, in Soames, ed., *Winston and Clementine*.

p. 43   glad to have been relieved of responsibility: WSC to Clementine Churchill, 5 September 1945, in Soames, ed., *Winston and Clementine*.

p. 43   'Every day . . .': Sarah Churchill to Clementine Churchill, 8 September 1945, quoted in Churchill, *A Thread in the Tapestry*, p. 95.

p. 44   'incongruous': WSC to Clementine Churchill, 24 September 1945, quoted in Gilbert, *Churchill*, vol. 8, p. 152.

p. 44   bathes at Villa Pirelli: Gilbert, *Churchill*, vol. 8, p. 151.

p. 45   he spoke of how certain: WSC to Clementine Churchill, 24 September 1945, in Soames, ed., *Winston and Clementine*.

p. 46   his family understood: Lady Soames, author interview.

IV: Old Man in a Hurry

p. 47   'a new man': Lascelles, *King's Counsellor*, 26 October 1945.

p. 47   with a cold: WSC to Clement Attlee, 6 October 1945, quoted in Gilbert, *Churchill*, vol. 8, p.156; *New York Times*, 15 October 1945; WSC to Sir James Hawkey, 18 October 1945, quoted in Gilbert, *Churchill*, vol. 8, p. 159.

p. 48   'produced his greatest . . .': Robert Menzies, 'Churchill at 75', *New York Times Magazine*, 27 November 1949, p. 37.

p. 48   asked Churchill to lecture: F. L. McLuer to WSC, 3 October 1945, quoted in Gilbert, *Churchill*, vol. 8, p. 159.

p. 48   'This is a . . .': Harry Truman to WSC, 3 October 1945, in G. W. Sand, ed., *Defending the West: The Truman–Churchill Correspondence, 1945–1960*, Westport, CT: Praeger, 2004, p. 152.

p. 49   Churchill's reply: WSC to Harry Truman, 8 November 1945, in Sand, ed., *Defending the West*, p. 153; John Ramsden, *Man of the Century: Winston Churchill and His Legend Since 1945*, London: HarperCollins, 2003, p. 159; Gilbert, *Churchill*, vol. 8, p. 172.

p. 50   told a joint session: WSC, 16 November 1945, quoted in Gilbert, *Churchill*, vol. 8, p. 171.

p. 51   motion of censure: WSC, 27 November 1945, in *New York Times*, 28 November 1945.

p. 51   Conservative Central Council meeting: *New York Times*, 29 November 1945; *The Times*, 29 November 1945.

p. 51   'Master Fighter': *The Times*, 29 November 1945.

p. 51   'the gloomy vultures . . .': WSC, 18 November 1945, quoted in *New York Times*, 29 November 1945.

p. 51   shot down Churchill's motion: *The Times*, 7 December 1945.

p. 52   Clementine Churchill watched: *Ibid.*

p. 52   Truman confirms his offer: Truman to WSC, 16 November 1945, in Sand, ed., *Defending the West*, p. 153.

p. 52   press for a firm date: WSC to Truman, 29 November 1945, *ibid.*, p. 154.

p. 53   only because so many: The Dowager Duchess of Devonshire, author interview.

p. 53   addressed the troops: Sir James Bisset, *Commodore: War, Peace and Big Ships*, Sydney: Angus & Robertson, 1961, p. 436.

p. 54   'farewell to politics': *Ibid.*

V: The Wet Hen

p. 55   'rather like a governess . . .': Anthony Eden to Cranborne, 3 January 1946, quoted in D. R. Thorpe, *Eden*, London: Chatto & Windus, 2003, p. 340.

p. 56   struck many of the anti-appeasers: Lord Stockton, author interview.

p. 56   barred Churchill from their meetings: Lord Salisbury, author interview.

p. 56   'despised': Lord Carrington, author interview.

p. 56   spoken of his intention to resign: Channon, *Chips*, 3 October 1940.

p. 57   'losing his grip': Cadogan, *Diaries*, 4 March 1942.

p. 57   'failing fast': Alanbrooke, *War Diaries*, 1 May 1944.

p. 57   'Waiting to step . . .': Headlam, *Diaries*, 9 July 1948.

p. 57   'an unworthy hope': Anthony Eden, diary entry, 17 July 1945, quoted in Eden, *The Reckoning*, p. 632.

p. 57   out for ten years: Henderson, *Inside the Private Office*, p. 21.

p. 57   'and get everything wrong': Oliver Harvey, *The War Diaries of Oliver Harvey, 1941–1945*, London: Collins, 1978, 28 July 1945.

p. 58   'forever': Cranborne to Paul Emrys Evans, 19 January 1946, PEE Papers.

p. 58   'evil day': Thorpe, *Eden*, p. 340.

p. 58   'fed up with everything': Cranborne to Paul Emrys Evans, 19 January 1946, PEE Papers.

p. 58   'anxious': Lascelles, *King's Counsellor*, 8 January 1946.

p. 59   'the wet hen': The Dowager Duchess of Devonshire, author interview.

p. 59   Baldwin warned: Thomas Jones, *A Diary with Letters, 1931–1950*, London: Oxford University Press, 1954, 5–7 January 1946.

p. 59   'through with him': Quoted in David Dutton, *Anthony Eden*, London: Hodder, 1997, p. 232.

p. 59   encouraged Eden: Cranborne to Anthony Eden, 8 January 1946, quoted *ibid.*, pp. 232–3.

p. 59   'the backbone to . . .': Lord Carrington, author interview.

p. 60   incident at UN dinner: Lascelles, *King's Counsellor*, 10 January 1946.

p. 60   letter of rebuke: *Ibid.*, 11 January 1946.

p. 61   'made an ass': *Ibid.*, 14 January 1946.

p. 61   'strongly': Cranborne to Paul Emrys Evans, 19 January 1946, PEE Papers.

p. 62   Cranborne was pleased: Cranborne to Paul Emrys Evans, 19 January and 12 February 1946, *ibid.*

p. 62   Cranborne did not really believe: Cranborne to Paul Emrys Evans, 12 February 1946, *ibid.*

VI: Winnie, Winnie, Go Away

p. 63 'delicious': Clementine Churchill to Mary Soames, 18 January 1946, quoted in Soames, *Clementine Churchill*, p. 441.

p. 64 caught another cold: Clementine Churchill to Mary Soames, 18 January 1946, quoted *ibid.*; *New York Times*, 20 January 1946.

p. 64 message from Truman: Gilbert, *Churchill*, vol. 8, p. 189.

p. 64 Truman had had to cancel: *New York Times*, 9 February 1946.

p. 64 rough flight to Washington: *New York Times*, 11 February 1946.

p. 65 'an electric shock': The Earl of Halifax to Mr. Bevin, 17 February 1946, *BDFA*, part 4, series C, *North America*, vol. 1, *1946*, Bethesda, MD: University Publications of America, 1999, p. 64.

p. 65 Stalin obsessively pored: Vladimir O. Pechatnov, '"The Allies are Pressing on you to Break your Will . . .": Foreign Policy Correspondence Between Stalin and Molotov and Other Politburo Members, September 1945–December 1946', trans. Vladislav M. Zubok, Working Paper No. 26, Cold War International History Project, Woodrow Wilson International Center for Scholars, September 1999, p. 9.

p. 66 Churchill distressed by rumors re Stalin's health: Diaries of William Lyon Mackenzie King, 26 October 1945, Library and Archives of Canada, Ottawa.

p. 66 Harriman announced: *New York Times*, 27 October 1945.

p. 66 Stalin breathed fire and fury: Pechatnov, 'The Allies are Pressing', p. 11.

p. 66 'The appointment with . . .': *Ibid.*, p. 13.

p. 67 stay an additional night: *The Times*, 12 February 1946.

p. 68 complained on the phone: Mackenzie King Diaries, 28 February 1946.

p. 68   Soviet violation re Iran compared to Rhineland: *New York Times*, 12 March 1946; The Earl of Halifax to Mr. Bevin, 2 March 1946, *BDFA*, part 4, series C, vol. 1, p. 68.

p. 68   'the Long Telegram': The Chargé in the Soviet Union (Kennan) to the Secretary of State, 22 February 1946, *FRUS: 1946*, vol. 6, *Eastern Europe, the Soviet Union*, 1946.

p. 68   would do nothing but good: WSC to Clement Attlee, 7 March 1946, quoted in Ramsden, *Man of the Century*, p. 178; Mackenzie King Diaries, 25 March 1946.

p. 68   only if his presentation was well received: Mackenzie King Diaries, 25 March 1946.

p. 69   'This is certainly not...': WSC, 5 March 1946, quoted in *New York Times*, 6 March 1946.

p. 70   'notorious for his love...': The Earl of Halifax to Mr. Bevin, 8 March 1946, *BDFA*, part 4, series C, vol. 1, p. 25.

p. 70   claimed not to have read the speech: Harry Truman, 8 March 1946, quoted in *New York Times*, 9 March 1946.

p. 71   'a far more...': The Earl of Halifax to Mr. Bevin, 23 March 1946, *BDFA*, part 4, series C, vol. 1, p. 81.

p. 71   'the sharpest jolt...': The Earl of Halifax to Mr. Bevin, 10 March 1946, *ibid.*, p. 72.

p. 71   'warmonger': Full text of Stalin interview in *New York Times*, 14 March 1946.

p. 72   'the most violent...': Kennan to Byrnes, 14 March 1946, *FRUS: 1946*, vol. 6.

p. 72   As Molotov later said: *Molotov Remembers*, 60.

p. 73   scene at the Waldorf: The Earl of Halifax to Mr. Bevin, 16 March 1946, *BDFA*, part 4, series C, vol. 1, p. 77.

p. 73   dizzy spells: Mackenzie King Diaries, 25 March 1946.

p. 74   began to fall forward: *Ibid.*

VII: Imperious Caesar

p. 75   intent that that night: Cranborne to Paul Emrys Evans, 1 April and 5 April 1946, PEE Papers.

p. 75   precursors of a stroke: Mackenzie King Diaries, 25 March 1946.

p. 76   to set off another war: Dutton, *Anthony Eden*, p. 320.

p. 77   to keep the job from going to a younger rival: John Ramsden, *An Appetite for Power*, London: HarperCollins, 1999, p. 301.

p. 78   'in an ever-increasing . . .': WSC to Anthony Eden, 7 April 1946, quoted in Gilbert, *Churchill*, vol. 8, p. 227.

p. 78   'certainly one of . . .': *Ibid.*

p. 79   'to play my part': Anthony Eden to WSC, 10 April 1946, *ibid.*

p. 79   'happy unity': Cranborne to Paul Emrys Evans, 14 March 1946, PEE Papers.

p. 80   'imperious Caesar': Cranborne to Salisbury, 7 May 1946, quoted in Simon Ball, *The Guardsmen: Harold Macmillan, Three Friends, and the World They Made*, London: HarperCollins, 2004, p. 280.

p. 80   'take their courage . . .': Cranborne to Jim Thomas, 26 April 1946, quoted *ibid.*, p. 280.

p. 80   caught up in party strife: Mackenzie King Diaries, 30 May 1946.

p. 81   'Smuts and I . . .': Quoted in John Colville, *The Churchillians*, London: Weidenfeld & Nicolson, 1981, p. 175.

p. 81   'I was apprehensive . . .': Winston S. Churchill, *The World Crisis*, London: Odhams Press, 1938, p. 57.

p. 81   dinner party in honour of Mackenzie King: Mackenzie King Diaries, 8 June 1946.

p. 81   urged him to devote himself: *Ibid.*

p. 81   told Betty Cranborne: Cranborne to Paul Emrys Evans, 9 June 1946, PEE Papers.

p. 82   to stand down: Cranborne to Anthony Eden, 21 August 1946, quoted in Ball, *The Guardsmen*, p. 280.

p. 82   cared a good deal less: Lord Salisbury, author interview.

p. 82   had the luxury: Hugh Cecil, author interview.

p. 83   'Beware of rampant . . .': Channon, *Chips*, 5 May 1939.

p. 83   distressed by the perception: Lord Carrington, author interview.

p. 83   'rather as if . . .': Lord Stockton, author interview.

p. 83   Zurich speech: WSC, 19 September 1946, in *New York Times*, 20 September 1946.

p. 85   'Having possibly endangered . . .': Duff Cooper, *The Duff Cooper Diaries*, ed. John Julius Norwich, London: Weidenfeld & Nicolson, 2005, p. 420.

p. 85   'to retire gracefully': WSC, 5 October 1946, in Robert Rhodes James, ed., *Churchill Speaks 1897–1963: Collected Speeches in Peace and War*, New York: Barnes & Noble Books, 1998, p. 896.

p. 87   'rapidly losing ground': Cranborne to Paul Emrys Evans, 9 January 1947, PEE Papers.

p. 87   'by some resolute . . .': *Ibid.*

p. 87   'at all costs': *Ibid.*

p. 87   'like Lord Chatham . . .': *Ibid.*

VIII: Plots and Plotters

p. 89   fuel crisis: Violet Bonham Carter, *Daring to Hope: The Diaries and Letters of Violet Bonham Carter 1946–1969*, ed. Mark Pottle, London: Weidenfeld & Nicolson, 2000, 11 February 1947; Clementine Churchill to Mary Soames, 16 February 1947, quoted in Soames, *Clementine Churchill*, p. 456.

p. 90   could no longer afford: Report on the Meeting of the State–War–Navy Coordinating Committee Subcommittee on

Foreign Policy Information, 28 February 1947, *FRUS: 1947*, vol. 5, *The Near East and Africa*, 1947.

p. 90   12 March 1947 censure vote: *Hansard*, 12 March 1947; *New York Times*, 13 March 1947.

p. 90   Macmillan and Butler at Conservative meeting: *New York Times*, 14 March 1947.

p. 91   beginning in late February: Ball, *The Guardsmen*, p. 282.

p. 91   hernia operation: Moran, *Diaries*, June 1947.

p. 91   gathering at Crookshank's: Stuart, *Within the Fringe*, p. 145.

p. 92   disliked and distrusted: Lord Salisbury, author interview.

p. 92   lost interest in Bobbety: Hugh Cecil, author interview.

p. 92   affairs with other men: Lady Elizabeth Cavendish, the Dowager Duchess of Devonshire, Lady Lloyd, author interviews.

p. 92   rekindled her interest: Hugh Cecil, author interview.

p. 92   resented his lifelong affection: Lady Elizabeth Cavendish, the Dowager Duchess of Devonshire, author interviews.

p. 92   doomed him: Lady Elizabeth Cavendish, the Dowager Duchess of Devonshire, author interviews.

p. 92   Butler . . . threw in his lot: Headlam, *Diaries*, p. 487; Pierson Dixon, diary entry, 21 July 1947, quoted in Gilbert, *Churchill*, vol. 8, p. 341.

p. 93   blocked by a number of factors: Sir Nicholas Henderson, author interview.

p. 93   Stuart meets with Churchill: Stuart, *Within the Fringe*, pp. 146–7; Thompson, *The Day Before Yesterday*, p. 87.

p. 93   'Oh, you've joined . . .': Thompson, *The Day Before Yesterday*, p. 87.

p. 94   'rude awakening': Pierson Dixon, diary entry, 21 July 1947, quoted in Gilbert, *Churchill*, vol. 8, p. 341.

p. 94   1922 Committee appearance: Headlam, *Diaries*, 31 July 1947.

p. 95   to forsake politics: *Ibid.*, 2 August 1947.

p. 95   'of nothing except . . .': Cooper, *Diaries*, 24 November 1947.

p. 95   loathed Churchill: *Ibid.*

p. 95   to lure and coax his pet birds: Cooper, *Autobiography*, p. 391.

p. 95   'the most boring . . .': Lord Salisbury, author interview.

p. 95   By Macmillan's own reckoning: Lord Stockton, author interview.

p. 95   'political Siberia': *Ibid*.

p. 96   always manoeuvring, always watching: Lord Carrington, author interview.

p. 96   making up for lost time: Lord Stockton, author interview.

p. 97   'We need a Prime Minister . . .': *New York Times*, 5 October 1947.

IX: Before It Is Too Late

p. 98   'in attendance': Lady Soames, author interview.

p. 98   Churchill at wedding: Mackenzie King Diaries, 20 November 1947.

p. 98   'We shall not . . .': *Ibid*.

p. 99   Moscow decreed postwar world divided: *New York Times*, 23 October 1947.

p. 99   Bevin told the Dominion leaders: Mackenzie King Diaries, 24 November 1947.

p. 100   'If I were . . .': Quoted in Bonham Carter, *Daring to Hope*, 12 August 1948.

p. 100   lunch party for Smuts and King: Mackenzie King Diaries, 25 November 1947.

p. 100   'I am telling . . .': *Ibid*.

p. 100   the whites of his bulging eyes: *Ibid*.

p. 100   'The gleam in . . .': *Ibid*.

p. 101   'admirers and hangers-on': Headlam, *Diaries*, 7 March 1949.

p. 102   'always been too . . .': *Ibid*., 23 February 1949.

p. 102   'Will there be . . .': WSC, 23 January 1948, quoted in *New York Times*, 24 January 1948.

p. 103　'unless we are able to learn . . .': Editorial, *New York Times*, 16 April 1948.

p. 103　serial sparked outrage: Channon, *Chips*, 2 June 1948.

p. 105　Speaking at a mass rally: *New York Times*, 29 June 1948.

p. 105　'something practical to . . .': WSC at Conservative Party Conference, Llandudno, 9 October 1948, quoted in *New York Times*, 10 October 1948.

p. 105　'much heartburning': Salisbury to Paul Emrys Evans, 4 October 1948, PEE Papers.

p. 106　'criminal error': *Ibid.*

p. 106　delegates carrying the book: *New York Times*, 6 October 1948.

p. 107　manifesto: Salisbury to Paul Emrys Evans, 29 November 1948, PEE Papers.

p. 107　Kemsley makes public call: *New York Times*, 19 October 1948.

p. 107　'devised with the . . .': Dwight D. Eisenhower, *Crusade in Europe*, Garden City, NY: Doubleday, 1949, p. 396.

p. 108　worst crisis of faith: Philip Goodhart with Ursula Branston, *The 1922: The Story of the Conservative Backbenchers' Parliamentary Committee*, London: Macmillan, 1973, p. 146.

p. 109　'personal decks': Quoted *ibid.*, p. 147.

p. 109　fortunate he had not given the V-sign: Headlam, *Diaries*, 3 March 1949.

p. 109　read the Liberal press: Lady Soames, author interview.

p. 110　'great prestige': Quoted in Bonham Carter, *Champion Redoubtable*, 1 August 1944.

p. 110　'gladly exchange the . . .': Mary Soames to Clementine Churchill, 21 October 1945, quoted in Soames, *Clementine Churchill*, p. 439.

p. 110　'Very successful . . .': Channon, *Chips*, 27 January 1949.

p. 111　'I do not mind . . .': Clementine Churchill to WSC, 5 March 1949, in Soames, ed., *Winston and Clementine*.

341

p. 111   White House announced: *New York Times*, 22 March 1949.

p. 112   'like a schoolboy': Macmillan, *Tides of Fortune*, p. 171.

X: The Dagger Is Pointed

p. 114   'The dagger is . . .': Quoted in A. J. P. Taylor, *Beaverbrook*, London: Penguin, 1974, p. 122.

p. 115   Moran's conclusion: Moran, *Diaries*, 24 August 1949.

p. 116   rumours flew: Macmillan, *Tides of Fortune*, p. 179.

p. 116   According to Sandys: *Ibid.*

p. 116   In the days that followed: Moran, *Diaries*, p. 357.

p. 116   'The dagger struck . . .': Quoted in Taylor, *Beaverbrook*, p. 758.

p. 116   'notice to quit . . .': Moran, *Diaries*, 11 October 1951.

p. 116   'wasted': Denis Kelly quoted in Gilbert, *Churchill*, vol. 8, p. 487.

p. 117   worried press will notice: Moran, *Diaries*, p. 357.

p. 117   attended the Lime Tree Stakes: *New York Times*, 11 September 1949.

p. 118   'entranced': Channon, *Chips*, 28 September 1949.

p. 118   'Over all there . . .': WSC, 28 September 1949, quoted in *New York Times*, 29 September 1949.

p. 119   'like a soiled glove': *Hansard*, 29 September 1949.

p. 119   'I hope, sir . . .': Quoted in Kay Halle, *The Irrepressible Churchill*, London: Robson, 1985, p. 246.

p. 119   'I am prepared . . .': *Ibid.*

p. 119   'I heard there . . .': *Time*, 23 January 1950.

p. 120   'toil and moil': WSC telegram to Clementine Churchill, 16 January 1950, quoted in Gilbert, *Churchill*, vol. 8, p. 501.

p. 120   'immense programme': WSC to Clementine Churchill, 19 January 1950, in Soames, ed., *Winston and Clementine*.

p. 120 'When great events . . .': Quoted in Bonham Carter, *Daring to Hope*, 16 January 1950.

p. 120 'It must be nearly . . .': Quoted in Lord Butler, *The Art of the Possible*, London: Hamish Hamilton, 1971, p. 152.

p. 120 everything went misty: Moran, *Diaries*, 24 January 1950.

p. 120 'I am not . . .': Quoted in Archibald Clark Kerr Diary, 16 August 1942.

p. 122 Eden signalled the world: *New York Times*, 14 February 1950.

p. 122 'Still, I cannot . . .': WSC, 14 February 1950, quoted in *New York Times*, 15 February 1950.

p. 123 Labour reaction: *New York Times*, 16 February 1950.

p. 123 'Of course, as I am reminded . . .': WSC, 17 February 1950, quoted in *New York Times*, 18 February 1950.

p. 124 'the prelude to . . .': Macmillan, *Tides of Fortune*, p. 316.

p. 125 inevitable: WSC to Sir Alan Lascelles, 27 February 1950, quoted in Gilbert, *Churchill*, vol. 8, p. 512.

p. 125 Eden questioned the wisdom: Dutton, *Anthony Eden*, p. 236.

XI: Another Glass of Your Excellent Champagne

p. 127 Beistegui Ball: Susan Mary Alsop, *To Marietta from Paris*, Garden City, NY: Doubleday, 1965, pp. 182–90; John Julius Norwich, *Trying to Please*, Wimborne Minster, Dorset: Dovecote Press, 2008, pp. 140–2; Lanfranco Rasponi, *The International Nomads*, New York: Putnam's, 1966, pp. 193–200; Charlotte Mosley, ed., *The Mitfords: Letters between Six Sisters*, New York: Harper, 2007, pp. 272–4.

p. 128 sink into the Grand Canal: Rasponi, *International Nomads*, p. 200.

p. 128 'Anthony Eden nearly . . .': Halle, *The Irrepressible Churchill*, p. 255.

p. 129 Seeking to counter sentiment: Harold Macmillan, *The*

Macmillan Diaries: Cabinet Years, 1950–1957, ed. Peter Catterall, London: Macmillan, 2003, 11–14 June 1951.

p. 129   managed to extract: Malcolm Muggeridge, *Like It Was: The Diaries of Malcolm Muggeridge*, ed. John Bright-Holmes, London: Collins, 1981, p. 437.

p. 129   whether he might safely swim: WSC to Dr Russell Brain, 22 August 1951, quoted in Gilbert, *Churchill*, vol. 8, p. 631.

p. 130   Churchill in bathing trunks: *New York Times*, 25 August 1951.

p. 130   'I found him . . .': Cooper, *Diaries*, August 1951.

p. 130   'run interference': Lord Norwich, author interview.

p. 131   watched his mother grow desperate: *Ibid.*

p. 131   'I shall be . . .': *Ibid.*

p. 131   'lacking in dignity': Cooper, *Diaries*, December 1951.

p. 131   intended to lay down the burden: Macmillan, *Diaries*, 4 October 1951.

p. 132   'physically able': *Ibid.*, 27 September 1951.

p. 132   'to younger hands': *Ibid.*

p. 132   lost ground in recent months: Moran, *Diaries*, p. 361.

p. 132   'at his best': Lady Soames, author interview.

p. 132   Churchill confessed: Moran, *Diaries*, 11 October 1951.

p. 133   'I do not hold . . .': WSC, 8 October 1951, in Winston S. Churchill, *Stemming the Tide: Speeches, 1951 and 1952*, ed. Randolph S. Churchill, Boston: Houghton Mifflin, 1954, p. 135.

p. 134   'Do you think . . .': Quoted in Tony Benn, *Years of Hope: Diaries, Letters and Papers 1940–1962*, ed. Ruth Winstone, London: Hutchinson, 1994, 31 October 1951.

p. 134   'cruel and ungrateful . . .': WSC, 23 October 1951, quoted in *New York Times*, 24 October 1951.

p. 134   'It is the last . . .': *Ibid.*

p. 135   'One may say . . .': Churchill, *Great Contemporaries*, p. 63.

XII: White with the Bones of Englishmen

p. 136 'rather an ass': Salisbury to Paul Emrys Evans, 29 October 1951, PEE Papers.

p. 136 infringement on the royal prerogative: Randolph Churchill, *The Rise and Fall of Sir Anthony Eden*, London: Macgibbon, 1959, pp. 193–4.

p. 137 'bullying people who ...': P. J. Grigg quoted in Bonham Carter, *Daring to Hope*, 3 January 1957.

p. 137 'into one throw': Lord Salisbury, author interview.

p. 137 played havoc with his hearing: Moran, *Diaries*, 9 November 1951.

p. 137 'a sea captain ...': Lord Chandos quoted in Thompson, *The Day Before Yesterday*, p. 91.

p. 137 die during the new Parliament: Channon, *Chips*, 28 October 1951.

p. 137 in lieu of a hot water bottle: Rab Butler quoted in Thompson, *The Day Before Yesterday*, p. 91.

p. 138 high words were exchanged: Evelyn Shuckburgh, *Descent to Suez: Foreign Office Diaries, 1951–1956*, ed. John Charmley, New York: Norton, 1986, 27 October 1951.

p. 139 Churchill intervened: *Ibid.*

p. 139 'If he wants ...': Quoted in Alistair Horne, *Macmillan, 1894–1956*, London: Macmillan, 1988, p. 341.

p. 139 'in a most ...': Macmillan, *Diaries*, 28 October 1951.

p. 139 'either make or mar': *Ibid.*

p. 140 poured out his anguish: Lady Elizabeth Cavendish, author interview.

p. 140 far better campaigner: Lady Anne Tree, author interview.

p. 140 extremely cautious: Lady Anne Tree, author interview.

p. 141 'in great form': Macmillan, *Diaries*, 30 October 1951.

p. 141 quoting Machiavelli: Cabinet Secretary's Notebooks,

30 October 1951, CAB 195/10, The National Archives, Public Record Office.

p. 141   'up': *Ibid.*

p. 141   'almost certain': Memorandum by the Director of the Office of British Commonwealth and Northern European Affairs (Raynor), 18 October 1951, *FRUS: 1951*, vol. 4, *Europe: political and economic developments (in two parts)*, part 1, 1951.

p. 142   difficult for Truman to decline: *Ibid.*

p. 142   'hasty public': Paper Prepared in the Department of State, n.d., *FRUS: 1951*, vol. 4, part 1; The Acting Secretary of State to the Embassy in the United Kingdom, 25 October 1951, *ibid.*

p. 142   'Now that I am again': WSC to Stalin, 5 November 1951, Foreign Office 371/94841, quoted in Gilbert, *Churchill*, vol. 8, p. 659.

p. 143   'cursed old age': Quoted in Simon Sebag Montefiore, *Stalin: The Court of the Red Tsar*, New York: Vintage, 2003, p. 614.

p. 143   'finished': Quoted *ibid.*

p. 143   'persecution mania': *Molotov Remembers*, p. 324.

p. 143   Churchill reported to his Cabinet: Cabinet Secretary's Notebooks, 12 November 1951, CAB 195/10.

p. 144   Eden welcomed and praised: *New York Times*, 13 November and 14 November 1951.

p. 144   stomach spasms: Shuckburgh, *Descent to Suez*, 4 November 1951.

p. 145   kill himself in the bargain: Salisbury to Paul Emrys Evans, 29 October 1951, PEE Papers.

p. 145   travelled with a black tin box: Shuckburgh, *Descent to Suez*, p. 14.

p. 145   heard through the wall: *Ibid.*, 21 November 1951.

p. 145   Eisenhower read advance extracts: Eisenhower to Hastings Ismay, 2 October 1951, in *The Papers of Dwight David*

Eisenhower, ed. Louis Galambos and Daun Van Ee, vol. 12, Baltimore: Johns Hopkins University Press, 1989, p. 589.

p. 147 Eden breakfast with Eisenhower: Anthony Eden, *Full Circle*, Boston: Houghton Mifflin, 1960, p. 36; C. L. Sulzberger, *A Long Row of Candles: Memoirs and Diaries, 1934–1951*, New York: Macmillan, 1969, 13 December 1951.

p. 147 liked the current European army plan: Sulzberger, *A Long Row of Candles*, 13 December 1951.

p. 147 presented himself as: Dean Acheson to Truman, 30 November 1951, *FRUS: 1951*, vol. 3, *European security and the German question (in two parts)*, part 1, 1951; Memo of Conversation by Secretary of State with Eden, 29 November 1951, Rome, *ibid*.

p. 147 a more cooperative mood: Sulzberger, *A Long Row of Candles*, 13 December 1951.

p. 147 agreed not to attack: Gifford to Acheson, 11 December 1951, *FRUS: 1951*, vol. 3, part 1.

p. 148 conferred with Adenauer: *Ibid*.

p. 148 praising Shinwell: *The Times*, 7 December 1951.

p. 148 hoped to ease French fears: Gifford to Acheson, 19 December 1951, *FRUS: 1951*, vol. 3, part 1.

p. 149 'second string': Shuckburgh, *Descent to Suez*, 16 December 1951.

p. 149 'very considerably': The Ambassador in France (Bruce) to the Secretary of State, 19 December 1951, *FRUS: 1951*, vol. 4, part 1.

p. 149 could not last in office: *Ibid*.

p. 149 'vigorously': *Ibid*.

p. 149 expressed doubt: *Ibid*.

p. 150 drinking whisky: Shuckburgh, *Descent to Suez*, 16 December 1951.

p. 150 'deliberately grumpy': Sulzberger, *A Long Row of Candles*, 13 December 1951.

p. 150   'to give Churchill hell': *Ibid.*

p. 150   'Eisenhower blames Churchill . . .': *Ibid.*

p. 151   'to put the bite . . .': *Ibid.*

p. 151   'I want a . . .': The Ambassador in France (Bruce) to the Secretary of State, 20 December 1951, *FRUS: 1951*, vol. 3, part 1.

p. 151   'pounded': *Ibid.*

p. 151   'I am back . . .': Diary entry, 21 December 1951, in *The Papers of Dwight David Eisenhower*, vol. 12, p. 810.

p. 151   'penniless beggar': The Ambassador in the United Kingdom (Gifford) to the Secretary of State, 29 December 1951, *FRUS: 1951*, vol. 4, part 1.

p. 152   contacted the American Ambassador: *Ibid.*

p. 153   the Captain came in: Shuckburgh, *Descent to Suez*, 29 December 1951.

p. 153   'Your one value . . .': Lord Mountbatten, diary entry, 31 December 1951, quoted in Gilbert, *Churchill*, vol. 8, p. 673.

p. 153   New Year's Eve: Shuckburgh, *Descent to Suez*, 29 December 1951; Moran, *Diaries*, 1 January 1952.

p. 154   talked of his trepidation: Moran, *Diaries*, 1 January 1952.

p. 154   on the presidential yacht: Memorandum by the Secretary of State of a Dinner Meeting Aboard the SS *Williamsburg* on the Evening of January 5, 1952, *FRUS: 1952–1954*, vol. 6, *Western Europe and Canada (in two parts)*, part 1, 1954; Notes by the Chairman of the Joint Chief of Staff (Bradley) of a Dinner Meeting Aboard the SS *Williamsburg* on the Evening of January 5, 1952, *ibid.*; Dean Acheson, *Present at the Creation*, New York: Norton, 1969, pp. 597–600.

p. 154   'definitely aging and . . .': The Ambassador of the United Kingdom (Gifford) to the Department of State, 28 December 1951, *ibid.*

p. 155   'so that we . . .': Prime Minister Churchill to President Truman, 10 December 1951, *FRUS: 1952–1954*, vol. 6, part 1.

p. 155   agenda and advisers: President Truman to Prime Minister Churchill, 13 December 1951, *ibid.*

p. 155   'nervousness': Sir O. Franks, United States: Weekly Summary, Period 22nd–28th December 1951, 29 December 1951, *BDFA,* part 5, series C, vol. 2, *1952,* Bethesda, MD: LexisNexis, 2006, p. 206.

p. 155   'by sheer weight . . .': *Ibid.*

p. 156   he assured the President: Acheson, *Present at the Creation,* p. 597.

p. 156   talk as equals: Moran, *Diaries,* 5 January 1952.

p. 156   cut Churchill off: Shuckburgh, *Descent to Suez,* 5 January 1952.

p. 156   'different circumstances': The Acting Secretary of State to the Embassy in the United Kingdom, 9 December 1951, *FRUS: 1952–1954,* vol. 6, part 1.

p. 157   urged him not to concentrate: Moran, *Diaries,* 7 January 1952.

p. 157   'with British blood': Memorandum by the Special Assistant to the Secretary of State (Battle) of a Meeting Between President Truman and Prime Minister Churchill, 8 January 1952, *FRUS: 1952–1954,* vol. 6, part 1.

p. 158   'bravely and loyally': Shuckburgh, *Descent to Suez,* 5 January 1952.

p. 158   tell night from day: Moran, *Diaries,* 8 January 1952.

p. 158   distressed about press communiqué: *Ibid.*

p. 158   conversation with Makins: Colville, *The Fringes of Power,* p. 600.

p. 159   address to Congress: Sir O. Franks, United States: Weekly Summary, Period 12th–18th January 1952, 19 January 1952, *BDFA,* part 5, series C, vol. 2, p. 215.

p. 159   firm, strong voice: *The Times,* 18 January 1952.

p. 159   visibly relieved: Moran, *Diaries,* 17 January 1952.

p. 160   drafted a joint communiqué: Acheson, *Present at the Creation,* p. 601.

p. 160   rip up the text: *Ibid.*

p. 160   'Hurricane warnings . . .': *Ibid.*

p. 161   Churchill during drafting of communiqué: US Secretary of Defense (Robert Lovett) to Eisenhower, 24 January 1952, *FRUS: 1952–1954*, vol. 6, part 1.

p. 161   'majestic': Acheson, *Present at the Creation*, p. 602.

p. 161   'upon that western . . .': *Ibid.*

p. 162   raising the possibility of a conference: US Delegation Minutes of the Meeting of President Truman and Prime Minister Churchill, The White House, 18 January 1952, 3 p.m., *FRUS: 1952–1954*, vol. 6, part 1.

p. 162   Truman easily brushed aside: Minutes, 18 January 1952, *FRUS: 1952–1954*, vol. 6, part 1.

p. 162   Truman gave him several openings: *Ibid.*

p. 162   Churchill sent Colville: *Ibid.*

p. 163   'I accept': Secretary of Defense Lovett to the Supreme Allied Commander, Europe, Eisenhower, 24 January 1952, *FRUS: 1952–1954*, vol. 6, part 1.

XIII: Naked Among Mine Enemies

p. 164   spent much of the train trip: Moran, *Diaries*, 19 January 1952.

p. 164   intended to spend forty-eight hours: WSC to Clementine Churchill, 20 January 1952, in Soames, ed., *Winston and Clementine.*

p. 164   received the Archbishop and the Mayor: *New York Times*, 23 January 1952.

p. 165   dreamed that he was so sick: Moran, *Diaries*, 26 January 1952.

p. 165   waiting at Southampton: *The Times*, 29 January 1952.

p. 165   looked forward to: WSC to Clementine Churchill, 20 January 1952, in Soames, ed., *Winston and Clementine.*

p. 166   his intention to reply: Cabinet Secretary's Notebooks, 29 January 1952, CAB 195/10.

p. 166   'get away': *Ibid.*

p. 166   'very anxious': *Ibid.*

p. 166   'Let's see what . . .': *Ibid.*

p. 166   'more convenient': *The Times*, 30 January 1952.

p. 167   'tardy, timid and fatuous': *New York Times*, 31 January 1952.

p. 167   'irritated': Richard Crossman, *The Backbench Diaries of Richard Crossman*, ed. Janet Morgan, New York: Holmes & Meier, 1981, 5 February 1952.

p. 168   'I've got bad . . .': Quoted in Ben Pimlott, *The Queen: A Biography of Elizabeth II*, New York: John Wiley & Sons, 1997, p. 176.

p. 168   tried to reassure him: Colville, *The Fringes of Power*, p. 601.

p. 168   announcing that the King had died: Cabinet Secretary's Notebooks, 6 February 1952, CAB 195/10.

p. 168   filled Churchill with dread: *Ibid.*

p. 168   doubted that they would: *Ibid.*

p. 169   Commons filled to overflowing: *The Times*, 7 February 1952.

p. 169   'terribly disappointed': Crossman, *Backbench Diaries*, 6 February 1952.

p. 169   'No doubt we . . .': *Ibid.*

p. 169   'hard-boiled': *Ibid.*, 11 February 1952.

p. 169   'Directly you got . . .': *Ibid.*

p. 169   'being much tired . . .': Macmillan, *Diaries*, 7 February 1952.

p. 170   'In the end . . .': WSC, 7 February 1952, in Churchill, *Stemming the Tide*, p. 238.

p. 171   in no rush: Cabinet Secretary's Notebooks, 11 February 1952, CAB 195/10.

p. 171   'steadying effect': Quoted in Macmillan, *Diaries*, 11 February 1952.

p. 171   a paternal attitude: *Ibid.*, 6 March 1952.

p. 171   'a real love-match': Lady Elizabeth Cavendish, author interview.

p. 171 'I've seen the man . . .': *Ibid.*

p. 172 'the power behind . . .': Macmillan, *Diaries*, 8 February 1952.

p. 172 'Why was he . . .': *Ibid.*; Cabinet Secretary's Notebooks, 8 February 1952, CAB 195/10.

p. 172 Mountbatten had been heard: Colville, *The Fringes of Power*, p. 602.

p. 172 repeated the story: Cabinet Secretary's Notebooks, 18 February 1952, CAB 195/10.

p. 173 top-secret information: Acheson, *Present at the Creation*, p. 618.

p. 173 'naked among mine . . .': *Ibid.*, p. 620.

p. 173 'I can win . . .': *Ibid.*, p. 621.

p. 174 needed to focus: Cabinet Secretary's Notebooks, 21 February 1952, CAB 195/10.

p. 174 Eden disclosed: Acheson, *Present at the Creation*, p. 618.

p. 174 could not think of the words: Moran, *Diaries*, 21 February 1952.

XIV: I Live Here, Don't I?

p. 175 recounted the telephone incident: Moran, *Diaries*, 21 February 1952.

p. 175 her nightmare that someday: Anthony Montague Browne, *Long Sunset*, London: Cassell, 1995, p. 122.

p. 176 her demeanour: Moran, *Diaries*, 21 February 1952.

p. 176 meeting with Salisbury: Colville, *The Fringes of Power*, p. 603; Moran, *Diaries*, 22 February 1952.

p. 177 Lascelles concurred: Moran, *Diaries*, 22 February 1952.

p. 178 only his wife and doctor: Colville, *The Fringes of Power*, p. 603.

p. 178 dull and listless: Moran, *Diaries*, 29 February 1952.

p. 178 'cumbrous, ill-at-ease': Crossman, *Backbench Diaries*, 26 February 1952.

p. 178 cheers that greeted him: *The Times*, 27 February 1952.

p. 179 'He is looking...': Nigel Nicolson to Harold Nicolson, quoted in Gilbert, *Churchill*, vol. 8, p. 707.

p. 179 Churchill's speech: *Hansard*, 26 February 1952.

p. 179 'sat stunned and white': Crossman, *Backbench Diaries*, 26 February 1952.

p. 180 took turns pummelling Butler: Cabinet Secretary's Notebooks, 28 February 1952 and 4 March 1952, CAB 195/10; Macmillan, *Diaries*, 29 February 1952.

p. 180 taken the lead: Shuckburgh, *Descent to Suez*, p. 38.

p. 180 Moran's letter: Moran, *Diaries*, 12 March 1952.

p. 181 dismissed the letter: *Ibid.*, 13 March 1952.

p. 181 destroyed his medical records: Sebag Montefiore, *Stalin*, p. 202.

p. 181 conferring with Cabinet about Stalin message: Cabinet Secretary's Notebooks, 12 March 1952, CAB 195/10.

p. 181 Stalin proposed: *The Times*, 11 and 12 March 1952; Gifford to Dept of State, 11 March 1952, *FRUS: 1952–1954*, vol. 7, *Germany and Austria (in two parts)*, part 1, 1954.

p. 182 unnerved by heavy Conservative losses: *New York Times*, 10 April 1952; Macmillan, *Diaries*, 8–10 April 1952.

p. 182 mocked and taunted: Channon, *Chips*, 9 April 1952.

p. 182 assure the 1922 Committee: *New York Times*, 10 April 1952; Channon, *Chips*, 9 April 1952.

p. 183 'old brain': Anthony Eden, diary entry, 4 June 1952, quoted in Rhodes James, *Anthony Eden*, p. 355.

p. 183 met to formulate new ultimatum: Harry Crookshank, diary entry, 16 June 1952, quoted in Gilbert, *Churchill*, vol. 8, p. 736.

p. 183 he was desperately hurt: Lady Soames, author interview.

p. 183 incident in sitting room at Number Ten: Acheson, *Present at the Creation*, p. 662.

p. 184 Eden suddenly fell ill: *New York Times*, 30 June 1952.

p. 184   Foreign Office announced: *The Times*, 1 July 1952.

p. 184   'fairly pulverized . . .': Channon, *Chips*, 1 July 1952.

p. 184   flushed and furious: *New York Times*, 31 July 1952.

p. 185   Colville sent for doctor: Moran, *Diaries*, 30 June 1952.

p. 185   rather in love with her himself: The Dowager Duchess of Devonshire, author interview.

p. 185   'latest admirer': Cooper, *Diaries*, 24 November 1947.

p. 185   never stopped trying: *Ibid.*

p. 185   'dynastic': Alan Clark, *The Tories*, London: Weidenfeld & Nicolson, 1998, p. 334.

p. 185   'I thought it might . . .': WSC to Truman, 22 August 1952, *FRUS: 1952–1954*, vol. 10, *Iran*, 1954.

p. 186   'I do not . . .': *Ibid.*

p. 186   Eden was furious: Colville, *The Fringes of Power*, 22–25 August 1952.

p. 186   his best hope: *Ibid.*, 13–15 June 1952.

p. 186   'the best man': Sir O. Franks to Mr. Eden, 21 August 1952, *BDFA*, part 5, series C, vol. 2, p. 158.

p. 186   'cheap politics': Sir O. Franks, United States Weekly Summary, 30th August–5th September 1952, 6 September 1952, *ibid.*, p. 299.

p. 187   'For your private . . .': Colville, *The Fringes of Power*, 9 November 1952.

p. 187   'I send you . . .': WSC to Eisenhower, 5 November 1952, quoted in Gilbert, *Churchill*, vol. 8, p. 773; *New York Times*, 6 November 1952.

p. 187   Churchill very cross: Shuckburgh, *Descent to Suez*, 5 November 1952.

p. 187   'a sudden burst . . .': Channon, *Chips*, 5 November 1952.

p. 188   did not even mention Churchill: Shuckburgh, *Descent to Suez*, 20 November 1952.

p. 188   On the flight home: *Ibid.*, 26 November 1952.

p. 188   had been speaking to Clarissa: *Ibid.*, 28 November 1952.

p. 188 'begged': *Ibid.*

p. 188 'rejuvenating' pills: *Time*, 15 December 1952.

p. 189 unable to follow: Shuckburgh, *Descent to Suez*, 2 December 1952.

p. 189 'pathetic': *Ibid.*

p. 189 sounded out Lascelles: *Ibid.*, 4 December 1952.

p. 189 Eden told Churchill: *Ibid.*, 8 December 1952.

p. 190 'I am delighted . . .': Eisenhower to WSC, 17 December 1952, in *The Papers of Dwight David Eisenhower*, vol. 13, Baltimore: Johns Hopkins University Press, 1989, p. 1450.

p. 190 best work was still ahead: Crossman, *Backbench Diaries*, 5 February 1952.

p. 191 'completely fatuous': Diary entry, 6 January 1953, in *The Papers of Dwight David Eisenhower*, vol. 13, p. 1481.

p. 191 'would turn over . . .': *Ibid.*

p. 191 told an audience in Detroit: *New York Times*, 15 June 1952.

p. 191 'no political directive': Dwight Eisenhower to Forrest Carlisle Pogue, 20 February 1952, in *The Papers of Dwight David Eisenhower*, vol. 13, p. 1001.

p. 191 no role in political decisions: Dwight Eisenhower to Fred Kent, 17 April 1952, and Dwight Eisenhower to Richard Nixon, 1 October 1952, *ibid.*, p. 1183.

p. 192 'much vigour': Prime Minister to Secretary of State and Chancellor of the Exchequer, 8 January 1953, PREM 11/422.

p. 192 'quite welcome': *Ibid.*

p. 193 'certain power': *Ibid.*

p. 193 'in too great . . .': *Ibid.*

XV: If Nothing Can Be Arranged

p. 194 'a real man . . .': Colville, *The Fringes of Power*, 11 January 1953.

p. 194 seemed to listen: Prime Minister to Secretary of State and Chancellor of the Exchequer, 8 January 1953, PREM 11/422.

p. 194   rejected Churchill's suggestion: Colville, *The Fringes of Power*, 7 January 1953.

p. 195   'an increasing liability': Anthony Eden, diary entry, 23 January 1953, quoted in Rhodes James, *Anthony Eden*, p. 358.

p. 195   Lascelles assured: Shuckburgh, *Descent to Suez*, 19 January 1953.

p. 195   tempted Macmillan: Macmillan, *Diaries*, 17 January 1953.

p. 195   Walter Gifford: Diary entry, 13 February 1953, in *The Papers of Dwight David Eisenhower*, vol. 14, Baltimore: Johns Hopkins University Press, 1996, p. 43.

p. 196   For some twelve hours: Sebag Montefiore, *Stalin*, p. 640.

p. 196   'killer doctors': *Pravda*, 13 January 1953.

p. 196   To allay public fears: Sir A. Gascoigne to Foreign Office, 4 March 1953, PREM 11/540.

p. 196   'contorted': Quoted in Sebag Montefiore, *Stalin*, p. 642.

p. 196   joint leadership: Sir A. Gascoigne to Foreign Office, 7 March 1953, PREM 11/540.

p. 196   paunchy, unkempt: Sir A. Gascoigne to Mr. Eden, 19 March 1953, *BDFA,* part 5, series A, *Soviet Union and Finland,* vol. 3, *1953*, Bethesda, MD: LexisNexis, 2007, p. 52.

p. 196   compared to Machiavelli: Memorandum of Discussion at the 150th Meeting of the National Security Council, 18 June 1953, *FRUS: 1952–1954*, vol. 7, part 2.

p. 196   to come out on top: Sir A. Gascoigne to Foreign Office, 4 March 1953, PREM 11/540.

p. 196   failed to accord: P. Mason to Foreign Office, 7 March 1953, PREM 11/540.

p. 197   'like hawks': *Ibid.*

p. 197   'I remember our . . .': Prime Minister to President Eisenhower, 10 March 1953, PREM 11/422.

p. 198   to throw Eden together with Molotov: Prime Minister to Secretary of State for Foreign Affairs, 28 March 1953, PREM 11/422.

p. 198 'interim objective': *Ibid.*

p. 198 'very keen': Shuckburgh, *Descent to Suez*, 1 April 1953.

p. 199 jailed doctors had been released: The Chargé in the Soviet Union (Beam) to the Department of State, 4 April 1953, *FRUS: 1952–1954*, vol. 8, *Eastern Europe; Soviet Union; Eastern Mediterranean*, 1954.

p. 199 the most dangerous moment: Prime Minister Churchill to President Eisenhower, 11 April 1953, *FRUS: 1952–1954*, 199. 6, part 1.

p. 199 distressed that he had missed: Memorandum of Telephone Conversation with the President by the Secretary of State, 16 March 1953, *FRUS: 1952–1954*, vol. 8.

p. 200 'We do not know . . .': Prime Minister Churchill to President Eisenhower, 11 April 1953, *FRUS: 1952–1954*, vol. 6, part 1.

p. 201 claiming that had Stalin: Memorandum of National Security Council Discussion, 11 March 1953, *FRUS: 1952–1954*, vol. 8.

p. 201 'Well, maybe Churchill's . . .': Emmet John Hughes, *The Ordeal of Power*, New York: Atheneum, 1963, p. 113.

p. 201 'prayerfully': President Eisenhower to Prime Minister Churchill, 11 April 1953, *FRUS: 1952–1954*, vol. 6, part 1.

p. 201 Eden's operation: Thorpe, *Eden*, pp. 384–5; Rhodes James, *Anthony Eden*, pp. 362–3; David Owen, *In Sickness and in Power*, Westport, CT: Praeger, 2008, pp. 109–10.

p. 202 'slipped': Rhodes James, *Anthony Eden*, p. 362.

p. 202 agreed to tone down: President Eisenhower to Prime Minister Churchill, 11 April 1953, *FRUS: 1952–1954*, vol. 6, part 1.

p. 202 'massive and magnificent': Quoted in *New York Times*, 18 April 1953.

p. 203 'In my opinion . . .': Prime Minister Churchill to President Eisenhower, 21 April 1953, PREM 11/422.

p. 203 'If nothing can be arranged': Prime Minister Churchill to President Eisenhower, 21 April 1953, PREM 11/422.

p. 204   Lord Swinton: Moran, *Diaries*, 24 April 1953.

p. 204   'extraordinarily well . . .': Bonham Carter, *Daring to Hope*, 15 April 1953.

p. 204   Moran warned: Moran, *Diaries*, 24 April 1953.

p. 205   spoke of not rushing: President Eisenhower to Prime Minister Churchill, 25 April 1953, PREM 11/422.

p. 205   'who could take up . . .': CC (53) 29th Conclusions, Minute I, PREM 11/422.

p. 206   'hadn't started this . . .': Cabinet Secretary's Notebooks, 28 April 1953, CAB 195/11.

p. 206   sent Eisenhower his draft: Prime Minister Churchill to President Eisenhower, 4 May 1953, *FRUS: 1952–1954*, vol. 8.

p. 206   advised him not to go: President Eisenhower to Prime Minister Churchill, 5 May 1953, *ibid.*

p. 207   'It is the . . .': *New York Times*, 12 May 1953.

p. 207   'the diplomatic leadership . . .': *New York Times*, 18 May 1953.

p. 208   'faculties and judgement': Memorandum of Discussion at the 145th Meeting of the National Security Council, 20 May 1953, *FRUS: 1952–1954*, vol. 15, *Korea (in two parts)*, part 1.

p. 208   'Sir Winston Churchill . . .': *Hansard*, 29 July 1953.

p. 209   pretended not to hear: Eisenhower phone call to Churchill, 20 May 1953, *FRUS: 1952–1954*, vol. 6, part 1; Cabinet Secretary's Notebooks, 21 May 1953, CAB 195/11.

p. 209   'in a mood . . .': Macmillan, *Diaries*, 21 May 1953.

p. 209   'frankly sceptical': Lord Salisbury to Prime Minister Churchill, 11 June 1953, PREM 11/428.

p. 209   'a quiet time . . .': Lord Salisbury, *Hansard*, 29 July 1953.

p. 209   'Eisenhower has followed . . .': Cabinet Secretary's Notebooks, 21 May 1953, CAB 195/11.

p. 209   'a direct result': Lord Salisbury to Prime Minister Churchill, 11 June 1953, PREM 11/428.

p. 210   'completely negative attitude': *Ibid.*

p. 210   'Yes, sir, it . . .': *New York Times*, 22 May 1953.

XVI: The Abdication of Diocletian

p. 211   the detective suggested: Edmund Murray, 'The Churchill I Knew', paper presented at the Churchill Centre, Surrey, England, 9th International Conference, 13 June 1992.

p. 211   encounter with Bevan: *Ibid.*

p. 212   leaned on the Soviets: WSC to Vyacheslav Molotov, 2 June 1953, PREM 11/420.

p. 213   'big game': Macmillan, *Diaries*, 1–7 June 1953.

p. 213   'would not trust . . .': *Ibid.*, 1 September 1953.

p. 213   'through': *Ibid.*

p. 213   Churchill late: Colville, *The Fringes of Power*, p. 666.

p. 213   the race: *The Times*, June 8, 1953; *Time*, 15 June 1953.

p. 214   'a most serious . . .': Macmillan, *Diaries*, 1–7 June 1953.

p. 214   'an understanding attitude': Lord Salisbury to Prime Minister Churchill, 11 June 1953, PREM 11/428.

p. 214   'great temptation': *Ibid.*

p. 214   'I am sure . . .': *Ibid.*

p. 214   agreed to a firm set of dates: WSC to Eisenhower, 20 June 1953, in Peter G. Boyle, ed., *The Churchill–Eisenhower Correspondence, 1953–1955*, Chapel Hill: University of North Carolina Press, 1990, p. 78.

p. 214   held forth with brio: Colville, *The Fringes of Power*, p. 625.

p. 215   'I want the . . .': Quoted in Kenneth Clark, *The Other Half*, New York: Harper, 1977, p. 128.

p. 215   leaning heavily: Colville, *The Fringes of Power*, p. 626.

p. 215   spasm of a small artery: Moran, *Diaries*, 24 June 1953.

p. 216   'Harold, you might . . .': Macmillan, *Tides of Fortune*, p. 516.

p. 217   He wanted to attend: Moran, *Diaries*, 25 June 1953.

p. 217   walk unaided: Lady Soames, author interview.

p. 217   no one was to be told: Colville, *The Fringes of Power*, p. 626.

p. 218   Had he left London: Lady Soames, author interview.

p. 218   In defiance: Colville, *The Fringes of Power*, p. 626.

p. 218   thrombosis spreading: Moran, *Diaries*, 26 June 1953.

p. 220   Salisbury and Butler visit: Butler, *The Art of the Possible*, pp. 169–70; Moran, *Diaries*, 26 June 1953; Macmillan, *Diaries*, 4 July 1953; Cabinet Secretary's Notebooks, 29 June 1953, CAB 195/11.

p. 223   live through the weekend: Soames, *Clementine Churchill*, p. 475.

p. 223   Beaverbrook visit: Moran, *Diaries*, 28 June 1953.

p. 224   Cabinet meeting: Cabinet Secretary's Notebooks, 29 June 1953, CAB 195/11; Macmillan, *Diaries*, 4 July 1953.

p. 224   'intermediate': Cabinet Secretary's Notebooks, 29 June 1953, CAB 195/11.

p. 224   'As he had . . .': John Wheeler-Bennett, ed., *Action This Day*, New York: St Martin's Press, 1969, p. 44.

p. 225   'Four years ago . . .': WSC to Eisenhower, 1 July 1953, in Boyle, ed., *The Churchill–Eisenhower Correspondence*, p. 82.

p. 225   'I have had . . .': Macmillan, *Diaries*, 2 July 1953.

p. 226   two key goals: WSC, 'Policy Towards the Soviet Union and Germany', 6 July 1953, PREM 11/420.

p. 226   read the Prime Minister's statement: Cabinet Secretary's Notebooks, 6 July 1953, CAB 195/11.

p. 227   news from Moscow: First Tripartite Foreign Ministers Meeting, 19 July 1953, *FRUS: 1952–1954*, vol. 5, *Western European Security (in two parts)*, part 2.

p. 227   He nimbly argued: Opening Public Statements at First Tripartite Meeting, 10 July 1953, PREM 11/425.

p. 227   'an unknown quantity': *Ibid.*

p. 227   'when practicable': First Tripartite Foreign Ministers Meeting, 10 July 1953, *FRUS: 1952–1954*, vol. 5, part 2.

p. 228   cabled London for instructions: Message from Lord

Salisbury to the Chancellor of the Exchequer, 11 July 1953,
PREM 11/425.

p. 228   'They've bitched . . .': Moran, *Diaries*, 14 July 1953.

p. 228   'Meanwhile, I am . . .': Prime Minister Churchill to President
Eisenhower, 17 July 1953, *FRUS: 1952–1954*, vol. 6, part 1.

p. 229   great hopes: *Hansard*, 21 July 1953.

p. 229   'the lesser men . . .': *Ibid.*

p. 230   impatient to hear: Moran, *Diaries*, 21 July 1953.

p. 230   'I like to . . .': President Eisenhower to Prime Minister
Churchill, 20 July 1953, *FRUS: 1952–1954*, vol. 6, part 1.

p. 230   'violently Russophobe': Colville, *The Fringes of Power*,
31 July–4 August 1953.

p. 231   'by every possible . . .': Meeting Between President
Eisenhower and Leaders of the Three Delegations, 11 July
1953, PREM 11/425.

p. 232   'triumphal': Shuckburgh, *Descent to Suez*, 21 July 1953.

p. 233   would not like to be asked: *Ibid.*, 23 July 1953.

p. 233   'two invalids': Colville, *The Fringes of Power*, 31 July–4 August
1953.

p. 233   'What! Can't you . . .': Clarissa Eden, diary entry, 27 July
1953, quoted in Clarissa Eden, *Clarissa Eden: A Memoir–
From Churchill to Eden*, ed. Cate Haste, London: Weidenfeld
& Nicolson, 2007, p. 142.

p. 234   'Anthony must get . . .': *Ibid.*

p. 234   vowed beforehand: Colville, *The Fringes of Power*, 31 July–
4 August 1953.

p. 234   to beard Churchill: Shuckburgh, *Descent to Suez*, 28 July
1953.

p. 234   'I have been . . .': *Ibid.*

p. 235   'I noted with . . .': *Hansard*, 29 July 1953.

p. 235   conversation with Aldrich: The Ambassador in the United
Kingdom (Aldrich) to the Department of State, 11 September
1953, *FRUS: 1952–1954*, vol. 6, part 1.

p. 235 racing to orchestrate: Colville, *The Fringes of Power*, 31 July–4 August 1953.

p. 236 'He is a . . .': Clarissa Eden, diary entry, 27 July 1953, quoted in Eden, *Clarissa Eden*, p. 142.

p. 236 had better sleep on it: *Ibid.*

p. 237 Violet Bonham Carter visit: Bonham Carter, *Daring to Hope*, 6 August 1953.

p. 238 recites Gibbon: Moran, *Diaries*, 8 August 1953.

p. 238 'more charming and . . .': Macmillan, *Diaries*, 10 August 1953.

p. 238 Clementine sure Eisenhower does not want to see WSC: Moran, *Diaries*, 16 August 1953.

p. 239 presided over his first Cabinet: Cabinet Secretary's Notebooks, 18 August 1953, CAB 195/11.

p. 239 'dazed and grey': Soames, *Clementine Churchill*, p. 477.

p. 239 wondered aloud: Moran, *Diaries*, 19 August 1953.

p. 240 quarrelled bitterly: Soames, *Clementine Churchill*, p. 478.

p. 240 on an ebb tide: *Ibid.*, p. 479.

p. 241 'fit and ready . . .': *The Times*, 2 October 1953.

p. 241 look as if he were not fit: Shuckburgh, *Descent to Suez*, 1 October 1953.

p. 241 Churchill's dinner: Anthony Eden, diary entry, 1 October 1953, quoted in Rhodes James, *Anthony Eden*, p. 371; Clarissa Eden, diary entry, 2 October 1953, quoted in Eden, *Clarissa Eden*, p. 147; Shuckburgh, *Descent to Suez*, 2 October 1953.

p. 242 initially saw Eisenhower: Shuckburgh, *Descent to Suez*, 5 October 1953.

p. 243 sent off a message: Prime Minister Churchill to President Eisenhower, 7 October 1953, in Boyle, ed., *The Churchill–Eisenhower Correspondence*, p. 89.

p. 243 Churchill rehearses: Moran, *Diaries*, 9 October 1953.

p. 244 Eisenhower icily refused: President Eisenhower to Prime Minister Churchill, 8 October 1953, in *The Papers of Dwight David Eisenhower*, vol. 14, p. 458.

p. 244   on the spot: Shuckburgh, *Descent to Suez*, 9 October 1953.

p. 244   'I haven't got . . .': *Ibid.*

p. 245   'What subjects are . . .': Colville, *The Fringes of Power*, October 1953.

p. 245   'I am very . . .': Prime Minister Churchill to President Eisenhower, 9 October 1953, in Boyle, ed., *The Churchill–Eisenhower Correspondence*, p. 91.

p. 246   'whether he would . . .': Edward Heath, *The Course of my Life*, London: Hodder, 1998, p. 158.

p. 246   'If I stay . . .': WSC, 10 October 1953, quoted in *New York Times*, 11 October 1953.

p. 246   'triumphant return to . . .': *The Times*, 12 October 1953.

p. 247   'would be walking a tightrope . . .': Memo of Conversation, 14 October 1953, *FRUS: 1952–1954*, vol. 7, part 1.

p. 247   dinner party for Dulles at Number Ten: The Secretary of State to the President, 16 October 1953, *ibid.*

p. 248   'loyally': *Ibid.*

p. 249   farewell luncheon: The Ambassador in the United Kingdom (Aldrich) to the Department of State, 19 October 1953, *ibid.*

p. 250   whether he wished to respond: President Eisenhower to Arthur Hays Sulzberger, 11 September 1953, in *The Papers of Dwight David Eisenhower*, vol. 14, p. 511.

p. 251   'The Soviet answer . . .': Prime Minister Churchill to President Eisenhower, 5 November 1953, PREM 11/418.

p. 252   must not be billed: President Eisenhower to Prime Minister Churchill, 7 November 1953, PREM 11/418.

p. 252   'I shall go . . .': Halle, *The Irrepressible Churchill*, p. 274.

XVII: I Have a Right to Be Heard!

p. 253   'Ike': Moran, *Diaries*, 3 December 1953.

p. 254   to douse press expectations: Sulzberger, *A Long Row of Candles*, 23 November 1953.

p. 254 forced: *New York Times*, 5 December 1953.

p. 254 'trotting behind . . .': Shuckburgh, *Descent to Suez*, 4 December 1953.

p. 254 'pirated': Colville, *The Fringes of Power*, 4 December 1953.

p. 254 broached the possibility: Diary, 4 December 1953, in *The Papers of Dwight David Eisenhower*, vol. 15, Baltimore: Johns Hopkins University Press, 1996, p. 729.

p. 254 convened that evening: Minutes of First Plenary Meeting, 4 December 1953, PREM 11/418.

p. 255 laid out the strategy: Policy of Soviet Union, 4 December 1953, PREM 11/668.

p. 255 'vulgar': Shuckburgh, *Descent to Suez*, 4 December 1953.

p. 255 'very violent': Colville, *The Fringes of Power*, 4 December 1953.

p. 255 a woman of the streets: *Ibid.*

p. 255 'pained looks': *Ibid.*

p. 256 'I don't know . . .': *Ibid.*

p. 256 squared off on atomic policy: Bermuda, 5 December 1953, Meeting Held 11:30, Notes Written by Admiral Strauss, Dwight David Eisenhower Library.

p. 257 'I have been . . .': Moran, *Diaries*, 7 December 1953.

p. 258 'kind': Shuckburgh, *Descent to Suez*, 18 and 19 January 1954.

p. 258 'gaga': *Ibid.*, 31 March 1954.

p. 258 Soames concluded: Moran, *Diaries*, 7 February 1954.

p. 258 'atheistic materialism': President Eisenhower to Prime Minister Churchill, 9 February 1954, *FRUS: 1952–1954*, vol. 6, part 1.

p. 258 'for the struggle': *Ibid.*

p. 258 even more alarmed: Shuckburgh, *Descent to Suez*, 1 March 1954.

p. 259 'start out': Memorandum of a Meeting of President Eisenhower and Prime Minister Churchill at the White House, 25 June 1954, *FRUS: 1952–1954*, vol. 6, part 1.

p. 259   He believed that: Prime Minister Churchill to President Eisenhower, 9 March 1954, *ibid.*

p. 259   cryptic message: Christopher Soames to the Prime Minister, 17 March 1954, PREM 11/668.

p. 260   Eisenhower checked in: President Eisenhower to Prime Minister Churchill, 19 March 1954, *FRUS: 1952–1954*, vol. 6, part 1.

p. 260   made things worse: Press conference, 24 March 1954, in *New York Times*, 25 March 1954.

p. 261   'more statesmanlike': Julian Amery, *Approach March*, London: Hutchinson, 1973, p. 434.

p. 261   Attlee spoke first: *Hansard*, 5 April 1954.

p. 262   Churchill's performance: *The Times*, 6 April 1954; *New York Times*, 6 April 1954; *Hansard*, 5 April 1954.

p. 262   'I have a right to be heard!': *New York Times*, 6 April 1954.

p. 262   Macmillan guessed: Macmillan, *Diaries*, 6 April 1954.

p. 262   White-faced: Montague Browne, *Long Sunset*, p. 180.

p. 262   swayed slightly: Crossman, *Backbench Diaries*, 6 April 1954.

p. 262   Woolton relieved: Moran, *Diaries*, 5 April 1954.

p. 262   The doctor worried: *Ibid.*

p. 262   Boothby walks out: *The Times*, 6 April 1954.

p. 263   Boothby later claimed: Robert Rhodes James, *Robert Boothby*, New York: Viking, 1991, p. 373.

p. 263   Two ministers: Montague Browne, *Long Sunset*, p. 180.

p. 264   no later than Whitsun: Shuckburgh, *Descent to Suez*, 6 April 1954.

p. 264   must not under any circumstances: *Ibid.*

p. 264   'warrant': WSC to Bernard Baruch, 29 August 1954, PREM 11/669.

p. 264   Eisenhower asked Churchill: President Eisenhower to Prime Minister Churchill, 4 April 1954, in *The Papers of Dwight David Eisenhower*, vol. 15, p. 1002; Cabinet Secretary's Notebooks, 7 April 1954, CAB 195/12; Eden

Memo to Cabinet, 7 April 1954, CAB 129/67 post war memoranda.

p. 265 'air action': Cabinet Secretary's Notebooks, 7 April 1954, CAB 195/12.

p. 266 'very much like . . .': Prime Minister Churchill to President Eisenhower, 22 April 1954, in Boyle, ed., *The Churchill–Eisenhower Correspondence*, p. 139.

p. 266 Eisenhower naturally assumed: Eisenhower to Dulles, 23 April 1954, *FRUS: 1952–1954*, vol. 13, *Indochina (in two parts)*, part 1.

p. 266 Churchill wrote to inform Eden: WSC to Anthony Eden, 12 May 1954, PREM 11/291.

p. 266 told the Cabinet: Cabinet Secretary's Notebooks, 5 June 1954, CAB 195/12.

p. 267 'precipitate action': Cabinet Secretary's Notebooks, 24 May 1954, CAB 195/12.

p. 267 'prize noodle': Salisbury to Anthony Eden, 9 May 1954, quoted in John Charmley, *Churchill's Grand Alliance*, New York: Harcourt, 1995, p. 284.

p. 267 'a strong deterrent . . .': Cabinet Secretary's Notebooks, 24 May 1954, CAB 195/12.

p. 267 to counter any arguments: Cabinet Secretary's Notebooks, 5 June 1954, CAB 195/12.

p. 267 'a very perfect . . .': WSC to Clementine Churchill, 5 June 1954, in Soames, ed., *Winston and Clementine*.

p. 267 asked Churchill to step aside: Anthony Eden to WSC, 7 June 1954, quoted in Gilbert, *Churchill*, vol. 8, p. 989.

p. 268 'see what emerges . . .': WSC to Anthony Eden, 11 June 1954, quoted *ibid.*, pp. 989–90.

p. 268 'terrified': Quoted in John Young, *Winston Churchill's Last Campaign*, Oxford: Oxford University Press, 1996, p. 266.

p. 268 'like squids or . . .': Quoted *ibid.*

p. 268 Eden and Dulles: Memorandum of Meeting of Secretary of

State Dulles and Foreign Secretary Eden, 25 June 1954, *FRUS: 1952–1954*, vol. 6, part 1.

p. 269   three-quarters of an hour: Editorial Note, no. 465, *ibid*.

p. 269   Eisenhower's answer: Colville, *The Fringes of Power*, 25 June 1954.

p. 269   put his proposal in writing: Memorandum of a Meeting of President Eisenhower and Prime Minister Churchill at the White House, 25 June 1954, 3 p.m., *FRUS: 1952–1954*, vol. 6, part 1.

p. 270   until he was back in Britain: Memorandum of a Meeting of President Eisenhower and Prime Minister Churchill at the White House, 26 June 1954, 11 a.m., *ibid*.

p. 270   'reconnaissance in force': Memorandum of a Meeting of President Eisenhower and Prime Minister Churchill at the White House, 25 June 1954, 3 p.m., *ibid*.

p. 270   'You are to . . .': Macmillan, *Diaries*, 6 July 1954.

p. 270   Dulles expressed doubt: Memorandum of a Conversation by the Secretary of State, 27 June 1954, *FRUS: 1952–1954*, vol. 6, part 1.

p. 270   'very carefully weighed . . .': *Ibid*.

p. 270   reported the conversation: *Ibid*.

p. 270   rooting for Butler: Memorandum of a Conference at the White House, 5 May 1954, *FRUS: 1952–1954*, vol. 13, part 2.

p. 271   in the hope of extracting: Colville, *The Fringes of Power*, 2 July 1954.

XVIII: An Obstinate Pig

p. 272   incident in the grill room: Moran, *Diaries*, 1 July 1954.

p. 272   'bashful': Colville, *The Fringes of Power*, 2 July 1954.

p. 273   raise objections: *Ibid*., 16 July 1954.

p. 274   offered to personally deliver: *Ibid*., 2 July 1954.

p. 274 out the porthole: Clarissa Eden, diary entry, 8 July 1954, quoted in Eden, *Clarissa Eden*, p. 164.

p. 274 'in principle': Colville, *The Fringes of Power*, 2 July 1954.

p. 274 'I propose to ...': From Secretary of State on Board RMS *Queen Elizabeth* to Foreign Office, 2 July 1954, PREM 11/669.

p. 274 Eden did not: Cabinet Secretary's Notebooks, 8 July 1954, CAB 195/12.

p. 275 Eden pouted: Colville, *The Fringes of Power*, 3 July 1954.

p. 275 Churchill grumbled: *Ibid*.

p. 275 'Presume my message ...': From RMS *Queen Elizabeth* to Foreign Office, 3 July 1954, PREM 11/669.

p. 275 Butler in Norfolk: Chancellor of the Exchequer to Prime Minister Churchill, 21 July 1954, PREM 11/669.

p. 275 suggestions for minor edits: From Foreign Office to RMS *Queen Elizabeth*, 3 July 1954, PREM 11/669.

p. 275 Hayter went to the Kremlin: From Moscow to Foreign Office, 4 July 1954, PREM 11/669.

p. 276 'Your idea about ...': To the Prime Minister, Mr. W. Churchill, From V. M. Molotov, 5 July 1954, PREM 11/669.

p. 276 summoned Salisbury and Macmillan: Macmillan, *Diaries*, 6 July 1954.

p. 277 'In the light ...': Prime Minister Churchill to President Eisenhower, 7 July 1954, *FRUS: 1952–1954*, vol. 6, part 1.

p. 278 messages from Foreign Office colleagues: Shuckburgh, *Descent to Suez*, 6 July 1954.

p. 278 Cabinet meeting: Cabinet Secretary's Notebooks, 7 July 1954, CAB 195/12.

p. 278 'bombshell': Macmillan, *Diaries*, 7 July 1954.

p. 278 'blithely unconscious': *Ibid*.

p. 278 'must, however, inform ...': Cabinet Secretary's Notebooks, 7 July 1954, CAB 195/12.

p. 278 'tacitly': *Ibid*.

p. 279   'blank surprise': Macmillan, *Diaries*, 7 July 1954.

p. 279   'disgust': *Ibid.*

p. 279   Eden spoke: Cabinet Secretary's Notebooks, 7 July 1954, CAB 195/12.

p. 279   Salisbury put Churchill on notice: *Ibid.*

p. 279   'temper': *Ibid.*

p. 279   'critical or hostile': *Ibid.*

p. 279   'The United States can't veto . . .': *Ibid.*

p. 280   cavalier: Macmillan, *Diaries*, 7 July 1954.

p. 280   conversation at Ismay dinner: *Ibid.*

p. 281   Eisenhower regarded it as proof: Notes of Telephone Conversation between Eisenhower and Dulles, 7 July 1954, *The Papers of Dwight David Eisenhower*, vol. 15, p. 1167.

p. 281   'only another stroke': *Ibid.*

p. 282   'went fishing': Sir Roger Makins to Anthony Eden, 7 July 1954, PREM 11/669.

p. 282   'could not prevent . . .': *Ibid.*

p. 282   'You did not . . .': President Eisenhower to Prime Minister Churchill, 7 July 1954, PREM 11/669.

p. 282   'I hope you . . .': Prime Minister Churchill to President Eisenhower, 8 July 1954, PREM 11/669.

p. 283   'better': Cabinet Secretary's Notebooks, 8 July 1954, CAB 195/12.

p. 283   paint himself as blameless: *Ibid.*

p. 283   stakes so high: Colville, *The Fringes of Power*, 16 July 1954.

p. 284   'absolute right': Cabinet Secretary's Notebooks, 8 July 1954, CAB 195/12.

p. 284   remedy of ministers: *Ibid.*

p. 284   Action, he conceded: *Ibid.*

p. 284   'He could have . . .': *Ibid.*

p. 284   'in mind': *Ibid.*

p. 284   'Only two days . . .': *Ibid.*

p. 285   'What was the . . .': *Ibid.*

p. 285 'I may have . . .': *Ibid.*

p. 285 'If I found . . .': *Ibid.*

p. 285 'Of course I . . .': President Eisenhower to Prime Minister Churchill, 9 July 1954, PREM 11/669.

p. 285 'I am very . . .': Prime Minister Churchill to President Eisenhower, 9 July 1954, PREM 11/669.

p. 286 'I am unalterably . . .': Cabinet Secretary's Notebooks, 9 July 1954, CAB 195/12.

p. 286 'Other members of . . .': *Ibid.*

p. 286 'dead white': Macmillan, *Diaries*, 9 July 1954.

p. 286 'puce': *Ibid.*

p. 286 'I should greatly . . .': *Ibid.*

p. 287 visit to Hatfield: *Ibid.*

p. 287 thought he would cite: Shuckburgh, *Descent to Suez*, 12 July 1954.

p. 287 'You, of course . . .': President Eisenhower to Prime Minister Churchill, 13 July 1954, PREM 11/669.

p. 288 'minimize': *Ibid.*

p. 288 'glum and worried': Macmillan, *Diaries*, 13 July 1854.

p. 288 'give a damn': Colville, *The Fringes of Power*, 16 July 1954.

p. 289 'Yes, I do . . .': Clementine Churchill to John Colville, quoted in Gilbert, *Churchill*, vol. 8, p. 1038.

p. 289 all the cards: Macmillan, *Diaries*, 16 July 1954.

p. 289 constitutional niceties: *Ibid.*

p. 289 resignation would be foolish: *Ibid.*

p. 290 such a fuss: Colville, *The Fringes of Power*, 16 July 1954.

p. 290 Only now did Churchill: *Ibid.*

p. 290 'this stickler for . . .': For Secretary of State from Prime Minister, 17 July 1954, PREM 11/669.

p. 290 'compound the sins . . .': *Ibid.*

p. 291 disputed him in writing: Chancellor of the Exchequer to Prime Minister Churchill, 21 July 1954, PREM 11/669.

p. 291 'gravely concerned': Memorandum by the Under Secretary of State (Smith) to the Secretary of State, 26 July 1954, *FRUS: 1952–1954*, vol. 6, part 1.

p. 292   'I am an obstinate pig': WSC to Eisenhower, 8 August 1954, *ibid.*

p. 292   expected Eden's support: Minute to Prime Minister, 22 July 1954, PREM 11/669.

p. 292   went home without her: Clarissa Eden, diary entry, 22 July 1954, in Eden, *Clarissa Eden*, p. 168.

p. 292   in the middle of the night: *Ibid.*

p. 292   on reflection he would not: Minute to Prime Minister, 22 July 1954, PREM 11/669.

p. 292   'white and tense': Macmillan, *Diaries*, 23 July 1954.

p. 292   'no message need . . .': Cabinet Secretary's Notebooks, 23 July 1954, CAB 195/12.

p. 293   'On reflection, I . . .': *Ibid.*

p. 293   'During this period . . .': *Ibid.*

p. 293   Salisbury thought he saw a way out: *Ibid.*

p. 294   'No word was . . .': *Ibid.*

p. 294   'If it is . . .': Macmillan, *Diaries*, 23 July 1954.

p. 295   'stag-party': Colville, *The Fringes of Power*, August 1954.

p. 295   'air of crisis': *Ibid.*

p. 295   'new event': Cabinet Secretary's Notebooks, 26 July 1954, CAB 195/12.

p. 295   said he was satisfied: *Ibid.*

p. 296   'I don't regret . . .': *Ibid.*

p. 296   happy to assent: *Ibid.*

p. 296   Molotov expressed astonishment: The Prime Minister, Mr. W. Churchill, From V. M. Molotov, 31 July 1954, PREM 11/669.

p. 297   fresh set of arguments for bilateral talks: Two Power Meeting with Soviet Government, Note by the Prime Minister, 3 August 1954, PREM 11/669.

p. 297   Salisbury's response: Lord Salisbury to Prime Minister Churchill, 20 August 1954, PREM 11/669.

p. 298   'In peace or war . . .': Prime Minister Churchill to Lord Salisbury, 21 August 1954, PREM 11/669.

p. 298   French would not be ratifying: WSC to Dulles, 24 August 1954, *FRUS: 1952–1954*, vol. 5, part 1.

p. 298   wrote to Eden: WSC to Anthony Eden, 24 August 1954, quoted in Gilbert, *Churchill*, vol. 8, p. 1050.

p. 299   'It has gone . . .': WSC to Clementine Churchill, 25 August 1954, in Soames, ed., *Winston and Clementine*.

XIX:. The 'R' Word

p. 300   'This is to . . .': WSC, 30 November 1954, quoted in 'On the Occasion of Churchill's 80th Birthday', The Churchill Society, London.

p. 301   'just the moment . . .': Lord Salisbury to Paul Emrys Evans, 28 November 1954, PEE Papers.

p. 301   'That is something . . .': *The Times*, 1 December 1954.

p. 302   'It is in . . .': Prime Minister Churchill to President Eisenhower, 7 December 1954, in Boyle, ed., *The Churchill–Eisenhower Correspondence*, p. 180.

p. 302   'play tough': President Eisenhower to Prime Minister Churchill, 14 December 1954, in *The Papers of Dwight David Eisenhower*, vol. 15, p. 1444.

p. 303   general election in the spring: Anthony Eden, diary entry, 21 December 1954, quoted in Rhodes James, *Anthony Eden*, p. 392.

p. 303   told Eden on the phone: Eden, *Clarissa Eden*, p. 181.

p. 303   Clementine Churchill expressed alarm: Anthony Eden, diary entry, 21 December 1954, quoted in Rhodes James, *Anthony Eden*, p. 392.

p. 303   'What do you . . .': *Ibid.*

p. 304   'one against the . . .': Macmillan, *Diaries*, 10 October 1954.

p. 304   'I know you . . .': Quoted in Anthony Seldon, *Churchill's Indian Summer*, London: Hodder, 1981, p. 51.

p. 304   no one contradicted: Anthony Eden, diary entry, 22 December 1954, quoted in Rhodes James, *Anthony Eden*, p. 393.

p. 304   'But if this . . .': Quoted in Seldon, *Churchill's Indian Summer*, p. 51.

p. 305   'in despair': Macmillan, *Diaries*, 22 December 1954.

p. 305   Stuart opined: Anthony Eden, diary entry, 22 December 1954, quoted in Rhodes James, *Anthony Eden*, p. 393.

p. 305   until he died: Macmillan, *Diaries*, 22 December 1954.

p. 305   reconvened at the home: Seldon, *Churchill's Indian Summer*, p. 51.

p. 305   rise to the great occasion: Norman Brook quoted in Gilbert, *Churchill*, vol. 8, p. 1084.

p. 305   Colville admitted: Colville, *The Fringes of Power*, 29 March 1955.

p. 306   'tired of it all': *Ibid.*

p. 306   sending for a calendar: Anthony Eden, diary entry, 1 February 1955, quoted in Rhodes James, *Anthony Eden*, p. 396.

p. 306   tell the Queen quietly: Clarissa Eden, diary entry, 2 February 1955, quoted in Eden, *Clarissa Eden*, 182.

p. 306   convinced that he finally: Clarissa Eden, diary entry, 14 February 1955, *ibid.*, p.184.

p. 307   he told Moran: Moran, *Diaries*, 21 February 1955.

p. 307   'What ought we . . .': WSC, 1 March 1955, quoted in *New York Times*, 2 March 1955.

p. 307   'a very fine . . .': Moran, *Diaries*, 1 March 1955.

p. 308   'It is absolutely . . .': *Hansard*, 2 March 1955.

p. 308   trembled for fear: Macmillan, *Diaries*, 2 March 1955.

p. 308   Soames chewed his thumb: *Ibid.*

p. 308   'slid successfully past . . .': *Ibid.*

p. 309   'At least not yet': Moran, *Diaries*, 3 March 1955.

p. 309   go to Sicily: Clarissa Eden, diary entry, 8 March 1955, quoted in Eden, *Clarissa Eden*, p. 194.

p. 309   Eden expressed confidence: Macmillan, *Diaries*, 9 March 1955.

p. 309   Clementine gave Clarissa a tour: Clarissa Eden, diary entry, 10 March 1955, quoted in Eden, *Clarissa Eden*, p. 194.

p. 309   tested the new Rolls-Royce: Colville, *The Fringes of Power*, 29 March 1955.

p. 310   changed his mind: *Ibid*.

p. 310   'lay plans for . . .': WSC to Anthony Eden, 12 March 1955, quoted in Rhodes James, *Anthony Eden*, p. 401.

p. 310   'the first time': *Ibid*.

p. 311   'The magnitude of . . .': *Ibid*.

p. 311   'full crisis': Clarissa Eden, diary entry, 11 March 1955, quoted in Eden, *Clarissa Eden*, p. 194.

p. 311   'would justify the . . .': Anthony Eden to WSC, 12 March 1955, quoted in Rhodes James, *Anthony Eden*, p. 402.

p. 312   might not be able to stand the strain: Macmillan, *Diaries*, 13 March 1955.

p. 312   'I don't think . . .': Cabinet Secretary's Notebooks, 14 March 1955, CAB 195/13.

p. 312   'Does that mean . . .': Macmillan, *Diaries*, 14 March 1955.

p. 312   'This is a . . .': Cabinet Secretary's Notebooks, 14 March 1955, CAB 195/13.

p. 313   'All this is very . . .': Macmillan, *Diaries*, 14 March 1955.

p. 313   'new offer': Cabinet Secretary's Notebooks, 14 March 1955, CAB 195/13.

p. 313   'It isn't against . . .': Clarissa Eden, diary entry, 14 March 1955, quoted in Eden, *Clarissa Eden*, p. 197.

p. 314   Aldrich delivered: WSC to Clementine Churchill, 15 March 1955, in Soames, ed., *Winston and Clementine*.

p. 314   insisted on going back: *Ibid*.

p. 314   'a gesture of . . .': Macmillan, *Diaries*, 16 March 1955.

p. 314   'It's the first . . .': Quoted in Soames, *Clementine Churchill*, p. 493.

p. 314   no 'next time': *Ibid.*, p. 492.

p. 315   'But Ike won't . . .': Quoted in Bonham Carter, *Daring to Hope*, 1 April 1955, p. 147.

p. 315   gaffed: Quoted in Seldon, *Churchill's Indian Summer*, p. 53.

p. 315   landed: Colville, *The Fringes of Power*, 29 March 1955.

p. 315   just to gratify: *Ibid.*

p. 316   the young sovereign said no: *Ibid.*, p. 661.

p. 316   Colville sent word: *Ibid.*, 29 March 1955.

p. 316   inquired how his niece: Eden, *Clarissa Eden*, p. 198.

p. 317   scene in Cabinet Room: Butler, *The Art of the Possible*, p. 176.

p. 317   'to die in . . .': Winston S. Churchill, *Marlborough: His Life and Times*, vol. 2, London: Harrap, 1936, p. 1036.

p. 318   'I don't believe . . .': Colville, *The Fringes of Power*, p. 662.

p. 318   'I have decided . . .': Cabinet Secretary's Notebooks, 5 April 1955, CAB 195/13.

INDEX

WSC indicates Winston Churchill